Liars Go To Paradise?

M. H. Woodscourt

For the fans,
because I can't offer gerani.

– M.H.W.

Prologue
The Liar?

Tears blinded her vision. Her tires dug into the pavement as she swerved around sharp curves on the mountain road. Hard rock music blared through her speakers, adding to her hurt and frustration.

Viciously she wiped at the tears shimmering in her deep blue eyes. Still they fell and she rubbed at them again. In the moment she took one hand from the wheel the car hit a deep pothole and jerked toward the right. The front of the vehicle slammed against the guardrail, tearing through the metal with a horrible screech heard even over the loud music. The car seemed to hover in the air for a moment and she felt her anger vanish as she realized what she had done. The car dropped. The woman's scream split the air as she plummeted toward the creek far below.

She did not survive.

Which really doesn't matter, as this story isn't about her —thank goodness. Though I must admit it would be entertaining to fall from such a height. At least, up until the part where one actually crashed into the water. That might not be so enjoyable. Unless, of course, one is a masochist—which, I hope, one is not. Or was not, seeing as how one is dead now. You may think me callous; that's your call.

Moving on.

Hi there, I'm Key. Pleasure. You're probably asking, "What kind of name is Key?" Trust me, you'll think it pretty normal by the end of my story, in comparison with a few others. Of course my proper name is Jason Sterling, but I prefer Key. As do my friends.

I want you to know here and now: I am a huge liar. Nearly everything I say is a lie. Though the fact I almost always lie could be a lie, and you'd never know. Especially since liars always lie, which means they lie about lying, but because it's a lie that doesn't really work, and you get all jumbled up trying to figure out exactly what I'm talking about and why. Not to mention why you're even attempting to understand the mind of a lying liar who doesn't not lie about lying or not.

Now that we've covered that, I want to commend you. You obviously haven't stopped reading yet, and that means some twisted part of you actually gets amusement from reading what I have to think. I'm impressed you comprehend me, or at least, you're making a good effort.

My mom once said my favorite pastime, aside from lying, was making long rants that made very little sense. I could be lying. Maybe she didn't say that, but you can decide for yourself whether or not to disbelieve me. I don't mind either way.

I just want you to know one more thing: Read on at your own peril.

Shall we begin?

Part One:
Strange Coward Boy?

1
To Touch a Furapintairow?

Luck was against me as usual. Freezing drops of rain fell mercilessly from the dreary sky, soaking me to the bone. Lightning flashed, followed closely by a clap of loud thunder. I'd like to say the sound didn't make me jump, but it did. In fact, everything was making me jump this particular Monday morning; it wasn't because I was afraid of thunder (though I might be), or that the gloomy atmosphere made shadows around every corner and beneath every leaf-dripping tree. It was something else.

I'd dreamed of yellow eyes.

Unusual, you'll agree. A cause for jumpiness? Not likely. But for me, it was. I never recalled my dreams—ever. Occasionally I had fleeting images or vague sensations left from dreams, but this was different. This time I recalled both a pair of intense yellow eyes and a prominent feeling of dread.

The dread stuck like glue. Thus, jumpiness.

A dog barked and I jumped again. Recovering, silently chastising myself for being stupid, I scowled and trudged on through the miserable rain, determined to focus on anything but the persistent dread twisting my stomach in knots, or on the stupid rain dripping from my lashes into my eyes.

My thoughts, oddly enough, turned to my family. There were times I thought I might be adopted. Doesn't every child? But I figured my reasoning was pretty legitimate. After all, I was the only blond in my household. Every single head of hair, minus my own, was dark brown (except my white-furred American Eskimo pet affectionately dubbed Beastie). They all had brown eyes (doggy too). Mine were light gray. They were all tall, while my own height was five-foot-six (with shoes), though I was nearly eighteen years old.

I'd asked on more than one occasion if I was adopted. My parents laughed it off and assured me that my genes came from my grandmother on my father's side. I asked for pictures. Sure enough, she was blond. Perhaps my melodramatic mind just demanded a much more mysterious answer for my unique appearance. It wasn't that I was unhappy; my family was the best and I couldn't be prouder to be a member (though they would never know it). I just craved something *different;* something as "out there" as my fibs.

I shifted my backpack strap from one shoulder to the other. Textbooks were heavier than bricks; of that I was thoroughly convinced. *Only a few more months,* I silently consoled myself. I was a senior, destined by the State to graduate in May. Only two months away. Two months of the ultimate juvenile hall and then I would be free to consider four years of prison life known as college. It's true, I had no ambition in life. I was just getting by like so many others my age.

Amid my ambling thoughts I heard a voice calling from down the street.

Glancing up, squinting beneath my dripping bangs, I caught sight of a fellow student. A local jock named Chas. He was waving at me—whoa; was he seriously waving at me? I stopped trudging through the murky water, waiting as he ran toward me. To be certain he was actually coming to talk with me, I glanced behind my shoulder to find the street empty.

Chas sprinted down the sidewalk, hoodie flapping out behind him, short light-blond hair slick from the rain, name-brand tennis shoes slapping at tiny puddles of water. He slid to a graceful halt in front of me, trademark smirk plastered to his clear-complected face. Even the male population of my high school had to admit he was undoubtedly handsome. But, instead of following his every whim for his God-given gift, we despaired at our misfortune and loathed him for his supposed perfection. Truth was, he was as arrogant as a man could possibly be (reason in itself to loathe him, even if his face had resembled a dog's instead of a Greek god).

"Jason, isn't it?" he asked, not short of breath despite his sprint. Stupid jock.

"Yeah," I muttered, stuffing my hands deep into my cargo pants pockets and hunching against the cold rain and biting wind.

"Seems a shame to rain this late in the spring," he commented, glancing at the sky as though to double-check that it was actually raining. He took a deep breath of the crisp freshness, basking in the clean smell.

I shuffled my feet, annoyed that my socks were getting increasingly damper thanks to the stupid chick magnet.

Slowly Chas lowered his gaze from the overhead gloom, his bright green eyes catching my gray with their sudden intensity.

"Let's walk," he said after an awkward moment. Turning to face the route toward school, he sauntered through the wet. I grudgingly followed, not thrilled at the prospect of running into his groupies. Shoulders slouched, I tried to stay a pace behind him, but Chas slowed to match my shorter strides.

"What are your plans after you graduate?" he asked, running a hand across his wet brow, removing strands of pale hair from his vibrant eyes.

I shrugged. "Not sure, really." Was I seriously having this conversation? Maybe my alarm hadn't rung after all and I was still fast asleep, stuck in a nightmare. Politeness kicked in after another awkward silence and I forced a convincing smile. "Yourself?"

"I'm leaving," Chas said, his tone odd.

"Where to?"

"Far away. I'll probably never come back."

"Hate it that bad, huh?" I asked.

"No." Chas shook his head, droplets of water trailing down his face. "I just won't have any reason to return."

What about your family, moron? I thought, but this I kept to myself.

Frowning, I wondered if there was more depth to Chas than I'd assumed. It seemed risky to entertain such thoughts; start believing in people and you end up disappointed. Still, Chas had everything in the world a high schooler craves: popularity, looks and smarts. What did he have to gain by leaving his familiar world?

"Will you go to school?"

Chas shrugged; a surprising gesture, as he always seemed so sure of himself. "I don't need to."

Still an arrogant cuss, deep or not. "Oh? Plan to charm your way through life?" I was startled that the words came out so easily; startled that I felt comfortable enough to insult him out loud. Still, I didn't care much if he was offended. Mr. Popular could afford to be affronted now and then.

A strange smile stole across Chas's face. "Something like that," he answered simply.

Again, silence. It wouldn't have been so bad, except he seemed to think I needed to fill the gap, and I somehow felt obligated. Stubborn, as I always was, I sealed my lips and kept quiet. It wasn't hard, really. I usually kept quiet around my peers.

"Do you ever feel like you don't belong here," Chas asked as we reached the end of the block, rounding the corner to view the school in the distance. The brick structure was ominous against the gloomy backdrop of the sky.

"Doesn't everyone, sometimes?" I slipped one hand from my pocket to wipe a droplet from my nose.

"I wonder," he murmured, gazing at the school. I studied his face several inches above my own; somehow he seemed mature as he pondered the mysteries of the universe (or something). I knew better than to think he was usually so reflective, but it was intriguing to watch his single 'ah-ha' moment in action. Finally he released a weary sigh and turned to face me fully. "Well, Jason. I can't say it hasn't been interesting."

"Huh?" I managed stupidly, blinking, both in surprise and from water trickling into my eyes.

An startling glint appeared in Chas's eyes and I involuntarily stepped back. A grin spread across his face, making me take another. Instinct I hadn't known I possessed screamed for me to run. Unfortunately, I didn't obey as my legs were frozen to the sidewalk.

"Bye-bye, Jase. See you around."

Chas's arms shot out from his sides with lightning-fast agility. I felt more than saw him shove me backward. I flung my arms out to the sides to counter my fall, hands groping for purchase. It might have been enough to keep my balance, had the sidewalk not been slick as ice from the storm.

Time seemed to slow. Water fell toward me from the dark sky, one arm was extended before my body; it almost didn't feel attached anymore, though I knew it still was. My breath appeared in a puffy cloud.

Distant sounds of scraping feet against pavement. Laughter. Golden light.

The last thing I saw were frightening yellow eyes in a familiar face.

Water filled my ears, swallowing me. My head slammed against the pavement and stars collided with my eyes, bursting like thousands of fireworks in a grand finale. Consciousness slipped away, though I grasped desperately at it. The last sensation I experienced was a strange tangy, sweet scent as it filled my nostrils.

I was acutely aware of the pain, first.

The second thing I was conscious of was the wind. It rushed around me; pleasant, warm, sweet-smelling. Moaning, I tried to open my eyes. It didn't work. I wasn't even sure if my eyes were still in my head (all my head knew at the moment was agony).

Working my mouth to stop from feeling panicked, I tried to pry my eyes open again. This time I could actually feel the effort, but they were still glued shut.

I raised my hand to my face, feeling for my eyelids; found them; rubbed. My fingers were wet. I decided to sit up, as I became aware of water surrounding my head and upper-torso. Gingerly, I sat. Water rushed from my ears and I shivered, despite the warm breeze. Pressing my palms to my face, I rubbed vigorously, then tried to open my eyes once again. This time, it worked.

Red sunlight burned my retinas and I cringed, shutting my eyes quickly. Gritting my teeth, I squinted with one eye and waited for it to adjust. After managing that, I babied my other eye and finally (through rapid blinking) I could see the world around me.

It was not what I expected.

I was sitting in the middle of a meadow. Tall trees surrounded the clearing and a bright-red sun filtered through the gaps between them as it set behind distant mountain peaks. Wild flowers bobbed in a warm breeze, while tall wild grass danced around the small buds. I found it rather peculiar that the sky was devoid of clouds and the grass was perfectly dry, yet I sat in the middle of a massive puddle.

How in the world—?

—Chas.

With a rush I recalled what had happened.

Disbelieving, bewildered and aching, I sat in the puddle for a long time, trying to devise a logical explanation for my predicament.

Either I was dreaming or I was insane.

I chose option one. It was the lesser of two evils.

I climbed to my feet, wobbled for a moment, head swimming, then reached up to investigate the egg-sized bump on the back of my head. The slightest touch caused pain to blossom and spread through my brain. I held my breath until the throbbing passed, then I released the air from my lungs carefully.

Another breath; now release.

I repeated the exercise a few times, then turned my attention back to my make-believe meadow. Happily chirping birds swooped around, gathering who-knew-what before dark came, then flew back to the trees. Three small butterflies danced around the wild flowers, swirling, flipping and gliding.

What the freak kind of dream was this, anyway?

I studied the trees, intrigued to find that while the trunks resembled a pine's in height and branch layout, instead of evergreen needles maple leaves adorned the branches throughout. I looked up and down the largest tree, trying to wrap my head around this particular insanity.

It was then that I saw them for the first time: two small creatures that couldn't possibly be real, sitting beneath the maple pine tree I had been studying.

They were covered completely in thick blood-red fur, giving the appearance that they were merely foot-high balls of fluff. A jagged tail, almost as though it had been broken multiple times along its length, protruded from the fur, and a smaller ball of fluff hung on its tip. The only other feature visible amid the fur were two huge (and I mean *huge*) pink eyes that watched me unblinkingly.

I couldn't help myself—either my curiosity took over, or their pink eyes were strangely alluring—and I slowly approached the furry things and knelt in front of them. My head didn't swim too badly as I moved.

They didn't stir. Carefully I reached toward one. Just as my hand touched its downy-soft fur, lancing pain shot through my fingers. I drew back in surprise and my gray eyes rested on the trickle of blood running down my right hand. I looked up sharply at the furry thing and gasped. It was grinning, displaying two rows of sharp, pointy, blood-covered teeth. The other creature was also grinning, its teeth pearly-white.

I scrambled to my feet and backed away, pressing my injured hand against my red jacket to ease the growing ache. I admit the furry things scared me, but not nearly so much as the fact that my hand was throbbing with pain.

Dreams were not supposed to hurt, right?

"It's too late to run," a soft voice said from behind me.

I spun, heart pounding, head banging, fingers throbbing, and came face to face with a woman.

She was beautiful, but frail. Her frame was slight, though she was quite tall. A shimmering silver shawl wrapped around her slender shoulders, covering her simple brown apparel. Strips of gray cloth wrapped around her wrists and feet. I stared as I spotted long sharp nails adorning the tip of each slender finger, and even her toes.

"You are peculiar," she said, voice still soft, as though she spoke to herself.

Pulled from her deadly nails, I looked up into her face. She was pale. By pale, I don't mean she had a light complexion; by pale, I mean her skin was almost white, like she'd never stepped foot out into the sunlight in her life (although she obviously had or she wouldn't be standing in front of me while the sun was still up). Apart from sickeningly light skin, she had a pretty face; it was angular, sharp yet alluring; framed by glossy black hair that reached just below her shoulders, parted in the center of her head. It was all one length; no bangs. And—I gawked—protruding from her hair were two long pointed ears, like something from a fantasy game.

"Can you understand me?" she asked.

I opened my mouth to speak, but the words were loathe to come out. My vision was starting to swim.

She cocked her head slightly to one side, arching a slender eyebrow, pursing her pale lips. "To touch a furapintairow is to incur its wrath. Are you not aware of the consequences?" She stepped forward, reaching out a clawed hand.

I stepped back, flinching. As I realized that I was reacting so, I felt myself blush with embarrassment; which only made me more embarrassed; which caused me to blush deeper. (An endless cycle.)

"It's all right," the woman said soothingly. "I will help you."

Stepping back again, alarmed without understanding exactly why, my foot found water. I glanced down, feeling the liquid seep into my already-sopping shoe. I was back at the puddle. Maybe, if I jumped I could get back home.

It was a wild thought, certainly. But I was in no fit state to comprehend that. Desperate to gain my senses once again, eager to wake up, I stepped backward into the puddle and jumped.

Pain exploded in my head and numbness spread up from my bloodied fingertips. I gasped, stumbling.

How exactly the woman got from standing before me to catching me as I fell backward, I couldn't say. She was surprisingly strong; that, or I'm just really light. Probably both. As I glanced up into her pale face, she smiled, flashing her pearly-whites. My blood froze.

Her teeth were pointed too.

"Relax, stranger," she said, easing me to the ground. I felt like I was floating. "Did you come from the puddle?"

I tried to nod. It didn't work. "Y-yeah," I croaked.

"You *do* speak. English, too."

What *else* would I speak? Chinese? My sight was fading completely now; inky blackness spread from the corners of my vision, seeping inward. I fought to stay conscious, but my brain and my fingers all protested.

"Rest now," the woman said, voice gentle. "Sleep, Vendaeva."

The pain seemed to melt away, dissipating like a cloud. My muscles relaxed, tension leaving my body. It was easy to let it go; to just forget the freakishness. Everything was fine, was safe.

"This is what death feels like," another voice whispered, this one dark, lulling yet bone-chilling. It filled my mind, drowning out the last of my consciousness. I didn't try to struggle.

2
A Tiny Misunderstanding?

Waking up had never been such a pain. Literally.

For a second time I was acutely aware of a pounding headache. That wasn't what pulled me from my sleep, though. Shivering, I tried to pull my blankets over me only to find a thin sheet my only source of warmth. What the—? Oh, I wasn't in my bed.

It was dark now. Stars glittered overhead and for a moment I stared. I came from a town where there were a lot of stars on a clear summer night, but this view put those to shame. It was so lit up with tiny white lights that they all seemed almost to touch.

I tried to raise my head, but the attempt only made me feel like puking. With a loud moan, I stayed still, willing my head to stop banging and my stomach to settle. I squeezed my eyes shut until the nausea passed, then shivered again.

"Take care, Vendaeva," a gentle voice, oddly familiar, said from overhead.

Opening my eyes, I recognized the alien woman from before standing on my right side. From what I could tell I was laying in soft grass, far beneath her lithe form. It hurt to look up in the gloom and, almost as though she sensed that, she knelt beside me.

"You are awake. That is a good sign," the woman said, her voice low. "Still, your body has experienced a good deal of trauma. Stay still and recover."

Trauma? Oh, red furry things, right. I remembered them. What I couldn't understand, however, was why I was still dreaming. This was ridiculous. Things like this don't happen in real life to real people. Sure, books, comics, movies; in modern fictional media such an adventure was plausible; the key word in that being 'fictional.' There was just no way this could actually be happening. What I meant when I wanted "out there" was winning a million bucks in the lottery, or taking a Caribbean cruise. I didn't actually want to live a video game life.

The woman stirred, reaching beyond my view. Slick black hair fell in her face as she worked; I heard water drip. She turned, pulling her hair back with her free hand as she held up a damp cloth. I didn't protest as she laid the cloth across my forehead. It alleviated some of the pain, though it made me shiver more.

"Are you cold?" the woman asked. She reached forward, claws flashing in the moonlight (I like to think I didn't wince), pulling the glistening sheet closer around my neck.

—Wait, glistening? I tried to look down, nearly going cross-eyed in the attempt. I was highly suspicious that I was wearing the woman's silver shawl. Glancing at my savior, I sighed. Her shawl was conspicuously missing, from what I could tell in the dark.

"So," I croaked. Horrified by how like a frog I sounded, I decided the questions could wait.

The woman watched me for a moment and I realized something was wrong with her eyes. One was silver, the other was gold. Was I imagining this? —Of course, I had to be. This wasn't real, after all, so why was I concerned? (Aside from the fact that my imagination had never been this wild in my life and I highly doubted I could conceive a world like this on my own.)

The woman seemed to decide I wasn't going to speak and she turned again. I heard water slosh in something, then the woman produced a leather flask.

"Thirsty?" she asked, shaking the flask to slosh the water more.

My mouth was suddenly drier than a desert. "Yeah," I said hoarsely.

She scooted closer and carefully slipping her deadly nails beneath my aching head. Thankfully she avoided my massive bump, and she lifted me up enough that I could take a sip from the flask.

"Slowly," she said.

Despite her warning, I drank greedily, determined not to sound like a frog ever again. Naturally I choked and swallowed wrong. Sputtering, I scrambled to sit up completely. The woman helped me, keeping a hand on my back as I wheezed and coughed the water from my lungs. Remembering her inch-long claws, my spine stiffened away from her touch. She withdrew her support. I fell backward, weaker than I'd thought. She caught me again before I hit the ground, lowering me carefully down, resting my head gently in the grass. I caught the scent of dew and peppermint.

"I warned you," the woman said.

I tried to shrug. Big mistake. "I was thirsty," I argued, ignoring the renewed pain in my head. I was pleased to discover that my voice was at least understandable now.

"Sips quench thirst best," she replied, slowly rising to her feet. "Sleep now."

I wanted to, badly, but the fact that she'd told me to made me want to resist.

She exhaled slowly and shook her head. "You would be headstrong, naturally."

What was that supposed to mean? "What's that supposed to mean?" I growled. The coldness I'd been feeling up till now was gone; instead—maybe thanks to my blood boiling—I was feeling very warm. On top of that, I felt like I was floating.

"Take it as you please." Her metallic eyes flashed in the moonlight as she glanced right, staring at something in the distance. After a moment she turned back to me, meeting my eyes, holding me captive with her intensity. "Rest. Your body is weak."

She struck the wrong chord. Gritting my teeth, I bolted to my feet, determined to show this slender (albeit tall) woman that I was every bit as strong as she. "I'm not weak!" My voice cracked with the strain on my nearly-drowned lungs. I began coughing raggedly, doubling over under the pain and sudden shivers that racked my body. My legs gave out and I fell forward, once again humiliated as the woman speedily caught me and lowered me to the ground.

"It's all right," she soothed. "You will not be so hot-tempered when your fever has fully fled."

I had a fever? That might explain a few things...

"Now, rest. Please." She covered me with her blasted shawl. "I will build a fire to keep you warm."

I nodded slowly, careful not to make my head worse. "Th-thank you," I murmured as my consciousness began to slip. She had only been trying to help, in her strange, alien way. I, on the other hand, was being extremely rude. My excuse was that it was in my nature, but that, like most of what I said, was really a lie.

"There is no need for thanks," the woman said, offering a flash of pointy teeth.

I tried not to panic. Luckily, I was feeling a little drugged now (I wondered if the water had something in it to calm my nerves) and I couldn't seem to care about this creature's inhuman appearance.

"Key," I offered as the stars flickered out of my sight.

"Key?" she repeated, but I didn't answer as sleep overcame me. I willingly gave in. I almost swear I heard myself snoring before I even finished falling asleep.

"If you sleep any longer, I will throw you into the puddle and leave."

My eyes snapped open.

"Awake now, are you?"

I freaking was now. But there was no way the voice I was hearing was actually real. Right...?

"Your fever broke last night, but you will still be weak for a few days. If you push yourself, you will become sick once again. I advise you lie still and keep your temper in check."

I didn't think I was going anywhere of my own accord, anytime soon. My headache seemed to have spread throughout my entire body, making me feel like one large purple bruise. I didn't even want to know how I looked at the moment. Still, one good sign of my improvement was, despite her taunting, I wasn't extremely angry with the lady who was aiding me. Just annoyed.

"Are you hungry?" the woman asked.

Unsure how my voice had held out during my fever's tirade, I instead managed a minuscule nod and hoped she recognized my efforts. I heard rustling to my right and waited as patiently as my roaring stomach allowed while she rummaged for breakfast.

She appeared above my head after a moment. In the morning light, without the shadows of evening or night, she was more pale than ever. Striking mismatched eyes studied me. "I will not give you anything solid to start. Your stomach cannot handle any more heaving."

Any more? Had I thrown up already? Considering the acidic taste in my mouth, probably. Man, that was one wicked illness.

She seemed to read my thoughts, or, at least, my expression. "You have no immunity to the sicknesses of this place; I'm not surprised that the venom affected you so savagely. If you dare to touch a furapintairow again, it will not be so bad, although, you'll probably die. I won't treat you again."

Her bedside manner was one of a kind.

"Furapin—what now?" I whispered, grateful when it didn't come out as "ribbit."

"Fur-uh-pin-tie-row," she said slowly. "The sacred animals you disrespectfully touched, two days ago."

Two days? Hadn't it been yesterday? Had I seriously been out that long? Was the fever really that bad? Did I have anything left of my body, or did I resemble a skeleton more?

"Relax," the woman said, gently touching my shoulder to calm me. Maybe she *could* read minds. "Two evenings ago you spoke of a key. I looked around the meadow and inside the puddle, but there was nothing there. It isn't in your pockets either. Do you have any idea where else I might look?"

Key? Oh, wait. I remembered now. I had been trying to tell her my name, so she'd stop calling me weird names. "No," I said. "Not a physical key. It's my name. Key."

She blinked, then smiled sadly, no teeth showing. "Is that so? Then it is true."

True? Well, not really, but I preferred Key to Jason. There were already five other Jasons at school, and none of them seemed to appreciate me having any sort of association with them. I had decided on Key (for whatever reason), but it didn't seem to stop the bullying. If anything, I was treated worse.

"And you came from the puddle," the woman said, breaking me from my thoughts.

"Er, well, it certainly seems that way."

"I can hardly believe it, but..." her smile grew a little brighter, "...I shouldn't question fortune."

I certainly could. Fortune was apparently not on my side, like always.

Feeling brave, I tried to sit up and the black-clad woman helped me. The shawl slipped from around my neck and shoulders, into my lap and I stared at the shimmering material. "Uh, thanks," I said when my head ceased swimming again.

"There is no need for thanks. I did what I would want in return, if I were foolish enough to touch a furapintairow."

I gritted my teeth to prevent a retort. There was a chance, slim though it was, that she didn't know she was goading me. Maybe it was in the nature of sharp-toothed, shawl-wearing, mismatched-eyed, pointed-eared, alien-women to throw out insulting remarks two-hundred words per minute.

I forced a smile on my face and turned to meet the woman's eyes. "You know my name, but I don't know yours."

She hesitated, glancing at the maple pines. "My name is Jenen."

Jenen, huh?

"Nice to meet you," I said, uncertain myself whether I meant those words.

She inclined her head, black strands of hair falling in her pale face. She didn't bother brushing them away, instead twisting to her left and lifting up a steaming bowl of...something. "Drink this. It will help you gain your strength back."

Obediently I took the proffered bowl and raised it to my lips. My mistake was to take a whiff before I tasted it. The smell was terrible; like rotten fish or garbage that's been sitting in the sun for days. I gagged, bile burning my throat as I dropped the bowl, spilling its hot contents all down my front. I gasped, wheezed and clamped my mouth shut to stop from vomiting.

Was this Jenen lady *trying* to kill me?

Ignoring the pain from being scalded, I twisted to my side, just in case I heaved up the roiling acids in my stomach. Finally I decided it was a false alarm and let out a moan, sitting up again to deal with the burns forming beneath my clothes. From bad luck to worse. What had I done to deserve this fate?

Jenen stayed silent as I patted my broth-stained t-shirt. It used to be white, but now a huge brown stain splotched it. My red jacket had mysteriously disappeared, unless...I glanced behind me and spotted it where my head had been resting. Case of the missing jacket solved. It had been my pillow.

Turning back to Jenen, I found her considering me, eyes glistening with the eastward sunlight. "The broth tastes very bitter—"

Didn't she mean "rotten"?

"—and it smells unpleasant—"

She seemed to have a knack for choosing all the wrong words. The proper choice here would be "foul".

"—but it would have helped sooth your pain."

Probably because it would kill me and end my pain entirely.

"Look," I said, grabbing my jacket and dabbing at the damp spot on my shirt. I took a moment to move the shawl aside, and Jenen snatched it from my hands before I could blink. "I really do appreciate all your efforts to make me feel better, but I'm pretty sure that broth would've done more damage than the poison in those red...things ever could."

"No wonder you're short," the woman said, shaking the wrinkles from her shawl then fluidly wrapping it around her shoulders with a swift motion of her arms. "The most healthy things are often distasteful to the tongue. No doubt your diet sadly lacks the proper nutrition to help you grow."

I scoffed. "What? Are you saying that sugar has somehow stunted my growth."

Jenen knitted her brows. "Sugar?"

"You know, the sweet white powdery stuff that makes food taste good?"

Jenen's eyes dropped as she considered my words. "Is that what you call it? Here, we call it swensie."

She brought up an interesting point. "Where exactly is *here*, anyway?"

"You have no idea?"

"None," I admitted, not bothering to lie. There are moments (few and far between) when the truth is better. This was one of those times.

"You are on the north-eastern side of Paradise, in the Resej meadow where medicinal herbs grow."

I nearly choked. Paradise? Was she kidding? ...Not that this was real, despite the pain, despite the whacked layout I couldn't possibly imagine on my own. And if by Paradise she didn't mean Heaven, there still hadn't been anything peaceful or serene about my time here; it wasn't well named. Sickness in Paradise wasn't possible.

"You look ill again," she stated, eyes intent.

Point in case.

I shook my head, both to assure her I was fine and to break my thoughts. "I'm fine," I lied smoothly, meeting her metallic gaze.

Again we sat in silence, probably both wondering the same thing: Now what? I was pretty well recovered so long as I took it easy for a while, and we couldn't very well just sit in the meadow and hear the birds twitter. —Actually, we probably co

uld, but I wasn't a fan of that option.

"Now what?" I asked at length.

"Rest," Jenen said simply.

My eyes narrowed. "Again? I just woke up."

"I siphoned the venom from your blood stream—"

How'd she manage to do that?

"—but there are still traces that will only leave with time. Exert yourself too soon and the venom will heat with your blood, causing a relapse."

I gave her a sharp look. "How long is 'with time'?"

"Only time will tell." I could have sworn I caught a mischievous glint in her eyes as she replied. It was gone before I could confirm anything.

Scowling, I returned to my shirt stain, rubbing only for something to do. I doubted even bleach could take this sucker out. What was in the nasty stuff anyway?

"Are you going to rest?" Jenen asked after a while.

What was she, my mother? "Look, lady, not that I don't appreciate what you've done—" I was about to ask her to back off, to let me take care of my own body, thanks, but mid-speech I noticed a drastic shift in her presence. I shrank before what looked like a terrible storm brewing over her head. Her face had darkened, glittering eyes narrowing, and she slowly rose to her feet, towering above my sitting form.

"I. Am. *Not*—" she hissed, enunciating each word carefully.

Mind racing, I tried to understand what I had done to offend her. Whatever it was, I was about to die.

"—A WOMAN!" she — excuse me — *he* screamed.

Have you ever jumped into a river in the dead of winter? Neither have I, but I imagine it can't top the chill that swept through my body and shook me to my feet as her—his words sank in. Panic drove me, and I didn't register that I was running until I'd already broken away from the meadow and plunged into the forest. The deeper I went, the darker it got and I had trouble seeing as I whipped through brambles and ducked under thorny branches. The scent of peppermint and damp earth caught in my nose several times. I tripped more than once, but kept running; adrenaline flooded my body, not allowing me to stop if I wanted to—though I didn't.

After what felt like centuries of endless running, tripping, and running some more, I heard the snap of a twig. Jenen was chasing me. I was going to die.

My mind raced with horrific deaths; most including inch-long claws or two rows of glistening pointed teeth. But how was I supposed to know he was a man? He didn't *look* like a man! He was prettier than my freaking sister, and she hadn't been one of the most popular girls during her high school career for her intelligence.

And, aside from a sickeningly pretty face, how could he expect people to know he was male when he wore a bloody shawl? It was preposterous! What the heck sort of man wears a silver shawl, anyway? Maybe it was some sort of order; like an elite group of girly ninja men with brightly colored shawls.

Right. Get a grip, Key. You sound like a moron.

Another twig snapped, bringing me sharply back to reality. This time the sound didn't come from behind, or ahead, or even from either side. It came from above.

Was he seriously leaping from branch to branch just to kill me over a tiny misunderstanding? He *was* a ninja—what other explanation was there? (Never mind that a ninja was a far-fetched explanation all on its own.) Sweat dripped from my chin. My breath was short. I tripped again, face planting in a puddle.

Another friggin' puddle? Give me a break!

Desperation surged through my body with another adrenaline rush as I heard more rustling coming from behind me. Pulling myself from the murky water, I groped in the tiny puddle for a door knob, something, anything that might get me out of this insane place and away from the man-lady.

I didn't find a door knob. I did, however, find a foot. It had long sharp claws at the end of five toes.

Jenen had caught me. I was going to die.

Heart hammering, I stayed very still. Not because I thought it would help, but because I couldn't seem to get my legs to work. Whether that was from fear or too much strain on my weakened body, I didn't want to know.

"Well, well, well," a gleeful voice hissed in the forest's gloom. "Look what we find here. Tell us," I felt clawed fingers wrap around my shirt collar and I was pulled gracelessly to my feet, "where is Sick Nasty Dog?"

3
Sudden Servitude?

This wasn't Jenen. That, or he was a schizophrenic psycho whose other personality had a speech impediment. Either way, instinct assured me I was a goner. The fingers holding me up by my collar flexed. I cringed.

"Answer us or we kill, yeah?"

Reluctantly I looked up from the ground, which I had been studying with wide eyes, scared stiff. Swallowing, silently chiding myself for being a coward, I met the gaze of my captor. Though it was too dark to make out most of his features—that, or my vision was fading—I could easily see the mismatched eyes, one vibrant gold, the other molten silver. It was Jenen—or did all the people in this make-believe world have eyes like these?

He shook me, then grabbed my chin with his free hand, thumb-claw pressing into my cheek. I felt something warm trickle down my face.

Oh yeah. He asked me a question. Remembering, but at a loss on how to answer, I tried shrugging, but found my body too weary to oblige. "Who?" I finally asked, voice cracking.

"Sick Nasty Dog," Jenen, or whoever, repeated.

Still at a loss, I offered a sheepish grin. "I...don't know who—" Wait. If he was looking for someone—besides me—then this couldn't be Jenen. Which meant, logically, he might be looking for Jenen, which would put Jenen off my trail if she—er, he was still chasing me. Except, what if this guy wanted to kill Jenen? I owed Jenen for helping me, even if he wouldn't repeat the same kindness again (but hadn't he already assured me he wouldn't, even before I insulted him?). And, to save my own hide, wasn't it worth risking Jenen's? This was a dream, after all.

The man holding me up was growing impatient. I felt him shift his weight from one leg to the other, and his grip on my chin tightened marginally. My eyes trailed to his mouth where—my spine popped as I stiffened—pointed teeth glittered in the trickle of daylight that danced before the man's face. He was grinning wickedly.

I was now convinced that I had landed myself in a worse circumstance than I'd been in with Jenen. And, yes, that was apparently possible.

"S-Sick Nasty Dog's by the fire i-in the clearing," I said, allowing myself to stammer for a more convincing effect. I had no way of knowing if Jenen was still at the fire, or if he had chased me into the trees, but if this maniac believed me, maybe he'd let me go and—

"Quiet Sneaky Thing," the man barked, making me jump involuntarily. "Go check fire."

I heard a rustle in the brushes behind me, then silence. So, then, this guy wasn't alone. He had minions. That meant my chance of getting out of this was gone. I slumped my shoulders slightly, thoughts wildly groping for any sort of escape, even as part of me wondered what the point was. This wasn't real.

"Strange Coward Boy sit." He pushed me to the forest floor. Several twigs snapped beneath me as I hit the ground. It smelled like dirt and mold, with that faint scent of peppermint.

—Wait, what did he call me?

I was strange, no question there. And considering I'd run from an effeminate man for my life, I could understand coward. But I wasn't a boy, no way. I had outgrown boyhood before I was a teenager. Opening my mouth to snap a retort at him, I reconsidered as he stepped into a large sliver of light. Shadows from dancing leaves overhead cast patterns on him, but I still got a good look. My breath got lost somewhere between my lungs and my nasal passages.

He wasn't Jenen, but he certainly looked similar; just less...girly. He was probably in his twenties, had the same narrow mismatched eyes, angular face and dark black hair—except this guy's was pulled up into a lopsided ponytail on his left. He was perhaps the same height as Jenen; probably approaching six feet. His outfit was black underneath a tattered red cloak that covered one shoulder and wrapped under the other. His feet were bare (with claws), but for tattered dark-gray wrappings that ended just before his toes. Similar wrappings ran along the uncovered arm, and I guessed the other arm was the same. All this was highly alien, but what caught my breath was his presence.

Despite his tatters, he stood like he owned the world, and I could somehow believe it. He wasn't built like a wrestler, or even a football player. Considering his six-foot-height, he was actually not well built, or it was well hidden beneath his layered apparel. He wasn't scrawny, either, just slim and lithe. The way he stood—shoulders erect, towering above his prisoner (a.k.a. me), pointy grin so self-assured—spoke of a sort of power that had nothing to do with muscle-mass. His mind was his weapon, and it could do more damage than an atom bomb.

I had encountered bullies in my eighteen years who all thought themselves superior, but they couldn't hold a candle to this guy. He knew the difference between intimidation and terrorization.

Suddenly I wasn't feeling so gung-ho about defending my manhood.

For the next few minutes nothing happened; I just sat on the damp earth and focused on coaxing my lungs to work again. During this time I also concluded that my reluctant breath wasn't only caused by fear, but probably by revitalized illness.

At length a form stepped from the shadows to my left; this man was older and looked like he had seen several battles in his lifetime; his pale face had several distinctive scars. He wore similar apparel to that of my captor, minus the red cloak. Black, with strips of cloth wrapped around his arms and legs, up to the knees and elbows. Also wrapped around his limbs were leather cords and several poaches. His hair was black with hints of silver from age. Like both Jenen and my captor, this man had inch-long claws on both hands and feet.

He stepped up to the man towering over me, and leaned in to whisper something quickly in one long pointed ear. My captor's ear twitched and his disturbing grin faltered, then widened. As the warrior stepped back and disappeared in the gloom, the Jenen-look-alike's metallic eyes slowly found me, holding my gaze for several eternal seconds. He snapped his fingers and I was hauled to my feet by two more towering shadows flanking me.

"Sick Nasty Dog not at fire, Strange Coward Boy," the obvious leader of the ninja people said coldly. I shivered, not sure how to respond. For the first time in my life, I didn't think lying would help me, but if not that, what could I say?

"Tell us, Strange Coward Boy, where is Sick Nasty Dog, yeah?" the man said again, his voice affable now. Somehow this change scared me more. Yes, I admit, I was scared. I knew the consequences for being ignorant would not be pretty, but what could I say? Honestly, if Jenen wasn't at the fire, how could I know his location any better than them?

Taking a faltering breath, I decided innocence was the best approach. Which, in this case, was sincere. "I don't know where he is now. I left him at the fire. If he moved how could I possibly know? I've been with you." Perspiration was gathering on my forehead.

The ninja-leader observed me for a moment. "Very well."

I released a sigh of relief. Too early.

"Strange Coward Boy's use has run dry as village well. Kill." He turned away.

Eyes widening as his words sank in, I found my strength and jerked out of the grasp of the two men. "W-wait a minute!"

He turned his head and raised his brow, mildly interested. "Yes, Strange Coward Boy?"

"Why kill me?"

"You heard. Use is dry like empty cloud."

"Yeah, I heard that part," I whispered, biting back a retort about his mix-up in phrases. Now was not a good time for sarcasm.

The leader seemed to appraise me for a moment, then he turned completely and stepped near. "Tell us, Strange Coward Boy, why you run from Sick Nasty Dog?" He leaned close to my face and looked into my eyes.

"Well, I," my cheeks flushed, "I called him a girl."

Silence reigned over the small clearing and then he burst into laughter. It was an almost insane laugh, malicious, yet delighted. I managed a weak smile, unable to find my situation humorous in the slightest.

"Sick Nasty *Girl*, yeah?" He barked laughter once again.

Everyone else in the group seemed as uncomfortable as I felt.

"You amusing, Strange Coward Boy. Too bad you must die." He clapped my back jovially. "Kill."

A clawed hand rested on my right shoulder, another took my left. Heart faltering, I bent forward, hands over my head to try and block the killing blow.

I'm going to die!

"Do not kill him." The voice came from the trees.

The hands that held me disappeared and cold fingers grabbed my throat, digging nails in far enough to draw blood.

"Show yourself, Sick Nasty Dog!" called my captor. "Or we will kill. You know we will."

For the first time in my life I prayed. I mean *really* prayed. Something had to save me. Anything. I needed divine protection from both the ninja order *and* Sick Nasty Dog—er, Jenen. It seemed both parties wanted the privilege of sealing my fate.

Jenen jumped from the trees, landing on his bare feet without a sound, metallic eyes narrowed, glittering like his silver shawl. "Release him, Crenen," he said, stepping forward. Even though there were at least a handful of my captor's minions circling the area where we stood, no one got in Jenen's path.

"Ah, not so easy, Sick Nasty Dog. You have him on one condition, yeah?" the man named Crenen said, sounding gleeful.

I scowled. I did not appreciate being a bargaining tool.

"What is the condition?" Jenen said patiently, his pallid face a mask of calm.

"You know it," Crenen answered simply. "Become leader of Yenen Clan, Sick Nasty Dog."

It took a moment before I realized what he said. When I finally did, I gawked. He was *threatening* Jenen in order to make him a leader?

"I told you before, I will not," Jenen said with a sigh. "Now, release the boy."

I scowled. Boy? Were they blind? So I was short, so what? It hardly made me a boy. (I was starting to suspect that my illness-induced hotheadedness was returning.)

Crenen started to laugh again. Then he stopped abruptly. "No. Strange Coward Boy belong to us, yeah?"

Jenen's mouth twitched upward, probably in amusement at my new nickname. I suddenly wanted to hit him. (My hotheadedness was definitely back.) After kicking down my violent urge, I tried to look up at Crenen's face to read his sincerity. I could barely see him from my awkward position.

I was hardly his. Never mind I was obviously captive. Never mind his clawed hands were wrapped around my throat. Never mind his men surrounded me on every side. Never mind that if he did release me, I'd be at the mercy of Jenen and his wrath. I was still my own property, regardless. It seemed my mind was so set on lying, I even deceived myself.

"He belongs to no one," Jenen replied, echoing my thoughts. I was beginning to think he could read minds.

"We think he does." I could sense Crenen's presence darken somehow. I decided if Jenen was psychic, Crenen was psychotic.

"I don't know why you're doing this, but release him now." Jenen took another step forward; Crenen's nails pressed more sharply against my throat, causing me to inhale sharply. I felt blood trickle down my neck.

"We'll kill. Don't think we won't," Crenen hissed. From the corner of my eye I saw his long, pointed ear twitch, probably in warning.

Jenen sighed and shrugged. “What makes you think I care if you do?”

“Would Sick Nasty Dog demand Strange Coward Boy’s release, unless cared?”

Jenen seemed to think the matter through for a moment. “His survival might be beneficial, but I don’t necessarily need him.”

Beneficial? I nearly screamed out that I was not a tool, not some useful device at their disposal, but Crenen’s claws were too freaking close as it was, and I doubted if he would hesitate to 'kill' if I so much as squeaked.

The ninja-leader growled deeply. “Buying time, yeah? Won’t save Strange Coward Boy.”

I was getting a little antsy. I didn’t want to die.

“All right. Kill him.” Jenen folded his arms, his expression that of mild interest.

Wha—? I wanted to wring his throat.

Crenen watched him for a moment and then he laughed. “Very well, we spare.”

I gawked again. Why in the—?

Jenen raised an eyebrow, half-curious. “Why change your mind?”

“Because servant recently die of Paradisaical Disease. Need new one,” Crenen replied, releasing my throat and flinging me to the ground before him.

I scrambled to my feet and decided to speak my mind (I blame my sudden stupidity on the venom running through my veins). “Now, wait just a freaking second—”

Crenen raised his clawed hand for silence and I faltered until he lowered his hand. “Okay, has been second. Now, Strange Coward Boy, Tall Strong Jerk take you to camp. You make comfort for our re-arrival.”

Another figure—this one taller than the others—stepped from his place among the minions and seized my arm. “Come,” he said in a low whisper, pulling me away from the gathered group. I scowled for the hundredth time, disturbed by this turn of events. How in the world did I end up in this mess? Would I ever wake up? As I was dragged from the small clearing, I heard Crenen demanding in broken English once again that Jenen assume the role of leader of his clan. Then I was beyond hearing range.

It was not too far to Crenen's camp, but the undergrowth and overhanging branches slowed us down quite a bit. I stumbled a few times, but received no help from my warden. The ominously tall figure Crenen had ordered to take me to camp was silent the entirety of our walk, which suited me fine since I doubted if I had anything to say anyway. Instead my thoughts dwelt on the strange circumstances I found myself in as I picked myself up the several times I tripped.

My false hopes that this was just a dream were at last beginning to falter as the sun climbed high into the sky and the trees began to thin. Such detail, such pain, such length. How could it possibly be a dream? Then again, what other logical explanation was there?

My eyes widened as the thought struck me for the very first time. Was I dead? Was it possible that when I slipped into that puddle, some random car slammed into my body and crushed my every bone? Or perhaps I had hit my head so hard it caused some kind of complication to the brain, and I died during surgery. Could this strange, mystical, pain-filled, tree-infested, furry-critter-populated, sharp-toothed wonderland possibly be Hell?

After all, I was a very good liar, and my mother always told me where liars went when they died. Now I had reason to believe her—when it was too late to change.

Was God really this cruel?

—Wait. Jenen had called this place Paradise. What was the definition of Paradise, anyway? Did it have to mean something pleasant? I was pretty sure it did.

While I was swarmed with these dizzying thoughts, I and my silent companion left the trees and entered a new clearing. This one was puddle-free. Instead, it had dozens of rawhide tents pitched in a large circle around the outskirts of the large clearing, along with more tents inside the protective circle. Weaving around the inner tents were wide paths and camp fires. Several black-clad ninja-men tended to the fires or patrolled just outside the circle of tents, carrying an assortment of weapons; some with bows and arrows, others with long spears, still others with nothing more than flexing claws—a formidable weapon all their own

One patrolling ninja-man came toward us wielding a nasty looking spear. Its jagged, twisting tip looked like it wasn't meant to kill quickly. The man holding this ugly specimen was rather ugly himself. Broad, tall and muscular, he bore jagged, twisting scars along his unwrapped arms to match his spearhead. He had a permanent frown plastered to his flat face, and his matted black hair looked like it hadn't been washed in a month. His foul scent confirmed it.

He barely spared me a glance, then turned his orange eyes up to my tall, better-smelling warden. In comparison with Mr. Ugly, my personal guard was very slender, but he still towered over his friend by a good inch or two.

Mr. Ugly spoke. —I was pretty sure. But, I had no idea what he was saying. His voice was deep, harsh, and I cringed with every syllable. He gestured to me as he babbled on, then, thankfully, he stopped.

The one Crenen referred to as Tall Strong Jerk took over their conversation, setting his right hand on my shoulder. He babbled, too, but his voice was soft and low—blessedly harmless. I didn't mind the babbling nearly so much. I did catch snatches of familiar words—or names, rather. Not English, but still recognizable. Obviously Tall Strong Jerk was explaining to his frog-faced companion the details of Crenen and Jenen's confrontation.

Mr. Ugly looked especially grim as Tall Strong Jerk finished his narrative. He shot me a grimace (or was that his normal expression?) and turned to take up position on the encampment's edge once again. Wordlessly Tall Strong Jerk guided us into the camp proper, passing Mr. Ugly and his nasty weapon.

We weaved through camp, smoke heavy in our nostrils from the noonday fires. Clan members glanced up from their respective chores (some sharping deadly-looking weapons, others stirring cauldrons), then returned to their work, eyes alert but indifferent.

"What sort of camp is this?" I asked, doubting I would receive an answer.

"We are at war," came the unexpected reply.

I glanced up at Tall Strong Jerk, but he kept his head straight, eyeing our route. I had been afraid that would be the case. The absence of women and children had been another clue. Though I'd never once walked through an army encampment (have you?) it didn't take experience to tell me this was what it was like. These men, young and old alike, were tired, suspicious and determined. One wrong move and I would die.

We reached the center tent fairly quickly, for which I was grateful. Keeping up with Tall Strong Jerk's lengthy strides was a chore I didn't want to repeat any time soon. The tent was erected before a half-naked tree. Tall Strong Jerk threw the musty flap aside, allowing me a full view of the lavish layout within.

Though lavish isn't the right word, per se.

I had expected to find exotic foods spread out over several tables, with generous lighting revealing every corner. Instead, it was as plain within as the camp was without. A pile of furs lurked in a dark corner near the entrance, and a low table sat in the center of the tent, on which were piled various rolled scrolls of yellowed parchment, a bottle of what looked like red ink and a single quill. An unlit candle was the only potential light source I could spot in the gloom.

Tall Strong Jerk set a callused hand on my back and nudged me inside. I stumbled forward. Glancing down, I noted the dirt floor beneath colorful rugs. How quaint.

The imposing man closed the flap, leaving us in thick darkness. I felt him pass me, then listened to his indiscernible noises until a light flashed before my eyes. Blinking, I watched as he lit the candle. The room brightened considerably.

He moved to the far side of the room and tossed whatever he had in his hand into a bucket I hadn't noticed before. Curious despite myself, I moved toward him and the bucket.

"Come," he directed, stepping away from the bucket before I had a chance to investigate. Reluctantly, I halted and waited for him to pass me. He headed for the pile of furs in the corner; I moved to follow him, grimacing at the idea of trying to drag those things around, weak as I felt.

Tall Strong Jerk lifted one fur easily, then nodded at the second. Sighing, I bent down and tried to lift it. It was even heavier than I'd expected. It had to weigh a good fifty pounds at least. Discarding the idea of lifting it, I resorted to dragging the dratted thing to where Tall Strong Jerk indicated—near the table, not far from the mysterious bucket (which didn't carry a foul scent, so I was fairly certain it wasn't a chamber pot or its crude equivalent). Tall Strong Jerk left his fur in a pile next to mine and ordered me (in five words or less) to make Crenen's bed.

Smoothing the furs out proved to be difficult, but I tried my hardest because I really didn't want to feel claws rip open my flesh. If I truly was dead, it meant I wouldn't die, but my mother had also informed me that in Hell the pain is eternal.

When I finally managed to untangle the various layers of Crenen's furry bedding (why couldn't the stupid man use a hammock instead?) Tall Strong Jerk returned (I hadn't noticed that he had even left) and made me cut several gooey, sticky, smelly fruits that slightly resembled mangoes into a bowl and mix it with a strange nasty-smelling liquid. (I thought it was fruit.) I was told to dish the fruit into two smaller bowls. (I hoped it was fruit.) Then I was told to eat the fruit from one of the smaller bowls. (I prayed it was fruit.)

One thing was certain. It didn't taste like fruit.

I sat feeling slightly ill in a dark corner of Crenen's quarters, on my own one-layer rawhide bed, by the time Crenen arrived that evening. He threw aside the door flap, stomped into the tent and flung himself onto his rawhide bed, his demonic grin replaced with a pouty lip. After several moments of huffiness and angry mumbling in his native tongue, he glanced at me through his long bangs and his grin slowly crept across his pale face.

"You make decent bed, Strange Coward Boy," he said after a moment. "Even though small and we thought furs suffocate when you try."

The furs would what now? "Pardon?"

"Pardon?" Crenen repeated. "Pardon what?"

"Er, what did you say?" I asked, hoping I wasn't going to die for not understanding him.

"Oh, you so small, thought you would die under heavy furs," Crenen said casually.

I scowled. "I may be small, but I'm not weak."

"Could have fooled," Crenen replied, unfazed. He turned his attention to the door. "Tall Strong Jerk. Come!"

In entered the strong silent guy, and he bowed his head to Crenen. I was struck again by his considerable height; he was at left six-foot-four. His hair was the same black as everyone else's, short, except for two long pieces looping around his ears. His bangs were longish, hanging slightly in his eyes. I stiffened. His irises were blood-red, glimmering eerily in the torchlight. He seemed in complete control of himself, utterly emotionless.

"We hungry," Crenen announced, and Tall Strong Jerk produced the second of the bowls of foul fruit I had prepared.

Crenen took the bowl and sniffed. Then he wrinkled his nose and tossed the bowl onto the dirt floor. "This not fit for even Small Red Fuzzy."

At least I wasn't the only one who thought so.

Tall Strong Jerk gazed unfazed at the fallen bowl as he spoke. "Master, the Small Red Fuzzy must be addressed as furapintairow, for it is sacred."

"Small Red Fuzzy not fitting of being sacred. *We* bite too, yeah?" Crenen ran his tongue along his pointed teeth. I was impressed that he didn't cut himself in the process.

"Master, you do not have *venomous* fangs," Tall Strong Jerk reminded quietly.

"Don't need poison to get point across, yeah?" Crenen scoffed, folding his arms and looking very affronted that his servant dared to believe differently.

"Of course." Tall Strong Jerk inclined his head again.

"In any case," Crenen looked at me once more, "Sick Nasty Dog refuse leadership, but still demanding Strange Coward Boy's return. Sick Nasty Dog stupid, yeah?"

Who was stupid? Didn't it stand to reason that if this Crenen guy gave up his right to lead these people, he wouldn't be able to order them around like he was obviously used to doing? Why give up his privileges? Was it merely a game to him? If so, it was the most retarded game I'd ever heard of.

"Yes, Master," Tall Strong Jerk politely agreed, bowing his head again. I figured it might be easier on the guy if he just got down on all fours and stayed there to grovel at Crenen's feet.

"Stop, Tall Strong Jerk," Crenen growled suddenly. "Bowing stupid."

"Yes, Master." Tall Strong Jerk hesitated, unsure how else to react, since his normal reaction was suddenly the issue.

Crenen rolled his eyes and scooped the gooey fruit off the ground, reached up and smeared it on Tall Strong Jerk's face. I gawked (something I seemed to be making a habit of).

"What we say, we say, yeah? No bowing, Tall Strong *Stupid* Jerk."

Tall Strong Jerk did well to hide his irritation. I only saw his clawed hands twitch for a moment, and then there was no sign of resistance. "Of course, Master." He did not bow.

"Now, Strange Coward Boy need decent nourishment. Come to think, *we* need decent nourishment." Crenen clapped Tall Strong Jerk on the back. "Get decent nourishment before Strange Coward Boy show signs of dying. Weak already, after all."

I decided in that moment I despised him, not that the feeling would help me in the least.

4
Menial Chores?

It was true I felt weak. It hadn't been that long since the furapin-whatever had bitten me , and before I could make a full recovery, I was chased through thorny woods by half-crazed ninja people. Suffice it to say, I was still feeling feverish. The adrenaline rush was long gone now, and I was determined to spend what little strength was left in my arms on picking up my crude spoon and devouring my food.

Tall Strong Jerk had brought each of us a sort of broth, along with a piece of stale bread and a flask of water. Crenen grumbled about this meal even as he ate it. When Tall Strong Jerk left us to dine alone, Crenen addressed me.

"Strange Coward Boy sick, yeah?

"I'm fine," I lied smoothly.

Crenen watched me with one raised brow and then shook his head. "Bandaged fingers not lie." He put his bowl to his lips and drained its contents.

I glanced down at my right hand where Jenen had carefully doctored my bite mark, and sighed. “It’s just a cut. That doesn’t make me sick.”

“Excellent.” Crenen tossed the empty bowl aside and stood as we heard a significant crash. “Come. We show what morning duties are belong to you.” He beckoned me with his hand. “Come, come. Sleep comes to you who lays down after long hard day and closes eyes.”

I decided not to speak.

I followed him outside and through the encampment, enjoying the night air. No one was around and, though each tent glowed dully from within, everything was silent. He took me just beyond the camp, past the sentries (I didn't spot Mr. Ugly), to a small spring that gurgled happily in the moonlight. I glanced around for some sign of sharp teeth, maybe in the form of river rocks, since everything else that was happy around here seemed to share that trait.

“Strange Coward Boy bring fresh water in Dead Animal Bag.” He raised his tan-colored flask. “We like water cold, yeah?”

“Yeah,” I acknowledged grumpily.

“Excellent.” He grinned, flashing pearly fangs in the full moon whose light made the spring glisten.

“So, tell,” Crenen said as he scouted around the spring’s edge. At last he found a big rock and plopped down on it. “How Strange Coward Boy know Sick Nasty Dog?”

“I just sorta met him,” I answered, unsure how to explain everything and feeling slightly annoyed that I was stuck explaining my predicament when all I wanted to do at the moment was sleep.

“Bad luck,” Crenen said with a heavy sigh.

It was my turn to raise my brow. “How?”

He seemed to contemplate for a moment and then shrugged. "Sick Nasty Dog is stupid. Bad luck meet him like accident."

I struggled to understand his meaning. "*On* accident?"

"Yeah." Crenen nodded absently, his eyes gazing up at the yellow moon. I followed his gaze only to discover there were two moons. "Strange Coward Boy believe in balance?"

I kept staring at the moons. "I suppose so."

Crenen went on. "Day, night. Sun, moons. Black, white. Good, bad. Boy, girl. Predator, prey. Love, hate. Nature, yeah?" He counted on seven fingers as he spoke, then held them up for me to see. "Nature is law; govern us whether we like or not, yeah?"

I nodded wordlessly, trying to figure out where he was headed with this. I grimaced slightly as I knelt in the squishy mud beside Crenen's rock, too tired to stand anymore.

"Excellent. Strange Coward Boy not too stupid."

Considering the source, I decided to take that as a compliment.

"Why Strange Coward Boy here?" he asked, glancing at me before turning to gaze at the moons again, metallic eyes glowing in their light.

"I don't know," I replied, feeling no desire to lie at the moment. I was just too exhausted. I listened to the wind rustle the leaves nearby. After a moment I decided I had better ask the question weighing heaviest on my mind. "Uh," I began rather stupidly, "am I dead?"

He blinked. "Is Strange Coward Boy ghost?" He leaned over to where I knelt and poked my arm with his claw. "Feel whole enough, yeah? We not kill you, so why be dead?"

"I'm not from here," I managed, wondering if everyone else was unaware of the fact that they might be dead. "I slipped and landed in a puddle, and then—"

"Puddle?" Crenen straightened abruptly, eyes intent, pointed grin gone. "You come by Small Wet Puddle?"

I nodded slowly, surprised by his sudden interest. "Yeah, I slipped and fell into a puddle, and then I was here."

"No wonder!" he exclaimed, springing lightly to his feet, easily managing to stay on the rock. "Sick Nasty *Stupid* Dog cannot have Strange Coward Boy ever, now. He knew, and yet…" Crenen started to pace, mumbling under his breath again in his native tongue, looking very angry.

What in the heck was going? I decided I'd better ask out loud, whether he was in a bad mood or not. "What in the heck is going on?"

Crenen stopped and leaned close to my face, balancing precariously on his rock. "What this 'heck' Strange Coward Boy speak of?"

"Uh..." I smiled blandly. How does one explain slang to a person who can't even speak properly? "Never mind."

"Strange Coward Boy come from Heck, yeah?" He seemed certain that was what I meant.

Well, if I came from Heck, I had certainly landed myself in the real Hell now.

"So, what does a puddle have to do with anything?" I asked again.

"You come from Small Wet Puddle, enter here, and speak Stupid Nonsense Language. All bad signs."

"Oookay. How is that bad?" Aside from my own dilemma, which he seemed to care little about.

"Vendaeva," he replied, pacing once more.

"Ven-what now?" The word was familiar.

"Vendaeva, Vendaeva!"

It didn't help, but I decided not to press the issue. "So, what does this puddle mean?"

Crenen looked at me in such a degrading manner that I felt like an insignificant worm.

"Simple, Strange Coward Boy from land of Heck," he finally said. My name kept getting worse. "Vendaeva say of traveling through Small Wet Puddle bring great big change in Paradise, yeah?"

"Paradise."

"Paradise *here,* dolt," he said, mistaking my tone for an inquiry, his expression more degrading that before. "Anyway, Small Wet Puddle is transport from other place—like Heck, yeah?" he finished.

"Just how does that work?" I asked skeptically.

"Don't ask pointless question, Strange Coward *Dolt.*" He nimbly stuck out his foot and kicked my forehead just hard enough that it hurt.

I prayed "dolt" wouldn't stick, ignoring the new pain in my head, but it seemed only more insistent the more I tried to think less of it.

"Now," Crenen stood, "you look like Sick Dying Person. Up. We go back."

I wondered if Sick Dying Person was real, or just another of his nonsensical comparisons. Standing, I felt dizziness overtaking me, and I fell back down, landing in the mud, unable to gather the strength even to catch myself. Before I could attempt to stand again my eyesight dimmed and I lost consciousness without the chance to fight it off at all.

"Stupid Strange Sick Coward Dolt Boy from Heck!" was the first thing I heard when I woke up. Quite the greeting. I moaned softly, trying to ignore the splitting headache that seemed to find my head the perfect home. Crenen was kneeling before my furry bed, looking down his nose at me.

"Had to carry back to camp and find out Stupid Strange Sick Coward Dolt Boy from Heck really is sick. Liar," he spat contemptuously.

"I never lied," I lied.

"Did so," he answered. He whipped away the cloth I hadn't known was sticking to my forehead and flung it into a bowl of water, sending droplets into the air. Several landed on my face. "Bandaged hand mean nothing? 'Only scratch,' say Stupid Strange Sick Coward *Lying* Dolt Boy from Heck."

Oh boy.

"You never said you were dumb enough to get bitten by a crazed furapintairow. Lucky thing you're not dead, though that may have been easier to deal with in the long run," he grumbled under his breath. Something seemed different about him as he spoke.

I mulled over everything he had said and gawked. (Stupid habit.) While his accent was still there, it was considerably less noticeable, and his English was nearly as good as my own. Perhaps it was a fluke?

He slapped the cloth back on my forehead none too gently and water trickled into my gray eyes. I decided in order that I not be harmed I should try an unusual tactic. "I'm sorry."

"Come from Small Wet Puddle and bring bad fortune, yet expect we forgiving you? Useful as dead dog, yeah?"

I refrained from pointing out that if I really was dead, and this really was Hell, a dead dog might actually be of some use. Instead I quietly wondered why my arrival was such bad fortune—aside from that Ven-whatever thing. Knowing I wouldn't get a straight answer, I held my tongue for the moment.

Now, it seemed, Crenen was speaking as before. That was one question I was determined to ask. "So, how come everyone speaks English really well but you?" The instant I finished my sentence I realized I had made a mistake. Crenen's gold and silver eyes flashed with such anger I felt my breath retreat and I knew I was going to die (if that wasn't already the case). What for? I couldn't say. Perhaps he was sensitive about his accent. Or—

Before I could think further, he dumped the entire bowl of water over my head. I gasped. Icy water seeped down my neck and ran along my torso, forcing another gasp from my lungs.

When I turned my head to give Crenen my own withering glare, I was just in time to see him stomp through the door flap, leaving me alone in his rawhide tent. I forced myself to sit up, shivering as the water ran further down.

"What the *freak* did I do?"

"Crenen doesn't like English," a familiar voice said from the shadows of the tent.

Jenen.

I watched him emerge from the darkness, his metallic eyes flickering in the light from the torch. A torch? I studied the hole in the top of the tent I hadn't noticed before, which allowed the torch's smoke to escape without much difficulty. The torch itself was held up on a slender wooden stick jutting from the ground.

—Back to Jenen.

He moved closer to the bed and handed me a small cup. I glanced at its contents. It appeared to be water. He could have killed me by now, if he'd wanted to, so I doubted the water was poisoned. Or was I being too optimistic?

"So," I asked tentatively, looking back at the newcomer, "why doesn't he like English?"

"It's only a second language to We of Paradise," he said quietly, "but we've all taken to it for the coming of Vendaeva—all except Crenen. He's...very stubborn."

"What is Vendaeva?" I put the cup to my lips for a sip. It didn't smell at all and it tasted like water, but I was pretty sure most liquid poisons were scentless and tasteless.

"Well, in one sense Vendaeva is prophecy. In the other sense, Vendaeva is you."

I swallowed the water wrong and began to cough. *Me*? What was he talking about?

"It was required—in order to read the prophecy we needed to learn the language of English, and in that prophecy, it said we needed to know the language of English in order to communicate with Vendaeva—the coming of One from the Puddle."

My eyes narrowed skeptically. This was sounding more and more like something from a typical fantasy game.

"Of course, the coming of One from the Puddle," —couldn't the name be at least a little bit cool?— "spells possible doom for We of Paradise. There are some who desire to kill you —furapintairow included. I'm not sure how Crenen feels of your arrival—he refused to learn English, so it is possible he will have you executed." He paused, allowing the idea to sink in. "But not yet. He believes he needs you to convince me..." He trailed off, turning his mismatched eyes to the flickering torch.

I raised my eyebrow, too curious to resist asking. "Yeah, about that. Why does he want you to take over leadership of these clan people, or whatever?"

Jenen frowned and turned his mismatched gaze to the torch's dancing flames. "These 'clan people' have a name, you know. They are of Yenen Clan."

I was beginning (yes, just now) to wonder what the significance was between Crenen, Jenen, and now this Yenen thing. All three names were way too alike to be mere coincidence, that much was *obvious*. What was it that tied them together? I was well aware that Crenen and Jenen resembled each other in a remarkable way, but Tall Strong Jerk also looked similar upon reflection, and I had seen no other Yenen clan members closely enough to know if that was the general appearance of their people or not (except Mr. Ugly, who was probably adopted, and originated from a clan of frog people).

"So, are you part of Yenen Clan, too?" I ventured, trying to sound casual.

"No." His tone was sharp, clearly telling me to back off.

I did as suggested, casting about for a topic change. "Um, so, I'm supposedly this Vendaeva thing that's got everyone concerned—what's Vendaeva mean, anyway? I mean, do I have some kind of significant role to play in the lives of, uh, You of Paradise? Do I have some bad guy I need to slay, or some terrible curse to prevent?"

"You have good instincts."

Yup. Definitely something from an archetypal fantasy game.

"So, what's my mission?" I decided if it remained true to the usual rules, once my task was complete, back home I went. Unless I woke up first. (Call it optimism, but I preferred a long-drawn-out-dream to being permanently-dead.)

"It's not so simple as that," he replied. "And I'm not the one to tell you..."

A predictable response. It just couldn't be easy, could it?

Jenen seemed ready to say more, but he turned his head toward the tent flap, one pointed ear perking up. He glanced at me, put a finger to his lips, and stepped into the shadows. Just as he vanished Tall Strong Jerk entered the tent and rested his red eyes on me.

"Come." He motioned toward the open flap. "I'll show you your morning tasks."

I thought about reminding him that I was still not feeling well, but his stature alone made me hesitate. I concluded the healthy choice was to keep my mouth shut. I got out from under my furs and followed him silently from the tent.

For only the second time since landing myself in this place called Paradise, I was bathed in sunlight (at least, when I was conscious enough to appreciate it). Never before had I been so happy to see the sun. I breathed in the fresh morning air as I felt the light rejuvenate me.

"Feeling better?" Tall Strong Jerk asked.

I looked up at him and nodded, unable to suppress my wide smile. "Much."

"Master Crenen thought you might."

I watched him thoughtfully, wondering if perhaps I could get a few answers from him. I was hesitant because of his height, but what if he could supply me with all I needed to know? That way I wouldn't bother Crenen and get another bowl of water dumped on my head, and it seemed that Jenen wasn't willing to give much away.

It was worth a shot. I opened my mouth to ask my first question when Tall Strong Jerk began walking. "Let's go," he commanded. I had to run to catch up.

We wound our way through camp, and I took the chance to get a closer look at Yenen Clan. The first thing I noticed was that every clan member had black hair done up in varying, strange styles. I also noted that most wore black, with some loose, colored garb wrapped around them. Today they continued with their chores; some of them stitched up rawhide; others polished daggers; yet others still bent over cauldrons of boiling water, occasionally dropping dirty clothing into it and stirring with long metal paddles.

My tall guide took me to the stream, handed me a "Dead Animal Bag" and silently watched as I filled the flask to the brim while wondering how clean this water really was. I capped it, and made to hand it over, but he shook his head and gestured for me to follow him. Biting my tongue to keep from grumbling, I trailed after him back into camp.

Again we circled the the tents until we arrived at a huge bonfire. I thought it ridiculous that they were burning so much wood in the heat of day, but then, they appeared to have plenty of forest to spare.

On the other side of the bonfire Crenen was sitting in the shade of a rawhide awning, his expression bored as one clan member fanned him with a giant red-tipped leaf. Yikes.

Crenen's cheek was propped against his hand and he looked ready to sulk. As I neared him, he caught sight of me and immediately perked up. I felt panic threaten to take over, but I forced my legs to move forward. Rapt attention from an evil maniac was bad, instinct made certain to assure me. Too bad instinct couldn't help me escape.

"What Strange Coward Boy got?"

Tall Strong Jerk bowed his head, apparently not recalling the chastisement he had received the previous evening for such an action. "He brings fresh stream water, Master."

As opposed to...?

"Excellent," Crenen said cheerily. "Our favorite." He beckoned me into the shade with a clawed finger and pointed at the ground. "Sit." I promptly knelt, grateful for the shade. I handed the flask to Crenen and he shook it close to his ear. "Very fresh," he said contentedly, and I decided that was as close to a 'thank you' as I would get.

He undid the cap and drank deeply, his eyes closed, his features relaxed. Finally he took a breath and glanced at me. He blinked in surprise and cocked his head to the side. "What you still here for?"

"Uhm." I glanced at Tall Strong Jerk, who waved me over with a quick motion of his hand. I got to my aching feet and stumbled back to his side.

"Be off," Crenen ordered. He returned to his drink of water.

I scowled as we walked away from the Yenen clan leader. "At war?" I mumbled under my breath, recalling Tall Strong Jerk's comment the day before. "He looked like the definition of 'at peace' to me..."

Tall Strong Jerk looked down in my direction. "We are at war, but we choose not to panic about it."

Blinking, I grinned sheepishly. "You heard that, huh?"

He tapped his ear with one clawed finger. "How could I not?"

"Right..." I made a mental note not to talk to myself out loud anymore. After a moment I spoke again. "So, what other 'tasks' do I have?"

"You will do Master Crenen's laundry," he answered simply.

I froze on the spot, staring after Tall Strong Jerk in horror. "L-laundry?"

He stopped and looked back at me. "Is *laundry* the wrong word to describe the washing of clothes?"

I laughed forcefully. "Nope, that's right..." Never before had I been forced to do laundry, and that was with a washing machine option. Washing laundry by hand or in one of those cauldrons was ludicrous.

"I thought so," Tall Strong Jerk said with a fleeting smile.

"Tell me you're joking."

He shook his head. "Come. I'll take you to your cauldron."

I moaned softly, not caring who heard. There was no way I could even pretend to be happy about doing that creep's laundry.

Not only was the water scalding hot and the steam thick enough to catch your breath, but the paddle was *not* made out of metal, as I had first thought. It was made with a heavy wood that was awkward to handle. Each time I turned the ragged clothes inside the boiling pot, another sliver worked its way into my skin. By the time I sat down in Crenen's tent for dinner, my hands were heavily bandaged. Tall Strong Jerk had been kind enough to remove all the slivers in a painful matter of minutes and then tightly wrap my hands and fingers with a rough white cloth. Lunch was not easy to eat, as I was having difficulty lifting my spoon. I finally resorted to sipping from the bowl's lip.

The meal was far from grand: a rather bitter soup, a clay cup of freshly squeezed juice (which tasted good, thankfully, despite the little floaties that resembled tiny bugs), and a day-old crust of flat bread. Crenen had nothing good to say about the food, which was fine, since he noisily voiced my thoughts on the subject for me.

As as I gulped down the last of my soup and shuddered at the taste, Crenen shoved his dishes into my hands. "Wash," he instructed. "Then nap."

I wasn't sure how I could wash the dishes with bandaged hands, but I was willing to attempt it for the sake of sleep. Considering I had nearly died recently, I wasn't getting anywhere near the pampering and rest I deserved.

With a quiet sigh, I got to my feet, precariously balancing Crenen's and Tall Strong Jerk's dishes, as well as my own, as I walked from the tent into a wind storm. Fighting the forceful torrent, I dumped the bowls and cups into a small simmering cauldron and stared at them as they soaked. Then I plunged my hands into the hot water, ignoring the pain as it seeped into my bandages. I figured I'd need re-bandaging anyway, so I used the wraps to scrub the dishes clean. Glancing around, I noticed that everyone else had stacked their own dishes beside their cauldron and extinguished their fire. I followed suit, dumping the water into the fire and swallowing smoke.

Still choking, I entered the tent again, grateful to be out of the wind. Crenen and Tall Strong Jerk looked up from a piece of paper they had been studying.

"Done?" Crenen asked.

I nodded.

"Excellent." He pointed to my bed. "Sleep."

I nodded again, turned toward the furry blankets and collapsed upon them, not bothering to climb inside. As I drifted into a weary rest I caught snatches of Crenen going over some sort of battle strategy.

I woke to the pungent aroma of wet dog. Moaning, I turned from the smell and buried my face into my bedding—only to get a better whiff. I jerked my head back and blinked the blankets into view.

Fur.

I moaned again, sitting up despite my stiff shoulders, and gazed around the dingy tent. Was it really real? Would it never end?

A drop of water splashed in my hair and I looked up to see a tear in the tent's top. Another drop fell on the blanket near my feet. Wet dog mystery, solved.

The tent flap opened, bringing with it dismal light and a very tall silhouette. "Good morning," Tall Strong Jerk said stoically. "Ready to work?"

I grimaced. "No." Still, I shoved my heavy furs aside and got to my unsteady feet. Had I slept the rest of the previous day clear through? I was surprised Crenen had let me get away with it.

"You still look pale," the tall man observed.

"I'm fine," I said, running a hand through my tangled hair and wishing for a comb.

"Excellent. You'll start by repairing the tent. It leaked last night."

"Yeah," I muttered, "I noticed."

I followed Tall Strong Jerk from the tent and my mood worsened. Rain pounded down from a gray sky, bringing out the vibrancy of the green forest around Crenen's encampment. Clan members milled around, ignoring the rain, barely registering each other as they splashed through the puddles, going about their business. Luckily the windstorm had mostly died out, even if the rain poured relentlessly.

"Here is what you need," Tall Strong Jerk said, motioning to a pile of sopping rawhide.

I stared at the heavy pile, waiting for the punchline to this highly elaborate joke. When I finally looked up into the man's face, he wasn't laughing—or even slightly amused (from what I could tell). I looked back down. "Don't I need needles or something?"

"Not unless you want to take the whole tent down to repair it," he answered.

I turned to look up at the tent. "Okay. So, how do I get up there to put this on?"

"Climb the tree. I'll be back later." He walked away and disappeared among the tents. I watched the spot I had last seen him for a long while, hoping he'd pop back up and offer to help. The rain still pounded mercilessly. Finally I focused on the rawhide, sitting like an island surrounded by muddy water.

"It won't fix itself," a soft voice observed.

I spun, kicking up mud, and faced Jenen. He stood calmly, also ignoring the rain, though it caused his hair to cling to his face. His mismatched eyes watched me mildly, hands clutching his ridiculous silver shawl.

"You seem at a loss for words," he said. "Again."

I scowled. "I know it won't fix itself. I just don't know how to get that," I pointed to the rawhide pile, "*and* me," I jabbed my thumb at myself, "both into the tree." I shot the offending tree a glare.

Jenen's eyes shifted from me, to the pile, and then up to the large naked branch hovering conveniently over the leaky tent-top. "That does seem problematic."

I waited for his offer to help, but he remained silent.

"Yeah," I snapped, "it is." I grabbed the heavy pile and lifted it, only slightly pleased than I could handle its weight better than last time. Struggling to keep a grip, I stumbled to the tree trunk.

"The leak was caused by the branch," Jenen said. "The wind brushed it against the rawhide through the night."

"That's a freaking strong wind," I muttered, gritting my teeth as I tried to raise the rawhide up into the tree.

"That won't work," he said.

I rolled my eyes. "Of course it won't. I can't do this by myself," I growled. "Nobody could." Except maybe Tall Strong Jerk.

"What will you do about it?"

Anger flared inside me and I chucked the rawhide into the mud. "I don't know! Everyone else seems so busy."

Jenen arched one slender eyebrow. "Are you blind, too?"

I stared at him, dumbfounded, rain thundering against my head and running down my freezing face. Was he offering? My eyes narrowed. No. He was waiting for me to ask him for help. But that wasn't going to happen. I would do this alone, if it killed me (figuratively speaking).

I bent down and heaved the rawhide into my arms, gathered my strength and threw the mass onto the nearest branch. Then I pulled myself up. I repeated the process—somehow keeping my balance—until I managed to reach the branch extending over the tent. Carefully I crept forward, then reached back and dragged the rawhide after me, trying to ignore the trembling limb I sat on.

Jenen watched from below, water running down his face, his body perfectly still as mud swirled around his bare feet.

The tricky part was getting the rawhide from behind me to in front of me, but after a few close calls, I finally managed it. From there I tossed the rawhide over the shuddering tent-top, covering the tears beneath the branch.

Smirking triumphantly, I looked down at Jenen's indifferent gaze.

"Now get down," he said.

I smothered a scowl and pondered my awkward situation. Should I shimmy backward toward the trunk, or should I somehow flip around and crawl? My dilemma was answered by a loud crack. Before I could react, the branch beneath me gave way and I, branch, and tent came tumbling down. I might have been short for my age, and built like a stick, but I still weighed more than any tent could handle, when crashing down on it.

Jenen rescued me from the smothering rawhide which had somehow gotten on top of me. As I was freed, sputtering, he only gave me a mildly smug expression (which I loathed). I turned to face the mess of muddy tent heaped before me, broken wooden poles jutting up amidst the rawhide.

"Impressive work," Jenen commented.

I gritted my teeth, barely keeping my temper in check. I had bigger issues to worry about: Crenen had chosen that precise moment to round another tent, and he halted abruptly when he spotted the fallen carnage.

I had two seconds to decide whether to hit the mud or shoot for the trees. Unfortunately I wasted those two seconds, frozen in place by thoughts of what Crenen would do when he found out how his tent had been destroyed.

It might not have been a big deal, except that the poles had obviously torn through the tent in several places. Without a lot of mending it would prove useless.

Crenen came to the same conclusion.

"What happening here?" he demanded, hurrying toward us, his eyes narrow slits as he stared me down.

I glanced toward Jenen for help, only to see empty space where he had stood two seconds before. That jerk had abandoned me. Reluctantly I looked back at the expectant Crenen and shrugged.

"It fell," I stated simply. "I turned away for a second, then heard a ripping sound, and—well, it looked like this."

His eyebrow arched. "That so, yeah?"

I nodded, meeting his mismatched eyes.

Tall Strong Jerk came up behind Crenen and stood silently, taking in the ruin.

Crenen stepped closer and raised one clawed finger, running it through my hair too quickly for me to react. He lowered his hand to my eyes so that I could see the tree sap oozing down his slender finger.

"Sticky Smelly Sap not lie like Strange Coward Boy," he said, his face carefully controlled.

I watched the sap drip to the ground, mingling with water and mud. Finally I met Crenen's eyes again. He was deadly calm. I almost wished that he would jump into a rage, but he only watched me.

I refused to budge either.

The rain kept pounding against us, little floods swirling around our ankles, leaking into the hole-filled tent. My shoes were sopping.

"Strange Coward Boy lie again to us, we kill," Crenen finally said, his eyes betraying nothing but terrifying sincerity. "Yeah?"

I found myself nodding more fervently than I liked.

"Tall Strong Jerk."

The towering man stepped forward, watching me with the same unreadable gaze.

"Show Strange Coward Boy how repairing tent is done."

"Yes, Master," the man said, inclining his head.

Crenen still held my gaze. "Strange Coward Boy learn to take responsibility, or wake up dead someday, yeah?"

I bit down my anger, trying to feel humble. It was an effort (especially with all the retorts going through my mind).

Without another word, Crenen spun around, kicking up mud (which splattered both Tall Strong Jerk and me), and he trudged away, tattered wraps dragging through murky pools behind him. I rubbed mud from my nose and glanced up at the tall man's now-disapproving face. I tried a grin, but was certain it came out as a grimace.

"If I leave for a moment to gather supplies, can you keep from causing trouble?" he asked quietly.

"Yes," I promised.

He took off through the rain, eventually disappearing in a tent down the way. Finally he returned, carrying several spools of heavy thread and four large needles, several rolls of rawhide hanging over one shoulder. He dropped these on top of the toppled tent and looked down at me.

"Working in the rain is difficult. We'll fish until the weather lets up." He turned again, and I made to follow him, nearly losing my shoes in the mud as I took a step.

"Fish?" I asked, finally catching up and matching his pace.

"Fish."

Having never fished in my life, I was both anxious and excited at the prospect. But I did have to wonder: In this strange, exotic world, what were the fish like?

I should've known.

"I should've known," I muttered as Tall Strong Jerk pulled one speared fish from the creek bed. It flopped wildly, baring its needle-point teeth, almost seeming to grin as it died. The scales were a shimmering orange-yellow; they flashed like firelight even in the rain.

Tall Strong Jerk pulled the fish from the spear after it wriggled its last and tossed the piranha-ish monster into the wet grass. "Never take the fish off of the spear until it has died. Otherwise you'll lose a finger."

I could believe it. "Right," I said aloud.

The other man handed me a second spear. "Rain brings the fish to the surface."

"Is this dinner?" I asked.

"Yes, though you may not get any." He thrust the spear into the rippling water, twisting the haft in his powerful hands.

"Because I lied." I didn't have to ask. Crenen's reaction to my little fib had left no room for doubt.

"Crenen despises liars," he answered, staring pointedly at the spear resting idly in my hands. Finally I sighed and plunged the spear into the creek, stirring the water absently. He could tell I wasn't trying, but he said nothing about it.

"He is disappointed," he continued, withdrawing the spear-tip, another piranha-fish attached. "If you truly are Vendaeva, he expects better of you."

I rolled my eyes. "I don't even know what the heck a Venday-thing is," I said.

"Ven-day-vah," he said slowly. "It is complicated. Suffice it to say, you fit the description, and Crenen cannot understand how you can be so foolish and still save us."

My face reddened. "I'm not foolish."

"Perhaps," Tall Strong Jerk said, his voice neutral. He pulled the fish off the spear and repeated the fishing process again. "You must learn to distinguish between the ripples caused by raindrops and by those of the fish."

The abrupt change in topic gave me a moment's pause and I turned my focus to the water. When I looked carefully I could just make out the lithe forms of fiery fish kissing the water's surface.

"Fyar," Tall Strong Jerk said.

"Huh?"

"It's their name," he answered. "Fyar."

The word almost resembled *fire*—with an accent, emphasis on the 'y'. I watched the fiery fish for a moment, carefully took aim, and stabbed the nearest one. It squirmed, but I held firm until it stopped wriggling. I pulled it from the water and dropped the fish besides the others.

"Good work," Tall Strong Jerk said, a tiny smile touching his pale face.

I found myself beaming until, on stabbing the water again, I startled a fish. It leapt from the water, engulfed in honest-to-goodness flames until it plunged into the depths again and swam away.

I was done fishing.

As the living tower predicted, I wasn't allowed to eat dinner. It hadn't helped when Tall Strong Jerk announced that the tent was beyond repair (no thanks to the water) and we would have to confiscate another. Luckily the occupants of the chosen tent relinquished it wordlessly, moving into another enclosure not far away. Still, Crenen found this change annoying. (It was more to blame for my fast than the lie was.)

As I sat in a dark corner of the new tent, absently picking at the damp fur beneath me, I thought of Jenen. He hadn't come back since the incident with the rawhide patch. I wondered where he slept in this wooded land when it rained. I also wondered, with some bitterness, how anyone that girly could stand to wear a shawl and still expect people to think them male.

After a while I shifted, sitting cross-legged on my covers, and stared at my bandaged hands. Laundry the previous day had given me blisters to compliment the slivers, and the haft of the spear today had added to both, even with the bandages. My palms throbbed dully.

The rain had turned to a drizzle now. Crenen and Tall Strong Jerk were poring over several damp papers rescued from the interred tent, talking in low voices, the torch flickering overhead. Dirtied dishes were shoved off to one side, forgotten.

I wanted to go home.

The thought occurred after what seemed hours of concentrating on absolutely nothing. With it came the images of my parents and siblings. I laid down, buried my face in my pillow, and wondered how any of this was possible.

And how I could make it all go away.

5
Before a Ninja Tribunal?

"Strange Coward Boy sleeping yet?" asked the dreaded voice of Crenen overhead.

My eyes snapped open and I realized with alarm that I had drifted off to sleep without permission. Not like I hadn't earned it, but I doubted he saw things the way I did. Turning from the tent wall, I blinked my drowsiness away and released a weary breath. "I'm awake," I mumbled, as much to convince myself as him.

Crenen leapt to his feet and motioned to Tall Strong Jerk, who approached my bed and grabbed my forearms, pulling me to my feet before I realized what he was doing. Swaying, I finally woke up enough to glower at Crenen and his trusty minion. What time was it anyway?

"Tall Strong Jerk take you to Gurgling Wet Water and make Strange Coward Boy smell decent, yeah?"

Now? This late at night? Or had I slept through to morning again? While I tried hard to get my internal clock to function, I was led by the tall man from the tent, where I got my answer. It was dark outside, the sky was clear, moons shining brightly, with very few ninja people around. Did Crenen want to punish me further for lying to him, so he concocted this cruel and *highly* unusual method? Or was this a primitive ritual and I was about to be sacrificed to save this psychotic world from its untimely end?

Grudgingly I followed after my warden, dreading whatever awaited me after I "smelled decent." We quickly reached the spring where I'd filled Crenen's flask before. Tall Strong Jerk instructed me to strip, and I willingly obeyed; now that I was about to bathe I realized it had been too many days since my last shower back home.

The water was cold, but I hardly noticed as I furiously scrubbed the grime and mud from my skin with a lye soap bar my warden provided. As I rinsed my honey-colored hair I was surprised to discover how much it had grown in a matter of days. Normally it was trimmed to my neckline, and my bangs reached my temples, but now they hung halfway down my face, tickling my cheekbones. I made a mental note to get my hair trimmed as soon as I could—assuming I didn't die tonight in a bloody ritual.

Tall Strong Jerk had taken the time I used bathing to sponge my clothes, making them slightly less dirty. As I'd suspected, the coffee-colored stain on my white t-shirt front stubbornly remained. My pants were in better order, though, for which I was grateful, since the mud had caked on the hems and crusted well up past the knee. He had had to immerse my jacket in the spring to get it clean, as the worst of the mud and sap had accumulated there. I decided, chilly or not, I would not be putting that on tonight.

Redressed, I glanced around for my socks and shoes. I spotted them in Tall Strong Jerk's hands. He was fascinated by my shoes; turning them over and over, lightly tapping the soles with pointed claws, tracing the traction-design.

"Hey," I said. As he looked up from studying my sneakers, his red eyes flashed in the bright moonlight. My heart skipped a beat. "I need those."

"Your feet must be very tender," Tall Strong Jerk said as he handed the shoes over.

I found a fairly dry patch of grass by the stream bank, where I sat to put them on, when I realized my socks were missing. "Where're my—?" I began, but the tall man was way ahead of me, dangling my dripping socks before my eyes.

"Thanks," I said with a humorless smile, far from appreciative that I'd been forced from my warm bed in the dead of night, taken a freezing bath in a stream with who-knew-what sort of alien bacterias, and now I was dressing in sopping clothing, possibly preparing for a pagan ritual where I had no say if I lived or died.

Can you blame me for being a bit upset?

"Are you ready?" Tall Strong Jerk asked as I got to my feet and stomped my shoes a few times to lessen the squishy sensation. I could only wring out so much liquid.

"Yeah," I fibbed, forgetting the lesson Crenen had taught me earlier about the bad things that happened to habitual liars.

Nodding curtly, the towering man turned and led me and my squeaky, sloshing shoes back toward camp. I fixed my gray eyes on my feet, watching the laces drag along through the mud left over from yesterday's storm. I hugged my soaked jacket to my chest.

"So," I tried, managing a smile that dripped with fakeyness, "what exciting wonder has Crenen got in store for me now?"

"You are being properly introduced," my warden replied with all the energy of a robot.

'Properly' boded ill. Feeling cold, tired and dejected, I stumbled after the tall man, noting that the patrol around camp wasn't actually around yet, including Mr. Ugly. Small blessings.

We weaved through the circular groups of tents and I kept my eyes peeled for ninja men. Everything to still and quiet. Peppermint-scented wind wafted passed me, brushing through my hair, making me shiver.

"Why does it smell like peppermint?" I asked as I caught sight of the glow above camp that suggested the bonfire was going full-force. Nothing like a huge fire in the dead of night to lead an enemy right here, but Crenen didn't strike me as the stealthy, fearful time who hides in the dark—unless he's the predator instead of the prey.

Tall Strong Jerk faltered, glancing down at me. "Peppermint?" he said, tasting the word like it was foreign—which it undoubtedly was.

"Uhm, yeah. That minty smell, you know?" I drew a deep breath through my nostrils to demonstrate, hoping he understood 'minty'.

He sniffed the air like an animal, carefully, head tilted upward. At length he looked back down, meeting my eyes. "I smell nothing out of the ordinary."

"Huh. Okay..." Which meant either I was delusional (which I wasn't writing off at this point) or Paradise smelled like this all the time, and he had no idea it was strange.

"Shall we?" he asked, moving again before I could respond. I trudged after him, returning my focus on the squeaking of my sneakers and squashing of my socks.

We rounded the last few tents before the bonfire and I halted, eyes taking in the massive group of men standing silently before their master and demonic overseer, Crenen. As we stepped into the generous light, Crenen turned his metallic eyes to us and his mouth split into the widest, most evil grin I could imagine—only worse. I swear my heart forgot how to pump for a full minute—that or seconds are longer than we think.

"Quiet Sneaky Thing," Crenen said, and a s black-clad man slinked from the darkness, soundlessly approaching my warden and me. When I first met Crenen a few nights back, I'd assumed the older fellow with the graying hair was Quiet Sneaky Thing, but apparently that had been another scout reporting to his master. This guy was in his late twenties, at the most, with the same black hair as everyone else. It was pulled back in a simple ponytail—the tamest hairstyle I'd seen yet. He didn't wear any accenting color either, sticking solely with black apparel. His eyes, though, were bright yellow. He was handsome—not in the feminine way of Jenen, or the imposing way of Tall Strong Jerk. If anything, he reminded me of Chas back home; clear-complected, though much paler.

He was smiling as he stepped before me. Reaching a hand up, he slid a clawed finger through a strand of my hair.

"Hey," I growled, annoyed that he touched me without permission.

He blinked his yellow eyes, sliding his gaze from my hair down to my face. After a moment, he set his hand fully on my head, patted it twice and, turning, spoke to the warriors at large. "Short," he pronounced, raising a smattering of laughter and hooting from the men, who all watched me with mixed curiously and hostility.

Anger jolted through me, and I stepped back, out of his reach. "Very funny," I snarled, shooting a glare first at Quiet Sneaking Thing (who should just stay quiet), then at Crenen, who now wore an unfitting neutral expression.

"Listen, Mighty Servant Men," Crenen said, speaking only loud enough for his voice to carry to the back of the crowd. He didn't scream or shout, but he had the group's immediate attention. "This," he motioned my way, so I assumed he was referring to me, "is great future of Paradise.

Bring with him only short self and heavy bag," he reached down to his other side and lifted my red backpack up to show the warriors.

I stiffened. I had completely forgotten about it. There was nothing valuable inside, just a bunch of textbooks, but I irritated that Crenen had taken my bag without permission.

Crenen went on: "Strange Coward Boy," —the group found my nickname amusing, judging by the muted chuckles and not-so-muted catcalls I received— "come by Small Wet Puddle, and now we being expected to aid Strange Coward Boy to save all. What Mighty Servant Men think? What thinking of this being Vendaeva?"

The crowd grew still, eyes sliding from their master to me, stopping, staring, unreadable. Needless to say, my cheeks turned a little red and I felt sweat trickle down my sides (I blamed the fire for feeling stiflingly hot).

Before the crowd responded, Crenen spoke again. "What say Strange Coward Boy?"

I stiffened, jerking my eyes to meet his, unsure how exactly I should respond. What did he expect? Some heroic speech of self-sacrifice? Some inspiring words about how much I cared about a people I didn't even know, who hadn't done anything for me but share bruises and stale bread?

I finally opted to say nothing, turning my attention to the bonfire, watching stray embers floating on the minty wind, listening to the crackle and pop of the logs being eaten up by the gluttonous flames.

Crenen hopped down from his throne, dragging my backpack through the mud and grass as he approached. Quiet Sneaky Thing bowed and stepped aside, only taking a second to offer me what might have been a supportive grin (or a malicious one—hard to say with sharp teeth flashing). Crenen released the strap on my bag and fixed his gaze on mine. He said nothing, merely keeping eye contact, daring me to hold still and stare back.

Gathering my nerve, determined not to let Crenen have the upper hand, I set my jaw and glared.

We stood like that a long time. My feet began to ache from standing still and, despite the massive fire, the midnight breeze was sending shivers down my spine. My toes were especially numb; I even tried to wriggle them, but couldn't tell if I'd succeeded or not.

It took a while before it finally sank in that Crenen could keep this up a lot longer than I could. That revelation may have actually saved my life—who could say how he might have reacted had I not finally surrendered?

Yes. I surrendered. Lowering my eyes, hating myself for doing it, hating Crenen more for making me.

Crenen seemed very pleased by this and he clapped me on the back, miraculously not scratching me. "Maybe hope for Strange Coward Boy yet," he remarked, grabbing my pack and swinging it over his shoulder. He sauntered back to his throne, sat, and fixed his intense eyes on the silent crowd.

As if he had been waiting for his master's attention, Mr. Ugly stepped from the throng, bowed deeply, and waited for Crenen's hand to wave his blessed consent. When it did, Mr. Ugly straightened and drew a deep, rumbling breath. Releasing it with a great whoosh, he spread his arms out, as if he were about to deliver a sermon.

Please let him not *be about to deliver a sermon.*

The frog man began, speaking in his horrible, croaking voice, once more jabbering words I couldn't understand. He spoke rapidly, throwing dark looks and jabbing fingers toward me at intervals, no doubt professing my demonic heritage and that I had no right to storm here through a puddle and save these people.

Hey. Who was I to argue? Ugly had a point. And if I could leave, I certainly would.

Crenen listened with the patience of a saint (oh, the irony), and when frog-face finished, the leader slid his narrow eyes to me. "Strange Coward Boy be accused of Bad Nasty Stuff. Want to defend self?"

I shrugged. How had I known? "What're the charges?" I asked, taking an unconscious step forward. I didn't want to be here; both Mr. Ugly and I agreed that I should go home. But the fact was, I *was* stuck here, couldn't go home and might as well accept it. For the moment. Because I hated to let the bullying type come out on top.

"You not from Small Wet Puddle," Crenen explained. "Instead, you from Yellow Sandy Place, come here to trick and make false hopes. Seem you too short for being Great Noble Hero, yeah? Although also too short for Yellow Sandy Place, come thinking."

I scowled. "Height has nothing to do with anything."

Crenen's grin returned. (It had never truly left, but I was beginning to tell the difference between his neutral grin and a wickedly delighted one.) He turned back to my accuser. "Hear that, Gross Smelly Man?"

I almost laughed outright at Mr. Ugly's nickname. Okay, I *did* laugh outright.

Gross Smelly Man had been about to respond to Crenen, but when he heard my snort he turned his cold gaze to me, his beady little eyes narrowed. Spitting at the ground, he crossed the muddy clearing, walking very near the hot flames, oblivious to the heat. He snatched me by my shirt collar and lifted me up, my toes only brushing the ground.

He smelled even worse up close and personal.

He shouted at me, still using words I couldn't understand. Nor did I believe I wanted to. Apparently he was sensitive about his Crenen-name. (Who could blame him?

Though I suspected he might have a relatively less offensive reference if he bathed a little more often.)

I sensed his fist before I ever saw it. For a split second I wondered why no one was coming to my rescue, then I remembered they had no reason whatever to help me. Except if I really was this Vendaeva thing, didn't that make me somehow important?

Oh, wait. I hadn't sold them on that yet.

Either way, the fist came charging fast. My eyes closed faster.

His knuckles connected with my cheek and pain filled my vision. My body jerked back, but I didn't fall as I'd anticipated, because Mr. Ugly was still holding my collar. Snapping my eyes open, I looked up and saw that he planned to strike again, same fist, same cheek.

I cringed, one eye squeezed shut even as my other eye watched the fist flying toward me. For one wild millisecond I thought about fighting back, but he was insanely muscular compared to me, and I had the feeling I'd only get him madder if I tried to defend myself.

"Enough," Crenen's voice interjected, and the fist halted, hovering almost comically a mere inch from my face.

Saved by a demon. Who'd have thought?

"Fenik," Tall Strong Jerk said quietly, placing a big hand on the bully's.

Mr. Ugly spat at the ground again, flung me from him and trudged back into the multitude, never glancing at me. That was fine, since I didn't want him to see me land clumsily in the mud. So much for bathing. My warden bent down and hooked one hand under my left arm, helping me stand back up. I allowed him to assist me, too busy rubbing my throbbing cheek to care. It would be a nice bright purple color come morning.

"Strange Coward Boy attract Bad Troubling Things like mud sticking to pants, yeah?" Crenen commented, his pointed smile as lopsided as his ponytail.

"Are you all right?" Tall Strong Jerk asked, gently turning me toward him for a better view of my cheek in the firelight. He touched the bruise. "It will hurt for a while."

How kind of him to show concern *after* the fact. "Yeah, it will," I muttered, looking down and brushing the mud off my pants, only managing to smear it more.

"Are you really Vendaeva?" a thickly accented voice inquired, reminding me of Quiet Sneaky Thing's presence behind me.

To cover my instinctive jump, I quickly turned around to face him, scowling. "I don't know. Maybe."

"Maybe?" he repeated, and I wondered if he knew what the word meant, or if he thought I was stupid for not being certain *what* I was.

"Yeah, maybe." Let him wonder away. I was so tired, my vision was beginning to blur in and out, and my cheek felt like I'd leaned into the fire. Turning back to Crenen, I asked, "Can I go back to bed now?"

He regarded me silently, and I shifted between my feet, trying to stay standing.

"Strange Coward Boy have pleasant sleeping, yeah?"

"Yeah," I said, taking that as a dismissal. Tall Strong Jerk seemed to agree, and he fell into pace beside me as I left Crenen and his minions behind. "*Right,*" I added, mumbling under my breath. How could I have a pleasant sleep under these conditions?

I barely remember reaching the tent and collapsing on my bed. I do remember wondering why I was so tired—aside from recent traumatic experiences (e.g. venomous bites, feminine shawl-wearing men, tyrannical megalomaniac demons, facing a tribunal of sorts and being clobbered for finding a brutally honest nickname as funny as it was).

I can be so bright, sometimes.

"He drools," an amused voice said from somewhere above and to my right.

"So do you," another voice murmured softly.

"What?" the first voice hissed.

"Nothing, Master."

"He sleep long time. Get water pouring, yeah?"

"If you wish, Master."

My eyes snapped open as I heard water being poured into something. Jerking my head to the right with a sharp snap, I saw Crenen sitting nearby, pouring water from his flask into a large bowl.

Tall Strong Jerk watched me without expression from his place on the table's far side. The lit torch cast shadows across his face. "He's awake, Master."

Crenen looked at me, his mouth twisting in annoyance. "Not supposed to wake 'til we dump water."

"I wasn't about to let that happen," I muttered, sitting up. At some point I'd been placed under my covers and my hands were freshly bandaged. I glanced at Tall Strong Jerk inquiringly, who nodded once. I smiled my gratitude.

"No fun," Crenen pouted. He grabbed the half-filled bowl and tossed its contents at Tall Strong Jerk, who closed his eyes as he was drenched. His expression was very patient as he wiped his face with his green wrap.

Crenen turned back to me as Tall Strong Jerk collected himself. "You drool," he informed me with mischief glistening in his gold and silver eyes.

"Thanks. I had no idea," I replied, wiping at the side of my mouth as I spoke.

"Welcome," he said with a toothy grin.

I turned to Tall Strong Jerk. "Need a towel?" Not that I knew where to get one, but I felt like offering. Of all the people I'd met in this hellish Paradise, he was the only one who hadn't angered me yet.

He shook his head. "I'll be fine."

I shrugged, then yawned. "What're my chores today?" I had decided to do them right this time, to avoid further embarrassment.

"Not today," Crenen said. "Still night."

I halted mid stretch and gazed at him with narrowed eyes. "Say what?" He had woken me up *again*?

Crenen waved his hand at Tall Strong Jerk, who walked to the tent flap and opened it to reveal darkness beyond.

"Then what did you wake me up for? *Again*." I barely kept myself from shouting.

"We dilemmaed."

I raised an eyebrow. "Dilemmaed?" Was that even a word?

"He means *troubled,*" Tall Strong Jerk said.

"That, yeah," Crenen agreed.

"I see." I stifled another yawn. "And how do you expect me to help you?" Not that I wanted to, but if it allowed me to go back to sleep, I was willing to do whatever it took.

"Here," Crenen crawled on all fours, back to the paper laying on the table in the tent's center.

I grudgingly, groggily stood up, walked to the torch, a flopped down at the table next to Tall Strong Jerk.

"Tall Strong Jerk and *we* have discord," Crenen said, tapping the map with a claw.

"About a map?"

"Basically," Tall Strong Jerk muttered.

Crenen scowled at us. "About strategy on map."

"Ooh." I glanced at the map. "Then I suggest not fighting on the map." I couldn't help myself; I was irritated and tired and I wasn't about to let Crenen's bad English get him by.

Crenen reached out and hit me upside the head with his hand. "Not joking time," he growled. "We have enemy close."

"Sorry," I lied, rubbing my newest bruise. He was stronger than he looked.

His gold and silver eyes narrowed, but he let me off the hook. Returning to the map, he tapped an area with his claw. "We here." His claw moved along the map, miraculously not tearing the paper, and then stopped at another area. "Kirid *here*." His claw punctured a hole on the spot he tapped.

"'Kay," I said, guessing that Kirid was the enemy.

"Quiet Sneaky Thing report that Kirid vanish from *here*. Tall Strong Jerk guess that Kirid move *here*." He tapped a clearing to the east of the Yenen encampment, leaving another puncture. "*We* say they *here*." He tapped a spot to the west, leaving yet another hole, and then he looked into my eyes. "What say Strange Coward Boy?"

I stared at him blankly, then gave the map the same expression. "Uh..." I tapped the area to the east. "They're *here*." Not that I had a clue, but I figured I had little to lose by siding with Tall Strong Jerk. He was the sensible party.

Crenen scowled. "Too hard!"

Tall Strong Jerk cleared his throat. "That's the point, Master. No one in their right mind would make it easy to guess where they were located."

Crenen hissed between clenched teeth. "Exactly. Tall Strong *Stupid* Jerk think we deal with those in right mind. Well, not so. Kirid crazy, yeah?"

"But not *that* crazy," Tall Strong Jerk said calmly.

Crenen scowled again and turned his head from us. "This is why *we* in charge, not Stupid Dolt Heads."

Even though I was very annoyed that he didn't care about my opinion, yet he'd woken me up to get it, I decided it wasn't worth arguing about. Instead I yawned loudly, stood up, and shuffled back to my bed. “Good night,” I said as I climbed under my covers. It took only a second to fall back to sleep.

6
A Moonlit Clearing of Blood?

For the third time that night I was awakened before sunrise. I bolted up and glanced around in a daze, wondering what had alerted me. The tent was dark, the torch was cold and Crenen's bed was empty.

I threw my blankets aside, slipped my shoes on and tiptoed to the flap. It was deathly quiet outside. The hairs on my neck tingled in warning, but I pushed the flap aside and squinted into the night. Light still came from the center of camp, while the rest of the tents stood in shadow. I decided to investigate.

Bracing myself, I wended my way around the silent campsites, eyes fixed on the glowing light from the bonfire. As I neared my destination cold dread washed over me, making my hair stick up more, prickling painfully now.

The warriors of Yenen Clan were still gathered around the bonfire. Glowing ashes floated high in the air above the giant flames. The scent of smoke and peppermint filled the air.

I pushed my way through the throng, which seemed wholly indifferent to my presence. This wasn't a second tribunal—it was something much more serious. Glancing at the faces of the men, I saw a grimness in their eyes that only heightened my dread. Swallowing hard, I pushed aside another dark-haired someone at the front of the group and spotted Crenen standing before the bonfire.

He wasn't alone.

A second man stood across from him in the clearing. He was tall, muscular yet slender (which seemed to be normal for these people), and his clothing was layered, long and flowing; dark with accents of gold, silver and blue. This man had no tatters or wrappings; he wore a type of light, cloth shoe, from which his clawed toes protruded. The night breeze teased his long, black hair. He was taller than Crenen, and definitely older. He was in his late thirties, at least; with the physique of a fully formed adult.

Glancing at the man beside me, I wondered if I should ask what was going on, but then I recalled how hostile Mr. Ugly had been and decided not to take any chances with this stranger. That, and he didn't seem to care that I existed. How typical; I should have been used to this sort of behavior. It wasn't much different from high school.

Returning to the center of attention, I felt discord between the two men like an almost tangible force. It was a stare-down from a spaghetti western—minus the dramatic background music and guns in holsters. Instead, claws flexed and feet shifted minutely. Crenen wore his permanent grin of doom, while the other man wore only a penetrating glare (or what might have been penetrating had he been glaring down anyone but Crenen). I almost felt sorry for the foolish stranger who dared to stand against the master of demonic-ninja. But then, this man didn't strike me as particularly foolish. He was the portrait of calm, especially his black eyes.

The multitude was holding its collective breath and I felt like gulping air for all of them. Or shouting. Anything to break up the tension.

Fortunately I was smart enough not to draw the attention of the whole. I didn't really want Crenen to shoot me his trademark grin and exclaim, "Tag! You're it," then lead me out to face off with Mr. Creepy in his stead.

I kept my lips sealed.

Exactly how long we all looked on while both men withstood the attention with calm indifference, I wasn't sure. I only knew that the perspiration from apprehension and anticipation (not to mention the blazing heat of the pine-scented bonfire) was very sticky as it trickled down my sides, neck and forehead.

Crenen moved first.

As he lunged, claws extended, some bestial part of me stirred, blood quickening at the prospect of watching this duel almost certainly to the death. My face was flushed with dread and excitement.

The opponent stepped back with one leg and deflected the attack, then retaliated, knocking Crenen's right arm aside at the same time that he thrust his knee into Crenen's abdomen. The latter man doubled over, instantly recovered, then jumped back, hissing.

In movies, the crowds always cheer.

The deathly silence emanating from this particular crowd was eerie.

Even despite the foreign excitement pacing through me, I couldn't make a sound. If I was breathing or not, I didn't know and didn't care. Despite the heat I shivered, understanding that something huge was taking place; something that meant everything to these people; that meant something to me, though I didn't understand why or what.

Crenen's opponent moved with the agility of a cat, shoulders rotating up and down in succession as he stepped lithely to his right. Crenen watched him, showing no sign of injury.

The offender dropped to a crouch, then sashaying forward still low to the ground, ankles and toes taking the brunt of his weight. He threw his arms up, claws spread wide to catch anything in their way while he dropped one knee to the ground, pivoting on it and shooting out his free leg to kick Crenen.

Crenen jumped.

Yes, as simply as that. Despite his opponent's swift, agile movements, he only waited until the very last second and jumped effortlessly, coming down silently after his foe had lost his momentum.

"Who is that?" I murmured, only half aware that I asked.

"Kirid," came the hushed reply from somewhere above me (because pretty much everyone stands above me).

Then, Kirid was a person? I had assumed it was an army. Or, did this single individual represent a larger force? Was he an assassin sent to murder Crenen, but caught in the act and forced to duel? Always only questions.

Kirid, or Kirid's representative, whichever, stood. He brushed the long strands of hair from his eyes, and nodded in respectful acknowledgment of Crenen's dodge. Crenen's grin only widened in reply.

This time they both struck at once, toes pushing them forward until they clashed, locked arms and then whirled around one another too speedily for me to keep up. I saw a blur of red as Crenen circled his dark assailant—or, I assumed that's what he did.

Their actions slowed marginally and I watched Kirid dodge Crenen's side-swipe and make his own fluid slash, catching the frayed edge of Crenen's red wrap. The latter spun, not bothering to dislodge Kirid's claws from his clothing before he thrust his pointy-tipped hand at Kirid's neck.

Kirid bent his waist a lot further than I could ever manage and knocked Crenen's hand off course with his elbow.

Crenen recovered, jutting out his left leg and catching Kirid's billowing clothing between his sharp toes. With a triumphant grin, he whipped his leg back behind him, dragging the robe with, flinging Kirid to the ground in the process. Black hair sprawled around Kirid's form as Crenen threw his right leg on Kirid's back, just between his shoulder blades, keeping him pinned. Snatching up Kirid's considerable length of hair, he tugged until Kirid's head was tilted up to view his victorious opponent. The felled man fixed his dark eyes on Crenen, fire blazing in their depths.

"Deal is deal, yeah?" Crenen whispered, then dropped the hair. Kirid's head snapped forward, face-planting in the mud. The Yenen leader looked like he would let Kirid go, and I almost told him not to, instinctively. I'd seen movies where the hero (not to say Crenen was exactly the hero-type, but it fit him in this particular moment) foolishly let the villain live, and only got himself hurt for his trouble.

Before I could decide whether or not to warn Crenen, he lashed out one last time, pressing hard against Kirid's back with his right foot, while his left hooked around Kirid's throat and jerked instantaneously. A sickening snap cut the muted stillness and acid bile rose in my throat.

Kirid's body remained still, but it was different from before. Now, he would never rise again. As Crenen's foot slid from under his victim's neck, the body shifted, strangely alien. Lifeless.

Dead.

Icy heat stole over my body and I bent down, vomiting into the mud. Without a second thought, without any show of mercy, Crenen had finished the man off. But even as I condemned Crenen for his atrocious act, my mind attempted to justify his actions. Maybe he had simply known that any show of mercy, any speech of civility and moral standing would fall on deaf ears; that Kirid would only stab him in the back, so he had stabbed first.

It was possible. Even probable.

But I couldn't block out the gruesome sound of death. The memory played again and again in my mind as I heaved and heaved, until I had nothing left in my stomach.

I knelt in the pasty mud, shuddering for breath, limbs shaking with sickness. My head was bowed, hair hanging in my eyes, quivering arms trying to support my weight.

Someone screamed.

It wasn't the sound of loss, of mourning. This was the sound of war. My instinct knew it.

Jerking my head up, I saw men pour through the crowd like raging water, leaping inward on Crenen standing over Kirid's corpse. Only now did I notice that these men who pounced on Crenen wore different apparel from the rest. Instead of wraps and cloaks, they wore flowing robes, much like the dead man, who must have been their leader only moments before.

I caught Crenen's eye just before he vanished under a sea of bodies, a fleeting smile crossing his face. I looked away.

Pandemonium exploded. As I scrambled to my feet, I was shoved forward and back; all I could do was focus on not getting trampled as warriors clashed in the names of their respective clans.

At one point I tripped, arms flailing to keep balanced. Strong arms snatched me up before I could hit the putrid ground and I was shoved under one arm and carried like a sack of potatoes. (I wondered vaguely if Paradise even had potatoes.)

Glancing up, trying very hard to ignore the agony in my stomach from being jostled, I spotted Tall Strong Jerk carrying me. I had suspected as much, considering the only other person with the physique to manage such a feat was Mr. Ugly, and I doubted he would have bothered.

"Hey," I greeted, voice wavering as my warden and I bumped over the ground.

Tall Strong Jerk said nothing as he headed for the thick forest of maple pines.

"What's going on?" I asked, pretty sure I already understood the situation, but figuring this was the best question I could ask to get more details under the circumstances.

"Kirid challenged Crenen to a duel," was the brief explanation.

So, Kirid *was* the dead guy then. There was a sick twisting in my gut as I again pictured the scene of death.

Either because Tall Strong Jerk felt he should elaborate, or because he was nervous and thought talking would help, he continued. "Kirid is the leader of Kirid Clan, the enemy of Yenen. He challenged Crenen to a duel to settle issues in a civilized manner. Crenen felt that something was suspicious about it, but he accepted the terms honorably."

"What were the terms?" I asked.

"Naturally, the victor commands both clans, while the loser dies."

Ah, yes. So civilized.

I turned everything over in my head as we passed the last of the rawhide tents and made our way into the forest, brambles and sticky leaves brushing against my face and tickling my nose. "So, lemme get everything straight. Kirid is dead," I swallowed hard, "so his clan—also Kirid—wants revenge, disregarding the set terms, just as their former leader probably instructed, should something happen to him. Crenen won, but now he's getting trounced by Kirid Clan as revenge for killing their leader, while *you* are removing me from the scene of battle and chaos—why?"

"Master Crenen ordered me to grab you and retreat if anything happened."

I paused, intrigued and horrified by this revelation. "Okay, so you're leaving your master behind because Crenen instructed you to save me, even though I'm just a lowly servant — Oh, but really I'm a prophesied being with some great secret purpose in Paradise. That about cover it?"

Tall Strong Jerk nodded. "Yes, I believe so. Master Yenen would have been proud of Crenen, despite this madness." He used his free hand to slash a thorny branch, which fell to the forest floor with a muted thud.

I blinked. "Yenen?"

"Crenen's father."

"Okay..." I glanced up at him. "And what's your name?"

"Menen."

I gawked, unsurprised but still astounded. Someone had taken their rhyming fetish too far. "Put me down," I said.

The world whirled by for a moment as he stood me on the ground. His red eyes turned toward camp, glistening in the near-full moonlight.

"You wanna rescue him, so go rescue him," I shooed, hoping this was finally a chance to escape.

"I can't. His other command is that I find Jenen."

I shot him a startled look. "Is Crenen right in the head?"

Menen arched his brow. "Does it matter?"

"I would hope so. Why do you need to find Jenen?"

"In case Master Crenen doesn't make it out alive. I am to locate Jenen and force him to take charge of Yenen Clan."

"Why?"

Menen sighed, looking a bit harassed. "There is a reason that Crenen does not go by Yenen though he is leader of the clan."

"'Kay?"

"He refuses to take on the name Yenen as a reminder to his clan that he will not stay its leader. He is desirous that Jenen take on that duty."

"But *why*?"

"Because as Crenen's twin, it is his right, should Crenen abdicate or perish."

Okay, so that—I didn't see that coming. Relatives, yeah. Brothers, sure. Twins, not so much. "So, what's your relation to them? Just a servant with a coincidental name similarity?"

Menen shook his head. "I am their cousin." His eyes trailed again toward camp, his expression concerned.

I bit my lip and gazed at my bandaged hands. I owed him a lot, but I hesitated to help. This was my chance to escape, my sole chance to put miles between me and Crenen's murderous whims. "Hey, don't worry about it. I doubt if anything could kill off your master, if it tried." It was probably true, though the odds were certainly stacked against him. And considering what he'd done, could anyone blame Kirid Clan for fighting back?

Menen frowned. "The Kirid aren't known to kill. They only torture cruelly until you take your own life."

How pleasant. I was liking this Paradise place more and more.

I straightened, setting my jaw and swallowing my pride. Crenen was a barbarous person by nature, so far as I could tell, but hadn't it been self-preservation to destroy his enemy first? Who could say Kirid would not have done the same, had his skills been superior to Crenen's?

"Well, what're we waiting for?" I gave Menen the most heroic look I could muster, which probably looked like a grimace. "Let's find Crenen and rescue him."

He looked startled, but then he shook his head. "No, my orders are to protect you and to locate Jenen."

I offered a grin, looking more confident than I felt. "Okay, tell you what. I'll go after Crenen and therefore force you to chase after me—that way you really *can* protect me—and then, after we rescue Crenen, we'll go find Sick Nasty Dog."

"It will be dangerous and we will probably die," Menen said solemnly.

Oh, great. Forget that then.

Unfortunately my nicer side was kicking in, and I forced a rather limp smile (deceptive abilities aren't always dependable). "That's okay," I lied. "We all die someday, right?" (So why not let Crenen croak now and leave us to die in a less painful manner much later in life?)

"I did not know you were so heroic," a new voice said.

My eyes narrowed as I turned to face the effeminate Jenen, who always seemed to come from behind. He was standing in the trickle of moonlight filtering from overhanging branches. Leaves danced in the mild breeze, casting shadows across his pallid skin.

"Well, aren't you coming? I mean, he is your brother, right?"

Jenen gave Menen a chiding glance—probably for telling me the truth of their relationship—before answering. "Crenen fights his own battles. I've no desire to become involved."

Crenen was terrifying, certainly, but Jenen was just as creepy; his own brother, and he'd let him die. I wasn't sure which twin I disliked more.

"Said like true dog, eh, Sick Nasty Dog?"

We all three spun on our heels to face the pitch-darkness to my left, and saw—nothing. It was too dark.

"Master?" Menen asked the trees.

"Yes, Tall Strong Jerk?" It was faint, but it was definitely Crenen's voice.

Menen dove into the trees after his master, while Jenen and I hung back, less than thrilled to see the trouble-making murderer return. A gasp from Tall Strong Jerk, however, sent me crashing through the undergrowth to see why he had made such an uncharacteristic sound. My eyes were slowly adjusting, but I didn't need to worry as I broke through the foliage; Crenen was sitting in a small moonlit clearing—

Drenched in crimson blood.

Crenen, meanwhile, appeared unconcerned by his condition. He grinned evilly and chuckled, then coughed up blood. "Matter, Strange Coward Boy? Blood scare you?" He raised his dripping hand into the direct path of the streaming moonlight, his bloody teeth glittering. "Come."

Riveted by his expression, unable to fight his commanding tone, and haunted by the image of Kirid's broken neck, I stepped forward.

Then I was there; standing before the sharp-toothed maniac, gazing at him in fear. I had felt fear before—felt the overwhelming numbness as it took over my body. But this was in a whole different league. I was terrified. Truly, honestly terrified.

"Vendaeva," he whispered, sending a chill through my half-numb body. "Swear you will serve me, Vendaeva. Swear you will not betray me. Swear you will not aid the Kirid in their cause."

I stared, unable to speak.

Why should I...? What could I do...?

A million questions flooded my overwhelmed brain, with theories about being Vendaeva, and that Crenen might kill me for it, most prominent in my mind. So he wanted to ensure that I would not use whatever I had against him? Why would I agree to such a thing?

"Kneel," Crenen ordered.

My knees buckled and I knelt before him, shaking like the leaves overhead.

"Swear," he growled, still whispering.

Rage welled up, breaking through the numbness. I was kneeling, but I would not be forced to swear allegiance to him. I was stronger than that. I wasn't a coward.

"No," I spat, closing my eyes.

"For the sake of my people, swear!" His voice changed now; it was suddenly desperate.

Eyes snapping open, I met his gaze and saw the pleading in their depths. Was it really not about him? Was this not the same man who had murdered his enemy without pause? Or had his cause been right?

"You hold the fate of Paradise within your unstained hands. Look." He beckoned to Menen, who knelt beside his master. Crenen brushed aside his thick black hair, smudging blood on his servant's cheek, to reveal a scar weaving along the side of Menen's face. "Scarred." Crenen pointed to Jenen. "He, too, carries scars. Not one person in Paradise, man, woman, or child, is without blemish. But you," he turned back to me, "are without permanent injury."

I wasn't about to ask how he knew that, but he was right. I had always found it odd that while other boys compared their scars, I had none to speak of. Every injury inflicted upon me had vanished with time; nothing lasted after the scab fell off.

"Swear, Vendaeva. Save my people from the Kirid. Save my people from our torturous end."

I remained silent. The facts were too few. Who was to say his side was right? From what I'd seen thus far, Crenen and his cronies weren't exactly angelic.

Finally I sighed and gave him a rarely-used expression of sincerity. "I swear to help Paradise however I can—but that's all I can promise." I was no fool. Liar or no, backstabber or no, there are some things you don't swear to unless you plan to keep the oath. "And," I continued, "I will serve you until I think it's just plain stupid to keep doing so." I didn't know why I pledged that. I knew I would regret serving Crenen.

Sometimes I could just kick myself.

7
A Misty Vision?

"Well said, Strange Coward Boy!" Crenen clapped my back with his bloody hand, then turned his toothy grin on Menen. "East, Tall Strong Jerk."

East? I decided not to ask. I had the impending feeling I would find out sooner or later.

Menen climbed to his feet, bent down, and scooped his master into his arms as carefully as he could. Crenen cried out in pain.

"Master, your injuries are severe."

"Tell us something we don't feel already, dolt," Crenen hissed, taking the time to clonk his cousin on the head. "Not worthy of carrying. Not worthy even of touching."

"Shall I put you down then, Master?"

Crenen glanced at me, probably noting my small build, and then at Jenen, probably aware that he wouldn't carry him if his life depended on it. Then he scowled at Menen and hit him again. "Dolt. No thinking, just do."

This was some family reunion. Twins that loathed each other (at least on Jenen's part), and a cousin used as a personal slave. I felt gratitude for my own family back home increase tenfold as homesickness twinged in my stomach.

We headed east after Crenen finished abusing Menen. Not that I could tell which direction was which. I'm no sailor, and stars are hardly my thing. As we began to walk, I glanced back and saw Jenen following at a distance. Turning back to the front, I wondered what had happened to Crenen's encampment.

Knowing the only way I'd find out was if I asked, I decided to brave Crenen's devilish reply. "What about your people?"

Menen halted and turned to give Crenen a full view. He wore the predicted degrading expression. "What about?"

"Well," I shrugged, trying to appear nonchalant, "you wouldn't leave them behind to face the Kirid alone, so...?"

Crenen arched one dark eyebrow. "Why not?"

"Why not?" I repeated. "B-because they're your people."

"They be always fine against Slimy Bad Kirid," Crenen assured me, smiling. "Best warriors in all of entire world."

Menen turned back around, apparently sensing that Crenen was finished, and they kept walking, leaving me to mull over his words. So, in his twisted, megalomaniac way, he did care. That, or he knew exactly the sort of words to use to sound awe-inspiring.

But then, so had Hitler.

We trudged through thorny brambles and over giant roots for what seemed like hours. The sun had risen forever ago, and we never stopped. An age had passed since I made the pledge to serve Crenen.

I gathered more information about the events of that night as Crenen and Menen discussed it in low tones. Apparently the Kirid army had come from the west, just as Crenen predicted. The clan leaders, Crenen and Kirid had met and discussed the terms of the duel, and then they faced off, which was about the time I showed up. Crenen never brought up how he escaped from the Kirid warriors after they pounced on him—probably because he wanted us to imagine the most impressive means possible. All I could conjure up was him gnawing everyone's arms and legs off with his sharp teeth. That gives some idea how tired I was trudging on and on.

The sun was high in the sky as we stepped from the dense forest and found ourselves in another Yenen Clan encampment. I stared blearily

Crenen flashed me that irritating grin of his and pointed at the rawhide tents. "Sleep. Food. Drink. Welcome to Paradise."

I nodded and dragged my feet toward the tent.

"Sa Vais," a large man cried out from the center-most tent, voice booming. He rushed forward to greet us, and I grudgingly halted, glowering at the man who dared to stop me from claiming my rest. The man looked breathless, though he had only jogged a few yards. He seemed fit enough. Perhaps it was just excitement at seeing his master in one piece that made his breathing short. *"Eyia sovei cir hej slovej. Veys irefen ii cran yas."*

Crenen offered the babbling man his evil, toothy grin. "We relieved, too," he said in English, and I wondered if he spoke it for my benefit. "We tired now, so taking Breathless Noisy Dolt's tent and going for nap, yeah?"

On cue, Menen carried his master toward the large center tent, and Jenen and I trailed after them, the former a bit reluctantly. Personally I was just looking forward to sitting for a bit.

Glancing back at Breathless Noisy Dolt, I expected to see some kind of dismayed expression; either at his nickname or the fact that his tent was being confiscated. Instead his expression was gentle, a tiny smile on his seasoned face.

Everyone in this world was demented.

As soon as I entered the darkness of the dingy tent, I plopped down on the dirt, legs burning, and closed my eyes. Sleep had never beckoned louder…

"—ward Boy!"

My eyes snapped open and I found Crenen across the tent, his form lighted by a single candle. "Yeah?" I managed groggily.

"Eat. Then sleep." He motioned to Menen, who set a plate of grapes before me with a frown.

Wait—grapes? Sweet, heavenly, beautiful grapes? No way. There was something wrong. There had to be. This place was hellish; it didn't have pleasantries. Only slimy fruit and stale bread.

Tentatively I picked one plump grape from among the rest, put it in my mouth, and chewed. Once. I winced as the sweet flavor exploded, overpowering my taste buds. These were *good* grapes—scratch that. *Amazing* grapes. *These* I liked.

"Ha! He likes."

"Yes, Master." Menen's tone sounded somehow disapproving.

I pulled my eyes from the luscious grapes long enough to take in Crenen only five feet from where I rested, sitting cross-legged on his new rawhide fur. His black shirt and red wrap were gone, and bandages had taken their place in covering Crenen's torso. Tape covered his left cheek, and one hand was wrapped like a mummy, though the blood still soaked through. Menen was just finishing his medical duties, tying one final knot behind his master's back. Cousin, slave, and doctor all in one. How come I'd never been so lucky?

"Paradisaical Purple Fruit—tasty and healing. The best medicine we ever need, yeah?" Crenen said, batting at one of the dangling ties on his hand.

I nodded contentedly as I savored another little morsel. Healing? Yeah, my soul felt like singing.

"Also known as gerani," Menen said as he raised Crenen's hands above his head.

Gerani was a beautiful word.

He slipped Crenen's tattered shirt back over his head. "This fruit is healing to a certain point, but it's also very addictive."

Well, duh. Nothing this good couldn't be.

"Tall Strong Jerk not like Paradisaical Purple Fruit—think it bad for body. *We* say if good for mind, good for body. Tall Strong Jerk have different attitude." Crenen pulled his shirt down over his bandages and allowed Menen to drape the red cloth over both shoulders, then lay him down on the fur and cover him with another rawhide.

"It's not good to eat it often," Menen said.

"So say servant. Not so say master."

"Yes, Master." Menen bowed his head and stood. "If you'll excuse me, I must attend to duties outside. Don't eat any, Master."

"Yeah, yeah. Leave," Crenen said with a dismissive wave of his uninjured hand.

Menen left and I returned to the most important matter at hand: my Purple Fruit.

"No need ferment Paradisaical Purple Fruit. Already plenty strong, yeah?" Crenen chuckled.

I stopped chewing. Was this like some sort of alcohol and that's why I felt so…intoxicated? "I'm too young to drink," I said after swallowing. I gazed at the fruit longingly.

"Technically Strange Coward Boy *eat* instead," Crenen said as he wriggled out of his covers, reaching with one clawed hand and snatching a single grape from my bowl. He popped it in his mouth and flashed me his toothy grin as he gnashed the fruit to bits, miraculously keeping the juices from dribbling down his chin.

He did have a point. I took another.

"Excellent." Crenen nodded his approval as he dipped his hand into the bowl for another helping.

"Master."

Crenen snapped his hand away from the grapes and guiltily looked up at Menen. "Yes, Tall Strong Jerk?"

"No gerani. Consider your condition," Menen growled, entering the tent wholly and scooping my bowl off the ground. I watched him in horror. Those were *my* grapes.

"Our condition hardly dictate if we eat Paradisaical Purple Fruit or not, Tall *Stupid* Jerk."

"Your condition dictates just that, whether you like the idea or not, Crenen."

Crenen's metallic eyes narrowed at Menen's use of his name. "Leave!" He pointed to the door flap. "Get out!" He tossed his pillow at Menen. "Banished! Never return."

I stared.

Menen stood there for a moment, and then bowed low. "As you wish, Sa Vais."

Crenen growled, eyes dancing with anger. His claws flexed and his sharp teeth clenched tightly. For a moment I saw a wild beast about to lunge at its prey, but then a ragged cough broke his stance and he doubled over, hacking up blood.

Menen dropped the bowl, grapes scattering across the dirt floor, and knelt beside his cousin. He placed his hand on his shoulder, as though mentally urging the cough to desist. Crenen attempted to shove him away, but another fit took him and he collapsed, landing on his face. He curled into a ball, hugging his ribs tightly.

I stared as Crenen continued to cough. Menen whispered to him, soothing his panic as he ran a hand along his back. At last the fit ceased and Crenen gasped for air, sweat trailing down his face. Menen turned him over and helped him sit up, propping Crenen against himself.

"It's all right," Menen said softly as he held Crenen in place. "You'll be fine now."

It seemed almost routine, as though recent injuries were only the icing on the cake. Tall Strong Jerk was very practiced; perhaps it was his doctoral side coming out.

I don't know how long I sat there, gazing at the ground before me. Darkness had fallen outside before anyone stirred. It was Jenen who broke our silence as he entered the tent. (When had he left?) "The Kirid are on their way," he announced, glancing at Crenen's sleeping form for only a second. "I'm taking the boy before they arrive."

I was startled. These Kirid were certainly persistent, but then, I might be too if my leader had been cut down by a creature like Crenen—assuming I had a leader whom I cared about.

I glanced at Menen, then up at Jenen. Then I stood. "I'm staying here."

"You've little choice in the matter," Jenen said coldly, eyes like ice.

I nodded to Crenen. "I'm his servant. You witnessed me swear an oath to serve him. Are you going to make me break that oath?" I didn't really want to stay with Crenen, but I wasn't about to head off someplace with Sick Nasty Dog in the dead of night either. I didn't trust him.

Jenen nodded. "Yes. I am."

I stared. "You're kidding?" So much for my honor approach. I made a mental note that in a war-torn, primitive world, honor didn't mean much.

"Strange Coward Boy speak true," Crenen spoke up, apparently now awake. Pain lined his face, but his eyes were focused. "You not take him, yeah?" I came to the definite conclusion that 'yeah' did not constitute as a question, but more as a command to concur.

"I don't have to listen to you, Crenen," Jenen said, snapping his hand out lightning-fast and grabbing my rather muddy red jacket, pulling me closer to him.

"Try it, Sick Nasty Dog. Try, and we show you true meaning of torture—future leader of Yenen Clan or no, yeah?" Crenen's hand flexed, as though he was determined to vent his frustrations and his bloodthirsty desires on the one person who dared defy his will. Which was just fine with me, since I wasn't the one trying.

Jenen tugged again on my jacket, and I scowled. This was no time to get possessive—and why the heck did he want me, anyway? What use was I to him?

As though in answer, Jenen spoke. "Vendaeva is no good to you. I will use this boy to change things in the best way possible. Don't be selfish, Crenen. This isn't the time for it."

Oh. Vendaeva again. Stupid prophecy.

"Won't!" Crenen shouted, jumping to his feet, ignoring the blood seeping through his bandages just as he dismissed the pain.

Menen moved as quickly as Jenen had when grabbing my jacket. One second he was kneeling behind Crenen, the next I felt the other side of my jacket being tugged on. I considered pulling free of the jacket and running away from all of them, but a second glance at the claws surrounding me made me stay very still.

"You can't keep him, Crenen. He's of no use to you—you haven't a clue how to even use him."

"True," Crenen said with a grin. "But we have in possession *Seer*."

My gut tightened as I felt something bigger taking place—something I had no clue about that held my sorry fate in its big, twisted hand. Stupid hand.

Jenen's expression darkened. "However did you manage that, Crenen?"

The other man's grin widened evilly. I began to worry that in the moment I pledged my loyalty to him, I had sold my soul to the Devil. Oh well. If this really was Hell, who better to swear allegiance to than its overseer?

"Never mind details," Crenen said. "The point, Sick Nasty Dog be both you and Strange Coward Boy come with us or never fulfill Vendaeva. Sick Nasty Dog must speak with Seer, yeah?"

Jenen frowned, knowing full well he had been manipulated. He was in too deep to turn back now. I suspected that had been Crenen's main reason for keeping me: to make certain Jenen would stick around, so he could be properly coerced.

The sound of distant thunder jolted me.

"Kirid," the three men hissed as one, sounding very much related. I kept this thought to myself.

Distracted, both Jenen and Menen released me, and I glanced around for a chance to escape. I caught Crenen's eye and he shook his head with a smile. Even in his weakened condition, I knew I'd never make it before he captured me again.

Menen turned to his master. "We must leave."

"No, we fight," Crenen said even as he swayed on his feet.

"You're in no condition—"

"Stop," Crenen hissed angrily. "We feel plenty well enough."

Menen sighed, bowed his head, then seized Crenen, somehow *gently* swinging him over his shoulder. "You'll forgive me," he murmured to Crenen, then grabbed me by the collar and swung me over his other shoulder despite my own protests. Strong was right; this guy was amazing. He appeared slender, but I credited that to his height, which seemed to hide the massive muscles that had to be under his clothes.

Jenen led the way from the tent just after the Kirid struck.

I had played my share of video games, so I thought I was prepared for the scene of battle—but I was very wrong. The view before us filled me with a horror I could never forget. In a matter of seconds bodies littered the ground, laying in their own blood. The clash of weapons filled the air with the sound of death, while the smoldering of several burning tents blanketed the sky with thick black smoke and an awful stench.

Several men were engaged in close-combat not far away, and I watched as one man jammed his clawed hand into the other's eyes. Blood sprayed into the offender's face. A scream rent the air, joining a chorus of others.

I turned my eyes from the battlefield, too sick to watch. The flap was still open to the tent we had just left and, desperate for a distraction, my eyes found the discarded grapes cluttering the dirt floor. Casting a farewell look of longing at the fruit, my stomach growled its own goodbye.

Jenen chose an escape route and sprinted into the smoke, Menen and his cargo (us) at his heels. I glanced at Crenen hanging down the other side of Menen's back. His eyes watched everything around us as we raced for the forest, his expression too complicated to guess what he was thinking.

We ran through the night. By the time Menen let me down, my stomach had bruises purple as gerani from being jostled against his shoulder for so long.

He had been much gentler with Crenen, for obvious reasons, but you wouldn't know it the way Crenen complained the whole time his cousin lowered him onto the grass. As soon as Crenen was free of Menen's grip, he raised his claws and slashed at Menen's cheek with a sharp hiss, just missing flesh.

"Disobey order again and we *kill*."

"Yes, Master." Menen bowed his head.

I glanced around and spotted Jenen sitting on a fallen tree, his arms folded, his eyes dancing with shadows. I considered taking a seat beside him and prying for information about the Seer, but thought better of it.

Crenen's voice brought me back to him. "How come *we* have to sleep when Strange Coward Boy still up?"

"Go to sleep," Menen whispered to me before turning back to Crenen. "Better?"

Crenen growled sulkily.

I had no argument. I was just grateful for the chance to get the rest I'd been wanting so badly. I searched in the gloom for something to prop myself against, but finally gave up and looked instead for the softest bit of grass. I finally found it and, laying down, fell toward sleep.

I dreamed.

At least, I hoped it was a dream. Chances were it was just another world I had stumbled into where I would discover more evil, sharp-toothed monstrosities lurking in wait to chomp on my hand and bend me to their will as they pulled my mind apart in my struggle to comprehend my outrageous situation. And I wasn't thinking of Small Red Fuzzies.

I stood in a dark field shrouded in oppressive blue mist, unable to see more than five feet in any direction. My eyes stung from straining to see through the aerosol vapor, and moisture clung to my hair and dripped to the ground. It was dark and muggy; bitter cold. I shivered, my jacket doing little good against the biting wind that churned the mist in a bizarre dance before me.

It seemed a little too real to be a dream. It was too freaking cold.

I wondered what to do as I hugged myself. Move, I decided. It would be warmer at least. I walked without a destination, mist still churning at my feet and wisping through my hair. Chances were, with my increasing bad luck (it had always been horrible, but never like this), I would never find an end—or, if I did, there would only be grinning, pointed teeth ready to gnash me to tiny bits until I resembled a mutilated gerani.

I kept going. Perhaps in this misty expanse I could find a puddle that would take me home. Mist creates puddles, right?

I lost track of time as I searched in vain for an exit. Forever had come and gone since I found myself in the vast emptiness; since the Kirid had attacked and slaughtered Crenen's people while we just ran away. Or had it just been a few seconds? This place felt as though time had little to do with it; as though the mist would haunt the plains forever, yet at any second it would disperse to reveal something wonderful—like maybe sunlight.

Despair seized me like a hand squeezing my lungs. Would I remain alone in this gloomy place, shivering with cold and fear, unable to find shelter or food? My stomach was growling for sustenance, but I had nothing to eat, and the ground beneath me was frozen solid, devoid of any life.

The mist was thickening. It shifted and slithered like strange creatures. I spun on my heels to run, only to see mist; mist everywhere. It was like death, heavy and bitter and dark. I was trapped, unable to escape as it choked me. I wanted to scream.

Falling to my knees, I bit my lip and tried to reason with myself. "C'mon now, Key, think. This isn't the end. Some stupid blue mist can't kill you just by being there. After all, it's pretty much nothingness, right? You can't be afraid of nothing..." Never mind that the vapor was, in actuality, *something*.

"A very wise conclusion," a clear voice said.

I jumped to my feet and whipped around, jaw dropping as I laid eyes on her for the first time. She was the most beautiful woman I had ever seen in my life. Long, flowing golden hair framed an angelic face and deep violet eyes deterred the mist around her. She was a young woman, probably only a few years my senior, and she was taller than I (which wasn't too hard). She was slender and graceful—perfect in every possible way as she stood before me, sweeping white gown trailing behind her.

Only after I memorized her by heart did I remember she had spoken. "Pardon?" I asked.

She smiled warmly and raised her hand. "Not only wise, but very careful."

Careful? I decided to ask. "Uh, how?"

She laughed softly. "You think before you speak, dear friend." She curtsied to me and offered her flawless hand again. "Come. I will give you leave of the misty plains."

I took her hand and the mist curled away, taking the darkness with it. Brilliant golden light filled my vision. I stumbled forward and closed my eyes, teeth clenching as I sucked in air.

"Are you all right?" the woman asked as she cupped her smooth hands over my face. When she finally took them away, I could see perfectly, a subtle ache the only sign I had nearly been permanently blinded. "I'm so sorry," she whispered. "I forgot to adjust your eyes."

I might have responded but I was too busy gawking at the strange place before me. Everything was made of gold, yet it flowed as smoothly as if it were a real valley. Golden water gurgled happily in its gold-bedded stream, and gold-flecked leaves danced happily on their golden branches. The mountains surrounding the valley were dark shades of gold, capped by gold-colored snow while gold-hued clouds floated across a white-gold sky. It was breathtaking.

"Welcome to the Golden Valley, Key," the woman said.

Appropriately named—a little obvious though.

I turned my attention back to the woman, surprised that she knew my name. "And you are?"

"Oh." She raised a hand to her pink lips and laughed. "I am so sorry, once again. My name is Veija." She curtsied. "It is an honor to meet you, Key."

"And why is that?"

"Because you are Vendaeva."

Yeah, that. I figured as much. "And why are we in the Gold Valley?"

"Golden," she corrected.

"Whatever. You gonna answer my question?" I didn't necessarily mean to sound short-tempered, but I was tired from walking for who-knew-how-long and, while this might have been a dream, it felt as though I hadn't slept in days.

"Oh, of course." She was a little absentminded, I decided then. "I wanted to meet you and so I brought you here."

I decided to take a wild, if predictable guess. "And I had to enter the misty plains before you could take me here, to this little world of yours?"

She blinked in surprise. "How did you know? You're most incredibly perceptive."

I might've slapped my forehead, but that would have been bad manners, and my mother trained me better than that.

—Okay, that's a lie. I *did* slap my forehead, mother or no mother.

"Mosquito?" Veija asked worriedly.

I refrained from slapping my forehead again. "Uh, yeah."

"Oh dear. I didn't know we had any of those in here." She glanced around with concern, hair rippling down one shoulder. "I'll have to get them exterminated. I'm sorry it disturbed you."

Okay, so her naïve sincerity and concern were cute.

"It's fine," I assured her, putting my best lying face to use. She fell for it.

"Wonderful." She beamed, her pretty face radiant. "As I was saying, I..." She trailed off and frowned.

"What?" I asked.

"I forgot what I was saying," she said, giggling.

I stifled an exasperated sigh. "That's okay. Did you have an important reason for bringing me here, or can you take me back?"

"Yes." She smiled brightly.

Yes to which part? "Okay..." I said vaguely, waiting for more.

"I want you to see something, but we're nearly out of time."

Gee. I wondered whose fault that was.

Veija turned toward a tall, golden tree hovering over the gurgling stream. She waved her hand before her. "You must understand." The tree wavered and then disappeared, replaced by the same blue mist as before, though it kept the same shape as its predecessor. "This is a sickness."

Gah! And I'd breathed it in. I stepped back and felt my heart fail for a moment, wondering how long it would be before my hair started falling out.

"It is not contagious to you, Key," Veija said. "It can only affect Paradisians. This is the dreaded Paradisaical disease that has been killing our people over the last decade. Half the population of our world has been destroyed by it." Her violet eyes shimmered with grief.

"So, what caused the disease?" I asked, willing my heart to work again as I eyed the twisting mass of mist.

"A good question. We believe Kirid Clan created it."

My eyes narrowed. "But why would they create something that can cause them harm too? Or are they immune to it?"

She shook her head. "They didn't mean to create it. It was their greed. Paradise is a beautiful, peaceful place, but the curse of Kirid has taken the form of destruction. In order to cleanse Paradise of greed and malice, the core of our world has created this disease to stop the wickedness of Kirid Clan from spreading. Unfortunately the core cannot stop from destroying other lives in the process."

I decided to take another guess. "And this is where I come in?"

She smiled sweetly. "Very good, Key. This is the purpose of Vendaeva. You must stop the disease from overcoming the entirety of Paradise. This is the reason you were summoned by the great Phudel."

"You mean the *puddle*?" I asked with a raised brow. I didn't mention to her that the great Phudel hadn't been responsible for my presence here—that I'd only come because some idiot teenage jock had pushed me in. The puddle had only taken it from there.

"Well, yes, you could call it that," she said with a blush.

I was beginning to suspect that every non-English word I had heard thus far was just a glorified term for something less-than-amazing that they didn't want you to see for what it really was.

"Okay, so how am I supposed to stop this deadly illness?"

"Uh," she raised a finger and then lowered it again, looking dejected, "I don't know."

My eyes narrowed. "Aren't you the Seer?"

She gasped. "How did you know?"

Too predictable. "Wild guess," I said aloud. "So, you really don't know?"

She shook her head. "I'm—" She broke off and spun around, her back to me now. "Oh no. I must leave. Our time is done."

Before I could respond, the images all blurred and fused together, then dripped like wet paint on a canvas. My mind began to spin and I teetered, fell, and lost consciousness. When I opened my eyes again, my first sight was of Crenen's mismatched eyes only four inches from my face.

8
The Realm of Yenen?

"Aaahh!"

I scrambled to my feet, twisting to avoid colliding with the very man I wanted to escape.

Crenen was kneeling on the ground beside the soft patch of grass I'd been laying on, watching me with wry amusement. "What matter, Strange Coward *Girl*? You scream like woman." He put his finger (claw and all) in his ear as though to stop the ringing.

I scowled. "What d'ya mean, 'what matter'? You were this close to my face." I held my hands out to show the close proximity. "What the freak?"

He was still smiling. "Strange Coward Boy mumbling funny words from dream and we was wanting knowing what was muttered. No 'freak' was present," he assured me casually. "You mention something of dying persons and tried hitting self while scrunching nose—like this," he wrinkled his nose to demonstrate. "Strange Coward Boy need hear self some time. Would get great laugh."

I stared at him, trying to comprehend not only his words but his sense of humor. How were 'dying persons' funny?

"Just, never get that close again, okay?"

Crenen's expression turned haughty. "We do as we please. Sooner you and Tall Strong Jerk know that, sooner you last long."

I said nothing about his obscure phraseology. Instead I looked around for Menen and Jenen, recalling what had been happening the last time I was awake. It was a wonder Crenen was acting so nonchalant after the attack—or, considering what sort of devil Crenen appeared to be, perhaps it wasn't so much of a wonder. "Where're your cronies?" I asked, not finding my fellow slaves.

Crenen blinked and then laughed his most maniacal laugh, sending shivers down my spine. Apparently he knew what 'cronies' were. "Lowly Cronies One and Two, yeah? Very clever Strange Coward Boy." He gestured off into the trees. "You been sleeping long time—two days. Yesterday, Sick Nasty Dog offer to use sharp nose and scout ahead for signs of Slimy Bad Kirid and to prepare for re-arrival, and we send Tall Strong Jerk along to make certain Sick Nasty Dog not foolishly run off."

"But didn't Jenen want to stick around because of me and this...Seer of yours?" I recalled Veija and managed a strained smile. She had been as helpful to me as a textbook—which meant none at all.

"Sick Nasty Dog think he very clever," Crenen said, lounging back in the shady grass, folding his arms behind his head. His movements were surprisingly lithe, considering how injured he had been before. His lopsided ponytail splayed across the dewy grass, probably catching all sorts of gnats, while his red wrap darkened as it soaked in the morning moisture. "He probably thinking he can outwit us and claim Strange Coward Boy, then find his own Seer. Maybe."

"So Menen is a sort of precaution against that; a way to make Jenen think twice about doing anything rash." Frankly, of the two twins, Crenen struck me as the rasher type. Jenen was a lot more subdued (though definitely as evil as his brother).

Crenen nodded wordlessly, fixing his eyes on the branches overhead. "We almost to Realm of Yenen. Be there in a matter of some time."

His sense of time was astonishing. "Realm of Yenen. Is that, like, your headquarters or something?"

"Yeah. Many of Order of Crenen won't re-arrive this time. Too many die at Slimy Bad Kirid attack." His eyes were distant for a moment. "Tall Strong Jerk and Sick Nasty Dog be coming back soon, and we travel then, yeah?" He raised one clawed hand to the sky. "Anyway, surprise, Strange Coward Boy."

I looked up—

—And my jaw dropped. The trees around us were packed with thousands upon thousands of Paradisaical Purple Fruit. I felt my mouth water as I recalled the scrumptious taste of those perfect grapes—er, gerani.

"We dwell in most fertile part of Paradise. Here grow most best Fruits of Paradise. We lucky enough to hide in Large Ample Grove last night, yeah? " He rose to his feet, perhaps a little slower than normal, and reached up to the branches, plucking a bunch from the tree.

Wait a second—

A tree? I thought grapes grew on vines.

Ah well. Who was I to argue?

"Eat. Tall Strong Jerk not like Paradisaical Purple Fruit, so he not see, yeah?"

I nodded consent and took the precious bundle from Crenen, staring at the spherical delights, each flawless and unspoiled. I popped what I thought was the largest of the bunch into my mouth and allowed the flavorful fruit to burst, juices spurting from my mouth and dribbling down my chin. Dang, these were good.

"In dream, Strange Coward Boy mention something of Seer, yeah?"

As I wiped my chin with my jacket sleeve, I tried to remember more of the strange dream I'd experienced. It was a little vague, but still clearer than any dreams I'd had before in my life. "Oh, uh, earlier you mentioned something about a Seer. I guess that entered my dreams." I was potentially telling a lie, but I didn't *know* for sure if it was a dream or something more.

A familiar voice spoke from the trees. "Eating gerani causes you to be more in tune with supernatural elements. Isn't that right, Crenen?" Jenen stepped into view, followed closely by Menen, who was eyeing the fruit in my hands with disdain.

Crenen flashed them both an evil grin.

Jenen continued. "Whilst under the influence of gerani you might even be visited by persons of tremendous power." He shot Crenen a suspicious glance.

"But only so say crazy persons, yeah?" Crenen said.

"I met her," I admitted, deciding it was best not to let the two of them start arguing again.

Crenen burst out laughing—again showing that either the rest of us had lost our respective senses of humor, or his was far different from ours. "Seer waste no time, yeah?"

"You saw the Seer?" Jenen asked sharply, ignoring his twin.

I nodded, too happy with my non-berry tree-clinging out-of-season grapes to care about whatever politics plagued the brothers.

"Did the Seer mention being in the possession of Crenen?" asked Jenen.

I shrugged as I munched away.

"Hardly in condition to give detail, yeah?" Crenen cackled wickedly. "Paradisaical Purple Fruit only good for mind that sleeps, or Small Red Fuzzies."

"Now he admits it," Menen muttered in the background.

Wait a second. Had Crenen intoxicated me to keep me from thinking too clearly? ...Because it had worked. I was being toyed with and I found myself unable to care.

Jenen scowled.

"Win again, yeah? You come back with Tall Strong Jerk. Tells us you need Strange Coward Boy enough to serve us, yeah? Make us wonder why Sick Nasty Dog need Vendaeva so much. Make intriguing situation, in which we have upper hand."

The effeminate twin's face darkened considerably, strongly reminding me of when I had stupidly called him a girl to his pretty face. The fear attached to that memory was almost enough to pull me from my stupor—but not quite.

"Let's go," Jenen said, then turned his back on everyone and walked the way he had just come through the trees.

"What did he do?" Crenen asked, his attention now on Menen, trademark grin replaced by a sober expression.

"He stared at the ground the entire time," Menen answered. "He refused to look around unless he couldn't help it at all, and he would not enter the Realm."

"Still foolish," Crenen growled, digging his claws into his other hand until blood was drawn.

"Master, there is no need for self-abuse," Menen said tersely.

Crenen released his hand and let his arms drop to either side of his torso, looking dejected. "What will it take? Must I actually give him the Seer for his consent?"

"Master, why try? This boy is the real Vendaeva, is he not? Why not use him yourself? Then the need for Jenen is—"

"No," Crenen snapped, baring his fangs in a snarl. "This boy's only use is for Jenen's acquiescence, is that understood?"

I noted that something was different in Crenen's speech.

"Then why did you make him swear to serve only you?"

"To make Jenen stay. Look at this boy!" Crenen pointed one claw at me while I watched silently, still cradling my precious fruits, munching away. "Do you truly believe he has what it takes to save Paradise? He acts like a little girl; does nothing but sleep; *lies*."

I opened my mouth to retort, but then decided against it. Let them pretend I couldn't hear. Just so long as I had my grapes....

Wait. That wasn't right. I shook my head, trying to clear it.

It was finally starting to click inside my groggy head. Crenen had given me those grapes earlier so I could be visited by the Seer; that way Jenen would grow more anxious and would have to stay put a while longer. Crenen had known Jenen would stick around while he waited for me to dream, just to see if I really would be visited. Of all the sneaky, insensitive, down-right wrong, manipulative, jerky things to do.

"I don't get it," I said, aware enough to defend myself now. "Why can't I do it? The Seer said it was my responsibility to sssave everyone, so why not let me try? Obviously, when I save everyone, you won't need Jenen for whatever reason you did before, right? Ssso, what would it hurt to let me try?" It was an effort to keep from slurring my words, but I managed. Mostly.

"The boy has a valid point, Master. Where is the harm —?"

"Time! Time, you dolts! We're nearly out of time. Both of you are useless! Kill! Kill all and be done with dolts." He wheeled around, bare feet stirring up dust, and buried his face in his hands.

I considered his back, then took a deep breath and walked forward, rounding the man until I stood face-to-face with Yenen Clan's leader. "Crenen, look. I vowed to serve you, but I'll do it in my own way. I gave you my word that I would help your people, and that's what I plan on doing. I'm gonna fulfill this Vendaeva thing if it kills me, and you're not going to stop me. Got it?" Part of me prayed he would argue, though my more prideful side was adamant about saving the bloody world just because he thought I couldn't.

He slowly spread the fingers of his left hand apart and his golden eye viewed me thoughtfully, saying nothing.

"So," I continued, feeling slightly braver. "Let's go see this Seer of yours so that she can give me a straight answer about what I'm supposed to do. Okay?"

His hands slid from his face and, before I could respond, he slapped me hard across the face. "Well, yeah!" he hissed and stomped after Jenen into the heavy foliage.

I watched him go with mixed feelings of anger, unexplainable pleasure and relief that he hadn't killed me. Finally I sighed, shaking my head as I rubbed my reddened cheek. "Let's get going, Menen. His Royal Worship has spoken." I plucked the final gerani grape from its vine, stuffed it into my pocket for later, then started walking. Menen fell into step beside me.

"You have grown, somehow," he said.

"Really? I don't feel taller." I raised a hand to my head and measured as though it would tell me something. Perhaps the gerani was helping me to grow.

"Not physically," he said with a small smile. "Anyone who can handle Crenen as you just did—well, you've matured." He wrinkled his brow in thought. "I don't believe I know your name."

"Just call me Key," I said, a warm, comfortable feeling settling in my stomach. It nearly countered the sting of my cheek.

"It suits you," he stated, leaving me to wonder if he meant the new color of my face or my self-appointed nickname.

We walked for only a few minutes before Menen and I caught up with Jenen and Crenen. From then we walked in silence, two in our party brooding.

We made camp early at Crenen's request. He claimed it was because Jenen looked like he would "fall down and become Dead Smelly Dog if not rest soon," although I suspected it had more to do with his own injuries.

My mother had warned me on more than one occasion to keep a civil tongue in my head. Luckily, either because of Menen's sudden faith in my maturity, or because I was still feeling the effects of the gerani, I didn't debate Crenen's reasons for an early rest. That, and I was perfectly willing to kick back and rest my own blistered feet. I had thought my sneakers capable of handling most terrain—but that was back when 'most terrain' entailed paved walkways, topsoil gardens and graveled driveways—not peppermint scented foliage-infested rock-strewn Crenen-paved (or, rather, unpaved) trails through treacherous forests with the potential threat of Small Red Fuzzies. Now my sneakers were without their tread and it was only a matter of time before I wore holes in the soles.

The only good that had come from all this pain was the grove of gerani trees we had tragically left behind. And the fact that I felt this way probably meant I was hooked for life. Make way for the new, inebriated Key. Mom would be thrilled.

For dinner, Menen passed out a handful of what I assumed was jerky. Again, Crenen was quick to inform the world of how horrible the food was and what he thought of Menen for daring to feed it to him.

Jenen and I ate in silence, the former chewing his dinner methodically on the far side of the group, beneath a tree whose roots acted as a sort of chair. Crenen and Menen were to my right, the latter enduring Crenen's harassment with the patience of a saint.

I sat watching Jenen without realizing it until he stiffened, eyes narrowing as he turned his head, one ear tilted as he listened. I turned my own focus in the direction he was intent upon, and after a moment I heard a rustling coming from the leafy brambles. Crenen's distinctive voice trailed off as he too heard the sound, and he and Menen eyed the same spot.

A figure appeared just outside our encampment, a dark splotch against darkness. We hadn't started a fire so our presence wouldn't be noticed, in case enemies lurked nearby; all I could see by was the light from the moons overhead, and they did nothing but further shroud the figure standing among the trees.

Jenen leapt to his feet, making no sound, hair falling in his face as he flexed his claws, ready to attack our visitor.

"Sa Vais." The phrase was familiar, as was the heavily accented voice that said it, though I couldn't quite place who its owner was. (I only knew it wasn't Mr. Ugly. Not croaky enough.)

Crenen perked up, eyes widening. "Quiet Sneaky Thing."

Jenen relaxed, sitting again as the Yenen warrior entered our campsite, walked to Crenen, and knelt on one knee, bowing low, black hair falling into his face. "*Sa Vais, eyias deshe ii cran yas.*" He lifted his head, but remained kneeling.

"*Cra yas en veikes,*" Crenen said, smiling with what might have been relief. "*Teishne.*"

"Keis lavun taka lem," Quiet Sneaky Thing said, then turned his head toward me, a strange glint in his dark eyes. "Vendaeva," he said, nodding slightly. "You live." He pronounced it like it was some sort of miracle.

I offered him a dirty look, still remembering his 'short' references. "You, too. Wow. Amazing how everyone here is alive."

His smile only widened, and he turned back to his leader, continuing to blather in the Paradisian tongue. I tuned him out, watching Jenen as he proceeded to eat his last piece of jerky. I then propped my head against the tree trunk I had chosen as my own seat-back.

"Strange Coward Boy," Crenen said after a while of rattling off Paradisian words with his minion.

I turned my head, keeping it against the trunk, arching a brow quizzically. "Yeah?"

"Quiet Sneaky Thing bring Bulky Heavy Bag. Wanting?"

I blinked, surprised as I recalled that my backpack had indeed been left behind somewhere after that first encounter with the Kirid. "Yeah," I said, leaning forward. "Where is it?"

Quiet Sneaky Thing stood, towering over me, and offered a playful smile. He turned, leaving wordlessly. I could only assume he was getting it, and I was to wait here. Whether that was actually the case or not, I had no inclination to follow him alone to wherever my backpack was stowed.

Crenen seemed of the same mindset, because he didn't question the fact that I wasn't moving.

After awhile, the stealthy man returned, but this time I didn't hear him at all until he sauntered into camp, backpack in hand. I could only assume that meant he had intentionally made noise the last time to announce his arrival, in case Jenen lashed out before he could probably reveal himself.

He threw the bag at my feet and plopped down beside me, eyeing it curiously.

"What is inside?" he asked slowly, enunciating each word.

"Books, mostly," I answered as I fumbled with the zipper until it finally gave. I unzipped it with a smile, remembering the chips and cookies my mom had packed for me that morning so long ago. It was a good thing my bag was waterproof.

"What sort of books?" Quiet Sneaky Thing inquired, dark eyes intent, one hand hovering near as though anxious to help me disclose the bag's contents.

"Textbooks," I said, pulling a particularly cumbersome volume from the largest pocket. "This, my friend," I said, patting the hardcover, "is the history of my world." The real world. The one I wanted to get back too.

He took the book without permission, flipping through black and white pages, stopping and studying the occasional pictures throughout. "English," he said with awe in his voice.

"Um. Yes." I dug into the bag deeper and withdrew the smashed baggies which contained the beat up contents of my school lunch. Disregarding the flat sandwich with its growing mold, I focused on the bag of chips, probably only powder now, but still edible. As I opened the chip bag, I glanced at my Paradisian companion still flipping through the pages of history, occasionally touching the illustrations with reverent fingers. "That's a gun," I explained, referring to the picture of a black-powder pistol from the 1800's, before I had time to consider whether I wanted to explicate about such weaponry to a claw-toting ninja.

"Gun," he repeated, but didn't press for more. He only continued flipping through pages, going one direction and then the other. Crenen, his twin and his slave-for-a-cousin watched us silently, the first eyeing my bag of chips with a strange glint in his mismatched eyes.

"Want some?" I asked, offering Crenen the bag.

He shook his head, probably more interested in the noisy bag itself than what lay inside.

Shrugging, I returned to the history book in time to meet Quiet Sneaky Thing's yellow eyes. "Vendaeva," he said softly, a hand resting on the open tome. "You must be he."

I offered him a twisted smile. "I dunno about that. Knowing English doesn't make me a hero; there're lots of people who speak English where I come from."

He eyed me for a moment, disbelieving, then a mischievous smile spread across his face. "True. The prophecy did not say Vendaeva to be short."

I scowled. "Ha. Ha."

He closed the textbook and handed it back. "I am Hiskii."

"Key," I answered automatically as I shoved the book inside my bag, all the while wondering why I bothered to protect it.

"Sometime," Hiskii continued, "I will let you read our history. After you learn Paradisian, yes?"

I laughed dryly. "Right. Sure. Okay." Like I cared about Paradisian history; I had enough trouble learning my own world's timeline, thanks.

We stood before a wall of trees; they resembled Red Pines, so far as I could tell, and grew so close together that I couldn't see beyond them. I wondered how we planned to get through them, and prayed Crenen wouldn't make me squeeze between the close-knit trees. Still, I knew this had to be the way into the Realm of Yenen. Could there be any question?

We had gotten up earlier than I would have liked, and continued on foot through the forest; me dragging my heavy backpack along and wondering how I managed it all those years growing up. Either I was entirely out of shape now, or my body was exhausted. Probably both.

"Strange Coward Boy goes first, yeah?" Crenen said, grabbing my arm and shoving me ahead of him.

I decided against arguing. After everything else, what did one more adventure up a tree matter? I reached out and poked the towering pine before me. "So, just climb any tree?"

There was no answer.

I turned to investigate the silence—

And found myself completely alone.

"Uh, guys?" I looked back and forth, trying to spot any flash of non-green in all the greenery. "This isn't funny!" I called, expecting to hear my own voice return in an echo, only to discover that the foliage was too thick.

I scowled at the area at large, feeling abandoned.

When I was young, my family and I had gone camping in the mountains. While we all hiked early one morning, my brother Jeremy and I had wandered off the path, scouting out rare bugs and shiny rocks. My parents told us to get back on the trail or they would leave us behind. Jeremy headed back after a while, but I was too engrossed in a caterpillar weaving its cocoon. When I finally did turn around I didn't see my brother anymore. Thinking it was some kind of joke I called out that it wasn't funny, only to receive silence in response. I wasn't stupid, and so I stayed put, waiting to be rescued. It was several hours later that my father found me, telling me he was sorry for leaving me behind. Somehow it hurt more to know that they had forgotten me; that it hadn't been just a mean joke.

I shook off the memory and turned back to the wall of trees. Sighing, I tried to wriggle my way between two. The only results I got were scratches, a few purple bruises and some sticky patches of sap on my palms, pants and jacket.

"Just perfect," I muttered, throwing myself onto the ground, snapping several twigs beneath me.

As I sat staring at the leering trees I noticed that the gaps widened higher up. Terrific. That meant I had to climb. Sighing, I stood and examined each tree closely. I spotted the least imposing and decided to attempt the climb just once. I jumped, grabbing hold of the closest limb, pulling myself onto it after a lot of effort and scraping of shoes against the bark. It was hard work, but I slowly made my way up the trunk, heading for the gap, occasionally trying to squeeze through the two trees as I went.

After what seemed forever, and when I was pretty much covered in amber sap, hair jutting wildly in every direction, I reached the wide gap and slid through it.

I found myself standing on a wooden bridge strung from the gap I'd entered by and stretching over to a large tree in the most amazing afforest metropolis imaginable. Hollywood would have been jealous. The wall of trees must have circled the Realm, but I couldn't see past the throng of tree-houses crowding one another in order to know for certain. Countless bridges crossed from tree to tree at varying levels. The ancient trunks were wide enough to carve multiple rooms within, and at the bottom of each tree were carved stairs and a wooden door leading inside. Windows dotted the trees as well; some were glowing from light within despite the early afternoon, as the canopy above shrouded the city in eternal gloom.

Between the wood planks under my feet, I could just make out the forest floor a good thirty feet below, where a multitude of people stared upward—probably looking at the sap-saturated guy who had just invaded their city. Me. If they were worried or confused, I couldn't tell. They considered me with somber faces, each one pale, black- or brown-haired and depressive. I was beginning to think Crenen was in a class all his own, no matter where we went. These guys all looked much more like Jenen's kind of crowd.

"Behold, Yenen Clan!" a loud, familiar, irritating voice cried from the other side of the bridge. I spotted Crenen standing on the platform there. "Behold Vendaeva!"

Muted noises below drew my focus and I watched in stunned silence as the crowd bowed, never making a sound but for the rustling of their clothes and the shifting of their feet.

Gee. This was great for morale. They looked so exuberant...

The bridge began to wobble and I whipped my head up to view Crenen ambling along, one hand sliding along one rope that served as a handhold strung along either side of the unsteady, hovering walkway.

I stayed where I was until he reached me, halting as he regarded my disheveled condition. (I swear his grin deepened in morbid satisfaction.) "We welcome you to Realm of Yenen, Vendaeva."

I lowered my voice to respond, in case it carried to the throngs below. "Could'a warned me, *yeah*? Were you watching the entire time I tried getting up here? I bet you enjoyed that."

His continued smirk assured me that he had. "Must make good entrance. Wouldn't spoil big welcome, would Strange Coward Boy? Made special for arrival of Vendaeva."

Such a warm greeting, too. "I thought you didn't believe in me."

"Don't. But Yenen Clan do." Crenen gestured to the still-bowing crowd, as if that would somehow convince me they were glad I was here. "Bow better for Strange Coward Boy or for Vendaeva?"

Was he doing this to mock me? Or was it to give his downtrodden people something to cling to, to hope for? Crenen had a twisted soul, no question there, but was he really in it for himself, or did he care about his followers enough to give them something he, himself, had given up on?

His character was a difficult one to read.

"Where are Menen and Jenen?" I asked.

"Cannot walk on Holy Bridge Thing. Only special persons walk on Holy Bridge Thing, and they too insignificant."

I cocked an eyebrow. "There are hundreds of bridges here. Why is this one special? Besides, I thought you wanted Jenen to be your leader?"

"Not leader yet, yeah?" he laughed, clapping me on the back, not answering my first question. "Come. Meet Seer." He turned and padded along the bobbing bridge, back the way he had come.

Apprehension crept through me as I thought of meeting that ditsy woman again. Pretty as she was, I doubted very much if I could handle the personality attached. Still... "Hey, before I meet her, can I take a bath? I'm sticky." I gestured at my clothes as I plodded behind Crenen.

"No bath prepared. Will be ready when done with Seer, yeah?" he said as he bounded further along the bridge. I followed carefully, attempting to maintain my balance.

Finally I reached the massive tree at the other end of the overpass, and was relieved as I stepped onto the firm platform. It felt like stepping on dry ground after a long ride on a storm-tossed boat (or what I think it would be like). Crenen led me inside, where my eyes had to adjust to the dim natural lighting. I followed him down a set of carved stairs that eventually led to open ground outside of the tree. Everyone was still bowing silently when I emerged from the dank enclosure, and Crenen let them grovel.

He took me to a wide pathway between the crowds, and we headed toward the largest tree in the metropolis. The tree was at least two hundred feet around, with countless branches reaching toward the hidden sky. Leaves twice the size of my feet fluttered in a gentle breeze. As we approached, I spotted two figures standing at the top of the massive, carved steps that led to a widely-arched, rune-decorated opening into the grandfather tree.

We climbed the steps and I counted each one I passed until we reached the top. Exactly fifty. I looked up as Crenen halted beside me, and saw her: Seer Veija.

Her golden locks tumbled down her shoulders and along her back, nearly reaching the ground, and her stunning violet eyes were shining with pleasure. She wore a sweeping pink gown of satin material, enhancing her slender, curved body. A patch of cloth was intentionally missing on her right sleeve, revealing a strange tattoo: a black sword caught in a red circle. A pink veil covered Veija's nose and mouth, though it could not hide her striking beauty.

Beside her stood a man with intense blood-red eyes, utterly unreadable, fathomless; after a searing instant, I broke eye contact with him, stung. His face was impassive, angular and handsome, like he had been chiseled out of stone. He also had long golden hair, reaching his ankles, though it was pulled back into a thin ponytail trailing down his back. On his cheek was the same tattoo that adorned Veija's shoulder. The tattoo was also embedded twice on each of his arms, visible through intended holes in his silk periwinkle shirt. He wore a blue waist-long cape that was caught behind each shoulder to avoid hiding his tattoos. A strange silver and black skirt of metal armor hung at his waist, under which were baggy black pants that tucked into knee-high black leather boots. To top off his bizarre wardrobe were jeweled armbands and a neck ring that strongly resembled a metal choker.

"Welcome, Vendaeva." Veija's sweet voice said, recapturing my focus. She curtsied, a hint of a smile in her singsong tone.

I bowed back, managing to make it appear natural. At least, slightly natural. Okay, so I stumbled a bit, but no one laughed (because Crenen's snicker doesn't count). "Thanks," I said, refusing to think on my awkward dip, though my cheeks felt slightly warm.

"We have much to speak of," Veija said, voice growing serious as she motioned inside the giant tree. "Please, follow me."

I glanced to my left to get Crenen's blessed permission, and blinked as I recognized two other familiar faces. Somewhere along the line Jenen and Menen had joined us and were standing just behind Crenen.

The latter nodded his head, and I took that to mean it was okay to go with the Seer. We all made to follow her, but as we took a step forward, Veija halted, glancing back at us.

"Please, only Vendaeva may come within." She turned around fully, pretty eyes apologetic. "Even His Highness must remain here."

Crenen blinked, but shrugged and plopped down onto the wooden landing, adopting a bored expression. Jenen's eyes narrowed, but he also sat. Menen kept his place behind Crenen and remained standing.

I turned back to Veija, who nodded, and I entered the structure with her, noticing that her silent attendant had come along. "I thought only us two—" I began without thinking, but she cut me off.

"Lon comes with me, no matter the reason. Even if I told him to stay behind, he would not."

She was acting a lot less ditsy.

"So, does Lon speak?" I asked, watching the stone-faced man. We were standing in darkness, the dim light from outside barely giving me sight to make out his expressionless features.

She turned, face just visible in the gloom, and Lon slipped next to her without a sound. "Only when he needs to," she said, the smile back in her voice.

"Okay." I shrugged, allowing her to continue our walk. "When we last spoke you mentioned that you had no idea how I was supposed to save Paradise. Do you know now?"

She hesitated and shook her head. "It has not yet been revealed."

"Huh," I said for the sake of responding. What the heck was I supposed to do in the meantime? "So what are we talking about, then?"

"I wanted to speak with you."

"But we did that already," I reminded, torn between jesting and mild annoyance.

She blinked and then giggled like a little girl who doesn't really get the joke. "Of course we did."

Now she was acting like herself. Apparently all formalities were finished.

"Okay, speak with me about what?" I stepped closer in my attempt to adjust my eyesight to the dimness, not really aware that I was doing so.

Instantly Lon was in front of Veija, holding his arm out protectively. His red eyes were locked on mine, daring me to approach again. I took two steps back.

"Lon," Veija said sharply. "It is okay—he is Vendaeva. He will not harm me."

I didn't think he would listen, but Lon stepped aside, still glaring.

"You'll have to forgive him," she said. "Lon is my brother, and he is more protective that he need be." She tossed the last bit at him reprovingly.

"It's fine. I'd probably do the same for my sister," I lied.

"It is still unforgivable. Come. Lon will walk behind us both." She spun on her heels only after shooting a pointed look at her brother. I smirked at her revenge on my behalf. Ditsy or not, she certainly was cute.

"Nice skirt, pretty-boy," I whispered as I brushed past Lon.

Perhaps that comment began the next chain of events, but I couldn't be certain. In any case, that was the beginning; that was what started our eternal feud.

9
The End?

Would the stairs never end?

Veija led me down and down a stairway spiraling into the oppressive gloom. From somewhere—I couldn't pinpoint where—a little light trickled through; just enough to keep me from tripping over my own feet, or on Veija's trailing skirts.

Then there was Lon, following closely behind me, eyes burning into my back. If we walked much longer, I was worried I might fall down dead. If looks had any chance at all of killing, his murderous glare would find a way.

"We are almost there," Veija said after what seemed forever. (Maybe all these forevers were the reason this place was called Paradise, instead of any aspirations toward peace or salvation.)

"Okay," I said, at a loss for anything more constructive, let alone eloquent.

'Almost', apparently, meant another fifteen minutes. The spiraling steps gave way to an unadorned vestibule, at the end of which were two giant wood doors, intricately carved with swirling symbols and runes. Blazing torches rested in sconces on either side of the doors, lighting the details of the etched doors and casting long shadows behind us. Veija approached the doors, then turned, skirts swishing.

"Prepare yourself. You will walk on sacred ground." Her voice was amplified by the room's natural acoustics.

With her pronouncement, the air became heavy, still. I watched her for a moment, waiting for the punchline, knowing it wouldn't come. *This isn't a dream,* I admitted to myself, understanding at last how much this mattered to these people. How much they needed me. Why else would they put up with my whining? My weakness?

But what could I possibly offer them? How was I supposed to help?

I just wanted to go home.

"Are you ready?" Veija asked.

I nodded, lying.

She nodded back, then turned and waited as Lon walked past me, then her, and rested his bespangled hands on either door. Muscles tightened as he pushed inward, and the doors finally gave, silently moving aside as Lon stepped forward.

Blue light flooded the vestibule where Veija and I stood, and the shadows fled as darkness retreated to the room's furthest recesses. I held up my arm protectively, momentarily blinded, but I pried my eyes open and lowered my arm again.

Something was moving in the room beyond those open doors. As I watched closely, gray eyes squinting against the light, I thought I saw countless glowing orbs floating about, scattered across an enormous chamber. The source of the light.

Veija drew nearer to the gaping entrance, her outline bright, hair shining. She turned after a moment, beckoning with one graceful hand. "Come, Vendaeva."

I hesitated, frightened without understanding why. "What is this place?"

Her eyes danced with shifting light from the moving orbs. "Are you prepared to be Vendaeva?"

Again I hesitated. How could I answer? I wasn't sure what it entailed. And, aside from coming through the great, muddy Phudel, what proof was there that I was their guy?

I opened my mouth to respond, but still couldn't answer.

"I see." Her tone was soft, disappointed. She stepped from the chamber, and Lon followed behind her, allowing the doors to close with a ominous boom and resounding echoes across the vestibule. The torches were oppressively dim and terribly cold after the brilliance of the orbs, yet an emptiness I hadn't known I was feeling was gone now that the doors had closed. A strange relief washed over me.

"You may return to your companions, Key," Veija said into the gloom.

I felt a stab of guilt, knowing I had failed her test. Bowing, because I wasn't sure how else to exit, I turned and retreated up the stairs, leaving Veija and her over-protective brother behind.

When light from above appeared in the winding stairwell, I jogged until I finally reached the top, gasping. Hands on my knees, back arched, I drew deep breaths, focusing on them to keep from reflecting on Veija's disappointed gaze. It wasn't really working.

I straightened, running a hand absently through my hair until it snared in the sap. With a scowl I freed my hand, ignoring the mess of hair I'd just made worse. I fixed my eyes on the tree's exit and hurried toward it, desperate to see my alien companions. The repressive feeling I had experienced when I saw the orbs had returned, lingering now like a weight on my body, mind and soul. If there was one person who could distract me from this, it was Crenen.

I stepped into the fresh air of Yenen Clan's Realm. Evening was descending, casting a deeper gloom across the city.

Crenen and his cronies were missing. Searching for them, I gazed down the fifty steps to where the bowing crowds had been. Now only a few dozen people milled about, heads bowed, pallid faces drawn. A city this large should have been bustling with constant activity, yet now it resembled a ghost town, complete with roaming specters.

"They do not believe you can save them," Hiskii's silken voice said from just behind me.

I turned, startled. "I can't save them," I said quietly. "I'm not Vendaeva." Despite my adamant claim yesterday that I would save Paradise whether Crenen liked it or not, I knew better than to believe myself. I was a liar. Liars weren't trustworthy. Up until now everything had been a crazy dream; a bizarre, freakish nightmare with a few perks—like being ultra-important. But it was different now. I was not the heroic type; I couldn't save people from a terrible disease. Doctors did that—not teenage boys with penchants for lying.

Quiet Sneaky Thing frowned at me, yellow eyes boring holes into my head. "I see," he finally said. "Very well, boy. Sa Vais wants you. Come."

Knowing he was referring to Crenen, I followed after the silent figure, descending the steps with leaden shoes.

Justifications ran through my head as I walked. I couldn't be Vendaeva. It was ridiculous to believe otherwise. And if I was—if that were even remotely possible—did it matter that I had failed the test? Could people really blame me for being hesitant? Part of me wanted to be the prophesied hero. Ensure my survival and, sure, I'll do whatever you want. I'll even try to destroy the Paradisaical—or whatever—disease.

As if that could happen.

The emptiness seemed to be deepening, and it wasn't until I reached the tree Hiskii was leading me to that I understood what it really was. I was homesick. I'd had enough of this world. I'd had enough of feeling pressured to heal the dratted place.

I mentally reiterated that it was impossible.

"Go," Hiskii ordered, nodding to a flight of wooden stairs that ran up the length of trunk. "They are on the second level. Sa Vais is waiting. Go."

Despondent, I obeyed, and without taking note of anything, I walked up the quavering steps. When I reached the second story, I pulled the door open.

"Well, well," Crenen said cheerily from within, where he sat at a long table laden with several varieties of food. Menen and Jenen were with him. "Come, eat."

I stepped inside, closed the door and planned to sit back and think miserable thoughts when my eyes caught sight of several bowls of plump, juicy gerani. My mouth traitorously began to water and for the moment all my cares melted away.

"Sticky Sap Boy smell like tree, yeah?" Crenen observed, his fanged smile stretching wide.

"You're the one who didn't let me take a bath first, *yeah*?" I retorted, gesturing with my spoon between mouthfuls of food. After eating a few gerani, I had discovered I was famished.

Crenen raised one dark eyebrow as though questioning my word—which he had a right to do. "In any case," he turned to Menen, "he smell like tree."

Menen merely nodded, chewing his food quietly. Apparently annoyed his servant wasn't being vocal, Crenen leaned toward him to insist he speak. I took that moment to glance over at Jenen.

As I suspected, he was watching me with unreadable eyes. As I kept his gaze I again noted that he was decidedly less friendly now than when we first met—and I felt a little regret in losing that strange kindness he had shown me. As I chewed my food—most of which I refused to ask the ingredients of—I offered Jenen a smile, hoping it wouldn't make him furious. Immediately he tore his eyes from mine, focusing on his own food.

I admired his ability to block out all the noise Crenen was making as he prodded Menen's shoulder with a sharp knife, demanding that he "sniff Sticky Sap Boy for self, since nose is broke."

As Crenen rattled on, my thoughts threatened to turn down dreary paths again, and I reached for another gerani to drown my sorrows.

"What Sticky Sap Boy think of Mysterious Girly Guy?" Crenen inquired, giving my hand pause as it hovered over the nearest bunch of gerani. I was convinced by this point that I was the only one who shifted from one Crenen-name to another.

"He means Lon," Menen supplied, receiving a glare from Crenen.

"Sure, speak to Sticky Sap Boy but not when Master order so talk, yeah?" he growled.

"As you wish, Master," Menen bowed his head obligingly.

Crenen blinked, speechless for once. Then he shrugged it off and swiped the Paradisaical Purple Fruit I had been aiming for as he gazed at me expectantly.

I stifled a scowl, selecting a different gerani. "Well." I recalled the loathing gaze Lon had given me since my remark on his skirt and his continued disdain below ground. "I don't much like him." Nor he, me, chances were.

Crenen cackled and nodded. "Seem arrogant and cold, yeah? Much like Sick Nasty Dog."

I nodded fervent agreement before I could stop. I only prayed Jenen wouldn't take offense.

Speaking of Jenen... "Hey, Crenen, you always have a reason for everyone that you name, er, what you name them..." So I could have phrased that better. "What I mean is—Tall Strong Jerk's name is obvious. Mine...is...also obvious," I admitted grudgingly, denial aside for time's sake. "But what about Jenen? Why 'Sick Nasty Dog'?"

Crenen glanced at Jenen, as though he was no more than an insignificant bug. I could still clearly remember how it had felt when he looked at me that way. "When little, Sick Nasty Dog get sick lots."

"And when I betrayed Yenen Clan, I became a 'nasty dog,'" Jenen added with a sardonic smile.

"Exactly," Crenen said.

"You betrayed your clan?" I asked.

Menen cleared his throat, gaining my attention, and shook his head in answer, but Jenen and Crenen shot him withering glares. He took a bite of food and became silent. I made a mental note to ask Menen the facts later. In the meantime, I decided to inquire into as much as they would allow. "If you betrayed your clan, how come Crenen wants you to be the leader?"

Jenen glanced at Crenen with a calculating look and then scooped food onto his wooden spoon. "I wish I knew," he murmured.

I turned to Crenen, putting on my best inquisitive expression.

He sighed after a moment and then glared. "No business," he said sharply, and swiped another gerani.

Before I could try another approach, the door into the tree opened and Mysterious Girly Guy—Lon—entered. His stony red eyes fell on me.

"Yes?" I asked coolly.

"Her ladyship desires another conversation," he answered.

I stood, glancing back at Crenen, who had somehow managed to get his hand caught in Menen's grasp, a large gerani clutched in his arrested claws. Neither of them were focused on their silent battle any longer, but instead watched Lon and me, curiosity written clearly on their faces.

"I'll be back," I said, sparing a fleeting glance at Jenen, who watched his food intently, raven hair hanging like a curtain in his face.

I followed Lon into the darkness outside. We walked down the wood-planked steps until we reached the ground, but instead of heading to the grandfather tree, Lon guided me through the city, heading in the opposite direction from where I had entered. I took the opportunity to study my surroundings. Lights shone in many of the tree-houses, though more than double that were eerily dark and silent. No one was out now, save us. As we passed one tree, I thought I heard sobbing coming from within the dark abode. A chill ran down my spine, and I walked just a tad closer to my guide, feeling nervous.

It was a while later, as the trees thinned considerably, that we reached a wide, deep, black pool of water. Here the canopy of leaves relented, revealing a breathtaking view of the nighttime sky and two full moons directly above us. The scene was reflected in the pool, glistening with the luminous celestial wonder.

Lon approached the water, eyes studying his stony reflection.

"Come here," he said. "Look."

I stepped up to the bank and gazed into the depths. The moons' reflections were so clear in the still pond, I almost believed they were the real thing; that somehow I stood on top of them.

"What do you see?" Lon asked.

I knew this was one of those profound, rhetorical questions, and I knew the answer he wanted me to state. "Me," I supplied as I glanced at my reflection. I did a double-take then, meeting my own gray eyes, somehow different from before. My honey-colored hair was much longer now than I'd thought, and tangled, sticking wildly in all directions because of the tree sap. Despite this, while I hadn't shaved since my arrival about a week ago, no stubble showed on my face. Longish hair, but no beard? That made no sense. Especially since my hair had grown at an amazing rate in such a short time.

"Is there something wrong, Vendaeva?" Lon's voice was mocking.

Why was it that everyone gave me the urge to hit them around here?

"No," I said coldly, finally looking up.

"Do you like Paradise?" he asked.

I shrugged. "Sure," I lied with ease. It wasn't a complete lie, though. A part of me, small though it was, did like it here. Did want to help. But I couldn't, could I? Was it possible? Even just a little bit?

"You are homesick," he remarked.

I clenched my fist, angry at his words. But the more honest part felt the longing for home return. It was a battle of longing versus pride—not an easy fight. Finally I sighed.

"Yeah," I admitted. "I kind of miss my family." As soon as I said it I regretted doing so. My cheeks warmed.

Lon laughed outright, a peculiar light in his blood-colored eyes. "Well, then, *Key*—what say you? Shall I send you *home*?" I stared as Lon's eyes changed color, glowing a brilliant metallic gold.

"W-what?" I stepped back as his words sank in. My heel touched the water, and I halted. "Drat." I tried to scramble from the pool, but Lon was too fast. Though his slender fingers pushed me almost delicately, as though he only grudgingly touched me, it was enough to make me lose my balance.

I fell back, flailing my arms as though to make them wings. A splash sounded in my ears, somehow distant. Sparkles of water flashed among the stars, while the man in the moon laughed with glowing, golden eyes.

Just one moon.

I awoke on my dreary neighborhood street. I sat up and gazed at the gloomy houses lining the suburban lane, at the school not too far away, at the potholes littering the paved road, ignoring the pounding rain that was flattening my hair against my head and causing my bangs to hang in my eyes.

Gingerly I picked myself up and rubbed my sore head, moaning softly. "What the heck?" I whispered.

I recalled, then, that it had been raining on the Monday morning that I went to Paradise. Was it possible that it had been a dream? Had Jenen, Crenen, Menen, Veija, and that stupid Lon only been a crazy dream?

Surely not. Not after I had accepted that it might actually be real.

"Hey!" a voice called.

I turned and recognized my sister Jana standing underneath her pink umbrella, waving at me from the other sidewalk. She was mostly dry in her black trench coat, brown hair trailing softly down one shoulder. I hurried from the side of the street, sneakers squeaking with water, and joined her, rubbing water from my burning eyes.

"Are you okay? Your head is bleeding," Jana said, reaching her hand up to touch my hair.

I would have brushed her off, but I was too exhausted. Instead I nodded numbly as her fingers inspected the wound, focusing on keeping my head above my feet.

"Jason, are you okay?" she repeated, her eyebrows furrowed with concern. "You've been missing for hours. What happened?"

"Nothing," I murmured, and I stumbled as I tried to walk in the direction of our house.

"You're bleeding and soaked, and you call that nothing? I knew you were mental, but this is stupid." Jana grabbed my arm to steady me as she spoke. "Let's get home and take care of that bump, and you can tell me exactly what happened."

I didn't know how to explain. What could I say? 'Well, you see, I slipped in the rain; landed in a strange world of sharp-toothed ninja-like pretty-boys; was treated like some hero; swore an oath to the freakiest ninja of all; met a beautiful woman with no brain—and finally ended up back here just as I was beginning to believe it had all happened.' I think not. No way was I going to let her know just how mental I really was.

As I concocted the elaborate story I would have to tell to keep her happy, we reached the house; a two level, white paneled structure large enough to comfortably hold my three siblings and me, as well as our parents.

Jana guided me through the living and dining rooms to the floral kitchen, where she pulled out a first-aid kit from a bottom drawer near the fridge, and began doctoring me up. "So," she said, "you gonna give details now?"

I shook my head. "Look. I'm in no mood for lies, let alone the truth. So, how about we skip the elucidation and just finish this. I'm…really tired."

It was true, my body screamed with weariness, and my head pounded so loudly I could hardly hear. But, more than anything, I just wanted to be alone. I knew of no one who gets pushed by the local jock, falls in the middle of the street, goes unconscious and dreams of an exotic world full of realistic (if strange) people and very realistic pains, then wakes up to remember it with perfect clarity. It was absurd to consider my adventure more than fiction, but something kept me from writing it off as a fantastical dream of outrageous proportions —though it was certainly outrageous.

At long last Jana finished with her bandaging (I swear she got a little band-aid-happy with my face) and took me up the stairs toward my room.

"Just a second. I need a shower. The sap…" I mumbled, switching directions in the hallway, slipping from my sister's grasp.

"Sap?" Jana asked, looking even more concerned than before. Big sisters tend to worry over stupid things.

"From the tree," I said crossly. I closed the bathroom door behind me and locked it. But instead of hitting the shower, I went to the mirror. As I had both suspected and feared, my hair was short once more, and very flat from the rain. Any and all signs of sap were gone, and my clothes were soaked and soiled, but not torn. I glanced at my hand, examining every inch—but the furapin-thingy's bite was nowhere to be found.

For all my urges to return home I couldn't help but feel like a piece of my heart had been torn away. It was over. I had done nothing to save them, and though it must have been a dream, I felt like I had deserted them.

And it was all his fault.

"Stupid jerk," I growled, slamming my fists against the counter-top, not caring what Jana thought.

Terrible realization struck me as I pictured the man responsible: I couldn't remember his name. Her brother. Wait—

What was her name? I tried to picture the Seer, but it was vague, like the passing vision of a late-night dream. I was trembling, and I gripped the sink to steady myself. I had forgotten. Somehow it was all fading—even as vivid as it had been a few minutes before.

Pitiful as it was, tears filled my eyes and I fell to my knees, shoulders trembling. "No," I whispered, filled with unexplainable horror. "Can't I at least keep the memory? Do I have to lose that too?"

Jana was knocking on the door, calling to me, rattling the knob—but I hardly heard. My world seemed somehow to have shattered.

I tried to tell myself it was only a dream. Only a passing nightmare full of freakish ninja people with sharp teeth and evil agendas. Only a horrible dream with red furry critters—or were they pink? No. The eyes were pink. Or were they yellow?

I ran my hands through my hair, pressing my palms hard against my head, as though that would help me to recall everything that was lost.

Surely I could remember his name. "Cren…something," I ventured. "Cren…en." But the name only forced me to admit it was a dream. Like all dreams, most events, names, and faces had faded; all but the most significant parts. And Crenen had been significant.

I hadn't even said goodbye. I tried to stop the tears yet again, but something was lodged in my throat, and the sobs came. Like a small child, I cried, feeling remorse and regret too strong for words to convey.

I stayed there for a long time, until I finally collected myself. Then I slowly got to my feet and opened the door to reveal a worried Jana.

"I'm okay," I said quietly, moving past her.

"You were crying," she said, holding a screwdriver in one hand. Apparently she'd been removing the hinges from the door when I opened it.

"Was I?" I reached my room and entered, walking arduously across the plush carpet to my bed.

Jana walked in after me and opened my dresser drawer. "Here's your pajamas," she said, handing them to me. "Did something happen at school?"

I shook my head. "I'm okay," I repeated, sounding remarkably like a robot.

Jana didn't look convinced. "Well, just get some sleep. I'll make you some chamomile tea." She hurried from the room and left me to change my clothes.

When I finished changing I pulled my covers down and chucked my soaked clothes on the floor. I was about to climb into bed when I noticed something out of the corner of my eye. Turning back to my clothes, I noticed an object by my discarded pants. I knelt beside them and picked up the little ball from the carpet.

A grape.

Part Two:
Vendaeva?

10
Panic Attack?

A storm shook my windowpane, stealing sleep. As I tossed and turned to make more noise than the rattling pane, I knew there really was no point. Either way sleep would not be attained.

Finally I threw my covers off and sat up, cupping my head in my hands, groaning. The storm was just an excuse. The real reason I couldn't sleep was the same reason I hadn’t slept in several months.

At first my family had assumed that I was just nervous about graduating; however, my ability to lie also encompassed the awesome power of cheating and I passed the exams with ease. Now the family contributed my restlessness to my mental health and had sent me in for counseling. The result was a bottle of pills (which I promptly flushed down the toilet).

Even before graduation they'd been concerned. Who could blame them? My parents had a son who changed drastically when he slammed his head against the pavement. Truth be told, I still believed I'd been swept away to a fantastical world, but I refused to tell my counselor of the event because the only proof I possessed was a single, solitary, insignificant gerani, and who was going to believe that it wasn't just some ordinary grape?

That ended up quite the issue at the house.

I placed the precious gerani in the fridge, to preserve it as long as possible—but I ended up having to sleep near the refrigerator each night, while my entire family attempted to chuck it so that I would get my 'head screwed on straight again.'

Jana was the most concerned. She made sure to relate the events of the evening when I had returned home—including my sob-session on the bathroom floor—to each member of my family. Of course, Jana, like everyone else in the house, had the ability to exaggerate—which was suddenly to my detriment.

Now I was psychotic. I needed pills. Pills would solve everything. They would make my sudden "depression" evaporate, leaving me whole and well and happy.

Right. Pills—meet toilet. Toilet—pills.

I didn't tell my family about Chas shoving me into the puddle, nor had I confronted him about it. I knew it would avail me nothing to tattle, and it hardly explained away my emotional state—not unless I was prepared to share everything.

I wanted badly to ask Chas why he pushed me, why his eyes glowed yellow, but the opportunity hadn't arisen quickly enough, what with exams swamping my life; and then Chas moved away right after graduation.

I counted the days since my return from Paradise. Then I counted the months. It was over six now. In my attempts to get back there, few though they were, I had splashed through puddles, ponds, and rivers. I had purposely slipped and hit my head several times, with the only result being a very powerful headache. There were times I also questioned my sanity, but then I sought the gerani to comfort my troubled mind.

I wasn't crazy. No matter what everyone thought, I wasn't crazy.

Lifting my head from my palms, I gazed at the bedroom door. With a sigh, I slid from my bed and headed for the stairs. I'd made my family promise to leave the "grape" alone, since I still felt I 'needed it desperately.' If they wanted a psycho kid, I would give them a psycho kid. Still, while they had agreed, I didn't fully trust them. They might not be as good at lying as I, but that didn't mean they wouldn't try.

I walked down the stairs and entered the kitchen; a cozy little room with floral décor on every available surface. My mother loved flowers so much that the rest of the family despised them.

I reached the fridge and hesitated. I'd often been tempted to eat the Fruit, to see if it might let me dream of the Seer again, but I was too afraid. I was terrified that it wouldn't work and that my one link to Paradise would be gone forever. I couldn't take that chance. Besides, by now the gerani looked a bit too shriveled (more like a raisin).

I gripped handle and pulled the door open. My eyes sought the gerani's usual spot, and my heart froze. I searched every shelf desperately and my stomach clenched. Something caught in my throat and I felt my hand tremble with horror. The gerani was gone.

I searched again, and again, and again. I moved things, opened things, tossed things—still there was no gerani.

"No," I whispered, kneeling down and hanging on the fridge's door handle, shaking my head. I had suspected, had feared, but I hadn't actually believed they would remove it.

There was no getting the gerani back now.

There was no proof of Paradise.

But there was a way to get even with them, even if the consequences were severe. As the idea crept from the depths of my sinister mind, I thought of something Crenen had once said of me. 'Weak already, after all.' The family believed that to be the case now. So let them think they'd gone too far. It would only serve them right.

I stood back up, watched the contents of the icebox for a moment, cleared my throat—

And screamed.

The response was instantaneous, as though the entire family had already braced for any kind of reaction. So I had only one option open to me: Make it worse than they could fathom.

I collapsed to the floor, not sparing myself the bruises such a move was sure to cause. I curled into a ball, hugging my knees to my chest, lying on my side and breathing erratically. My father reached me first, and he lifted my head off the tiled floor as he spoke in soothing tones. I ignored him.

It wasn't too hard to act panicked. In reality it was only an amplification of what I really felt. My one link, the one possible chance of remembering Paradise, had been taken from me—cruelly ripped away at the first sign of independence from said object.

The pain I felt at their betrayal was sharp. They tried to communicate with me, but I pretended not to hear.

Dad ordered Jacob to search the fridge for my "grape," and this perked my interest. I remained supposedly oblivious to my surroundings, but my ears focused on the events that unfolded.

"It's not here," Jacob finally announced, sounding a little frightened.

I shoved my guilt way down deep.

"Check his hands," Mom said, her voice quavering.

My hands were pried open.

"Nothing," Dad said.

"Who took his grape?" Mom asked accusingly.

It was a silly situation if one were to watch it; an eighteen-year-old boy, lying helpless in his father's arms, awaiting the return of his precious comfort object—a grape. But I didn't care. If the family didn't collaborate against me, who had taken the gerani?

"I did," Jana said.

I felt a fire ignite inside of me, both with anger at her actions, and severe guilt at what I had put my family through. But I did not move; I couldn't.

"You knew better," Dad scolded.

"I know," Jana said, and I pictured her hanging her head like a child.

"Why?" Mom asked, and I noticed the weariness in her voice.

"I didn't think he'd actually react like this. I thought that if I removed the stupid grape, he would snap out of it. I'm tired of tiptoeing around him all the time," she said, her own voice full of emotion. "I don't know what made him like this suddenly—all I know is that I want my brother back."

Another stab of guilt cut me, but I continued to breath unsteadily; in truth, I was having trouble breathing anyway. I couldn't move. My limbs were weak, and my mind felt heavy.

I don't remember falling asleep in my father's arms. In fact I remember only snatches of conversations and a few fleeting images of the next few days. It was as though the furry critter from Paradise had bitten me all over again; only, it hadn't.

I went from hot to cold to hot, over and over, and I tossed and turned in my twisted bedding. It was an eternity of discomfort, and I wondered about my sanity during those long, torturous days and nights.

What caused the fever? I didn't know.

While I couldn't often grasp the words being formed around me, half of the time I felt an incredible sense of urgency from the tones that circled my bed. In those moments, I struggled to free myself of my smothering blankets. It felt like I was swimming through murky waters without light and with only fleeting sounds. Then the urgency would leave and I tiredly sank into the depths of my dreams.

When I finally managed to pry my tired eyes open, only a little light streamed in through my curtained window. I attempted to blink my weariness away, but it stubbornly stuck to my eyelids and forced them closed. Again I blinked my eyes open and managed to sit up. A wave of dizziness slammed into my head and I fell back on my pillows, grasping for some secure portion of my blanket to keep from spinning out of control. Darkness threatened to overcome me again, but I resisted.

"Key?"

I finally conquered the vertigo and looked around the room for the source of the voice. I would have assumed it to be a family member, but no one in my family called me Key. I was the only one who called myself Key, except a few creatures from Paradise.

"Crenen?" I couldn't recall if the voice was male or female, so I had to take an uneducated guess, and though I knew Crenen called me 'Strange Coward Boy,' none of the other Paradisian names would come to mind.

"Very *good*, Strange Coward Boy," the voice remarked in an amused tone.

"Why'd you call me Key?" I mumbled. My eyes scanned the empty room yet again.

"Strange Coward Boy named Key, yeah? Tall Strong Jerk tell us."

The image of a tall, masculine man with black hair and bloodred eyes flashed through my mind. "Menen?" I asked, feeling stupid for forgetting a name that rhymed with Crenen.

"Well, yeah!" the chipper voice said. "Oh, by the way, swim like fish on land flopping as you die."

"Gee. Thanks."

"Pleasure," he replied and I could imagine his sharp teeth split into a malicious grin.

Through the remnants of my fever the questions I should have been asking were only slowly coming to the surface of my brain. "Why're you here?"

"Slow, yeah? Come to visit. Missed feeding Paradisaical Purple Fruit against better judgment of Tall Strong Jerk."

"That's so kind," I muttered. The annoyance I felt was real, but I had to wonder about the person I was supposedly hearing. Was I just crazy?

"We know," he agreed, bringing my focus back to him.

"Why can't I see you?" I asked, annoyed at my inability to spot him in my bedroom's gloom.

"Not left Paradise, *dolt*," he said.

"Oh…" I murmured, feeling my mind shift toward sleep-mode.

"Longer I stay, more you see, yeah?"

"Yeah." I nodded as the light faded and flashes of strange people blazed in my head. I was starting to dream already.

"Sleep, Key," a different voice whispered. My heart stopped and I felt fear seep into my stomach. "Soon…all… destroyed…last…vanish…" It faded in and out, so I couldn't understand, but I grasped enough.

"Lon!" I cried out, remembering the traitor's name. But then I fell into a fitful slumber and remembered no more.

When my fever broke, I awoke, feeling shaken and horribly sweaty. My father was sitting beside the bed when I opened my eyes, and he smiled brightly, though he looked weary. Dark circles had formed under his brown eyes, and his dark hair was tousled. Stubble adorned his normally clean-shaven face.

"You gave us quite a scare, Jason," he said, leaning forward and resting a hand on my head.

I appreciated his quiet tones, because even that was enough to hurt my head.

"How long was I out?" I croaked, which made me suddenly aware of how thirsty I was.

Dad perceived my dehydration, poured some water into a glass, and helped me sit up to take a sip, then another. When I was satisfied that my parched throat would be okay, I attempted the question again. "How long?"

"After you were out for three days, we took you to the hospital, because your condition was worsening. You've been here for six days."

The hospital, huh? That would explain the smell of antiseptic. But had I really been out for nine days? Ridiculous. "Why…?" I asked, hoping he would understand my question.

"The doctors think it was a kind of nervous breakdown."

I nodded; then, realizing what being in the hospital entailed, I glanced down and saw that I was in the normal white patient gown. Great.

Looking up, I met my father gaze evenly. "Dad. I'm fine, really." Staying here anymore wasn't an option; not when I was required to wear a dress. Besides, I couldn't have had an actual break down. It had been pretend. A means of forcing the gerani thief into the open. I wasn't actually crazy.

"I sure hope so, son," Dad said, ruffling my hair affectionately, like he used to do when I was much younger.

He didn't believe me. That was fine. I wasn't sure I believed myself.

I stared down at my thumbs for a while, but my eyes widened as I remembered the voice I thought I'd heard—the mischievous voice of Crenen. Had that been just a figment? Was I really insane?

"I…" I cleared my throat and tried again. "I didn't…say anything, did I?"

Dad raised an eyebrow. "You've always talked in your sleep, Jason."

That was why I asked. "That's why I asked," I repeated aloud.

"You mumbled a few things."

"Oh." I looked at my hands to find them clutching the white blankets as tightly as they could. I pried my fingers loose and forced a smile as I met my father's brown eyes. "So, I'm okay now. Can we go?"

Dad glanced at my hands and frowned. "What do you think?"

My eyes traveled down to my hands again, to find them gripping the blankets just as before. For a moment I stared, then frowned, despairing. Was I really sick? "I think we've got a ways to go," I finally admitted.

"You've taken the first step, son," he said as he again ruffled my hair. "You've acknowledged that you might need some help."

I nodded vaguely, trying to find something to occupy my busy hands. There was silence for several moments.

"Where's Mom?" I asked at last.

"Resting. She was worried sick," he said.

"Literally?" I felt a lump growing in my throat.

"She just needs some sleep. She'll be happy to hear that you're up." He smiled encouragingly.

"When...?" I trailed off.

"When what?"

"When do you think I can leave?" I had to know if there was the remotest chance I wasn't crazy; that I hadn't heard voices in my head—at least, not fake voices. When I returned to my room, if Crenen contacted me again...

"Doctor Rush will be the judge of that," he answered. "Although, if I can convince him to release you, maybe you can sleep in your own bed tonight."

I managed a smile. "Good. I want my own pajamas back." And I wanted to know for sure whether Crenen was-real or not.

"What is it, Jason?" Dad broke into my thoughts, watching my expression.

"Nothing," I said with a crooked smile, lying easily.

He watched me suspiciously for several moments and then nodded. "I'll go get your mom. Rest until we come back, okay?" He stood and headed for the door.

"Key," I mumbled.

"What?" He glanced back, hand hovering over the doorknob.

"Call me Key," I said, meeting his eyes.

He stared, hesitating a moment, and then nodded. "If you want."

"I do," I affirmed without looking at him.

"Okay. Get some sleep. Key."

Only when the door closed did I lay back on my pillows and close my eyes.

The memory of Lon's words echoed in my head. Was he real? If so, was it his intent to kill me, even still? Why then hadn't he done it while I was in Paradise? Or had he just intercepted Crenen's telepathic visit and found that I still remembered some things, if only vaguely?

"Is it possible to return?" I asked the ceiling, amused by my own desire for the world called Paradise to actually exist, despite every sign that it didn't.

Laying there, I tried to recall everything I could of my adventure in Paradise. I remembered Crenen well enough, and Lon was fairly vivid now, and flashes of the tall man called Menen also played in my mind's eye; but there were two people missing—two important pieces to the Paradisaical puzzle.

Could something this substantial really be only a crazy hallucination?

I could make out the hazy images of fuzzy critters, though the colorization escaped me. I absently rubbed my fingers and remembered a cloud of blood in murky water.

And a shawl. Something about a silver shawl.

"You would be headstrong, naturally."

The voice that had said those words was familiar, but I couldn't quite grasp it…

"If you sleep any longer, I will throw you into the puddle and leave."

The icy sensation of plunging into the murky puddle returned, almost as though I was there now.

"I. Am. Not. *A. WOMAN!"*

A very real fear gripped me and I felt the urge to bolt, but my mind reasoned with the fright. The voice was just a memory—and probably just of an illusion, like everything else.

Still, the memories persisted.

"Tell us. Where is Sick Nasty Dog?" Crenen's voice now.

"Sick Nasty Dog…?" My eyes widened. "Of course! Jenen!" The image of the man I had mistaken for a woman came clearly to my mind, and I grinned at my forthcoming memories. How could this possibly be a fantasy conjured by the mind of a psychopath?

Jenen was the effeminate twin brother of Crenen, just as pale and just as tyrannical, though much more subdued. He wore a silver shawl draped across his shoulders, and while he had a sharp grin like Crenen, it was more solemn.

I felt the overpowering urge to discover why the brothers had such a rift between them.

"I've gotta get back," I told myself. Determined, I pulled the I.V. from my arm, tossed my blankets aside and jumped out of bed, flinging the provided robe folded on the nightstand around me as I did so. Instantly my knees gave way and I met the floor, wincing at the forming bruises as my knees tingled. "Good job, dolt."

The door swung open, and my parents walked in, hands linked.

"Jason!" Mom cried out, halting as she saw me, no doubt resembling the living dead.

"What're you doing out of bed?" Dad demanded.

I pushed myself up with my wobbling arms and met their gazes evenly. "Mom, Dad—I'm not crazy." I grinned. "I'm Vendaeva and I need to get back to Paradise. I have some people to save."

They were dumbfounded, utterly speechless. Finally my father opened his mouth to talk, but before he could find his voice, a wicked laugh ripped through the air.

"'Bout time, yeah, Strange Coward Boy?" The voice thundered through the room.

The laughter was contagious. I joined in. "Hey there, Crenen. You gonna take me to your home now?" I asked the ceiling.

"We think on this…Okay, yeah. Why not?" Again the malicious laughter, once so frightening, ran down my spine and I thought it a beautiful sound.

Golden light surrounded me and I laughed with sheer delight. I was going back to Paradise.

—I wasn't delusional.

11
Stolen In The Dark?

The golden light faded to a dim glow around the edges of my vision, and I found myself standing waist-deep in a silvery lake that reflected the full moons above. A breeze scattered ripples across the water's surface and I felt myself drawn to the center of the translucent water.

I wader deeper, sensing that something beneath the surface was waiting for me to touch it. The water crept up until I was shoulder-deep in the silvery fluid. My eyes scanned the water carefully.

It was too dark to see anything beneath the surface.

The lake was somehow familiar. Just as I reached its center I knew why it felt like I had been here before. It was the same pool of water that Lon had pushed me into to send me home. A cold shiver ran up my spine and I spun around, gazing into the shadows for any sign of glowing eyes. Something had to be done about that traitor. As soon as I returned to the tree where the others were I would tell them what he had done.

I laughed softly as I realized my memories had returned.

My eyes widened. Had time passed here? If not, how could Crenen have spoken with me? And wouldn't Lon be standing beside the lake, laughing evilly? But if it had passed, what were the chances that I would arrive on the night of a full moon, with the same soft breeze blowing through my long hair?

—Wait. Long hair? I touched my head and ran my fingers through the locks that hung in my eyes, then down my neck. It was as long as it had been before I returned to Earth. Someone had some explaining to do (assuming they had an explanation to give).

Remembering the something that lured me to the middle of the lake, I turned around and gazed into the murky depths again, but its presence had vanished. Feeling annoyed that my curiosity hadn't been sated, I began wading toward dry ground.

"For all you learned, you yet remain unfocused."

My eyes narrowed and I halted, feeling my anger flare at the familiar voice. Whirling to my left, I gazed at the man who had betrayed me—no, who had betrayed everyone, including his sister. Lon stood calmly before the lake, gazing down at me with an unreadable expression. I wanted to punch that pretty face in.

"What do you mean, 'unfocused'?" I demanded.

For a moment he watched me impassively, but then a subtle smile broke through his masked features, and he softly laughed. At first I felt my body shake with uncontrollable rage, but then I saw the sincerity in his expression. Where before he had stood coldly—an imposing figure of indifference—now he was...good. There was no other word to describe it.

Baffled at the change in this strange man, I gawked (the nasty habit was returning) and finally raised my hand. "What's so funny?"

"You," he answered, the soft smile fading away, replaced once again by coldness.

I was still very annoyed. "Me?"

He watched me for a moment, then gently smiled. Gently? Something was wrong. Had I landed myself in an alternate Paradise where the inhabitants looked the same, but acted entirely different? Did that mean Crenen would like flowers and hearts, and Jenen despised shawls?

"It's all right, Vendaeva," he said quietly, voice carrying on the breeze as he took a step into the water. I noticed then that his apparel differed greatly from before. It used to be an armored skirt, but now he wore long silken robes of rich purple. His arms were completely bare now, sporting the same tattoo that adorned his cheek: a red circle through a black sword. The tattoo was both on his upper and lower arms. His gold hair was loose, flowing like liquid in the nighttime draft. I squinted to be sure that I hadn't mistaken Veija for her brother —only to sadly determine it really was Lon, acting out of character. I was still wary. He could very likely be trying a new tactic.

"How is it all right?" I asked.

"It was a test, and you passed."

I folded my arms. "Oh, yeah?"

Lon continued, face serene. "You were homesick; Crenen also knew this. You had to be sent back so that the choice to return here was entirely your own. Only then would you take your appointed task as seriously as you must. Only then could you become Vendaeva."

I made a cutting motion with my hands. "Whoa, time out." I ran through everything that had happened since I returned home.

Lon seemed to read my thoughts. "You recall placing the gerani into your pocket when Crenen shared a bunch with you in the orchard? Crenen made certain it remained there. We were fearful of what would happen after the gerani was stolen by that girl—which is why Crenen intervened. We had no intention of driving you mad, and so we had to let you know that we were quite real."

"But," my eyes narrowed, "what about when I heard your voice? You were talking about my destruction. What was that?"

He halted in the pool, robes floating on the water's surface, and met my gaze evenly. "Shall I repeat what I said?"

I nodded, my eyes still narrowed suspiciously. "'Kay."

"'Sleep, Key. Soon you must return or all will be destroyed. You are our last hope, for without the coming Vendaeva all of Paradise will vanish…'"

It seemed far-fetched, yet thinking back, his voice hadn't been malicious. There had been no evil laughter, no taunting monologue. If anything, the whisper in my ear had been gentle, comforting, soothing. "So, you're telling me that you and Crenen have been in league all this time to make me want to become Vendaeva?"

He nodded. "Yes, basically."

If Crenen's manipulation riled me, and if Jenen's taunting angered me, this man's supposed good intentions were truly infuriating.

"You'll catch cold if you remain in there any longer."

I glanced down and tried to wriggle my toes. No good. I was half numb. As I started for the shoreline, an earlier observation on his part returned to my mind. "What did you mean, unfocused?"

He sighed. "When the time is right, you will reach the center."

I raised an eyebrow and shook my head. I hated riddles. As I dragged one foot forward in the water I remembered another question. "Has time passed here?"

He nodded. "Six months."

"Dang, usually it's not supposed to work like that," I muttered. Once the hero returned to his own time, the fantastical world was always supposed to halt; remaining paused until he was ready to come back.

Lon sighed again. "This is not a game, Key. This is real. If you don't know this by now, I suggest that I return you to your home so that you can play on your game console and ignore the reality of fact."

He knew about consoles and videos games? "How—?"

"Answers later. Come. Dry clothes, warm food and sleep await you, along with several eager individuals."

"Jenen, too?"

He shook his head. "After you were gone for three weeks, he gave up and departed. Of course, he attempted to take Veija, but I put a stop to that."

He offered me his hand and I grudgingly accepted it, surprised to feel its warmth. I allowed him to haul me from the lake, frowning. I had wanted to see Jenen. "So, why did you act like such a creep?"

"Crenen thought it best at the time. I believe that means he is the real 'creep'."

I had to agree. As my bare feet touched the dewy grass along the edge of the pool, I felt my body tremble. Fatigue fell over me like a pounding waterfall, and I collapsed to my knees.

"Vendaeva?" Lon asked, voice still impenetrable.

I tried to look up, but the effort only drained what little strength remained in my bones. I tumbled forward, into the soft, damp grass, smelling peppermint faintly. My vision blurred, and I was only half-aware of anything.

"Side effect…wear…eventually…rest…get Crenen…" Lon whispered, voice fading in and out with my vision.

I tried to nod, but couldn't move at all. The sounds of the night were loud in my ears as I laid there, unable to see anything but the grass before my eyes. Shivers tried to rack my body, but even those couldn't break through my immobility. I felt the desperate need to cough...

Something warm wrapped itself around me and I was turned over onto my back. Mismatched eyes peered at me through my hazy vision and I attempted a smile. It didn't quite work.

"I would tell you to remain still, but I doubt that will be an issue," a quiet voice whispered near my ear.

Wait. That wasn't Crenen. Then, who?

...Oh.

As I felt myself lifted from the grass, I mentally laughed. Once again, I was at Jenen's mercy.

I might have called for help, had I been able. But, then again, I wasn't so sure. During my last escapade in Paradise I had run away, destroying any chance of knowing Jenen. As far as I was concerned this time would be different.

I wasn't running anymore.

I woke to the smell of smoke. Wrinkling my nose, I attempted to roll over, but found my body loathe to acknowledge my subconscious command. Moaning softly, I tried again, this time receiving limp results. My leg kicked up for a second, and fell again, tingling with the promise of more bruises. Better, but not good enough. I tried again, but this time my leg didn't bother responding. It took a few seconds to remember why I was having trouble, then memories rushed back, shoving a headache in as a side effect.

Ouch.

I recalled Lon; the silvery lake; Jenen carrying me away before I could meet with Crenen. I recalled that for some reason I was quite immobile, and I tried to figure out why.

"Your body is in shock from the journey back to Paradise," a familiar voice, not far away, answered my mental question. I was almost positive that Jenen really could read minds.

Gathering my limited strength, I decided to venture a vocal question now, fixing my eyes on the rising sun and the branches silhouetted against its brilliant light. "Why am I paralyzed this time, when my first time entering Paradise was just fine?"

"Because last time you were summoned. This time you came entirely by your own choice."

"I did?"

"You invoked the power of Vendaeva and came back of your own will. No one brought you this time."

I wondered who had brought me here the first time.

"You're an accident in the making," Jenen commented, his voice nearer now.

I smiled. "That's for sure. My mom always said I attracted accidents, but until now I couldn't see why…"

Jenen appeared above me, dark hair framing his pallid face. His expression was quizzical. "No violent urges?" he inquired.

I shook my head slightly, feeling tired but satisfied with the effort. "What's the point. It's the stupid truth."

"This coming from an innate liar…"

"Yeah, but it's a liar's prerogative to tell the truth from time to time, just to shake things up. When will I be able to move again?"

"I cannot say for certain," the Paradisian replied. "Lon mentioned that it would wear off soon, but what that means I can only guess at."

"Speaking of Lon," I ventured, "is he a traitor or a good guy?"

"Define 'good guy,'" Jenen said dryly.

"Right." I thought for a moment. "Lon shoved me into the lake. Was that at Crenen's request, or was it independently executed?"

"I don't know," Jenen whispered, disappearing from view. I heard him sit near me, dirt grating beneath his wrapped feet. "I doubt he did anything without Crenen knowing of it, however Crenen might not have intervened only because it coincided with his own agenda. Honestly, I would not trust either of them."

Thinking about it now, I wondered if what Jenen was saying was the truth. In all my time spent in Paradise only Jenen had really helped me out. When I was poisoned he prevented my death; then I was captured by his enemy, which forced him to come along. Both of us were pawns in Crenen's twisted game.

While I somehow liked Crenen, I wondered about his motives. What was he after? Certainly he employed many people on the basis that I was Vendaeva, but he had made it very clear that he didn't really believe in me and he dragged me along only as a means of getting Jenen to remain and, eventually, become leader. But to what purpose? Why would such a self-centered creep like Crenen want to give up his position as leader of Yenen Clan to his twin brother? What possessed him? What were his real motives? Was he friend or foe?

"Jenen?" I asked, keeping my gaze on the dawn sky.

He said nothing, so I decided to assume he was listening. "Why do you hate Crenen?"

Deathly silence rose between us and then I heard Jenen stand. I listened to the sound of his footsteps until they were too far away to hear. Sighing, I closed my eyes and tried to sleep, but my mind was too full of calculations and questions. It took an age before I drifted into an uneasy rest.

It seemed only seconds before I was startled out of shadowed dreams. Feeling disturbed, but unable to pinpoint why, I forced my aching body to sit up. Shuddering, I climbed to my feet and gazed into the darkness. Wait. Nighttime already? Was that possible? Glancing at the black sky, I noted that no stars glittered above and, try as I might, my eyes refused to adjust to the pitch-colored void around me.

"Jenen?" I called, hearing my voice crack nervously, not carrying very far, as though smothered by the darkness. Nothing, not even the whistling of the wind, reached my ears. That was what had awakened me: utter silence.

I took one step forward, ignoring the aching of my half-numb body. Adrenaline pumped in my veins, giving me the strength to move. My internal clock was usually broken, but something told me that this blackness wasn't natural. It should be closer to noon, not midnight.

"Jenen!" I willed my voice to cut through the endless shadows. For a split second I thought I heard a response and I took that as a sign. Veering left, I followed the memory of that distant sound, praying it was Jenen and not something fouler.

I stumbled, but caught myself and forced my legs to hold my weight. Moving forward again, I strained my ears for any more sounds. "Jenen, where are you?" I cried out, trying not to panic. It would be fine. This was probably a dream and I would wake up any second—but I knew that wasn't true. I could now clearly tell the different between reality and dream. While this was certainly a nightmare, I was very much awake.

Mid step, something halted me, as if a hand forced me to stop, though nothing was there. I distinctly smelled peppermint. Somehow I knew that a body was sprawled on the ground before me. Raising a hand instinctively, I whispered, "Liitae," and a ball of blue light formed above my hand. I blinked in surprise, then lowered the light to see the ground.

As weird as a source of light springing from my hand was, it felt natural and I remained calm.

As the blue light illuminated the ground I saw the body's face. Jenen. I had known it would be him. Kneeling before the limp form, I placed my free hand on his face and felt his cold skin. He was dead.

Panic started to spread through my mind, but the peculiar calmness inside batted it away. I had no time to cry. There was no reason to.

Grasping the ball of light with both hands, I shoved it against Jenen's chest and watched as it was absorbed. Immediately breath returned to his lungs and his eyes fluttered. I grasped his hand and dragged him to his feet. He stumbled for a moment, then straightened. While I had surrendered my source of light, I wasn't worried. Jenen was glowing with near-blinding radiance; even the whites of his eyes were radiant blue.

He turned his striking eyes to me and stared. "Vendaeva," he whispered in awe.

Overwhelming power coursed through my body at the word, but then it was gone, taking with it the last of my waning strength. I collapsed, and he caught me, easing me to the ground without any effort, though seconds before he had been dead.

"What is this blackness?" I asked.

"Kirid Clan," he explained, rancor in his tone.

"What?" I asked, trying to grasp what he meant. How could the Kirid do something like this?

"Somehow the Kirid have gained their own Seer, and they used the power such a Being provides to destroy me."

I felt my awareness wavering, but I urged my mind to comprehend his words. "Why you?" I wasn't trying to sound conceded. Just...it really didn't make sense why they were out to get him, instead of me.

"I wish I knew," he answered, gazing into the distance, and I recognized his lie for what it was.

I decided not to press the issue until I had the mind for it. Instead I forced the blackness around us to dissolve. The sun broke though the shadows and warmed us once more, and I allowed a different darkness to overcome me.

Sleep.

12
Deadly Venom?

I was forced abruptly from my rest yet again, but it wasn't hard to place why this time. Heated voices ascended from somewhere below. The tones rose and fell, making my ears ache with the effort to catch the exchange. I peeled open my eyes and stiffened as I saw branches hanging not an inch from my nose. Oh, please, not a tree.

I looked down.

—Great, a tree. Precariously balanced as I was, it was a miracle I hadn't fallen in my sleep. Now that I was coherent, I felt the limb beneath me palpitating in the crisp breeze. Easing into a sitting position, I grasped the trunk and hugged it. What had Jenen been thinking, putting me in a huge freaking tree?

Only when I felt sure I wouldn't fall did I measure just how many feet I would have dropped before my sudden demise. Too many.

Recalling the voices that had awakened me, I tilted my head down to catch snatches of the argument. I caught more than snatches.

"You know where he is, so tell me," a hoarse voice demanded in a thick accent.

"Don't get so upset, it won't help you," Jenen calmly answered.

"Easy for you to say. You aren't—" He broke off, coughing violently.

"...Running out of time?" Jenen suggested.

"You're only cocky because you have the boy," the raspy voice said between gulping breaths. "Just wait until you're overpowered by the Kirid. When that time comes—" He began coughing again.

"I'll have you distract them," Jenen said.

By this point I was brave enough to venture away from the trunk, creeping out onto the quivering branch, to catch a glimpse of the stranger. His fit ceased and he gulped air again. "Your time for humbling is coming, Yenen traitor."

"Your prediction is dismissed," Jenen said laconically.

Yenen traitor? Yet again he had been accused of that offense. My eyes narrowed. Really, when everything was laid out, who was on my side? I could only think of one person who, while under the orders of Crenen, could still do what he needed to, and stood his ethical ground. Menen. I decided the only person I would trust was Menen.

"All I want is to see him," the stranger said, changing his tactics.

"Only to betray him to the Kirid for your own sake."

"Why would I do that when I desire Vendaeva to save us all from this disease?"

"Yourself, you mean."

While I didn't entirely trust Jenen, I was definitely cheering him on.

I'd climbed out as far as I dared on the limb, but it wasn't far enough to get a clear view. The only thing I could make out was a blood-red shoot of thick hair jutting out in every direction possible. Apparently this guy hadn't heard of a brush before, or he'd had a run-in with an angry barber and a dull knife.

"Leave, Sikel," Jenen said in a commanding tone.

I held my breath and waited for the stranger to depart, stalking noisily through the brush as he went. Releasing the air from my lungs, I nimbly grabbed the branch and swung down to the ground—

Okay, that's a lie.

I actually found myself stuck, unable to crawl backwards, and well aware of the distant between the branch I clung to and the hard ground. After contemplating what to do, during which time my mind stayed perfectly blank, I craned my neck to catch a glimpse of Jenen.

"Uh, hey, could you give me a hand?"

I heard footsteps beneath me, and the crack of a twig. Then Jenen appeared, gazing up at me. A smile crossed his face. "But I need my hands, the both of them."

I moaned, rolling my eyes. I was stuck a good twenty feet from the ground, unable to move for fear of falling, and Mister Always Serious decided to take this moment and poke fun. I swear, Paradise was a freaking, living, breathing *nightmare*.

"That's very funny," I said, trying to ignore the imagined sounds of cracking branches. "Why'd you put me up here?"

"Sikel wanted to steal you."

"Okay, I gathered that much. But who is Sikel?"

Jenen sighed. "A backstabber, a cheat, and a liar."

That sounded pretty familiar. "So why do you associate with him?"

"I don't."

"You were talking with him."

"That's different."

The branch swayed, forcing me to cling tighter still. My knuckles were white. "He had the Paradise-whatever disease, didn't he?" They say fear has a way of making one ramble. I can vouch for it.

"Paradisaical. Yes."

"How do you get it? I mean, is there some way to pre—"

"It strikes at random," Jenen snapped, his eyes glistening.

"Okay, all right," I said, backing off. The branch swayed again. "So…uh, can you get me down now?"

"Find your own way."

I scowled. "You put me up here—what happens if I fall?"

"You get hurt."

I had come to the conclusion that 'They of Paradise' took turns making me hate each of them most—but I was certain Jenen took the cake for the most irritating of all. For now.

"I really could use some help…" I said again.

Jenen opened his mouth, most likely to retort, but a new voice, oozing with arrogance, beat him to it. "Don't worry, I'll take it from here," it said from directly behind me.

Jenen stiffened, his eyes wide with alarm. The fact that Jenen was surprised at the appearance of the newcomer behind me was unnerving enough. Put that with the recognition I felt at his voice, and I was downright dumbfounded. I might have dreaded Crenen's return, I might have cheered Menen's rescue, I might have kicked Lon out of the tree, or smiled warmly at the ditsy Seer, Veija—but this man was none of them. In fact, the very idea that he was in Paradise made no sense.

Hesitantly I turned my head and looked at the bane of my existence: the young man called Chas. The very same idiot who had shoved me into the great Phudel with a maniacal smirk on his pretty-boy face.

Before I could move, the blond young man leaped from the branch he stood on, grabbed me by the collar of my hospital robe, then jumped to the grass so many feet below. I hardly knew what had happened until I was already safely, if shakily, standing on the ground. I allowed myself a sigh of relief before I refocused on the strange situation I found myself in. Well, the strang*er* situation.

I stared at the guy I had known for several years during high school. He stood six feet tall, with all-black clothing that slimmed him down but didn't diminish his well-toned physique. He smiled back, with that usual smug expression of his, then his green eyes flicked to Jenen and his smile broadened.

"Well, if it isn't the little lost prince," Chas said in a mocking tone.

Jenen's gold and silver eyes narrowed, and then he reached forward, grabbed my robe collar, and pulled me backwards. "You cannot take him."

"Wouldn't dream of it. I was only sent to be sure he was protected, since you seem unfit to manage even that much," Chas drawled, walking back to the tree trunk and resting against it, folding his arms and crossing his legs.

"We're managing fine," Jenen said coldly, dragging me back another few feet.

My mind was racing five times faster than the speed of light. At the very least. He *knew* Jenen; he was somehow here in Paradise; I was in my hospital apparel. My eyes widened. I was still in my hospital apparel. Thank goodness I had a *robe*, but still...

I forced my mind to focus again on the present. By now Jenen had dragged me a good fifteen feet from the tree and the arrogant man leaning against it.

"Well, Jason," Chas finally addressed me, "seems you're having quite the adventure."

I could have sworn I heard Jenen hiss. "How do you know this boy?" he demanded of the blond.

Chas shrugged, his vibrant green eyes dancing. "We were at the same school, though our roles were significantly different. Jason was a nobody, while I was what Earthlings label the resident 'heartthrob,' isn't that right, Jasey?"

I scowled, my loathing for the most popular senior at my school returning, even though we had both since graduated. It wasn't that the girls adored him, though that might have had a little to do with it. More than anything it was Chas's acceptance of it—in fact, he had reveled in it, playing the strings of every girl's heart like a harp.

"Still," I said aloud, "I wonder at your knowing my name. It wasn't like we ever talked..." Except once. When he had pushed me into the puddle. Did he even remember that? Since he was here, did that mean he hadn't merely been toying with me, but had sent me here intentionally?

"Ah, but I would never forget the face of my rival."

I scrutinized him, judging his sanity. He considered me his rival? Every male student had declared him the rival of each of us, but it was only at a distance. No one dared to actually say it to his face.

"You have questions, so many questions, running through your head," he said quietly.

"What were you doing in the land of Earth?" Jenen asked, his voice betraying his confusion.

"You might say it was my assignment," Chas said with a casual shrug.

My eyes narrowed.

"You're with Kirid Clan," Jenen said.

Chas tossed his head back and laughed, a clear, singsong sound. "Well now, Prince, I wouldn't—" he broke off and turned to his left, suddenly alert. "Not now."

I blinked. What was coming? Then I heard it, as clearly as if it had been standing before me—thousands of feet, marching across the ground in perfect synchronization. They was a little way off, but still too close. "What is it?"

"You're human. You wouldn't hear," Chas said dismissively.

"I hear it fine," I retorted, "but I don't know what it is that's coming."

Jenen and Chas gazed at me in surprise.

"You can hear that?" Jenen asked in disbelief.

"Well, yeah."

"But…it's at least thirty miles off," Jenen whispered.

"Actually, twenty-two," I corrected, then blinked. "Uh, wait…" How in the world had I known that?

"The boy's right," Chas said. "And quickly approaching. We have fifteen minutes, at the most."

Jenen still had his eyes on me, though one long ear was cocked toward the impending sound. "...Yes. We must move."

"You didn't answer my question. *What's* coming?" I demanded. It was especially important, since whatever it was had to be going roughly the speed of a car on the freeway, and that was pretty dang fast.

"The Paradise Warriors," Jenen answered. "They're coming to kill you."

That was enough motivation to get me moving. "Right then," I said. "Let's go."

Chas leaped back into the tree. "They come from the west. We'll head east, then." He looked down.

"He can't travel by tree," Jenen said, and I considered it the funniest thing to yet come from his mouth. Who ever heard of traveling by tree? I smiled to myself, but was also resigned to my fate. The fact that I hadn't heard of it just bolstered its chance to exist in this crazy place.

"Carry me, I don't care," I said docilely, though my heart hammered with the prospect of approaching doom.

Jenen raised an eyebrow. "I am *not* carrying you."

"Nor I," Chas said, suddenly dangling by his legs from the tree's branch, his hair sticking every which way.

"Fine, but you'll be considerably slower with me walking beneath the blasted trees," I growled, spinning around and trudging in the direction I guessed was east.

"It won't do," Chas remarked.

"Agreed," Jenen said.

Suddenly they acted like best buds. Terrific. My day was now complete.

As I stomped off, my ears began to thunder with the sound of the approaching army. They were moving faster than Chas had estimated. Suddenly the crash of feet halted, and the sound of silence reigned in the forest like the promise of death.

They were here.

"Vendaeva! Find and destroy Vendaeva!" a deep voice cried in my head. I doubled over as a sharp pain shot through my head. Gasping, I straightened just in time to catch a blur of red.

"Jason!" a familiar voice called, but it was far away, too far to reach. Then arms encircled me, and I was pulled up. Trees bounced around me. No, wait, that had to be me. *I* was bouncing. Not that that consoled me in the least…

Slowly reality crashed back into place around me. My face flushed with the understanding that I was being carried. Still, I had to smile (if only to salvage my pride). So they had ended up carrying me after all.

—I thought too soon. An instant later I slipped from the person's arms and tumbled to the forest floor below, branches snagging at my face and clothes as I plummeted. I hit hard but managed to stay conscious. Getting to my feet, I limped out of the thicket I had fallen into and began walking, though to where I didn't know. I just let my feet lead the way.

It wasn't long before the noise of a fight met my ears and I hurried faster, ignoring my twisted ankle. Branches whipped by, and undergrowth reached out to trip me, but I was determined not to fall.

Unexplainable urgency filled my stomach with sickening dread.

"C'mon, let me through, dang it!" I screamed at the forest, and in response the trees bent away from me to clear a path. The undergrowth lay flat. I didn't stop; I could reflect on the wonder of that later. Right now, for some unknown reason, I had to get through. My robe was tattered, and I felt several stinging cuts bleeding along my arms, but the previous taunting of the forest had desisted, and I made better time. The sounds of battle were fast approaching.

Then I was there, breaking through foliage to find a dimly lit clearing, the scent of peppermint strong in my nose. I stared at the scene before me. A half dozen red furapintairow were facing off against Jenen, who was fighting them with bloodied claws, dark hair clinging to his face.

Unthinking, I rushed forward, determined to destroy our foes. As I neared, I felt a tingling in my hand and I raised it to find out what it was. The need to point it at the enemy filled my thoughts, and I obeyed. "Liitae," I whispered, the word foreign yet familiar.

A bluish light shot forth from my palm and slammed into one of the small creatures. The red animal rolled over, and its pink eyes closed, the jagged tail laying limp beside it. I raised my hand to destroy another. Again the light appeared and it killed the second furapintairow. I repeated this four more times, giving the critters only a second to realize what was happening, and soon all six Small Red Fuzzies were laying on the ground. As fast as they had been before, in this moment I had been faster still.

Jenen, soaked in sweat and blood and gasping for breath, stared at me, and I thought I saw a smile touch at his ashen lips.

"Are you okay?" I asked, absently rubbing the palm that had, literally, single-handedly defeated six Paradise Warriors.

He nodded, then staggered. I sprinted forward and grabbed him before he had time to reach the ground, and I carefully laid him down. He was hot with fever.

"They bit you, didn't they?" I asked as I searched for signs of bite marks. I found more than one set. There were at least twenty bites along his arms, legs, and neck. "Holy mackerel, Jenen, how are you still alive?" There was no way a man should live more than a few minutes with that many noxious bites.

He managed a smirk. "It takes more than that…" He moaned, and didn't finish his sentence.

"Just hang in there," I said, trying to quell my panic as I wondered what I could do. "Where's Chas?"

"He went to save you," Jenen answered in a hoarse whisper.

I touched his forehead and cringed. He was burning up. "He did a terrific job," I muttered, recalling the person who had accidentally dropped me. Or perhaps he had deposited me there to keep me from harm. Who could say?

Jenen was dying. As though a voice in my heart had spoken, I knew he wouldn't last long. Much as I appreciated the tip, it wasn't hard to guess that already.

Jenen hissed as his body stiffened. I grabbed his shoulders. "Hey, I said to hang in there."

He was shivering violently, and his head tossed from one side to the other before he nodded his understanding. "I… know."

"I'm going to get this poison out, okay?" I said, wondering at the same time how I was supposed to do that.

The tables were turned. When I first came to Paradise, Jenen had saved my life. Now it was my turn. He'd told me he was only doing for me what he would want done for him, if he were foolish enough to touch a furapintairow. "You touched one," I told him quietly.

"We all have…our moments…of…foolishness…" he replied arduously, smiling. Apparently he'd been reflecting on the same thing.

I touched one of the bite marks. *I need to withdraw the poison,* I thought desperately, wondering which plant might draw it out. A violet fluid shot from the wound to my hand, where it hovered before it like a bubble. For a moment I stared, shocked, then shook myself and and touched another puncture mark, silently reiterating the same thought. Again the fluid emerged from the bite, hovering near my hand. I continued the process until I had withdrawn the venom from each wound. As I finally pulled my hand away, the bubbles popped, splashing into the grass, where the venom soaked into the ground.

Jenen had lost unconsciousness. I felt his forehead again. It was still on fire. Nevertheless, something inside me whispered that he would live. "You'll be okay now," I told him gently. "Just rest."

He moaned softly in response, and I smiled. It felt really good to help.

"Where are you going?" the boy asked, his voice distant as an echo.

"Leave me be!" the other youth cried out.

"Are you coming back?" the first boy asked quietly.

"…No. I'm not."

"Oh…" The adolescent hung his head, but then he looked up again. "Before you go…" He ran off, but returned a moment later, clutching something to his heart. "Take this." He extended the object toward the other boy. "To remember."

"Don't you understand? I want to forget!"

"Not forever. Someday you will want to remember."

I awoke with a start and the chill night air seized the chance to slap my face. Wincing, I pulled my robe closer to keep the worst of the cold out. It did nothing for my frozen legs. As I gazed into the darkness, I tried to figure out what had awakened me from my dream.

That dream.

I attempted to recall the details, but even the faces were a blur now. Still, the ache inside from whatever had occurred was as powerful as it had been in my sleep.

Yawning, I turned to check on Jenen. My left hand was resting on his shoulder, where I'd placed it to keep him from tossing during the worst of his fever. At some point I'd drifted into a heavy slumber, but it seemed Jenen was resting peacefully. I was relieved, but I touched his forehead to be certain he was out of the woods. He was still feverish, but not roasting.

His metallic eyes fluttered open, reflecting the dim light from the moons filtering through the branches above us.

"…Key?" he whispered.

"Right here."

He managed a nod before returning to oblivion.

I shivered from the cold and touched his arm. It was freezing. There had to be some way to warm him.

I stood. Jenen had a shawl somewhere around here. I walked the length of the clearing, attempting to locate the silver cloth. A shining something caught my eye, then vanished. I approached the shadowy area and bent down to grope for the shawl.

Pain shot across my fingers and I jerked back from the darkness. Gazing at my hand I saw teeth marks.

Oh, come on! This had to set a record or something. Couldn't I avoid fainting for just one day? Grasping my fingers tightly, I hissed with irritation. I didn't want to be poisoned, darn it.

The pain stopped. Blinking, I again looked at my hand and found no sign of the injury. Had my fingers healed in response to my subconscious thoughts? ...This meant I wouldn't die. That was good.

But the little fuzzy who had given it to me was still in the vicinity, and the little fuzzy had to die. I scanned the gloom again, lifting my hand. A ball of blue light appeared at my fingertips and I held it out to scatter the shadows. There it was, a single furapintairow, growling at me with bared fangs, its back against a gnarled tree.

"Oh, shut up," I said as its growling grew more incessant. I'll admit I was more than disappointed when that didn't quiet it. Apparently this strange ability of mine to conjure and control did not pertain to creatures and humans. Drat.

"My, my, the boy does know how to use powers," a familiar voice said from behind me.

I turned around and glared daggers at Chas. "Where have you been?" Then I got a clear view of him. His black apparel, so flawless before, was now a clawed and bloodied mess.

"I was off taking a nap," he said with a casual shrug, though I caught the wince as he moved his shoulders.

"Were you bitten?"

"No," he said.

I raised a brow. "You sure? 'Cause I just learned this new trick, and I thought some practice could make perfect." I held up my hand to find the blue orb still hovering above it. "How do you shut it off?"

"Good question," Chas said, strolling over and thrusting his hand at the orb. His fingers slid through the light, not touching any solid substance. "Apparently that won't work."

I shook my hand to try shutting the light off, but it stayed.

"Tell it to disappear," the blond suggested.

"Go away," I told it. Instantly the light vanished. I shook my head in disbelief. "At least it's easy. So, you weren't bitten?" I asked again.

"I wasn't. Clawed a good deal, certainly, but I avoided the mouths—at least, when I couldn't kick them in."

"If you're sure," I said, glancing back at the growling fuzzy. "Wanna kick his teeth in, too?"

"Not particularly," he said with a yawn.

"Get some sleep. It's not everyday you fight an entire army of little red things." I forced a smile.

"Maybe for you," he said before leaping into the treetops.

I decided not to ask, though I still had to wonder whether this guy was from Earth, or if in reality this was his home.

Unwilling to ask, I turned to the growling Small Red Fuzzy and grinned in a manner I thought even Crenen would be impressed by. I knew exactly what to do with the vile little thing, if only it would work.

After dispatching the creature, I finally found sleep.

"Take this." He extended the silver cloth toward the other boy. "To remember."

"Don't you understand? I want to forget!" He tossed the shawl to the ground.

"Not forever. Someday you will want to remember," the black-haired youth said, mismatched eyes glinting in the orange light of the evening sky.

"You fool, how can you stay?" the other boy demanded.

"Our people, they need me. I have to save them—I swore I would save them..."

"Swear, Vendaeva. Save my people from the Kirid. Save my people from our torturous end."

"I swear," I mumbled, turning over in my bed. Wait. I touched the bed. There was no mattress. Instead I felt grass, wet and cold. Forcing my eyes open, I stared at the ladybug creeping along on a blade of green grass, mere inches from my face. It turned toward me and my eyes widened as I saw its unusually large mouth opening to reveal needle-point teeth stretched into a grin. Unsure whether I was seeing things or not, I sought a bug-less blade of grass to stare at instead. Then I recalled where I was.

Groaning, I forced myself to roll over, sit up, then stifle a yawn before taking in my surroundings. It was morning now, and the sun was working to drying the dew sparkling across the foliage.

I glanced at Jenen. He was curled up, his legs tucked beneath his folded arms, his breathing regular as he slept. I frowned. I hadn't been able to find Jenen's shawl, but because of some dream I could barely recall I knew it was important that I locate it.

I climbed to my feet and stretched, ignoring the soreness in my muscles. When I'd gone back to Earth after the first visit to Paradise, I'd decided to work out and get in shape—but after my family diagnosed me with insanity, my exercise became less frequent. Still, the muscles weren't as sore as they could have been.

I took a pebble from the grass and chucked it up at the trees.

"Yes?" a voice called down.

"Shh," I said, putting a finger to my lips. I beckoned with my hand and Chas jumped down from the branches. "I need water," I told him.

He stared for a moment and finally sighed. "You're taking this Vendaeva thing to your head," he muttered before walking into the dense foliage.

"Thanks," I whispered after him, though it galled me. Chas had proven himself last night against hundreds of Paradise Warriors. The least I could do was show him my gratitude for that—and take advantage of his services in the meantime.

It wasn't long before my rival returned, toting a leather flask of stream water. He handed it over wordlessly, then jumped to the lowest branch where he watched me give Jenen a drink.

As I helped Jenen sip slowly, I glanced at Chas. "Weren't there thousands of furapintairow that attacked?"

"Yes."

"Then, why did they retreat?" The question had occurred to me in the night..

"Oh, well, they weren't very keen on facing the two of us. They'd been under the impression that you didn't have the use of your powers, and, besides, they were being controlled. The spell didn't last long."

"Controlled?" I repeated, frowning. "By Kirid Clan."

"That's the one," Chas confirmed.

I fell silently, reflecting on the idea that somewhere close by were people who wanted me dead for no other reason than a stupid prophecy I had yet to read for myself.

"What did you do with fura?" Chas asked after a moment, bringing me from my thoughts.

"I gave it a second chance at life," I answered.

"That sounds dangerous, coming from you." He swung his legs in the air.

"I just decontaminated him."

"You what?"

"I took the poison out," I said, looking up and meeting his gaze.

He blinked, then smirked. "You're a cruel one."

"Why? I just spared us any further trouble from at least one stupid fuzzy. 'Sides, it's not like it'll die, so we're all happy, right?"

"So naïve."

Anger flared inside of me but I gritted my teeth and gazed at him inquiringly.

"A fura can hardly defend itself without venomous fangs. It will soon die," Chas said.

"I doubt that," I replied, though I wasn't sure why I felt so certain.

"A mystery, as always," he commented.

"What do you mean by that?" I asked. Again I felt curious about Chas's knowledge of me and the fact that he was actually from Paradise.

"Since you were this big," he said, holding his hands vertically, three feet apart, "you've always known things no one else could even fathom. But then, I suppose that makes sense." As he spoke his voice took on a different sound, deeper and older than eighteen.

"Since I was…?" I stared. "You never knew me before high school, Chas. You moved there when I was fourteen…"

His mouth twisted into a vague, mysterious, almost gentle smile. "Ah, Jason, I knew you would forget—each time, I knew. But, I still…hoped."

Each time? I shook my head. "I don't—"

"'I'll beat you,'" Chas's voice was young like a ten-year-old. "'No matter what, no matter where, no matter how—I swear, I'll beat you at everything.'" He smiled fondly.

A chill ran along my spine, but not from the cold. I recalled saying those words, but when, and to whom, I didn't know. "What are you?" I whispered, staring at the young man before me.

In answer his features changed, making him appear around twenty-five. His blond hair grew long and spilled off his shoulders, and his green eyes danced with a strange yellow light. He was taller—I could tell even though he was still sitting on the lowest branch—and more muscular. No longer boyish, Chas appeared as a full-grown man.

I took a step back, trembling, not understanding.

"Reincarnate," another voice said.

Whirling around, I spotted Crenen standing in the clearing, lopsided ponytail bobbing in the morning's breeze, tattered red wraps flapping. Menen stood just behind him, like a sentinel.

"Also called shapeshifter, yeah?" Crenen explained with a dark smile.

13
A Painful Midnight Excursion?

Distracted by the arrival of some familiar faces, Chas's transformation was forgotten for the moment. These were the people who had haunted my mind the past six months; it was an incredible relief to see them living, breathing and undeniably real. "Hey guys! What took you so long?"

Crenen arched an eyebrow. "What take *we* so long? Strange Coward *Dolt* ask dumb questions sometimes, yeah?"

It was great to see him too.

He went on. "We wait on Strange Coward Boy. What take *you* so long?"

I blinked, then scoffed. "What?" If he dared to lay into me about not returning to Paradise sooner, I was prepared to defend myself. I'd splashed through more puddles and rivers than I could count in my attempts to get back.

Menen stepped forward before Crenen could reply, red eyes resting on the sleeping form near me. He crossed the clearing and knelt before Jenen.

"Six of those furapintairow things got him," I explained.

"Six?" Crenen asked, gazing at his twin. "Why not have buried the body by now?"

"He's not dead yet," Chas spoke up, reminding everyone of his presence. He was still in his new form, which startled me again when I glanced at him. Apparently he was *not* originally from Earth.

"Sick Nasty Dog fight good, we admit," Crenen commented.

"He had help," yet another voice broke in, this one female. I turned to find the voice's owner. My eyes beheld the one person I had been hoping to see since I was forced from Paradise. I had forgotten what she looked like, and though my memories had come back to me upon my return to this world, it wasn't the same at gazing upon the real thing. She was absolutely gorgeous.

Crenen's lip curled upward into a smirk. "So say Seer, yeah?"

The woman nodded in reply, then her violet eyes sparkled as she rested her gaze on me. "Key!" she cried happily, her voice as a song from Heaven. She rushed forward, her silken skirts of pink flowing behind her as she ran straight into my arms. Somehow I managed to keep on my feet, and I returned her embrace.

"Hello, Seer Veija," I whispered, taking in the sweet fragrance of her long golden curls.

Crenen, apparently irritated by all the interruptions, grabbed Veija's arm and pulled us apart. "Now not time for reunions, yeah? Now we have many questions and many answerings."

"Such as?" I asked.

"You ask, we answer. And vice…something."

"Vice versa," Menen supplied from his spot next to Jenen.

"That, yeah."

"Great, sounds like a plan," I said, throwing Veija a reassuring smile. "Just pick a spot on the grass and we'll start."

Crenen scowled at the only seating option and circled the clearing, seeking something else to sit on. The rest of us sat in the grass and waited. Finally the Yenen clan leader gave up his search and turned back to the rest of us. "Well, ask, Strange Coward Boy."

"Okay." There were so many questions, how could I possibly find some place to start? "I guess I want to know how you found us so quickly?"

Menen answered. "You've made a circle around the Realm of Yenen for several days now. It's been a wide circle, certainly, but far from untraceable. It was almost as though Jenen wanted us to follow."

"Maybe Jenen was trying to lure Veija," I mused. The image of a shoot of blood-red hair flashed in my mind. "Hey, you guys didn't happen to run into anyone while you were following us, did you?"

"We did, as a matter of fact," Veija said, her expression full of surprise. "How did you know?"

"Was his hair red?"

She gasped in astonishment. "Yes!"

"You know him?" Menen asked me.

"Well, no, not really. I just saw him," I said. "Where is he now, do you know?"

"Lon is watching him," Veija said.

"You captured him?" I asked, relieved to know it. "Seems to be a favorite hobby of yours, Crenen."

The prince's reply was a toothy grin.

"Where did you see him?" Menen asked.

"He was talking to Jenen, but I missed most of the conversation…" I remembered my wake-up call in the massive tree. And to think, that had only been yesterday morning.

"What he say?" Crenen asked, finally appearing halfway interested.

"Well," I tried to remember, and then it rushed back with perfect clarity, "his name was Sikel. He was dying of the Paradisaical disease…"

"We thought so," Crenen nodded. "Was coughing like Teetering Last Legs."

Again I wondered if the name was in reference to a real person. "He wanted to see me," I said.

"Kirid spy, yeah?" Crenen said.

"Jenen seemed to think it possible."

"Sick Nasty Dog stupid, but not dense," he admitted. No one bothered to point out the problem with his choice in words. We knew what he meant.

"How is Jenen alive?" Menen asked.

"Oh, well, I kind of…" I glanced at Jenen. "I kind of took the poison out."

They stared.

"Is possible for one Fuzzy Poison Bite, but six?" Crenen said in disbelief.

"It's quite possible, even with six, when it's done by Vendaeva," Chas said, jumping from his tree branch. "Show them your little orb friend." He brushed his long hair away from his face. It was still disconcerting to see my high school rival as a twenty-five year old.

Shaking off the feeling, I raised my hand and urged the orb to come out. Immediately the blue ball of light returned, floating above my hand no matter how I waved it back and forth.

Veija gasped with delight, Menen blinked in surprise, but Crenen's eyes danced with something unreadable.

"He's got more than just this trick up his sleeve." Chas smiled at me reassuringly, and I couldn't help but smile back. It was bizarre, but welcome to think that the source of much resentment since entering high school was suddenly on my side.

"No one speaking of sleeves, yeah?" Crenen snapped, finally sitting in the grass, then laying flat on his back. "Speaking of fates," he whispered, his voice faint.

"Someday you will want to remember..."

I shook my head as the child's voice replayed in my mind.

"Is something wrong, Key?" Veija asked with concern.

"No, I'm fine," I assured her before she could assume there was another bug flying around my head. I stood and walked over to where Crenen lay in the grass, and crouched down beside him. "You said something about me taking too long. What did you mean?" I inquired, gazing expectantly into his eyes.

"You swore," he said quietly.

I thought back. "I...what?"

"You swore to save my people."

Oh. The kind of swearing. "I did, yes, a long time ago..."

Crenen nodded. "At that time, in this clearing, you swore to help Paradise, but not save its people. To help Paradise could mean so many things."

It was still and quiet all around us as I looked about the clearing, hardly seeing the people as they watched us silently. Was this really the same place where I'd found Crenen soaked in blood? Was that really so close to the Realm of Yenen?

He continued. "When you were dreaming, I asked again. And you swore, Vendaeva. You swore to save my people."

A tingling sensation ran along my fingertips, as thought confirming the truth of his words. I glanced at my hands and saw them glowing with a blue hue. "I'm turning into a nightlight," I observed.

Chas chuckled, while everyone else dismissed my words as incomprehensible.

That reminded me.

"Hey, Crenen?"

"Yes, Strange Coward Boy of Many Questions?" Crenen asked, smiling almost patiently. (At least, as close as he would ever get to looking patient.)

I lowered my voice, rubbing at the side of my mouth to smother any carrying sound. "Is Chas a good guy, or does he work for the Kirid? I mean, can we trust him?"

"What do you think?" he asked me, cocking his head to the side.

I smiled. "Yeah, guess you're right." I looked up at my former rival and considered just how much I had changed in a short amount of time.

That night we camped in the clearing, as Jenen was still recovering. I fell asleep swiftly, then woke with a start. Again. (Why couldn't I ever get a decent night's sleep?) Sitting up, I gazed at the small blue orb that had somehow come out of my hand again. It was flying back and forth in front of my vision excitedly. Rubbing the sleep from my eyes, I pushed to my feet, instinctively aware that the orb was trying to get my attention for a reason.

It danced above my head, giving me the light to make out each sleeping form around me. Jenen slept nearby, and I saw that his breathing was deeper and more regular than it had been. Veija was covered in Menen's green cloak, sleeping near the coals of what remained of the fire. Menen was resting against a tree stump. Chas was presumably somewhere in the branches above. I swept the clearing again, and my eyes narrowed. That was the problem.

No Crenen.

The orb touched my shoulder to get my attention, and when I looked, it floated off to my right, leading into the undergrowth. Glancing one last time at my companions, I turned and crept after the ball of light. Soon I lost sight of it and quickened my pace to catch up. Occasionally I glimpsed the light between the brambles and overgrowth of the forest, but soon I was completely lost and only darkness surrounded me. Frustrated, as well as nearly frozen, I raised my hand and muttered, "Liitae." The blue orb shot forth from the brush and rested in my palm. "Don't do that again," I ordered.

I couldn't be sure, but I thought the orb bobbed a nod.

"Now, Liitae—that is your name, right?"

It bobbed up and down.

"Take me to Crenen, only slower. Okay?"

Liitae rose above me and inched forward as swiftly as a snail.

"Very funny, Smart-Alec. We don't have long, let's *go*."

The orb set a steady pace, remaining four feet ahead of me at all times. We traveled as silently as humanly possible until I heard the faint hum of voices. Creeping closer, I attempted to listen in, but while I had earlier been able to detect the distant thundering of many furapintairow feet and judge their distance, my hearing now seemed worse than ever in my life.

The hairs on my neck tingled as I inched a little closer. Suddenly something slammed against me. The pressure increased as I was pushed back and forward all at once. Overwhelming pain squeezed in on my lungs, and I gasped for air, possibly screaming. Liitae fell limply to the ground beside me.

"Vendaeva!"

The cry broke through the deafening pain and the smothering force departed instantly. Collapsing to my knees, I gulped in air more greedily than any gerani.

A hand rested on my shoulder. "Key?"

I blinked and then slowly looked up, meeting the blood-red gaze of Lon. Never before had I been so happy to see him. I smiled but didn't speak, determined to keep all the air I could to myself.

"What are you doing here?" he asked.

I didn't answer, still set on protecting my precious oxygen.

"I'm amazed you aren't crushed. A person doesn't generally walk into a barrier and live afterward."

Wheezing, I wished he would shut up. At last I felt confident I'd reclaimed all the oxygen I needed, so I met his concerned gaze. "What was a 'barrier' doing there, Lon?"

"I put it there," he said.

"Why?"

"That, Key, is none of your business." He helped me to my feet, golden hair rippling as he stepped back.

"Where's Crenen?"

"Over there, speaking with our captive," Lon said, pointing somewhere beyond the tree trunks.

"About what?" I wondered aloud.

"They share one common motive," he answered. "And I think Crenen has been particularly bloodthirsty lately. He's kept from killing solely for my sister's sake, but…" he trailed off.

"...Now that she's not here…"

"Exactly."

"Liitae thought something was wrong, so I followed it here," I explained. Then I remembered the orb falling to the ground. "Liitae," I said, turning to look for it. I found it nearly lightless, just where it had landed.

"You called it Liitae?" Lon asked, watching as I knelt down again and scooped the orb into my hands. I was surprised it was solid.

"Yeah."

"Interesting…"

"Okay, so it's unoriginal," I muttered, gently tapping the ball.

"What do you think it means?" he asked.

"Light, duh," I said, still attempting to revive it.

"Hardly," Lon said. "Something much more important, actually. Strange that you would name it without knowing its meaning."

I scowled. "Do you mind? That barrier may have killed my orb." I turned back to it, prodding it gently, determined to keep it alive.

"Don't worry, it can't die. That would defeat its entire point, don't you think?"

"What are you talking about?" I snapped, glaring up at him angrily.

He met my gaze evenly. "Liitae is Life, Key. You created this orb, and it cannot die unless you do. Which means, this thing is nearly immortal."

I stared at him. "Immortal?" The way he said it, it came across as more than just a way to express the orb's existence. Unless I'd missed my guess, he was saying…

"According to prophecy, Vendaeva is half immortal," Lon said, kneeling down beside me.

"Whoa, wait just a second here," I said, making a cutting motion with my hands, nearly dropping Liitae in the process. I quickly snatched him before he fell. "Are you saying…" I leaned closer and looked him in the eyes. "How can anyone be *half* immortal. Either you are, or you're not."

Lon smiled patiently, and I wanted to strangle him for pitying my ignorance. "It's simple," he said, reminding me even more of my former loathing of him, "but I'd rather not explain it right now."

I could've throttled him, but Liitae's light flickered for a moment, and I turned my attention to the orb.

"It responds to your anger," Lon commented.

Sure enough, as soon as he said that, and I gritted my teeth, the little ball lit up yet again. I rubbed its surface, attempting to revive it, when a thought struck me. "Hey, Lon, when Chas tried to—"

"Chas?" Lon interrupted, suddenly interested.

"...Yeah..." I nodded, a little annoyed by his disruption.

He stood abruptly, and I got to my feet as well. Before I could say anything else he took off in the direction I'd come from. So many questions were left unanswered already, and he only added more to the blasted list. I ran after him, holding Liitae carefully in my hands. All thoughts of Crenen had fled.

We crashed through the same foliage I'd seen far too many times already, and I wondered if I would ever be rid of it. It seemed to take less time than before to reach the clearing, and for that I was grateful. Already my legs were screaming from the exertion the last few days had provided.

Lon halted in the middle of the clearing and his eyes rested on one tree. "Chasym!" he called, making Veija jump in her sleep.

Menen awoke, on his feet in a second, his claws before him, sharp teeth shining with light from the moons. His gaze fell on Lon, and then me, and he finally relaxed. In that moment I was grateful I wasn't his enemy.

Movement came from the tree Lon had addressed, followed by the rustling of branches. Then Chas jumped down, his green eyes vibrant in the light from the heavens. A few leaves fell around him, settling in the dewy grass. He was still in his adult form, familiar yet alien to me.

He and Lon studied each other for several moments before they both broke into smiles and then started laughing. Lon approached and gripped his friend's arm. "It is good to see you."

Chas clapped Lon on the back. "It's been far too long."

"You've been well, I hope?" Lon glanced at Chas's tattered apparel. "Furapintairow attack, from the looks of it…?"

My rival nodded.

I was completely at a loss, so I plopped down in the grass and glanced at Menen, who watched the two men, seated once again. Then my eyes rested on Veija, who turned over in her sleep and murmured something about mosquitoes. I smiled in spite of myself.

Crenen's irritated voice interrupted the happy reunion. *"Cra vener eyia baskyne, Lon!"* he growled, making me jump. I turned to watch him storm into the clearing. Then I stared. He was covered in blood. What was it with this clearing and him? He walked over to the robed pretty-boy, completely ignoring Chas. *"Vener miek diay kryn,"* he growled. *"Daja vener soraj ihi kryn keis levieshna jaer lanya deirsh eyia baskyne liish cra liiv, Domi Libin Kag? Se braryr hem."*

Lon blinked before he glanced at me, then back to Crenen. He sighed. "I'm sorry, I was distracted."

I opened my mouth to ask what was going on, but Crenen turned on me. "And you—almost killing your Essence! What possessed you?"

I also blinked. "E-Essence?"

"Yes, Essence!" he shouted, causing Veija to sit up, startled awake.

"Wha—?" she began groggily, but one look at Crenen made her clamp her mouth shut.

Chas stepped from behind Lon and Crenen to address me. "Crenen is upset because Lon left him abruptly to rescue you from the barrier they created to keep people away, and he never returned."

"Oh," I managed.

Crenen, once again, did not acknowledge Chas's presence. "Well?" he demanded.

"Uh…" *Well what?* I wondered.

"Leave him alone," another voice said.

We all turned to see Jenen sitting against the tree he'd been sleeping under. His breathing was heavy, his pale face beaded with sweat, but he was awake. Relief washed over me, seeing him conscious. I'd managed to save him.

Crenen's frown turned into an evil smirk as he regarded his twin. "Beneficial, indeed, Sick Nasty Dog, yeah?"

Jenen considered him, then smiled. "Yes, I believe so." He turned his gaze to me. "I owe you my life."

"No," I shook my head, "we're even."

He frowned. "That's twice you've saved me and I will repay you."

For the first time, I recalled that Jenen had died and somehow I'd summoned Liitae to save him from the darkness. How I forgot such a thing to begin with was beyond me. I puzzled over this, wondering what the extent of my powers were, until the conversation drew my attention again.

"Why are you bloody?" Jenen asked Crenen.

Crenen glanced at his stained clothing. "Had long talk with Bloody Dying Man."

Jenen raised an eyebrow. "You killed Sikel?"

"Not dead yet," Crenen replied, flexing his claws as he spoke.

"Good. He has something I need," Jenen said, attempting to stand. Menen stepped to his side and helped him up.

"Hey, I have some questions," I said, wondering if anyone would listen.

Chas and Lon looked at me expectantly.

My mind went blank, but I forced myself to latch on to one of the many questions I had. "Okay, why did Chas's hand go *through* Liitae, while to me the orb is solid."

"Because you're the only one who can touch your soul," Lon explained.

My *soul*? "…Okay…" I glanced at the glowing ball. "Next question." I caught Crenen's gaze and held it. "Why in the world do you want Jenen to take over Yenen leadership." I wanted to know about their rift, too, but that was a personal issue and I didn't want to pry. Yet.

The entire clearing was deafeningly quiet as each member of the strange group regarded Crenen curiously. The manipulative man's expression darkened.

"Vendaeva."

I glanced around the group, wondering which of them had spoken, but they were still watching Crenen, who, for once, seemed to have clammed up.

"Did…you guys hear that?" I asked, shattering the thick silence.

"Hear what?" Chas inquired.

"That voice." I'd heard it before, when I was being crushed by Lon's barrier. At the time I assumed it was his voice, but thinking back, it was different from Lon's; perhaps a little deeper. Plus, that wasn't the first time I'd heard it, either. The same voice entered my mind when the furapintairow army attacked, and I was almost certain there was least one other time, though when escaped me.

So much for questions getting answered. The list was endless.

14
They Of No Identity?

"What voice, Jason?" Chas questioned, raising an eyebrow.

I frowned and shrugged. "My imagination, I suppose." I knew it wasn't; no way had I heard it without good reason. I decided to change the subject entirely. "So, now that we're all here, what next? I guess I could just stand here and let you guys pull me back and forth to see who gets me this round."

"What talking about, Strange Coward Boy?" Crenen asked. "You *my* servant, you stay with *me*."

I couldn't help but smile. "Right." Apparently Crenen's memory was not impaired by his poor English; not that I expected otherwise.

Crenen considered my response good enough, since he then dismissed me and turned back to his twin. "You stay with us, since you owe Strange Coward Boy much, yeah?" He smiled the most victorious smirk I'd ever seen. "Besides, if wanting something from Bloody Dying Man, only we can supply Sick Nasty Dog with location, yeah?"

Jenen watched Crenen for several moments before he sighed resignedly and, without a word, walked across the clearing and stood beside me, aided by Menen.

"Are we going to visit Jenen's friend?" Chas asked.

Veija laughed. "Jenen has a friend?"

I smothered a laugh of my own. How anyone could be so clueless I would never know.

"What does that man have that you want?" Menen asked, curious.

I was wondering the same thing, so I threw in my own questioning expression.

Jenen held my eyes, but remained silent, ignoring Menen entirely. I, on the other hand, suddenly desired to pull Tall Strong Jerk aside and drill him for as many answers as I could think of. Knowing my luck, I doubted it would ever happen. Crenen pretty much ran the show and he had invisible strings attached to each of us, keeping us from doing anything without his blessed permission.

"Come," Crenen said, as though reading my thoughts and acting accordingly.

We moved out of camp and I bade farewell to the place I had mentally christened the Clearing of Blood. Crenen kept a fast pace, and we struggled to keep up in our battered conditions. It was only now that I realized that I hadn't eaten for several days—too many things had happened to make time for it. I didn't even know how many days it had been since I returned to Paradise. Two? Three?

My robe snagged on a bramble, and as I jerked it away from the thorny bush, realization hit me again—I was still wearing my hospital clothing. Looking down at the formerly white gown, I winced. It was a muddy mess. As I continued walking, I ran a hand through my hair and felt the tangled locks as they tickled my chin. Not only was I wearing a dress, but my hair was long, too. Something had to be done about this. I determined that I needed a bath and a new wardrobe as soon as possible—though not anything from Lon.

Speaking of which—

I glanced around for the pretty-boy, but he wasn't among the traveling party. I looked back at Chas, walking just behind me, and raised an eyebrow. He also looked at each person, then shrugged.

Frowning, I wondered where Lon had run off. Was he really working with Crenen, or would he again come out suddenly and pounce another betrayal on me? I decided there was little I could do about it. Fate had taken over my life, and I could only brace for whatever he threw at me next.

"When is Kiido coming?"

"Soon, my Master. Soon."

I halted and shook my head, tapping my palms to my ears.

"Something wrong?" Chas asked.

"No, it's nothing," I whispered even as I reflected on the voices in my head. I almost saw images—a man bowing before his lord, the latter shrouded in shadow. It was the perfect picture of something sinister.

We arrived at the place where the barrier had nearly killed Liitae and me. Crenen motioned for us to remain where we were while he went to get Sikel. I sat in the wild grass and pulled my orb from the pocket of my hospital robe, gently stroking it, watching as the pulsing light brightened and dimmed, brightened and dimmed.

"Is it going to be okay?" Veija asked, taking a seat beside me.

"You're the Seer, you tell me," I said with a smile.

She blushed and looked away. "I…I have a confession to make…"

Suddenly Lon jumped down from the treetops, causing my heart to leap involuntarily. What were these people, monkeys? He walked over to me and knelt down, meeting my gaze.

"Such perfect timing," I told him sourly, watching as Veija got up and scurried away.

"Let me see Liitae," he commanded even as he took the orb from my hands.

"Help yourself," I muttered, listening to the murmurings of my stomach.

Lon glanced up from the ball of light and gazed at my abdomen pointedly. "Hungry?"

"No," I said sarcastically. "I've just not eaten for days, I'll be fine."

A fleeting smile crossed his features as he pulled a bunch of gerani from his pocket. "I found these on my way back. Eat."

Scratch that 'eternal feud' bit. Lon was now my best friend.

I snatched the Purple Fruit from him, downing the grapes three at a time.

Chas shook his head. "How can you eat so many? I can only handle one—tops."

I blinked, surprised. After swallowing another gerani I looked at him. "They're not that potent."

He snorted. "For you, maybe. But I'm not the only one who has dizzy spells after the first swallow."

"What are you talking about, Chasym?" Lon gazed at his friend wryly. "You don't get dizzy spells; you pass out completely."

"Even so, no one can handle more then four before it's too much."

My eyes narrowed as I considered that Crenen could not have known how well I handled gerani, yet he offered them without any kind of warning. The jerk.

While eating my breakfast, I glanced at Menen, wondering if I could pull him aside for questioning while Crenen was away. He was still sitting by Jenen, though neither said anything. As I watched them it struck me that whatever caused a rift between the twins, it had torn Menen in two. But if there really was a rift, what possessed Crenen to willingly hand over clan leadership to his reluctant twin? One thing was certain: Power wasn't the motive in this matter, regardless of Crenen's megalomaniac tendencies.

The rustling of bushes brought me from my thoughts, and I looked up to see Crenen reappearing with a deep frown on his face. "Not there," he said to Jenen.

"He escaped?" Lon looked startled. "Impossible."

Crenen glanced at him. "No Bloody Dying Man there," he said with a hiss.

I looked at Jenen who was watching Crenen with a penetrating stare. "You lost him?"

Crenen nodded casually.

"Master?" Menen asked gently as he got to his feet.

Crenen stepped back, watching Menen with a wary expression. Then he doubled over as a fit of coughs racked his body. Blood splattered his hands as the coughing grew worse, and Menen ran to him with terror in his red eyes—but before he could reach him, something shot out from the trees and tackled Crenen to the ground.

We were all on our feet now. I gawked at the newcomer, and my eyes widened as I saw that it was Crenen. But—two Crenens? Heaven help us all!

I wasn't the only one who noticed. Lon and Menen dived in to stop them from killing each other. They held the

Crenens back firmly while the rest of us stared in absolute shock.

"Triplets?" Veija suggested.

"Certainly not," Jenen said coldly.

"Let go," both Crenens hissed together.

"Interesting," Chas mused, stepping forward. "I wonder if this means pigs can fly now." He glanced at the sky.

"Probably already could in Paradise," I muttered.

He chuckled, then grew serious.

"So, if not triplets, one is an impostor?" Veija said.

"I would assume as much," Lon replied.

"Tall Strong Jerk!" both Crenens cried in warning tones, struggling hard against their living bonds.

Menen looked at the Crenen he held in an arm lock, and then at the other. He remained still and silent—probably thinking that was safer than helping the wrong Crenen and hearing about it later.

Chas strolled forward, casually gazing at each Crenen in turn. "An intriguing situation, to be sure."

"Do something to fix this or move out of the way," Jenen growled.

"Maybe we could ask them which is real?" Veija suggested.

I attempted to hide my smile, and succeeded for two seconds at the most.

"We real one, yeah?" the Crenens snarled.

"This is easily taken care of," Chas said.

"Kill 'em both?" I suggested.

"Well, there's one possibility."

"What's the other?" Menen asked, showing no signs of budging as his captive continued squirming to break free.

"Well, I know who the real one is." Chas's eyes danced with mystery.

"Spill it," I ordered.

"Neither."

Everyone stared at the blond, not comprehending. Chas just laughed.

"Explain," said Lon.

But suddenly both Crenens acted, and Lon and Menen found themselves face-first in the grass before anyone knew what had happened. Crenen and Crenen pounced on Chas, slashing with their sharp claws.

Once, I ordered the forest to part for me and it obeyed. Now, desperate to stop the impostors before they hurt Chas or anyone else, I mentally urged them to cease. Nothing happened. "Stop, dang it!" I yelled.

On command the clearing froze, and everyone in it. Everything glowed faintly with an icy-blue sheen.

"Uh…that's not what I meant," I said.

Someone applauded behind me, and I turned from the halted scene and gazed at—Crenen?

"Very good, Strange Coward Boy," he said with a smirk. "You get grasp on power more full each day, yeah?"

I looked at him warily. "Are you the real Crenen?"

He rolled his eyes. "Don't be dolt, Strange Coward Boy. We only real Crenen."

Still, I wasn't so sure.

"So, how do I fix it?" I asked, waving a casual hand at the stalled clearing.

"Good question," he said, and I recognized that his voice was strange; dark and cold like ice. This wasn't Crenen.

"Crap," I muttered, wondering what I was going to do now that any form of protection I might have had was currently a statue.

I backed up. My eyes gazed into the impostor's and for a moment I saw their contrasting depths waver and change to orange. Gathering my fleeting nerve, I decided to try out this new-found ability yet again. "Show yourself."

The transformation was instantaneous. Crenen blurred as the illusion melted away to reveal a man with flame-colored hair and striking orange eyes—the only features going for him. He was shorter than I, and heavyset. He couldn't be younger than forty and his face was just plain ugly. I figured Crenen would be insulted that such a homely guy would try and impersonate him.

"Well done, Vendaeva," he said in a scratchy voice.

"Thanks," I replied dryly. "Tell me who the freak you and your friends are."

"We are They of no identity."

"Uh huh. Okay." I glanced at his clawed hands. "So, what now? You gonna kill me or something?"

He chuckled. "I'm afraid you'll not be that lucky."

That promised pain. I grimaced and backed up again. "I could freeze you, too, you know."

"Could you?" He stepped forward.

I nodded solemnly.

Before he could move another figure jumped in, and—surprise, surprise—he looked like Crenen. My shoulders drooped with weariness. Would this ever end?

As my energy ran dry, the invisible ice around my "icy" friends did as well. Suddenly the first two impostor-Crenens were again wrestling with Chas, while Lon and Menen picked themselves off the ground. Veija and Jenen watched with worry (in her case) and mild interest (in his). They didn't seem to notice any time lapse.

I only had a second to note all of this as my attention was again drawn to the orange guy and the newest Crenen. The latter raised his claws and lunged at the former. I watched in awe as Crenen gracefully, yet powerfully forced the man back, not allowing even a second for his enemy to return a blow, hands slashing inward, blood flying out. I'd never seen anything so impressive as his fluid, precise motions. The fight didn't last longer than a moment, but I would never forget it.

The illusionist fell to the ground before Crenen, who drew himself up and looked every bit majestic. I had to give it to him; he'd earned the satisfaction he felt.

"You haven't lost your touch," Jenen remarked from just behind me. (I hoped no one noticed me jump.)

"'Course not," Crenen sniffed, his eyes still on his new prisoner.

I turned to see both of the Crenens unconscious beneath Chas. He was sitting on them with a self-satisfied look that nearly rivaled Crenen's arrogance. What were they, long lost brothers?

Veija ran over to Crenen and hugged him. I laughed out loud at his startled expression.

"You're okay!" she exclaimed needlessly.

"Naturally," he answered, batting her away while regaining his dignity. She stood beaming beside him.

"Would someone care to explain what happened?" Jenen demanded, looking very cross.

"I would be happy to," Chas spoke up.

We all turned to face him.

"Reincarnate," he said simply.

"Huh?" I was lost.

He smiled. "They are those with no identity."

"I got that part," I remarked, recalling the orange guy's words.

"Honestly, Strange Coward Dolt, need to pay more better attention," Crenen chided. "We already mention Reincarnate."

I wrinkled my brow, but the memory didn't return. What was the use of my abilities if they weren't reliable?

"Patience," Lon whispered from across the clearing. How I heard him, and if he was actually talking to me, I couldn't say.

Chas continued. "The term you would know better is shapeshifter. Although these are of the lowest caliber. You might have noticed how easy it was to see through the deception once you knew what to look for. A true shapeshifter doesn't cast illusions—he literally molds his body into a new form. Still, these are from my people."

"You're no longer one of us," the orange guy growled.

"Shut up," Crenen hissed, kicking the man hard in the face, causing the man's gnarled nose to bleed as he fell backward with a painful grunt.

"It's true, I was banished for my...choice," Chas said. "In any event, that's how I knew these Crenens were impostors. This one," he poked at the Crenen just beneath him, "is Sikel, if I don't miss my guess."

"You guess right, Shifty Cocky Man," Crenen said.

I snorted at Chas's nickname.

Jenen swiftly knelt before the unconscious Sikel and began fishing through his robes and pockets. I watched with curiosity until he pulled forth a shimmering cloth: his silver shawl. So that's where that went.

"When did he—?" I began.

"Just before Crenen caught him, after we were attacked by the fura, I imagine," Chasym guessed. "Sikel must've sneaked off with it—though what possessed him to do that is completely beyond me..."

Jenen scowled at Chas as he drew the shawl around himself.

"No more time for chat," Crenen hissed. "We kill Reincarnates and move on, yeah?"

"Kill?" Veija whispered, looking pale.

Crenen hissed again, realizing his mistake. "Another word for sleep sometimes, yeah?"

She blinked twice. "R-really?"

Poor thing. She just didn't get it. Lon grabbed his sister by the wrist and led her away from the prisoners.

I found it rather a shame to kill them—at least before I could find out why Sikel had stolen Jenen's shawl. I smiled wryly as I realized how calloused I'd become. But then, Crenen could certainly make a person that way.

Still, I turned away as Crenen slit their throats with a single claw, a little disturbed that I wasn't as disturbed by their deaths as I ought to be.

15
In The Dark?

Since I never remembered my dreams after I woke up, I had no problems with nightmares in my childhood. Even if I was jolted awake by phantom horrors, my groggy mind couldn't recall any real details of the bad dream, and so I drifted into a blissful sleep without much delay. Only vague images of nighttime visions ever prodded at my mind in the day.

Perhaps that's why it got under my skin when I drifted into sleep that night only to awaken in a cold sweat as I reflected on the images of my dream, the remnants numerous, and as clear as water. As I shivered in the cold and glanced around the campsite, checking every sleeping face, I tried to focus on anything but what I 'd seen. It wasn't any use.

Liitae bumped against my hand, as though to ask if I was all right. I looked down and smiled at it.

When we made camp earlier, Lon slipped the orb into my hand and whispered to be more careful. Then he walked away and sat under a tree while the rest of us worked to build a fire and spread bedding around—the rest of us minus

Crenen, naturally. (Okay, so the only ones setting up camp were Veija, Menen, Jenen, and myself. The other three lounged.)

"I'm okay," I said as Liitae brought me from my thoughts with another touch to my hand. But my mind returned to the nightmare I still remembered with perfect clarity.

It began with screams.

I'd found myself standing in a foggy field tinged with bitter cold. Wails of pain and mourning haunted the field, though the figures were shrouded by the aerosol covering. A child cried sharply, then fell silent. Fear gripped me and I ran toward the awful sound, feeling a strong desperation to save it, though I knew already the child was dead.

As I ran I began to hear other sounds more distinctly; the clash of blades, the pleas of the helpless, and the cruel laughter of men turned savage. Still, I only sought the child. I felt a vibration in my throat and realized that I was calling for someone, though I couldn't hear the name. Was the dead child someone I knew?

Plunging deeper into the swirling mists of blue, I swiped at the fog, trying to clear the path before me. A body fell before my feet and I stopped short, staring into the near-lifeless eyes of a beautiful woman. Her dark brown hair lay all around her and she clutched at a whimpering child even as the blood flowed from her body, stealing her life. She spoke, and though I heard no words, I knew what she asked. I knelt and took the child from her icy grip.

I ran on.

The child looked up into my eyes with tears in its own, but it made sound as we hurried on. Instead, it only turned its head forward and watched the mist before us.

Carnage was piled on either side of us, and pools of blood splashed into our faces, but I kept my gaze straight ahead, refusing to see the horror around me. The child stirred after a while and glanced up at me, staring with a sorrowful expression as it reached its tiny fingers up and ran them along my cheek. It was wiping my tears away.

I spoke to the child comfortingly, though I couldn't hear my words. I continued to talk soundlessly until we were forced to stop before a giant wall. Searing, horrible laughter rang in our ears as we studied the wall despairingly. I knew in the dream that breaching the wall meant freedom. And I knew we had to climb it.

Cradling the child under my black robes, I touched the wall and tried to climb, but there were no flaws or indentations to grab to hoist myself up. I groped in the gloom even as I felt some great darkness coming toward us from behind.

I shouted something at the child as I leapt into the air, then grasped the wall with razor claws. It hurt more than I could stand, but again I dug into the stone, arduously climbing upward as my fingers bled.

I'd almost reached the top when I slipped and nearly fell. As I forced my nails into the stone yet again, wincing in agony, a new horror struck me—the child was gone. Panicking, I craned my neck and gazed hopelessly into the abyss of mist beneath me. My sharp ears caught the cry of a child as it fell.

Darkness enveloped me then and I felt tears slide down my face. I saw no more.

Stirring from my recollection I realized Liitae was trying to wriggle out of my tight grip. I released the orb with an apologetic smile, then stared into the darkness around me. The dream made no sense, but the feeling of hopelessness remained even now, when I was awake.

"What is wrong, Vendaeva?" a soft voice floated across the cool breeze.

I jumped and raised my orb into the air to see better. In the diminishing darkness I caught sight of Lon leaning against a gnarled tree.

"Bad dream?" he asked

I nodded, feeling no desire to lie.

"What was it about?"

I shrugged at the same time that I shivered.

"Clasp the orb in both hands and desire warmth," he instructed.

I obeyed, then sighed as heat bathed my body and my goosebumps dispersed.

"What was it about?" he prodded.

"A child," I whispered.

He raised an eyebrow. "Truly terrifying."

I sighed, not willing to explain. "Tell me something, Lon."

"Hm?"

"Are you a good guy?"

He smiled, amused. "I reverse the charges."

I chuckled, feeling the weight of my dream lifting just a little. "Okay, I guess I deserved that."

"My question for you, Vendaeva, is, is there really only good and bad in this world? The color I see is gray."

"You mean, like various shades?"

He shrugged. "It's still gray."

"Fascinating," a new voice spoke blandly from above.

"Come down, Chasym," Lon invited.

A few twigs snapped and fell to the ground as our resident shapeshifter landed on his feet and bowed sweepingly, long hair slipping into his face, then falling away as he straightened.

"So," I addressed Lon, "are you a cool gray, or more like a dark gray?"

Chas chuckled as he knelt in the grass. "He's as close to black as they come—aren't you, my friend?"

Lon brushed a strand of golden hair from his face. "In most respects."

"We have a bunch of melancholy morons in this group," Chas remarked.

"I'll say," I said.

"I'm just moody," Lon assured us, as though that was any different.

"Let's see." Chas tapped his chin. "Melancholy Moody Moron. I'd say it's not too bad a Crenen-name, eh, Jase?"

I smirked. "I can do better."

"Can you now?"

"No sweat. Moronic Moody Man suits Lon more."

Chasym snorted. "Score one for the short guy."

"Hey, I'm growing."

"Yeah, soon you'll reach Veija's shoulders."

I rolled my eyes. "I'm not that short."

"You're still shorter than her."

"By an inch. Tops."

"Gentlemen," Lon said. "Keep it down."

We glanced at the others sleeping blissfully under their covers.

"You said you dreamed of a child," Lon reminded.

"Uh huh."

"Got any aspirations to play mommy?" Chas asked with a smirk.

"Go drown yourself."

"What? You're short like a girl," the blond shrugged, his grin widening.

I rolled my eyes. "Face it, Chazzy—if anyone's the woman in this group, besides Veija, Jenen takes the prize. Followed very closely by pretty-boy here." I jabbed a thumb at Lon, who watched me with a wry expression.

Chas snickered. "Good point. But you come in third."

"Not when you have long hair," I stated, reaching out and yanking hard on his yellow locks.

He grimaced and pulled away. "Oh, c'mon—if we're going to get technical let's face reality. The only real man in our presence is Menen."

There was no disputing that. "Agreed."

We had called a truce for the moment.

Lon sighed and got to his feet. "I'm taking a walk."

"At this time of night?" Chas asked. "You really are loony." Lon ignored him and walked into the trees. I turned to Chas and considered him.

"You irk him sometimes, I can tell," he commented, watching the trees.

"Serves him right," I answered, also peering into the foliage.

"Such a heartless lad."

I bowed my head graciously. "You flatter me, sir. Now, answer me this. Why does Lon call you Chasym? Is that your real name?"

"It is," he said. "But you can call me whatever you want."

I pondered that. "Chasym suits you better." Here, where he wasn't so much my rival, it felt right to refer to him by a different name. It made it easier to set aside my prejudice.

Silence fell between us. In my head I could hear the cry of a falling child, and I tried to block it out.

I didn't remember falling asleep, and if I dreamed again I couldn't remember that either. I felt myself shaken awake and when I pried my heavy eyelids open I looked into the beautiful violet eyes of Seer Veija. She smiled brightly, put a finger to her lips and, gently taking my hand, helped pull me to my throbbing feet.

I yawned, stretched, and gazed at her inquiringly as she guided me away from camp, where, upon glancing back, I saw that no one was yet awake, though the sun was rising. Feeling deprived of much-needed rest, and jealous that everyone else could continue in uninterrupted bliss, I trudged after Veija, somewhat reluctant. As my mind began to wake up, I wondered why she was leading me away. Then I recalled that before the attack of four killer Crenens she'd been about to tell me something.

We halted among the trees and she glanced around before meeting my eyes.

"I need to tell you something important. It's about my brother," she whispered with a frown.

"About Lon?" I repeated, my mind concocting a thousand different possibilities.

She opened her mouth to speak, but the crack of a twig made her jump, and she clamped her mouth shut, peeking around fearfully.

"I wondered where you'd gone off to, Jason," Chas—no, *Chasym* said as he stepped out from behind a thick tree. He paused as he gazed upon Veija. "Excuse me for interrupting." An odd smile played at his lips and a light sparkled in his eye. His smile grew wicked as he turned his gaze to me.

I scowled. "What do you want, Chazzy?"

He chuckled as he stepped nearer. "I don't recall." He extended his hand to Veija. "I believe we've not met properly before now."

If Chasym was Lon's friend, how was it he'd never met her?

She smiled. "I am Seer Veija."

Chasym smiled darkly. "Ah yes, a Seer. Lon told me of you; it's good to meet you at last. I am Chasym."

"I know," Veija said, and I noticed that her smile didn't reach her eyes.

Chasym noticed too. "Come now, let's forget *what* I am, and try to see *who* I am. I can't help what I was born, but I can choose who to be."

She relaxed a little. "True, though I'm afraid you will have to prove yourself."

"Lon trusts me."

"Lon trusts Crenen," she returned.

"Point," I added.

He grinned. "I understand. Allow me to begin proving myself. Care to take a walk, fair lady?" He bowed and offered her his arm. She hesitated and then slipped her arm through his, allowing him to guide her toward camp. Chasym glanced back and winked at me, though I ignored his taunting. Let him flirt.

I took a step after them, feeling like some breakfast, but stopped as a strange feeling entered my gut that had nothing to do with hunger. I gazed at my pet orb was floating around the high grasses by my feet, chasing pointy-toothed bugs. "Something's wrong," I whispered, touching my temple with a finger. I scanned the trees and noticed that everything appeared darker—as though the shadows of evening had overcome the dawn.

The crunch of fallen leaves behind me brought me from my thoughts. Before turning around I knew it was Lon. "What is it?" I asked, facing him.

"The Kirid are marching," Lon said quietly, his red eyes studying the gloomy sky. "They're backed by tremendous power. They come from their home in the west."

I frowned. "How fast?"

"The darkness will be complete before they strike. It could be days."

I recalled a darkness so thick that I couldn't see anything at all as I sought out Jenen. It felt the same now as then, and at that time someone had died. "Where will they strike, Lon?"

"The Realm of Yenen, if they can penetrate its defenses."

I thought for a moment. "Jenen said they were after him. Why?"

Lon's eyes caught the light of the sun and shone. "Their Seer is afraid."

"Of Jenen?" I couldn't really blame the Seer, honestly.

"Of what the Seer helped bring about by trying to prevent it."

I cocked an eyebrow. "Care to explain?"

Lon took a step nearer, his lavender robes dragging through the moist grass. He reached for Liitae and drew the orb toward his face. "Your dream..."

I thought of the child falling through the darkness.

"No, your other dream," Lon said blandly.

I pictured two children standing in a sunset; one pleading, the other defiant. The first handed the latter a shimmering silver shawl.

"Yes, that one," Lon said.

I wondered how he knew what I was thinking, but decided not to ask. Yet. "What about it?"

"Why did you dream that?"

Good question. "Who cares?" I mumbled.

"You do."

I bit back a retort, recognizing that I needed to know his point.

"Very good," he whispered. "You're slowly learning focus."

Can you read minds? I thought very hard.

"When I feel the need to," he answered.

My jaw dropped. I thought Jenen was supposed to be the psychic one.

"Come now, Key, don't be silly."

I scowled, but held my tongue, waiting for his explanation about the dream.

"Very good," he commended, smiling gently now. "When that darkness came before, Jenen was supposed to die in order to prevent the very thing that occurred. The Seer did not take into account how you would be bound, and therefore unwittingly created just the situation needed."

"Bound?" I ventured.

"When you found Jenen laying dead on the ground, you acted on instinct, summoning Liitae, correct?"

I nodded, recalling vaguely.

"When that happened, you thrust the ball of light into his heart, bringing Jenen back to life. In this way, you shared a piece of yourself with him, binding the two of you."

I frowned. "What do you mean exactly?"

Lon thought for a moment. "This binding allows you to share each other's thoughts and emotions occasionally. While Jenen was delusional with fever you shared his dream—the one involving a much younger Jenen and Crenen. Likewise, it is possible that he shared your vision of the child."

"So," I considered quietly, "so, how deep does this connection go, and...is it permanent?"

"The orb was placed into his heart, so it runs very deep. In a sense, I suppose, this makes you brothers." Something flashed in his eyes. "As for its endurance, I believe the length of time in which you share this bond is entirely up to you."

"But why would the Seer be concerned with our bond?" I asked. "What're they afraid of?"

Lon shrugged. "You would need to discuss that with a Seer."

My eyes narrowed. "How do you know so much?"

He smiled mysteriously. "You'll have to ask a Seer about that, too."

I rolled my eyes, recognizing that I would get nowhere now. "We better go warn the others about the Kirid."

"An excellent suggestion."

We began walking through the trees, following the path left by Chasym and Veija.

"Why do the Kirid and Yenen clans fight? What caused it?" I asked, for the sake of breaking our silence.

"How long have you wondered that?" he mused. "If I told you it was for the sake of fighting, would that be answer enough?"

I shook my head. "There's more to it."

"Years ago—" He broke off, listening hard.

I knew the history lesson was off for a while. Darkness was cradling around us much more quickly than Lon had believed. The Kirid were coming fast.

"Come," he whispered, seizing my wrist and dragging me swiftly through the trees. "We must reach the others."

"Lon, are they after us?"

"You're a much bigger prize than even the Realm of Yenen, and it seems they have found you."

Prize, huh? I'd been called worse.

We crashed through the brush, giving no regard for the thorns scratching at our legs; me in my stupid hospital vesture. I felt numb, both from fear and from the intense cold that the darkness was bringing. A blur of blue on our right caught my eye.

"Liitae," I called. "Go on ahead and warn the others."

It sped up, passing us in an instant and vanishing in the gloom. I urged it on in my mind.

"Lon," I said.

"Yes?"

"Who was the child?"

We were moving faster now, but the sounds of breaking branches were distant in my ears as I waited for his reply.

Before he could respond—or, perhaps, *would* respond—we broke through the trees and entered the clearing where Crenen held an excited Liitae in one hand.

"Wanting translate Stupid Round Light?"

"The Kirid are coming," I offered.

"Good summary," Lon said.

"Thanks."

Crenen blinked. "Is certain?"

Lon nodded, pointing at the stretching shadows. "We could be dead in minutes—we have to leave now."

"But where will we go?" Menen asked, glancing around.

Crenen hissed. "Doesn't matter, can't stay, that matters, yeah?"

"Exactly," Lon agreed. "Anywhere is better than here."

"Where is the Seer?" Jenen asked.

I turned around, looking for Chasym and Veija. "I thought they came back."

Lon tensed.

Crenen handed Liitae back to me and glanced around as well. "No time. Must get Vendaeva out of here before Slimy Bad Kirid attacks, yeah?" He grabbed my arm and pulled. "Do as wanting, but we leaving."

I forced my arm out of his grasp and backed up. "I'm not going to leave those two out there to be captured and tortured. Save yourself, for all I care, but I'm gonna find them."

Crenen rolled his eyes and then sighed. "Very well, but not alone, yeah? We go with." He again took my wrist and forced me to follow. "All split up, but stay in groups, yeah?"

Menen followed us while Lon and Jenen took another route.

"Liitae," I whispered. "Show me where they are."

The orb floated above my head for a moment and then shot off into the brush before us. "Follow it," I said, now dragging Crenen.

"Slow and silent," Crenen hissed. "Kirid are here."

Sure enough, the darkness was complete.

The stillness of the trees was maddening. After searching for Chasym and Veija for what seemed hours, I was ready to scream, if only just to make some noise. I felt like a plastic bag had been laid over the forest and the air was running out. Too much longer and I knew I'd snap. The panic was steadily building inside.

Crenen halted me by sticking out his arm, and I smacked against it. Even though he was only a few inches taller than I, he was significantly stronger—that, or his arms were made of rock. I winced and rubbed my bruised collar bone.

"Thanks," I growled.

"Strange Coward Boy need to stay calm or Kirid sense position, yeah?" Crenen replied in a quieter voice than I'd thought he could manage.

"How can I stay calm when the air is getting thin?"

"Tall Strong Jerk," Crenen said.

Before I could make any sound, I felt myself lifted by the collar of my robe, through the darkness, up into the branches of the trees. The front of my hospital gown was suddenly choking me, and I struggled to break free so I could breathe. After a moment I was released and dropped to my feet, rubbing my throat and swallowing air.

"Breathe better now, yeah?"

I scowled. "Very funny."

"We think so, too."

"Master, we need to move," Menen urged.

"Yeah, yeah. We go." He poked my arm to prod me forward.

So much for our quiet search. I'd be surprised if the Kirid hadn't located our exact position by now. Still, no matter how much longer we walked on, and regardless of my nervousness, the forest was still.

“How long has it been?” I whispered, making sure I was barely audible.

“Too long,” Crenen said shortly.

I was afraid of that. Glancing around, I shivered in the bitter cold and strained my eyes to make out any signs of our comrades. Liitae's glow barely cut a sliver of light before us to illuminate our path, so it was almost pointless to peer into the darkness as we wouldn't seen anything anyway.

“Pointless,” Crenen voiced after a while, causing me to jump.

“Agreed, Master,” Menen said.

A sharp hiss escaped Crenen's lips and he stopped abruptly. I ran into him again and barely kept myself from crying out (more from fright than pain).

“Master?” Menen whispered.

“Menen—stay with Vendaeva,” Crenen ordered, his voice deadly.

I stared. He had just called Menen by his name. Fear pricked at my neck as I felt the stillness shifting around us. Menen caught my arm and dragged me away from where Crenen stood. Liitae followed. “No,” I told the orb. “Stay with Crenen.” Liitae bobbed for a moment, as though deciding whether or not to obey before it floated back to the Yenen clan leader. “Good...orb thing,” I said, smiling despite the fear in my gut.

Though the darkness closed around us completely as we wended our way through the trees, I was more afraid for Crenen, because whatever he was about to face was worse than suffocation. Maybe.

“I'm sorry,” I whispered, the nearness of my voice a little startling.

Menen's grip on my arm loosened as his focus returned to the present. “It's not your fault.”

“Still...” My presence kept Menen from staying with his master.

“You left him your Essence,” Menen said. “That is enough.”

Was it? Lon had told me the orb was a portion of myself. When I thrust it into Jenen's heart, he became bound to me. Would the same principle apply now? Would this, if only on a smaller scale, link Crenen's life to mine? Would it do him any good?

So many freaking questions.

I've found you.

I stiffened and my back popped at the sudden movement.

Menen turned to face me. “What is it?”

“He's here,” I whispered, trembling.

“Who, Key?”

“The voice,” I said. “The Seer.”

Menen hissed softly, then placed a hand on my shoulder. “He won't claim you.”

I nodded, but the terror I felt had turned into icy fingers with razor-sharp claws tearing at my insides.

It is too late to run away, Vendaeva.

I shuddered, closing my eyes. Menen guided me onward, forcing me to run, leading me, stumbling, around trees and through brambles. I didn't argue. I felt numb from head to toe and I knew I couldn't run without his support.

“Oy, Menen!” The voice shattered the stillness and froze my heart mid beat.

We stopped yet again and I forced my eyes open. It didn't help.

“We've been looking for you.” Chasym's voice.

“How did you know it was us?” Menen asked warily.

In answer two floating lights in the dark appeared: Chasym's yellow eyes. “Built-in night vision.”

“Where's Veija?” I asked, locating my voice.

“In the tree. We hid there when we sensed the Kirid.”

I sighed. “And we all split up to look for you. Why didn't you just go to camp? Why are you both so far out here?”

“That was my fault,” a female voice said from above. “I wanted to speak with him in private.”

“Are you okay?” I asked her.

I could picture Veija's smile as she answered. “Yes. Sorry to worry you.”

“Where are the others?” Chasym asked.

“Lon and Jenen went off together to search for you. And Crenen...He's back there.” I pointed to the general area behind me.

You're too late.

I stiffened again.

“What's wrong?” Chasym asked.

“Nothing,” I said, managing a weak smile. “Just a voice in my head again...”

“We're in the Seer's domain,” Veija said. “It's very easy to enter a person's mind when the Seer has complete control.”

“That's wonderful,” I said.

“Sounds like it,” Chasym agreed.

“There's got to be a way to get all of us back together,” I said.

“This is rather a big forest,” Chasym said flatly. “How do you propose we go about it?”

“Well,” I hesitated, “I'm not really sure.”

“Thought not.”

My eyes widened as I thought of something. “Scratch that. I've got an idea.”

“Really?” Veija asked excitedly.

“Be fast,” Menen said.

I closed my eyes and focused on Jenen. If what Lon said about our bond was true, he would sense my thoughts and, quite possibly, my emotions. They just needed to be strong enough. I didn't know our present location, but if I could keep a strong enough connection, surely I could weave a trail for them to follow. Or something.

Clever, but it won't work.

A horrible, agonizing pain shot through my body like electricity, and I screamed.

"Jason!"

I pried my eyes open and the pain ebbed.

"I take it your idea failed." Chasym's voice was wry.

I chuckled. "Something like that."

"Still," an unfamiliar voice joined in, "an impressive attempt."

Our small group spun on its heels to face utter darkness.

"Who are you?" Chasym demanded for all of us.

"Never mind that." The voice's owner was definitely male, no question there. "I'm here to collect what is mine."

"Unless you're talking about the grass, I think you've got your directions crossed," Chasym said. "There's nothing here you could own."

"I'm afraid you're mistaken, Chasym Verenvey of They." A rustling of the grass informed us that he was moving nearer.

Chasym scoffed. "You're mistaken if you think I am. Leave us alone."

"I'm afraid it's far too late for you to make demands of me. Several hundred years too late." Such a cliché line, yet at this moment I couldn't knock away the fear in my heart. I knew this man was after me; there was no question. This was the Seer.

"Ha! You think a couple hundred years is a long time?" Chasym inquired, sounding amused.

"No. It is a very short time. Now, step aside, Verenvey."

"I don't answer to that name anymore," Chasym said flatly, "so, no."

With a howl, wind rose up from the grass, and while I could only feel its biting cold, I knew it hit Chasym full force, knocking him to the ground with a muffled gasp. The wind's icy fingers wrapped around my throat and covered my nose.

"I would release him, Menen of Yenen Clan, before the boy dies."

Menen hissed. "Better to let him die now than in your clutches."

I reached up with my hand, trying to knock the wind away even as I struggled to breathe. "M-Men...en..." I gasped.

He hesitated but let go of my arms. Immediately the wind vanished and I coughed, gulping the air as quickly as I could. Though my lungs ached, I straightened my back and focused on the man who stood before me in the darkness.

"You're not going to take me," I stated firmly, all my fear gone away. There are only so many attempts you can make on one's life before the thought of suffocation loses its effectiveness.

"You've little choice in the matter, Vendaeva. The master desires your presence, and I must accommodate."

"Tell your master I don't give a care what he desires."

The Seer laughed. "As charming as I thought you might be."

My mouth twisted wryly. "Yeah, well, we can't all be angels."

"I agree," he said in a soft voice. "Come now, we've wasted enough time. The master grows impatient."

"Poor baby. It must be hard not getting what he wants right away." I backed up and felt Menen set his hand reassuringly on my shoulder.

The man laughed again (which was really getting on my nerves). "Stop,"he whispered. My limbs froze, and try as I might, I couldn't break free. "Come. The shadows wish to kill your friends—a sight, I have no doubt, you loathe to view yourself."

I gritted my teeth and willed the ice to melt away. It gave a little, but I still couldn't move.

"Very good. You impress me with your calm." The man's hand touched my cheek and I winced as his icy fingers numbed my face. "Now, sleep."

It was as if my brain had been replaced by an ice cube. Everything blurred together and if I was falling I didn't know it. It was cold, so very cold.

"Snap out of it, Strange Dolt Boy! Now not time for napping, yeah?"

My eyes snapped open as I heard the familiar taunting voice and the ice cube melted with a pop. I fell hard on my knees, as I'd been half-way through my faint when Crenen spoke up. Wincing, I shakily got back to my feet.

Crenen was standing with his back to me, his inch-long claws dripping with crimson blood, staring down the man in magenta robes.

—Wait, there was something wrong with this picture.

Oh. I could see.

The darkness had receded to the edges of our tiny clearing. Shadows danced around, eager to get back in, yet unable to pass an invisible barricade to reach us.

I turned my attention back to the stare-down.

The Seer was scowling, his own clawed hands quite bloodless, while he clutched his chest area, as though to cover a wound. He had long vine-green hair that reached down to his feet and sea-foam green eyes that blazed with anger. He was slender, and taller than Crenen, by an inch or more, and his presence spoke of authority. Still, his presence didn't proclaim it quite as loudly as Crenen's did.

"Best you leave now, before we gut you, yeah?" Crenen said, his tone dangerous.

The Seer smiled unpleasantly. "I'm not through here."

"So says Delusional Broken Man," Crenen sneered.

"Broken?" The Seer frowned. "Hardly."

As they began what promised to be a long verbal duel, I swept the small clearing for the others. To my right I found Menen guarding Veija, who had climbed down from the tree and was watching Crenen intently. Lon was here now, standing beside Menen. Still, there was no sign of Jenen.

"Define broken," the Seer ordered.

"Delusional Broken Man redefine broken—hard to put into words when exemplified so well, yeah?"

Something silver caught my eye and I turned my head to see Jenen kneeling before Chasym. My eyes widened. The latter was sprawled limply on the forest floor, his long yellow hair spread around him. His eyes were closed, mouth slightly open, and blood seeped through the corners. A large icicle protruded from his stomach and two smaller ones jutted out of his shoulders, pinning him to the ground. The voices of Crenen and the Seer were drowned out by the horror I felt as I stared. Was Chasym dead?

I took a step toward him, but Veija gasped loudly. Spinning back around, I saw the Seer appear just behind Crenen and swipe his nails to slash him.

"Stop!" I cried, focusing the rage I felt toward the man before me.

For a moment the Seer faltered, but he didn't freeze as the others had last time. Still, it was enough. Crenen turned with lightning agility and dug his claws into the other man's stomach and, just as quickly, slashed them across the Seer's throat. The man staggered and fell backward. Instead of blood seeping from his wound, a black mist poured onto the ground and the body disintegrated. The dark mist slithered off into the shelter of the trees.

You will have to do better than that, Vendaeva...

"Only an illusion," Lon whispered.

"Too bad," Crenen sighed. He turned to face me. "Strange Coward Boy okay?"

I nodded feebly as I turned back to where Chasym lay motionless. "How is he?"

Jenen's ear twitched and he looked up at me, metallic eyes ablaze with noonday light from the sun. "He's alive...for now."

Lon brushed by me and knelt on the other side of Chasym. "We need to remove the ice, but when we do, the bleeding is going to be hard to stop."

"Can I do anything?" I asked.

They ignored me and conversed quietly as Lon inspected the wound.

"Let them do it," Crenen said as he stifled a yawn."We take nap..." He walked over to a tree, plopped down beneath it, and stretched out comfortably.

"Wait," I said, walking up to him.

He opened his silver eye and peered at me in annoyance. "Yes, Strange Coward Boy?"

"What happened?"

He smirked. "We slash gut and he turn into Black Misty Stuff. You see as well as we, yeah?"

I scowled. "No, before. When we left you behind."

"Didn't so," Crenen said, opening his other eye now. "We left you ahead. Not left us behind, yeah?"

I rolled my eyes. "Whatever. So, what happened then? After...you left us ahead."

He nodded, appeased. "Well, Delusional Broken Man send Nasty Shadowy Dragon and we quickly kill, yeah?"

"Nasty Shadowy Dragon?"

"Yeah," Crenen said as he stifled another yawn. "Big Stupid Thing. But we kill, and it turned into dark mist too."

"Also an illusion?"

"Always was illusion."

"Right. So it was sent to kill us?" I guessed.

"Uh huh, but we remove obstacle from Vendaeva's path." He winked his silver eye.

"Much appreciated."

"Welcome." Crenen snapped both eyes shut. "Now, be quiet or we gut Strange Coward Boy, too, yeah?"

"Yeah." I turned and walked away from him, ignoring the trembling in my legs. I headed over to where Veija and Menen stood watching the operation.

"Are you alright?" Veija asked, reaching a hand to my face and gently touching my cheek. "That's an awful cut."

I touched my cheek where the Seer had placed his fingers and felt warm blood. It had been cold at the time but it hadn't hurt at all. I wiped the blood away with the sleeve of my robe. Glancing down, I grimaced. The hospital robe was no longer white, nor was it completely whole. The edges were frayed and tattered, and the cloth was covered in dirt, grass, and blood stains.

"I need a new wardrobe," I muttered.

"Yes, you do," Menen agreed. "I'm glad I do not dress as they do in your land."

I shivered, ignoring his comment. "Anybody got a blanket?"

Menen shook his head. "We left them all at the camp."

That reminded me. "When did it get light again?"

"Around the time Lon and Jenen arrived, just before Master Crenen came."

"Why?"

"Perhaps he lost his concentration," Menen suggested.

"...Maybe." I wasn't convinced. Something else had caused the darkness to recede, especially since they'd seemed blocked by some hidden barrier.

"You look really pale," Veija said, interrupting my thoughts. "Go lay down."

I shook my head. "I can't sleep until I know if he'll be alright." I gestured toward Chasym's unconscious form.

"We'll wake you when we know something," Menen promised.

"Can't I do something to help?"

"Yes, shut your mouth and get some rest," Lon ordered without looking up from his doctoring.

I huffed, almost shot back a snide retort, reconsidered, and took to sulking.

"Ready?" Lon asked, glancing at Jenen.

"Yes," Jenen said quietly.

My eyes trailed down to the large icicle in my rival's stomach. I felt my own stomach clench in sympathy. Lon and Jenen placed a hand on the object and pulled hard. It slid out of the wound, glistening red, and the blood began to flow.

The icicle was tossed aside and they stuffed the wound with Lon's outer robe.

"I wish we had some hot water," Lon murmured.

My eyes trailed back to the icicle.

"Do you have something to heat water with?"

"At camp, with our water," Jenen said flatly.

I glanced around the sky above me. "Liitae, c'mere." The little blue orb danced into view and swooped down into my open hand."Make yourself useful. Turn into a pot." The orb bobbed its acknowledgment and reshaped itself into more of a bowl than anything, but it would do. "Make yourself really hot."

It flashed purple.

I walked over to the large icicle, well aware that every eye was on me. I nonchalantly wiped the blood from the icicle onto my soiled robe, tossed the icicle into the makeshift pot and watched as it melted into water. Within seconds it was boiling.

"There you go, Lon," I said, smirking.

He gave me an appraising look and finally smiled. "Very well done."

I bowed my head, still smirking, then walked over to the nearest tree and plopped down. "If you need me for anything else, I'll be napping," I said as I stifled a big yawn.

16
The Healing Pool?

It didn't surprise me when I was shaken awake. I couldn't recall the last time I'd come out of a deep sleep gradually, but my aching body assured me it had been a while. I grudgingly forced my tired eyelids open and peered into Crenen's face, again only inches from my own.

"I thought I told you not to do that," I mumbled.

He grinned as he backed away and stood up. "We wondered if Strange Coward Boy remember."

"How could I possibly forget? Your face is rather...inexpungible, when it's that close."

Crenen looked confused, but shrugged it off. "Strange Coward Boy use very odd words sometimes."

"If you'd take the time to learn English properly, you might not need to complain so much."

Crenen's eyes narrowed. "Why we need learn different language for likes of you? We move now, yeah?"

I rubbed my face. "We're leaving?"

"What we said, yeah?" He spun around and walked away, and I thought I saw a small storm cloud hovering above his head.

"Snappish twit," I muttered as I struggled to my feet.

The area was thick with evening shadows and a frost had settled on the bracken around the clearing. I could see the last of the sun's rays as it set beyond the sea of trees.

Turning to the others I saw that a makeshift stretcher had been constructed out of long branches and Lon's under robe. Now he was only wearing a thick, baggy black shirt and black pants, with lavender wrappings up to his knees and around his wrists. Chasym was laying inside the stretcher and it appeared Jenen had been generous enough to lend the injured man his shawl for warmth.

Veija walked over to me, skirts rustling, a radiant smile on her pretty face. "Did you sleep well?"

"I hardly remember," I answered, not bothering to smile back, as I was too tired.

"Good," she said brightly. "That means you slept soundly."

"I guess so. So, why're we leaving when it's almost night?"

"Lon ordered us to pull out as soon as he and Jenen stopped the bleeding." She glanced back at the stretcher. "Chasym has lost a lot of blood, and Lon is really worried. Reincarnate blood is really hard to get a hold of, so I don't know if he'll live."

I frowned. "Is it really that serious?" I brushed by her without waiting for a reply and walked to the stretcher, gazing into it. Chasym's face was pasty-white, his breath shallow, his skin clammy. "I'll help carry," I said.

"You're too tired," Lon remarked, coming up behind me, red eyes glittering in the dim light. "And you were touched by Seer magic. That leaves a mark. You can't possibly..." As he spoke I walked over, grabbed the makeshift handles of the stretcher, and glared at him.

"I'm carrying him."

He watched me and then nodded. "Very well. Suit yourself."

"That I will."

"I'll take the other end," Jenen said.

Since he was probably the closest to my own height, I was grateful. With anyone else, except maybe Crenen, it would be too lopsided to carry comfortably, and poor Chasym would have blood rushing to his head.

As we trailed out of the clearing, Veija explained to me that Menen had gone back to gather our supplies at the other camp only to find everything gone. Apparently the Seer's shadows had taken off with them.

"No need worrying," Crenen said from beside Menen. "We only few days travel back to Realm of Yenen."

"A few days?" I glanced down at Chasym's pale face. "Can he last that long?"

"What else can we do?" Veija whispered, her own eyes fearful.

"There is a pool," Jenen said quietly.

Crenen halted, turning to gaze at his twin. "And...?"

We all stopped—save Lon—and fixed curious stares on Jenen.

"I often go there," Jenen continued without meeting his brother's eyes. "The water has certain healing properties."

Lon turned around now, interested. "There shouldn't be any healing pools left, Jenen."

"I'm aware of that. I can't explain how it exists, but I can take you there."

I cleared my throat. "Question."

Crenen found my eyes. "Yes, Strange Coward Boy?"

"I gather that the healing pools heal, obviously. But why did they once exist, but shouldn't anymore, even though they apparently do?"

"You ask questions in a very confusing manner," Lon chided.

"You know what I mean," I said, shrugging. The stretcher bounced lightly with the motion.

"We keep walking well talking, yeah? Only, Sick Nasty Dog leading way now," Crenen ordered, jabbing a nail in Jenen's direction.

After Jenen took the front, still carrying his end of the stretcher, we continued walking, changing routes.

Lon explained: "A few hundred years ago, the healing properties in several pools throughout the land were a gift from Paradise, but when the Paradisaical disease struck, the pools changed, and when those who had the disease came to heal themselves, it instead caused the inflicted to die more quickly and more painfully."

"But this one didn't change?" I asked.

"No, it did," Jenen said from the front.

We all watched his back quietly, waiting for more.

He sighed. "I live near the pool."

"Ha, Tall Strong Jerk, we know where he live now!"

"Yes, Master."

Jenen ignored them. "Once...someone came to kill me."

"You're popular," I drawled.

"I injured him very badly but he continued to fight me. So I drew him close to the pool, intending to shove him in the water. Not only does it increase the speed of illness, but also injury. He would have died instantly."

"But he didn't," I finished.

"Exactly. Instead he was healed of his wound." He paused. "I had a hard time killing him after that, as his energy had been repleted."

"You did kill him though, that's impressive," I said.

"Afterward, I experimented with the pool, throwing in small injured animals."

"Not injured before, we think," Crenen chuckled.

Veija blinked, but said nothing.

"The water had regained its medicinal properties." Jenen finished his narrative, pretending that he hadn't been interrupted a hundred times.

"I wonder why," Veija said, tapping her chin.

I felt eyes on me and I looked up, glancing left, to find Lon watching me without expression, his red eyes impenetrable. I thought I could guess what he was thinking, but I couldn't be sure. It made me more curious than ever though. I needed to know who Lon really was. What his motives were. What everyone's were, come to think.

Maybe someday I'll tell you, a whisper drifted quietly through my mind.

We traveled well into the night, and my body ached with the strain I was causing it. I refused to complain, or even flinch though, because I knew that one sign of weakness and they would force me to be carried while someone else took the stretcher. This was something I could do, so I would do it.

It was strange, really; before I came to Paradise I would have gladly given such a menial task to anyone else. But now, it was as though I felt some great weight on my shoulders, like there was a lot expected of me, yet I was helpless. So I found myself eager to jump at anything that might ease the burden, anything that could make me forget that helpless feeling.

A few hours until dawn I finally stumbled, my newly blistered hands slipping under Chasym's weight. As suspected, they'd been watching for this. Menen grabbed my arm to steady me while Lon snatched the handles of the stretcher.

"Rest, Key," Menen whispered, lifting me up in his arms. "You've done enough."

I raised my hands to my eyes and inspected the blisters, too tired to protest how I was being carried. “Got a band aid?” I mumbled, though I knew he had no idea what I was talking about.

He regarded me blankly.

“Heh. Never mind.” I curled my throbbing hands into fists and closing my eyes. “Wake me up when we get to the pool, 'kay?”

“Of course,” Menen said, a smile in his voice.

If time flies on Earth, it's a freaking bullet train in Paradise. I felt myself set on my legs all too soon and pried my eyes open to see the rising sun's reflection glistening in a silver pool of water.

“Ow,” I mumbled, rubbing my eyes to reduce the glare. When I looked up again I saw Crenen prodding the pool with a stick.

Menen guided me toward the pool. Lon glanced my way and started walking toward me, making me stiffen. Last time I'd walked toward a pool with him in the vicinity I'd had a rather unpleasant experience.

“Relax, I'm not going to send you home,” he said, a slight smirk on his lips.

“Yeah, you better not, pretty-boy,” I said, my tone not as firm as I would've liked. I watched curiously as he took my hands and examined the blisters.

“This will work,” Lon said after a moment.

“Do you know that for certain?” Jenen asked, coming up and gazing at my hands too. “He's not from Paradise. How do we know it will have the same effect on him?”

Lon didn't answer. “Come, Key. We need to test the water.”

“With my hands?” I asked, following him to the muddy bank.

His red eyes glistened. “Thank you for volunteering.”

I sighed. "Sure, anytime."

"Did someone feed him gerani? He seems very docile," Menen observed as he gazed at Crenen, who was munching on something.

Crenen grinned wickedly, displaying pointed fangs. "We had no time, but can be doing now, yeah?"

I perked up. "I'm really hungry."

Crenen only laughed, the creep.

"Kneel."

I obeyed Lon, kneeling in the squishy mud, feeling the unpleasant warmth through my thin, worn robe. He placed my hands into the water and searing pain exploded in my palms. I screamed (I admit it). The pain was excruciating, and even though Lon jerked me back, the agony only intensified. I curled into a ball, clutching my hands to my chest, biting my lip hard against the burning sensation.

"Are you certain this is the pool?" Lon demanded of Jenen.

"Yes, but it seems the properties have changed again." His own voice was concerned.

"Are you all right, Key?" Veija asked, and I felt a gentle hand touch my cheek. "Let me see."

Several pairs of strong hands sat me up and pried mine away from me. I didn't bother to hide the tears streaking my cheeks. It hurt too freaking much to care. I avoided looking at my palms even when the others gasped.

"Oh, Key," Veija whispered breathlessly.

Finally I forced myself to look, and my own eyes widened. My hands were horribly torn and burned, but where there should have been blood, silvery-blue fluid, pulsing with light, dripped from the wounds.

"Told you I was turning into a nightlight," I muttered, trying to ease the pain by joking.

"If this isn't proof enough that he is Vendaeva, then nothing is," Lon stated, unwrapping a strip of cloth from his arm and wrapping it around one injured hand.

"Glad I could sacrifice my hands so you'd know," I said, gritting my teeth as he tightened the lavender bandage. "Though I assure you that up 'til now I've never once bled anything but blood."

"It's a magic wound, Key. Of course it's going to be different."

I scowled. "Well excuse me for never having seen a magical wound before to compare it with."

"We seen plenty magic wounds, but never bled anything but red blood," Crenen mused, standing just behind me.

Lon began bandaging my other hand. "As I said, it's proof that Key is Vendaeva."

"Hm." Crenen stepped to my side, bent down, and ran a hand across the small puddle of glowing liquid on the ground before me. He hissed, wiping his fingers on the grass. "Very hot."

"So." I drew a shuddering breath. "So. What made the pool go bad again?"

"Few can say, but it is a bad sign," Lon said, glancing at Veija. "What do you think, Seer?"

She jumped, as though caught off guard and then grew very still, her eyes unfocused for a moment. "The Paradisaical disease is spreading. More Paradisians have been infected." She frowned. "Time grows short."

"The question should be, what made the pool heal itself and then become poisonous once more?" Jenen said quietly from beneath the shadows of a large gerani tree.

I hesitated, eyeing the grapes with longing, and then sighed, shaking myself of the desire. There were too many other important things to think about.

Ugh. But not the pain; focus on anything but the pain.

"What do we do about Chasym?" I asked, shifting my gray eyes to the stretcher.

"If he stays here he will die," Jenen said. "He needs immediate treatment."

"Which means we haven't the time to take him to the Realm of Yenen," Veija said.

"Then we go and catch help for immediate treatment," Crenen announced.

"Whom do you suggest catching?" Lon said.

I stupidly tried to wiggle my fingers but the searing pain flared worse. I winced, closing my eyes to stop the tears from coming back.

"And Key must have his hands looked at, in case they are seriously damaged."

I imagined myself trying to eat supper with my toes. I didn't think I was flexible enough. "Don't worry about me." I forced a smile. "Chasym's life is on the line."

Crenen spoke up. "We the nimblest, so we go—and Vendaeva come with us."

I blinked. Didn't that kind of defeat his point. "Uh, doesn't that defeat the point? I mean, if you're the nimblest in the group, then I'm the stumbliest."

Lon chuckled, covering his mouth to hide it.

Jenen raised an eyebrow. "Key poses a good point, and besides, who said you were the most nimble?"

Crenen pointed at Lon. "Too much hair and too much clothes. And," he pointed at Veija, "she is girl. Tall Strong Jerk have too much length, and you, Sick Nasty Dog, would fall down dead if pushed yourself too hard. This leaves us."

I smirked. "But, uh, taking me would only slow you down and you'd be as bad off as someone who is either female, has too much hair, or is... lengthy—none of which are decent arguments anyway. Though I can see where you're coming from about Jenen."

I pretended not to catch the scathing glare Jenen sent my way.

Crenen ignored me. "So, we go with Strange Coward Boy and return with Screechy Hurting Doctor, yeah?" (That sounded so reassuring.) "Come back by nightfall."

I looked up sharply. "Tonight?"

"If we leave now, won't be too hard, yeah? We take Shifty Cocky Man, but is too heavy and too hurt." Crenen beckoned me with his hand. "Come, and bring Stupid Round Light."

I glanced at Liitae, who was hovering above me, and shrugged. "You heard the guy, let's go." The orb bobbed its understanding and perched itself on my shoulder as Menen helped me to my feet.

"You'll be fine," he assured me before releasing my arm. "Probably."

"I hope so," I whispered as I watched Crenen pick some gerani from the tree.

"Want some?" Crenen asked, dangling a bunch out to me. My stomach growled and I nodded. Crenen's mouth split into a vicious grin. "Good! When we reach Realm of Yenen we give you some, yeah?" He popped one in his mouth.

"Jerk," I snarled.

"Come, Strange Coward Boy." He turned and headed for the trees.

"Isn't it about time you give me a different name?" I asked, beginning to follow him, pleased to note that my legs were mostly steady.

Jenen scoffed from behind me. "I've had the same one since I was sixteen. You'll not get a name-change so easily."

I shrugged. "Ah well. Could be worse. I mean, *I* could be the nasty dog."

"True," Lon murmured.

"Well," I turned and waved my hand once, wincing at the flaring pain, "see you all later."

"Take care of yourself, Key," Veija said.

I smiled. "As much as Crenen will allow." I turned back around and saw the impatient Yenen clan leader tapping his clawed fingers.

"Not have all day," he reminded.

"Right," I said, catching up to him. "By ground or by tree?"

Crenen scoffed now. "What you thinking we be, monkeys? We walk on ground like was intended."

That worked for me. "Works for me," I said, my mind already made up not to let anything get to me.

Of course, that was before I met the doctor.

17
The Doctor?

It was everything I could do to keep up with Crenen, but I managed it. Of course, I was too out of breath to think of conversation, so my thoughts dwelt on Chasym's condition—better that than to reflect on the horrible pain in my hands.

Finally Crenen called a halt, and I rested flat on my back, gasping for air in a small, green clearing. Liitae plopped in the soft grass beside me and pulsed erratically with light. I had the distinct impression it was mocking me. I reached over to give it a gentle flick, but cried out with the effort as my hands flared with indescribable pain.

"Make us wonder if *dolt* should be permanent name, yeah?" Crenen commented as he plucked a gerani from its bunch and popped it in his mouth.

"Ha, ha," I managed, still cringing with pain. "You try burning your hands raw sometime, and then move them." I tilted my head to view Crenen sitting on a large mossy rock, from an upside-down angle.

"That our point, yeah? Wouldn't."

"Yeah, well." I decided to change the subject. "How close are we?"

"Not far."

I raised an eyebrow. "Well, that's helpful. How many more hours, Crenen?"

He selected the largest gerani and took his time chewing. Finally he swallowed. "We arrive in short time, maybe even less than...that time..."

"An hour?" I supplied helpfully.

He nodded. "Exactly."

I glanced at the noonday sun. So his estimation about getting back by nightfall *was* plausible. "Hey, Crenen, I've been meaning to ask you..."

"Which question?"

"About this doctor...?"

"What about?" Crenen stashed the gerani bunch in his pocket.

"Won't that smush them?" I asked.

Crenen looked at me and blinked. "The doctor?"

I nearly laughed, but managed to contain it. "No, the gerani."

His lip curved into a half-smile. "What about Screechy Hurting Doctor?"

"Well, Veija said Chasym's blood is hard to get. Can the doctor save him?"

Crenen's eyes caught the light of the sun and flashed. "Worth trying, yeah? All one can do, we think."

I smiled softly. "That's true."

He leaned forward. "What is it, Key?"

How he sensed my troubled thoughts I couldn't be sure. I looked back up and saw that the mocking presence normally surrounding him had considerably lessened.

"Am I Vendaeva?" I asked, meeting his metallic eyes.

"Are you?"

I sighed. "This disease. Somehow I'm supposed to stop it, right? But...I mean, how in the world am I supposed to do that? I'm not a doctor, or a wizard, or a fairy. I'm just a high school kid with an overactive imagination and a penchant for lying. Suddenly I'm swept up in something way over my head; something that only happens in video games and cheesy films. But this is real. We're real. I'm here. And somehow I have to cure a world-wide epidemic, with no knowledge of how to do it—and my only source? A ditsy lady who thinks mosquitoes can enter her visions at random." I raised my palms above my head despite the pain. "And I can't even use my hands now."

Crenen's mouth lifted into an almost gentle smile. "What is your point, Key?"

I lowered my hands. "What would you do?"

"Question. As you are doing. There are thousands of other people in Paradise, even with this disease. Think. If you have one hundred questions, certainly there are one hundred people, each with an answer to give."

I smirked. "You have an interesting outlook on things, Prince." At first I hadn't been sure, but it was true. Crenen was once again speaking in perfect English.

He blinked and then his smile returned. "All right, Key. I'll give you two free questions. I may not answer them completely, but I will give some kind of truthful reply. Fair?"

"What'd I do to deserve this?" I asked, turning my eyes to gaze at the shifting branches above me. The sun's light splayed dancing shadows across the ground, and its rays sparkled through the leaves overhead.

"You grew."

I looked at him.

"Only a little," he assured me.

"Not physically, though," I sighed.

He scoffed. "Does that really matter?"

"No," I said honestly. "Not anymore." There were too many important things going on to let a simple matter like height bother me.

"Now, ask your questions before I change my mind."

I thought for a moment. There were so many things I could ask, so many directions I could go. But I could get answers from Menen later. I must be careful what I selected now.

"Okay, first. Why do you want Jenen to take over Yenen Clan?" It was one of the questions that had plagued me the longest, and just asking it, knowing he had to give an answer, was satisfying.

He hesitated, his eyes growing distant as he calculated what to tell me. "When we were young," he finally said, "even though I was the older twin, I followed Jenen as a loyal pet follows his master. There were moments I would attempt to take charge, but Jenen's levelheadedness was much more suited for leadership. I taught him the ways of fighting, of survival. And he, in turn, shared with me the meaning of love for one's people. In those youthful days we never considered who would become leader one day, because we didn't have to. We had an elder brother to lead us."

"Elder brother?" I repeated, surprised.

Crenen nodded, his eyes still distant. "Yenen, named after our father. He was to be the clan's next leader, but the Paradisaical disease struck him down when he was only sixteen. It was the first tragedy in our family, but not the last."

I was still. Even the wind in the trees was muted, and the forest creatures seemed content to listen in silence.

"Jenen had always been a solemn child, but when Yenen died he grew *very* distant. We were fifteen at the time, and though he and I were twins, I think Yenen and Jenen were closer somehow. Both were more like my parents; somber. I was different from them."

I found myself breathing shallowly, almost fearing that any sudden movement would startle Crenen out of his reverie.

"After our brother's funeral, it finally occurred to me that I would be next in line for leadership when my father died. And I knew I wasn't suited for it."

"But your people respect you," I told him.

"Respect, yes. Love? No." He looked up. "It's not that I can't lead, just that Jenen is better. He is levelheaded, remember? You know I'm not."

"But I still think you're wrong, Crenen."

He looked down and met my eyes. "Oh?"

I nodded. "I think your people do love you."

He chuckled. "As if you could possibly know that, Key. You've never seen me interact with them."

"Something I have a feeling you made sure of," I said, shifting to carefully rest my right arm under my head. "But, you only explained half the question."

Shrugging, he said simply, "Jenen is better suited for it."

"Yeah, except that he's not willing."

Crenen stood up on the rock he'd been sitting on and reached up to snap a twig from its branch. "Jenen has a deep wound. He is afraid to care again for fear of making it deeper. I want to show him that wounds do heal." He tossed the twig at my feet. "That even though a part of him will never be whole again, he is still the majestic tree. Will you help me show him, Key?"

I gazed at the twig, and then looked back up at him. "Yes. I'll help you."

His smile broadened. "And in return, let me take some of that weight from your shoulders." He jumped from the rock and took my arm, pulling me to my feet. "We'll go twice as fast if you aren't doing the work." He wrapped my left arm around his shoulders and slid his arm around my waist. I gratefully accepted his aid, knowing I couldn't run on my own anymore.

Crenen crouched down, grinning. "Hold on," he advised as he leaped into the air and landed on a branch. I did as instructed and soon we were gracefully leaping through the air, from branch to branch. I barely felt a thing.

"I thought you said you weren't a monkey," I reminded him.

"I'm not," he assured me. "Only birds can fly like this!"

We reached the high wall of trees surrounding the Realm of Yenen before another hour was up, just as Crenen had said. This time I was shown the easy way in. One tree among the many had a hidden door. One could easily pull it open if one found the right knot, then could walk into the Realm.

Six guards met us on the other side of the door and Crenen relinquished his arm, passing me to another guard, who easily lifted me in his arms. I was surprised by how weak I was—I couldn't even stand on my own before the guard picked me up.

"Careful," Crenen ordered the man holding me, and I was grateful for his unusual show of kindness.

We proceeded directly toward the largest tree. I recalled that on those beautifully carved steps I'd first laid eyes on Veija in person, as well as Lon. This time, however, we went around the large tree and climbed down a short set of stairs, entering through a less impressive door. The room we entered was warm and brightly lit. A fire crackled cheerily in a hearth and I wondered about the safety of fire inside a tree.

I was laid on a soft bed and covered with a fur. Sighing contentedly, I closed my eyes and began drifting into a deep sleep.

"No, Strange Coward Boy," Crenen said, rapping me on the side of the head with his bony knuckles. "Can't sleep yet."

I moaned, but forced my eyes open. "I know."

"Screechy Hurting Doctor be here soon, yeah?"

"And for the record, I only cause people to hurt when they squirm a lot," a crisp female voice said from somewhere to my right.

I sat up, or tried anyway, but found myself tangled in the heavy fur, unable to move my hands or feet. I didn't need to worry, though, as the woman appeared above my head only a second later. She was beautiful, perhaps twenty years old, with pale skin and dark brown hair pulled into a loose bun behind her head, several long strands hanging free. Her eyes were a clear, sapphire blue color and her lips were deep red. She wasn't smiling.

"What a mess," she commented, wrinkling her nose. "And when is the last time you had a bath?"

I thought back. "A while."

"Well that much is obvious," she said, tearing the fur away. "You need to bathe before anything else."

I wouldn't argue. I knew better than she how much I needed one.

"And what is that horrible garb you're wearing?" she asked, pinching the collar of my muddy robe between long claws. "That needs to be burned."

"Please, burn it."

The woman doctor motioned a servant over. "Prepare a bath. Hurry, before the stench lingers too long in the air and sticks."

I sniffed my robe. It smelled more of pine than filth, really.

She whirled on Crenen. "And where have you been?"

"Busy," he replied, utterly unconcerned.

She scowled, her eyes glistening dangerously. "One of these days you're going to end up dead, and when that happens, don't come crawling to me for help."

"By the time he's dead," I interjected casually, "he'll have no need for a doctor, no matter how adept."

She turned her withering gaze on me. "And what is this child?"

Ignoring the reference of 'child', I raised an eyebrow. "What's with you constantly saying 'and' at the beginning of all your sentences?"

Her scowled deepened, distorting her fair features. She turned a questioning stare on Crenen, who ignored her as he rummaged through his pockets.

"Here," he said, pulling forth a single gerani, miraculously not smushed. "As promised, yeah?" He offered the precious morsel to me, and I eagerly accepted it, ignoring the burst of pain in my hand.

I was about to pop it in my mouth when the doctor snatched it from my fingers. "This is *not* an appropriate food to eat when one is injured."

I could handle snide remarks about my clothes, my appearance, or my odor, but take away the gerani I had worked so hard to earn and she was going too far. "That's mine. Give it back, lady."

She dropped it on the floor and stomped on it, before resting her degrading gaze on me. "If you really want it now, go ahead and eat it."

I stared down in horror. What kind of creep would do that?

Crenen stiffened. "That was his," he said with a sharp hiss.

"And it still is," she replied.

The servant entered, bowed, and announced the bath was ready before Crenen could react.

"Good," the doctor said, turning back to me. "Go clean yourself up."

I attempted to get up, but my body felt like it weighed two tons and I only fell back against my pillow.

She raised an eyebrow. "Well, are you going, or must I carry you?"

"Yeah," I answered.

Crenen shoved the woman aside and lifted me into his arms. "Come," he whispered. "I will carry you."

As we followed the servant into the next room, steam hit me in the face and I grinned. Then my thoughts returned to the woman doctor and my good mood faltered.

"Crenen?"

"Hm?"

I frowned. "She has no respect for anyone. Why don't you kill her? You've disposed of people for less—not that I'm condoning your executions, but...I'm a little surprised you put up with her."

He sat me down on the wooden floor. I glanced over and saw that the bath's edge was at ground level; it was an large, rectangular tub dug out of the ground and covered in smooth river stones, then filled to the brim with clean, hot water.

"She is the best," he answered, removing my filthy robe as he talked, "and we need the best to save Chasym."

I sighed. "Somehow I have a feeling Chasym'll never forgive us for having a wench like that save his life."

Crenen stood, leaving the rest of the undressing to me. "Even so, you and I both know he can't afford to be choosy in his condition."

I nodded and then remembered. "Hey, I never did ask you that second question."

Crenen laughed. "Save it. I'll let you ask your question later."

"Okay."

"I'll find you a decent wardrobe," he added, raising the muddy robe up to inspect it. "Scrub hard, yeah?"

With a parting wink of his silver eye, he closed the door and left me to ponder recent events on my own. Well, almost on my own. A male servant took that moment to step into the open and remove my hospital gown, then aid me in entering the water.

I sighed at the instant soothing the water gave my aching muscles, and then watched in fascination as clumps of mud detached from my body and floated to the top of the water. I kept my hands out of the bath, for the sake of my wounds, propping my elbows against the tub's edge.

"Please soak for a while," the servant said, bowing. "I shall return with food."

I smiled my appreciation, then slid further into the water, tilted my head back against the bath's edge, and basked in my moment of peace.

"This is what Paradise should be," I said to no one, closing my eyes .

18
The Threat Of A Shadow?

I was the type of high schooler who always fell asleep in class. My days wore away while I napped; at my desk, at the lunch table, on the bus (when I actually rode it) and under the old oak in my backyard (though not when it was snowing outside).

I desperately wanted those days back. The days when I *could* sleep.

The weariness I had collected over the last two weeks seemed to have caught up with me. I didn't wake up as the servant scrubbed me clean, toweled me dry, dressed me, and hauled me back to the good doctor's bed.

It wasn't until my hand flared with pain that my eyes snapped open and I gasped. A few blinks of my eyes and the doctor came into focus, her mouth twisted in a sardonic smile.

"Sleep well?" she asked as she pulled more of the bandages away from my hand. Apparently keeping it out of the water had been a bad idea, as now the bandages were stuck to my dried magical blood.

"Yeah, while it lasted," I snapped even as I winced. "Where's Crenen?"

"There," she said, pointing to a chair by the fire.

I squinted and just made out the sleeping form of my captor, his lopsided ponytail jutting up over the wingback. I imagined he was nearly as tired as I felt.

I fixed my gaze on the doctor. "Do you know why he goes back and forth between broken and non-broken English?"

She pulled the last of the bandage off and began examining my hand by the afternoon light streaming through a carved window. "He hates English."

"So I've heard, but why does he switch back and forth?"

She picked up a wet cloth and slapped it onto my palm. I bit my lip to keep from crying out. "Simple, really. When he is serious or very angry he lets slip just how good he is at speaking it. Otherwise he puts on a front. He's always putting on a front. Stubborn, selfish, demented..." She trailed off.

Tears leaked from the corners of my eyes. "That really hurts," I whispered. "What are you using?"

She glanced up and smirked at my tears. "Crenen said you got into some bad water. So I'm washing it away with good water."

"It's just water?" I asked between clenched teeth.

"Hot water, yes," she answered, removing the cloth. I watched her dip it in a bowl of crystal water and then she slapped it again on my hand.

"Ow," I snarled.

"The blood needs to circulate," she informed me coldly.

We both watched the cloth.

"Who taught you English?" I asked after a moment.

"You ask a lot of questions."

"I figure the only way I'll get a straight answer is by asking a straight question."

She removed the cloth. "Look."

I looked down at my hand and blinked. "What's that?" I asked, lifting my hand to the light to better see.

"You tell me," she replied.

The burn marks and blisters on my hand created some kind of elongated shape stretched lengthwise along my palm; the sort with too much precision to be mere coincidence. It was still too swollen to make out what the shape might resemble.

"Take it away from the light," she said.

I obeyed, too curious to argue. As I moved my hand into the shadows of the corner by my bed, the shape shimmered silvery-blue.

"That's an interesting wound," she remarked.

I nodded, my mouth agape.

"Give me your other hand," she said.

I obliged her, bracing myself for the awful pain I knew would come. "I'm Key," I told her more for something to say than because I thought she cared.

She looked up, her mouth twisted again in that annoying smile. "*Who* was it with the broken English?"

I scowled. "No, it's my name."

She began peeling the bandage away. "Ah."

"What's yours?" I asked through clenched teeth.

She pulled the last bit off and examined the wound. "Sasha," she said after a moment. Then she mercilessly slapped the cloth onto my palm.

I bit my lip hard. After a moment I dared to breathe. "Sasha," I repeated.

"That's what I said."

"Well, for what it's worth, it's nice to meet you."

She arched a brow. "Nice? You really are mental, aren't you?"

I shrugged. "Heck if I know."

"How did you get these wounds?" she asked after another awkward silence.

I tried a shrug, but received a scalding glare from the doctor for my efforts. Apparently she didn't like wiggling patients. "Like Crenen said, I got into some bad water."

"And that caused identical afflictions on both palms."

I met Sasha's icy eyes and held them. "Yes."

Her mouth twisted into scowl once again, but she said nothing.

We sat in silence for the rest of the time it took to doctor my hands. I tried to think of something to say, but she only poked and prodded harder each time I drew breath to speak. I finally took the hint and shut up.

Once she finished bandaging my hands, she stood. "You'll live," she pronounced in a tone that nearly sounded disappointed.

"Thanks so much."

"Any time." I knew she was only offering an encore of the painful parts. "Now," she walked over to the fire and shook Crenen's shoulder, "I understand I've got another patient, yes?"

Crenen cracked his silver eye open and looked up at her. "We need be getting back by night."

"You realize we haven't much time until then. Is it far?"

He shook his head. "Not if we take theshers, yeah?"

"Theshers?" I asked, though I had a sneaking suspicion I would be sorry I inquired.

"We show, but first need to be redressing." Crenen stood and pointed to some clothing draped over the foot-board of my bed.

I glanced down and noticed that I was currently wrapped in a loose white tunic that reached my knees. I glanced at the doctor. "Your patient apparel?"

She nodded curtly.

"You get acquainted, yeah?" Crenen asked.

I threw the doctor a resentful glance. "Somewhat."

She walked back to her chair, turned it to face the window, and sat down, her back in my direction. "Hurry and get dressed. I'll respect your privacy."

It seemed rather oxymoronic; a doctor respecting one's privacy. I shrugged the thought off and peeled the tunic from my body, then grabbed the garments Crenen had pointed out. And stared. "Er," I said. "How...do you get this thing on?" I couldn't tell the sleeves from the neckline.

Crenen chuckled and separated the different layers of clothing, handing me what appeared to be a Paradisian version of an undershirt. I already had on what looked like boxers, and they had even supplied my feet with a pair of very itchy socks. Both were black, as was the undershirt.

"You guys sure like black," I commented.

"Easier to make many of one color than many of five," Crenen said, handing me the black, long sleeved shirt that went over the first one. It was much softer than the socks.

It wasn't easy work, attempting to dress myself with two bandaged, very sore hands, but with Crenen's unexpected aid, coupled with my determination, I managed to get the matching baggy, black pants on, tie them around my hips, then watch Crenen wind leather wraps around my arms and lower legs. He removed the itchy socks and continued winding the soft leather around my feet. I had to admit, it was much more comfortable than the hospital wardrobe I'd acquired before.

"And finishing touch," Crenen said, flashing a proud toothy grin. He returned to the chair by the fire and lifted a long, cerulean-blue cloth in his hands. "Keep Strange Coward Boy more warmer," he explained, in case I had any complaints; which I hadn't.

I allowed him to drape the cloth over my shoulders, and around my neck, making the cloak hang long on the left side, and allowing my right hand movement by draping it shorter on the right. He stepped back and examined me, nodding in approval.

"Look better. Less girly," he stated.

It was probably true, so I couldn't argue. I felt so much better anyway. I was clean, well dressed, and very warm; three things I'd missed desperately. Now I only needed food and some more sleep and I'd really believe this was Heaven.

"That won't do," Sasha said when she turned from the window and looking me up and down.

Crenen raised an eyebrow inquiringly.

She scowled and crossed the room, her strides long and graceful. She reached a shelf covered in parchment, vials and herbs, and grabbed a wooden comb, a hand-held mirror, and a small leather cord. She grabbed my elbow and sat me down on the bed, which suited me fine, as I felt too weak to stand much longer anyway. She began combing my hair. As I felt the comb's teeth fight the tangles, I realized that my hair was much longer than I'd accounted for. I reached back and brushed my fingers against the locks. They just brushed against my shoulders, easily covering the nape of my neck.

"When'd that happen?" I mused aloud.

"Been growing all this time," Crenen explained.

"Yes, hair has a tendency to do that," Sasha said dryly.

I gave my own scowl. "Yeah, but it's never grown as quickly as it does in this place."

Sasha hesitated, and then took a thick strand of my hair which tended to defy gravity, and wound the cord around it, tying it off at the end. She handed me the mirror.

I studied my honey-colored hair, now long and sleek, hanging like a curtain around my face. Only the one lock was caught in the leather cord. "I thought you were tying it all back."

"It's not long enough for that yet. It would slip out," she explained. "But it's not tangled now, and you look more natural."

"More Paradisian," Crenen enlightened me.

I couldn't help but smile. I had to admit I was thrilled to wear the traditional garb of a strange and magical people.

"Was difficult finding outfit small enough to be fitting on Strange Coward Boy," Crenen remarked thoughtfully.

I wilted slightly. "Thanks."

"Now," Crenen said cheerily, "we go get theshers!"

Theshers turned out to be horses, or like unto, at any rate. My thesher was a massive, black beast with—you guessed it—sharp teeth. My bet was these were carnivorous horses. And they all had creepy yellow eyes that looked a bit too intelligent for my taste. It took some coaxing to get me near the animal, even with as little strength as I had. Finally Crenen dragged me over to where our mounts were chained to three stumps and threatened to gut me should I remain stubborn.

After I was securely tied to the horse (so I wouldn't jump off) Crenen mounted his meat-eating monster and Sasha climbed up behind me in the huge saddle that was strapped around the equally huge belly of my steed. Now I was not only stuck with the horrible beast (who might breathe fire at any second) but I was also stuck with Screechy Hurting Doctor (who had yet to prove one part of her Crenen-name, which worried me).

"We go now, yeah?" Crenen said, urging his thesher forward.

Sasha reached around me and gripped our reins. "Hold on."

I scowled. To what? My hands couldn't clutch anything. (I guess that might be the other reason they tied me up.)

My family had once owned horses when I was very young, but I would never go near the stables because I was terrified the animals would bite me. Though I eventually understood that horses don't eat people, I remained uncomfortable around them. And now I had good reason.

As soon as Sasha urged the thesher onward, the nasty beast growled. It was a deep, predatory sound, and I felt my spine stiffen. Never mind wanting to get off the creature. I knew the second I slid from its saddle I would consumed.

The Paradisian horse was fast; extremely fast. It was everything I could do to keep from falling back against the lady doctor, but my pride and my fear kept me from jostling about too much. I could only pray it would end soon; if only for the sake of my backside.

Crenen and Sasha didn't take pity on me. We rode harder and faster than I thought I could handle, yet still we pressed on. The last rays of sunlight stretched across the edge of the sky as we tore through the everlasting forest. The stray light had taken on a purple hue, reminding me of the constant chill in the air lately.

"Is winter coming?" I managed to ask regardless of the rough ride and the blasting air in my face.

"Naturally," Sasha said, her tone suggesting my stupidity.

"Hey, give me a break," I defended. "I'm not from around here, you know."

"A desert dweller then?"

"No," I replied, glancing at Crenen ahead of us. Apparently he hadn't informed her of who I supposedly was. It was unusual for him to keep quiet about Vendaeva, but I wasn't going to argue.

"Then where did you previously reside?" she asked, sounding only half interested.

"At my house."

"Suit yourself," she snapped.

I frowned. Such a touchy person. "Look, I'd tell you but it's really not that important. I'm unfamiliar with this place, that's all anyone needs to know."

The thesher leaped over a fallen maple pine, and my face paled by several shades as we nearly fell off. Sasha's arms wrapped around me to keep us both steady, then she pulled away, maintaining a firm grip on the reins all the time.

As the thesher returned to a steady, speedy gait, Sasha took a deep breath. "Why is Crenen so interested in you? What does he have to gain by keeping you alive?"

I blinked. When she put it that way, it sounded incredible—more incredible than before. Ridiculous, in fact. "...That's a good question. I don't really know his motives." I shrugged. "You've known him longer, you tell me."

She twisted the reins in one clawed hand. "Who is the injured person?"

"Chasym. He was attacked by a Seer." I winced, realizing I might have given her too much information. Crenen probably had his reasons for not telling her.

"A Seer?" she whispered. "Suddenly they all come crawling out of the woodwork."

"Tell me about it," I muttered.

The thesher jumped over another fallen tree, and I glanced down as Sasha's arms against held me. A shadow flickered across the ground beneath us. I would have thought nothing of it and assumed it was the thesher's shadow, but it seemed to have eyes. Glowing eyes. Last I'd checked, normal shadows didn't.

"What is it?" Sasha asked, glancing down to where I was staring as we steadied again.

I looked back up. "Oy, Crenen. We're being followed!"

I felt Sasha stiffen at my words, but I didn't offer an explanation. Crenen glanced back at me, his eyes narrowed.

"Certain?" he called back. I nodded. The sound of a hiss caught in the wind and was carried back to us. Crenen gazed at the ground. "Speed up, Screechy Hurting Doctor. We got little time, yeah?" With that he snapped his reins and the huge beast lurched into a lightning-fast gallop. Sasha followed suit, saying nothing as the thesher raced to keep up with its companion.

It was only a twenty minutes further to the pool at neck-breaking speed, but that time seemed to stretch on for hours as I watched the ground beneath for any more signs of pursuit. Occasionally Crenen glanced back, making sure I was keeping a close watch, and he would nod in satisfaction when I looked up and shrugged my report.

When we pulled the theshers to a halt before the glistening pool of evil water, I waited impatiently for Sasha to untie me, then slid from the saddle with little thought of what the horse might do if I got too near. I couldn't care less about carnivorous beasts when we were under possible threat of another Seer attack.

"They're back!" a female voice cried happily.

I looked around and saw Veija standing in the shadows of the gerani tree. Jenen stepped out from behind her and walked quickly toward us. He looked strange without the silver shawl usually wrapped around him.

Crenen slapped his thesher's flank and both creatures took off, disappearing in the forest gloom. He and Sasha neared me, the latter gasping.

"Jenen?" she growled, stomping forward. She slapped him across the face, eyes sharp as icicles. "Where did you go? Why didn't you ever come back?"

Jenen touched the sore spot on his face and watched her calmly. "If you're a doctor now, you should be more concerned with your patient."

She looked ready to slap him again, but finally nodded. "Show me where he is."

They started back toward the gerani tree, but before we followed, I stopped Crenen.

"What was that all about?" I asked.

Crenen shrugged. "Sick Nasty Dog never say goodbye to Screechy Hurting Doctor before he leave. She stewed for Long Hurtful Days about it."

I blinked. "So, she, I mean...were they...a couple?"

Crenen laughed. "No, but many Big Scary Rumors circulated around Realm of Yenen, yeah?" He winked and pulled away from me. "Come, we go watch."

The way he said that indicated I would be watching more than just a doctor saving someone's life. I followed, curious.

"Hey, Crenen? What about that shadow?" I asked as I caught up and walked beside him.

"Nothing can be doing but wait, yeah?"

I supposed that was true.

Hidden just out of view, thanks to the gerani tree, was the entrance to a cave. How quaint. As Veija directed us inside, I swiped a bunch of gerani from the tree and hid it under my blue cloak, ignoring my throbbing hand.

The cave entrance was a three-foot-wide, seven-foot-high tunnel that lasted for a hundred yards and then opened into a massive room brightly lit with several torches. A cold draft swept down from above as we entered and playfully carried my hair around my face.

The stretcher was discarded and Chasym had been placed in a bed carved from the rock. The mattress looked surprisingly soft, and when I investigated I discovered that it was stuffed with thousands of down feathers. Where Jenen had acquired this luxury, I could only guess.

Chasym was ghastly pale, his breathing quieter than ever, his strength waning. It was definitely a good thing we traveled by thesher. Though I was less than fond of the creatures, it had been worth the sacrifice.

Sasha neared the bed and gazed coldly at the man inside it. "You're joking. This is the creature you want me to save?"

I glared at her. "What of it?"

She folded her arms. "You can't expect me to help an enemy."

"Of course not." Lon's voice carried across the room. I looked toward the entrance and saw him looking very ominous against the shadow of the tunnel. "We're only asking you to aid a dying friend."

She scoffed, but when no one disputed Lon's claim, she stared. "You can't be serious. This creature? You can't possibly be his *friend*."

"Sasha," Jenen said, his quiet voice penetrating the tension. "It's exactly this attitude that has put our people at odds with all of Paradise. Such prejudice has killed more than any sword ever could—and it created swords to begin with."

"But he's of *They*," she hissed, showing her own sharp teeth.

I grabbed the shawl on Chasym and whipped it away to reveal the blood-soaked bandages. "I don't care what he is," I said. "Only *who* he is."

She narrowed her blue eyes on me, baring her teeth. "You expect me to listen to you—a foreigner?"

Crenen and Veija had watched in silence on my other side, but at her words Veija stepped forward.

"He's not a foreigner! He's Vendaeva."

"We're wasting time," Jenen murmured.

Sasha didn't hear him. She was staring at Veija as though she was insane (which might be a disputable point). "Ridiculous," she said. "Vendaeva doesn't exist. That's only a myth."

"It's true," Crenen said seriously.

Her eyes focused on Crenen for a moment, then lighted on me, their depths flickering with the light from the torches. "This *boy*?"

I bit back a retort about her not being much older. My height probably threw off her judgment anyway.

"Please focus," Jenen said with a sigh. "Vendaeva isn't the issue, Chasym is."

I nodded. "Exactly."

She broke off eye contact with me and gazed at the still form in the bed. "But—"

"Help him, Sasha," Crenen said, his tone authoritative. Glancing at him, I saw the commanding presence that his antics usually tended to hide. His eyes were bright with a strange regal bearing, and his body was erect.

The lady doctor hesitated for a moment, then inclined her head, though I caught a glimmer of defiance in her eyes as she bowed. "As you command, my lord." She knelt beside the bed and touched Chasym's forehead. Then she moved some of the bandage aside. "There isn't enough light. I can't work in here."

"Yes you can," I assured her. "C'mere, Liitae."

The little orb floated down from the ceiling where it had been playing with the drafts of air. It flitted above my palm and pulsed contentedly.

"Give us some light. And no goofing off."

The orb bobbed its understanding and, floating into the air, focused all its light down on Chasym, scattering the shadows.

"Better?" I asked.

She glanced warily at the orb. "It'll do."

"Excellent," Crenen said. "Now, Strange Coward Boy, get sleep."

I shook my head. "Not yet."

"Don't be foolish, Key," Lon spoke, still at the cave's entrance. "Chasym is in capable hands, you may rest."

"No." I shook my head again. "Not until I eat." I raised the gerani bunch before me. "And don't anyone try and stop me."

"You tell 'em, Jase," Chasym mumbled.

I jumped, heart missing a beat, then looked at him. Sure enough, he was wake, a smirk on his white face.

"Hey there."

"I want one," he said, his green eyes resting on the grapes in my hand.

I knelt down and plucked one from the bunch. "Here, but only one."

"Wait a—" Sasha began to protest.

"Hurry, she steps on 'em," I warned. He opened his mouth and I quickly tossed it inside.

"Do you mind?" Sasha asked, shoving me aside.

I stood back up and smiled as I watched Chasym go back to sleep, the effect of the gerani already taking its toll. "He really *can't* handle them."

"Smart move," Lon commented from beside me, making me jump yet again. "Now he won't feel a thing while she works." His eyes glittered as he observed his friend.

"Probably his intention all along."

"Now, eat," Lon directed me, "and then get some sleep. If those dark circles are any indication, you'll fall down dead if you don't get a full rest."

I nodded, plopping down on the ground and munching on the Paradisaical Purple Fruit contentedly. "Believe me, no one knows better than I."

19
Nothing Left?

This time I didn't even get a chance to fall asleep. I was only half way through my gerani bunch when an icy blast of air shot through the cavern, blowing out the torches and sending a layer of frost up the rock walls. I jumped to my feet as the frost tried to seep beneath my clothes.

Several of my companions hissed at the cold presence in the room. With Liitae's light still focused on Chasym, the rest of the cave was cast in shadow. Still, one shadow stood out. A shiver colder than the frosty walls ran up my spine as I stared at the green eyes in the dark silhouette. Those calculating eyes gazed back at me, filling me with terror. It was the Seer, but this time he'd come in person. Without proof, I simply knew it.

Instantly Jenen was before me, his claws extending toward the shadow threateningly. Then Lon was beside him, protecting me as well.

A cold laugh erupted from the darkness and, like a heavy mist, the layer of shadow folded away from him, and the Seer stood before us in human form, his entire body glowing faintly. He looked very much the same as before; tall, draped in maroon robes, with long vine green hair and sea-foam eyes boring holes wherever they peered.

"You think your petty abilities can withstand mine?" he asked, amused.

"Sounds like he admitted that his are petty, too," Chasym's arrogant voice spoke up. Glancing back, I saw him sitting up. Sasha was too busy gawking at the Seer to notice her patient's reckless behavior.

I smirked. "That's what I heard, too."

The Seer's smile faltered for an instant and then his eyes rested on Chasym. "You don't know when to die."

The Reincarnate smiled dryly. "Sorry, living's a nasty habit I picked up once—can't seem to drop it."

The Seer chuckled. "You've always thought yourself very clever."

"I've always had your reassurances to back me up," Chasym replied.

I blinked. So, the evil Seer and Chasym knew each other? I needed to stop thinking things could get more confusing—it had already been proven numerous times that they could, and usually did.

"Delusional Broken Man know Shifty Cocky Man?" Crenen asked, sounding as confused as I felt, doubtless annoyed about being in the dark.

"We've met," Chasym said vaguely, a strange smile on his lips.

"Enough of this," the Seer snapped, his patience gone. "I'm here to collect Vendaeva for my master, and you're wasting my time."

"You're really the Vendaeva?" Sasha asked, her voice a whisper.

I shrugged. "Like I know? They're the experts," I said, not really sure who 'they' were.

Crenen tapped his cheek. "We say he Vendaeva only to lure Delusional Broken Man here so we can fight him many times and finally capture and make our slave, yeah? Really not any Vendaeva at all."

"Somehow," the Seer said, "I'm unconvinced."

A crackling sound came from the rock floor and I saw cold rising like steam. A strange aura surrounded the Seer and his eyes began to glow. I felt my body step forward, completely against my will. Panicking, I tried to stop myself, but no conscious thought could keep my feet from walking toward him.

Lon grabbed my arm as I unwillingly tried to push past him.

"No, Key," he whispered, and I felt myself freed of the Seer's working. I stepped back, scrambling behind Lon, trembling with cold.

"You leave me no choice," the Seer said, his voice tight with anger. He flicked his hand, and suddenly the shadows released themselves from the walls and shot toward us, giggling shrilly. In an instant they pounced on everyone, except me.

I turned and saw Chasym weakly struggling against several shadows as they strangled him, shoving him against the wall, pressing against his bleeding wound. Sasha was slashing at the shadows with her claws, but having no effect. I glanced around for Liitae and spotted the orb lying frozen on the ground. Angry, I raised my hand and, even through the bandage, my palm lit up, forcing the attacking shadows to flee. I raised my other hand and pointed it toward where Lon, Veija, Crenen, and Jenen struggled against their own shadowy assailants. Again the shadows fled back to their master.

Gasping, Chasym leaned forward, his green eyes flashing with dark amusement. "Looks like...you were right, Seer—your abilities...*are* pathetic," he said. His neck already showed signs of bruising and his hands held his stomach, but he didn't seem to care.

The Seer scoffed. "Never fear, Chasym Verenvey, I'm not done yet."

Crenen let out a laugh, drawing everyone's attention. "Delusional Broken Man have to try much hard if even Strange Coward Boy easily deflect Weak Sissy Attacks."

I sighed. "So much for due credit."

The Seer opened his mouth to respond, then closed it, reaching up with a clawed hand and touching his temple. He closed his eyes and seemed to listen for something. We stared in confusion for a second—everyone but Crenen, who took that second to walk forward and clonk the Seer upside the head.

I snorted.

"Stupid Dolt Head shouldn't close eyes like we not important!" Crenen growled.

The Seer slowly opened his eyes and gazed impassively at Crenen. "Move," he said sharply, and Crenen flew sideways, slamming against the cave wall.

The Yenen clan leader wasn't through yet, however, and he quickly jumped to his feet, claws extended in an attack position. "You not throw us like unimportant either," he spat, flexing his fingers for emphasis.

The Seer turned his head from Crenen and met my gaze. "I have to hand it to you, Vendaeva; you and your comrades have fought bravely. But I've seen the future—something your dear Veija lost the ability to do long ago. Let me assure you—I do win."

I glanced at Veija, whose face hung in shame, her eyes shimmering with tears. Then I scowled and stepped forward—this time of my own will. "I don't freaking care what you saw through your stupid crystal ball. Nobody but me writes *my* future."

The Seer burst into mad laughter, his entire body shaking. Finally he gained control of himself, but his smirk stayed in place. "Oh, you're amusing, Vendaeva—no question about that. But then, I doubt if you were ever told the truth, so of course you're naïve. And why would you be told? You're only a tool, after all. A tool and a cover up. Merely something to hide the mistakes of your—"

"That's enough, Haeon," Chasym said, his voice harsh.

I blinked, turning to view my injured rival. His eyes were yellow instead of green, and they blazed with hot anger. He was half standing, ready to fight the Seer. I glanced at his half-bandaged torso and saw blood seeping between his fingers and dripping onto the floor.

The Seer's smirk widened. "Half dead and still blathering on. Why try to hide the truth? He'll find out eventually, don't you think?"

"It's not your place," Chasym replied, slapping Sasha's hand away as she finally tried to push him back into bed.

"Fine," Haeon said with a shrug. "I really don't care. I have different plans for your Vendaeva."

Crenen had taken being ignored for as long as he could handle. With a snarl, he rushed forward and thrust his claws into Haeon's arm, but the Seer merely grabbed his other arm and twisted it, forcing the lighter man to slam against the ground. Again Crenen rose, jumping back to avoid being thrown again. He hissed, spat on the ground, and then lunged forward yet again.

This time the Seer snapped his wrist and a shadow shot forward, colliding with Crenen's claws. As shadow and man began to duel, Haeon stepped beyond their range and walked toward me, his eyes unfathomable, alluring.

"Come, the master awaits," he told me, though his lips didn't move. His words echoed in my head and I felt coldness seep through the corners of my sight, draining me of my will to

resist, or even to stand. I struggled to remain conscious, knowing full well that if he got me now I might never wake up.

"You are strong, but I will overpower you," he said, his voice lulling me into drowsiness.

I watched vaguely as Jenen made a stand, and was blocked by another shadow. Veija went next, her eyes still haunted but her jaw set determinedly. Another shadow kept her from her target. Then it was just Lon, standing in front of me protectively.

"Sleep, child. When you wake, you will meet the master," the pensive voice assured me.

I still fought sleep, even as I witnessed five shadows jump on Lon. He knocked them away but more came, driving him back. I felt arms grab me, pulling me to the ground and when I looked for who had done it, my eyes collided with Sasha's. She kept a firm grip on my arm and spoke to me, but no sound escaped her mouth. I tried to read her lips but my vision was beginning to blur.

"Pathetic. You haven't fought five minutes and already you are tired." The voice was taunting now, but still somehow alluring. *"Come now, rest. You haven't slept properly in days. You need to sleep."*

I couldn't keep my eyes open. Even as Sasha shook my shoulders, screaming silently to get my attention; even as Chasym gripped my wrist and turned me to face him, talking quickly and alertly; even as several shadows were suddenly upon them both, prying them away. I couldn't fight sleep any longer. As darkness spotted my vision and I felt myself slump against the cold wall, a sense of panic and a distant voice rang in my mind.

There was nothing I could do. I had no strength with which to fight. I simply had nothing left.

20
Vendaeva?

"You can't be serious! Have you lost your senses completely?" the man cried out, grabbing the other man by the arm and turning him around. A heavy fog clung to the air, making it impossible to see their faces.

"Yes, I think that I have. But what else can I do?" the voice pleaded. "I'm open to suggestions, if you have them."

The first man sighed. "I know how you feel, but I doubt if this will help."

"I know. But I've got to try something—and it must be my sacrifice. I'm at fault."

"No. I won't let you. I'll do something instead. I owe you that much."

The second man laughed sadly. "Don't be foolish. You paid that debt long ago."

"Yes, but it never made anything better, did it? So what's the point now?"

"Hope, my friend. If that's all I can give to Paradise, it will be enough."

"False hope isn't hope," the first man said darkly. "Believe me when I say that your sacrifice will be in vain."

"I'm sorry, but I can't. I won't. Because...I want hope, too."

"Can you really go through with it? You'll have to live with the consequences."

"And that will enable me to do it."

My mind felt like a solid block of ice. As I awakened from my deep slumber, I felt myself laying on something that moved rhythmically, up and down, up and down. I tried to feel what I was on with my wounded hand, but I couldn't move my body.

After a moment I forced my eyes open and gazed upward, into a gray sky. I couldn't turn my head at all, so I just stared overhead, watching my breath escape my lips in a puff of cloud that evaporated in the air. It was very cold, but I felt something heavy and warm on top of me—probably a fur.

I tried to recall where I was—why I couldn't move—but my mind was too numb to think clearly. I finally gave up, and instead merely focused on the sky. As I looked, a snowflake appeared above, and I watched its gradual descent as it twirled about like a feather dancing on the bitter wind. Finally it landed on my forehead and melted into water that trickled down my face.

Another snowflake came down, and several more trailed after it, dancing a similar dance as they fell. Soon the sky was completely covered with waltzing snow, gracefully descending from the clouds above.

I felt sleep come over me again, and I allowed it to drag me back to my dreams, too tired and cold to heed the urgent feeling tugging at the back of my mind. Whatever it was, the urgent feeling could wait. And even it it couldn't, it would anyway.

"I hope he wakes up soon. I want to speak with him."

"He is stirring now, Master," a familiar voice said from somewhere to my left.

"May I speak with him now?" the first voice asked timidly. It was a young voice, almost gentle in its tone.

"Let me speak with him first, and then I'll call you back in—if that is all right, my master?" the man said.

I pried my eyelids open and blinked to make the blurriness go away. It was fairly dark, wherever I was, but I saw flickering shadows on the ceiling and I guessed a torch was lit somewhere.

"Are you coherent yet?"

I moaned in response as I attempted to sit up, and only managed to lift my head for a second.

"The paralysis will finish wearing off soon, but then the pain will begin. I'd sit quietly and enjoy your numbness in the meantime."

"W-where...?" I managed.

"You're in the Kirid lands now."

When had that happened? At my mental command to recall the events that brought me to this point, my mind rushed with memories.

"I've been captured?" I whispered hoarsely.

"Yes, you have."

My mind raced with questions, but one was more important than the rest. "Where are the others?"

The Seer chuckled somewhere overhead. "You never need worry for them again."

A coldness clutched at my heart. "What?"

"My shadows finished them off before I brought you here. I couldn't have them begin some sort of quest to save you, now could I?"

I listened to his tone, searching for any hint of a lie. If anyone should be able to tell a lie from the truth, it was me. But I found nothing but the heartless truth: they were all dead. The numbness in my body was beginning to wear off and my limbs ached painfully from the binding, but I hardly noticed. The pain in my heart overpowered all else.

"Now, Vendaeva. I want you to meet the master. Be polite or I will be forced to make your pitiful existence more pitiful."

I doubted if he could do much worse than he had done already.

The footsteps of the Seer faded as he walked away, and then I heard lighter footsteps walk toward me. A dark form appeared above my head, hovering. I squinted to try and see the face better, but it was just too dark.

"Did you come here through the Phudel?" the quiet voice asked.

A thousand retorts went through my brain, each crueler than the last, but the numbness was giving way to grief now and I felt like crying. So I turned my head away and shut my eyes tight, wanting everything to disappear and leave me alone.

They died because of me.

The thought played over and over in my mind. It was a hard realization, but a true one. If not for my appearance in this place, none of those people would have died—at least not this way. Sure, maybe they would have died of the Paradisaical disease instead, but...at least then...I wouldn't have known them. And it wouldn't hurt.

I smiled wryly. What a selfish twit I was. The others had suffered worse pains than this. They'd lost important people, too. I really was a coward if I couldn't accept this pain.

"I'm sorry," the boy whispered. "I heard about your friends. Haeon said they died honorably."

I bit my lip, determined not to cry. "You're Kirid, right?"

The boy hesitated. "Yes."

"And Prince Crenen killed your father a few months ago, right?"

A longer hesitation this time. "Yes."

"Then why are you sorry?" I spat, still not looking at him,

"Because I understand what it's like to lose someone you care about." His voice was so gentle and sincere, it made me want to reach up and strangle him; to scream for him to shut up; anything to make that pitying tone disappear.

"Go away," I whispered.

The boy didn't leave. "You're stuck here, Kiido. Haeon won't let you leave, so, treat this like your home—if you want."

I wanted to laugh; a hard, mad laugh. One that told him how naïve he was, but I hadn't the strength. "How can a prison be a home?"

"Very well," Kirid said quietly. I heard him walking away.

"Wait," I said.

The footsteps faltered.

"Why did you call me Kiido? What does it mean?"

"I've always liked the word," Kirid said quietly. "Get some more sleep, Kiido. Haeon won't let you grieve for very long."

When his footsteps were too far off to hear anymore I faced the ceiling again, letting the tears come.

"Let it all out," I told myself. "Just...let it out."

For the next two days I slept, cried, slept, ate, cried, and worked on getting my body to move again. In that time, I didn't see Seer Haeon or the young Kirid. The only person I did see was a servant who quietly brought my food and then quietly left with the last meal's dishes.

My prison was a stone room with a straw-stuffed mattress and dirty fur blankets. It was a tiny space, freezing cold. My mood changed frequently during those days. At times I felt scared and wished for company. At other times I was angry and wanted to pummel something. And other times still I was completely numb, oblivious to anything around me.

When Haeon finally appeared and told me to follow him I climbed from my bed and obeyed. He guided me down a dark passageway lit with feeble torches, and then turned down another. As we walked, the décor changed, and I understood that they had placed me in the resident dungeon. Not surprising.

The walls were still made of stone, but more torches lined the halls and carpets ran along the center of the flagstone floor. It reminded me of a medieval castle. I wondered vaguely if that made me the heroic knight, captured by the dark lord. More than likely it made me the damsel in distress. I frowned as I considered that no one could rescue me, but tried to push back the images of my comrades. I had decided, in those two miserable days, that I wouldn't allow myself to feel guilty about their deaths. I couldn't afford to give up now and let Seer Haeon do as he pleased with my powers. Not unless I wanted them to have died in vain—and I would rather die than let that happen.

While I'd once taken no side in this strange war in Paradise, I would rather take my chances with Crenen and his cronies. I would rather risk another betrayal from Lon. And I would rather discover the mysteries of Jenen and Chasym. Never mind that all the forces in this fantastical realm were against them, and therefore me. Now, even though they were dead, I would fight for them—and pretend to fight *with* them.

Haeon pushed open a set of enormous double doors and led me into what could only be the throne room. I gazed at the ornate decoration of the chamber. The intricately carved stone dais and the plush carpet leading up to it. Several lit candelabra rested on tables positioned on either side of the carpeted path leading to the throne. And shrouded in darkness, the young Kirid sat, only his outline visible.

"Before we step nearer," Haeon said, turning his cold eyes on me, "be warned. You are about to realize a harsh truth." His mouth twisted in a malicious smile as he spoke. With that, he turned and walked toward the throne, his magenta robes trailing behind him. I followed, taking his advice and bracing myself for whatever was about to happen.

As I neared the dais something flew past me and I turned to see what it was. My eyes widened as I saw Liitae hovering near a candelabrum, dancing around the flames as though teasing them.

"Liitae," I called, feeling warmth spread through me. I recalled that Lon once said it couldn't die unless I did. Thank goodness for that.

The orb bobbed up and down a few times and then raced toward me, nearly knocking me to the ground as it slammed into my hand. My palm throbbed dully, mostly healed. Liitae left my hand and circled me excitedly, its center glowing more brightly than normal.

"I'm happy to see you, too," I told it, laughing at the orb's energy. Somehow, it felt like the sun had finally risen after a long nightmarish sleep.

"He followed Haeon's dragon all the way here," Kirid's voice said softly. "No matter how many times he tried, Haeon couldn't get the orb to stop following you."

I turned to face the boy master stepping from the shadowed dais. As my eyes fell on him, I stared, breath caught somewhere in my throat.

Kirid smiled brightly, his gray eyes dancing with excitement. "Hello, Kiido. Or, should I say, my other half?"

It was like looking into a mirror, with only two flaws. His hair was long and black—a deeper black than any hair I'd ever seen. And his ears were long and pointed, like that of Yenen Clan. But his eyes were mine, his face was mine, and he stood at exactly my height. He was skinnier than I, and his skin was pale as though he had been deathly ill for a long time. But, despite these differences, we could be twins. No—the same person.

"Don't confuse him, Master," Haeon said, breaking through my thoughts. "We ought to explain the truth—that he is merely your copy, not your other half. He was meant to replace you, though it would never work."

I blinked. "What do you mean?"

Kirid smiled—my smile. He raised a clawed hand, and my orb flew to him, lighting in his palm. "It's true, Kiido. When I was lost, you were meant to take my place. Somehow, you were given the powers of Vendaeva, but they are only a copy—a shadow of the power I possess." His voice wasn't arrogant, only factual. And honest. That was another difference we had; he told the truth.

I shook my head, trying to comprehend. "You were lost?" And, as if in answer to my own question, my mind remembered the dream of that infant child. My eyes widened. "You—you're...?"

"That's right," Haeon said with a smirk. "Master Kirid is the real Vendaeva, while you are only a false hope."

"But...I-I came through the puddle."

"A rewriting of the prophecy. Few had heard of it before it was rewritten, and so it was easy to fool them." He shrugged. "Now you know, Jason Sterling. You are only a lie."

It was as if reality was crashing in around me. As if my lies had caught up with my fantasy and I had no more room for imagining. It was over.

"It's all right, Kiido," Kirid said gently, stepping closer and holding out Liitae. "That doesn't mean you can't stay here." He smiled. "I want you to stay."

"Of course we'll have to take your powers," Haeon said. "You won't need them, after all."

I looked up at him sharply. "No."

"It's the only way. Because of your powers, Master Kirid can't access all of his. If you really want to save Paradise, you'll cooperate."

I backed up. "No. You don't want to save Paradise. Kirid Clan made it sick in the first place. You can't take my power."

"Don't be a fool," Haeon said. "You don't have a choice." He raised his palm and I felt myself restrained, unable to move. "It won't hurt. Besides, you won't miss it." His eyes were blazing with delight.

I looked at Kirid. "Please stop him."

He shook his head, gray eyes sad. "Haeon knows best."

Before I could respond I felt a tingling in my head. As I watched through my mind's eye, I saw our conversation play before me in rewind. Then it was dark, and I couldn't remember what I'd just seen. I saw the fight with the shadows, but that was suddenly gone too. Lon, pushing me in the puddle. Chasym, before him. In a matter of seconds, I saw my life play in reverse—and then I forgot what I'd seen. As everything became darker, I saw a blur of my life with my family. And finally, the last fleeting image was of being held, and I gazed into the loving eyes of a strange woman.

I could move, and I fell to my knees, then collapsed to the ground. I laid there, staring into nothing.

Who was I?

Part Three:
Key?

21
A Stranger In The Wine Cellar?

Thunder rumbled somewhere close by. I sat up in bed, running a hand through my hair as I listened to the pounding rain and howling wind outside. Tucking my knees under my arms, I buried my face, pretending I couldn't hear the sounds of the ferocious storm.

I wasn't sure why it scared me so much, but I desperately wanted the winter snows back, because thunderstorms never happened in the winter.

I considered finding Kirid, but my heart was racing too wildly. I didn't dare move. As I sat there, waiting for the harsh winds to change and take the storm away, I rocked back and forth and concentrated on something less frightening.

It wasn't hard to recall memories, both good and bad. My life had begun only three months ago when I opened my eyes and saw a young man smiling down at me with kindness in his eyes. I didn't know who I was, nor why I felt so empty inside. I didn't remember anything before that day and every time I tried to think of something from my past, my mind nearly burst with agonizing pain. The young man, Kirid, always reprimanded me softly when I tried to recall things.

It was a strange place where I lived—but then, everything was strange to me. Especially myself. The only thing that seemed at all familiar was Kirid. His smile, his voice, his mannerisms—I felt something stir in my mind each time I watched him, like a distant memory, but never so much as when I studied his eyes.

Why Kirid took me in and helped me, I didn't know. When I asked if he was family, or if I inquired about anything that related to my past, he would grow sad and ask if I wanted to leave. Of course I didn't, and I assured him as much. While I wanted to remember my past, I hated to lose his friendship or appear ungrateful for his generosity.

The one thing that made this life imperfect, besides thunderstorms, was Kirid's servant, Haeon. His presence sent a chill down my spine and so I always knew when he was lurking around the corner. Haeon hated me; I could feel it. Whenever I brought this concern before Kirid, he acknowledged my observation but wouldn't explain why Haeon felt as he did.

I lived in Kirid's castle all through the winter, with only Kirid, Haeon, and the servants for company. And while I found ways to entertain myself, something always pushed at the back of my mind, as if memories were trying to surface but didn't yet have the strength.

I once asked Kirid if I would ever get my memories back. He told me that there was little chance of remembering my former life ever again, and he told me it was for the best. A dull ache in my heart confirmed that he was probably right—like always.

As I grew accustomed to my new life, the seasons decided to change and I watched as winter grew into spring. And thunderstorms kept me awake at night.

With another loud boom of thunder, I scrambled from my bed, shot from my room and raced down the flagstone hallway, aiming for Kirid's chambers. I reached the door before I stopped short, hesitating.

"It's all right, Kiido. You may come in," the soothing voice of Kirid murmured from the door's other side.

I tried to straighten out my haggard appearance before I opened the door, determined not to let him know I had been afraid. I stepped into his brightly lit chamber, glad of the blazing fire and the cheery torches on every wall. Kirid was sitting in an armchair near the fire, a stack of papers before him on a round table. A cup of steaming liquid was balanced in one hand, while a quill rested in the other. He eyed me with a delighted smile.

"Care for a warm drink?" he asked, motioning toward a steaming pitcher on the other end of the table. "Come. Sit and enjoy."

I came forward, taking the seat opposite my host, and poured myself a glass of the warm liquid. Its pleasant, sweet aroma teased my senses.

"Why are you up so late?" I asked, glancing at the stack of papers.

"Sometimes I find it difficult to sleep," he answered before taking a delicate sip. He winced, setting the cup down and licking his lips. "Still hot," he warned.

I blew into my cup, watching him scribble a note on a piece of parchment. "What are you doing?"

"I'm writing thoughts as they occur to me," he answered, dipping his quill. "It helps to jot it down. Then my head feels much less full." He stopped mid dip and looked at me apologetically. "I didn't mean to—"

"It's all right," I assured him. "I don't have memories, but my head can be just as full sometimes."

His smile returned. "Of course." He took to scribbling again and I sipped my drink, welcoming the warmth as it trickled down my throat and took the chill away.

After a moment I ventured another question. "So...why haven't you asked why I'm up so late?"

"Do you mind if I ask?"

I pondered that. "No."

"Very well." He set the quill in the ink bottle. "Why are you up so late?" he asked gently.

I hesitated, trying to decide whether to be honest or not. "I couldn't sleep."

"Too many thoughts?"

I shook my head. And then nodded. "Well, yes and no."

He laughed softly, then took a sip from his glass. "Please, share if you like, Kiido."

I stared into my amber-colored drink, trying to remember. "At first I thought the thunder had scared me awake," I said sheepishly.

"At first?"

"I think it was a dream," I answered.

"Do you remember it?"

I shook my head. "Every time I try recalling the images, they slip further away."

"Those are the most frustrating kind," he said sympathetically as he got to his feet and walked to the fire. He stirred it and then gazed into the flames, his gray eyes dancing with the light. So familiar. "Was it a bad dream?" he asked without looking up. "Did it make you afraid?"

I nodded, taking another sip. "Yes," I said after I swallowed. "It...made me feel like I do around Haeon."

Kirid chuckled.

"It isn't funny," I informed him blandly.

He shook his head. "I know, I'm sorry. It's just...I remember when he used to scare me, too, when I was little. My father and Haeon would speak for hours on end, and I felt very afraid each time I had to enter this very room and speak to my father, because I knew Haeon would be here as well."

"Did he make you feel like prey he'd soon be feasting on if you couldn't run away fast enough?" I muttered.

He turned around and faced me, his eyes serious now. "No." He sighed softly. "I am sorry, Kiido. I can't stop Haeon from disliking you. Maybe...perhaps you should confront him about it?"

I shook my head, smirking. "Nah, my knees'd be knocking together too loud for him to hear what I was saying."

Kirid chuckled again. "You have a certain way with words."

I shrugged, feeling the weight on my mind lifting gradually. Kirid's calming presence usually quieted my concerns. "I do talk funny," I conceded.

"Don't reflect too much on your dreams, Kiido. Only Seers need to worry about seeing the future. To us, dreams are only illusions."

I nodded drowsily, feeling so relaxed and warm that sleep was beginning to take me. "I sleep too much," I commented as I stifled a big yawn.

"Then you need it," Kirid said, walking to his massive bed and peeling a blanket from the rest. "Have my bed. I'll keep this blanket with me, in case I sleep tonight."

"You're going to keep writing?" I asked, standing up and approaching his bed. I climbed onto it and laid down, grabbing a blanket and rolling myself up.

"For a little longer," he answered quietly, letting me drift to sleep. "Goodnight, Kiido."

"...Night," I mumbled as my eyelids shut and my world plunged into foreign dreams.

I awoke with a start.

Sitting up, I rubbed my head and tried to remember what had jarred me from my sleep. Blinking to clear my vision, I yawned and glanced around Kirid's room. It was bright with the morning light flooding in through the large window. While the castle was always cold, this room seemed warm no matter what, yet it had the largest window I had ever seen (that I recalled).

Throwing aside the blanket, I slid from the bed and walked to the window, glancing out at the grounds. The rain of late had done them a world of good, and green plants shot up out of rich soil. The sky was a vibrant blue, beckoning for people to come and bask in its splendor.

Turning from the view, I walked to the table by the hearth. The fire had long since gone out, and the ashes were cold. The glasses and pitcher had been cleared, and all of Kirid's notes were removed. I sat down in the same chair I occupied the night before and yawned again.

"Did you sleep well?" Kirid's serene voice said from the doorway.

I turned around, smiling in greeting. "Yeah, wonderfully."

"Excellent." Kirid flashed me a sharp-toothed grin, and I felt something stir in the back of my mind.

"So, what are we doing today?" I inquired, feeling the same excitement I did each morning at the prospect of learning something new from my friend.

Kirid's smile faltered and he walked across the large room, taking his own chair. "Something has come up. Haeon informed me that there is a border breach. I need to investigate."

"Border...breach?"

"Yes, a rival clan to the east has been up in arms of late. It blames us for the death of its leader." Kirid sighed. "War is an ugly thing."

I frowned, feeling an ache in my heart like I did every time I considered death. "Will there be war?"

"Well," Kirid said quietly, "our clans have been at odds for many years now. It's been more cold warfare than anything, but occasionally the fire sparks and we battle. The last time we fought, the leader who just died killed my father." He stood back up. "Haeon and I are going to try and appease them. We're going by dragon, so hopefully we'll return by nightfall, should negotiations go well. Can you...? Will you be all right by yourself?"

I nodded. "Sure, I'll probably take a walk or something."

Kirid smiled. "All right." He walked toward the door, then hesitated. "You had better not wander about the castle too much. Just stay to the areas you're familiar with. You could get lost."

I nodded. "Sure." I turned my eyes to the window as the door closed. "Where's the fun in staying safe?" I mumbled. I had wanted to explore the lower levels of the castle for a month now, but Kirid had always come up with some excuse why we couldn't. As much as I trusted Kirid, my curiosity could be abated no more.

I stood up. First I would eat some breakfast, and then, when I was certain Kirid and Haeon were gone, I would descend the stairs to explore.

After donning my clothes and pulling my shoulder length hair back with a strip of cloth, I made my way to the kitchens. There I was given a hearty meal, and a bundle of food for lunch, per my request. When I finished breakfast I grabbed the bundle and headed straight for the nearest set of stairs leading downward. It was the one I'd been eyeing for a while now, as though it beckoned for me to please come and make use of it.

It was pitch black when I reached the bottom of the steps. I ran my hand along the wall and found a torch. Apparently they hadn't felt the need to light it since no one visited this level. Turning around I headed back up the steps, until I reached the landing. Grabbing a lighted torch from its place on the wall, I turned back around and descended the stairs once more, this time with plenty of light.

The corridor I found myself in was cold and damp. I knew it was below ground level, so it seemed possible that the night's rain had leaked into the hallway. The castle was carved from the mountain, and centuries of hard labor had gone into its intricate structure. Now, the castle's height nearly reached the top of the mountain. Kirid had told me that he thought it ridiculous to create a building so large when only a few dozen rooms were actually in use. I had silently agreed with him. Still, when I finished exploring the lower regions, I planned to make my way to the top of the mountain castle, one level at a time.

The rhythmic dripping of water on the flagstones followed me as I continued along the lengthy corridor. Twenty minutes passed, yet nothing struck me as particularly interesting. I kept my eyes peeled for doors or other connecting hallways, but it appeared the set of stairs I'd chosen led down into an isolated area. I was considering heading back and taking a different stairway when my torch's light caught on something ahead of me, causing whatever it was to glint.

I moved forward, increasing my pace with every step, until the fire's light revealed a wooden door. Grinning, excitement hammering at my heart, I reached the door and grasped the brass handle, mentally noting that it was probably what I'd seen flashing before. I pulled on the door, but it didn't budge.

Determined not to let it keep me from whatever was beyond, I replaced a cold torch in its sconce with the lit one in my hands, and then rubbed my palms together before taking another crack at opening the door. For a moment I thought it was no good, that it must be locked, but finally with a loud creak the door gave way and flung open, causing me to fall and slam my back against the ground.

The wind was knocked from my lungs, and I lay there, stunned. Then I remembered that breathing was a good idea, and I coughed for a moment, then started gulping air. When the sharp ache in my back subsided a little, and I felt like my lungs might recover, I dragged myself back to my feet and gazed through the open door.

The room beyond was dark, smelling of dirt, rancid water and sweet wine—a bad mixture. I retrieved my torch and raised it before me. Blinking, I stepped into the room, waving the torch around. Crates were piled high against the back wall, while shelves to the left and right held dusty bottles, and barrels were stacked on either side of the doorway in columns.

"That's it?" I said to myself, disappointed. "Just a wine cellar?"

In response I heard a vague sound coming from the crates in the back of the room. Tilting my ear toward the sound, I listened hard. Humming? Curiosity took over and guided me toward the crates as the noise increased. Someone was humming—no, singing a song.

"...gently down the stream..."

The familiar words brushed something in my mind, but I dismissed it, too curious to know what sort of drunkard had found himself such a nice place to live.

"...merrily, merrily, merrily, merrily, life is but a dream."

I jammed my torch between two barrels and shifted a crate only to find another crate behind it.

"Row, row, row—"

"Hello?" I called.

The singing voice halted. "Well, if it isn't a human being."

I blinked, feeling a strange sensation creep up my spine. "Where are you?"

"If I said I was just a talking crate, would you believe me?"

Definitely drunk. "No."

"Well, at least there's that. Though, for as long as I've been down here, I think I'd be rather joyous to hear even a crate speak."

I shifted the next crate, to find yet another one.

"How'd you get in here?" I asked.

"I was put in here."

"Punishment for stealing wine?" I mumbled.

"No. Nothing so...amusing." The voice paused long enough to cough raggedly. "And for the record, it isn't just any wine. In fact, I have a strange suspicion that you would find it particularly delightsome."

I rolled my eyes. "I doubt that. How long have you been in here?"

"Good question. Is it winter out there?"

"No," I said, sliding the crate forward and moving it aside.

"Hm, then at least three months."

"With only wine to live on—no wonder you're half mad."

"No," the voice said with a laugh. "Though, I admit the lack of food has been...torture."

"I bet," I said, staring at the stone wall before me. "So, where are you?"

"Down," the voice said.

I climbed onto the crate and walked across the other two, gazing down. There, in a space only three feet wide, beneath the stacked crates and the wall, was an opening covered by thick metal bars. Below that was darkness.

"You're in there?" I asked.

"Exactly," the voice said.

I went back and got my torch, returned, and lowered it to view the prison under the floor. "Why were you put there?" I asked, now seeing that there was no way he could sneak wine into that place. As the light gave me a view of the room below, I saw only the man's feet.

"Because I wouldn't die," he said with a chuckle.

I raised an eyebrow. "Oookay."

A rustling came from beneath me and I watched the man's feet disappear. Then he crawled into view. He was filthy, his pants were tattered and a tangle of greasy blond hair trailed down his back. Dry blood covered his bare chest, but for a few filthy bandages half-covering an ugly wound in his stomach.

"Well, well, well," he said with a laugh. "It's been forever since I've had any light. What took you?"

My eyes met his green-eyed gaze and something jabbed at my mind sharply. I winced. "Do...I know you?" I asked.

He blinked slowly. "You're hilarious, Jase," he mumbled flatly.

That name. "Who are you?"

He snorted. "Have any food?"

I glanced at the food bundle I'd tied to my waistband. "Yeah."

"Mind sharing?"

I untied the bundle.

"I must admit, as long as it took you, I was beginning to think you were dead—even with Liitae's reassurances."

I halted at another familiar name.

"Can you go a little faster?" the stranger asked, leaning against the stone wall.

"No," I answered. "Not until you tell me your name."

He raised an eyebrow. "You really don't know?"

I shook my head.

"Are you sure?"

I nodded.

"Boy, you just keep getting your memory messed with, don't you?"

My eyes narrowed. "What do you mean?"

"I mean I can't count the times you've forgotten who I am." He sighed heavily. "Fine. If it'll get me a long overdue supper—I'm Chasym."

I dropped the torch and it died with a hiss. I hardly noticed, though. Clasping my hands to my temples, I bit my lip as the pain in my head exploded. Swirls of memories were trying to get through some kind of barrier, but the pain was too intense.

"Jason! Are you okay? What happened?"

Jason. What was it about that name? The pain intensified, and I felt myself falling forward, off the crate. I hit the ground with a sharp thud and knew no more.

22
Secrets of They?

"Farewell. Until we meet once more." The voice was misty, an echo from some distant place. A place impossible to reach. "You will be looked after." The voice grew more distant. "I'm sorry."

"Jason! Are you okay?"

I wanted to bat the voice away, but my head hurt too much.

"What happened?"

I moaned softly.

"Jase? You were in pain. What happened?"

I was *still* in pain and his incessant talking was only making it worse.

"If you don't answer me..."

"Shut up," I muttered.

"Thank goodness," he breathed. "What happened?"

Did he not know how to stay quiet?

"I fell," I said, getting up and rubbing my head. Then I recalled the pain. Something about this man had stirred the memories I hadn't been able to, but whatever was trying to reach the surface of my mind had failed. I groped for the fallen torch, picking it back up.

"That was some fall." He paused. "So, do you remember anything?"

His tone sent fear through my spine. I climbed onto the crate and sought out the bundle. When I found it, I climbed back down and stuffed the bundle through the bars, letting the food drop to the prison floor with a soft thud.

"Food?" the man who called himself Chasym asked, and I heard him shuffle around until he found it. "Thank you."

"I have to go," I whispered, too afraid of his familiarity to stay. Kirid had told me I didn't want to remember, and I believed him. Somehow, this man promised me more pain if I stayed.

"You'll come back?" the man asked.

"I—I don't know," I said, clambering back onto the crate and making my way down the other side.

"Jason—do you remember anything?"

"...No," I said quietly. "And...I don't want to." I walked to the cellar door.

"Please come back," he called after me.

I slammed the door hard and darted down the hallway, determined to leave that place and never return. Things were fine as they were; Kirid was a wonderful friend, and even if Haeon hated me he would never hurt me. It was a blissful, pleasant, predictable life.

If that's what you want, something inside me said quietly. No matter how much I desired to have things remain as they were, a part of me yearned to know about before, no matter how painful.

"Don't be stupid," I told myself. "Kirid knows best."

For the next few days I kept myself occupied with thoughts of anything but that cellar. Kirid hadn't suspected anything when he and Haeon arrived home that night and he informed me of the temporary truce the clans had formed.

On the third night after my discovery of the prisoner, I sat in the library, reflecting on his words and on the familiar names he had used. Something was urging me to return, but I hadn't the courage. I didn't want things to change, though, deep inside I knew they had the second I'd ventured to the lower levels.

"Is something on your mind, Kiido?" Kirid asked, bringing me from my thoughts.

I turned and shook my head. "Not really. Well. More like a lot of things."

"I can sense it," he said with a knowing nod. "If you care to share, I will listen."

I smiled my appreciation. "If I ever get it sorted enough for words I'll be sure and dump my load on you."

He chuckled. "That's fair."

"I'm...going to bed," I said after a moment, getting to my feet. "I'm really tired."

"Certainly," he said, looking up from his book, gray eyes reflecting the nearest candle's light. "Sleep well."

"You too," I said as I headed for the door leading out of the library.

Walking along the hall, I stared at my hands, tracing the scars on both palms with my eyes. The scars looked like they had been purposely branded into my skin in shape of skeleton keys. It was a mystery Kirid was also surprised about when I had shown him. For the first few weeks after waking up with no memory, I had difficulty using my hands, but eventually the pain ceased and I was able to move them freely.

As I neared my room, something tugged at my mind, and I found myself continuing past the door, heading further down the dim corridor. I blinked as I stopped before a flight of stairs leading into pitch darkness. Absently, my hand found the burning torch and I pulled it from its sconce.

After a familiar walk down the steps and through the long corridor I reached the cellar door and pried it open. Walking across the room, I climbed up and over the crates and my torch lit up the grate leading down into the prison.

Angling my head to see the cell better, my eyes rested on the filthy figure leaning against the wall, his head raised and his green eyes blinking to adjust to the light. "Jase?" he called, his voice hoarse.

"Why do you call me that?" I asked.

He chuckled, but it turned into a ragged cough. "Because it's your name—well, one of them."

"And you knew me...before?"

"Yes," he replied, raising a hand to shade his eyes.

"Well, I don't care about what happened," I said. "So, I don't want to know about it."

"Did you come here to tell me that?"

I hesitated and then nodded. "...Yes. So, I'll leave now." I started to turn away.

"No! Wait. Please?"

I halted, resting my gaze on him. "Why?"

"Well," he shifted his feet, "it gets pretty lonely, and...we don't have to talk about your past. I could... Well. I just want to talk to somebody." His voice was weaker than when I last spoke with him, and I heard the desperation in his tone.

I bit my lip, but nodded. "Fine."

A pained smile spread across his pallid face. "Thank you." We were silent for a moment, but then he spoke again. "So, what are you called now? ...If I might ask?"

"I'm Kiido."

"Kiido, eh? Interesting. Any idea what it means?"

"No."

"Ah. Well, it's...nice to meet you, Kiido. As you know, I am Chasym."

A dull pain started in the back of my head. I ignored it. "Why were you put down there? And how the heck are you alive?"

He chuckled again, managing not to cough. "I told you, I wouldn't die. I...manage to beat death a lot."

"Are you given food?"

He shook his head. "No, but I still live."

"That's impossible."

"Yes, well, I've always been called impossible—maybe it rubbed off and became a part of me."

I glanced around until I found a small gap between two crates and wedged the torch between them. "Oh yeah?"

"Yeah, but, much as I've cheated death," the strange man continued, "I wonder how much longer that will last." He doubled over, coughing violently.

"Are you...?" I trailed off. Of course he wasn't all right. How could he be, in the state he was, coughing like that?

"I'll...be fine," he said between gasps of air as he leaned back against the wall. "It's just...all of Paradise is...shuddering."

I blinked. I knew Paradise was what Kirid called our world, but what was Chasym talking about?

He saw my expression as he looked up. "The world is sick, Ja—Kiido. It's dying. And us with it."

A feeling tugged at my mind. I brushed it off. "We're dying?"

"Some are, yes," he said quietly. "Others are causing it—but then, they'll die, too, in the end."

"But...how?" I asked, trying to grasp the concept.

"Well." He hesitated. "It happened about eighteen years ago—no, that's when it became noticeable. It had been building up for centuries, but everything spiraled out of control eighteen years ago."

"What happened?" I asked, intrigued despite myself.

"A clan split in two. You're seeing the results of that. Eighteen years ago, one of Lord Kirid's right-hand men opposed him and took his own followers to the east. The rebel's name was Yenen. Rather than leave them alone, Kirid grew furious, and attempted to wipe out his new enemy, but Yenen's clan was more powerful than Kirid had supposed. Kirid Clan had split almost exactly in two, so they were equal in power.

"It was a gruesome fight. Before that point, most of Paradise had lived in considerable harmony for a few centuries, but it's said that with the shedding of blood—with the sudden slaughter among brothers—something happened to the core of our world. Paradise is not perfect as a whole and it never has been. But at that point some say something changed and Paradise became cursed. A horrible disease struck the land, killing off most of the elderly and many young children. If you took a walk through any village, you'd find few of either anymore."

I shivered at his words. "Is...that what you're dying of? This disease."

He smiled. "Yes and no."

Like that answered the question. "What do you mean?"

"Seers were once prominent in Paradise."

I blinked, startled by his sudden change in topics. "What...?"

He went on, not hearing me. "But they weren't its rulers. They were more...caretakers, if you will. Another force ruled Paradise and kept it in order. They watched over the living: people, animals, plants."

"Another force?"

"They Clan," he said. "That's what it was called. But when the Seers grew too independent, They Clan forced them to mostly vanish; to step aside for other caretakers—the Kirid. Then They Clan, through a series of events, mostly died out. Needless to say, Kirid Clan messed things up badly, and when Paradise grew ill and created the Paradisaical disease, They Clan got it even worse. It went mad."

I was beginning to grasp his point. "You're...?"

"I am Chasym of They."

"So, you're mad?"

He shook his head. "Through...circumstances...I am the only one of They left with my mind perfectly intact."

"So, even though you ruled Paradise, the world opposed you and created this illness, driving your people crazy?"

"We weren't gods, Ja—Kiido. But our heads grew too big. We thought ourselves invulnerable. And we suffered for it."

For the next few nights I visited Chasym. Sometimes we didn't speak of anything but what I did that day with Kirid. Chasym never touched on my forgotten past, and I appreciated his consideration. I told myself everyday that it would be my final visit, but something kept taking me to the stairwell and I always returned to the cellar. Every once in a while I smuggled food to him. Even though I knew he had gone months without it, I doubted he was very comfortable with an empty stomach.

I often wondered why I felt so drawn to the man in the prison. What was it about him that made my curiosity overcome the terror I felt? I finally concluded that it was exactly this wonderment which kept me going down there, night after night.

As I pushed the door open and entered the wine cellar for a sixth time, my eyes fell on the back wall. I found it strange that while I usually shared everything with Kirid, I made it a point not to mention this new friend to him. With surprise, I realized that I considered Chasym a friend—and I'd thought of him as such for several days now.

"Kiido, is that you?" Chasym's voice called up weakly.

Who else would it be? I crept across the room and climbed over the crates, placing the torch in its usual spot as I shoved some food through the bars. "Catch," I said.

I saw him grab the bundle and untie the binding as quickly as he could, tearing the fresh bread apart as he took big bites. After he finished the whole loaf he sat back and looked up gratefully. "Now that you feed me, it's hard to cope without it."

I smiled grimly. "No problem."

"Did you do anything interesting today?"

I shook my head. "Kirid locked himself in his room. He goes through strange moods; sometimes he's really social and other times he keeps to himself for days on end."

"I'd imagine being a leader so young could do that to a person."

"True," I said, pulling a piece of dried meat from my pocket and chewing as I considered. "He always apologizes when he comes back out, though I really don't mind. It gives me time for myself, too."

"Mm." Chasym rummaged through the bundle and pulled forth a ripe fruit. "What about this Haeon person?" he asked casually, but I sensed spite in his tone.

"His room is on a higher level, so I don't know what he does most of the time. I'm not supposed to explore," I answered sheepishly.

He laughed. "What's with that tone, Jase? You were never apologetic befo—" He stopped abruptly, then sighed. "Sorry. I forgot for a second... I won't do that again."

I shifted uncomfortably and scratched behind my head. "It's okay. I slip up too, sometimes. I mean, about other things."

He smiled again. "Who doesn't? Still, I need to be more careful. There are things I understand which would tear the world apart if people knew. Not that it isn't already being torn apart, or anything."

I snorted. "Right." I wasn't entirely convinced about the world's end, but I didn't bother to argue with things I couldn't understand.

Chasym swallowed another bite. "If you're not supposed to explore, pray tell how you managed to get all the way down here?"

"I was bored," I said with a shrug.

"Boredom can be deadly, but in this case I'm grateful." His expression grew pained. His body stiffened and he hissed through his teeth.

"Chasym, are you okay?"

After a moment his body relaxed and he nodded slowly. "Yes...I just..." He trailed off, and my eyes caught his hand gripping his stomach. Something dark and moist was seeping between his fingers.

"Your wound is open again?" I asked.

He nodded. "It never fully closed." He clenched his teeth. "I'm pretty certain it's infected."

"Drat it all, Chasym, you should be dead by now," I said, grabbing the bars and pulling hard on them. I was more than surprised when they actually budged, and I fell backward against the crates. I recovered, tossed the bars aside, and crawled back over to the opening. "Just a second."

I jumped down, not daring to consider how far the drop might be. I hit the ground quickly, landing on my feet, toes smarting from contact with the hard floor, though it couldn't be more than eight feet from floor to prison ceiling.

"Shouldn't have done that, Jase," Chasym mumbled weakly. "Now you'll have trouble getting back out."

"I'll manage somehow," I assured him more than myself. I knelt down, prying his hand away to see the damage. "It's too dark," I muttered as I narrowed my eyes to try and focus.

"Raise your hand and say 'Liitae'," he instructed.

"Why?"

"Just do it."

Rolling my eyes, I lifted my hand, palm up, and whispered, "Liitae." Instantly a ball of brilliant blue light flared up from my scarred hand and I cried out with mixed fear and awe.

Chasym chuckled. "No wonder..."

I blinked, shaking my hand and staring as the little glowing ball followed my every wave. "No wonder what?" I asked.

"No wonder you're still alive, Jase," he said with a grin. "Oh, how Haeon must be writhing with anger right now. It's no surprise you think he hates you."

His words struck me and I stared at him, the ball of light forgotten. "'Still alive?'" I said sharply. "What do you mean?"

But Chasym didn't answer. His eyes were closed, his face horribly pale, his breathing ragged. Holding my right hand in the air, I used my free hand to shift the filthy bandages aside and peered at the wound. It was deep and ugly. Signs of serious infection covered half his torso and the smell was pungent.

"Dying because of Paradise's disease, my friggin' foot," I muttered, grabbing the cloth I'd used to tie his food in, and pressing it against the injury. "I can't leave you like this. We've got to get Kirid." I stopped, looking up at the orb warily. "Hey...can you understand me?" Such a stupid question, yet I knew somehow that while this thing was just a ball of energy, it could think on its own.

The orb bobbed up and down in reply.

"Great, I need you to get my friend."

The orb rolled over in the air, as though cocking its non-existent head in question.

"His name is Kirid," I supplied. "He's got—" But the orb didn't wait for a description. Instead it zoomed toward the prison's entrance and disappeared from view. "Here's hoping that worked," I muttered.

"Jase."

I looked down at the strange man and met his green eyes. "Yes?" It wasn't my name, at least not anymore, but he probably wasn't aware enough of his surroundings to recognize his mistake.

"Did you know I was in love once?"

I blinked. How could I know that? As far as I was concerned I'd only known him for a few days. Something as personal as his love life never entered our conversations. "No, I didn't know."

He laughed softly. "Well, I was. She was beautiful—the very vision of the sun's brilliant rays peeking over mountain ridges on a warm spring morning."

"I didn't know you could be so poetic." I fought the urge to roll my eyes.

"Pretty good, huh?"

I didn't reply. "...What happened?"

"She went crazy."

That would certainly put a damper on things. "So, she was of They, too?"

"No. Nothing like that. She was a Seer, actually."

"Like Haeon."

"Only nice," he replied.

"Right."

His body shook with the need to cough, but he was too weak. After a moment he relaxed and raised his grimy hand to my forehead. "Here. I'll show you."

The prison vanished, replaced with a stunning forest clearing and a gurgling stream only yards away from where I found myself standing in the soft spring grass.

Sweet laughter came from my right and I turned to investigate the beautiful sound. When my eyes fell on the figure sitting beneath the apinaikeal tree, her blue skirts spread over the ground like gentle water, I felt my jaw fall open as a dull pain started at the back of my head. The woman was gorgeous, with soft golden hair tumbling down, reaching mid back, and striking golden eyes. Her lips were stretched in an amused smile as she gazed at a bouquet of wild flowers in her arms.

Somehow, somewhere before, I had met this woman. I knew her.

"Her name is Veija," Chasym's voice came from my other side, and I turned to face him. His yellow eyes watched the woman forlornly. "I placed the bouquet under the tree an hour prior to her visit here. She has yet to meet me, yet to fall in love, yet to have her heart broken and, as a result, lose her ability and desire to see into the future. All that, for a few months of joy."

I turned back to the young woman, studying her fair and carefree features. "Why do I know her?"

"Do you really want me to answer that?"

I hesitated, unsure, and finally decided to change the subject. "This is your memory?"

"Yes, I've brought you into my mind's eye. As you can see," he motioned to his stomach, "I'm perfectly whole in this place—or, I appear so. I still feel the pain, but it's less...persistent." He was clean, his long blond hair was smooth, his black clothing was intact, and his eyes shone with a life that hadn't been there in the prison.

I blinked as something hit me. "If this is your memory, how come you aren't here?"

He chuckled. "I gave her a bouquet of flowers—don't you think I'd stick around to watch?" He pointed to a berry-laden bush just behind us. "Besides, I had every intention of introducing myself to her."

"Did you?" Before he could answer a rustling sounded from the bush and a figure stepped out from behind it. I stared. "But that isn't—"

"I am Reincarnate—a shapeshifter. I didn't dare come to her as one of They, so I took the form of one from Kirid Clan. There were few Seers, and fewer still she didn't know by name, and Yenen Clan hadn't been formed yet. They Clan wasn't trusted, and if she'd seen me in my true form, I would—well, never mind." He smiled dryly.

I kept my eyes on Chasym's new, past form. He looked similar to the man I knew, though his hair was a little longer and very black. His eyes were still green, but his pointed ears had a different shape, resembling Kirid's ears. He wore a simple blue garb, probably used by the common class of Kirid Clan.

My eyes trailed back to the woman called Veija. "She looks different."

"Is it her hair?" Chasym asked softly.

I nodded after a moment. "Yes, it's too short." But there was something else, too.

The disguised Chasym bowed before Veija and asked her if she liked her flowers. She laughed delightedly before answering.

"You must understand, Ja—uh, Kiido. The Veija you know—knew is eight hundred and eighty-three years old. This memory takes place four hundred and seventy-four years before that. She's only four hundred and nine."

Only? I had never asked Kirid how long an average person stayed alive, but I instinctively knew that four hundred plus was not average. So much for my observation of 'young' woman.

"Kiido?"

I met Chasym's grim gaze.

"Do you trust me?"

I hesitated, knowing that his question was leading somewhere I didn't know if I wanted to follow. "I think so."

"If I told you that getting your memories back is the only way to save Paradise, would you believe me?"

I frowned, watching as Veija laughed, motioning for the disguised Chasym to sit beside her. He spoke softly, introducing himself as Reji. I turned away from the peaceful view and stared at Chasym hard. "Setting aside the part about saving Paradise—do I want my memories back? Be honest."

Chasym's mouth worked as he pondered what to tell me. Finally he sighed. "There is some pain—"

"Some?" I pressed my hand against my heart. A strange, desperate anger filled me. "Just some, Chasym? How much is some? It feels like my heart is bleeding with a grief I can't remember. It screams in agony at the very thought of death. I feel like crying myself to sleep, but I don't understand why. Is that some?"

"Jason, maybe it wouldn't hurt so much if you knew?"

I paused, then shook my head. "How could that possibly help?"

"Though the mind forgets, the heart will always remember." Chasym walked to the gurgling stream and knelt down, placing his hand in the water. "It's cold. Details like that are forgotten with time, but because my heart recalls all of this with perfect clarity, it makes up for that which my mind can't remember. It's more real to me now than it was at the time it occurred, because this place is created through the memories of my heart. The feelings I still retain create this place in a more glorious sphere."

He stood up and held my gaze. “Likewise, the pain in your heart is intensified because the mind cannot understand and balance the grief.” A gentle smile touched his lips. “Besides, Jason, I promise you there are more than only painful memories buried in your mind. Don't you want to know your family? In this half-life you live, there is only unexplained grief and terrible fear. Fear of whatever your little life doesn't include—and even in your supposed bliss, aside from your bleeding heart, there's also Haeon. Maybe, instead of asking Kirid about your former life, you should ask the man who took it from you. I doubt anyone could explain it better than him.”

I stared at Chasym, holding my breath, my eyes wide with the truth in his words. Was Haeon was the reason my mind had forgotten? What was it he wanted? I knew he hated me—and Chasym had suggested that there was some reason I was 'still alive.' Did Haeon...? Did he really want my life?

“I think,” Chasym said after a moment, “that you owe it to your grieving heart to remember what it is you lost.”

His words stung. I felt like I'd been slapped. Something told me that my denial in the last months had been a betrayal of whatever I'd lost. As I bowed my head and thought on what he'd said, I noticed that everything had grown quiet—no laughing voices, no trickling stream. I looked up and saw that we stood in a vast plain with blue mist swirling all around. Moisture formed in my hair and dripped down my face.

“There is so much I want to tell you,” Chasym whispered, “but I fear you're far from ready, and I wonder if it's even my place.” He laughed, but it was a sardonic sound. He raised his head and looked up. A tear slid down his face. “I know your pain, Jason.” He clutched at his clothes just over his heart. “I have the same pain. I lost the same thing you did.” As the single tear fell from his chin, it dissolved into the mist, never reaching the ground. “Pain never becomes easier to bear in life. Never. War is never beautiful. Peace is never lasting.

Death brings tears. Life brings agony. Love creates loss. But," he looked at me, "if we didn't know all this, how could we ever understand and appreciate happiness? How could we ever truly live?"

"Kiido!" an echoing voice pierced the mist.

I stiffened. "Kirid."

Chasym smiled weakly. "He's been trying to get through for a while now. I've said my piece. Now, the choice is all your own."

Everything gave way like puzzle pieces and I felt dizzy as the prison fell into place all around me. I was still kneeling in front of Chasym, one hand holding the cloth to his stomach wound. Chasym was unconscious and barely breathing.

"Kiido," Kirid's concerned voice said from overhead.

I looked up and tried to smile, but suddenly my strength was spent and I dropped my hand, using what little energy I had to stay kneeling.

"I'm coming down," the boy said even as he dropped to the prison floor and stepped near. "What are you doing down here?" His eyes rested on Chasym for a moment and then he reached down and touched his burning forehead. "Let's get him up to my quarters." The little orb swooped down from the prison's opening and hovered over us. Kirid addressed it. "Liitae, go get the doctor."

The orb bobbed its understanding and shot off once more. I looked at Kirid. "What is Chasym doing down here?"

Kirid met my gaze evenly. "Would you believe me if I said I didn't know?"

I wasn't sure how to answer him. The only world I could remember had been turned upside-down and I found myself questioning everything and everyone.

Kirid sensed my confusion and dropped the issue, wrapping Chasym's arm around his shoulders. "If you have any strength right now, might you help me?" he asked gently.

I got wearily to my feet and placed Chasym's other arm around my neck, then glanced at the tiny opening above us. "How will we—?"

"That can't be the only entrance into this place." Kirid's gray eyes swept the room. "Ah. There it is." He pointed to the wall.

"I don't see anything," I said, squinting in the darkness. A light streamed into the room, probably from a torch Kirid had brought, but it wasn't nearly enough to get a good view of anything.

"It's a barrier. Haeon's magic, from what I sense."

So Haeon *was* responsible for Chasym's capture and imprisonment. "Kirid?"

"Yes?"

"I have a lot of questions when we get out of here."

"I have no doubt," he said softly, a sad tone in his voice.

Kirid managed to walk right through the wall, as if it had been only an illusion. He explained that if Chasym or I had attempted to do the same on our own we would be torn apart from the inside out. Luckily Kirid knew how to break the barrier down, and with a casual flick of his wrist, he instructed me to come through with Chasym.

Once through the false wall, we went up a short stairwell and turned a corner, opened a wooden door, and found ourselves back in the wine cellar. The door had been hidden behind numerous barrels and several crates, which we had to shift to get out of the cellar. We hauled Chasym down the long corridor and up the steep steps. We then headed for Kirid's bedchamber, where we laid the unconscious man on the bed and undid the rest of his soiled bandages.

Kirid left and returned moments later with a basin of hot water and fresh bandages, along with his personal physician. The orb, Liitae, followed them into the room and then took to the ceiling, floating about as if chasing shadows. The doctor shoved me aside and shooed Kirid away, so we went to the table by the fireplace and sat in silence.

It was Kirid who spoke first. "When did you find him?"

I glanced at Chasym, pondering what to say. Then I met Kirid's intent gaze. "When you went to stop that breach as the border."

He nodded. "You've seemed very preoccupied since that day. Haeon told me to ask you about it, but I thought you would eventually tell me."

I drummed my fingers lightly against the table. "I was planning to, eventually. I guess...it was sort of exciting...having my own little secret." I winced at my apologetic tone. Why did I have to be sorry? Why was I the guilty party in need of chastisement?

Kirid smiled patiently. "It's all right, Kiido. I'm not angry with you. It's natural to want to keep things to one's self. It's understandable that you would want some independence. It means you're finding a part of yourself that you need."

I frowned, wondering if that was all I needed of myself. "Kirid, who is this man?"

Kirid's gray eyes focused on Chasym and I thought I saw a flash of ice in them. "He is from your past, Kiido. Do you like him?"

I paused. "Well, I... He's a good person."

"Some might say otherwise," he whispered.

"What was he doing in that prison?"

Kirid's eyes slid back to mine. "He wanted to take you away."

I blinked. "He...what?"

Kirid stood abruptly, rounded the table, and came to stand before me. He placed a clawed hand on my head. "You're like a brother to me, Kiido. Sometimes you're so innocent that I think of you as the younger, while at other times you seem to guide me as the elder. When he appeared at the gates, demanding that we return you to him..." He shook his head. "What could I do, Kiido? I knew he would not go away if I asked, and I couldn't kill a friend of yours. Haeon said he would take care of him, and I left it at that. I didn't want to be responsible..."

A fire sparked inside of me and I jerked away from his hand. "How the heck do you assume giving him over to Haeon made you not responsible?" Did you think the problem would just vanish? That if Haeon killed him or hid him from view you wouldn't be as much at fault?"

Kirid watched me blankly, then a strange smile crept up his face. "This is what I mean!" he cried out, but his tone was happy. He knelt on the floor before my chair, meeting my stare with bright eyes. "Now you play the part of the older brother, teaching me, scolding me when I do wrong." His face saddened. "Have I, Kiido? Have I done wrong?"

I watched him in horror and confusion, wondering how a person could be so—what? I didn't know what was wrong with him, but I knew in that moment that Kirid needed help. He was like a tiny child playing adult and failing at it.

"Yes, Kirid," I said firmly. "You've done wrong."

He blinked, worked his mouth, then hung his head. "I see."

I grasped his shoulders, waiting until he raised his head and met my eyes. "It's okay," I said softly, ignoring the self-consciousness I felt. "You know better now, right?"

He shook his head. "I don't understand. Not at all."

"Nor do you have to," a chilly voice said from the doorway.

I stiffened as I looked up and glared at Haeon. "Go away," I growled, pushing down the fear trying to grip my heart.

The Seer smiled, flicking his gaze to the bed. "I hope you've enjoyed your moment of freedom, Chasym Verenvey, as it's the last you'll ever know."

I stood, sidestepping Kirid as I made my way to the bed. "You can't touch him."

Haeon chuckled. "I don't have to *touch* him." He lifted his hand and pointed it towards us.

"No," I stated, and my voice rolled like thunder across the room.

Haeon stumbled backward and stared at me in horror. "Impossible."

"You should be used to the impossible happening by now, Haeon," a familiar voice drawled. I glanced behind me and saw Chasym propped up on his elbows, a smirk on his face. "After all, you're dealing with Vendaeva."

I hissed as a sharp pain erupted in my mind. I clasped my hands to my head, trying to stop the ache.

Haeon laughed outright. "That's where you're wrong, Verenvey." He pointed his long nail at me. "He is not Vendaeva—and *you* know it well."

The pain was increasing. I fell to my knees and released my head to hold myself up. I glanced at Kirid, who watched me with a concerned expression. He was still kneeling on the ground by my chair.

"If he really is a fake, how do you account for his ability to restore his power all by himself?" At Chasym's voice I glanced up at him, then followed his pointing finger to the ceiling. Liitae was no longer chasing shadows, but appeared to be watching the proceedings. "Looks to me like you miscalculated somewhere, eh, Haeon?"

I turned my eyes to Haeon, who was glaring furiously at Chasym. After a moment he spoke, his voice still calm. "He may still have some power, but he cannot replace Kirid as the true Vendaeva."

"Define true," Chasym said smugly.

Kirid got to his feet and walked to where I knelt. He grabbed my arm and pulled me up. "This doesn't concern you, Kiido." He pressed his hand against my forehead. "Just go to sleep, okay?"

My vision wavered as I felt pressure in my mind.

"Jason, no! Stay awake. You need to know the truth!"

I was falling, but Chasym's shout stirred an urgent memory and I thought I heard other voices calling to me. I needed to stay awake. Fighting against the desire for sleep, I raised my hand. "Liitae!".

Brilliant blue light exploded all around me. Something warm surged through my hand and I felt all weariness rush away as adrenaline surged through my body. I got to my feet again and gazed around the room. The light had receded enough to see. Haeon was watching me in stunned silence, his mouth agape and his fingers twitching. Chasym was laughing, though no sound came from his mouth. Kirid was staring in shock, his eyes alight with wonder. In my hand rested a small sphere of swirling light.

What now? I had the advantage somehow, but what could I do with it? As if in answer, another figure appeared beside Haeon. I couldn't make out the figure's features, but its hand rose above its head and then thrust it forward, as though throwing something. My hand tingled and I copied the figure, raising my hand and throwing the orb hard at the ground. Sound burst in my ears like a rushing waterfall and the orb shattered into thousands of pieces.

"Where?" a voice whispered in my ear.

"Somewhere safe," I answered.

"No!" Haeon screamed.

"Who?"

I smiled. "Bring Chasym, too." As swirling winds surrounded me, pulling every which way, I made eye contact with Kirid. He was smiling sadly.

"I know you'll come back, Kiido," he said.

I hesitated, then I shook my head. "No, Kirid. You'll have to come get me." The wind engulfed me and I allowed myself to be lost within it. Then, suddenly, the wind's deafening roar ceased and I felt myself laying on the cold ground.

"Well, well, look what Shifty Cocky Man drag in, yeah?"

23
Two Mistakes?

I blinked, somehow recognizing the voice that had spoken. Wincing, I sat up and rubbed my throbbing head. Opening my eyes again I saw a tree trunk, and as my eyes slid down, I found Chasym's unconscious form beneath the tree. Turning to take in the rest of my surroundings I saw several strange faces —all somehow familiar.

The nearest to me was very tall, and he stepped nearer, offering me a hand. I didn't feel threatened by his towering presence so I allowed him to haul me to my feet. He clapped my back once before letting me stand on my own.

Just behind the tall man was another figure. His mismatched eyes gazed at me solemnly as he clutched a silver shawl wrapped around his slender frame. "Are you alright?" he asked quietly. I might have thought he was a woman, with his feminine features, shawl, and silken voice, but something deep inside me insisted he was male.

I wasn't sure how to respond. I knew these people, but... "You're alive?" I couldn't remember their names or how I was connected to them, but I knew that they were supposed to be dead. The ache in my heart assured me these were the people I'd lost. So, "How?"

"Shifty Cocky Man not only one hard to kill, yeah?" the first voice I'd heard said. I turned around to face the voice's owner, grinning from ear to ear though I couldn't understand why I felt so eager to see him. The man lounged in a hammock dangling between two trees. His right hand was propped lazily under his chin as he rocked with the spring breeze. He was wrapped in red robes, and his messy hair was pulled off to the top, left side of his head. His mismatched metallic eyes watched me with mischief twinkling in their depths. "Welcome back, again, Strange Coward Boy," he said, flashing glistening white teeth.

My grin widened as I felt a weight lift from my shoulders. Everything was going to be okay now, even if I didn't remember these people. The ache I'd felt since I woke up in Kirid's castle fell away; the hole inside me was filled.

"Tall Strong Jerk get Screechy Hurting Doctor," he waved at the tall man. "Save Shifty Cocky Man before he almost die *again*." The tall man bowed low and then turned and headed for the thicker trees. "Now, Strange Coward Boy, sit and explain all happenings since entering Slimy Bad Kirid lands, yeah?"

I hesitated. What could I tell him? I didn't know the details; I didn't really know anything.

"He's in no frame of mind to explain anything to anyone," Chasym said, sitting up with the help of the tree trunk.

"Take only catnaps, yeah?"

"I've had plenty of time for long naps in the past few months. Right now," he winced as he rested against the trunk, "I should like an explanation of my own."

"Oh?"

"How *are* you all alive?"

I looked between the two men, but before they could exchange more words a third voice entered the fray.

"It's about time." A woman's voice. It sounded angry.

I jumped guiltily, unsure what I'd done wrong, and spun around to face the threatening tone. The beautiful woman, with dark brown hair pulled back in a long ponytail and icy blue eyes, stormed across the clearing, pointing a sharp nail in my direction. I glanced around for a place to hide, but she stopped in front of me before I could spot a large enough bush to conceal myself in.

She glared me down for a moment, making me feel like a lowly worm, before a smile broke through and she slipped her arms around me and embraced me gently. "We've been so worried about you. How did you escape?"

Dumbfounded, it took a moment before I relocated my voice. "Uh." Well, at least a sound came out, pathetic as it was.

"Screechy Hurting Doctor should be happy she get patient back, too!" the man in the hammock said cheerily as he pointed to Chasym, who seemed to be making an effort to blend in with the tree, eyes glued on the doctor in terror.

The woman released me, turned, and loomed before her cowering patient. "I'm afraid your appointment is long overdue," she hissed, showing her own set of razor teeth.

Chasym gulped and shot me a pleading look. I only shrugged, feeling too overwhelmed to lend him a hand. As the frightening lady knelt down to examine her victim, I turned back to the hammock-lounging man—who was obviously in charge—and decided to venture a question.

"So, what's your name?" I asked.

He chuckled at what he assumed was a joke, but his eyes scanned my expression and his smile disappeared. "Shifty Cocky Man. What being wrong with Strange Coward Boy?"

Chasym shooed the doctor aside. "His memories are suppressed."

"Which memories?"

"All of them, though he's making a good effort of getting them back. Aren't you, Jase?"

I continued to watch the leader, not bothering to answer.

"We Crenen," he said after a moment.

The ache in my head doubled, but I continued to ignore it, determined not to let any more keep me from the answers I sought.

—I thought too soon.

"Key!"

I knew that voice; knew it better than just a vague semblance of a memory. I looked past the man called Crenen and my eyes rested on the angelic form of Veija. Unlike Chasym's memory, her hair was long and flowing, but everything else was the same.

Except—

I frowned and glanced at Chasym, who was watching her with a soft smile. Her presence was different. Whatever occurred four-hundred and seventy-four years before had changed her. He said she'd gone mad. Was it true?

She ran forward and threw herself into my arms, golden locks of hair encircling us before falling into place around her shoulders. "I missed you!"

"Wait, Seer Veija," the tall man said, stepping next to us and placing his hand on her shoulder. "He doesn't remember you."

She met my gaze, concern in her eyes. "Key, you've forgotten?" She reached her hand up and touched my forehead. "Did he take your memories?" Her voice was bitter, her eyes dark with anger.

"Yes," Chasym said before I could answer. "Haeon took them from him when he sealed his powers. He underestimated him, though, because Jason managed to break the seal—but he still has to unlock the memories."

Veija's soft hand ran along my cheek as she stared into my eyes. "Are you okay?"

I took a step back and nodded. "Yeah, I'll..." I cleared my throat, "I'll be fine. Um, thank you."

She lowered her hand and nodded. "Good. It's great that you're back."

"Yeah, yeah, now move, Seer," Crenen said, tapping her thigh from his hammock with a long stick. "We talk with Strange Coward Boy now."

As Veija moved aside, hovering near, I focused on the lounging man as I considered what I dared ask. He beat me to it.

"We introduce our servants, yeah?"

That worked. "Sounds good."

He cleared his throat and pointed with the long stick to the tall man. "That be Tall Strong Jerk."

"Menen," Tall Strong Jerk corrected.

Crenen ignored him. "And that Screechy Hurting Doctor."

"Sasha," she said.

"You meet Shifty Cocky Man already."

Chasym winked.

"And Seer."

How come she got a short name?

"And that Sick Nasty Dog."

The other metallic-eyed man nodded his head. "Jenen," he added quietly.

I flinched as the memories struck viciously at my mind again.

"And Mysterious Girly Guy is vanished. Again." Crenen chuckled. "We think he secretly shy or something."

Chasym snorted. "Sounds about right."

I went back through the names mentally, so I could keep them straight if I ever had to use them. If all else failed I could probably resort to their nicknames, but they were actually harder to remember, which rather defeated the point.

"We was hoping Strange Coward Boy come back and ask how we manage escape from clutches of Delusional Broken Man and Noisy Twitchy Shadows, but..." Crenen shrugged.

From somewhere indiscernible came a new voice. "I think Vendaeva needs to rest. The magic he used to bring Chasym and himself here takes an enormous toll on the user. He may not feel it now, but it won't be long before he will need nourishment and sleep."

I glanced around for the voice's owner, but I didn't see anyone save those I'd already met.

"Mysterious Girly Guy make mysterious entrance, yeah?" Crenen said with a grin.

"Does it hurt?"

I jumped, spun around, and looked up into blood-colored eyes. Blinking, I backed up to get a better view. I suddenly understood the "girly" part. The newcomer was very slender, with long golden hair reaching down to his ankles. He wore rich purple robes resembling a gown, with earrings in both of his pointed ears. While he seemed harmless enough, there was something about him that felt like Haeon's chilly presence.

"Does it hurt?" he repeated in a soft tone.

I wasn't certain how to answer so I shrugged. "Only a little."

His eyes narrowed as he searched mine. Finally he nodded, satisfied. "I am Lon."

Easy enough to remember.

"Do you mind?" Without waiting for a reply Lon raised his hand to my forehead and closed his unnerving eyes. I stood there, feeling uncomfortable, until he pulled away and stepped back. "It is not too difficult to undo the memory seal. I'm sure

Seer Veija could easily accomplish the task—when and if you feel ready."

I swallowed and nodded slowly. "Okay, yeah, I'll...let you know."

He stepped back and gazed at the sky. "Evening descends. After eating, I advise that you rest."

"'Kay..." I watched him turn and walk into the darkness of the trees. When I could no longer see him, I turned and glanced around for a place to sit. My eyes collided with Jenen's, and he motioned to the grass where he stood. I accepted his offer, moving across the clearing and sitting down. Jenen sat beside me.

"At least Kirid treated you well," he said quietly.

I blinked. "Yeah." For the most part I certainly had been well cared for.

"You don't remember us, yet you seemed alarmed that we were alive. Why?" he inquired.

"Well, I knew I'd lost something. Chasym said he had, too. When I saw all of you I...I just knew you were supposed to be dead."

Jenen nodded. "The heart never lies."

"How *are* you alive?" I asked after a moment.

Jenen looked up, meeting my gaze with an impassive face. "You saved us," he whispered.

"I...what?"

He took a deep breath. "This may be somewhat confusing, especially since you can't remember everything. Are you certain you wish to know?"

I nodded firmly. It wasn't a matter of wishing; I needed to know.

"Until today, were you aware of the power you wield?"

I shook my head.

"Well," he paused and took another breath. "To make it simple, you are Vendaeva—an individual with the power and responsibility to save Paradise from its own destruction. Paradise is—"

"Dying. I know," I said softly. "Chasym told me." Apparently it hadn't been his fever talking.

"Good." Jenen rested his head against the tree and watched the orange-hued sky. "Before you were taken to Kirid Clan, when Seer Haeon came to collect you, we all made a stand against him. He sent his shadows to hold everyone off while he focused on incapacitating you."

"And it worked," I guessed.

"Almost exactly how he had planned." Jenen's eyes fell on my hands. "However, he underestimated something." His eyes moved to mine and he held my gaze for a moment. "He forced you to fall asleep, and swiftly collected you. Then he gave orders to his shadow minions to destroy us. It would have worked, had Haeon not overlooked two very important details. Of course, there was also Chasym, who somehow slipped out of the cave and followed Liitae after you—or I assume as much."

I glanced at my left hand, remembering the little blue orb. "Liitae," I whispered. I didn't really mean to summon anything, but as soon as I said its name, the sphere popped out of my hand and energetically spun around my head a few times before hovering above my shoulder.

Jenen looked almost ready to smile, but he brushed it off and resumed his story. "What Haeon failed to notice was the absence of Menen, who had been guarding the entrance to the cave from a stealthy location outside."

I glanced at Tall Strong Jerk, who was speaking quietly to Crenen, and wondered how anyone could overlook his absence.

"The Seer's second mistake was actually a continuation of an earlier blunder," Jenen said, now allowing a soft smile to tug at his mouth. "On a past occasion, the Seer tried to kill me

—and succeeded. What he didn't count on was your intervention. You brought me back to life."

I started, then my eyes narrowed. "Wha—how?"

Jenen pointed to Liitae. "You pushed your Essence into my heart. From what Lon explained after we destroyed the shadows, you and I...share the same soul."

My head felt light as a new dimension pressed in around me.

Jenen continued. "Now, just like Liitae, unless you die, I cannot either. Lon said that it is possible to remove our 'bond,' but very painful and possibly fatal."

Oh, was that all?

Jenen didn't seem bothered by the idea. "Menen entered the cave and distracted the shadows, and...I really don't remember anything more. From what the others have explained, I began to glow faintly, and I stood up from where the shadows had knocked me down, raised my hand and...banished them." He reached forward and touched Liitae, stroking its surface. "Seer Veija said you had worked your power through me, as we are bound. Even though you were captured, you saved us."

Something caught in my throat. The idea that I helped to save them eased another ache; a guilt I hadn't known was clutching at my heart. I wiped at my face.

A slender hand rested on my shoulder and I looked up at Jenen's gentle expression. "It's all right," he whispered.

I didn't know that for certain. I wasn't sure of much. But his words were soothing and I heard sincerity in his tone. What reason did this man have to lie to me? I knew I could trust him.

"Thanks," I said, wiping at more stubborn tears. As I rubbed at my face, I caught a glimpse of Crenen still swinging in his hammock, reflecting on his peculiar speech pattern. "Hey, Jenen?"

"Hm?"

"Why does Crenen refer to himself as 'we'?" I glanced at the man beside me, surprised to find him smiling with amusement.

"You must understand, this tongue we are speaking—English—is only a second language to us. When we were little, during a very difficult lesson on nouns and pronouns, the instructor mentioned the 'royal we' or the majestic plural a king used often times when he spoke for his entire country. From that lesson on, Crenen has very rarely referred to himself as anything but *we*."

A smile pushed itself to my face. "He's a very interesting guy."

"Yes," Jenen murmured, face unreadable. "Very."

24
Verenvey?

Long after everyone drifted off to sleep I sat before the fire, staring into the flames as my thoughts wandered. Only vaguely did I hear the pop and hiss of the wood or feel the burning heat on my skin from sitting too near the fire for so long. Beside me, the little ball of light chased the night bugs creeping in the grass. Distantly I heard soft footfalls from the trees guarding our camp. Then the steps came from the grass. I lifted my head and met Lon's frightening eyes where he stood across the camp on the far side of the fire.

"Can't you sleep?" Though he whispered the wind carried his message clearly to my ears.

I exhaled slowly, causing my long bangs to flutter. "If I laid down, I think I'd enter a coma and never wake up."

"Is that why you're still up?"

I shook my head. "I just...don't want to. Sleep, I mean."

He stepped from the shadows and walked to the fire, sitting down across from me and the flames. "I find night is the best time to organize one's thoughts."

"Yeah." I shifted, propping my chin on my knees and wrapping my arms around my legs. "There are a lot of thoughts swimming in my head right now."

"Understandably," Lon said. "You've been through quite a lot, and, as I'm sure you already know, it's far from over yet."

"Yeah."

"Are you deciding whether to have your memories returned or not?"

"Yeah."

Lon lifted a stick from the ground and poked at the fire.

"Can I ask you something?" I asked.

He raised an eyebrow. "You can."

I smiled. "May I?"

"Very well."

I inhaled. "What are you?"

He stopped mid prod and looked up, meeting my eyes. "What sort of question is that, Key?"

"Well..." I glanced around. "There's something about these people, in a strange sort of way, that's...honest? I mean, I kind of know what to expect from them. Sort of. But, uh..." I scratched my neck as I considered how best to explain. "You're, well, different. Kind of like Haeon...only, not so..." I shrugged, "...scary."

"I see." Lon prodded at the fire again, though the flames were high by now. "I once told you—though I understand you don't remember—to ask a Seer that question."

I bit my lip, then caught his gaze, holding it. "I think I am."

His eyebrow rose again. "What do you mean?"

"I think I am asking a Seer. I think you are a Seer."

A smile crept up his face. "You have quite the imagination, Key."

I scowled. "If you're not one, explain to me how you feel just like Haeon does—and how Veija used to, before...before she changed?"

His smile dropped and he stared at me. "Before she changed?"

I nodded. "Chasym showed me a memo—"

He raised his hand, cutting me off as he glanced at the sleeping forms around us. "Come. We will discuss your...concerns...elsewhere."

"They can't hear us," I said firmly. Somehow, though at what point I wasn't sure, my strange little pet ball had begun emitting a pulse around us and the fire. It was a clear barrier, hardly noticeable, though I'd been subconsciously aware of it for some time.

"So they can't," Lon said. His expression turned steely. "Chasym showed you a memory?"

I nodded. "He said he was once in love with her, then he showed me a brief memory."

It was his turn to breathe deeply. "Did he explain the circumstances behind everything?"

I shook my head.

"Very well. You best understand how it all works."

"Chasym did mention They Clan, and how...the Seers...uh..." I wrinkled my brow to remember.

"He certainly explained it well if you can remember it that clearly," Lon said sardonically.

"Well, he was a bit out of it."

"Let that be a lesson: never attempt to teach when you aren't coherent enough to remember not to."

His statement oozed with contradictions, but I kept that observation to myself.

"Now then." Lon looked up at the star-infested sky. "The clan of They was more an organization, really. An organization within a single race. The race was Renocahn—

Reincarnate—shapeshifters. They could take the form of any living organism. Within the race was a group of alleged elite—mostly it was comprised of the rich and noble-born.

"The Renocahn race was the least primitive culture in Paradise at this point—this was about two thousand years ago. The legends say that Renocahn actually created all the other races and clans, but that is false. The Renocahn only helped shape the other cultures into less primitive civilizations. Of course, this became the downfall of the Renocahn later. Are you following?"

I nodded mid yawn. I was determined to stay awake, as I knew that this information was vital. I pushed down my weariness. "Keep going."

He watched me suspiciously before he continued. "As an experiment, the first race the Renocahn chose to educate was the Verenvey."

I winced as my mind throbbed. "Oww."

"Yes, you do know that name." Lon closed his eyes. "There is so much..."

"Just do your best. I'll try and keep up. I can ask questions if I don't understand."

"Chasym Verenvey. Does that sound familiar?"

I blinked. "But...isn't Chasym...?"

"He is of They Clan, and he is of the Renocahn race, yes. At least, partially. I'll come to that. The Renocahn discovered that the Verenvey race had an incredible gift—they could see the future. Taking them under wing, the Renocahn drew the Verenvey out of their primitive state." Lon lifted his hand and smiled to himself as he studied his palm. "The two races had considerable peace for a long time. And many within the races mingled, marrying one another. Unfortunately, the Renocahn grew jealous of the Seer-like powers of the Verenvey and felt threatened by the growing populace of said Seers. They banished the Seers to the eastern side of Paradise and kept the

West for themselves. At the time the East was only desert, but within a single century the Verenvey made it flourish and bloom.

"Enraged and jealous, the Renocahn declared war, and with their abilities of transformation they quickly overpowered the peaceful Verenvey. Forcing them into submission, the Renocahn made the Seers their slaves."

Something was wrong with this story. Something bothered me, but I couldn't place what.

"As you may guess, Chasym is actually half Renocahnian and half Verenveyan. Because of his Seer blood, he grew up a slave to his own father." A bitter smile played at Lon's mouth. "I, also, was born into slavery, though a few centuries later."

So, I had been right. He was a Seer. As I mulled over his words, something struck me. That was it. That was the problem. "There's something I don't get. I thought Paradise wasn't corrupt until the Kirid and Yenen clans fought, but this sounds a little bit bad to me. I mean, they killed back then, too. What made the conflict between Kirid and Yenen worse than enslaving an entire race?"

"Very good question," Lon said with a gentle smile. "That observation is exactly why the true story has been kept hidden."

I frowned, but stayed quiet. Lon also recognized the issue, so he would probably explain in time. I just needed to stay patient.

He went on. "While the Verenvey were oppressed, the Renocahn became aware of another presence in Paradise, one that was becoming very powerful. So they turned their attentions to Kirid Clan, determined to keep them from superseding Renocahn's grip on the land. There was nothing extraordinary about the Kirid—at least, nothing noticeable at first. But their bond to the land and their stubborn determination frightened the Renocahn. Still, they knew that enslaving the Kirid would only pose a threat. They did not have enough forces to keep two races at bay, and so they approached the Kirid peacefully and gave the western lands to them, keeping the more fertile eastern lands for themselves, still forcing their Seer-slaves to keep the forests alive.

"What the Renocahn didn't count on was the half-and-half, Chasym Verenvey." Lon laughed softly. "He did a most foolish thing, but somehow it was effective. He gambled, and, miraculously, he won. In a sense he lost as well, and it cost the Seers their hope for domination over the Renocahn, but that is just as well."

"What did he do?"

"He broke the one rule of a Seer: he manipulated the future. A Seer must never rewrite the future through vision, because it could have dire consequences. But Chasym was careful. He thought his plan out well and created self-prophecy. Afterward he lost his Seeric gift forever, as is the cost of such a crime. He was among first to attempt such a thing, but since then many Seers have followed his example, losing their Seership, as well as their immortality."

I stared. "Immortality?" I glanced at Chasym, then my eyes fell on Veija. "But...?" So many questions.

Lon smiled. "Let me answer these for you, and then I'll continue the story. First, yes, immortal, but not in the sense you think. We—" He sighed. "It's so complex, this universe, Key. I could discuss its secrets, and the history behind Seeric power all night, but I doubt if it is relevant to your own quest. Suffice it to say, the Verenvey cannot die of old age—they will never grow old. They can only die by the sword or by choice. It is a form of half-immortality. But, when a Verenveyan manipulated the future to suit his purposes, he lost his Sight, and with it, his Forever." He raised his hand before I could open my mouth. "Yes, I know, Chasym should be dead. And, as you have guessed, so should Veija. That is easily answered: I don't know."

I blinked. "What?"

He shook his head. "Chasym never explained how he managed to keep Veija alive, though I suspect Chasym's mysterious immortality stems from his manipulation. That is why I believe it was so effective. He did what no other Seer who lost their Sight thought to do. They seemed to believe they could only manipulate one aspect of the future, but Chasym, as far as I can tell, caused three changes through one action. He restored his immortality, forced They Clan to make him their leader, and thus caused the downfall of the Renocahn Empire."

"How long ago was all this?" I asked.

"About one thousand years ago Chasym took control of They. I was born toward the end of the Renocahn regime, and I grew up with stories of Chasym's supposed betrayal of our people." Lon smirked. "Chasym was a genius. He was intelligent enough not to mock fate, instead he worked with it. Before his outright loss of Seeric power, it was only speculation that one would lose the power by manipulation. Chasym recognized something no one else took into consideration. He saw how the removal of Seership would enable him to pay his Renocahnian brothers back for what they had done to his Verenveyan brothers." Lon extended his hand above the fire. "When he lost his power, he went before They Clan and announced that he had drained the Verenvey heritage from his veins and desired to prove his allegiance to Renocahn and They.

"He underwent horrible tests to prove the truth of his words, and then he spent the next eighty years under the tutelage of They." Lon sensed my next question somehow, because he said, "No, the Renocahn were not immortal, but they were long lived. Even if Chasym hadn't manipulated his immortality, he would have lived for another few centuries—though, he'd certainly be long in his grave now."

"How did he cause the Renocahn to fall?" I asked.

"He succeeded the third leader of They Clan, actually," Lon said, "as he had proved so well his faithfulness. The Verenvey were also convinced he was completely Renocahnian now. Chasym was smart enough to recognize he could not immediately change the condition of his Seer brothers, and so he played tyrant—albeit a rather lenient tyrant with many lazy Verenvey servants in considerable good health. Chasym bided his time and no one was the wiser. And then," Lon paused, "he met Veija."

The dates clicked in my head and I waved my hands. "Just a second. You said that Chasym took control of They one thousand years ago, right?"

Lon nodded.

"And he met Veija while he was still its leader?"

"Yes."

I blew my breath out quickly. "But Chasym told me that it was only four hundred-something years ago that he met her."

"Yes."

"What the heck took him so long?"

Lon smiled seriously. "While I should like to defend him, I also am quite aware of the nature of man. I believe that, no matter how noble his intentions, Chasym lost focus of his original goals for a time. He had beaten mortality and become head of an Empire—not an easy thing to give up. It took a woman to bring him back to his senses."

That figured. It was guys like that who gave men a bad name.

Lon chuckled. "I'll not mention your philosophy to our mutual friend." He cleared his throat. "When Chasym saw Veija he found himself intrigued, but he knew she was

Verenveyan. It was against everything his position entailed to even think of her as a fellow being. But her beauty was entrancing and her wise demeanor hypnotized him. He continued to watch her each day at her favorite spot to sit alone. And, inevitably, he fell in love. When he could take it no more, he transformed himself into a Kirid merchant and introduced himself as Reji. It was some months before I was even aware that anything was amiss."

"You—?"

"I am Veija's older brother. Forgive me, I forgot that you did not remember that fact."

It only made sense why Lon was a pretty boy, I supposed.

Lon raised an eyebrow. "I should warn you now, I can read your thoughts."

I had suspected as much, but hadn't dared ask the question. I decided to get back on topic. "So, how did you discover something was going on?"

Lon breathed slowly through his nose and shook his head. "Only through chance. I was given an afternoon off from my servitude, and so I took the occasion to visit Veija at her normal spot by the stream. I caught them talking and laughing, but thought little of it, as he looked like a Kirid merchant."

"I thought the Kirid were in the West."

"Most, yes, but not all. There were several small groups who traded with the Renocahn, and so Chasym posed as a merchant. It was a good ruse, and he a great actor. Again, only chance showed me the truth. There are moments I regret ever having found out..." His voice quieted as he turned again to watch the stars. "There are many things I regret now."

I allowed him two seconds of thought before I pushed for more. "So, how did you discover his identity?"

Lon turned a wry face to me. "A shapeshifter's true form is visible in his reflection. I caught a glimpse of yellow in the water when he neared the stream's bank. By this time I had spent a few afternoons with them both and didn't mind Reji in the least, but when I caught the flash of yellow I was surprised and followed him in the evening when he departed. From a safe distance I saw him transform into our hated tyrant master, and," he shrugged, "I was angry, honestly, but I didn't do anything then. I recognized my awkward position and realized that if the leader of They fancied my sister, he might do anything to get her. If I interfered, I might actually cause unnecessary bloodshed, or worse.

"What I didn't count on was Chasym. The next time he was due to visit I sneaked away from my servant duties and went early to the stream, only to discover him already there, in his merchant form. He told me there was something he needed to discuss with me, but I suspected what it was and beat him to it. I'm ashamed to admit that I exploded, and amidst the torrent of anger, I informed him that I knew who he was, but I didn't care what he did to me, and that I never wanted him to come near my sister again. I recall telling him that I would rewrite the future and kill him if he ever spoke to her again." Lon paused and grabbed a twig from the ground.

"What'd he do?" I whispered.

"He was the absolute picture of calm, Key. He took every childish word like a man, and when I had fallen into a breathless silence, he bowed and said he understood my wish, and that he had been selfish. He begged for me to let him see her one final time to say goodbye. The most startling and mortifying part of all was when he said he understood my prejudice and hoped that someday I could forgive him." Lon snapped the twig in two. "If I'd only known what he meant by those words..."

We sat in silence, listening to the swaying branches overhead and the popping fire between us, before he continued.

"Chasym devised a plan to murder his merchant self, using Renocahnian guards to actually skewer him for alleged thievery. For some reason he couldn't actually die, but he came close. As he drew what seemed his last breaths, he hurried toward Veija's glade, calling for her. She went to him, found him nearly lifeless, and then watched in horror as the guardsmen took him away.

"As Chasym healed himself in his domain, he must have thought his plan would enable Veija to go on with her life and eventually forget Reji's existence altogether. But he miscalculated badly. In desperation and with a breaking heart, Veija broke the Seeric rule. She foolishly rewrote the future, saying Reji would live. Of course, Reji the Merchant never existed and so her sacrifice was for not. Mortal now, and half-mad with grief, Veija grew ill—" Lon's voice cracked and he looked down at the ground as he struggled with his emotions, "—and has never been well since. She was once fair, and wise, and gentle, but though she remains fair and gentle still, her wisdom died with her sanity."

The fire crackled, but it was not a cheery sound. Something was caught in my own throat. Another spell of silence passed, until I couldn't take it anymore.

"What did you do, Lon?"

For a moment I wondered if he would answer, but finally he stirred.

"Foolishness, it seems, was contagious. In a mad rage I fought my way past Chasym's guards until I finally entered his chambers. News of Veija's act had traveled to his ears already, and he sat in his bed weeping. As I stared at the man who had caused my sister's madness, all the bitterness and anger bled away and I did not struggle as I was captured by the guards. Chasym lifted his head then and ordered them to leave me be. We sat in stony silence for hours before either of us had the will to speak. Chasym finally said he could not beg my forgiveness because he did not deserve it, but I was well aware that my own prejudice had also caused Veija's pain. We called an unspoken truce that day." A single tear slid down his cheek.

"There is an old Renocahnian custom. When someone betrays a friend, they take the other's name on until the offense is forgiven. Thus Chasym took upon himself the surname Verenvey, feeling he had betrayed his mission to save his oppressed people. He swore an oath to rectify his mistakes. After that, he vanished for several long years, and his disappearance caused the downfall of the Renocahn Empire. A strange madness swept over the Renocahn. The abrupt loss of leadership caused greed among its chiefs, and as well as members of They. After a millennial rule, the Renocahn Empire made its ghostly descent into the pages of history in just five years. At the first sign of disorder, the Verenvey rose against its master and wiped most of the Renocahn from Paradise.

"Chasym appeared at the end of the carnage to witness the worst of it. He found me and explained that he had made certain Veija would be immortal regardless of her blunder. He said it was all he could do to pay me back for what he had done.

"Only a small remnant of They Clan survives today, descendants of Chasym's betrayed followers." Lon's eyes found Chasym's sleeping form. "His noble intentions caused the fall of both races, in the end. The bloody swords of Renocahn mostly cut down the Verenvey, but those who lived followed his and Veija's examples and attempted to rewrite the future. They died after a short span of one hundred years. Now at history's end, bitter resentment and loss make Chasym both tyrant and hero, leader and slave, immortal and foolish man. The remains of They and the few Seers left hate Chasym with a vengeance they don't understand. And Veija, in her madness, does not even recognize the man she fell in love with. To her, he is only They."

"She doesn't know he was They Clan's leader?"

"Apparently not." Lon hovered his hand over the flames again, watching the smoke dance around it. "It is just as well. The prejudice against Renocahn has spanned the ages and the peoples. The Kirid and Yenen clans also hate They because when it fell, it forced the Kirid lands into poverty for many years. Now, while the poverty of centuries lost is forgotten, the hateful feud goes on."

I watched this man for a long time, amazed at his strength. He and the others had endured so much for so long.

"Why do you pretend not to be a Seer?"

Lon's eyes searched out Jenen, laying under the tree only three yards from where we sat. "Crenen told me to pretend I was a Lost Seer—one who foolishly lost his Seership. My appearance and relation to Veija made it impossible to hide the absolute truth, so we made due with that. Veija and Crenen, you might say, outvoted me. You see," Lon inclined his head toward Jenen, "he and Crenen are twins, with two completely different agendas—or so they believe—and to ensure that Jenen stays put, Crenen has Veija. Jenen wants a Seer, and *you*, so they decided on this ruse. That way, should Jenen lay his hands on the two of you, he still can't fulfill his purposes, as Veija does not have the information I possess. I disagreed with the idea, but Veija...insisted. Ever since she lost herself, the only driving force in her life is keeping me safe and my powers alive. If that keeps her conscious, I will not stand against her. Not unless I have to. She has only been aware of her surroundings for the past fourteen years and now she acts like a child." He paused. "I finally relented to her wishes; so, while she pretends to be a Seer, I guide her through telepathy." He tapped his temple.

"I'm sorry, Lon," I whispered, dropping my eyes to the ground.

"Why should you be sorry, Key? You've done nothing wrong."

I shook my head. "I've...been selfish. I was so concerned with my present reality, I'd decided already to keep my memories locked away forever. I was afraid...but...that's stupid." I wiped at the tears collecting in my eyes. "There's no reason to be afraid of what I don't know." I smiled at Lon through watery eyes. "I can't see the future to try and manipulate it, and for that I'm grateful. This way I can write my future any dang way I please."

"But, Key— "

I raised my hand. "Lon, I don't know about you, but I think some things are worth sacrificing. Sure, there are consequences, but doesn't that only make the painfully right choices that much more worth it?" I grinned. "I take it Veija wouldn't be the one to open those memories to me, right?"

Lon nodded. "I would, of course."

"Then get cracking. I'd rather sleep through all the coming pain anyway." I winked. "And you can inform Veija through telepathy that I'll pretend to receive them in the morning."

Lon's mouth twitched in a smile. "I'm afraid you may be out for days when I do this."

I grimaced. "Well then," a grin broke through, "I'm sure you'll find some excuse."

He sighed and stood up. "Very well." Rounding the fire, he helped me to my feet and touched my temples. "This *will* hurt."

I nodded bravely.

Like a key turning in a lock, it felt like something clicked in my head, and then the memories rushed in like a tirade of water from the other side of a freaking strong door that had suddenly burst. I barely felt Lon catch me as I fell forward, and then the memories swallowed me whole.

25
Going Home?

My movements were sluggish, as though I tried to run through water. Images flashed around me, tugging and screaming for my attention. Voices tumbled from above, crashing in on my deafened ears, while faces—so many faces—swirled before my burning eyes. Excruciating pain finally gave way to numbness and I fell forward on the puddled ground.

This place. This misty plain I continually came to, what was it? Was it significant? Veija. Yes, it was she who had said the mist represented the Paradisaical disease. There was something here, then; some key to open the door to all the answers. I just needed to find it.

Determined now, I clambered to my feet, running once again through the swirling fog. I raised my hands and summoned Liitae, who sprang from my palm and shot forward into the gloom. I tried to call the orb back, but my voice was gone. Irritated, I flicked my hand toward me and watched in satisfaction as the mischievous orb flew back. I caught it like a baseball and held it tight, raising my hand to let Liitae light the way. The mists peeled apart for us, and I walked forward, still resolute.

More memories slammed into my head and I stumbled, though I still clutched the orb so it couldn't escape. My knees collided hard with the cold ground and I hissed at the pain even as I recognized that no noise came from my mouth. Another wave of memories blanketed my vision.

Just as it felt the pain would subside, more memories rose up. I screamed, still hearing nothing. If this kept up I would go mad. Somehow I stood up unsteadily. I needed to stop the onslaught before I couldn't take it. I stumbled as the number of images increased.

Stop! I begged silently. *Please, stop.*

"Focus," a gentle voice said in my mind. *"Calm your thoughts and focus."*

That voice.

Lon! I cried mentally. The voice didn't return, but I thought of his words. *He's trying to help me.* I closed my eyes tight, barely registering the wriggling sphere in my hand. Then it clicked. I focused all my thoughts solely on Liitae and the orb grew still. The memories ceased and I felt my ears open back up. Breathing heavily, I got back to my feet and gazed down at my little Essence.

"Thanks," I whispered. "Feed them to me slower, Liitae. 'Kay?"

The orb pulsed its understanding and the memories came again. Much more slowly.

A presence appeared before me and I grinned at Lon's pleased expression.

"Very good, Vendaeva," he said.

"Thanks for helping."

"I did nothing," he said quietly. His eyes studied the mists. "Your memories will only slowly come now, but you may wake up more quickly for it. In any case," he met my eyes again, "it will be good to have Key back."

I smirked. "Missed me that much?"

"Yes," he answered.

I blinked and felt my cheeks reddening. "It's all a bit murky. I guess it'll take time to sort everything out again, huh?"

"Yes, the chronological order may take the most time to organize." Lon stepped forward and took Liitae. "When Haeon sealed your memories, he actually meant to destroy them, but Liitae protected them for you. When Haeon sealed Liitae inside of you to keep your powers sealed as well, his miscalculation was this." He took my hand and traced the marking on my palm. "You and water have an intriguing connection."

I stared at my palms. "Does that mean...? Did that healing pool...?"

Lon nodded. "It is very possible. I suppose we should test it. If the pool gave these marks to you for the purpose of protection, the healing properties could very well still be there."

I groaned. "Meaning we got Screechy Hurting Doctor for nothing."

"Nonsense. Another female presence will be good for this group," Lon said, still studying the key-shaped burn.

"What're you talking about? The majority of our group is female."

Lon raised an eyebrow, though he didn't look away from my hand. "These immature comments of yours are what prevent your final growth. Though I imagine they are also what has been missed most."

"Final growth?"

"Your final step into ultimate power."

I wrinkled my brow. "Yeah, about that...? You never did answer my question."

"Which one?"

"Um." I tried to separate the memory from the others. "Something about how in the heck it was possible that the Kirid and Yenen battle made Paradise sick, while the, uh, Renocahn and Verenvey thing didn't?"

"Ah. That one. I certainly wish I knew, but for the record, I believe Paradise has been sick longer than anyone is aware of. It only became apparent in the last two decades." He released my right hand and took the other one.

"Right." I separated more memories. After a moment I decided to ask something else. "What are you after, Lon? What is your agenda?"

He looked slightly amused. "What makes you think I have one?"

"Because everyone does."

"What a jaded observation."

I scowled and opened my mouth to retort when another memory forced its way to the forefront of my mind. "Wait—Lon!"

He snapped his eyes from my palm and watched me in concern.

I shook my head to clear it. "That dream..."

He frowned.

"Yeah!" The memory of the dream about the infant came back, along with Haeon's explanation. My happiness plummeted, replaced by a sick dread. "Lon." How could I say it? "I-I'm...not Vendaeva..."

He stared at me blankly, moisture dripping from his long bangs. "Why do you think that?"

Panic rose in my stomach. "Haeon—He—I saw..." I shook my head, looking at the ground. "He has the real Vendaeva." I ran my hand through my hair, swallowing hard. "I... Kirid...The baby in my dream. It was Kirid." When I looked back up, Lon's face was pale and his eyes were wide.

"Are you certain?"

I nodded. "He can control Liitae...He said I was just a tool...Only a—" the sick feel was getting worse, "—a cover-up. I'm...sorry, Lon. I wanted to help you guys, but...Kirid is the real Vendaeva."

Lon stared at me, then he shook his head. "Tell me you are only joking, Key. Tell me this is a dream." He looked as sick as I felt.

"I wish I could." I ran a hand through my hair again. "I should've brought Kirid with; gotten him out of Haeon's grasp. I could have at least done that, if I'd just remembered everything..." I blinked away the hot tears threatening to come. There was no reason to cry, none at all. At least the real Vendaeva was alive, at least Paradise still had hope.

"We...we can go and rescue him..." Part of me, the horribly selfish part, wanted Lon to grab my shoulders and firmly tell me that Haeon was mistaken, that I really was Vendaeva. That they needed me. But Lon's pallor, his obvious understanding, and the shocked look on his face—it was only further proof of what I knew already to be true.

Lon turned from me, placing his hand to his chin as his mind tried to digest what I'd told him. "I can't believe it," he whispered nearly inaudibly. "I thought..."

My stomach dropped. "You knew, Lon, didn't you?"

He spun around to meet my gaze, his face contorted in pain. "Oh, Key..."

That tone was sharper than a slap to the face. Tears spilled down my cheeks. "It's okay," I whispered. "Really. It's..." Anger flared inside, trying to fight off the hopelessness I felt. If Lon knew, why keep me in the dark? And he did know. His guilty expression plainly said it.

Something inside me snapped. Even as the tears kept falling, my fists clenched tightly. "Why did you pretend?" I yelled, voice cracking, vision blurring. "Why lead me on when you knew I wasn't real? How...? How did you know?" I wiped angrily at the tears. When my eyes cleared again Lon was watching me impassively. My temper flared higher. *"Answer me!"*

"I'm sorry," he whispered, tone impassive.

Before I knew what I was doing, I slammed my fist against his tattooed cheek, causing him to stumble. "Sorry doesn't cut it! You lied! To everyone! Does Veija know? Does Crenen?"

He held his cheek, stunned. Slowly his eyes met mine, then he looked away. "Key..."

"No! Shut up! No excuses, no lies. I never want to hear them again!" I backed away from him. "I'm going to tell them. And I'll help them rescue Kirid from Haeon. But never ask me to listen to a Seer again." The tears came back, and a bitter smile crept up my face. "I am glad, at least, that the real Vendaeva does exist." I laughed. "Unless Haeon was lying, too."

Lon released his cheek and straightened. He gazed at me as if he had never seen such a creature in his life. "You need—"

"Honesty?" I suggested.

"You're—"

"Acting like a child?" I supplied. "Yeah, maybe, but at least I know the truth now. At least..." What? There was nothing now. Nothing. "I want to go home."

Lon flinched as if those words hurt him worse than being punched. But he didn't argue. "Do you want to say goodbye to your friends?"

I hesitated, then sighed. "Yeah. I need to explain."

"Very well."

I thought, for a moment, that Lon's voice had cracked, but when I glanced up his face was stony.

The misty plains wavered, then vanished, a forest falling down before me in its place, as if a new backdrop had been lowered. The sun was just rising beyond the distant mountains and the camp hadn't stirred. It took a moment before I realized Lon was holding me up, and I quickly stepped back.

"They will awaken soon," Lon murmured, avoiding my gaze. "Call me when you wish to return home." He turned and headed toward the deeper woods, swallowed in their depths.

I sat back down at the fire, though only embers now glowed in the makeshift pit. I stared down in silence, feeling sickness, grief, and anger squirm in my stomach as I waited for my friends to wake up. I wasn't sure how I could say goodbye, only that I must. After all, I was useless to them.

"Morning, Strange Coward Boy!" Crenen said, giving no regard to those still sleeping. "Up early for change of habit, yeah?"

Startled from my thoughts, I managed to give him a weak smile, which he returned with an especially toothy grin.

"Show some mercy for the half-dead," Chasym mumbled, prying one eye open to attempt a glare from his spot beneath a shady maple pine.

"Shifty Cocky Man only can half-care then, since other half dead and not hear loud noises, yeah?"

"You would be surprised," Jenen's wry voice joined in, "what the dead can hear."

"So settled. No matter how, Shifty Cocky Man still hear loud noises!" No one bothered to point out that his latest argument didn't work with his last one—we knew what he meant.

Veija turned over, talking in her sleep, a smile on her face.

"Tell me you slept," Sasha said from behind me, where she'd slept propped against a rock near Chasym. I turned to view her and noted that her mid-length brown hair was slightly mussed from sleep.

I nodded. "Yeah, a bit."

She sighed and rubbed at her sleepy eyes. "What happened to my feisty patient?".

I smiled dryly. "Sorry. I just...have a lot on my mind."

"Considering Strange Coward Boy have lost memory, we think it would be opposite," Crenen mused, glancing around as he spoke. "Where Tall Strong Jerk?"

"Here, Master," Menen said from overhead.

We all looked up. The tall man was sitting on a branch, one leg dangling beneath him as his eyes watched the rising sun. Slowly he looked down and his eyes caught mine, holding them. I pried my eyes away after a moment, wondering if he overheard Lon and I when we reappeared—assuming we disappeared at all. If so, he probably knew what was coming.

"Get down from tree, Tall Strong Jerk. We hungry like in famish, yeah?" Crenen said.

"Famine," Jenen corrected.

Crenen scowled. "If Sick Nasty Dog knew what we meaning, what point in fixing?" He turned his gaze back to his cousin. "Come now, Tall Strong Jerk."

"Yes, Master." Menen gripped the branch he'd been perched on, shoved off, and swung for a second before dropping gracefully to the ground. He reached into his pocket and pulled out a very familiar fruit. I felt my mouth water as he handed Crenen a bunch of gerani.

I heard soft footsteps behind me and Jenen sat to my right, poking at the dying fire with a long stick. "Did you sleep well?" he asked.

I shrugged. "I don't really remember." I felt his eyes on me and I turned my head toward him. "Yes?"

He continued to watch me wordlessly. Lon once said that through our bond Jenen and I could occasionally feel each other's strong emotions and feelings. So then, it was possible he knew too. A smile tugged at my mouth. He and Menen seemed to understand what others missed entirely.

"Strange Coward Boy want some?" Crenen asked, dangling his breakfast toward me.

I shook my head. "Nah." I took a deep breath. "I need to explain something."

"We all ears," Crenen said, popping a gerani in his mouth. His brow creased. "That is Stupid Nonsense Saying. Who be only all ears?"

I couldn't fight the chuckle. Nor could anyone else—except Jenen (but considering his nature, a brief smile probably constituted as his idea of a laugh). But my mirth died under the weight of my guilt, and I grew serious again. Every eye was on me.

"I got my memories back."

"That's wonderful," Chasym said from his tree trunk, smiling.

"Well, it was," I said, determined to keep on topic, "but I remembered something...and..." I halted.

"We not good at filling in gaps," Crenen complained. "Explain better."

"I'm not Vendaeva." There. I'd said it. Now to expound. "Before Haeon sealed my memories, he told me the truth. His figurehead master Kirid is the real Vendaeva. I'm not sure how, but something happened and...I was used as Kirid's replacement after he vanished. But, I'm not the true Vendaeva. So," I met Crenen's gaze, "I'm going home."

The Yenen clan leader frowned, his eyes glittering darkly. "Certain?"

"Yes. About both. So I'm going home. Lon is sending me."

"Wait, Jase," Chasym said, sitting up straight and wincing. "You've misunderstood. It's not li—"

"Chasym," Lon's sharp voice cut him off. As a whole we turned to see Lon standing at the edge of our clearing. "That's enough."

"But—"

"No," Lon said. "Key is going home. It was his choice. That is final."

I glared at the Seer. Somehow his words made me feel like I was at fault, that I had betrayed everyone. But I didn't belong here. I wasn't even needed.

"Are you really leaving again?" Veija's sweet voice asked. She had woken up.

"Yeah," I said, refusing to meet her gaze. "I need to go back to my own world. I'm not important anymore."

"Don't be a—" Chasym began, but Lon must have shot him a look because he closed his mouth.

"When Strange Coward Boy going home?" Crenen asked, and though his tone was neutral, I felt as if his name for me had never meant anything bad until now. But I wasn't a coward. I *wasn't*.

"Right away," I said softly. "There's no reason to stick around. I think you guys can probably get Kirid. Of course, if he realizes what you're trying to do, he'll help you out. He's...a good person, just a little confused right now."

"Like you?" Chasym muttered.

I bit my lip and stood up. "Well..." I stopped long enough to collect myself before my emotions got the better of me. "Thank you. All of you. For everything. I'm sorry I wasted your time."

"You didn't," Menen said, meeting my eyes, holding them. "Thank you, Key."

I couldn't keep eye contact. Finally I turned to Lon. "Get me out of here," I whispered, too angry with myself to remember my renewed hatred for him.

"Jase," Chasym called. I turned to face him and saw his sad smile. "I'm afraid this is goodbye. I don't plan to return to Earth."

Swallowing hard, I nodded. "Yeah, okay. So long, then."

He tried a smirk. "So long."

"Goodbye, Key," Veija said, rising to give me a hug. Finally she let go and turned away, golden curls quivering, shoulders shaking with silent sobs.

My eyes fell on Jenen, but he was no longer watching me. His head was turned away and he watched the ground. The sick feeling washed over me again and I quickly turned to Sasha.

"You're an idiot," she said flatly, then her face softened, "and I'll...miss that." She really was pretty.

I laughed hollowly. "Gee, thanks." Finally I faced Crenen again. "I still haven't asked that second question."

He raised his hand. "Save it."

"But—"

He smiled seriously. "If you don't come back to Paradise, someday I'll visit you, and you can ask it then."

"Crenen, I'm not coming back."

"Okay." His face was serene.

"Stop it!" I clenched my fists. "Stop putting your trust in me. I—" As fresh tears formed I hurried to Lon's side. "I'm leaving."

The Seer placed his hand on my shoulder. "This journey will be different, Key."

"Just...let's go," I whispered, closing my eyes. I didn't want to see Paradise anymore. But I would miss its people.

26
Crenen's Secret?

As the golden light receded, a scream sounded before me, and my eyes fell on my parents. Mom had fainted and Dad was holding her as he stared at me. I was standing in the exact place I'd been just before I was swept off to Paradise the second time. Feeling a little shaken and disoriented, I stumbled back and sat on the hospital bed to keep from collapsing to the floor.

"Jason?" Dad whispered.

I smiled feebly. "Hey, Dad."

"Y-you..." He gently set my mother down and walked to me, reaching his hand out until he touched my head. Then he ran his fingers down my long hair. "W-what in...?"

I blinked, grasping my shoulder-length locks and tugging. The last time I returned to Earth I hadn't kept my Paradisian appearance. Was this what Lon had meant by a different sort of journey?

"Dad, how long has it been since I vanished?"

It took a moment before he found his voice. "Only a few minutes. Jason, there was a voice booming through the room, and then...you were surrounded by golden light. You disappeared, and...and then you were back. What—what happened? You've changed so much."

Was this Lon's idea of a joke? He brought me back changed, and with only a few seconds' time lapse. How was I supposed to explain it now? I wasn't sure whether to feel gratitude or anger toward the Seer.

"I'll explain in a little while," I said softly. Chances were since my family had always believed my lies, they would ironically not believe the truth. I stood up, feeling stronger now. I began pacing, but then stopped, turning back to see my father's worried, bewildered face. "No, I should explain now." I motioned to the bed. It couldn't hurt to try telling the truth. Much. "Sit. This...could take a while."

I didn't share everything, but there was little I didn't tell my father. I began at the first; starting with Chasym pushing me into the puddle, and ending only when I reached the present. I was in tears as I finished, but while my constant crying irked me I didn't bother to wipe at my face. I was too busy praying he didn't think I was crazy.

After a moment my father looked up. "Up until today I wonder if I could've believed you, especially with your habit of lying, but," he shook his head, "after that voice and all the light, and now," he waved a hand at my general appearance, "I can believe anything." He hesitated, then gathered me up in a hug. "I'm glad you came back. Key."

"Me too," I whispered as I choked on my tears.

I was released from the hospital the next day. Dad had promised to explain to the family what happened to me, and I wished him the best of luck. When morning came and both parents came to pick me up, my father reported the story had been hard for my siblings to digest, but with the witness of both parents, they agreed to hear me out before committing me. That was something anyway.

What really convinced my brothers and sister was my drastic change of appearance. Even they couldn't explain how my hair had grown so long in a six-day hospital stay. As I exited the backseat of the car and walked up to the house, Jacob peeled himself from the porch and ran into my arms.

"We thought you were crazy!" he said, punching my arm. "Why didn't you tell us what happened?"

I smiled. Jacob was just young enough to accept the possibility of my visit to a foreign world, or at least willingly pretend. My gaze trailed up to Jana, who was frowning as she watched me from just inside the front door. As I walked up the steps she came out to greet me, arms folded.

"How are you feeling?" she asked carefully.

I shrugged. "I've felt worse." It wasn't a lie.

She cast her eyes to the ground, then looked up again, biting her lip. "Jase, I'm the one who took your grape."

"Gerani," I corrected automatically, then smiled. "It's okay, sis. You just wanted to help." She stepped aside to let me through, but I didn't move. "Jana." I waited until she looked at me again. "I'm not lying. It really is okay."

A smile touched her lips, tentative but sincere. "Thanks, Key."

My third sibling, Jeremy, was just older than Jacob and several years younger than me. He was sitting at the table when I entered the house, and when he saw me his face lit up. "Hey! So, we're gonna hear all about this Paradise place you think you visited, right?"

I nodded. "Sure." I wanted desperately to forget Paradise, to stop the guilt I felt, but in honor of my friends I would relate the events as many times as it took to etch it permanently into my mind and heart. I would never forget my Paradisian friends again.

That evening, as my family sat at dinner, I related my adventure once again, much more concisely. As I spoke, Jacob and Jeremy laughed at Crenen's antics, while Jana defended Sasha's actions at our first meeting. My brothers tried to give the whole family Crenen-names through our dessert, and then I completed my tale with my time at Kirid's castle and the return of my memories.

"You left?" Jeremy asked in disbelief. "Just because you weren't Vendaeva?"

I stabbed at my empty plate with my fork, frowning. "What could I do? I wasn't needed anymore."

Jeremy and Jacob exchanged looks, but said no more.

Finally I stood. "I'm going to go shower." As I headed for the stairs I heard Jacob ask for more dessert, ending his sentence with a chipper "yeah?"

It seemed Crenen had a fan.

I suspected my family didn't so much believe me, but rather hoped that by playing along they'd help me return to the world of reality, of sanity. My father could not account for the bizarre turn of events at the hospital, but, give him enough time and he'd find some logical explanation.

It would be ludicrous to expect them to throw away reason for fantasy, no matter how appealing, no matter how apparent.

I stepped out of the bathroom in my pajamas, holding a brush in one hand as I walked across the hall to my room. I halted when I saw Jana sitting on my bed.

"What're you doing in here?" I asked as I stepped onto my carpeted floor.

"Let me brush your hair," she said, waving a brush in one hand as she pointed at the floor. "Kneel here."

I obeyed, turning to face the door as my sister started brushing through my honey-colored hair.

"I'll be honest," she said after a moment, "I just can't believe your story. I mean, it's like a fantasy book or something."

"Yeah."

She worked on a tangle and sighed. "Jase, I don't know how you grew your hair out...but...there must be some sort of explanation. Some sort of chemical imbalance, or...or something."

I turned around on my knees, regarding her with a mild smile. "Look." I raised my hands, showing the glimmering burns in the shape of skeleton keys. "They glow in the dark."

She clasped my hands, staring. "Oh, Jase, this is incredible. Did you do this to yourself?" She looked frightened.

My face fell. She thought I was a masochist? "Um, no. I didn't." A thought struck me and I perked up, grinning. "Jana, watch this. Liitae." I was worried it wouldn't work, but the little orb didn't disappoint. My Essence shot out of my palm, circling Jana excitedly as she gasped, and then it plopped down on the bed, pulsing contentedly.

"Unbelievable." Jana tried to touch the sphere, but her finger slipped through its surface. "I don't understand."

"You don't have to understand," I laughed. "You just have to accept it."

My sister was silent for a long while. Finally she looked up, studying my face closely. "If it really is true, what did you leave them for?"

I frowned. "I felt so useless. Besides, my presence made it so Kirid couldn't use his powers at their fullest. I had to leave."

She nodded thoughtfully, pursing her lips together. "Turn around. I'm not done." When I slid back to face the door she continued to brush my hair, but then yanked it hard and gasped loudly. "Jason!"

I jumped to my feet and turned around. "What?" My eyes snapped to Liitae, then back to Jana.

"Y-your ears! They're *pointed*!" As she emphasized the last word, her voice cracked.

My hands flew to my ears and my eyes widened. They weren't just pointed—they were *long*. Long enough to protrude from under my hair, like a Paradisian's. "How?" I gasped. "Liitae." The orb floated up from my mattress. "They're pointed." It bobbed in solemn agreement.

"They weren't like that a minute ago. What does it mean?" Jana asked, her tone a mixture of fear and awe. She stood and ran her finger along my ear until she touched its tip.

I shivered and sank onto the bed. "I wish I knew. If that stupid Seer—!" I clenched my teeth. If Lon thought this was funny—!

Jana sat back down beside me, evidently admiring what she'd probably dubbed my "elf ears."

"I...can't believe this," I moaned. How was I supposed to go out into public with ears like these?

Jana's third gasp was already half expected. "What now?" I whispered, closing my eyes.

"No, you have to open them!"

I shot her a sharp look. "What's wrong with my eyes?"

"They're silver!"

I blinked, then scrambled for the bathroom, flipped on the light and hurried to the mirror. Sure enough, rather than the dull gray they'd always been, my eyes had decided to turn metallic silver. It was strange, staring into those eyes and knowing that they were mine.

"You're turning into Legolas," Jana said from the hallway.

I turned and stared at her, one question on my mind: What the freak?

I could handle the ears (although the ability to hear things better than ever was a bit disconcerting), and I could live with the silver eyes, but when I woke up the next day with long nails I screamed outright and managed to cut myself on accident.

To make matters worse, my entire family was flabbergasted but utterly fascinated by the transformation, after the initial shock. (Jacob started yelling "It *is* real!" as he jumped around the house.) The only thing that consoled me was the knowledge that my family would never hand me over to anyone for scientific experimentation. I hoped.

Four days after my return from Paradise, I finally got some time away from my family, when all but my mother went out on some kind of errand. I retreated to the backyard with Beastie, my dog, where I sat in the swing Dad had made when my siblings and I were younger. I swayed back and forth, staring at my shadow as it shrank and grew beneath my feet, pondering what I was supposed to do now. I'd changed, and not just physically either. My mind worked differently than it had before my adventure and I didn't know if I could cope with this reality anymore. Was it really the best choice, coming back to Earth?

"Even if they don't need your power, is it possible they might need *you*?"

I jumped and looked up at Mom, who had somehow managed to sneak up on me despite my heightened hearing. "Hey," I said glumly.

"Don't you think?" she asked, smiling.

I sighed. "I didn't have to leave, Mom. I chose to."

She sat on the grass before me. "Would it be hard to choose again, then?"

I shrugged. "I dunno." I reached up and traced my pointed ear.

"Jason Sterling," she said. I met her gaze, stomach clenching. Her face softened and she smiled again. "I love you so much."

I blinked. "I...love you, too, Mom."

"Because I love you, I want you to be happy. I want you to be where you feel most like yourself." Her eyes welled with tears. "I don't want you to leave, Jason, but more than that I want you to make the right choice." She stood up and pulled me into a hug. "Please don't hold yourself back from what you want most."

I swallowed hard. "Thanks," I whispered as she released me, smiling.

She ruffled my long hair. "There's someone here to see you."

I felt panic attack my insides. "Mom, no one can see me like this."

She laughed and winked. "Oh, I think this someone will be okay to see." Turning to the house, she beckoned with her hand, and the back door opened.

I stood up sharply, jaw dropping. In the shade nearby I could hear Beastie's fluffy tail thumping excitedly against the ground. "Jenen?"

"You look changed," Jenen said by way of greeting.

"What're you doing here?" I asked.

Jenen glanced at Mom. "You should introduce us, Key," he said flatly.

"Er, right." I cleared my throat. "Mom, this is Jenen. Jenen, this is Lydia Sterling, my mother."

Jenen bowed his head, then straightened, still watching Mom. "I apologize for the intrusion. I would have given you notice if I thought your son would stay put with news of my coming."

Mom smiled. "I completely understand. Please make yourself comfortable. You can stay as long as you want."

"Thank you," Jenen said with the briefest of smiles.

"If you'll excuse me," Mom said, and with that she abandoned me.

We watched her enter the house and then Jenen flicked his metallic gaze back to me. "You've changed drastically. Chasym said there would be some difference, but..." he trailed off, and his eyes found my dog.

I followed his gaze and managed a smile. "This is Beastie. Funny that he seems to like you—usually he barks at strangers." My smile deepened. "Must be your Crenen-name."

Jenen scowled, then looked up from Beastie to gaze at the oak tree towering above us. "I was angry with you." His eyes flicked back to mine.

I nodded, not avoiding eye-contact. "I can't blame you."

He shook his head. "That is beside the point now. You must come back." The urgency in his tone scared me.

"What happened?"

Anger flashed across his face and for a second I thought he would lash out at me, but then he turned away, gritting his fanged teeth. Finally he answered, "It's Crenen."

"What happened?" I repeated.

He seemed to struggle for words, then turned back to face me. "Key, he's dying."

I stared. "What?"

"It's hard to believe, I know." He sighed. "That is the reason he wants me to take over leadership of Yenen Clan. He has the Paradisaical disease. I discovered the truth last night. He isn't aware yet that I know."

I realized my jaw was hanging open again. I shut my mouth. There was no freaking way. There had to be some sort of mistake.

Jenen started pacing. "In the middle of the night I heard him climb out of his hammock, and he and Menen left the clearing. I couldn't sleep so I followed after them. They were arguing about something quietly, and then—Key, Crenen was coughing up blood."

"How...how long has he had the disease?" I asked, feeling lightheaded.

He shook his head. "A long time. The horrible thing about this disease is that it takes forever for the victim to die. Considering how much blood he was vomiting I suspect his case is very advanced. He has been sick at least two years, maybe more."

"Two...?" I stared into space, trying to imagine Crenen having a terminal illness.

"Key, I need you. Please."

I cringed at his tone. "Jenen, you know I'm not—"

"I don't care who or what you think you are; all I know is that the power I've seen you wield is real and you brought me back to life. Please, Key, save my brother too."

My mind was reeling. Crenen's quest for his brother; his determination to force leadership on him; his refusal to believe in Vendaeva at first, followed by his complete support. This was the second part of the question I'd asked Crenen on our way to retrieve Sasha—the part I'd felt he was hiding. It all made sense now. If it didn't, and if this wasn't Jenen telling me, I would've thought it only a ruse to get me back to Paradise. But the truth rang too loudly to ignore.

"But...Jenen, why can't Kirid—?"

"Kirid is Seer Haeon's puppet, not Vendaeva. I do not believe in fate. If you want to be Vendaeva then be Vendaeva.

You know already that you have the power, whether intended or not."

A fire flare within me as he spoke. He was right. No way in heck was I going to let a couple of Seers keep me from what I knew needed doing. I set my jaw and clenched my fists. "Okay, Jenen. Take me back."

"I'm afraid we'll have to wait until the morrow," he said.

I blinked. "Why?" My determination wavered.

"Chasym sent me here and said he would open the portal back to Paradise in the morning. I told him I could convince you in a few moments, but he insisted that just in case I needed more time, he would wait until morning."

Convince me in a few moments? Drat, Jenen was as manipulative as his twin. "Well, since we have to wait 'til then…" I nodded toward the house. "Come on in?"

"Very well."

I must admit I was kind of excited, despite the news Jenen brought. In the few hours we had I would get to show him my world.

"This is what we call a washer. We just load the clothes into it, add soap, and start it up. When it finishes the cycle you take the wet clothes out, stick them in the dryer, and it takes care of the rest."

"And thus laziness reaches new heights," Jenen commented as he opened the dryer door and stuck his head inside. "Machines for cooking, machines for washing dishes, and more machines for cleaning clothes." He closed the door and straightened. "What happens when the machines break down?"

"We get them fixed or buy new ones."

"Expense," Jenen said softly. "No wonder your people are not warriors."

"Hey, we have warriors."

"Do they fight with machines?" he asked.

I shrugged. "Come on, I'll show you my room." Jenen followed me up the stairs. When we entered the bedroom he walked across the plush carpet and approached the bed.

"Go ahead, test it out."

Jenen hesitated and then carefully sat on the mattress. He blinked in surprise. "This is soft."

"Yeah, it's pretty comfortable." I gazed around the room, wondering if I would ever see it again.

"Key."

"Yeah?" (I was convinced that before I met Crenen I hadn't uttered that word even half as much as I did now.)

Jenen kept his eyes averted, staring hard at the wall across from him. "I was coming for you even before I discovered Crenen's secret."

I smiled. "I'm glad." After an awkward moment I broke the silence. "He'll be okay. If there's one person who could cure the disease all on his own it's Crenen."

He laughed softly. "That is certainly true."

"And, somehow, I'll find the cause of the illness."

"The cause?" He looked at me. "You say that strangely."

I sighed, sitting down on the floor. "Before I got my memories back Lon told me the real history of Paradise. The world isn't sick because Kirid and Yenen fought. It's...something else. I have to find out what."

"Lon is a Seer, isn't he." Jenen said. It wasn't really a question. His voice was sure.

"Yep."

"I had suspected as much. When Haeon mentioned that Veija had lost her abilities I knew Crenen wouldn't have settled for that. Lon seemed the only logical explanation. Besides, whether Crenen likes the idea or not, I know him well."

I chuckled, but then grew serious. "Jenen?"

"Yes?"

"What caused the rift between you and Crenen?"

He sighed heavily. "It is not a simple answer."

What was anymore? "I'm a good listener," I assured him.

He continued to stare ahead, eyes unfocused. "We never had an argument, if that is what you want to know. We just...went separate directions."

I arched my brow. "Details, Jenen. Or I'll probe Menen for 'em."

"Your slang does not suit your appearance anymore," Jenen observed.

I shrugged. "My slang was here first." I snapped my fingers in front of his face. "And don't change the subject."

The Paradisian's eyes trailed to the window and he focused on the oak tree visible beyond the glass. "When was I fifteen," Jenen began quietly, "my older brother Yenen died after two years of suffering with the Paradisaical disease."

"Two years?"

Jenen's eyes dropped to the floor. "He couldn't take the pain anymore, and he...killed himself."

I closed my eyes, feeling the pain of his loss. "I'm sorry."

"After that, many more victims fell to the disease, and my mother caught it. By that time it was said there was no cure, and so my father killed her at her own request." He closed his eyes, as if that would block the grief. "My father was murdered only months after the funeral. We never caught the Kirid assassin."

So many tragedies all at once. I shifted, unsure what to say, all too aware of my loud breathing in the somber atmosphere.

"By the time Crenen and I were sixteen we had lost our entire family," he whispered. "Perhaps it was foolish, but I couldn't take anymore. I didn't want to see something happen to Crenen, I didn't want to witness any more death... So I ran away. Before I could leave the Realm of Yenen, Crenen caught me." He paused, pulling his silver shawl closer. "He gave me this shawl. It was my mother's. When I was little she would wrap it around me when I was sick. Crenen told me..." he trailed off, unable to speak.

"'Take this. To remember,'" I whispered, recalling the dream that had occurred so long ago.

Jenen stirred, focusing his metallic eyes on me. "Yes, exactly."

"You said you wanted to forget and he said, 'Not forever. Someday you will want to remember.'" I smiled sadly at his startled expression. "I shared your dream when you were delirious."

"I see," he whispered, then shrugged faintly. "I couldn't understand how Crenen had the strength to go on. I wanted to curl up and die. But when he gave me this shawl, I almost felt my mother's spirit with me. It was easier to go on somehow."

I inhaled. "When...when I thought Haeon had killed all of you, I remember wanting to die. But then I thought of what you guys would do to me if I gave up." I hesitated. "Like when I came back here. That was...stupid."

"You were confused by the two lives you had led, and your judgment was understandably impaired. No one blames you."

"I do." I stood up. "We need to go back." There was no question now. "So what are we waiting for?"

"Chasym?" Jenen suggested flatly.

I turned, grinning at him. "I went back by my own power before, so what's stopping me now? Come on, Jenen. We've got a world to save." I'd said similar words before, but this time I meant them—because I knew where I stood and I knew who I was. I might not be the prophesied Vendaeva, but that wouldn't stop me from doing what it took to make things right. Who cared about some foretold destiny anyway? I 'd once told Haeon I was the only one who wrote my future, and now it was time to show him I meant every single word.

Jenen smiled, showing his sharp teeth. "Yes, we should go."

A cold chuckle sounded from the doorway. "I'm afraid you can't go anywhere."

A shiver shot up my spine. Spinning around, I glared at Haeon's illusory form. "You think you can stop us?"

"No," he said simply, propping himself against the door frame, his vine-green hair trailing down his shoulder. "The only power that can rival Vendaeva's is...hm, let me think." He tapped his chin. "Ah, yes! Vendaeva, naturally." He laughed and waved his slender hand. "Master Kirid?"

Kirid appeared before him, smiling as his eyes rested on me. "Hello, Kiido."

"Kirid, are you really going to fight me?"

He shook his head. "No. Not if you cooperate. Haeon told me that you are very confused, and he assured me this is the only way to help you. Until I've accomplished my mission in Paradise you must stay here, in your world."

"I'm afraid I can't do that," I said.

He shook his head, black hair slipping into his pale face. "You won't have a choice, I'm afraid." His smile grew cold. "Unless you would like your family to suffer an instant but very painful death."

I stepped forward, gritting my teeth. "Kirid, this is stupid. Haeon is lying to you, he's using you as a tool."

Anger flashed across the boy's face. "How dare you, Kiido?" His eyes softened. "I see what you mean, Haeon. He *is* confused." His gray eyes flicked to Jenen. "And I believe this is the one to blame." The air grew cold.

"No, Kirid!" I moved to get in front of Jenen, but found Liitae barring my way. "Liitae, move!" The orb quivered, as though fighting some invisible hand.

"Kill him, Haeon," Kirid said softly.

The Seer stepped forward, raising his hand toward Jenen.

"NO!" I screamed. Lifting my palms, I felt heat flare inside the scars.

"Him or your family? Decide."

I halted, staring in horror. What could I do? I closed my eyes, hanging my head in feigned defeat. *Focus,* I thought silently. Liitae appeared in my hand. "Kick 'em out, Liitae."

Haeon raised his hand to strike, but he didn't get his chance to shine.

Exclamations of surprise came from the door as blinding blue light filled the room. Then all grew silent and Liitae absorbed the light back into himself. Opening my eyes I saw Jenen standing in shock, and then I looked to the door. No one was there. "I didn't think that would work," I said, then looked at Jenen. "Are you okay?"

He turned to me, looking a little dazed. "That...was amazing," he said, and a full-fledged smile broke across his face. "Even if you're not Vendaeva, you might be something better."

I felt my face color, so I focused my eyes on Liitae. "C'mere, little troublemaker," I said. The orb floated slowly toward me, looking dejected (if such as thing is possible to see on a little ball of light). "You need to stop listening to Kirid, 'kay?" It bobbed its understanding. "Good." I sighed and flopped down on the edge of the bed. "I wonder if we can go back to Paradise now, or if the portal has been blocked."

"There is another way through," Jenen said softly.

"Oh yeah?"

He nodded. "Come with me."

Wearily I stood back up and followed him down the stairs and out the back door. He walked past the swing and halted before the irrigation ditch running along the border of our yard.

"I saw this when we conversed earlier," he said, watching with satisfaction as the water moved along in its little bed.

I moaned. "I do not like traveling this way."

"That's too bad," Jenen said as he knelt down and dipped his hand in the water. "It is not too swift, so we will not appear in a river or something of the like."

I blinked. "So, the rapidity of the water decides where in Paradise we appear?"

"I have no idea," he said. "I'm just being careful."

I laughed nervously. "And how do you propose we make this ditch transportable?"

"Not we." He straightened and held my gaze. "You."

"Do I have to?"

"Yes."

I sighed and gazed at the water. "Here goes nothing." I lifted my hand and waited until Liitae perched on my palm. "Well, make it a portal." The orb shot eagerly forward and plunged into the water, making it glow faintly. "Better hurry." I stepped closer and felt hands press against my back, and I was suddenly falling forward with flailing arms. With a splash I felt water seep into my earthly clothes. My Paradisian outfit was being mended by my mother, which meant I'd have to get a new wardrobe—again. But at least this time I wasn't going in a hospital gown.

27
The Muddy Battle?

"Apparently it didn't work."

I opened my eyes and came face to face with a water skipper. "We're still in the ditch?" I asked, blinking to uncross my eyes.

"No. *You're* still in the ditch. I never jumped in."

I groaned. "Jenen, tell me you at least thought that might work, and that you didn't do it because you were bored?"

"I thought it might work and I didn't do it just because I was bored," he repeated boredly. I was less than convinced.

"Liitae?" I said, and felt something under my arm wiggling to break free of the weight and the mud. "Okay, this just sucks," I mumbled. "How're we supposed to go back?"

"Wait until Chasym comes for us?" my companion suggested mildly. "I'm afraid we've tried everything else."

Lifting myself up, I stood in the muddy water, dripping wet. "I guess you're right. If I couldn't open a portal in the water I doubt very much if I can open up that other thing like before."

"That was quite a clear description." Jenen offered me his hand.

I hesitated, gazing at my muddy fingers. "Sure you want me to—?"

"It's fine," he said sharply. "I'm not afraid of getting dirty."

"Oh, good." I raised my other hand and chucked a mud ball. Startled, he didn't move in time. The mud splattered him directly on the forehead and oozed down his face. "I just wanted to be sure," I finished.

He ran his hand along his face, removing the worst of the mud. "Was that for pushing you in?"

I shook my head. "Nah, that wouldn't quite be payback." I reached forward to grab him and pull him in the water, but his reflexes were fast and he dodged at the same time that he kicked out with his leg and sent me sprawling back into the ditch water. "That's it," I growled, grinning as I spat mud from my mouth, "you're dead now."

"You're in no condition to make threats."

I scrambled onto the ditch bank and whipped the long strands of muddy hair from my face, rubbing the muck off my shirt—smearing it horribly—as I smirked at my opponent. "We'll just see about that."

Jenen looked unimpressed, but his eyes widened as he felt Liitae pushing him forcibly from behind. He stumbled forward and I grabbed him, yanking him by the collar into the shallow ditch. As he fell headfirst toward the water I grabbed his shawl and tossed it to a dry bit of grass where it would be safe. I was taking enough of a chance getting Jenen dirty—I didn't want to feel his wrath if his comfort object got wet too.

He came up sputtering, hair hanging in his face as he scrambled up to the other side of the ditch. He turned around and gave me a cold stare. "Did you enjoy that?"

I nodded. "Uh huh."

"Good," he spat muck on the ground, "because that is the last good memory you'll have to take with you."

"Oh ho, I dunno about that," I cackled. "You gotta catch me first."

"Already done," he said, and even as he spoke he vanished from before me. Suddenly hands wrapped themselves around my throat from behind. "You see," he breathed into my ear, "I am very fast." He shoved me to my knees and dunked my head into the murky water. I struggled uselessly until he finally raised my head and allowed me a few short breaths before shoving me under again. Once more he lifted my head and I gasped for air. "Are you sorry?" he asked.

"Y-yes!" I cried out between laughter and coughs. My head shot down toward the water. "Sorry! Sorry!"

"Good." He released me and I fell back into the ditch. Spluttering, I pulled myself from the muck and turned to face Jenen, who was now lying in the grass with a contented smile on his feminine face.

"Man, for being so girly, you can certainly fight." I sat down near him and started wringing out my hair.

"In the defense of women, they often times fight better than men. But I would advise taking back what you said. I'm apt to drown you again should you suggest even once more the idea that I resemble a female." His eyes were closed as he spoke.

I bit down a retort about the scariness of "effeminate male feminists" and snorted instead. "Face it, Jenen, it's the truth. Like how Crenen is the devil incarnate, and Chasym is a chick magnet. You just have a pathetically pretty face."

He sighed. "No one has to keep reminding me. I've been aware of this fact since I was eight."

"Took you that long to see your reflection?"

He rolled over and regarded me flatly. "No. Up until then I hadn't realized it was strange to look this way. After all,

Crenen is my twin—we share the same face, yet no one ever bothers him."

He had a point. Why was it everyone teased Jenen while we never questioned Crenen's masculinity?

Jenen must have read my expression, because he said, "Crenen's personality distracts from his facial features."

It was true, thinking about it. Crenen really did have a feminine face; though he reminded me more of a cat than a woman. "Okay, so, you're more feline than female," I told him.

"That is *slightly* better," Jenen said after a moment.

"Your shawl does throw people off.""

He scowled. "It only tells you that people no longer put their eyes to full use."

I laughed. "No, it just shows how much you look like a girl."

Jenen seemed ready to retort, but stopped himself and turned his eyes to the setting sun. "We best dry off inside. The night's chill is coming."

I got to my feet. "Right. First thing is a shower. Since you're the guest I'll let you clean up first."

Jenen gracefully stood and walked toward the door, stooping down to snatch his shawl on the way. "Good. If you hadn't offered I would be forced to drown you again."

I laughed and then a thought struck me. "Hey, Jenen?"

"Yes?"

"How come the strangeness of my world doesn't have you freaked out?"

Jenen stopped at the door, his hand almost touching the knob. "For one thing, I do not easily 'freak out', and for another, along with our lessons on English, we were occasionally told about the ways of your people—I think, in part, to prepare us for your arrival."

"Who taught you English?"

Jenen opened the door and walked into the house. "A creature named Ter."

Despite the claim that Jenen did not easily freak out, when I showed him how the shower worked he leaped back and hissed at the water shooting from its head. I couldn't keep from laughing while I tried to explain that it wouldn't hurt him. Finally he got near and put his hand under the spout, his eyes narrowed suspiciously.

"It's hot," he said after a minute.

"Yeah, it's called a water heater. We don't have to boil the water before we bathe."

He withdrew his hand and turned to face me. "Only when we're on the move must we boil the water. The Realm of Yenen has several natural hot springs. We plumb these into our homes." That would explain the bath I'd taken in Sasha's domain.

"Just shower. The mud is drying." I pulled out a towel from the linen closet and hung it up. "Use that when you're done."

"Key?" Jenen murmured.

I glanced at him half way out the door. "Yeah?"

"Crenen's condition really doesn't make sense."

I watched him silently, waiting for more.

"His case is advanced, yet he can walk. By the second year the diseased are always bedridden. Something...bothers me. Something about his condition doesn't work."

"Are you certain he has the Paradisaical disease? I mean, he might just be severally injured or something."

He shook his head. "No. The way he was debating with Menen, and his odd behavior; the way he lounged in that hammock—and looking so diligently for me all this time. It all comes down to this answer."

I raised a finger. "Question. Doesn't Crenen *always* lounge?"

"Yes, but...not for so long. He's a very active individual." That was certainly true.

I frowned. "Drat it all, Jenen. There's so many questions. How're we supposed to find the answers with more questions piling up?"

"I wish I knew."

I sighed, deciding to change the subject. "You'd better shower. Hurry."

"All right." He turned his gaze back on the water and I could clearly envision his suspicious glare.

"It won't eat you."

"Of course not."

"It won't drown you either."

He turned, walked to the door, pushed me out, and snapped it shut.

"You're welcome," I growled, trudging across the hall to my room. I closed the door and leaned against it, closing my eyes and sighing wearily as I slid to the floor (leaving muddy smears on the wood behind me). "What a life."

"Jason!"

I shot to my feet, turning to face the door as it opened to reveal my brothers pointing across the hall.

"Jason, who's *that*?" Jacob asked, grinning with a wild light in his eyes.

I looked at Jenen standing just outside the bathroom in the blue pajamas I'd let him borrow; he was watching the boys with an indifferent expression. "That, my friends, is Jenen." I grinned back, proud to show them more of Paradise.

They turned and gawked (maybe it runs in the family).

"You look nothing like the rest of your family," Jenen commented, stepping toward the two boys.

I shrugged dismissively.

"Are you really Jenen?" Jeremy breathed.

Jenen blinked his metallic eyes and nodded once. "Yes."

"Cool!" my brothers exclaimed.

"Did Crenen come, too?" Jacob asked.

"Are you staying forever?" Jeremy said.

"Are you here to take our brother back with you?" Jacob added.

The Paradisian placed a clawed hand on each boy's shoulders and pushed them apart to walk between them. "Your brother and I are leaving in the morning," he answered as he motioned me aside. "You may *shower* now," he added above the joyous exclamations of the two youths.

"Right." As I gathered my pajamas and headed for the bathroom, I glanced back at my brothers and smiled crookedly. "Don't you dare say anything like 'I told you so', got it?"

Jacob laughed. "But we didn't say anything to begin with."

"Yeah," Jeremy piped up. "'Cause we knew you'd go back anyway."

I scoffed. "Sure." I pushed the door closed before they could respond.

"His light is dimmer," Jenen observed.

"How do you know it's a boy?"

We were kneeling on my bed, sometime toward midnight, watching Liitae floating in a circle between us. The bedroom light was off and the orb's glow was the only source of light to see by as we talked.

"Because it's part of your soul," Jenen said flatly.

"Yeah, but I dunno. I mean, you and I share the same soul, so isn't it possible Liitae's a girl because it took after you?"

Jenen raised his hand to strike me, his eyes flashing dangerously.

"Sorry, sorry! Couldn't resist," I laughed.

He lowered his hand and turned his mismatched eyes back to the sphere. "Even when you joke around or become annoyed, its aura does not increase."

"Now it's genderless again."

"Will you please take this seriously?" Jenen said with exasperation.

"Yeah, sorry." I smiled grimly. "Just...someone needs to lighten the mood. I think you're absorbing all Liitae's energy—you sure are mine. Thief."

Jenen sighed, closing his eyes to calm himself. "Listen, Key—Jason. Whatever your name is..."

"It's Key."

"Fine. Key." He opened his eyes. "If, by some chance, Chasym cannot open that portal tomorrow, what will we do? We need a secondary plan."

"Well, we already tried using Liitae. The only thing I got from all that is a mud bath and some protein. That bug was disgusting, by the way."

Jenen's mismatched eyes narrowed, glittering in the vague light cast from below. "*I* may look female, but *you* whine like a little girl," he said crossly. "My point is: it isn't you that has been blocked, it's Liitae."

"Who *is* me, and therefore that blocks my power, don't you think?"

"No." Jenen slid off the bed and started pacing. "Liitae is your Essence, but, if you recall, you summoned another Liitae before him—her—" He moaned. "—It. Anyway—you gave that Essence to me. So, if you can summon multiple Liitaes, they only carry a portion of your power divided between them. The real power still resides within you."

"Makes sense," I murmured, watching Liitae change direction and circle back the other way. "But I'm not certain how to access my powers without Liitae."

"You've done it numerous times."

"Yeah, but it was always on a whim and..." I shrugged. "Worth a shot, I guess."

"More than worth it. It's the only hope we have, should Chasym not come through."

"Yeah, about that. When and where will the portal be?" I asked.

"He said to go to your favorite puddle at dawn," Jenen answered, walking to the half-open window and gazing into the yard.

I blinked. "I'm afraid that puddle doesn't actually exist unless it's raining."

"Then we should hope it rains tomorrow." He turned back to me and the light from the moon cast shadows from the tree across his face. His eyes flashed vibrantly.

"That'd be a miracle in all this heat." But I wouldn't write it off as impossible. It seemed every time I did, it would happen just to prove me wrong.

"I never believed in miracles," Jenen whispered, and a tiny smile stole across his pale face. "Not until recently."

"What changed?" I asked.

He laughed softly. "I decided that not believing hadn't helped at all, so it couldn't hurt any worse to try having a little faith."

I couldn't sleep, and it wasn't because I'd taken residence on the floor. After a long debate about who should sleep where, I convinced Jenen to take the bed. He was angry about it up until he laid down and immediately fell asleep. While he may have procured himself a good mattress in Paradise, he wasn't used to the comforts of modern living.

As the night dragged on I tossed restlessly, turning things over in my mind. I'd reorganized most of my memories and I didn't feel like too much was still missing—at least nothing recent. I found it strange, though, that my childhood seemed a little scattered. It was weird recalling everything from my youth almost as vividly as the past few months, but with that clarity I noticed very large gaps in my memories. Was that when I'd known Chasym before? Why were those memories not there now?

And there was one memory I couldn't place at all. It was there, swimming in my mind, yet I didn't know where to put it in the chronological order of things. It was a woman, smiling kindly, her eyes full of wet tears as her soft, red hair lay in wisps across her pretty face. "I love you," she mouthed, and I could almost hear her angelic voice. Who was she? Why did I know her? And why was that the only memory I could find that had her at all?

The alarm clock started beeping, jolting me. It was almost dawn and I hadn't slept a wink. Throwing my covers aside, getting to my feet anxiously, I walked to the bed and found Jenen still dreaming. I shook him gently.

"Jenen, it's morning. Get up." He seemed the type to always be up with the sun, so I found it rather comical that he was having trouble even stirring. I shook harder.

He moaned softly, turning over and laying on his back. "Did I sleep late?" he muttered, his eyes still closed.

"Yeah, it's nearly noon. We slept in big time." I kept the laughter from my voice.

He shot straight up, brushing his black hair from his face as he blinked sleep away. "Did we really?"

I laughed. "Nope, but you would've if I didn't do that."

He exhaled slowly and brushed me aside so he could get off of the bed. "I will never sleep on that thing again."

"Aw, but it gives you a full night's rest."

"No, it gives one too much rest. You do not need to sleep forever," he grumbled, rubbing his eyes and yawning at the same time. He sat back down on the bed, his eyes half closed.

Chuckling, I began raiding my closet for some clothes. "I wonder if my mom finished fixing up my Paradise stuff yet."

"I'll go see," Jenen mumbled sleepily.

"Uh..." I turned from the closet to find him already gone. I wondered how he would react to a gerani if a mattress did this to him. "Maybe Crenen would know," I mused aloud. Forgetting the closet, I hurried down the stairs in search of my half-dreaming comrade.

I went straight to the kitchen where I found him sitting in a daze at the table, staring at my brothers and sister, who were all bombarding him with questions. My mother was setting a plate of eggs before him. "Eat up," she said kindly.

Torn between laughter and wonderment I walked to the table. "What's everyone doing up so early? It's the weekend."

"Morning, Key," my siblings chorused.

"Yeah, hi, now answer my question."

"We knew you were leaving early so we got up to say goodbye," Jana explained, not tearing her gaze from Jenen's face.

"Okay, enough drooling," I said. "We really need to head out. You awake, Jenen?"

He slowly looked up at me, as though silently asking how he'd gotten down here. I grinned as I grabbed his arm and pulled him to his feet. "We gotta go." I turned to Mom. "Are my clothes ready?"

"Yes, I finished mending them last night," she said. "And your friend's things are clean as well."

"Thank you," Jenen said with a bow of his head.

"No problem," Mom said cheerfully. "You'll find your things in the laundry room, folded on top of the dryer."

"Thanks," I said as I pushed Jenen from the kitchen and down the hall.

"What was I doing in there?" Jenen asked as we entered the laundry room.

"Sleep walking," I explained. I grabbed our clothes piles. "Here." I handed him his things. "You can change in the bathroom. Go ahead and shower again if you want to."

He nodded, turning and heading for the stairs, probably still pondering the strange situation he'd woken up to. I laughed as I followed him up the stairs.

Fully dressed and fed, we stood on the front porch just as the first rays of day peeked over the mountain ridges in the distance. Already it promised to be hot. So much for our rain.

"Jason, take care of yourself, okay?" Mom ordered, her eyes teary. "Your dad wanted to see you off, but...he sends his love."

"No problem," I said, careful to keep my own emotions in check.

"Kill those bad guys," Jeremy said.

"Yeah, and say hi to Crenen for us," Jacob added.

"Sure thing," I winked. "We better hurry."

"Wait!" Jana appeared behind my family, smiling shyly as she gazed at Jenen. "Uh, good luck. Both of you."

Jenen inclined his head. "Farewell."

We headed down the walk, then turned one more time to wave a final goodbye. After that we took the route I'd often used in school.

"Your sister—what was wrong with her?" Jenen asked after a while. "Her face was very red."

I snorted, slapping my hand against my thigh. "Come on, you can't tell me you're that clueless."

He raised an eyebrow. "She...fancied me?"

"Well, yeah." I shrugged. "I don't know why, but some girls tend to be attracted to pretty-boys. I still can't grasp the concept of that since pretty-boys look almost female." I threw him a sidelong glance. "In some cases, *very* female."

He gritted his teeth but said nothing.

"You shouldn't be all that surprised. I mean, Sasha likes you, right?"

He stopped walking. "Sasha? Hardly."

He really *was* clueless. "I'm serious. Crenen was telling me something about it after Sasha slapped you."

"Crenen?" Jenen began walking again. "That makes sense then."

"What?"

"Crenen is the 'clueless' one," Jenen said. "He has been unaware of Sasha's affections since they were children. She's always angry with him because he doesn't seem to get it."

I stared. "Seriously?"

He nodded. "Yes. If I do not miss my guess, the reason she slapped me is because I abandoned my brother and left him to handle everything on his own." He looked thoughtful. "And, being a doctor, she is probably aware of Crenen's condition—another reason she was so angry that I had left."

Maybe I was the clueless one? Me and Crenen both. "I never would've guessed."

"I think in time you would have seen. Everyone except Crenen knows of her feelings for him. She has loved him for years."

"How come he hasn't noticed?"

"It is possible that he does know and that he pretends not to, for her sake."

That was reasonable, I supposed. If he knew he was dying, why give her any cause to think they had a chance? That, or he was just too self-absorbed to care. Who could say with that man?

I smiled dryly. "You know, life is pretty messed up."

"I agree," Jenen said. His shawl shimmered as he stepped from beneath the shade of a tree.

That reminded me. "Hey, Jenen, why did that Sikel guy steal your shawl?"

The Paradisian blinked, but seemed to be used to my abrupt subject changing by now. "I really wish I knew. It's odd, but a lot of people have tried to steal it."

"Silver shawls aren't rare and valuable or something, are they?"

"No. You remember that man I told you about, the one I fought with by the healing pool?"

"Yeah."

"He was after my life *and* the shawl."

I wrinkled my brow as I watched the still trees overhead. "Weird." It really was. Why were so many people out to steal it?

"Yes..." Jenen trailed off. "I assumed that was why Haeon wanted to kill me—and momentarily succeeded. I was convinced of it, until after Lon explained about our bond."

"That explains your lie," I murmured.

"Lie?" Jenen asked.

"Yeah, when I asked why the Kirid people were out to kill you, you said 'I wish I knew'. I sensed that you were lying."

"I see."

We trudged on in silence for a while.

"Still," I finally said, "I do want to know why Haeon is so afraid of our bond. And, more than that, I want to know what Haeon is after. Obviously his motives are different from ours, or we could all join forces to heal Paradise. So, what does *he* want?" What did *both* Seers want? I pictured Lon, his face panicked as he tried to speak through my angry onslaught. What had he been trying to explain?

"Perhaps we should ask Lon?" Jenen said quietly.

"Heh." I forced a smile. "Maybe."

"What is it?" Jenen asked, sensing my hostility.

"Well, I'm a little angry at him right now," I said, and stopped walking. "Here it is. The pothole where the puddle was."

Jenen knelt down to investigate, sliding one claw along the pothole's edge. "Do you find it strange?"

"What?"

"That there is no one around," Jenen whispered, placing his palm in the hole's center.

Blinking, I looked up and noticed that no cars drove by. I might've written it off as just too early for the public, but no dogs were barking, no sprinklers rotated, and the slight breeze had ceased entirely. It was dead quiet.

"What is it?" I whispered back. "What happened?"

"I think we're inside a Seer's domain."

28
Seership?

"Back for more?" I asked, turning and glowering at the form I suddenly felt behind me.

The Seer stood in all his malevolent glory; chin held high, broad shoulders erect, green eyes shimmering with cruelty, green hair trailing and twisting down one shoulder like a vine. "I've come to dispose of the both of you," he said.

"And Kirid will be okay with that?" I asked.

"Master Kirid doesn't have to know I did it." His smile stretched. "Thank you for uncovering the truth about Lon. I did wonder what part he had to play. Now I understand everything—yes, it all makes sense."

"Except your senseless chattering," Jenen remarked, standing up.

"Yeah, I agree," I chimed in, twisting a finger in one ear as if to clean it. "Mind expounding, Delusional Broken Man?"

"Yes, actually," Haeon said, "I do mind." He raised his hand, positioning his fingers like he was about to snap them together. "I despise you, Jason Sterling. You and Jenen have caused nothing but trouble for me from the start. But it will end now." He snapped, and the sound reverberated off invisible walls.

My eyes narrowed as a loud explosion sounded from somewhere beyond the barrier and fire and smoke billowed into the sky.

The Seer's grin turned wicked. "I'm so glad you said your goodbyes to your family already. Otherwise you'd never have had the chance!"

I stared in horror at the smoke until his meaning sank in. They were dead; he'd killed them. He'd destroyed my home, and everyone in it. "No!" I screamed, rushing toward the Seer in a blind rage. Something seized me from behind and I jerked back, stumbling, then turned to find Jenen grasping my wrist.

"Don't," he hissed. "I'm sorry, but no sort of revenge can bring them back now."

"Come now, boy, don't listen to him. How can he dare to talk? He hates the Kirid for what they did to his father. If he came within range of Master Kirid he would do all in his limited power to destroy him."

Jenen held my gaze. "He's right, but you would be there to hold me back, just as I am now."

I swallowed hard. "Jenen." Tears began to fall. "They...they're all..."

"I know," he whispered.

"Oh," Haeon said, startling me. "I missed one. It seems your father escaped. But that is easily remedied." Another snap of his fingers echoed through my ears.

My body trembled and I screamed again, spinning around and tearing my arm from Jenen's grip. "I'll kill you!" I raised my hand. "Liitae!"

"Key, no!" Jenen yelled helplessly as I bolted toward the Seer with nothing else on my mind but his destruction. Just as I reached him, an image flashed across my mind, causing me to stop short.

Haeon scowled in annoyance. "What's wrong, boy? Are you a coward?"

I took a step back, watching him in shock. "You're dying."

He raised his eyebrow. "Don't be ridiculous, I cannot die. I'm immortal."

"No." I shook my head. "You're dying."

Growling, he stepped forward and struck me across the face. "Are you stupid? You lost your only chance to kill me, and now your friend goes next." He raised his hand.

"Liitae! Save Jenen!" I grabbed the Seer's hand and pried his fingers apart before he could snap them. "I won't do what you want me to, Haeon." I smiled bitterly. "I know what you're after and I won't help you get it." Anger still boiled inside of me, smothering most of my pain. *He killed them, he killed them, he killed them,* intoned in my mind, keeping me focused.

"Insolent brat!" he spat as an icicle formed in his free hand. He stabbed my arm and threw me back, blood spurting from the wound. "You can't keep me from my goal."

"I believe," Lon's calm voice echoed across the barrier, "he already has."

Wincing, I sat up and turned to see Lon standing before Jenen, holding Liitae in one slender hand. His red eyes were focused on Haeon, but rather than cold indifference, his eyes were ablaze with hot anger. "This 'insolent brat' has revealed your secret and I know your weakness. Now, Haeon, I will kill you."

"I am not your lesser, Seer Lon," Haeon growled. "I have equal, if not greater power! You think you can destroy me so easily?"

"Yes," Lon answered mildly, though his eyes were still on fire. He released the orb and held his palm up. White fire sprang up from between his fingers. "Farewell, Haeon."

The Seer paled, stepping back. He waved his hand quickly and vanished just as the white flames streaked lightning fast across the barrier. As Haeon disappeared the sky around us wavered, then a cool breeze swept through my hair.

Lon lowered his hand, smirking darkly. "Who is the coward?" he murmured, then his eyes fell on me. He stepped forward and then halted, uncomfortable. "Are you all right?" he asked.

I nodded, feeling numbness creep through my shoulder. It didn't bother me. Nothing did. My family was dead. They were gone.

Jenen stepped around Lon and hurried to my side, kneeling down to examine my arm. "Thank you for protecting me," he whispered.

"That was quick thinking," Lon said, stepping nearer. "You handled the situation very well."

I looked up at him bitterly. "Thanks," I hissed, feeling my rage almost returning.

Jenen placed a hand on my shoulder to calm me as he turned to Lon. "Haeon murdered his family."

I cringed and bowed my head to hide the threatening tears.

"No," Lon said softly. "Key, he didn't kill them."

I jerked my head up to meet his intent gaze. "What?"

"I felt his barrier, so I contained it. He thought he killed them, but it was only an illusion that he felt and which you saw. I'm sorry I had to trick you as well, but I needed to keep Haeon distracted while I worked to get inside his domain." The Seer smiled gently. "They are all fine, including your father."

I trembled. "Really?"

He nodded. "I promise."

Relief washed over me and I finally felt the cold of the icicle. Hissing at the pain pulsing in my shoulder, I glanced at the wound. "Can we take it out?"

"Yes," Jenen said. "It's not too deep, but it will bleed."

"Well, go ahead. I'm ready." I braced myself as he slid the icicle out as carefully as he could. I gritted my teeth against the pain.

"What happened?" Jenen asked as he tossed the bloody icicle aside and pressed my blue wrap over the wound to stop the bleeding.

I watched a car drive past, marveling that it didn't seem to notice us in our strange apparel. "What do you mean?"

"You were going to kill Haeon. What stopped you at the last moment?"

Oh, that. I considered for a moment how I could explain. "He's dying."

"I caught that part," Jenen remarked dryly, dabbing at the wound.

"If I used Liitae to kill him it would have done the exact opposite, kind of like when you shoved that guy into the pool thinking he would die. Liitae would have brought Haeon back to his immortal state, just like when I resurrected you."

Jenen looked startled. "Why is that?"

I hesitated. "Haeon's lost his Seership, just like Veija."

Jenen paused. "Ah. And that made him lose his immortality as well?"

"Yeah," I said with a nod. "Haeon was trying to manipulate me into 'killing' him using Liitae, which would've saved his life."

"How did you discover this?" Jenen asked.

"Well, I saw it, somehow." I shrugged and immediately regretted the action as pain coursed down of my arm. Cringing, I continued, "...I saw me, thrusting the orb into his heart, and then he had tremendous power—and he was going to kill me."

"You saw it?"

"Weird, I know."

"Not really, no," Lon spoke.

Jenen and I looked up at him.

"Just as your appearance is slowly altering, so are your dormant abilities coming to light." Lon reached up and stroked Liitae. "It's only natural for you to See."

I opened my mouth to ask what was so natural about seeing like that when something else hit me. "Hey, how come you can touch my Essence? I mean, I know Jenen can because he's bonded to me, or whatever, but why can you?"

He hesitated. "I'm a Seer," he answered after a moment (either already aware that Jenen knew his secret, or just unconcerned about it).

"Yeah, but that's not the reason," I said. "Explain."

Lon turned his eyes to mine, looking reproachful. "One day I might, but for now I choose not to enlighten you." He cupped Liitae in his hands. "I understand that you wish to return to Paradise with Jenen, am I correct?"

"...Yeah."

"Very well." He waved his hand and the pothole filled with water. "You may return."

"But, Chasym—"

"Is recovering from severe injuries. I would much rather he reserved his strength until it's truly needed," Lon said, smiling coldly.

Jenen helped me stand and we walked to the puddle. As the Seer handed me Liitae, I met his gaze again. "Hey, Lon?"

"Hm?"

"Your eyes are supposed to be gold," I murmured, not sure how I knew that.

He blinked. "Oh?"

"Yeah. Oh, and Lon?"

"Hm?"

"Thanks. For saving my family." It pained me to say it, but this time he deserved my gratitude.

His smile warmed a little. "You are welcome, Key."

Jenen and I stepped into the water. Golden light welled up, enveloping us in a pleasant warmth. For a third time I was going to Paradise.

"I have never gotten wet so often in such little time," Jenen observed as he stood up and waded out of the little pond we'd appeared in. "I think I should blame you."

I coughed up some water and got to my feet. "How do you think I feel? I've been traveling like this a lot longer." I waded through the water after my companion, feeling the pond's murky floor beneath my bare toes.

"True." He sat in the grass and started wringing out his shawl.

I plopped down beside him. "Long hair sucks," I grumbled, brushing my dripping strands aside.

Jenen didn't comment, but lifted his head and gazed at our surroundings. "Why did Lon send us to a swamp?"

"Swamp?" I blinked and then noticed the frogs croaking and the potent scent of putrid water. Looking around I saw that the trees were more like willowy thorn bushes than maple pines and the air was muggy. "Wow, so Paradise isn't just a big forest?"

"Certainly not. We have deserts, mountains, prairies, forests, and so forth."

Thinking back I did recall Sasha asking if I was from the desert. I just never thought about it before. Come to think, I didn't even know how big Paradise was. "So, where are your swamps located?"

"Most of them are at the edge of the forest, just before the desert lands," Jenen answered, going back to drying his shawl. "We were heading this direction en route to rescue you. One must pass through the desert and climb the Hykyae Ridges before entering the Realm of Kirid."

"Is the forest really big?"

"Fairly, but not too extensive."

"Does it take three months to travel through?" I asked.

"No," Jenen said. He arched one slender brow. "Oh, you're wondering why we were not very far along after three months' journey?"

"Yeah."

Jenen sighed. "We were lost."

"Lost."

"Yes, lost." He shook the shawl before him and then spread it out on his other side. "No one is familiar with the terrain after a certain point beyond the Realm of Yenen. Menen was only nine when Yenen Clan headed for the East. Lon has always lived on this side of the land as well. We were lost." His tone was mild.

I stared with narrowed eyes. "You were lost. For three months?"

"No. Four days short of three months. Crenen sent Menen back for some maps."

I slapped my forehead. It took them that long to think of going for maps? "Some rescue operation," I mumbled.

"We didn't have to even try. We could have just gone back home, you know."

I knew. Sighing, I decided to change the topic. "So, Lon sent us to a swamp. Could it be near the others?"

"It is possible."

My shoulder ached more as we sat in contemplation, listening to the buzzing of insects around us. After a few minutes my stomach started growling. "Wha...? I just ate," I muttered.

"You are certainly full of complaints this morning," Jenen commented.

"I'm trying to figure out why I'm hungry again. We just ate."

"You used your powers and discovered a new gift. What did you expect?" Jenen asked as he gathered his hair from his face and started pulling it back with a leather tie. I gawked. As he finished tying it he resembled Crenen more distinctly.

"I dislike that expression very much," Jenen said without looking at me. "Even if you are startled, try not to look like an idiot."

I blinked and turned away, unsure whether to be angry or not.

"That's better. Quizzical expressions are less insulting."

I watched as a frog caught a fly with its long tongue across the pond. It swallowed the insect, and then belched fire. I jumped visibly as I stared. Fire-breathing frogs? "Uh. That's freaky," I said, pointing at the croaking frog.

Jenen glanced at the animal. "The freket?"

I slowly looked at him, eyes narrowed. "*Freket*?"

He nodded. "A fyar freket, more specifically. The waya frekets live near the ocean, never in a swamp."

"What to they do, spit acid?"

Jenen arched a brow. "Of course."

Fire-breathing and acid-spitting freket frogs. Paradise was such a charming place.

We watched the hopping critters for a while, neither speaking. My thoughts drifted to recent revelations as I worked to piece everything together. I was having little luck, as my head felt like it was swimming in a vast sea of hole-filled facts. "Is the Paradisaical disease contagious?" I finally asked, latching onto the first question I could formulate which might have a straight answer.

Jenen stirred. "No. While it is widespread, and eventually all Paradisians will be affected, it can't be caught through contact. And it will not spread to those not of Paradise."

"But how does it spread, then?"

"I'm not sure," Jenen said, frowning. "It has always seemed to strike at random. Though some have their own ideas of how the disease works."

My stomach growled again. After a moment I cast around for something else to say. "I know a person can wipe someone's memories. I've had enough recent experiences to ascertain that, but...is it possible to, well, create memories? False ones? And put them in a person's mind?"

"I'm not sure," Jenen said again. "I've never heard of anyone being able to do that, but I suppose if they can be taken, new ones can be given—in theory."

"Yeah, I think so too." I frowned. "Do you think Lon might know?"

"I would imagine he could answer more questions than most," Jenen said quietly, "but *would* he?"

I laughed. "Yet another question only he can answer, I guess." My smile faded away and I watched the murky pond without really seeing it. "I need to know things but I'm afraid to ask."

Jenen also regarded the water. "The creature who taught me English once said, 'it is not the knowing which makes us afraid, and if we took the time to actually find out that which we desired to know, we would find it isn't so scary as the not knowing to begin with.'"

"Sounds like an interesting fellow."

"He certainly was. I wonder where he went."

"You refer to him as a creature. Why?"

"At first we assumed he was of Earth, and that was why he taught us English, but when Crenen asked him, Ter said he came from a different land but knew English and recognized our need to learn it. He was from a place called Sirinhigha, if I recall." Jenen touched his ear. "He had long ears, but when he was sad or playfully annoyed, they drooped as if sopping wet. While he resembled a small child, he had the wisdom of the ages, and he assured us he was not as young as he looked. He called himself a woodelf, I believe."

I blinked. "Woodelf?" Jana would be thrilled to discover one existed. "And he just up and vanished?"

"Yes. He said he had more places to visit. He was a very cryptic soul more than half the time, and occasionally got his students flustered, but we were all sad to see him leave."

"How old were you when he left?"

"Crenen and I were thirteen. He first appeared one year after Yenen Clan arrived in the Realm of Yenen. I was five at the time."

I wrinkled my brow, thinking back. Finally I gave up. "How old are you now?"

"Nearly twenty-three."

I could see Jenen being twenty-three, but Crenen? He had the mentality of a ten-year-old.

Another thought struck me. "Did this Ter person teach the Kirid, too?"

"I don't know," Jenen said thoughtfully. "I never questioned how they knew English, but I wonder now how they learned it if not through him."

Great. Another unanswerable question.

"Here you are," a familiar voice said from behind us.

We turned our heads and I smiled up at Menen. "Hey," I greeted. "I take it Lon really did plan to reunite us with the group and not leave us stranded with only frogs to live on." Or frogs to live on us. Whichever.

Menen stared for a moment, undoubtedly startled by my altered appearance. Finally he returned my smile, not questioning the change. "We were a little concerned when he said he had sent you to a pond. There are well over a hundred small ponds in the swamps, but he assured me I would find you if I headed due north."

I watched Jenen climb to his feet.

"Yeah, well, I just wish I didn't always have to appear in water," I said.

"I've been assured that it's the easiest way," Menen explained, pulling me to my feet. "You look exhausted."

"When does he not?" Jenen asked curtly.

"A valid point," Menen said, and his eyes fell on my shoulder. "How did this happen?"

"Oh, we had a run-in with Haeon. But it's not deep, so we're good."

"And thus 'we' becomes contagious," Jenen said as he slipped his sopping shawl back around his shoulders.

"Better that than other things," I said, trying to sound optimistic. My shoulder was aching badly. "Let's get back to camp. I feel really—"

"Dirty?" Menen suggested. He was certainly talkative this morning.

"That too," I acknowledged, unable to suppress a smile.

Menen walked between the two of us, probably making sure that he could catch whoever fell first from some sort of injury.

"Hey," I said after a minute, "are we near any healing pools?"

"Do you want to see if you can get more scars to match your palms?" Menen inquired.

"Whatever it looks like, I want you to know I'm not a masochist," I said flatly. "When Lon and I were talking we realized the healing pools might not be toxic anymore. There's a chance I was just different."

"Did I not suggest that?" Jenen muttered under his breath.

"You did," I said helpfully.

As we walked, the thorny trees grew farther apart and the terrain became less swampy. I caught sight of a campfire ahead and smiled despite the pain. Even though I'd left them with the desire never to return, deep inside I'd known I would come back eventually. There was no way I could leave them after everything we'd been through together.

"Key!" Veija cried.

"Hey there," Chasym called from his perch on a large rock. He was looking much less pale. "What took you?"

I scowled. "Where was your portal?"

He grinned sheepishly. "Lon caught me mid summoning. Sorry."

I thought I'd feel awkward as I reunited with them, considering how I'd left, but the shame I felt was only glimpsing. I was too happy being back to notice it much.

"His shoulder is wounded," Menen said from beside me.

Sasha got up from her place on the ground and walked over. "Welcome back," she said softly as she removed the cloth wrapped around my shoulder. She scanned the wound with her icy eyes and frowned. "There's some sort of poison. Nothing serious, but enough to make it hurt."

I could've told her that.

"Poisonous ice shards," Lon said from behind us. "Rather tasteless."

I took a moment to slow my heart rate down. Why was it *always* from behind? Did these people not know how to begin a conversation when facing someone?

"Sit down, Key," Sasha ordered.

Obediently I sat. "Where's Crenen?" I asked, taking in our rather rocky campsite. I had to admit it was refreshing to see a different backdrop.

Menen looked around. "Yes, where did he go?"

Chasym pointed behind him. "He heard a noise, barked for everyone to stay put, and ran off in that direction."

Menen gave a small sigh and trudged off into the swamps after his master.

"Would that we all had such faithful servants," Chasym said ruefully, shaking his head. "It's a pity there aren't more Menens in the world."

"Yeah, but if there were, don't you think there'd have to be more Crenens for them to serve?" I commented. We all paused at the thought and shuddered. Our one encounter with multiple Crenens was not fondly remembered. My stomach growled again, impatient for food. "Got anything to eat?"

Sasha retrieved her bag from beside the large rock and came back, kneeling down and rummaging through it. Finally she pulled out a red fruit that strongly resembling an apple. "This is an apinaikeal."

"Yeah, I discovered them while I lived with Kirid." I snatched it eagerly. While it was not so tasty as gerani, it was much, much better than the slimy fruit Menen had first introduced to me upon my capture. Smiling, I reflected somehow fondly on that. So much had happened since then. It was like another lifetime. I'd changed so much—

—But not enough. I had yet to grow into a man. I determined that the next time Menen set a plate of slimy, smelly, grotesque fruit before me, I would eat it without a single cringe. (Would I ever live to be a man with such a goal?)

"Where did you get the ears?" Sasha inquired.

I blinked, brought back to reality. "They just appeared suddenly. Kind of like my eyes. And..." I raised my claws, flexing them, "*...these*."

She smirked. "Now who's the resident pretty-boy? We might need to vote."

I snorted. "Jenen still wins, no contest." I ignored the holes being burned in the back of my head by the dark figure sitting behind me. He was just going to have to accept his lot in life. I took a bite of my Paradisian apple, savoring the juicy taste.

"I really need haircut," I said.

29
An Overdue Declaration?

My eyes snapped open and I sat up sharply, biting my lip to keep from crying out. My shoulder was *burning* with pain. Sasha had assured me the poison was gone and slowly the ache would subside, but apparently she'd missed something.

Gazing around the campfire I found the sleeping forms of my comrades—all but Menen and Crenen. As evening had progressed into night, there was still no sign of master and servant. The group at large wasn't too bothered since Crenen was always doing mysterious, manipulative things behind our backs, but Jenen and I were a bit wary because of what the twin had discovered about Crenen. Still, we knew Menen would look after him, so we drifted off to sleep after a while.

A fresh stab of pain brought me back to the present, and I winced. Squeezing my shoulder, I hoped pressure would easy the ache. It worked for a minute, but then it flared up, worse than ever. My silver eyes located Sasha, tucked tightly under her blanket to keep out the nighttime chill. I wondered if I should wake her or not. Could she do anything about the pain? Probably not.

Drawing my blanket around my shoulders, I stood up and started pacing. There wasn't much to reflect on, or, at least I didn't want to try and bring everything to the surface of my mind. Instead I just let my feet carry me back and forth while I tried to ignore the pain.

I lost track of time while I walked until I heard voices coming from beyond Chasym's rock perch. Turning, I waited for further sign of our two missing companions.

"...can we do, Master?" The first voice carried to my ears though he spoke softly.

"I wish I knew," Crenen's voice was equally soft.

"What caused this so suddenly?"

Crenen laughed shortly. "Come now, Menen, don't you think it's a bit overdue?" They stepped from the shadows of the trees and boulders, and Crenen's glistening eyes fell on me. "Well, well, other nocturnal creature, yeah?"

Menen watched me in silence.

I shrugged. "I was restless."

A smile flitted across Crenen's face, then vanished. "Might as well tell Strange Coward Boy goings-on, yeah?"

Menen nodded. "He is as much involved as any."

I assumed Menen had already informed his master of my return; that, or Crenen didn't want to raise a fuss. Either way, he'd probably known I would come back anyway. Remembering his serene expression on the day I ran back to Earth, there was no doubt this strange man knew me well. It was disturbing to think he knew me better than I did.

Crenen drew a breath and slowly released it. "Kirid Clan has declared open warfare."

I stiffened. The cold war was over?

He continued. "Your friend, Prince Kirid, sent a declaration to me this afternoon. Apparently Seer Haeon discovered our survival and is rather annoyed." He smiled crookedly. "Shortly after I received the declaration, Hiskii came from the Realm and reported that a remote Yenen village has been demolished. The Kirid took no prisoners."

I closed my eyes, feeling sick. Haeon wanted to distract us. That fact hit me like a blow to the stomach. Up to now he'd been playing a game, holding both clans at bay until he was ready to strike. He created the cold war, and now, when he needed it most, he played his ace: To keep us from achieving our goal, he declared war.

I clenched my teeth and tightened my fists. That...! I couldn't think of a single word to convey my hatred for him strongly enough. Instead I locked my eyes on Crenen. "What's your move going to be?"

The clan leader sighed , shaking his head. "I must defend my people. I will fight."

I slid my gaze to Menen, who was watching his master with a complex expression. I saw worry, blended with anger and seasoned with determination. For his master, friend, cousin, and prince, he would also fight.

A shiver crept up my arms as I watched these two warrior men.

War. I knew about war. I'd glimpsed the attack on Crenen's two encampments. I'd heard Crenen slit the throats of his enemies. I'd watched movies, played games, read history. But something told me this would be different. It was frightening, truly frightening. But it was different. It was real, and it meant something. These men were fighting for a cause, fighting to protect what was theirs. And, I—?

"I will fight, too," I said firmly, again setting my eyes on Crenen.

He watched me for a moment, reading my sincerity. Finally he nodded. "Yes, and I will be glad to have you."

"He'll need proper training," Menen finally spoke.

A smile spread across the leader's face. "You want to, don't you, Menen? Very well, I leave his training to you, to Chasym, and to Jenen. He must be well rounded."

A strange giddiness filled my stomach. I was going to fight, I was going to learn combat. I was going to war. But, above the glee, I felt like a child undertaking a task too great. Could I handle it?

I reflected on Haeon again. Yes, he was dying, so he needed my powers to save his life. But why did that stop him from allowing us to save Paradise? What else was the mad Seer after, that he couldn't ally himself with us? As I pondered, I discovered that my eyes had wandered and I was staring into Chasym's piercing green depths. From his rock he was watching me with a strange smile, very much awake. I recalled now that somewhere before all this, sometime in the distant past, Chasym had been acquainted with Haeon somehow.

Then this man had answers. He even held ones which Lon lacked.

What do you know, Chasym? I wondered. *What aren't you telling us?*

"We going back to Realm of Yenen," Crenen announced in the middle of our breakfast of stale bread, apinaikeal and water.

"Why?" Veija asked, blinking her surprise, fruit hovering near her full lips.

"Crenen's homesick," Chasym supplied, smirking.

"Shifty Cocky Man needing stay shut up or we make insides become outsides, yeah?" Crenen said mildly. "No time for having jokes."

Chasym shut his mouth and watched Crenen with amusement.

"We're at war," Menen supplied. "Kirid declared open assault."

Sasha looked up sharply. "You're certain?"

Crenen nodded. "Before now all attacks been little fights over land and factions," he shrugged, "but now Slimy Bad Kirid got permission from Big Mighty Head to come full-force. We go back to Realm of Yenen, make army, fight back."

"But what about the disease?" Veija asked timidly.

"That will have to wait," Lon said from his place against a jutting boulder. "If the war is one-sided, there will soon be no need to worry about the disease, as everyone will be dead."

Way to say it bluntly.

Veija closed her eyes. "Can we not stop the war?"

Crenen scoffed. "How Seer propose we do that?"

"It cannot be helped," Jenen said from his spot under a shady tree, his eyes intense. "We must go to battle."

I felt Veija's despair and, looking at the rest of the somber group, I saw the same emotion in all of them. The only difference was they knew better than to think there would be peace. For too many years they'd been at odds with Kirid Clan. For too long their families had been killed, their lands stolen, their honor destroyed. They knew Kirid Clan felt the same. Even if they appealed for peace, it wouldn't be granted.

War was inevitable.

"Hurry and eat. We will then break camp and head East," Menen said.

I stood, done eating, and moved to gather my meager gear. As I grabbed my blanket, pain burst in my shoulder and I gasped.

"Key?" Menen asked from above me.

I forced a convincing smile and looked up. "I'm okay. Just moved it wrong; it's still a little sore." I patted my shoulder.

He watched me disbelievingly and finally nodded. "Very well."

I turned away, cringing. *Why?* I wondered. *Why am I always injured?*

We left camp about fifteen minutes later, and I was relieved to see Crenen pull out a map. At least he wasn't the type to insist on finding the way on his own. Or at least, those months of being lost had made him humble enough to consult a map.

Still, three months of being lost? I frowned. Had Haeon ever thought them dead, or had he only pretended while he somehow misled them? It was hard to say. I couldn't read that Seer at all.

"Hello, what's this?" Chasym's nonchalant voice came from ahead. "A little fuzzy, come to die?"

Curious, I moved forward and stood on my toes to see above Chasym's shoulder. As my eyes rested on the creature standing in our path, I blinked in surprise. How long had it been since I'd even thought of the furapintairow? The solitary red fuzzy stared up with its huge pink eyes, not blinking even once. Slowly its pupils slid from studying Chasym and landed on me. Sharp fangs flashed across its face and the fura bounded into the air, high above Chasym's head. Before I had time to think, the fuzzy was upon me, its teeth sinking into my injured arm.

"Key!" several voices yelled as I fell backward, crying out in pain. Squeezing my eyes shut, I swung blindly at my arm and the creature attached to it. I forced my eyes open for a more accurate aim in time to see a flash of purple robes as a booted foot kicked the furapintairow hard in the face. The animal whimpered as it released its hold and rolled several feet away. I sat up, clutching my new injury as I focused on my attacker. It was on its feet (presumably), growling deeply as it stared back at me.

No way. The creature was familiar.

"Let me see," Sasha said, kneeling beside me. She didn't wait for me to offer my arm, but pried my fingers away and examined the wound. "I need to extract the venom."

"There is no venom," I said flatly.

"Don't be ridicul—"

"I'm serious. This fura doesn't have any venom. Isn't that right, little guy?"

"You're kidding," Chasym whispered, stepping near the animal, which growled louder, fur bristling.

"Nope." I grinned. "This is the one I kept alive. Told you it'd survive."

Chasym shook his head, still staring in fascination. "Incredible. You really are something, Jase. I don't know what, but something." He folded his arms, regarding the furapintairow with awe.

"Would someone care to explain?" Sasha asked.

"I sucked the venom from this little guy when it bit me before. I was kind of annoyed with it at the time."

Crenen burst out laughing. "Strange Coward Boy very, very strange, yeah?"

Sasha sat back, shaking her head at the injury. "You must be right. There's no sign at all of the venom."

"I know." I got to my feet, crunching undergrowth, and pushed my sleeve down over the cut. "Let's keep going."

"What about this thing?" Chasym asked, jerking a thumb at the intently staring furapintairow.

I looked down at it, frowning as I considered. "Leave him. If he's that annoyed about what I did he can try following us all the way back to the Realm. Otherwise he can just sit there and growl. He's fairly harmless now."

As we traveled through the day I felt eyes on me. Glancing back every so often I glimpsed its pink eyes protruding from various bushes or behind large trees. Amused,

I said nothing about it. If the fuzzy wanted to kill me, he'd have a difficult time doing so. I wasn't worried.

"We're lost."

"Not lost," Crenen hissed.

"We *are*," Jenen snapped.

"Not lost," Crenen hissed again.

"Guys," I said from my spot on a fairly cool rock, "it's too hot to argue. You're making me tired." We'd stopped for the midday meal just as the heat was too unbearable to go on. Spring had suddenly decided to take on summer weather and so, while the twins could still fight (somehow), no one else had the strength to stop them. (Except Menen, who'd kept the peace until now, but was taking this opportunity to run off and discover our location, because apparently Crenen's map reading skills were lacking.)

"Not care about Strange Coward Boy. Care only that we not lost."

"Stop denying it. You have gotten us *completely* lost," Jenen growled, the heat making him more irritable than normal.

I moaned softly. It was too dang hot. Where did they even find the strength to talk, let alone move? I ran my sleeve across my forehead, wiping the sweat away. Even the shade was ten degrees too warm. I wanted—needed—a bath. Badly.

I attempted to ignore the twins' squabbling but it was too much effort to try. Finally I focused on them, wondering if I could at least put forth the effort to be amused. It seemed far-fetched, but it was something.

How could the heat become this sweltering so quickly?

Somehow the brothers were still pale, for all their anger and for all the heat. Neither had a hint of red to their faces. Did they even feel the change in weather, or was I the only one?

Chasym seemed miserable enough, and the two women were cowering in the shade, but they still didn't seem quite so heated as me. So I was a pansy; I couldn't help that my body wasn't able to handle two hundred degree weather (I was certain that's how hot it was).

A rustling sounded from the bushes behind my coveted rock. I turned wearily and blinked as my eyes collided with those of my stalker. The furapintairow was still determined to kill me, it seemed, but the heat was making its movements slow. Sighing heavily, I shook my head. "I feel for you, little guy."

The furapintairow growled in response even as its tail drooped and its eyes took on a glazed look.

"If you would just give someone else the map, we would be fine," Jenen snapped, bringing my attention away from the creature.

"No. We doing fine reading Stupid Squiggly Map, yeah?"

"Is that why Menen is scouting the area?"

"Tall Strong Jerk crazy like that."

"Just admit you hate being wrong," Chasym muttered under his breath.

I smirked. Even that made me exhausted. Slumping more, I moaned. "Just kill me now," I grumbled at the grueling sun.

"It's merciless," Chasym said woefully, following my gaze.

"Will you two stop it?" Sasha growled from her tiny bit of shade.

Chasym and I looked at her with mild surprise.

"Not you two. *Those* two." She jerked a thumb in the twins' direction.

Jenen and Crenen stopped arguing and threw withering glares at the doctor before returning to their spat.

"No good. While the rest of us suffer with heat stroke, they suffer from sibling rivalry...or something." Chasym heaved a dramatic sigh. "Alas! Will Menen ever return to save us from their energy sapping?"

I turned my focus back on the fura, who'd moved only an inch or two closer. "Almost there," I said, perfectly aware the fuzzy thing was aiming for my injured arm again, but unable to care.

"That thing's still following you?" Chasym asked, rolling onto his stomach to watch the critter's slow progress.

"Apparently. Is this heat normal?"

"No, not at all," the blond answered, brushing aside his sweat-soaked bangs. "I don't want to know what's causing it, but I have a sneaking suspicion we'll find out."

"Typical," I murmured.

The tree providing my shade shook, causing a few shriveled leaves to fall from the branches. Glancing up, I saw Menen perched on the branch, watching the twin brothers argue with a disbelieving face. He jumped to the ground before my rock and turned to me.

"Are you all right, Key?" he asked with concern.

"No. I think the sun is out to kill me, like everything else."

A smile played at his lips and he pulled a few (slightly shriveled) gerani from his pocket. "Here. Eat."

My exhaustion left just long enough for me to snatch the little morsels and stuff them into my mouth.

Chasym sighed from his place on the wilted grass. "I wanted some."

"You'd just pass out," I retorted as I munched.

"True. Then I'd be oblivious to the heat..."

"Oy, if I have to be miserable, so do you."

"Now *they're* going at it," Sasha said to no one in particular.

Menen looked around our pathetic group and his red eyes narrowed. "Where is Lon?"

Now that he mentioned it... "I dunno. He was here." A while back, but I couldn't pinpoint the last time I'd seen him.

"That guy. He's always off doing something mysterious." Chasym made the effort to turn over and sit up, wincing as the sun's rays reached his eyes. "I think he believes he can save Paradise all by himself."

"Mysterious Girly Guy wander off again, get left behind," Crenen said.

"Hey, Menen, did you find out where we are?" I asked, ignoring our would-be guide.

"I have some idea, but there is a high chance I'm wrong. Master, may I see the map?"

Crenen shook his head. "No."

"Oh. Come. On!" I snapped, irritated now. "The Kirid declared war two days ago. If we don't find our way soon there won't be any Realm of Yenen to go back to! Please, give someone else the map, or freaking kill me now."

Crenen stared at me, then shrugged. "'Kay." He pushed past his brother and cousin and offered the map to me. "Have fun reading map, Strange Coward Boy."

There were moments, very long moments, when I hated this man. "I can't read the stupid map."

Menen stepped forward to take it from me, but Crenen grabbed his cousin's arm and shook his head, lopsided ponytail bobbing. "No, Tall Strong Jerk. Let Strange Coward Boy try and read map, yeah?"

I rolled my eyes and unfolded the map, determined to prove how little I knew. I never thought I'd be so willing to show off my ignorance. As my silver eyes fell on the parchment, they widened. What was this? The map showed a large island surrounded by endless sea, but that wasn't the peculiar part. There was no question that the island was in the shape of a key—the exact shape that was burned into both my palms. Looking up sharply, I shoved the map toward Crenen. "This island is Paradise, right?"

The Yenen prince nodded his head, a strange sparkle in his metallic eyes. "Yes, Vendaeva. Paradise Island in shape of key. Make interesting observation, yeah?" He grinned, showing his sharp pearly whites. "We think it being time by now you know just how interesting name like Key really is."

"Are you trying to confuse the boy even more?" Lon's voice came from behind me.

I jumped, turning my head quickly enough to make my neck pop. Ignoring the pain, I stared up into Lon's serious face, wondering just what else this Seer wasn't telling me.

Lon turned from Crenen and rested his eyes on me. "It's true, Paradise is in the shape of a key. But do you really think that has anything to do with a nickname you chose for yourself?"

I nodded firmly. "Yeah, at this point, no question. After all the other seeming coincidences, I'm willing to bet that this is somehow very much connected to the rest of the puzzle." I stood, wobbling from the heat. "Lon, we've gotta find out the whole truth. I need to know how to save Paradise. I've gotta..." I wavered, feeling the heat press in on me like an iron. Spots formed before my eyes and I couldn't breathe. Struggling to stay conscious, I blinked my eyes, trying to shake off the attack. Suddenly my body shifted from overheating to freezing cold. I gasped as the cold stole over my body like I'd plunged into a raging river of near-frozen water. I fell to my knees, hugging myself, still trying to see, though my eyes refused to work.

"Key!"

"What's wrong?"

"Is it heatstroke?"

"He's freezing!"

The urgent voices were clear, but I couldn't respond. I was dying. That knowledge came clearly to my mind. Haeon's ice shard had left a poison and it was killing me now. With this realization came the shrill laughter of Haeon in my head, as if to pronounce his victory. Would it end? Just like this? What could I do?

A sharp pain shot through my injured arm and I cried out.

"Get it off!"

"What's it doing?"

"Move out of the way!"

I shot my hand toward the wound, but my fingers collided with something soft. The furapintairow. Was it trying to kill me too?

No.

All along the creature had been trying to suck the poison from my arm. It had been trying to save me, though I couldn't imagine why.

I felt other arms trying to pull the animal away, but I latched onto its fur, determined to let it suck my blood dry if that's what it took to get the poison out. I was in no state of mind to grasp that either option left me dead.

"Jason, let go of the furapintairow. It's killing you."

"L-leave it," I stammered.

"Don't be an idiot!"

"The heat's gotten to his mind."

"It's killing you, Key. Let go."

I shook my head. The laughter was still present, the voices still loud, but I focused my attention solely on keeping the furapintairow attached to my arm. "Th-thank y-you," I whispered, stroking its fur.

"Don't talk like that."

"Don't give up!"

The creature growled in response, but something told me this growl was more like a rough purr.

Finally my strength waned and I felt hands pull the creature away as the laughter abruptly ceased. Feeling dizzy with blood loss, I allowed myself to fall down into a deep well of nothing, feeling secure in the knowledge that I would wake up again.

Probably.

30
A Firm Resolution?

"Hey, Menen?"

"Hm?"

"What happens when you're injured? Who carries you?" I asked, not bothering to open my eyes. I knew who was carrying me.

"That is exactly the reason I do not allow myself to be injured," he replied. "I would be too large a burden."

"So it has nothing to do with the pain involved, eh?"

I heard Menen chuckle. "That's a good reason, too."

"Thought so." I was silent for a while, allowing my thoughts to drift. Eventually I latched onto one. "How many times does this make it?"

"You being carried?"

"Yeah."

"I'm not sure."

"Just curious." I pried my eyes open and blinked the bleariness away. I was so tired and so nauseated I wondered if I would ever be able to stand again. As the twilight view of the surrounding trees became more clear, a severe headache also made itself apparent. Wincing, I turned my head to see the others walking ahead of us. "Did Lon ever show back up?"

"You don't remember?"

"Uh..." I tried to recall. As was becoming common, the memories clicked into place clear as a bell and I remembered Lon's appearance, along with the map, along with the heatstroke and the furapintairow's bite. "Hey, where's the fuzzy?"

Menen motioned with his head for me to look forward. Turning to see toward the front, I sought out the red creature, and gawked. It was propped backwards on Crenen's shoulder, its tail twitching almost happily as it grinned with razor sharp teeth at everyone following our bizarre leader.

"What the—?"

"Exactly my thought," Menen whispered. "We were going to kill the furapintairow but Crenen stopped us, ordering Sasha to examine your bite. Somehow the furapintairow healed you of the poison."

I chuckled. "So, Crenen saved the Small Red Fuzzy, huh?"

"Yes. He said he will keep the furapintairow until you recover from blood loss. After that, Master Crenen dictated that you may do with the creature what you will."

I rested a hand on my injured shoulder, smiling at my recent good luck. "You know, Menen, there're a lot of things I don't understand and I really do feel inadequate to save Paradise from almost certain doom. But I can't help feeling something out there is doing everything possible to help me, regardless of my faults."

"You are mortal, Key," Menen said quietly. "No one can ask you to remove your faults. At least, not without sounding hypocritical."

"Yeah…" Even the Seers, with their supposed immortality, had succumbed to so-called *mortal greed.* I watched the furry critter turn around on Crenen's shoulder and thought I saw tiny paws beneath the thick fur. After a moment I spoke. "When I was in Paradise the first time, and you guys took me to the Realm of Yenen, Crenen announced to the people that I was Vendaeva. I'm sure they had their hopes up. What's going to happen now?"

"You will prove to them that the only difference between you and their prophesied Vendaeva is that you showed up."

I thought of Kirid and his role in Paradise. I considered Haeon's power over him. Maybe I had shown up, but Kirid didn't truly understand his significance, and that was the only reason he hadn't purged Paradise of its epidemic. For some reason Haeon didn't want Paradise to be healed; that or his agenda must be completed first. Whatever the case, Kirid needed to be rescued from the clutches of his two-faced servant.

"Menen."

"Yes?"

I shifted until I could meet his eyes. "I'm going to save Paradise. I'm going to save everyone in it. I'm going to make this place what it should've been from the beginning. But I'm going to have to do so in my own way. Even if it sounds crazy or completely pointless, I must do it my own way."

The tall man nodded, a slight smile on his face. "I know, Key. We would not expect otherwise."

"Good." I smiled back.

"You and he are not so different."

I blinked. "Me and who?"

"Master Crenen," he replied, his blood-red eyes fixed on his cousin. "I think he recognizes the similarities. I think that is why he wants to help you so badly."

I regarded Crenen's back for a moment. "Menen?"

"Yes?"

"...Never mind." I wanted to know if Crenen had the disease. I wanted to know that more than most anything else. But I was also afraid. I was terrified it would be true. I doubted I could handle the knowledge that my master, leader, and friend was dying. "You're incredible, Menen," I whispered. If it was true, if Crenen really did have the disease, then Menen knew it. And somehow he was able to handle that knowledge without betraying anything.

Menen said nothing.

I listened to the breeze causing the branches above to sway and the leaves to rustle. A bird flew overhead, casting a shadow across my face. A single leaf detached from a branch and danced on the wind. It reminded me of the snowy sky when I was captured by Haeon and rode his dragon to the Kirid lands.

It's dying.

Paradise was dying. Even the spring air was stale. The new leaves were already falling. The birds flew to what they hoped was safer ground, but there was nowhere left to run—or fly. This was the world's final stand—and I was part of it.

"How far to the Realm of Yenen?" I asked after a while.

"Two days more. Lon, it seems, found an old path traveled in ancient days. Traders and merchants used it when times were peaceful. Lon says it will take us directly to the Realm's main gate."

I nodded grimly. Once there, I was to train rigorously with Jenen, Chasym, and Menen. Along with that training, I had something else I must do. War was upon us. I had little time left.

"Menen."

"Yes?" I heard the patient smile in his tone.

"Let me sleep until we get there. So I can fight."

"Yes, Key." There was something different in his voice now. A tone he used only when addressing Crenen in times when the Yenen leader took things seriously. Whatever it was that made him speak so, my shoulders felt suddenly heavy with responsibility.

I was allowed to walk only when we were actually within sight of the wall of trees surrounding the Realm of Yenen. I'd slept clear through the first day with Menen carrying me, but when I attempted to sleep through the second day I found my thoughts too active. Still, Menen held me to my own words and I was forced to stay in his arms until we reached our destination. I was almost completely recovered from blood loss —but trying to tell Tall Strong Jerk that availed me nothing. Apparently he was more stubborn than even Crenen when he felt the need for it.

"Now, Sick Nasty Dog, we at Realm of Yenen. You become leader now, yeah?" Crenen said from the front of our train.

"Give it a rest," Chasym mumbled, turning to face me as he rolled his eyes. "Doesn't he ever get a clue?"

"Not if he doesn't want to," I informed him, grinning.

Jenen didn't even bother responding to his twin. Instead he pressed the knot in the tree and walked through the entrance. Crenen followed after him but reappeared seconds later, walked up to me, and plopped the furapintairow in my arms.

"Care for Small Red Fuzzy in any way wanting, yeah?" he said before hurrying after Jenen again.

I glanced down at the fuzzy, which watched me with those ridiculously huge eyes. "You know, Chasym, these furas bring new meaning to the whole 'pink eye' term."

Chasym snorted. "Paradise has a tendency to take everything a bit literally. In the extreme."

"That's certainly true," I murmured as Menen herded the remainder of our party through the entrance so the Yenen guards could take their posts again. We scrambled through the entrance and the tree fell back into place.

"Key." Sasha's strict voice said from my right. At least she didn't sneak up behind a person.

"Yeah?"

"I want to see you this evening for an examination. You remember where my home is?"

I tapped my temple gently. "They're all in here now, I know where to go. 'Sides, if I get lost, Liitae will guide me." (As if I would get lost going to the grandfather tree.)

She nodded curtly, then stalked off toward the mighty tree, her sleek brown hair bouncing in its ponytail as she went.

Chasym shook his head. "Bit moody, isn't she?"

"She still ignores you somewhat," I said, "but she's getting better."

"Can't say I blame her for what she thinks of me," Chasym said, and I caught a hint of sadness in his voice.

"Prejudice is ignorance," I whispered.

Chasym glanced at me. "What?"

"Huh? Oh. Prejudice is the product of ignorance. When a person is afraid of something they don't know or understand, they shun it. I'm convinced it's the number one cause of prejudice."

Chasym smirked. "There's hope for you yet, kid." He nudged my arm, then headed off, stretching his arms out and yawning.

"Kid?" I followed after him. "C'mon Chazzy, I'm not a kid anymore."

"We shall see," he replied without glancing back.

Menen followed behind us silently.

I stared at the furapintairow. It stared at me. We continued this for about five minutes, until I could take it no more. "Just give me the stupid bowl," I said, wiggling my fingers.

The furapintairow didn't budge.

"Technically gerani were only meant to be consumed by furapintairow," Chasym said between mouthfuls of food. "Of course it's going to protect its dinner."

We were lounging on several plush pillows inside a tree near the center of the Realm. Crenen had left us here before forcing Jenen to follow him somewhere else. Chasym and I were the only ones present anymore.

I raised an eyebrow. "You're telling me this thing is an herbivore?"

"Omnivore, actually."

Like I cared. "Just give me the freaking bowl, fuzzy," I demanded of the creature. It stared at me unblinkingly, its tail wrapped around its meal.

"If you get the bowl back, I want one," Chasym said.

"Why? Wanna go to sleep early or something?"

"You could say that. Just hurry, Key. Your training begins soon and you've yet to get that check up. I doubt Doctor Sasha will like you fighting without her blessed consent."

"With so many bosses in the world," I growled, "who's a person supposed to listen to?" I flicked the furapintairow's tail, causing it to twitch. "Don't make me use Liitae."

"I suggest listening to which ever boss scares you most," the blond man answered before biting into an apinaikeal apple.

"It's a toss up. Crenen and Sasha tie for first place."

"Followed by?"

I flicked the jagged tail again and the furapintairow released the bowl, which I snatched up quickly. I smiled and plucked the plumpest morsel, popping it in my mouth and chewing happily. "Lon."

He snorted. "Good choice."

The furapintairow scuttled toward me, its pastel eyes blinking rapidly.

"Beg," I told it, raising a single gerani in the air.

The creature's tail wagged back and forth. I could almost picture a lolling tongue to match. After several moments of its pathetic begging I relented and tossed the gerani toward it. The furapintairow snatched it up quickly, gnashing its pearly whites as it mutilated the hapless fruit.

"How in the world do the furapintairow climb up trees to get their food?"

"If you think their teeth are razor sharp you've yet to be introduced to their claws," Chasym said as he leaned forward and snatched a gerani from the bowl. "The only thing that makes their teeth more dangerous is the venom. Since you took care of that with this one, he protects himself using his claws."

"Before, you said it would die because I did that."

"Yes, well, furapintairow tend to kill the weaker of their kind."

"So how did this little guy survive?"

Chasym shrugged, tugging on a strand of blond hair hanging in his face as he rolled the gerani around in his other palm. "He probably understood the danger of reuniting with his pack. So he adopted you."

"Adopted me?" I glanced at the creature quizzically. "'Kay…"

"Strange as it seems," Chasym yawned, "he considers you family. Otherwise he wouldn't have removed that ice shard's poison."

I shifted my focus to the Reincarnate. "I noticed something after the poison was sucked away with half my blood. Even though the weather was excruciatingly hot before, it cooled down a lot by the time I went unconscious. So, did I have something to do with the climate, because of Haeon?"

"That's more than likely. Lon speculated that Haeon was attempting to gain control over you, and to resist him you subconsciously attacked with the weather."

"And made all of us suffer in the meantime."

"Everything has its consequences."

I frowned and gazed out the carved window across the room. "Still, even without my subconscious efforts the world is dying." I watched another leaf detach from its branch and descend slowly out of sight.

"Time is wearing down quickly. Paradise is in its final hours."

I turned to watch him. "What happens then, if there are still survivors of the disease?"

Chasym's lip curled in a sardonic smirk. "The world goes mad."

Too many thoughts occupied my mind as I made my way toward Sasha's den with the coming night. As I walked I glanced around at the thousands of ancient trees towering high above me. Most trees were dark and lifeless, while perhaps a few hundred gave off light from inside the carved homes. Were there really so few Yenen clan members left? Was it war or disease which had killed the greater part off? I wasn't sure I wanted to know. And whatever the case, I was determined to change it.

I rounded the tree I'd been occupying and set my eyes on the giant structure standing erect in the center of the Realm. Hundreds of years before these trees had been planted by a race of peaceful Seers, and then been forcibly taken over by They. Now this ancient place was the stronghold of the Yenen; a final protection against death. Still, as strong and formidable as its walls were, something more deadly fell upon its people to destroy them. Walls and bravery couldn't defend against disease.

A sharp gasp to my left broke my train of thought and I turned to see a woman staring at me in awe. After a moment she bowed low and backed away before turning on her heels and running. I stood in silence, blinking in surprise.

"They respect and fear you," Sasha's voice floated across the air. "You represent the fleeting hopes of Paradise, but the people are afraid to hope for much. Too long they've watched their loved ones suffer and die without rhyme or reason. Now you come, as the last of our people face war with more desire to die than to live and wait until the illness claims them. You offer them one last chance at life. But can you save them?" She stepped from the shadows and her striking blue eyes glittered under the perforated light of two full moons.

"I don't know what I can do," I said, "but I know what I *must* do."

"At least you've become honest."

I smiled grimly. "Lies are for people who are too afraid of truth to face it. But I've discovered that lying only makes everything more terrifying." A thought struck me. "How come you knew I always lied?"

"Jenen told me," she answered. "He also said you were changing."

"He told you that after I was captured by Kirid."

She nodded.

I shrugged. "I thought so. You hugged me when I came back. The Sasha I knew before that wouldn't be nearly so friendly. In fact, she'd be downright hostile."

She smiled a little sheepishly. "I was wrong, Key. I'm sorry. I prejudged you and misjudged Chasym. I don't really trust your shapeshifting friend, but if you trust him...I'm willing to give him a chance."

"Thanks." I smiled. It felt good to smile genuinely. Since Menen's respectful tone two days earlier I'd found it hard to be amused by anything. It was an effort to make a joke or enjoy Chasym's sarcastic comebacks. The weight on my shoulders was no less than yesterday, but it was somehow easier to carry. I met Sasha's gaze again after a moment and my smile turned mischievous. "So, how's your relationship with Crenen coming along?"

Her eyes widened and her cheeks turned red. "What are you talking about?"

My grin widened. "C'mon. It's obvious you love him. So," I folded my arms, "what're you going to do about it?"

Her cheeks flushed brighter. "Don't be ridiculous, Key. I do not love Crenen." She tried a scowl. "How could anyone love a man like that?"

"Deny it 'til your heart's content. I don't buy your bluff."

She narrowed her eyes and leaned closer. "I. Do. Not. Love. Crenen."

"That isn't what Jenen said," I laughed.

Sasha stiffened. "He told you…?" She spun on her heels and stalked toward the massive tree. Then she halted and turned around. "Well, are you coming or not?"

I followed after her, grinning from ear to ear. It was possible she would poke and prod painfully for my fun at her expense, but it was worth it.

When we reached the door leading down into her quarters the scent of herbs and spices filled my senses. Had these same smells been here before? At the time I'd been too tired to notice if they were. I walked down the wooden steps and took a seat when she motioned to the chair before the empty fireplace.

Sasha went to a cluttered desk across the room, shifting through papers and studying vials of various liquids. Finally she came back with a small bottle containing a translucent sort of substance. "Take your shirt off." I did as instructed, folding the blue garment on the chair's arm with one hand while Sasha examined my shoulder. She undid the bottle's lid and generously poured the ointment onto my near-absent wound. "This will stop any threat of furapintairow salivary germs creating infections in your injury. Be sure to keep your shoulder clean." She glanced at my appearance. "Along with the rest of you."

"Hey, I appeared in a swamp. That doesn't make it easy to keep clean."

"You've been in the Realm since this morning. What prevented your bathing then?"

"Chasym?" I suggested.

"And you claim he can be trusted," she muttered as she wrapped my arm. "Filth is a cause of disease. Even if you aren't of Paradisian decent, I wonder if you'll still somehow catch the Paradisaical disease because you can't stay clean."

I scowled and thought of a good five retorts, but held my tongue. Her words reminded me of another question, and my mood shifted downward. "Sasha, how quickly is the disease spreading?"

She finished tying the bandage and straightened her back before she answered. "Another clan member falls victim every month. Because it takes several years to die, I have many patients."

"Was Crenen's one of the first cases you treated?" I asked.

Sasha started, tearing her icy eyes from the vial she'd been studying to stare at me. "*What*?"

"Crenen. He has the Paradisaical disease, doesn't he?" I said quietly.

"H-how did y—?" She cut herself off and looked away.

My stomach clenched. So it was true. Jenen had been right; Crenen really did have the disease. "I've known for a while. Sasha, how long has he had it?"

She swallowed hard, still shocked at my knowledge. Finally she spoke. "He's had it since he was sixteen. His case is severe, yet somehow he can stand. Something is different about it, something allows him to stand when he shouldn't be able to even move his eyes by now."

Sixteen years old. And he was now twenty-two. Six years? It was twice as long as any victim had survived the disease, before or since, from what I'd gathered. "Do you have any idea why he's lived twice as long and is twice as healthy as any other victim?"

She shook her head. "I'm completely at a loss. He should be dead… And while he seems healthy outwardly, inside his body is a complete mess. He's in more pain than anyone else I treat, but he refuses to be bedridden."

"It's getting harder for him though," I guessed. "And soon his willpower won't be the master of his body anymore."

"Yes." Sasha's eyes were tearful. "That's why he's so determined to make Jenen Yenen Clan's leader. And that is why he puts his trust in you so fervently. You can save his people, though he doubts *he* can be saved anymore."

A lump was forming in my throat. "Who knows about his condition?" I whispered.

"Just Menen and myself, as far as I know." She knelt before my chair, staring imploringly into my eyes. "Key, please—if you can—save him." Her pleading tone, her trembling hands, and the fear in her eyes struck me deeply.

I took her hands in my own. "I promise you, Sasha, I will do everything in my power to save him." I was resolute. There were no 'what ifs' anymore. Paradise could be saved and I would see it done.

Tears filled her eyes and she bowed her head, lifting one of my hands and kissing it with her soft lips. "Thank you, Key," she whispered as her tears fell onto my hand. "I couldn't bear to lose him, too."

I watched her quietly, unsure how to comfort her. "Too?" I finally asked, hoping it didn't sound insensitive.

She nodded gently. "I have no family of my own. They died when I was nine."

"From the disease?" I asked.

"No," Sasha said, raising her head and staring into the cold hearth. "They were murdered."

I watched her, speechless. What could I say?

Sasha turned from the fireplace to meet my gaze, a sad smile on her pale face. "We were traveling from the Realm of Kirid to join Yenen Clan. My father had argued with Kirid and decided to leave. A few days out, when we were camping for the night, we were attacked by a group of Reincarnates.

"They killed my father first...laughing as..." She closed her eyes, suppressing her emotions. "...as they severed his head from his body." Her icy eyes opened as tears spilled down her face. "Then They violated my mother and finally killed her. The creatures turned to me next, but before they touched me..." her smile returned, "...Lord Yenen appeared, cutting through They effortlessly. Younger Yenen, Crenen and Jenen joined the fight, as well as Menen. It ended quickly. Lord Yenen took me in after that, treating me as his own child."

I returned her smile, though I felt cold inside. Her hatred for They was understandable now. The fact that she was willing to give Chasym a chance was admirable.

"I had a hard time...at first. I didn't want to play with the other children. I didn't want to live. The horror of seeing my parents murdered kept playing over and over in my mind. But Crenen came to my rescue. He didn't like to see me alone, sulking." She laughed softly, staring beyond me, seeing something I couldn't. "He told me I was stupid."

I had trouble seeing how that made her love him.

"He kept yelling as me," she said, "until I finally broke down and started to cry. Then he held me, telling me I had to let it all out now or I would stay broken. He said only after I shed all the tears I had inside would my parents be happy." She wiped at a fresh tear. "I still have a ways to go yet, but someday I will always be able to smile."

I realized my hand was still in hers. Slowly I shifted it, placing it over hers again and squeezing gently. "I'm an idiot," I said.

She gazed up at me inquiringly.

I smiled wryly. "I should've known Crenen wouldn't call you the best unless he meant it completely."

She blinked, then her smile grew fond. "Did he really say that?"

"Scout's honor," I grinned.

She wrinkled her brow, but didn't ask about the phrase. "It's silly," she said instead. "I've always loved Crenen—ever since he called me stupid. He can be immature and very self-centered, but...he's a great man. I do love him."

I watched her thoughtfully, taking in her angular features. She glowed when she spoke of Crenen—not just her eyes, but her whole body was somehow brighter. This wasn't just an infatuation.

Would that glow disappear if Crenen died?

I made a silent vow to never find out.

31
The Means Of Mourning?

All the way back to my quarters in the neighboring tree I reflected on my conversation with Sasha. Any walls still between us had crumbled as she bore her soul to me. The weight had moved from my shoulders to my heart; she trusted me wholly. It was overwhelming to think that while I wasn't the true Vendaeva, the prophesied one, people still believed in me. There was no rhyme or reason for their actions.

They could've gone to rescue Kirid; they could've done any number of different things. Yet they chose me even still. The trust instilled in my powers would *not* be in vain. Somehow, someway, I would find the source of the disease and stop it. My future, and that of everyone else, rested in my hands. I couldn't afford to feel inferior, even for a second. The time for cowardice was over. The time to face my fears head on had come.

It had been six years since Crenen was diagnosed with the disease. He was sixteen when it struck him. Somehow he kept it more contained than the others, yet he was still dying.

As a final act of leadership he was trying to make Jenen take control of Yenen Clan. All of this time I'd hurt my brain trying to figure out what his motive was, what he would gain through my powers. All this time I'd assumed he was acting for himself. While through our journeying I had come to see a deeper, more mature side to this strange being, I'd still been convinced that in the end he had some ulterior, purely selfish motive. All this time I'd been wrong. As Lon had observed, it was childish of me to suppose that everyone put his own personal agenda above all else. I really did need to grow up.

And I would, somehow.

I stopped before the giant tree, gazing at the ancient bark shadowed by numberless leaves so far above my head. As though something whispered to me, beckoning, I slid my newly-clawed fingers against the rough bark, feeling every groove and clinging bit of moss.

A jolt shot up my arm and I stepped back, inhaling sharply. Intrigued, I pressed my palm against the cool trunk and felt my burn mark pulse with tingling warmth. Something wet trickled down my palm and fell to the ground. Pulling my hand slowly from the tree, I examined the liquid on my palm. Blood. My eyes narrowed and I wiped the blood away with my other hand, only to witness more seep slowly forth from my scar.

"What in the world?" I whispered aloud, curious yet afraid. The mysteries of Paradise were unceasing, but rather than feel overwhelmed, I felt more determined to unlock each secret until the full tapestry was revealed. Somehow every question, secret, and motive would be clear, and when that day arrived I would welcome it, no matter what the ending then became.

Pressing my palms together to stop the bleeding, I turned from the trunk and gazed at the shadowed grounds of the clan's protective fortress. The wall of trees seemed impenetrable, especially in the dark. Still, those walls weren't enough to protect Yenen Clan from invasion for long. Haeon was desperate, and desperation led to reckless abandon. No matter the risk, he would move swiftly through our defenses.

An idea I'd formed earlier flitted across my mind. It seemed the only way, but was ludicrous by its own right. Still, it was worth the risk if there was even the slightest chance it would work.

I sprinted to the spiral set of carved stairs leading up toward the residential area of the tree, and ascended. I tried to ignore the silky strands of hair bouncing around my face as I jogged, but I was still not used to its length. Without my memories I'd thought little of my growing hair. Nearly everyone in Paradise had long tresses. But with my former self reestablished I was more than a little self conscious of the mop hanging in my face; the mop I hadn't thought to cut off when I was on Earth because I'd been so distracted by my guilt. I made a mental note now to chop it all off at the first opportunity.

Stepping onto the deck that circled the massive trunk, I walked quietly to the door and pulled it open. Warm light fell on my feet. I scanned the room's comfortable layout quickly.

The furapintairow was sound asleep in a dark corner, its jagged tail laying limply beside it. Chasym was still sprawled across his many pillows, now asleep with a nearly-full bowl of gerani beside him. His attempt to make it through at least half the gerani had apparently failed. Surprise, surprise.

"What did Sasha say?" Menen's smooth voice asked from my right.

Glancing in his direction, I did a double take. Sitting across from him at a finely polished table was a beautiful woman, with deep brown hair woven in several intricate braids, and light pink eyes. She wore a simple black garb, with a pure white shawl draped over her shoulders. A gentle smile tugged at her lips as she watched me.

My eyes slowly slid from studying her, down to the tabletop. Menen's powerful hands were resting over her slender fingers, as if he had been consoling her before I entered. I was certain I was gawking.

"Key."

Blinking to force my gaze off their hands, I pulled my eyes up to meet Menen.

"I have wanted for some time to introduce you to my wife."

If I hadn't been gawking before I certainly was now. Menen was married? In all his traversing of the land with his master I'd naturally assumed he was single. How could anyone have time to get married with a demanding master like Crenen around? This new-found knowledge made me wonder what else I was missing? Chasym loved Veija; Sasha loved Crenen; Menen was married. Who next?

A clear, bright laugh broke me from my whirling thoughts. I focused on the woman who was Menen's wife to find her the source of mirth.

"I am sorry," the woman said after a moment. "I do not make fun. My husband told your expressions were *vonenae havun*—one of a kind." She had a strong accent. "It is good to meet. Menen tells only good of you." She slid one hand from under Menen's, raising it up to me.

I wiped my hand quickly on my dirty clothes to remove any residue of blood and, crossing the room, took her hand, unsure whether to shake or kiss it. Instead, I squeezed it softly and let go. "Well, Menen tends to overlook the bad in people," I replied, smiling crookedly.

"It is also true," she agreed. "Ah! Sorry, I am forgetting to tell my name. It is Nithae."

Her mannerisms were gentle; her voice, angelic; her eyes, kind. This was no normal Paradisian woman. It made sense, though. Menen deserved someone special.

I sought out Menen's gaze and found him regarding me inquiringly. I grinned in response. "How come you never mentioned your wife before?"

"I thought it would be better to meet her first," he answered.

He thought right. If I'd known he was married I would've asked questions, and I doubted Menen would be able to supply the words to describe this woman. It wasn't just her beauty or kindness which struck me so deeply. There was something about her that nearly filled me with delight. She was rather like a walking, talking, breathing gerani. (But I wasn't about to tell Menen that. I knew how he felt about gerani.)

Nithae stood. She was tall and slender—though not nearly so tall as Menen. Still, they were perhaps the most suitable couple I'd ever seen (aside from my parents, of course). "I will be leaving. Menen told you were having lessons in fighting tonight. It grows late. I will not detain you."

"Uh, yeah. Um, see you later?" I hated to see her leave.

"Good night, Key," she said as she slipped past me and walked to the door. She paused, turning her pale eyes to Chasym. "He is so tired. Perhaps let him sleep? He may teach Key fighting tomorrow?"

"Very well," Menen said.

With a graceful incline of her head, she took her leave, slipping wordlessly out the door.

"She is incredible, isn't she?" Menen said softly. "She was not an easy catch."

Somehow I doubted that, considering this was Menen. "She probably went after you." I turned a smirk on him. "I'm right, huh?"

Menen looked startled. "H—?" He cut himself off.

"How did I know? Good question." I shrugged. "So, how come her English isn't as good as yours?"

Menen got to his feet. "To some it came more easily. The older we were when we started to learn, the harder it often was. English came to me more readily than most my age. She speaks it more eloquently than many others. Jenen is the most fluent."

I could definitely see that being the case. "And as for Crenen, you're not sure how quickly he picked it up because he's always pretended not to speak well."

"Exactly."

"Any kids?" I asked, suddenly curious.

He shook his head now. "No. I'm afraid I'm not home often."

"Right." I grew silent, not exactly certain what I was thinking about until another thought hatched. "Hey, how come Sasha and Nithae both have brown hair?"

"Females of our race have dark brown hair. Males have black," he answered.

"Well, guess that disproves the Jenen-being-female theory."

"Yes, but that doesn't stop even Yenen clan members from tormenting him over it," Menen said with a shake of his head. "At least when they're brave enough to venture a joke."

"Can't blame 'em. He *looks* female. I made that mistake when I first came to Paradise. The shawl doesn't help anything." Speaking of which— "Speaking of which, Nithae had a shawl too."

"A shawl is a woman's sign of mourning."

Why did Jenen choose to wear one, then? "Mourning?" I asked quietly. "Nithae is in mourning?"

"She lost her father."

Something tugged at my mind; a gut instinct insisting on being recognized. "Her father?"

Menen nodded seriously. "He was killed in a duel."

I drew breath sharply. "Kirid." Her father was the same Kirid whom Crenen had killed so many months before.

Menen walked to Chasym's sleeping form and stooped down to pick up the bowl of gerani. "When Yenen brought half of Kirid Clan with him, Kirid's daughter, then only eight, came with her mother."

"That's what really started the feud," I whispered. "Kirid's own wife took her daughter and came to the Realm of Yenen." I looked up sharply. "Did she have a younger brother?"

"...Yes," Menen said suspiciously. "Why?"

"What happened to him?"

"He was born shortly after we arrived here. During the battle against the Kirid he and his mother were killed."

The dream of the infant in his dying mother's arms; climbing up the wall; the blackness which swallowed the baby. It all came back in a flood. "Kirid," I whispered.

"Key. You look pale. What's wrong?"

I needed to sit down. Numbly, I walked to the table and took a chair, gazing at the polished wood as I tried to connect everything. "How ironic can you get?" I muttered under my breath. There was so much to fathom. —Something else surfaced. Another question. "How come the mother of Jenen and Crenen wore a shawl?"

"She was also mourning."

"What was she mourning?"

"Lord Kirid was her brother. When we left the Kirid lands, she considered him dead."

That made Nithae and young Kirid the cousins of Crenen and Jenen. "And how do you fit into the family?"

Menen took a seat across from me, his face a mixture of concern and curiosity. "I am the son of Yenen's brother. My father was Jekis. Key, what is wrong?"

At least Menen was connected through different means. "I-I'm just trying to grasp your genealogy. It's definitely fascinating." I forced a smile. "When did Haeon get involved, I wonder?"

"Key."

I took a deep breath, not listening. "Lemme get this straight. So Kirid-Senior married and had two kids—one is Nithae. His wife left him to join Yenen Clan. Kirid-Senior also had a sister, who married Yenen, who is the father of Crenen and Jenen. Your father is the brother of Yenen. Yeah?"

"Yes," Menen said, sounding confused and slightly concerned. "Key?"

I looked up, meeting Menen's red eyes. "I'm really okay. It's just a lot to digest."

"What is?"

I snorted dryly. "Oh, just that you're the brother-in-law of the true Vendaeva."

He blinked. "What?"

"Menen," I leaned forward, "Nithae's little brother didn't die. Haeon stole him away from the battlefield when someone else was trying to protect him. He's the new Kirid leader. He's the one who adopted me as his brother…" I shook my head, feeling dazed. "He was never supposed to stay with the Kirid. If Haeon hadn't stolen him, he would've been raised right here. He would've—"

—Saved everyone.

Before Menen could respond, I felt an arm wrap around my shoulders. Startled, I looked up and saw Chasym smiling down at me.

"Now, now, Jase. No need to get excited. That may be how it *should* have been, but it's not, and you're the only one who can fix the problem now. Right?"

"You really don't sleep, do you?" I remarked, shaking his arm off.

"It's all about catnaps," he said.

There was something different about him. I watched him sit on the ground and continue smiling at us almost creepily. Yellow-blond bangs fell in his yellow-green eyes, and sprawled down his shoulders, vibrant against the black backdrop of his clothing. Thinking back, he'd always worn black in high school, too, though it hadn't seemed that noticeable at the time.

"You're almost recovered then?" I asked, returning to the present.

He nodded brightly. "Feeling better by the minute, actually. Soon I'll be able to hold any form for any period of time again."

"Hurray for you." I really was relieved to see his improvement, but I found my energy nearly depleted.

"Chasym," Menen's voice broke into our conversation, "if you're feeling up to it, shall we begin the training?"

The shapeshifter nodded eagerly. "By all means. I doubt if I can sleep with as much energy as is coursing through my body. Might as well wear some away with a good fight."

"Very well." Menen stood. "Jenen is probably waiting for us."

"If he got away from Crenen, that is," Chasym said, jumping nimbly to his feet. "Ah! I feel so strong again." He turned to me. "Come along, Key! We've some abusing to put you through."

I winced. "Pretend I'm Veija," I moaned. "You wouldn't hurt her."

Chasym laughed and bounded for the door, swinging it open with vigor. "Come, me hearties! Time we teach this lad a thing or two about the unpleasantness of battle!" And he bounded more energetically down the stairs.

"Your friend is very odd," Menen commented as we descended more slowly, losing sight of our companion.

"Don't blame me. I had nothing to do with it."

Jenen was waiting for us, as Menen had predicted, but he wasn't alone. Crenen sat on a stump near a small pond at the edge of a large clearing. The clearing had a few shoots of grass, but most plant life had been trodden down, probably by clan members in training.

"Strange Coward Boy better not die, yeah?" the clan leader taunted, grinning widely.

"I don't plan on it," I retorted, stepping onto the training ground as I spoke. I turned to face my three mentors. "So, uh, who's first?"

"To test your skills we will all fight you. Then, when we have judged your potential, we will choose the safest course to carry out the training," Jenen answered.

I blinked, but nodded firmly. "Bring it on." I had no weapon. Would they give me one?

"Key."

I looked up at Menen.

"This is war. If you do not fight, you will die. Remember that."

"Right." Already I was trembling (whether from excitement or nervousness, I couldn't say).

"Begin," Jenen whispered. Somehow his words echoed loudly in my pointed ears.

All three warriors disappeared. I stepped back instinctively, but the prickling feeling on my neck made me second-guess—too late. Something hard slammed against my back and I stumbled forward as a burst of pain exploded in my spine. I threw my hands out and caught myself before I crumpled to the ground.

Jumping back to my feet, I flinched with pain in my back. I felt the air shift by my right ear and ducked to evade it.

Somehow I succeeded. Straightening, I caught sight of Chasym jumping high into the air above me. I made to step back, only to trip against something. I fell hard, wincing. Glancing under my feet I saw a branch. What rotten timing! Chasym landed before me then, pointing a twig at my face.

"You're dead three times over, Jase. Nice going." A mischievous grin crossed his face. "Still, you survived slightly longer than I'd bet you would. I'm impressed."

"Three times?" I tried to think back. "I dodged once."

"Ah, but tripping counts separately from my finishing move. Trip in battle, and that will be a swift death indeed. First rule: keep your footing." He offered me his hand. I took it and let him haul me to my feet.

"I'll try and remember that," I murmured, glaring at the branch that had been my downfall.

"Now then, Menen will kick things off." Chasym clapped his hands together and rubbed them energetically.

"I will what?" Menen asked.

Chasym turned with his heels. "Sorry. I spent too much time among Earthlings. Let me rephrase: you will train Key first, if you don't mind."

Menen's vibrant eyes caught in the moonlight as his gaze flicked to view me. "That is acceptable. Are you prepared?"

I nodded, feeling my old tendency to lie coming back strong. I wasn't the least bit ready. Still, better to start with Menen. Warrior or not, he would be gentler than the other two. I stepped forward. "Don't I at least get a weapon?"

"We are teaching you how to survive. That means bringing forth what is already available to you. When and if we have more time at a later date, perhaps I will teach you the use of weaponry." Menen shifted his weight and brought his hands, palms forward, to either side of him, his needle-sharp claws facing me. "Live or die. You choose." With that pronouncement, he lunged.

"L-Liitae!" I raised my arms over my face. A flash of blue light sneaked beneath my closed eyes. Silence surrounded me then, but for a distant wind among swaying trees. Slowly I lowered my arms and pried my eyes open; no one stood there. I could only see Crenen sitting on his stump a few yards away. He watched me curiously, as a child witnessing a show with torn emotions. He seemed ready to laugh; yet somehow he appeared bored.

"Got a problem?" I asked him.

He shook his head, a strange smile creeping up his face. "Amuse us, Strange Coward Boy."

My temper flared, but I shoved it down. Something about his tone told me he was asking for something different. He wanted me to show him how *I* fought. The question then was, where did Menen go?

In answer to my wondering, a clawed hand wrapped around my throat. "Dead again," Menen whispered into my pointed ear.

"Wrong." I smirked as I heard Menen hiss sharply in surprise. "Just in time, Liitae." The clawed fingers slipped from my throat and I was free. Spinning on my heels, I turned to face my opponent, who was surrounded completely with blue light, trapped in Liitae's barrier, his claws harmless within its perimeter. "I win."

Menen stared at me unblinkingly, unable to move more than a few inches. After a moment he smiled. "Well done. Your system has many holes yet, but your next two engagements should help to fill them."

"Excellent," Crenen said as he applauded. Quite frankly I wondered how he found our display the least bit entertaining, as my own skills lacked any refinement at all, but whatever floated his boat.

"My turn?" Chasym asked, stepping from among the closer trees to my right side. His long hair was pulled back now, and his outfit, while still black, had less layers for easier movement.

"Already?" I asked. "Menen and I didn't really fight yet."

"We wouldn't want you tiring too fast, eh?" the Reincarnate said with a wink. "Jenen needs his turn, too."

"Don't worry about me. I'm more fit now than I ever was in the past," I said.

"Yes, well," Chasym grinned mischievously, "that's the only reason you won't *die* from exertion."

I opened my mouth to retort but Menen cleared his throat. Turning, I found him still bound by Liitae. "That's enough," I said. The blue glow vanished from around the tall man and a small orb materialized near my palm, looking almost sheepish.

"Thank you," Menen said, raising his hands high above his head in a stretch. "That was not comfortable."

"I bet." I turned back to Chasym. "Okay, so you're next."

"Yeah. Oh, and, Jase?"

"Lemme guess—the same trick won't work twice."

Chasym laughed, tossing his head back as he did. "Right you are. Shall we commence?"

"Definitely." Even as I uttered agreement Chasym disappeared; he was incredibly fast. He would attack from the left, something inside me instructed. Gritting my teeth, I crouched, pivoting on one foot while kicking out with the other. I whipped my hand out from my chest, snatching Chasym's leg. I clutched his pant-leg as I kicked my foot into his knee from the back.

Chasym hissed with surprise, but recovered and snatched my hair, raising his own hand to strike. Moonlight flashed off his nails as they grew into sharp claws. His hand lunged, and I gasped, cringing, braced for the killing blow. For a second I forgot it was only practice.

"*Vais*! *Sa Vais*!" a deep voice cried out.

Chasym's claws halted half an inch from my face, and he glanced up. Releasing a quiet sigh, I glanced at the newcomer.

A middle-aged clan member dashed onto the training grounds and ran to Crenen. He got to his knees, arching his back as he bowed his head low.

"Yes, Loud Urgent Thing?"

The messenger remained unfazed by his master's mocking tones. "*Sa Vais, eyia Rydi veren—*"

"English," Crenen said, glancing to me even as he snapped at his servant.

The man hesitated only a moment. "Prince, the village Rydi has been attacked. Smoke rises higher than the Hierlek. There is no word for help; we think it possible none survive." His accent was heavy but I clung to every word. Another attack?

"Rydi," Chasym mumbled from overhead. "How near is that?"

"One day." Menen's eyes were ablaze with thunderous anger and his stance was tense.

I got to my unsteady feet as Crenen slid from his stump. "Lead." The servant bowed his acknowledgment and stood, turning wordlessly to lead us back toward the Realm's center. As we walked, Jenen joined our group, his mismatched eyes emotionless. Again I realized something was wrong. Aside from our female companions' absence, Lon was the only member of our party missing. Where had he gone now?

32
Into The Wild?

The Hierlek turned out to be a watchtower positioned near the top of the Realm's grandfather tree. It more resembled a tree-house than anything else, which made me nervous; it sat precariously among the frail branches of the ancient perennial. I could swear I felt the wooden structure shudder with every breath of wind. Still, the tree-house stood firm even as our large group filed into the tower after climbing a rope ladder.

Inside, a single guard was posted at one of the round windows opening up to the night air. He turned from his view and bowed low to Crenen. As he straightened, his eyes fell on the rest of our party and I recognized him as Mr. Ugly, the frog-like man who'd tried to kill me the first time I'd come to Paradise; this time he was clean and didn't smell like his Crenen-namesake, Gross Smelly Man. As his gaze fell on me, he bowed respectfully. I tried to ignore the uncomfortable feeling his surprising gesture caused.

"My lord," he said in a much clearer accent than the messenger, "you can see the distant fire from here." I was surprised by his exceptional English skills, as I'd assumed he was among those who refused to learn it for the sake of some unbelievable prophecy.

Crenen stepped across the creaking floorboards and peered out the window, placing his palms on the window's ledge as he poked his head through the circular opening. He sniffed the air and then drew his head back inside. "So, Slimy Bad Kirid come to fight us now." He turned and his glistening eyes fell on me. "Reach here tomorrow. Feel ready for fighting?"

I managed a strained smile. "Nope." There was no sense lying; no amount of skill could keep the fear from my eyes and the nervous crack from my voice.

Crenen nodded solemnly. "Many times Strange Coward Boy nearly die. Many times he somehow make it out fine. Now we test mettle once again, yeah?"

With a nod I stepped closer to the window, setting my silver eyes on the glowing forest in the distance and the thick smoke clouding the night sky. Not far away a bloody battle waged and there was nothing I could do about it. I took a deep breath. "Assuming the battle is over and the Kirid are marching this way, how long?"

"Arrive by evening time, we think," Crenen answered.

I nodded, turning. "I have something to do. I was going to wait until morning, but I don't think there's enough time for that now."

"What's your plan?" Chasym asked.

"I can't tell you. You'd think I was crazy."

"You *are*," Jenen said darkly from the back wall. "Now, share your insanity."

I shook my head. "I just need a map. And some food—preferably gerani."

Crenen slid his sharp eyes from me to the messenger. "Hear? Get supplies." The servant bowed and hurried toward the ladder.

"Do you want someone to go with you?" Chasym asked, looking concerned.

"No. I'll be fine." The faces of my comrades remained unconvinced. "I'm not facing the Kirid, I swear. I just have a little errand to run. Besides, I'll have Liitae with me, and I'll bring the little furapintairow, too. That ought to be plenty of protection, don't you think?"

"Are you certain about bringing the furapintairow?" Menen asked.

"I don't see any harm in it." I grinned. "Don't worry so much. Honestly, I'll be fine. I just have to do this thing before we fight."

"You're certain it will make a difference?" Jenen asked.

"No. But it's better than doing nothing at all." I looked at Crenen. "Can I go?"

He hesitated only a second, perhaps surprised I was asking permission. "We not stop you. Go if wanting."

The servant returned, carrying a pack and a rolled parchment. I took the parchment and unrolled it, scanning the immediate area around the Realm of Yenen. Smiling, I slid the map into the pack. "Okay, I need to get going."

Chasym blocked the doorway. "Is this really all right? What if something happens to you?"

"Nothing can be worse than the threats already hanging over my head. I'll be back by noon, I promise." I could've explained my idea, but the mischievous part of me whispered that it was high time I got my turn to wave secrets in *their* faces and keep the answers all to myself. I brushed past Chasym and descended the rope ladder, the pack swung over my shoulder.

"Take care, Strange Coward Boy. Wouldn't want to bury before battle even happen. That make for pathetic storytelling, yeah?"

I laughed. "Yeah, that'd be rather pathetic."

Chasym poked his head from the tower. "You can't read maps, Jase, remember?"

"Liitae can," I assured him. And with that I blocked any further protests from my ears. Luckily my destination wasn't far away. It could easily be reached by dawn, and I'd be back before noon, should all go well. There was an eighty percent chance I wouldn't come back alive. Still, it was worth the risk if there was even the slightest chance of success.

"And after this," I murmured as I eventually stepped onto solid ground and started running for the tree where my little furapintairow lay sleeping, "I'm coming for you, Kirid."

The forest to the north of the Realm was denser than any I'd yet encountered. It didn't surprise me really; if there was any way to slow me down, this fantastical world would accommodate. It didn't help that my two companions were less than, well, helpful. Liitae kept zooming off ahead and out of view, while the furapintairow stuck to my shoulder and growled at anything that moved (including me). I began to wonder if furapintairow suffered from extreme paranoia.

After several hours of trudging I could hear the taunting of 'Sticky Sap Boy' coming from an invisible Crenen somewhere up in the trees. Of course it was only my imagination, but that didn't stop it from annoying me. Perhaps it was because I knew upon returning to the Realm I'd be faced with the real Crenen, continuing the taunting where his imaginary self left off—if he left off.

"Gotta be getting close by now," I sighed, wiping sweat from my forehead. I was grumpy, but I knew better than to blame this on anyone else; it had been entirely my choice. The biggest issue (even more than the imaginary taunting or sappy trees) was the splitting headache trying to rip my head in two. These blasted, newly pointed ears of mine could hear noises for miles and every croak of a freket frog, coupled with the sharp hum of crickets and the rattle of dry leaves, collided in an orchestra with not a single instrument tuned. It was sheer, chaotic madness.

Amidst the onslaught of forest music I heard another sound. Curious, I pushed forward a branch, peering beyond its reddened leaves, and gazed at the new scene before me: a lake, shimmering crystal clear in the early morning light. There was no real shore around it; the trees merely halted at the water's edge all around the lake. Both my furry companion and I stared, somehow mesmerized by the beauty before us. I wasn't sure why I was so entranced, but something drew me toward the water.

Brushing past the branch and letting it swing back into its original position, I slid my wrapped toes into the very edge of the lake. It was warm as I stepped further into the water, and I smiled contentedly as I waded out toward the center of the pool. I remembered the first time I'd returned to Paradise; the strange light leading me to the water's center. But I'd become distracted. This time I wouldn't let that happen. Whatever was drawing me held answers I desperately sought. The answer, the key to Paradise's condition, lay in the water. On the misty plains in my visions stretched countless puddles. My entrance into Paradise was through puddles. The healing pools, the shimmering lakes—everything was connected by water.

"What are you telling me?" I whispered, staring into the glistening depths. A small glow pulsed beneath the surface and I shivered with its power. "Tell me." I felt something brush against my ear and I jumped, breaking eye contact with the watery sphere. Liitae brushed against me again, as if to make certain I was finally paying attention. "*What*?" The orb bobbed around, insulted. "Sorry, sorry. What is it?"

Liitae circled twice and shot into the sky. After a moment it returned, then headed off into the forest to my left. Moaning, I glanced at the water longingly before wading toward land where I followed my obnoxious companion, hoping this was important enough to drag me from my answers. At least the furapintairow rested silently on my shoulder now, only making its presence known by its claws digging gently into my layered apparel for balance.

I pursued the little ball of light for several minutes, barely keeping it in view until it vanished altogether. My soul or not, the little orb irked me. (Or maybe that's why it irked me.)

By now the sun's rays could only peek through the heavy foliage above, and my vision was impaired. Stumbling through the thick undergrowth, I felt my way around several massive trunks, several times getting thrashed in the face by a stray branch. The minimal light shone on patches of ground here and there, throwing my depth perception off. I started grumbling under my breath as though that would help the situation.

On my shoulder the red fuzzy stiffened and its tail thumped against my back. Alarmed, I stopped mid step and listened to the wild hum of the woods. It took a moment to sort through the various sounds but finally my ears pinpointed the low growl that welled up from all sides. I was surrounded.

"Liitae," I whispered softly. My orb flew back into view and came quickly to my side, hovering on my right. Its light fell across the bramble and I saw a least two-dozen oval-shaped eyes the color of strawberry milk peering up at me unblinkingly. Rows of sharp, glistening teeth grinned beneath the many pairs of eyes. This was it; I'd found the nest of the furapintairow. Now to carry out my plan.

The growling ceased as I stepped into the center of their nest. Bracing myself, I felt deafening silence fall around me but I remained calm, fixing my gaze on the set of pink eyes directly before me. The creature stared back, looking almost intrigued. Perhaps it was the presence of a furapintairow resting on my shoulder which kept the other critters at bay—whatever the reason, I was grateful.

I raised my hands, palms forward, and smiled. "I come with a proposition."

At first I wondered if the furapintairow could understand me. From previous encounters it'd seemed they did, but how well was another matter. As I stood there, holding my breath and bracing myself for whatever came next, a shuffling movement came from the furapintairow before me and then it stepped out of the shadowy bramble and padded forward. Its teeth still gleamed and its eyes still glittered evilly, but I remained motionless, watching.

The creature's large pupils slowly moved from me to the guest on my shoulders. It blinked and my pet responded in like. The first growled; the second copied. More growling welled up from the group and I felt panic start from my toes and quickly climb to my head. We were dead. They sensed the missing venom in my companion and realized it was no longer of their nest. The visible creature lunged, but I sensed it and stepped back just in time to evade its attack. Another furapintairow pounced; I avoided this as well, only to feel another set of razor fangs sink into my leg.

Crying out, I stumbled, catching myself on a branch only to find another fuzzy waiting. It bit into my hand, determined not to let go. More furapintairow struck and I felt the venom begin to take effect with alarming swiftness; I was lightheaded and the world spun and tottered.

I had to do something. Fast.

Liitae was racing around, knocking furapintairow on their backs, revealing tiny paws that waved in their efforts to get back up. One creature pounced—its jaws wide open—and swallowed the orb whole.

"Liitae!"

Staggering back to my feet, ignoring the five creatures clinging to my limbs, I held my palm toward the other furapintairow and felt warmth tingle in my raised hand. *"Stop."*

The nest fell still. The furapintairow released their hold on my body, dropped to the ground, and scuttled back to the ring of fuzzies.

I continued, "Listen up. Whether you like the idea or not, I've come for your help and I freaking expect to get it." I couldn't know if they understood my words, but I was certain they understood my tone.

Dizziness clouded my vision and I nearly stumbled again. I heard shuffling feet. "Don't even think about it," I growled. Clapping a palm to a bite mark on my arm, I focused hard and felt the venom shoot from my wound. I repeated the process several times, shaking my head to keep the lightheadedness away. When I was certain I'd removed all the venom from my body I turned my attention back to the creatures. "Now you know you can't kill me. I'm in charge, got it?"

Stillness resumed in the gloom.

Finally the largest creature padded toward me; its expression almost appeared humble this time, tail drooping and eyes downcast. The animal stopped at my feet and rested its jagged tail's balled tip on my toes. It stared at me with huge eyes, blinking innocently. I wasn't convinced yet, but the furapintairow was making progress. The others stared at their leader until it turned to them and growled. Suddenly submissive, the creatures all came forward and added their fluffy tail-tips to the growing pile covering my feet.

"Ookay." So this meant they would obey, right? Slowly a grin stole over my face. "Excellent. Now, spit Liitae out."

"It's not exactly pleasant getting poisoned," I informed it flatly.

The lead furapintairow sniffed its indignant reply.

"I don't care what you think," I said. "You're the reason we're running late."

After making certain the furapintairow were on my side, I felt unconsciousness take over. Only after several hours of sleep did my full strength return. Now we were on the march: me, Liitae, and over two thousand Small Red Fuzzies. The thunderous pounding of paws boomed through the afternoon sky as we made our way toward the Realm of Yenen.

Liitae was scouting ahead, dodging trees playfully as it went. Occasionally the orb came back and made circling motions to indicate who-knew-what. I only nodded my acceptance of the vague report and carried on my argument with the leader.

"It's really not nice to bite someone before you know his intentions, don't you think?"

The fura grunted reluctantly.

"From now on I want you to give people a chance. This whole misunderstanding has caused excessive superstition among the Paradisians. Do you realize they all seem to think your clan is sacred?" The critter snickered. "It's not funny. I want you to set the record straight just as soon as we reach the Realm, got it?"

The fura sighed and blinked its understanding.

"Good. Now, considering the time you've lost us—"

It sounded in protest.

"—No excuses. Just listen. Because of the time you've lost us we could arrive when when the fighting's already started. If so, separate your, uh, troops into several groups and think of a strategic attack. If we're early, I'll show Crenen what we've got here and he can help plan."

It grunted.

"So, it's settled." I looked up as my orb returned. "There yet?"

It bobbed a shrug.

"Close then?"

It nodded now.

"Good. Any sign of the Kirid yet?"

Liitae shrugged again.

I sighed. "Go there, wait until you can tell for sure, and *then* come back and report."

It jerked forward an inch (probably its attempt at saluting) and shot off again. One day away from people and I was already going mad. By the time I got back I'd be begging to hear even Crenen's broken English.

We trudged through the forest for another twenty or so minutes before my not-so-reliable flying soul reappeared. To save Liitae the trouble of pointless gesticulating, I held up my hand and decided to pose yes-or-no questions.

"Are the Kirid at the Realm?"

It bobbed up and down vigorously.

My stomach clenched. "Are they fighting?"

Again the sphere nodded.

I turned to the furapintairow leader. "Pick up the pace. We need to be there *now*."

It growled its agreement and the entire furapintairow army sped up marginally. I did my best to keep up.

I was panting heavily as we broke through the thicker trees and caught sight of the giant wall of pines protecting the Realm. Or, what was left of it. Heavy smoke streamed into the sky and the loud clash of steel and cries of warriors filled the murky air, while smoldering stumps and felled trees scattered the terrain. A great portion of the formidable wall was completely gone, other parts of it still burning. The fighting clans didn't notice our arrival. I motioned for my Paradise Warriors to stay in the trees as I backed up. No sense blowing our cover just yet.

From the safety of the forest I turned to Liitae and the furapintairow leader, my two Generals. "Okay." I took a moment to slow my racing heart. "As I said before, split into groups. Circle the Realm stealthily and attack where defense is weak. The element of surprise is on our side, so this is our chance to give Crenen the upper hand. Bite, claw, kick—I don't care what you do, just make it count. Oh, and try not to kill *all* of Kirid Clan."

The furapintairow leader gave me a mischievous grin.

"I mean it."

Its grin fell.

"Sulk all you want, but I'm not budging, Grump." I always had a knack for obvious names. "Let's get this show on the road. Grump, divide your men—furapintairow. Liitae, with me. Oh, and," I gave Grump a pointed look, "don't attack until I call for you."

I turned back to the battlefield, blocking the death cries I could easily hear. Swallowing hard, I took a single step. "Good luck," I added, more for my own sake than anything else. I knew the furapintairow could take very good care of themselves, but it was another matter altogether for my own fighting skills. Still, it was far too late for such thoughts now; live or die—those were my only options. And since life sounded much more pleasant than death, I must fight.

The haziness around the Realm kept the scene of battle from my eyes for several yards. As the distance closed, the scent of blood filled my nostrils and I nearly gagged. The smell was something movies and video games hadn't included, probably the first among many realistic horrors I was about to face.

A sharp cry ended abruptly somewhere in the smoke to my right. I halted, terrified. This was like the dream. Here I was, walking in carnage, not yet caught up in the heat of battle; searching. Only this time there was no Vendaeva child crying in his mother's arms. This time I sought my friends—hoping, praying, they were alive.

I caught movement from the corner of my eye. Bracing, I spun to face the enemy, grabbing Liitae as I pivoted, holding the orb out toward the figure. A young Kirid warrior stared at me with terrified eyes; he was covered in soot and blood. His only weapon was a bloodied dagger clutched tightly in a shaking hand. He couldn't be older than fifteen.

I relaxed a little. "Hi there."

His mouth worked but he said nothing.

"Where's your master? I need to find Kirid. I need to stop this war."

I realized too late how he must have interpreted my words. Suddenly he sprang into action, leaping on me with a glistening dagger in hand. On impulse I shoved Liitae into his face as I fell beneath his weight. Landing in a pool of reddish water, I blinked in shock before I recognized the limp body pinning me down. Struggling to lift the boy, I managed to roll him to my left. I sat up, ignoring the sticky mud dripping from my hair as I stared at the motionless boy. I placed a hand on his face; it was already cold. Liitae suddenly appeared by my shoulder, pulsing.

"I-is he…dead?" I whispered, knowing the answer already. Shoving the orb into his brain had finished him instantly. "I…killed him." I should've been horrified, but numbness was creeping into my mind. Later. I could freak out later. Right now another, calmer part of me was telling me to stand and find Crenen.

I stood, knees shaking with terror. I turned from the lifeless form and staggered through the mud, searching desperately for the Yenen prince. The idea of unleashing the furapintairow horrified me now. No more bloodshed. One life lost by my hands had been enough.

I slipped in the mud and barely caught myself. Despite the numbness, I retched. My arms shook, straining to support my weight as tears slid down my face.

The distraction kept me from seeing another Kirid warrior lunge at me until it was too late. Through the corner of my eye I saw the form, and I rose to dodge, slipping again and tumbling backward. The attacker's blade grazed my cheek and then slashed through my right arm.

"Stop!" I screamed, focusing on the warrior before he could try a second assault.

Blood splattered in my face and my heart hammered in my ears. Had I killed him? Panic surged through me and my stomach lurched as I clambered to my feet. My would-be killer lay unmoving on the bloody ground, frozen into place.

"No," I gasped, staring in horror. I hadn't meant to—!

"It's okay, Kiido," a meek voice brushed by my ear, carried on the wind.

I looked up and my eyes fell on the man who looked so like me, standing only feet away. "Kirid, did you—?"

"Yes, I killed him. My warriors were ordered to spare you. Direct violation of that order ends in punishment of death." Kirid smiled pleasantly. "I missed you, Kiido. How have you been?"

"You killed your warrior because he was doing what he thought was right?" I whispered hoarsely.

Kirid's smile fell. "Did I do wrong again?"

The last time I'd seen him he was convinced I was confused, yet now he sought my guidance as a child seeking his mother's view of the world.

I shook my head to clear it, gripping my injured arm tightly. "Kirid, you have to stop this battle. These clans are brothers—you have family here. It's senseless. Stop the fighting. You have the power to end it."

"No." Kirid's gray eyes lost their light. "Haeon says this is the only way to save you, Kiido. I will destroy Yenen Clan and take you back where you belong."

I clenched my fists. "Do you want me to hate you? Do you want to hate yourself? Don't be a fool. Stop the fight. Your father only created this feud because he was hurt and greedy. Don't let it spread like a disease anymore." I trudged quickly to him and placed my hands on his shoulders. "If I go back with you, will you stop this battle?"

"No." Kirid's smile returned, but now his presence was cold and his eyes stared past me. "As long as your friends survive you will not be happy."

"If you kill them I won't be happy!" I gritted my teeth. "Look at me!"

His vacant gaze slowly met my eyes.

"Kirid, I appreciate your care and concern, but please don't do this. I'm not worth death." My hands trembled. "Haeon is using you… Please, Kirid, fight his stranglehold. You have the power to save Paradise. Help me. Maybe if we combine our power we can heal the world together?"

"The world is beyond healing, Kiido," Kirid whispered. "Haeon showed me. The core has disintegrated. It's too late, and it's your fault."

I felt as though I'd been stabbed. "No. That's not true—there's still time. Paradise isn't past saving. And I'll freaking prove it!"

Kirid shook his head. "If you had stayed, maybe we could have discovered how to heal it together, but Paradise is only a bloody battlefield now. Even the trees are bleeding their last. The leaves are dead. Spring can't run its cycle because as each bud blooms, another shrivels."

"Yes, Kirid, but still the bud pushes to live, even just for a single moment." I smiled encouragingly, despite my fear and anger. "Even in the face of death, we struggle for life. Don't you get it, Kirid?" I turned to face the battlefield, hearing the defiant screams of the dying. "Until the last ounce of life leaves our bodies, we will fight. Until the very last soul leaves Paradise, there will still be hope."

"No," Haeon's sickly-smooth voice said from behind me. "No, I'm afraid you're wrong, Jason Sterling. *Dead* wrong."

33
Finally Overcome?

I turned to face the Seer, my expression calm. "Hi again," I said, shoving my trauma down to face my enemy. I was almost grateful for the distraction.

Haeon smiled darkly in reply, saying nothing.

I released my arm, ignoring as its bleeding quickened. "Aren't you the one who should be concerned about death? After all, your time is coming. I can *See* it."

If my words bothered the Seer, he hid it well. His face was impassive. "I hope you've said your farewells, boy. Your friends will die this day." Or maybe I'd really upset him after all.

I tacked on a smirk. "Oh? Did you *foresee* that? I'm disinclined to believe you have, since you're not a real Seer anymore."

"Don't be ridiculous, Kiido. Haeon *is* a Seer," Kirid said, laughing. "How else could he know of you? Or about your bond with Jenen? Think carefully. Who has deceived you?"

"I'm sure Haeon has his ways of knowing, but I know he's not a Seer. Not anymore. He lost that right by doing something stupid." I folded my arms.

"Something stupid? You know not of what you speak," Haeon scoffed.

"But you admit you lost your Seership," I said flatly.

His face darkened more. "Learn your place, Jason St—"

"I know my place, *Hae-Hae,*" I interrupted. "But obviously you forgot yours. You've been demoted, O Seerless One. For some reason you felt justified enough to rewrite the future, but things didn't go as planned because, suddenly, you're as good as dead. So much for those immortal desires. Your sacrifice was wasted because you won't live long enough to see it done."

"You have no idea what—!"

I laughed, cutting him off. I'd hit a nerve.

Pain shot through my head as images flashed before my vision; mostly of things I couldn't comprehend. I saw Chasym flick among the images, though what part he had to play in Haeon's past was unclear. Then the images slowed down and I saw Haeon kneeling before Chasym, his hands clasped together as he pleaded. The blond man loomed before him, his expression angry. As Haeon cowered, bowing his head, a smile crept across his face. The distant screams of a wailing infant rang in my ears. I couldn't grasp what this vision meant, but the echo it left made me feel both ill and enraged.

"Kiido! Stop it!" Kirid's voice cried, its closeness causing my ears to throb.

As the vision faded away, I found myself grasping Haeon by the throat. He was struggling, but something kept him firmly latched in my hands. A faint blue aura glowed around his body. Liitae was holding him bound. Haeon's eyes were wide with fear.

"Kiido!" Kirid cried again.

"He deserves to die," I growled, anger burning in my stomach.

"You said it's bad to kill," the boy said. "Was that a lie?"

"Some people have to die, Kirid," I said, squeezing harder. "Sometimes it's the only way to stop bad things from happening." Besides, wasn't I already a murderer?

A familiar voice chimed in. "That doesn't mean *you* have the right to do it." My heart stopped for an instant. Turning my head slightly, I saw Lon standing a few feet away; his red eyes danced with the flames rising high above the Realm, but he stood serenely. "Release him, Key."

I gritted my teeth, anger still searing inside. "No. He's done too much. If I let him go he'll cause more pain."

"Release him," he said again.

Haeon gagged and dug his claws into my wrists desperately. With the pain came the realization of what I intended to do. Horrified, I pried my hands from his throat and backed up, stumbling in the mud. Suddenly Lon was behind Haeon, jerking the man's hands behind his back.

"You're now our prisoner, Haeon," Lon whispered. "Liitae holds your powers captive, so don't try anything foolish." Lon's eyes turned to Kirid. "You will do as we say, or I cannot guarantee the safety of your servant."

Kirid's eyes were wide with fear. He nodded. "Don't hurt him."

"As long as both of you behave, there will be no reason to harm anyone," Lon said. His eyes flicked to me. "Are you all right?"

I started to nod, but changed mid motion and shook my head instead.

Lon's expression softened. "Seeing can sometimes blind us. Just be grateful you're more sensible than you think."

I nodded soberly.

"Now, *Kirid,*" Lon said, "call off your hounds." Kirid blinked in bewilderment, causing Lon's frown to falter. He was serious again very quickly. "Let me rephrase that. Stop your army from attacking. Enough blood has been spilled."

At his words I remembered the battlefield, and I turned to view my surroundings. Bodies littered the ground, blood clouding inside muddy puddles. The desperate cries of dying warriors filled my ears. In the haze I could make out the forms of many Paradisians still in close combat; the thunder of death rang loudly in the smoky sky, blending with terrible screams.

War. It was something I never wanted to see again.

Kirid raised his trembling hand to the sky, emitting a blueish glow. "Halt," he whispered. A rippling tremor pulsed through the air; I felt a strong desire to stop, to just stand still, but I knew better than to succumb to the sensation. Glancing at Lon, I saw his face showed no signs of submission either. The sounds of battle faded as Kirid and Yenen warriors alike stopped fighting, gazing around them in a daze.

"Most of the fighting will have ended," Kirid said quietly.

"Very good."

"Lon, do you know if the others are okay?" I asked.

"I haven't seen all of them," he answered, still holding Haeon prisoner. "Chasym is fine—but you could easily guess that."

The guy with the incurable penchant for living against all odds? Yeah, I could definitely guess that.

"Veija is safe. The others—I'm unsure of their present condition," Lon said.

I glanced at Haeon, held both by Liitae and Lon. Raising my palm, I silently urged another Liitae forth. The new orb bounded from my hand and shot toward the sky. Sighing patiently, I waited for the glowing ball to come back down.

Finally it complied with my wishes and settled near my shoulder.

"I'll be back," I said, heading off in a random direction.

"Be careful," Lon said.

I waved casually, assuring him I was feeling up to the task. Haeon had been captured; all other threats seemed minuscule by comparison. Trudging through the muck, I made sure to steer clear of the carnage at my feet. The smell of blood was heavy, my glances at the ground made my stomach lurch, but something about this scene was familiar—too familiar. Like I'd been here before.

It wasn't the dream about Kirid that made it feel familiar either. Something else...something deep in my subconscious... made the scene bearable, yet all the more frightening. Even before I would glance down at the face of some fallen fighter I knew it in detail. This bloody battlefield—I'd seen it before. And, somehow, it felt like home.

The images pushed forward in my mind once again. Tumbling words rushed like waterfalls; faces, all familiar, pummeled my vision. I cringed, falling to my knees, sinking deep into the mud as I covered my face. What was happening? Why did I have to see these confusing scenes? I wanted it to stop—wanted it to all go away. But unlike the natural world around me, my mind didn't obey. The tirade of words continued.

"Focus. Push the Visions back; allow only one at a time."

Easier said than done. The pressure was incredible; I felt it wrap around my lungs and my stomach. I started coughing violently, trying to rid my body of the excruciating pain.

Hands gripped my shoulders firmly.

"I'll take it away this one time. The next assault will be yours to tame."

The pressure lifted. The images ceased. The world was quiet.

With trembling breath, I opened my eyes and gazed at the ground. My hands were holding me up. As I looked at them, I saw blood splattered across my knuckles. Was it my blood?

"If you don't soon learn to control your Visions, they will consume you."

I glanced back and saw Lon standing behind me, his gaze disapproving. I was too weak to feel defensive; too ill to feel much of anything. As reality settled into place around me, a question surfaced.

"Lon. What were those? They weren't mine."

"Your...?"

"My memories."

"They weren't anybody's," he answered. "What you Saw has yet to be. I told you, your powers continue to grow."

"Why?" I whispered.

"Why do your powers come like this?"

I nodded weakly, still too sick to climb to my feet.

"Because the world is nearing its Apocalypse. With Paradise's end, your powers increase."

That was it then. I had to transfer my powers to the world's core to restore its life.

"Not quite," Lon said, reading my thoughts. "But you're getting closer to the answer."

"Why can't you tell me?" That was the biggest question of all. Why wouldn't anyone explain how it all worked?

Lon circled around to face me, unimpaired by the mud. I looked up into his face. He sighed, bending down and meeting my eyes. "Because if we give you all the answers, your journey will be meaningless."

My body shuddered as I shook my head. "It's not about my journey. It's about saving Paradise."

"Both are one and the same, Vendaeva."

I swallowed hard. "I don't understand. Anything."

"You're not expected to understand everything at once, but never belittle yourself by saying you understand nothing. I do not believe *any* being is incapable of comprehending at least one thing."

I tried a smile. "You know what I mean."

Lon smiled back. "Yes. I do." He straightened, offering a hand to me. "Come. I will help you search for Crenen."

I took his hand, pulling myself up with his help. Pain flared in my stomach and I coughed raggedly. Blood splattered the ground. I blinked, but smiled again. "Sasha's gonna love this."

"I will take responsibility for it."

"But you didn't do anything...did you?" I looked at him suspiciously.

"No. But she doesn't have to know that.".

It was probably best Lon was blamed. There was no way Sasha would dare to get mad at him. Probably.

"Your vote of confidence is reassuring," he murmured.

I remembered something. "Weren't you guarding Haeon?"

Lon inclined his head, motioning to where Haeon and Kirid still stood. Another figure was with them: Jenen. He was holding Haeon in place with one delicate hand pressed against his back, just where the heart would be.

When did he get here? I wondered.

"Just a moment ago. He will watch the prisoners while we find the others."

That mind-reading thing of his was admittedly rather handy (if slightly annoying).

I nodded, relieved to know Jenen was safe and sound. But I still had the others to worry about (though I was fairly certain my fears were a complete waste). Finally I acknowledged the newly-born Liitae. "Find Crenen."

With an energetic loop around my head, the orb shot off to the west, into the glare of a bloodred sunset. Lon and I followed after Liitae, fighting the mud as we hurried to keep up (at least, I fought it).

"Those Visions I Saw," I said as we went. "I could See the faces of the dead before I looked down at my feet. It was...really disconcerting."

Lon was silent for a moment. "The gift of clairvoyance. To See the future is one thing. To See a moment ahead is quite another. No wonder you had trouble keeping your feet."

"That sort of thing isn't normal?" I glanced at the Seer.

Lon shook his head. "Not at all. Few who can See as you or I have the gift of clairvoyance. A skill like that is one to use sparingly. Otherwise, you might act rashly."

"Rashly?" I knitted my brows together. "Wouldn't it stop me from acting rashly?"

I broke free of mud and entered the forest, Lon at my side.

"Consider this," Lon said. "To see five seconds into the future, you might See an action which looks appealing. But that sixth second, the one you couldn't See, might turn the tables against you. It's wisest not to rely on Seeing too often. In a fight, it could cost you your life."

I nodded, saying nothing more as Liitae led us toward a steep hill. We jogged, cresting it quickly.

And stopped.

Just when I was beginning to think my quest for the furapintairow might have been a waste, the scene before me swept that doubt from my mind. While Kirid had ceased the fighting within the Realm, either he hadn't been aware of the fighting out here, or these warriors were particularly good at warding off commanding magic.

Two dozen Kirid warriors, adorned in distinctive magenta robes to show their allegiance to Haeon, were swarming around a single individual. Crenen was soaked in crimson blood from head to toe, but his eyes were focused and his claws were drenched in what was probably not his own blood. Already five Kirid bodies littered the ground, while at least a dozen of those still standing were in some sort of pain.

"No matter how good he is," Lon said, "he won't last against so many for very long. Especially with those injures."

Squinting, I realized most of the blood covering his body *was* his own. Deep gashes in his side and along one leg bled openly. "We've got to help."

"Agreed, but we cannot be reckless."

I smirked. " Of course not. That's why I brought backup."

Lon raised a questioning brow. "Will this 'backup' explain where you ran off to?"

"Just watch," I said with wide grin. I closed my eyes. *Grump. Now.* The words echoed, as though traveling a great distance. I opened my eyes in time to see Lon staring at me with wide eyes. Apparently he'd heard.

"You know telepathy now? Your instincts are impressive."

I smiled. "There's more where that came from." Though I wasn't sure myself what that meant.

It was only a few seconds before the forest trembled with the thundering of many paws. The warriors before us halted, listening to the familiar, dooming sound. Crenen glanced across the meadow at me, understanding in his eyes, before he seized the opportunity and lunged at a distracted warrior. Startled, the other fighters tried to save their comrade, but were once again distracted by the arrival of several thousand furapintairow encircling the battlefield, razor rows of teeth glittering wickedly.

That was my cue.

"All right, listen up," I said, stepping onto a half-rotted stump as I struggled to make my voice carry. "Either you surrender, or my fuzzy friends here will have you for dinner. Your choice."

Three guesses what they chose.

As Lon conducted an orderly line of new prisoners, setting up the furapintairow as guards from a safe distance (and still shaking his head in disbelief at what I'd somehow managed), I walked down the slope toward Crenen.

He wore a smirk on his bloodied face and his eyes sparkled with delight. Apparently he'd quite enjoyed my show.

Up close, he looked even worse for wear. The gashes were deeper than I'd thought, and more injuries adorned his shoulder and carried down his back. His hair was a tangle; most of it had slipped out of the usually-lopsided binding, and it was matted with blood. My analysis proved one thing. He shouldn't be standing. How did he and Chasym manage to evade death so narrowly, and so...loudly?

"Strange Coward Boy not so cowardly, we think, yeah?" he said, grinning.

"So, do I get a different name?"

He chuckled. "We think on it."

It was something anyway.

I turned to watch Lon walk widely around Grump, eyeing the creature with obvious distrust. (Grump seemed to feel the same way about Lon.) The Seer approached us after making certain he had put a few yards between him and the furapintairow. "I must learn how you managed to tame the wild," he said.

I grinned. "Sorry. That's a secret I intend to keep for a while. Call it just desserts for all the things you kept from me."

Lon smiled wanly. "I don't think even this would be justice enough."

His statement intrigued me, but I decided to press the issue later. My gut instinct was telling me to get Crenen to Sasha as quickly as possible. I turned back to the Yenen prince. "Ready to go?"

He grinned. "Ready when Vendaeva ready, yeah?"

I nodded. "All right. Let's go." I started forward, but my gut twisted, so I stopped. "Crenen, Lon, go ahead and walk in front of me."

They gave me perplexed expressions, but didn't question. Lon started out, still giving the fuzzy army a wide berth. Crenen limped ahead next and I followed close behind him. As we walked I examined the claw marks on his back. Ample blood had been lost, but I knew that wasn't what worried me.

My eyes widened as I saw Crenen stumble and fall. He caught himself with his hands, but remained kneeling on the ground. His shoulders shuddered and I heard his ragged breathing. Hurrying to his side, I knelt and put my hand on one trembling shoulder.

The disease.

"It's nothing," he whispered. "We just tired." He tried to push himself to his feet, but all his energy was gone and he only breathed harder for his effort, shaking worse than before.

I glanced ahead and saw Lon watching with a fathomless expression.

"A little help?" I snapped.

He came back and offered his hand to Crenen, who scowled before accepting it. Lon pulled him to his feet. Crenen wavered and would've collapsed again, but Lon caught and held him up.

Crenen hissed in frustration.

I frowned. "We need to get you to Sasha."

He nodded grudgingly.

I grabbed one arm and slung it over my shoulder, motioning for Lon to do the same on Crenen's other side. We would make slow progress, but there was little else we could do. As we headed down the hill I glanced at Grump, who had at same point taken position near my feet.

"Find the others."

With a parting growl the critter disappeared in the foliage.

"You make interesting friends," Lon commented.

34
To Find The Answer?

Grump's task proved very easy. And pointless. When Lon and I managed to bring Crenen into the Realm, we found everyone already gathered together. A prison had been constructed from several charred tree trunks, and Kirid sat quietly inside, his long dark hair hanging limp and tangled over his bowed head. Haeon was still in Jenen's grasp, though it appeared Chasym had taken it upon himself to be a second guard—just in case.

The Kirid troop had been gathered together in one large space, their prison guard made up of furapintairow warriors. I would have to congratulate Grump later on a job well done. Speaking of which—I spotted the furapintairow standing near Kirid's makeshift prison. He wore a rather frightening grin.

"Master," Menen said, frowning at Crenen's appearance. He looked a little bedraggled himself.

Sasha broke away from the group and hurried to where we'd halted. "What happened?" she demanded even as she gently touched Crenen's wounded shoulder.

"Either Crenen was ambushed, or his own attempt failed," Chasym remarked lightly.

Sasha shot the Reincarnate a deadly glare and held it until he managed to plaster on a remorseful expression. Turning back, she placed one hand on Crenen's cheek. "You're burning up. I need to get you inside."

Crenen jerked away from her hand, growling. "We fine, yeah?" He tugged against my own supporting hold.

The doctor looked stung. Then her face darkened. "*No.*" She snatched his shirt-front. "You're not fine at all. You're bleeding all over the place and you're a running fever. *You're anything but fine*!"

Crenen stared, bewildered by her outburst, but then he scowled. "Let us go, Strange Coward Boy."

"No," I said, feeling remarkably calm despite the situation. I tightened my grip.

He hissed, pulling against my hold, but his strength was waning. Beads of sweat trickled down his face. He feebly pulled against Lon's grip, then stopped struggling, glaring at the ground.

"That is better," Lon murmured. He set his eyes on Jenen. "Take care of your brother. I must speak with Key privately."

Jenen released his grip on Haeon, stepped forward and, with only a second of hesitation, slid Crenen's arm over his shoulders. Menen came forward and linked his arm with Crenen's other arm for extra support. They headed toward the blackened grandfather tree, Sasha following close behind them.

"Chasym, keep watch over our prisoners," Lon directed.

"Of course." Chasym smirked, twisting Haeon's wrist. The captured Seer winced.

"Don't kill him," Lon said.

"Wouldn't dream of it."

"Don't maim him either."

Chasym scowled, but recovered and shrugged. "Fine."

Before turning away I caught Kirid's eye. He watched me almost vacantly as I started after Lon. I glanced back twice as I followed Lon toward the grandfather tree.

"Don't worry so much," Lon said. "It helps very little and hurts very much."

I nodded slowly. "I just wish I could get through to Kirid. He's a good kid, Lon. Just very confused."

"The same ailment which afflicts most worlds," he remarked. "Perhaps one day you might teach him what he now lacks. This, however, is not the time."

"I think it's the perfect time," I said, halting in my tracks.

Lon turned to face me, mildly surprised. "Oh?"

"Yes. Whatever the real reason for the Paradisaical disease, I know it's caused by confusion."

"What makes you so sure?" he asked, folding his arms.

"Gut instinct. I've learned to heed it quite a lot lately, and so far it's been pretty reliable."

"I advise caution, boy," Lon said, his voice stony. "This gut instinct you trust so much has led others down paths they will regret forever. It isn't always wise to pursue a course with such reckless abandonment as you have recently shown." He turned and started walking again, faster now.

"I'm aware of that," I said, hurrying after him. "Be that as it may, there are times when it *is* right, and this is one of them."

He scoffed but said nothing.

We climbed the fifty steps to the platform of the ancient tree in a matter of minutes. I found myself huffing less as I crested the top than the first time I'd taken these steps so long ago.

"Where are we going?" I asked as we entered the dark tree trunk.

"You will know soon enough," he answered.

I wondered if I should feel panicked, being alone with this unreadable figure. If he wasn't on my side, what would he do? I wanted to trust Lon, but past experience and recent discoveries made me leery. Still, as I began to descend with him down more steps toward the same room Veija had taken me many months previous, I felt calm. Even Crenen's condition didn't worry me at the moment.

We entered the vestibule, then approached the two massive doors, standing side by side. The same swirling, graceful runes adorned the giant doors and from inside I could feel the pulsing of a thousand entities. My eyes widened as I remembered what had been behind these doors before—and undoubtedly still would be.

"Lon," I whispered.

In answer, he pushed open one heavy door. Beyond was the blue glow of thousands, no, millions of souls, floating as tiny orbs all around the room. "They...they aren't dead," I whispered. "They're just trapped." The disease didn't kill. It merely captured. Which meant Crenen wouldn't die! That his family wasn't dead! That—

"You're wrong," Lon said quietly. "...Well, you're not completely right, I should say."

I turned to him, anxious to understand.

"I meant to have Veija explain this before, but you weren't ready. That is why I sent you home. Even now...I wonder if you can handle the truth."

I frowned. What was he get at?

"What I'm getting at," he said coolly, "is that these souls are trapped, yes. But they aren't alive. The disease ravaged their bodies; these souls cannot come back now. It is your duty, as Vendaeva, to free them of their captivity so that they can move on to the next world. So that they can have rest at last."

I gaped at him, feeling somewhat numb. "You mean...?" I turned to face the numberless orbs glowing and pulsing in their enormous prison. "They've been stuck in this state for years?"

"It will not last much longer," Lon said. "Whether you succeed or fail, their time in this domain will end when all is said and done."

"But if I fail..." I hesitated. "If I fail, they...?"

"Won't exist, yes. At least, not in any fit state. Their souls will become lost, forgotten."

I set my jaw and gazed at the souls for a long time. Finally I met Lon's red eyes. "How do I save Paradise?"

He watched me for a moment. "You know the answer to that, Key."

I didn't yet. Not completely. But I did know where to start. "I have to go." I turned and headed for the exit, my steps steady.

"Where are you going?" he called after me.

"To the water," I answered without looking back.

After a climb I barely registered, I passed the entire Kirid army and its furry guard; passed the remaining Yenen people, who bowed as I walked by; passed Chasym and his prisoners; passed the training field—and finally halted before the pond Lon had once pushed me into. I studied the reflections cast by the water; smoke still rose from smoldering trees that had once been houses. Then I saw it, the glowing something beneath the surface. I stepped into the water and waded toward the light. My resolve had never been stronger. Today, I would discover the secrets of Paradise.

I reached the center of the pool and gazed at the shimmering object. Reaching into the water, I cupped my hands around the white aura. Warmth exploded in my body as I felt myself dragged into the depths. I opened my eyes in the water and saw an orb in my grip. The orb was the same size as Liitae, but instead of pulsing blue, it was purest white.

"Vendaeva?" it whispered in my mind.

Yes, I answered silently.

"I have waited for you."

What do you want with me? I asked.

"What do you want of *me?"*

I need to know how to save Paradise. You can tell me, can't you?

"Yes."

Will you?

"Yes."

Then...how?

"Close your eyes and I will show you."

I closed my eyes.

I walked back to the grandfather tree, too distracted with my thoughts to notice the chill night wind blowing through my sopping clothes. Shivers racked my body, but I was oblivious to them as well. I walked by the steps and found the path leading to Sasha's quarters in the back of the tree. Reaching her door, I pulled it open and stumbled numbly down the steps. My actions were stiff from cold, but that barely registered. As I stepped off the last stair and entered the light of Sasha's hospital wing a collective gasp was my greeting.

"Key, you're soaking wet! What happened?" Veija asked, standing up and rushing to my side. "Sit down by the fire." She guided me to the chair by the fireplace.

"You look worse than usual—which is saying something," Sasha remarked. "Although, you *are* clean this time. That's impressive."

I managed a weary smile in reply.

Sasha walked out of my view and I heard her rummaging around. After a moment she stepped to the side of my chair and set clean clothes on the arm. "Change," she ordered sternly. "You'll catch your death in those clothes." She turned away. "Come on, Veija. Let's give our savior his privacy."

I listened to their footsteps as they left the room and closed the door behind them.

"Why are you wet?" Menen's voice drifted across the air.

I sat forward in my seat and turned to face the bed I'd occupied months before. Menen sat beside it. Under its covers Crenen lay sleeping.

"I went swimming," I answered casually, then nodded toward the sleeping form. "How is he?"

"Very weak." He seemed about to say more, but stopped himself and gazed at the floor thoughtfully.

"It's okay, Menen," I said. "I already know he has the disease. Jenen told me."

He looked up sharply. "*Jenen* told you?"

I nodded. "He overheard you and Crenen speaking and put two and two together." I got to my feet and starting unwrapping the strips of cloth from my feet. "Sasha confirmed it yesterday."

He looked almost relieved to hear it. "I've...been hoping you would find out. Crenen ordered me not to say anything..." He frowned again and watched his sleeping master.

"He'll be okay," I said, and pulled off my shirt with a shiver. "I'm going to save him, Menen. I swear it."

"I certainly hope you can," he whispered, "but Crenen has been very sick for a long time. I doubt if he can last much longer."

I'm going to stop the disease tomorrow."

He blinked. "How?"

"I have to go to the Realm of Kirid," I answered.

"That's weeks away from here, Key—"

"Not the way I travel, it isn't." I grinned. "I just have to going swimming again."

"Can you transport yourself within Paradise?"

I shrugged. "I don't see why not. I did it once before." And not even in water either. I quickly dressed, welcoming the warmth of my clean, dry clothing. "Where's Lon? Chasym, too?"

"They were here for dinner, but left together shortly thereafter."

I tied my hair back with a strip of cloth. "I'll go find them." I stooped down and rummaged through my wet clothes until I found what I was looking for. I pocketed the object carefully. "Be back later."

I wanted to speak with Kirid, but that would have to wait until I informed Lon and Chasym of my plans for the coming morning. I felt my pocket, just to make certain the object was still there. Opening my palm, I summoned Liitae softly.

"Locate Lon and Chasym," I told it.

Bobbing excitedly, it shot off into the night. I sighed and trailed slowly after it. Eventually the orb came back and hovered contentedly above my open palm. I took that to mean I was going in the right direction so I kept straight, heading for the forest gloom.

As I quietly approached the trees my pointed ears picked up whispering voices. I strained to hear better and finally distinguished the words.

"...took us all by storm," Chasym was saying softly.

"I know. But I can't afford for that to happen," Lon said in frustration.

""It's already happened. Can't you just admit to it?"

"Chasym," Lon whispered helplessly, "I wasn't supposed to love him."

"Why not? We're all proud of him, all rooting for him. He's grown so much."

"Not enough. He shouldn't have to yet."

I halted, just beyond sight of the two men. I stared into the gloom with growing apprehension.

"He's a man now, Lon. Not a child. Believe me, I know. I've watched him grow from a toddler. Watched him experience all the things you couldn't—no—wouldn't see."

"You know the risk my presence posed," Lon snapped.

"A risk any normal person would take to see their child!"

"He's not my child!" Lon shouted angrily, then his voice lowered. "...Not anymore."

Cold washed over my body, sharper than a winter's night. I stepped forward, hesitated, and stepped back. I barely registered Liitae circling around my limp hand; barely felt the wind rustling the dead leaves overhead. I wasn't who they were talking about. It was impossible. It was some kind of mistake. I had misheard—

"Don't give me that," Chasym snarled. "You're still his father whether you gave him away or not. You chose to accept the responsibility of your actions fourteen years ago, yet here you are—running away every time you can't stand looking at him anymore."

I cringed, feeling a pain inside I couldn't comprehend.

"I can't watch..."

"You don't have a choice anymore. I tried to stop you; tried to make you understand. But you chose this path and there's no walking away now. Just tell him, Lon. Tell him the truth."

"No. I will not destroy Key's life more than I already have."

"It's already destroyed! No wonder the boy turned into liar. His whole life has been a great facade!"

"It must remain so."

"He'll figure it out," Chasym whispered. "He's smart. He already knows about Kirid. He just can't figure out why he was the second option yet." He sighed heavily. "Lon, if you won't tell him, then I—"

"You will do nothing! I forbid you to say anything to him."

I was trembling. It couldn't be true. But while my mind denied it, my soul was filled with the terrible, resounding confirmation: Lon was my father.

"How can you be like this?" Chasym hissed. "You love that boy, yet you deny him everything he deserves to know."

Lon was silent for a moment, then he sighed softly. "Chasym, I can stand for him to be cautious of me, but I could not stand for him to hate me."

"What makes you think he would?"

"You hated your father for making you a slave."

"That is entirely diff—!"

"*No*. Not from the perspective of a young man. When you were young, did you ever stop to consider why your father did that? Was it really his choice? ...Whether that is true now doesn't matter. At the time you only felt hurt and betrayed."

"Then explain the whole thing to him."

"Even if I did, he would have every reason to hate me. What I did was wrong and nothing can change that fact now." Lon's tone was bitter.

"So, to save yourself, you'll keep the truth from him?"

"Yes. And to save him from an all-consuming hatred."

Chasym laughed humorlessly. "You really don't know him, Lon. Not at all."

I heard the crunch of dead leaves. One of them was walking toward me. Quickly and silently as possible, I dove for the undergrowth, grabbing Liitae as I concealed myself. "Hide me," I told the orb softly. While nothing about me changed, I felt suddenly invisible.

Seconds later I saw Chasym walk by my hiding spot. Eventually his footsteps wore away. I stayed where I was, knowing very well that Lon was still standing there in silence. My eyes widened. Could he read my thoughts? Was there a chance he knew I was there? Or did he have to see me in order to connect to my mind? Whatever the case, I barely dared to breathe, as if that would make a difference.

What seemed an eternity later Lon followed after Chasym, crunching the same dead leaves. His lavender robes raked the ground as he headed for the Realm. I waited a few more minutes before pushing to my feet. Brushing the twigs and bits of bramble from my clothes, I gazed thoughtfully after the man who was my father.

The walk back to Sasha's quarters was a slow one. I tried to digest the news I'd received; tried to recognize what exactly I felt inside. I didn't know all the facts, but I already knew I couldn't hate Lon. Whatever his reasons for sending me away as a child, I didn't understand them, so it wasn't my place to judge. Beyond that, it was hard to recognize exactly what I felt inside.

I opened the door at the bottom of Sasha's stairs and entered the cheerfully lit room. As warmth enveloped me, I took in all the people inside. Every member of our party was present. Veija smiled at me in greeting. Sasha raised an eyebrow at my leaf-infested clothing. Menen watched over his master with the patience of an angel, while Crenen slept peacefully. Chasym sat near Jenen, both looking preoccupied. And Lon—he gazed at me with an impassive face, hiding away all of his feelings for fear of revealing anything that might hurt both of us.

I scowled at him. "There you are. Menen said you and Chasym were out there, but Liitae and I couldn't find you anywhere." I walked to the empty chair by the fire and threw myself into its comfort.

"Did you discover your mission?" Lon asked quietly.

I leaned forward and gazed into the flames. "Yeah. I'm going to the Realm of Kirid tomorrow. I'll find the core there."

"How will you travel?"

"By lake."

"Ah."

I waited until I felt his eyes leave my face and then I glanced at him, studying his profile. Was I really the son of such a pretty-boy? Our hair was similar, comparing it now. His was more gold, mine more blond, but still quite alike. But he was so tall. Had I gotten my slight build from my mother?

My mother. Where was she? *Who* was she? Had she been a victim of the disease as well? Could Seers catch the disease? Was she even a Seer? I sat back and exhaled slowly. So many questions and still no real answers. I pushed myself from the chair and stood.

"I'm going to retire, gotta leave pretty early... I'm taking Kirid and Haeon with me."

"Is that wise?" Veija asked.

I looked at her. If Lon was my father, that made her my aunt. I smiled. "I don't know, but I've got to do it anyway."

"What being with so many I's, Strange Reckless Dolt?" Crenen's almost-cheerful voice spoke up. I turned around to find Crenen sitting up in his bed, propped against the pillows for support. "We going with you. We *all* going with you, yeah?" He grinned toothily, though his eyes were full pain.

"Yeah," I answered, smiling.

We would all end, or begin this, together. As I felt my spirits bolstered my eyes returned to Lon.

Where was I?

"You are in your memories, within a dream."

I glanced around, bewildered. "I don't remember this."

I stood on a strange circular platform of smooth stone which rose above flowing lava far below. Around the platform was a ring of blue stone, in which were carved intricate characters—some form of ancient writing that felt familiar, though I couldn't read it.

"There are many memories unattainable through your conscious mind. Only if Liitae or I unlock these memories can you view them."

"But they are my memories?"

"Yes and no," the voice answered.

"Who are you?"

In answer I felt pulsing coming from my pocket. Reaching in, I withdrew the white orb and gazed into its crystal depths.

"I am a Remnant of Paradise. A guide, historian, Seer, and soul."

I smirked. "Sounds more like several remnants to me."

"You might look at it that way."

I glanced around the strange, hazy atmosphere. "If this is part of my memory, where is this place located?"

"This is the core of Paradise."

"My destination." I simply knew it.

"Yes," the orb replied.

"Where in the Realm of Kirid is the core?"

"I will guide you tomorrow, Vendaeva. Now, we watch."

I was about to ask what we were watching when a movement caught my eye. Glancing up, I saw a figure falling from the misty sky. It landed on another platform some distance away. After a moment I saw the form stir and finally stand.

"Who is that?"

"Shall we get closer?"

I nodded and suddenly we were standing on the other platform. I stood face-to-face with Lon. Gasping, I stepped back but knew instinctively that he couldn't see me. He was younger; his face was softer, his eyes brighter, and his hair wasn't so long. He hesitated, then knelt on the cold stone surface, pressing his forehead to the ground.

"Vendaeva, I come before you to ask for help." Lon's voice was humble, pleading, desperate.

Vendaeva? "What does he mean?"

"You will know."

"Why are you showing me this?"

"Because your desire is to know."

Frowning, I watched my father groveling. The blue ring of stone around the column began to glow brightly and light spilled across the surface, bathing everything in blue. Lon raised his head, staring in awe at the glowing characters.

"What would you need of me?" a distant voice whispered.

"I've made a grave mistake," Lon replied somberly. "I have lost the child who was to be your heir."

Silence reigned for what seemed eternity. Finally the voice returned. "Then Paradise is doomed."

"Is there no other way?" Lon asked, bowing his head. "Please?"

A soft sigh, blowing through the air like a breeze, ruffled Lon's hair. "None other which you would be willing to risk."

"I will do anything to save Paradise. It was my miscalculation that caused this. I must see it undone. Take my life if you must." His eyes flashed with determination.

"It isn't your life that you would risk, Seer."

Lon blinked, then paled. "No. You don't—?"

"Your child, Seer. I give you three days. After that it will be too late. Consider carefully."

"Will it save Paradise?" Lon asked softly.

"There is little chance anymore. But it is one last hope."

Lon faded away along with the core.

Wet mist kissed my face.

I glanced at the hovering white orb beside me. "When Haeon stole Kirid, Lon had to replace him with something. But why me?"

"Perhaps you will remember this next memory. You saw it once in a dream."

I was standing in a forest glade now, facing two men. Lon and Chasym.

"You can't be serious! Have you lost your senses completely?" Chasym growled, grabbing the other man by the arm and turning him around.

"Yes, I think that I have. But what else can I do?" Lon pleaded. "I'm open to suggestions, if you have them."

Chasym sighed. "I know how you feel, but I doubt if this will help."

"I know. But I've got to try something—and it must be my sacrifice. I'm at fault."

"No. I won't let you. I'll do something instead. I owe you that much."

Lon laughed sadly. "Don't be foolish. You paid that debt long ago."

"Yes, but it never made anything better, did it? So what's the point now?"

"Hope, my friend. If that's all I can give to Paradise, it will be enough."

"False hope isn't hope," Chasym said. "Believe me when I say that your sacrifice will be in vain."

"I'm sorry, but I can't. I won't. Because...I want hope, too."

"Can you really go through with it? You'll have to live with the consequences."

"And that will enable me to do it."

Again the two men faded away, leaving me alone in a sea of blue mist.

"Kirid, the original heir to Paradise, was chosen by the sacrifice of his mother. In this case another sacrifice had to be made. Lon gave up his child."

I frowned. "But why a sacrifice?"

"Anything worth attaining has its price. Other sacrifices were given at the Alter, one such by your friend Crenen." The orb pulsed. "But that is tale for another night. Dawn approaches and you've yet to find true sleep. Rest now, Vendaeva. You have a task to complete."

I hesitated. "Wait."

"Yes?"

"Both Chasym and the core said there was little hope. Can I...can I really save Paradise?"

The orb pulsed. "That depends on you."

The morning dawned dark and dreary. Not the best kind of mood-setter in the world, but it could have been worse. Our group set out for the lake in the light drizzle with a determination that set us apart from all the dying world. We meant to make our departure a silent one, and it was, even with all of Yenen Clan assembled along the path to bid us farewell. They said nothing, only watching with mixed sadness and indifference. It was almost depressing.

I stopped at the lake, staring into the shimmering pool. Fingering the object in my pocket, I turned to the others. "Ready?"

They nodded somberly; all but Crenen, wrapped in many layers of blanket, and laying almost comfortably in Menen's strong arms. He was grinning from ear to ear. ""We go," he said with a surprisingly strong voice.

"Long live Vendaeva!" a woman's voice called from the despondent crowd.

Glancing behind my comrades, I spotted the shawl-clad wife of Tall Strong Jerk, standing a little apart from the masses. With her stood Mr. Ugly and Quiet Sneaky Thing, both wearing grave but resolute expressions. Nithae bowed to me and I bowed back.

There was still a reason to fight.

"Okay. Let's do this." I pulled the white orb from my pocket and threw it into the lake. Brilliant light shot forth from the water, causing our audience to gasp and step back. "Into the lake, everyone." I stepped into the magical transport, focused on my destination.

As the whirlwind of water and light swirled around me I caught glimpses of landscapes above my head. Forests, mountains, deserts, prairies. Instead of the splendor one might expect from such views, everything I saw was dead. Few leaves clung to their withering branches and mountain waterfalls were dry. Desert plant life had vanished, while the prairie grass was brown and crisp.

Finally the whirl began to slow and the water above me shimmered with sunlight. At least the sun wasn't gone from every place yet. I glanced around to spot the others. They were swimming quickly toward the surface as the last of the white light receded. Chasym had a firm hold on Haeon, while Jenen had taken Kirid as his prisoner. They dragged them upward, until they broke free of the water.

I stayed standing on the bottom of the pool for moment, closing my eyes and listening to the sounds above me. I smiled after a minute and walked toward the surface slowly along the lake-bottom. As I broke through the water, I saw several thousand Kirid warriors standing before our tiny group. They no longer held their weapons, as they were completely surrounded by another portion of my Small Red Fuzzy army.

"You've done nicely here, too, I see," Lon remarked.

I grinned. "Can't be too careful." I spotted my venomless friend at the head of the fuzzballs and waved. It smiled widely in reply.

I turned back to the water, reaching my hand out and summoning back the white orb. I pocketed it and summoned Liitae from my left palm. I allowed the blue orb to hover by my shoulder.

"What now?" Sasha asked.

I fixed my eyes on the mountain castle in the distance. "We head for the core."

"Kiido, the core isn't there," Kirid said. "If it was, don't you think I would know?"

"Of course it's not there," I said, glancing at him. "It's only one portal to get us there."

"Don't be ridiculous," Haeon sneered. "I searched the castle from top to bottom. Not the core, nor any portal to it, is within."

I turned a cold eye on him. "You think I'm going to trust you over *this*?" I patted the pocket where the white orb rested. "Shut your trap, Hae-Hae. Your opinion's been void for a while now."

He meant to scowl, but it turned into a wince as Chasym tightened his grip on Haeon's bound hands. The prisoner exhaled angrily through his nose and closed his mouth.

"Now that he's been properly cowed," Chasym said with a grin, "to the castle?"

"To the castle," I agreed.

We walked through the gap in the imprisoned forces, several in our party giving the fuzzies a wide berth.

"So, how did you get these little guys on your side anyway, Jase?" Chasym asked as he eyed a furapintairow who eyed him back.

I smirked. "Lon was wondering that earlier."

"What I want know is how you didn't get lost," Sasha said with an evil, pointy grin.

"I had a guide, naturally," I said, nodding toward Liitae, who perked up at the mention.

Chasym stopped walking and the rest of us halted, glancing at him curiously. He stared at nothing in silence, then laughed. "A guide! Of course he is. What were we thinking?"

We stared at him.

"Explain self or die like flopping fish on land," Crenen ordered.

"Remember when we were lost?" Chasym asked no one in particular. "Well. Imagine what would have happened if we'd thought to ask Liitae for help. Just think for a moment."

Our eyes slid toward the little orb, which bobbed excitedly at all the attention.

"Okaaay. Now I feel stupid," Sasha remarked for us all.

Veija chuckled nervously. "Well, better late to remember than never."

I smacked my forehead with a moan. "Of all the stupid things to forget..."

"Nobody perfect, yeah?" Crenen said casually, and our bewildered gazes focused on him. How could something like that even come out of his mouth? Wasn't he the biggest megalomaniac to ever live? He only grinned back at us, apparently amused by our surprise.

"The core," Lon said, bringing everyone back to our objective. I glanced back and considered Lon for a long moment. He was such a moody, standoffish guy.

As we once more headed for the castle I dropped back to walk beside Chasym, ignoring Haeon walking ahead of us. I needed to get some answers and he seemed able to give them. He gave me a grin.

"S'up?" he asked. The slang didn't quite work with his Paradisian appearance.

I tilted my head in Lon's direction. "Has he always been this moody?"

Chasym chuckled. "Well, yes. He was always a sober person—ever since I've known him anyway. Though he used to be cheerful a *little* more often."

Lon cleared his throat, obviously warning Chasym to shut up.

I was tempted to press more, just to annoy the Seer, but more important questions needed addressing. "...There's something I've been dying to know ever since I got my memories back. Before anything else happens—"

A deafening rumble filled the sky as the ground began to shake. (One of these days I would learn to stop jinxing myself.) I lost my balance and fell to the trembling earth. Looking up, I saw the others struggling to keep on their feet. Chasym grabbed my shirt sleeve and pulled me up, still gripping Haeon's wrists with one hand.

"Run!" he shouted at me, pushing me toward the distant castle. "GO!" he urged as I hesitated. "We'll catch up."

I turned and stumbled in my attempt to run. A loud cracking noise tore through the sky. Veija screamed. Halting, I spun around in time to see the ground break apart. Menen, Crenen, Lon and Veija were trapped on the other side of the new canyon. Forgetting my objective, I ran back toward them.

"No, Key!" Lon shouted. "Chasym, stop him."

I ignored him, determined not to let them stay behind. Just as I reached the gorge I felt strong arms drag me back.

"There's nothing we can do," Chasym whispered in my ear.

"We'll find a way across and catch up," Lon shouted. "Go now, Key. The core is almost gone. Go while there's still time."

Gritting my teeth, I allowed Chasym to pull me away from the giant rift and up the quaking hillside. Jenen pushed Kirid and Haeon after us, Sasha trailing behind them. I spared a last glance backward before I set my sights ahead. A dread I didn't understand settled in my stomach as we left the others further behind.

The earthquake only lasted a few minutes more, but the skies were dark now, as they had been in the Realm of Yenen. A light drizzle fell, as if mourning the final hours of Paradise.

The dreary landscape was colored only by the occasional emerald green plant not yet wilted with the world's destruction, as though defiantly standing up against impending death.

Tremors shook the ground now and then. Eventually I took position behind Sasha and steadied her when the ground shook. At first she was reluctant to accept my help, but finally she concluded that I wasn't going to stop for her pride's sake.

It took an age to reach the mountainous castle. We halted at the foot of the stone steps leading up toward the giant front door. I sat down heavily, slumping over, weary from our quick pace. Brushing aside my wet hair with annoyance, I closed my eyes to calm my nerves. That same something was still gnawing at me, whatever it was, but I couldn't afford to be distracted.

"You can't save Paradise now, boy," Haeon's sinister voice spoke up.

I opened one eye, shooting him a weary expression. "I'm not in the mood to spar, Hae-Hae."

He only smirked.

"Haeon is right, Kiido," Kirid chimed in, his eyes dark. "It's too late."

I sighed, straightening my shoulders and opening my other eye. "We're still alive, aren't we?"

"Key has a point," Jenen said, smiling softly. "There is hope even still."

"The world doesn't deserve to survive," Haeon spat. "This is its final judgment. Its corruption is being purged. You think you can fight justice?"

I met his glare evenly. "Says the guy who tries so desperately to live by any means possible? Regardless of what you might think, I happen to believe in a thing called mercy. Now, how's a world supposed to prove it's changed if it doesn't get a second chance?"

"It's had many more than one," he snapped. "Its people have outlived their chances. It is time for the end."

"What about people who don't deserve death?" Jenen asked quietly.

"Name one," Haeon growled. "Name one soul on this forsaken world who deserves life!"

"Kirid," I answered firmly, getting to my feet. "That's one. But there's more—many more. Who the heck are you to judge, Haeon? Do you think you're the only one worth sparing? Please. Don't be so arrogant. You're not God, last I checked."

He stared defiantly. "You're not God either, Jason Sterling. What can you do to alter fate?"

"I don't know," I said, "but I'm not about to die without a fight, that's for freaking sure."

"That goes for us, too," Sasha said, nodding toward Jenen and Chasym. "We're not planning to die so easily."

Haeon spat at the ground. "Either way, you will die."

"Feel special, then," Chasym said, grinning. "You're going down with us."

35
Betrayal?

We stared at the massive door to the looming castle, all frowning, most of us contemplating the same question. The wind picked up, whistling through the flawed face of the castle, and playing with our hair, whipping it into our eyes.

"Do we go in?" Sasha voiced at last.

"I'm...not sure," I said sheepishly.

"What exactly did you and that little white orb talk about all that time? I thought it was unraveling the secrets of Paradise—specifically the core's location," Chasym said in exasperation.

I shrugged. "It showed me the core, not the exact route there. I just knew it was in the Realm of Kirid, somewhere hereabouts."

"Some hero you make," Sasha remarked.

I scowled. "Sorry, I'm kind of new to the business. Perhaps you could give me pointers or something?"

"Ha. Ha. You're so funny."

"They're arguing," Kirid murmured. "We're facing the end of the world and they pick this moment to argue? It's incredible..."

I glanced at him and shrugged. "Makes it more interesting."

"Though I must point out that the boy has a point," Jenen said flatly. "We are wasting precious time."

I pulled the white orb from my pocket. "Where do we go?" The orb bobbed for a moment and then floated through the closed door, leaving us behind. "I'm gonna take a wild guess and say we do go in."

"I second that motion," Chasym said, grabbing the metal handle and pulling the heavy door open. "Everyone in. This isn't as easy as it looks," he said through clenched teeth. We filed in quickly and Chasym slithered in and released the door behind him. It swung back into place with a resounding boom.

We found ourselves standing in a massive entryway unlit by torches, illuminated only by the presence of my two orbs. Looking up, I thought the ceiling was vaulted, but I couldn't be sure. During my stay with Kirid I'd used other doors that led out to the grounds, never venturing far enough this way to discover the front door. I almost regretted not seeing it in good light; it felt grand.

"Will we run into anything unpleasant, like a welcoming committee?" Sasha asked, gazing around the darkness.

"Nah," I said just as the sound of padding feet came from down the hall. Holding up Liitae, I grinned at the approaching furapintairow. "I took care of things here just in case."

"Nice," Chasym said approvingly. "Though...a little anticlimactic, you know?"

"Sorry, I didn't think we'd have time for delays."

"Says the man who's managed to initiate two debates in the last twenty minutes."

"I didn't initiate them," I argued. "I was provoked."

"...And that's better?" Sasha asked, her eyes still on the little red fuzzball who was staring up at her with a playful grin, its tail wagging happily. "What's it doing?"

"It wants you to pick it up," I said, taking a second wild guess.

Sasha threw me a dirty look. "Right."

"I mean it," I lied. "Go ahead. It won't bite." Probably.

Tentatively she bent down and scooped the fuzzy into her arms. It only continued to grin, its tail rotating in a circle.

"It's so soft," she breathed, a slight smile touching her pale face.

I blinked. Of course it shouldn't surprise me to hear she'd never touched one before; furapintairow were considered both sacred and lethal until now. I stretched out my hand and patted the furapintairow's top as I glanced around. "All right, let's go." I'd spotted the white orb hovering near a set of stairs leading up into darkness.

Up we went, the two orbs our only source of light as we ascended the narrow stairwell. I'd taken the lead, with Kirid and Jenen following, then Sasha, Haeon, and Chasym last.

"Where does this lead?" I asked Kirid.

"It's one route to the throne room," he answered in a hoarse whisper.

Glancing back at him I was surprised to see his face flushed and beaded with sweat. "Kirid?" I turned and placed my palm on his forehead. "You're sick?" Instead of hot, his face was freezing cold.

His body trembled. "...It's...not me," he said after a moment. "Something...something up ahead."

Glancing ahead in the blackness I wondered what he meant. Curious and concerned, I wrapped Kirid's arm around my shoulders. "Let's go." I stepped forward and Kirid cringed. Hesitantly I took another step—

Pain fell upon me like an crashing weight. I felt like I was being crushed by the air. "L-Liitae," I stammered as Kirid slipped from my grasp and fell against the wall, his face contorted in pain.

A flash of blue light filled the passageway and the pressure lifted. I spun on my heels, glaring past the others into Haeon's defiant face. "You want to explain yourself?"

"I didn't do it," Haeon said.

"And just who the heck else did?"

A smile stretched across the man's face. "You're more Seer than I, boy. You tell me."

"That was a barrier," Chasym said quietly. "Liitae's binding is still around Haeon—he couldn't have initiated it, Jase."

"Then, who else?" I asked, glancing at the blond. Fear threatened to invade the clarity of my thoughts.

Chasym frowned, his face shadowed by the limited light. "I've been hesitant to bring this up, but...think about it. Haeon isn't a Seer anymore, right? Yet somehow he's had the powers of a Seer at his disposal—how else could he summon illusions and kill Jenen?"

"So, there's someone else behind all this?" I turned my silver eyes back on Haeon. "You're working for someone, aren't you?"

He scowled but said nothing.

"If that is the case," Jenen spoke up, "then we have yet to confront the real threat."

Way to make me feel better. "That doesn't matter now. Either way we have to go on."

"Of course," Jenen replied.

I knelt down by Kirid who leaned against the wall, his face turned to the ceiling. "Are you okay?" I asked gently.

His gray eyes shifted to me, vivid even through the strands of hair covering his face. "I'm confused," he whispered. "...So confused."

I smiled. "It's okay. If you follow us, I promise you'll get your answers."

He watched me blankly, then nodded. "Very well." He got to his feet. "Though the answers frighten me more than the secrets."

I understood well what he meant.

No further obstructions kept us from the throne room, and while we expected something foul to greet us there, the massive chamber was empty but for the unlit candelabra and sconces, and the ornate dais shrouded in deep shadows.

"...More anticlimax, eh?" Chasym sighed. He flicked his wrist and the candelabra flickered to life, their flames dancing in the air drafts. As the room was illuminated, it revealed the grand beauty of centuries' old artistry. Kirid's ancestors had been proud and regal, despite whatever faults they had. Stone surfaces were smoothed and carved, drawing vague yet alluring shapes and symbols. Arches overhead were decorated by plain magenta flags, which danced on the drafts of air.

Finally registering what Chasym had said, I lowered my head and turned to the blond. "Be grateful," I said, and my eyes caught the white orb floating toward the throne, Liitae following curiously. I also followed, studying the intricate carvings on the dais's surface as I walked. Several runes seemed vaguely familiar. My eyes widened. "Haeon, you said you never found a way into the core? You just didn't look under your nose."

"You found it?" Sasha asked, putting the fuzzy down and hurrying to stand beside me as I stopped a few feet from the raised throne.

I pointed to the dais. "Yeah." Gentle words, foreign yet familiar, brushed by my ear, whispering unintelligible instructions. "This is the gateway."

"It can't be. I've sat on this throne countless times," Kirid said in bewilderment. "I would think I might have sensed it."

"I visited this room too, Kirid. I didn't sense anything then either." Kneeling before the stone dais, I ran my hand along the carved glyphs. As I touched each engraving, it lit up, glowing blue. "...Anyone know the significance of blue, white, and gold?" I asked.

"No idea," Chasym replied, leaning down to examine the carvings as well. For the moment he'd relinquished his hold on Haeon, allowing Jenen to watch both prisoners. I glanced at the Renocahnian man, watching as he intently studied the stone surface. Behind him I saw both orbs floating around a candelabrum, teasing its flames.

"Hey, about that question I had earlier," I said, remembering suddenly.

A wry smile touched his mouth. "Yes?"

"Well," I turned back to the dais, "that day in the forest, just before the Kirid struck and Haeon showed himself for the first time, you disappeared with Veija. Later she said that was her fault. What happened?"

Chasym laughed softly. "Don't for one second believe she was confessing her love for me. One thing you must understand about Veija. All she has left in her world is Lon. The presence of one of They concerned her greatly, and so, even after my little speech about 'giving people a chance' she led me away from camp to make me swear I would never harm Lon or betray his friends."

I chuckled. "What did you say?"

His face darkened. "I never actually got to respond, I'm afraid. The darkness struck then and we ran for the nearest tree. The ground isn't a safe place to be with shadows around."

"I'll keep that in mind," I murmured. By this time I'd touched every rune on the dais's front. "There's got to be a way in."

"We're overlooking something," Chasym said. He glanced back. "Any thoughts, O Seerless One?"

I snorted.

"Even if I did, do you honestly think I would share?" Haeon sneered.

"...That would be the smart thing to do, so, no. I doubt it," Chasym replied.

As I considered what to do my eyes wandered to the two orbs still bobbing around the candle flames. My eyes widened. That was it. "That's it," I exclaimed aloud, making Sasha and Kirid jump involuntarily. Jenen, Haeon and Chasym watched me expectantly. "Kirid, come here," I said.

Kirid glanced at Jenen, as if asking for permission. Jenen nodded and Kirid approached, hesitantly kneeling beside me.

"Listen. You and I are both Vendaeva, so if we both touch these runes in succession we might get through."

He managed a limp smile. "But, Kiido, Vendaeva isn't the only one who can get into the core. Others have done it," as he spoke his eyes wandered to Jenen, who arched his eyebrow inquiringly, "so why can't we get in that way?"

I leaned closer to Kirid. "What way? Do you know, Kirid?" He nodded, and for a moment I felt like Kiido again; eager to learn from my more experienced friend and brother-figure. "You must intend to sacrifice something," he whispered.

Silence fell.

"No problems, then," Chasym finally said. "We'll just sacrifice Haeon and—" Kirid's sharp glare cut him off. "All right then, how about, um..." He trailed off, at a loss.

I smiled. I'd already been told that part. "All right. Assume for a moment that we have a sacrifice to give. What comes next?"

Kirid glanced at the white orb. "I think that opens the way."

I blinked.

"I think the orb appears in water for anyone with a deep desire for something; a desire for what they cannot gain alone," Kirid explained quietly. "I've...seen it in the water, too."

Of course. It only made sense. (In a magical, improbable sort of way.) Standing, I raised my palm. "Come on, both of you."

The two orbs reluctantly left their play and approached.

"Listen," I said, cupping the white orb. "Will you open up the way to the core?"

It bobbed in agreement.

"Thanks," I said, allowing the orb to float down to the dais.

"But, Kiido, we don't have a sacrifice."

"Kirid's right, Jase," Chasym added.

"Don't worry. I already knew that part."

Before anyone could question further the white orb finished touching each glyph. Instead of the carvings glowing blue, however, they began to glow brilliant white. A flash of blinding light burst through the throne room. I closed my eyes and shielded my face with one arm. After a moment I felt hot air rushing past me from beneath. I was falling. The sensation only lasted a minute and then I landed hard on the stones, knees smarting. A little bruised, but far more curious, I got to my feet and blinked the blindness away.

I was standing on a wide circular column of stone several hundred feet above a bubbling ocean of lava. Other stone columns rose up from the heat as well, evenly spaced in all directions, going on forever.

We had reached the core.

Still, something wasn't right. My instinct was trying to warn me, but I couldn't place why it felt so wrong.

Glancing behind, I saw the others gazing around in awe. Above them shimmered an image in the sky, showing the vague outline of the throne room. A way out.

"Well, now that we're here, what happens?" Sasha asked, turning her blue eyes to me.

"Uh," I began stupidly.

"Now, I'm afraid, you have to die."

I was about to snap at Haeon for his cliché and dooming answer when a chill ran down my spine. That voice—it wasn't Haeon's. I started to turn around, but my attention was caught by the vanishing image of the throne room. In seconds it was gone completely.

"You're trapped, Jase," Chasym said. "But I must thank you. You helped me in more ways than you can realize. I knew you had your uses."

Disbelieving, I whirled around to face my friend. While he still looked like Chasym in appearance, his yellow eyes danced with a cold insanity that shouldn't have been there.

"What—?" I began.

"What are you doing?" Sasha demanded, cutting through my version of the question.

He ignored her. "Make certain the portal is sealed, Kirid," Chasym said without taking his frightening eyes from mine.

I saw Kirid visibly jump out of the corner my eye, but he quickly raised his hand to the spot where the way home had been. "It is," he answered quietly.

"Chasym, please, tell me this is some sort of joke," I said, attempting a smile.

He ignored me, shifting his gaze to Jenen and Sasha. "Release Haeon."

"We won't," Jenen replied.

"You will." It wasn't a demand, just a strong assurance.

Jenen gasped as he suddenly released Haeon and watched in disbelief as the robed man walked calmly toward Chasym. Sasha tried to step forward but stopped mid motion, as if something invisible held her back.

Was this really happening? I felt my knees trembling.

"Chasym," I said again, "I don't understand."

"Jenen," Chasym said, "would you be good enough to give me your shawl?"

Jenen hissed. "I will not, *traitor*." He tightened his grip on the shimmering cloth.

Chasym sighed. "Now, now, let's not be stubborn." His face darkened. "Give me the shawl."

"No."

The Reincarnate stepped up to me more quickly than I could react. He grabbed a handful of my hair, jerking my head back with a painful jolt in my neck. "You may not die while the boy lives, but if the boy dies..."

I was bent awkwardly, only held up by Chasym's strong grip. I stared up at him, aware of the strain in my legs and spine but indifferent to it, focused only on one question: Why?

I heard Jenen shift and finally walk toward us. "No," I said quietly. "Jenen, that shawl is too important somehow. Besides, he can't kill me. I'm just as powerful as he is."

Jenen halted.

Chasym pulled my head back more. The pain surged. "Don't be so sure, Jase. You're only half Vendaeva."

I ignored his taunting. "Chasym," I whispered, "why?"

He glanced down at me, smirking. "Because, kid, Paradise can't be saved—I won't let it."

My legs gave way under the strain and I collapsed to my knees, slamming them sharply against the stone. Chasym still held my hair near my scalp and he jerked me up until I was half-dangling.

"Why?" I asked again.

"Right now, Jenen," he said, ignoring my question as he wrenched my head back more.

I hissed with the pain. "Don't," I said through clenched teeth.

"Kirid, get the shawl," he ordered.

"Kirid, please don't!" I called, unable to look at him but praying he would listen. I didn't know why they needed the shawl so desperately, nor did I want to find out. Blackness was invading my vision, trying to spare me the awkward pain.

"*Now,*" Chasym barked.

I heard the brief struggle as Kirid tried to take the shawl and Jenen fought back.

"Liitae," Kirid finally called.

Even without seeing I knew the fight was over. Jenen would be bound and the shawl removed. Through the corner of my eye I saw Kirid step beside Chasym, holding the precious cloth.

"Good work," Chasym said. "Now, Kirid, release Liitae's hold on Haeon." Releasing my hair, he reached for the shawl.

I fell to the ground, feeling every muscle in my body tingle with new-found freedom. Jenen knelt beside me, apparently freed from Liitae's binding, and helped me to sit up. I gratefully accepted his aid, massaging my scalp as I focused again on Chasym.

"Does Lon know?" I asked.

Chasym looked up from examining the shawl, meeting my gaze evenly. "As a matter fact, no. For being such a skilled Seer, he didn't have the foresight to suspect his own friends."

"That's called trust," I said.

"Yes," a creepy smile spread across his face, "a trait you inherited. Aren't you lucky?"

I watched him impassively, not letting any of my emotions show.

"I know that you are aware of your parentage now," he said. "I heard you coming toward us in the forest last night and I steered the conversation in that direction. Of course I had to shield your mind from him; otherwise he would have discovered you there."

I felt Jenen's confused eyes on me, but I didn't enlighten him. "Why would you do that?" I asked.

"To make you aware. To let you know that you're not special. Because you're not, Jase. You're just a replacement, like Haeon said. Your own father didn't want you. How does that make you feel?" He chuckled.

My eyes narrowed. His words now completely contradicted his words with Lon.

Chasym turned his focus on Jenen. "Oh, didn't you know? Lon is Jason's father." His yellow eyes flicked to Sasha standing behind us as she gasped. "That's right. He's not a foreigner. He's just as Paradisian as you and me. Well, almost." His eyes returned to mine. "There is the issue of your mother..."

I stiffened, feeling suddenly hungry to learn more—but I couldn't be distracted now. Something was bothering me; something about before. But when and what were unclear.

The blond held up the shawl. "Do you know what this does?"

Jenen and I exchanged blank glances, then shook our heads.

Chasym smiled coldly. "Allow me to show you."

"What are you doing?" Haeon demanded. "You don't have time to explain. They're going to die anyway. Leave them ignorant."

Chasym kept smiling. "Jason always wants to know the answers. I would hate to leave him in the dark now." He handed the shawl to Haeon and knelt before Jenen and me. He placed a hand to each of our foreheads. Instantly we found ourselves standing within a tree in the Realm of Yenen.

It was night, and the room was dark but for a single candle flickering on a small table beside a bed. Stepping closer, I peered into the bed. A young man of fifteen or so was covered in several heavy blankets. He was bathed in sweat, tossing in his fevered sleep.

"Jenen," I whispered. "It's..."

"Me," he agreed softly.

Younger Jenen wasn't too different from his older self; he still looked effeminate, had a very slight build and long black hair. But, as his eyes slowly opened to gaze around the room in confusion, I saw one feature which differed greatly.

"Jenen, your eyes," I whispered.

"What about them?" he asked.

"They're both gold," I said, squinting to make sure. Young Jenen's eyes closed as he settled back into sleep before I could confirm it.

"...Yes," Jenen said from behind me. "I remember that."

I arched one eyebrow. "I would hope so. Care to explain?"

"I would, if I knew, myself," Jenen said, approaching the bed and gazing down. "This is very strange, seeing myself like this."

"What the heck do you mean you don't know?"

Jenen glanced at me patiently. "Tell me. Are you aware of why you suddenly grew two pointed ears and why your eyes changed to silver?"

"I have my theories," I said.

"But that's all." He reached a hand down to hover above the boy. "I remember falling very ill like this. When I finally awakened I was stronger than I had ever felt. I discovered that my eyes had changed and thought them a sign of some great struggle my body had finally overcome. Then I saw Crenen. His eyes had changed like mine. We marveled at its mystery, but no explanation ever presented itself."

I thought back on the time-line I'd constructed in my head to keep track of Paradisian history. "So, you left the Realm of Yenen shortly after this?"

"That's right," he answered softly, still watching the unconscious form. "Crenen said I had nearly died..." His voice faltered for a moment. "...I knew that if either of us was to catch the Paradisaical disease it would be me. My body wasn't as strong as his. Afraid to hurt him, and even a little afraid that he might catch the disease instead and leave me alone, I did the only thing a foolish boy could think of. I ran away.

"It doesn't make sense now, I know. The idea of running away from the thing you can't stand to lose defeats the purpose. But after I had run for so long, I was too afraid to go back. I had hurt him, Key. Hurt him deeply. It is said that the disease can only penetrate a body when it has been weakened. Crenen was never weak. If he has had this disease for the last six years, it can only be my fault. By leaving him alone, both to endure the heartache of loss and the responsibility of his dying clan, I created the weakness which that cursed disease needed in order to infect him. I am to blame for Crenen's condition." He raised his eyes to the ceiling.

"Don't be stupid," I said sharply.

He turned his metallic eyes to mine, and a sad smile crossed his pale face. The flickering flame of the candle caught in his eyes and made them glisten.

I continued. "Jenen, I don't know everything, but I do know this: You and the others have to stop this self-blaming game. Lon blames himself for losing Kirid to Haeon. Chasym blames himself for Veija's insanity. Veija blames herself for

Chasym's supposed death. Menen blames himself for the rift between you and your brother. You blame yourself for Crenen's illness. Sasha blames herself for not having the skills to heal him. Even I'm blaming myself for not saving Paradise sooner. Crenen seems to be the only one not blaming himself, as far as I know. And why is that? Because he's just doing the best he can and he knows it. That's all we can do, Jenen: our best. So stop regretting and start forgiving. Until you do that, there's no way you can solve anything."

"It is much easier said than it is done," he whispered ruefully, "though I do see the wisdom in your words." He turned to face me fully and changed the subject. "What should we do, Key? I thought Chasym was our ally, but it seems that he really was with the Kirid all this time. Not only that; it appears he and Haeon are partners."

"I'm not so sure," I said thoughtfully. "Something doesn't make sense. Haeon hurt him, Jenen. He even nearly killed him. And then he threw him in that cellar. Partners and allies don't do that sort of thing and expect deals to continue working between them."

"Unless it was all a ruse. One that convinced everyone," Jenen said.

I shook my head. "To what purpose? No, it doesn't quite add up. Even in order to fool us they didn't need to take it so far. Can you see Chasym willingly getting injured nearly to death just to further convince us of what we already thought?"

"But you heard Chasym before. Veija confronted him because she was wary. It was just after that when the darkness struck and Haeon appeared. Perhaps they felt it mattered enough to injure him. Or perhaps he was never injured. He is a shapeshifter; a master of illusions."

I frowned. "I don't understand. I don't *want* to understand."

"But you must."

"Yeah."

Chasym's smooth voice interjected. "While I am thoroughly amused with your theories, I suggest turning your attention the doorway."

Jenen and I jumped and turned to face the dark corner behind the bed. Chasym's yellow eyes glowed in the gloom.

"No, no. The door is *behind* you."

We glanced at the wooden door just as it burst open. In stumbled an adolescent Crenen, his mop of black hair hanging in an uneven tangle around his shoulders. He wore a ragged black garb, with dirty white wraps around his ankles and wrists. He scrambled to the bed, oblivious to our presence.

"Jenen," he whispered. Placing a dirty hand on his twin's trembling shoulder, he slowly knelt beside the bed. "Please, no."

"Crenen?" The female voice spoke from the open doorway. Jenen and I turned to see a young Sasha step into the dark room. Even as a teenager she was beautiful, though her face was grave and haunted. She tentatively walked nearer. "I shouldn't have told you."

For a moment Crenen didn't stir, but finally he raised his gold eyes to the girl. "I would have found out."

"I know. But there's still a chance that it's just another bout of illness. It might not be the disease." Her tone was unconvincing.

The young man frowned. "You know as well as I that this is the disease, Sasha." He stood and his hand slid from young Jenen's shoulder. "I..." He closed his eyes to collect his emotions. "I can't lose him now, Sasha. He's all I have left."

I felt Jenen stir beside me.

Sasha hesitated, then placed a slender hand on Crenen's shoulder. "I know, Crenen. I wish there was something I could do."

"No more than I," he whispered. His face was full of helpless pain. He shrugged off her hand and walked by her, heading for the open door.

"Crenen?"

He stopped, but didn't turn around. "I just wish it was me instead."

My stomach clenched.

"What is the point of this?" Jenen hissed as he spun to face Chasym's shadowed form.

"This memory answers all the things you never knew, Jenen. Hush now, and watch," was the simple reply.

"Don't say that," Sasha said, her icy eyes fixed on Crenen's back. "You know Jenen's constitution is weak. We *don't* know he's dying."

A cold smile stole across Crenen's face. "I've seen it twice before in my family. I think I can recognize it for what it is." He walked to the doorway and stood in the streaming light from the full moon. "I'll be back later. Please watch over him until I return?"

"Of course."

His smile grew gentle. "Thank you." He closed the door behind him.

"Follow," Chasym said, "if you want to know the truth."

I walked toward the door without hesitation, passing through it as if it were intangible. Jenen joined me seconds later, his expression wary.

Placing a hand on his shoulder, I smiled encouragingly. "Let's go see what that creep has up his sleeve this time."

He nodded.

We followed after Crenen, keeping close since we both knew he wouldn't see us. This was a memory, nothing more. We couldn't alter what had already been; we could only watch.

The Realm of Yenen had changed little in six years. Even then the trees were tall, majestic, and protected. In the darkness many lights from the carved tree-houses cast a cheery glow from above. The sacred bridge, and others, stretched from tree to tree, swaying in the gentle spring breeze. The only difference between the memory-Realm and the one I'd first set eyes on was the number of people living in it. Six years had done much to destroy Yenen Clan's populace, judging by how many lights flickered from within the trees in this memory.

Crenen walked a familiar route and finally halted before a similarly familiar pool of water. He stared at the water's reflection for several minutes before he bent down and collected a handful of pebbles. Gently, showing none of the frustration he must feel, he tossed the pebbles into the water, one by one. Ripples spread across the glassy surface and slowly died away. Soon he ran out of pebbles.

I joined him at his side and glanced at his face. Tears slid down his dirt-smudged cheeks and his gold eyes shimmered. Finally he stirred and bent down to gather more rocks. Straightening, he tossed a flat rock into the lake and it skipped across the whole pool, rolling a few inches up the other shoreline. He sighed heavily and sat down, cross-legged. Propping one elbow on his knee, he rested his cheek on his palm and gazed into the pool's depths.

A heartbeat passed and he stiffened. He pulled his head from his hand and fixed his eyes on a spot in the dark water. I followed his gaze and found a pulsing glow. I started, recognizing it as the white orb. Crenen got to his feet and splashed into the pool, not taking his eyes from the glowing spot for a second.

"What is that?" Jenen asked me.

"A Remnant," I answered.

"Which is...?"

"I'm not certain," I said honestly. "I think we may be about to find out."

Crenen dove his head under the water and cupped his hands around the little orb.

"Crenen." The voice sounded in my head.

What? Crenen thought, sounding a little frightened. Somehow I could hear his thoughts. Glancing at Jenen, I knew it was the same for him. I wondered whose memory this was.

"I have waited for you."

You have? Crenen asked warily.

"You desire something, do you not?"

Crenen hesitated. *How do you know?*

"I am a Remnant. I know your thoughts, your feelings, your desires. What do you want of me?"

What do you mean?

"I will grant your desire, Crenen, if you so wish it."

How? Crenen was skeptical.

"There is a price. You cannot get something for nothing. Perhaps...an exchange?"

I felt my heart drop. I knew what was coming; suddenly everything was clear. I wanted to jump forward and stop him, but knew I couldn't. Besides, if not for this moment, Jenen would have died years before.

Name it, Crenen urged.

"You, instead of him. I would transfer the disease to your body. It is the only way. The disease cannot yet be annulled. Only moved."

Crenen frowned. *How would you save him? What if he contracted it again? His body is weak.*

"Choose an object. So long as he is its owner, he cannot succumb to the disease again. Do you agree?"

Yes.

"Very well."

But, Crenen thought suddenly, *I need time.*

"Time?"

Yes. Three years might not be enough.

"Why not?"

Because, I have too much to do. I need to set clan affairs in order. I need to ensure its future and place Jenen at its head. He is not easily convinced. More importantly, you must prove to me that he really won't become sick again. I can't trust you so soon.

"...Very well. Since you would not have become ill without this bargain struck, I will give you more time. While the disease will not slow down for you, I will make your body strong. You will live only until Jenen agrees to become leader, or, in the case that he does not agree, you will die exactly six years from this day. That is twice as long as any victim thus far. It is fair."

It is, Crenen agreed.

"Very good. Choose the object of Jenen's protection."

So long as he has it, he will never catch the disease?

"You have my word and the time to test it."

All right. I choose my mother's silver shawl.

I glanced back at Jenen, who reached instinctively for the shawl that should have been around his shoulders. His eyes were dark with emotion.

"It will be done."

One more thing.

"Yes, Crenen?"

Jenen can never break this bargain, even if he finds out. All right?

"Very well. You are a hard one to please, Crenen. But it will be so."

...Why?

"Why do I offer this deal?"

Yes.

"Because, young one, for every desire I fulfill, the world draws nearer to its close."

Its close? Crenen whispered fearfully.

"The end of all things old, and the start of all things new. You will see this close."

So, the world will end soon.

"The world, as it is now, will. Yes. But, what comes from that has yet to be decided."

Before I could hear Crenen's response, the scenery shifted and Crenen, the orb, and the pool disappeared. Jenen and I stood on the plains of blue mist. I felt Chasym behind me, and turned to view his smirking face.

"Do you understand now?" he asked. "Do you know the purpose of the shawl?"

"To keep me alive," Jenen said quietly.

"Yes, but besides that," Chasym said. "Jase?"

I brushed a stray lock of hair from my eye and met his yellow gaze. "To prevent me from getting the disease," I said. "Because when I bound Jenen's soul to mine, his shawl protected my Paradisian blood as well. It ensured that I wouldn't die before I fulfilled prophecy."

"Exactly," he said, grinning. "Sharper than ever, Jase. Trust you to figure things out."

I raised my brow, sensing something hidden in his words.

Jenen stepped forward once. "Chasym, why are you doing this? Why did you betray us?"

The blond paused to consider his response. He finally shrugged. "Once upon time I lost the girl I loved because she tried to rewrite history to bring me back from the grave. She would die mortal for her foolish sacrifice. Had she not done that, I could have won Lon's trust and eventually revealed myself to her. But I suppose I should be grateful. With her mortality, I grew desperate. It's amazing what desperation can cause a man to do. I found the core in my efforts to save her." He smiled. "Imagine, Jase. You stumble upon the core; ultimate power. The Essence of Paradise. With it you can control the very elements. But," he raised a finger, "as always, for a price.

"I interrupted that memory before you had a chance to see Crenen leave the mortal plane and journey to the core's Alter. There he sealed the bargain. It was in that moment that his left eye changed to silver; a physical manifestation of his sacrifice. Jenen's left eye also changed in that moment. When Jenen awoke—the younger one of course—he had no idea that he had been dying. Sasha was also startled, but delighted when, after a thorough examination, she discovered no sign of the disease. In the weeks that followed Jenen was stronger than he had ever felt before. With this strength, Jenen made the choice to leave, thinking it would not last. He didn't want to die in front of Crenen and was afraid that he might.

"As he left, Crenen stopped him, and gave him the shawl 'to remember.' Not a week after Jenen's departure Crenen fell ill and Sasha discovered his secret. She never knew, of course, how he had contracted the disease. After two years of outward health, but inner torment, Crenen began the hunt for Jenen so that he could end his pain. If Jenen would only agree to become clan leader, he could pass on in peace. But, while he wanted this, he knew from the words of the Remnant that he would not die before the world's close."

Jenen trembled. I placed my hand again on his shoulder comfortingly.

"I paid a different price four hundred years ago," Chasym continued. "When I confronted the core, I struck a deal. I desired nothing more than two things: Veija's survival and Paradise's judgment. I got both, though the price was a heavy one to pay."

"You created the disease," I whispered as everything fell into place. Visions swam in my mind's eyes. "You loathed the world for all its cruelty, and so you made the core sick. When it became sick, They went mad, the Seers despaired and broke their rule just to be able to die, and Kirid Clan lost its sense of honor and peace, becoming a violet people. You made the world worse, Chasym, not better."

"It is odd what grief will do, Jason," he answered simply. "Haeon was my servant at that time and he agreed with my philosophy. He drove me on in my search for revenge. It was he who knew the only price I could pay to get what I wanted."

"Was it worth it in the end?" I asked softly. "Was it worth the loss of your humanity?"

He smiled, insanity dancing in his eyes, but made no answer. Instead he turned to the mist. "I have won, Jason. Veija will live, the world will die, and you, my little friend, will fail. Haeon manipulated fate to see to that."

My eyes widened. "Is that why he's mortal now? He changed the future." More images flashed in my head; the answers. "He used his Sight to find Kirid, manipulated the future to steal him, and lost his Seership for it. What a foolish sacrifice."

Chasym shrugged, still smiling. "It worked. And he will certainly live now. He saw to that, too."

"What was your price, Chasym?" I asked.

His smile faded. "I *am* the disease."

36
Too High A Cost?

Realization dawned on me.

Of course Chasym couldn't die. He was feeding off the energy of the world, growing more powerful with the decimation of Paradise. It was a heavy price to pay—sacrificing life to attain power—but I doubted he would see it that way.

"How is that a heavy price to you? It renders you omnipotent. You have total control over whether this world lives or dies."

He smiled wryly. "Not quite, but nearly. Once this world is cleansed, I will have control over what next inhabits its lands. But I'm afraid there's no way I could stop the disease from spreading if I wanted to. That would, simply put, cause my own destruction. And, as you can guess, I'm not partial to that plan. Facing my own judgment is something I'd rather avoid."

"You admit your actions were wrong, but you're too afraid of your own damnation to rectify what you have done," Jenen said darkly.

Chasym considered his words. “Right. Exactly.”

Again something nagged at my mind, but I didn't know what. “Was it worth it?” I repeated.

Chasym merely smiled again, still making no answer. Then he stiffened and glanced above us into the mist. After a moment he looked at us again. “Time to return. We must finish. The world is waiting for its final judgment.”

The blue mist dissolved and we were standing on the stone column above a glowing ocean of lava. Haeon stood in front of Kirid and Sasha lay unconscious at the former Seer's feet. I ran to her, kneeling down and lifting her head gently.

She opened her sapphire eyes after moment and smirked at me. “I'm all right,” she assured me, gingerly sitting up. “I just tried to kill him, and he fought back.”

I laughed. “Well, thanks for trying.” I glared up at the Haeon, who watched me with cold indifference. I helped Sasha to stand and guided her back to where Jenen waited.

“Now what?” Sasha asked.

Chasym glanced at Haeon, who handed the shawl to the blond.

“Now,” Haeon answered, “we destroy Vendaeva.”

“...With that?” she laughed.

“With this,” Chasym assured her. “You see, this little shawl has been the only thing keeping me from killing Jason up 'til now. Isn't that right?”

I watched him wordlessly.

Sasha glanced between us, then threw Jenen a questioning look. He didn't respond either.

“End this,” Haeon said, a wicked smile spreading across his face.

“Of course,” Chasym said, grinning. “But let me play first.”

“You've had your fill of that,” Haeon said.

"No. I want Jason to understand. I don't think he believes yet that I've betrayed him. I want to drill it into his little head." He flung the shawl across one shoulder and, quicker than lightning, he was behind me, pulling my arms back and twisting them. I cried out at the unexpected pain. "Do you hate me, Jase?" he whispered into my ear, pulling tighter.

"No," I answered between clenched teeth.

"We'll have to rectify that, won't we?"

"Chasym," Haeon said, "stop at once. Just kill the boy."

"He can't die yet. We need his power."

"If we kill him the power will transfer to Kirid."

"We don't know that," Chasym said, twisting my right arm just a little more. I could feel the strain threatening to break my humerus bone. "Are you willing to take that chance? Let me play. I will get out of the boy what is needed."

With a sickening crack I felt my arm explode with pain. I screamed, squeezing my eyes shut as tears spilled down my cheeks. Chasym released me and I crumpled to the ground, clutching my twisted limb. I gasped for air, gulping it quickly to focus on anything but the agony that was my arm.

"Key," Sasha said, kneeling beside me. "Let me see." She gently reached for my broken arm, taking it carefully. I winced, but remained still.

"Step aside," Chasym said from overhead.

"I will not," I heard Jenen reply coldly.

"Suit yourself."

I turned my head in time to see Chasym wave Jenen aside with a brutal blast of icy wind. The raven-haired Paradisian slid across the stone, but was on his feet again in seconds. Several deep incisions bled along his arms, legs, and one cheek, but he showed no sign of pain.

"Stay there," Chasym said as he turned his attention back to me. "I'm busy right now."

Sasha jumped to her feet and flexed her claws.

Chasym sighed. "Sasha, you don't need to die here. Well —not yet. Not this way."

I gritted my teeth as I pulled myself to my feet, letting my useless arm dangle. I turned to face the blond, ignoring the tears streaming down my face. "Sasha, it's okay. This is between us."

She hesitated for only moment, then stepped to the side, understanding as only a warrior could.

"So noble, suddenly? I guess you really are growing up."

"Shut up, Chasym," I said, raising my left hand. "Let's just finish this. From what I understand, you need my power, so I can't die. Meanwhile all I have to do is kill you to stop the disease."

Chasym chuckled. "Stop it, yes. Cure it, no. Besides, I doubt you could kill me if you wanted to. No, Jason. I'm afraid your task is more difficult than you're willing to admit. But then, you've always had a knack for denying the truth; even as child." He raised his hand and another burst of wind shot forth, pushing against me and cutting into my skin. I winced but stayed standing.

Jenen rushed forward, jumping into the air and falling toward Chasym, his claws extended to strike fatally. Chasym flicked his wrist and Jenen flipped backward on the gust of wind, landing maladroitly on the hard stone, laying on his stomach. He attempted to get to his feet again, but couldn't seem to find the strength.

No. That wasn't it.

Looking closer, I saw the vague outline of air-formed chains keeping him face first on the ground.

"Be grateful I didn't send you over the edge," Chasym told him.

"Liitae," I said. The orb materialized above my hand and shot toward Chasym. The blond grinned and brushed it aside.

Determined, the orb came from behind. Again Chasym deflected it effortlessly.

"You're nothing but a pest, a mosquito. Surely you have more skill," he mocked.

"Stop toying," Haeon barked. "Just get his power and kill the boy."

Chasym sighed. "He's right, Jason. We need you to give your power over to Kirid so we can end this."

I shook my head. "No way. I'm not especially fond of suicide, so I'll pass."

He smiled patiently. "One way or another you're going to lose, why bother fighting?"

"Because in the unlikely event that I do lose, I'd rather go down trying." I reached out with my mind, searching.

"Ah, heroics. They've always amused me."

I felt my mind make contact with what I sought. *Lon, help. We've been betra—!*

The connection was suddenly severed and a jolt of pain.

"Uh uh uh," Chasym shook his head. "Tattling isn't a good trait, Key. Especially for a liar like yourself." He grinned and sprinted forward. Within a second he was on me, his fist connecting with my cheek. I lost my footing and slid across the stones.

I scrambled up again, still ignoring the terrible pain in my right arm, but before I could retaliate Chasym kicked his foot into my stomach. I flew backwards, summoning Liitae behind me. It barely kept me from flying over the edge of the platform, then pushed me forward. I staggered but kept my balance.

"Not too bad for only one lesson in defense," Chasym said, applauding me. "You're certainly an impressive boy to listen so well to your instincts. When we were children you trounced me pretty hard—though you shouldn't expect things to stay the same forever. People change, grow up, move on. It's life. And, unfortunately for you, life has given me every advantage."

I grimaced and rushed forward, summoning Liitae's energy inside myself to boost my speed. Instantly I was on him, slamming my left fist into his cheek. As he stumbled backward in surprise I smirked. "Maybe so, Chazzy, but life tends to keep things interesting by raising the stakes. I'm afraid we've both been dealt pretty impressive hands. And, you can rest assured, I'm gonna beat you."

Chasym ran his hand gently along his bruising cheek and chuckled. "'I'll beat you. No matter what, no matter where, no matter how—I swear, I'll beat you at everything..'" As he spoke, I heard my own voice—though younger—in his. "How interesting that even now, without your memories of back then, you say similar things." His eyes lit up with mad excitement. "This will be fun!"

His words stirred a memory. For an instant I was sitting in the grass, holding my own bruised cheek, glaring up at the taller, dark-haired boy gloating before me. "The only way to make you stop sulking is to beat you up. How pathetic!" the boy had taunted.

With a scream of rage I'd jumped to my feet and tackled him to the ground, throwing my fists randomly in the hope that I would deal him damage. When I finally stopped, he was just laying there, grinning up at me from a bloodied face.

"That's better. That's the man I know," he'd said, laughing.

It was then, in order to hide my own horror at what I done to him, that I had shouted out the promise that I would beat him at everything.

Now, looking at the form of Chasym before me, I managed a sad smile. "It's time to make good on my promise."

He raised his hands. "By all means, try."

As a child, I'd blindly fought because my pride was hurt. Now, however, something far more precious than pride had been injured. He'd betrayed my trust, and not only that; he'd betrayed everything and everyone that was important. For that he must answer.

I caught Liitae in my hand and shoved the orb into my chest, absorbing its considerable energy. "To keep everything, you lost it all, Chasym." I jumped aside as the blond whipped a forceful wind torrent at me. I landed a few yards away. "That was stupid."

"In order to gain this power, I had to," he said. "It was worth it." He brought his hands together and wind crashed into me from either side, cutting deep lacerations in my skin.

I kept from crying out, determined not to give him the pleasure. Bracing against the pain, I reached out to the wind, seeking its core.

—There.

I mentally stoppered the vortex and the wind died away.

Chasym looked startled, then smiled. "Well done."

"Don't patronize me." An idea came to mind and I reached out to grasp at the core of the lava below. Raising my hand, I pulled on the lava's tremendous heat.

"I really mean—" He broke off as something took form in my hand; a new orb, this one a swirling ball of red fire.

I released it, summoning another and firing it within seconds of its predecessor. Chasym barely dodged the first, but the second slammed into his stomach, tearing through flesh. He stumbled backward as he vomited blood. Hunching over, his shoulders shook with the pain, but he straightened. Now his eyes were lightless and his face wore no expression. He ran a hand across the hole in his stomach and the wound vanished.

Inhaling shakily, he fixed his eyes on mine. "That wasn't nice," he said in soft tones.

"I'm not sorry." Part of me was lying; the part that still couldn't believe he would really betray everyone. But that part was slowly dying.

He wiped the blood from his mouth and studied the red smear on his hand. His yellow eyes flicked to me again. "That will cost you, Jason Sterling."

I said nothing. I was tired of talking. Instead I considered how in the world I was going to kill him. A direct assault did nothing; besides, he was immortal—or, if what Lon once said of me applied to Chasym, he was only half immortal. Considering that an entire world was so easily plunged toward its own destruction, could it be much more difficult to kill a single man?

Probably. But I couldn't afford to entertain doubts.

Key. I'm coming.

Lon's voice in my head brought a wave of hope to back my determination. I perked up. He was coming; my father was coming. And with him would come Crenen and Menen—and Veija. My eyes widened. If she appeared, would Chasym be able to carry out his plan? Was there a chance she might still be his weakness? Could I use that?

"You should pay more attention," Chasym said.

I stiffened as Chasym disappeared from before me. Suddenly he was in front of Sasha and with a swift motion he plunged his claws into her stomach. I caught sight of a fiery orb in his fist as it entered her gut.

"NO!" I screamed as she cried out.

He slid his hand free, bloodied and empty. Sasha stood in shock for a moment and then, turning frightened eyes to me, she collapsed to her knees and fell backward. Blood pooled around her as her body jerked.

I ran to her, sliding to my knees and raising her head up, cradling her in my good arm. "Liitae." The blue orb appeared, but Chasym snatched my hair and tore me away. Sasha fell limply to the ground. "Let me go!" I screamed, struggling against his iron grip.

"No. You can't save her. I won't let you do that again," he whispered in my ear. He grabbed my right arm, twisting the broken bone. I didn't feel pain. I only struggled more, desperate to reach my dying friend, adrenaline pounding in my ears.

"Please, Chasym! She's dying."

"I told you I would make you pay."

Rage filled my body and soul at his words.

Die, I thought vehemently.

Chasym jerked back, gasping. He released me as he clutched at his heart with terrified eyes.

"What's wrong?" Haeon demanded.

"Kirid!" Chasym cried in a pain-filled voice.

I ignored them and rushed to Sasha's side. She was still breathing, and, surprisingly, still conscious. Her vibrant eyes opened and she smiled dryly. "Going to doctor me up now?" She tried to chuckle, but only choked on her own blood and started to cough.

I smiled grimly. "I figure I owe you one."

"It's...about time...someone realized that," she managed between trembling breaths. "I...only wish that...Crenen could be...h-here now."

I raised my palm and urged Liitae to return to me. "Don't talk like that. You're going to be fine." Liitae wasn't coming. Glancing behind me I saw Kirid standing nearby. Liitae was floating above his opened hand. "Kirid," I said, "please let me save her."

He shook his head sadly. "No, Kiido. I can't."

"Kirid! She can't die like this! Please." Vaguely I felt tears fall down my face.

Chasym laughed and stepped up to join Kirid. My violent thought hadn't been enough to destroy him; it had only momentarily halted him. "You've lost, Jason."

Almost as if in retaliation to his words a deafening peal, like a mighty bell, filled the hazy sky and the portal back to Paradise appeared. From the sky four figures fell, taking in the scene as they reached the ground.

"Sasha!" Crenen's voice was full of terror as he stared at the dying form beside me. He ran toward us, but Haeon blocked his path. With a vicious hiss the Yenen prince slashed his claws at the man, who managed to dodge. Menen rushed forward and knocked Haeon to the ground.

"Master, go," Menen said. I saw something in Menen's eyes I'd never seen before. Blood lust. Haeon was going to die.

Crenen didn't hesitate. He only sidestepped the fallen Verenveyan and quickly reached us, kneeling beside the dying woman and taking her head in his arms. She smiled up at him as if she weren't in pain; as if her life wasn't swiftly bleeding away.

"Y-you're here," she whispered.

"Yes," he said softly as his eyes swept over her fatal wound.

"I am glad. I...I wanted—" She coughed raggedly and blood seeped from the corners of her lips, "—to say goodbye." Her eyes were growing dim.

"No," he whispered. "Do not leave me. I was supposed die, not you. Do not go." A tear slid slowly down his face.

She laughed hoarsely. "Don't be...so selfish, Crenen. Y-you can't have all...the glory."

"What glory?" he choked. The tear fell from his chin and landed on her pale face.

"You're...you're crying for me? ...Thank...you..." Her eyes closed.

"Sasha?"

"I...love you, ...Crenen," she whispered with a smile and released her final breath.

"No!" he screamed, gripping her shoulders and roughly shaking her limp body. "You have to stay! I cannot lose you!"

My vision was blurred by the tears falling from my eyes, but I reached forward and placed my hand on his arm. "Crenen, she's gone."

"No," he hissed, jerking away from my touch. "No." His body grew lax and sobs began to rack him. He doubled over Sasha's body and cried into her bloodied stomach.

"I'm sorry," I whispered. "I...couldn't save her. I'm so sorry."

37
The Shawl's Defeat?

"I bid you welcome, Seer Lon," Chasym said, spreading his arms out in greeting.

I numbly looked up from Crenen's sobbing form and fixed my gaze on Lon. He stood in silence, his red eyes taking in everything: Sasha, dead; Crenen, weeping; Jenen, chained by the wind; Kirid, holding Liitae prisoner; Menen, fighting with Haeon—and finally he paused on me. His expression was unfathomable, but for a split second I could almost swear I felt his relief when he studied my tattered, but relatively whole appearance.

"Explain yourself, Chasym," he demanded.

The blond smiled blandly. "I think it's rather obvious."

"Fine," Lon said, "consider your chance to monologue over then."

"I did plenty of that while fighting your son." Chasym shrugged. "I'm finished."

Lon stiffened and glanced at me. I only smiled wearily back.

Chasym chuckled. "That's right, he knows. Now all the secrets are out! So, let's end this."

Lon continued to watch me and slowly his expression softened. A sad smile touched his lips, then it was gone, replaced with iciness as he turned back to Chasym. "Very well. As far as I'm concerned whatever reasons you have for your actions are invalid." As he spoke, tiny lights appeared in an oval around him and then burst into white flames.

"Be careful, Lon," Veija called. Chasym hesitated, glancing at the beautiful woman standing near the edge of the platform. She turned her violet eyes to him and her gaze turned frigid.

"Don't worry," Lon assured her. "This will not take long." The white flames rushed at Chasym, circling around him and pushing inward, engulfing him. A burst of light threw the flames back. Chasym turned an annoyed expression back to Lon.

"Don't be so impatient. We will fight when we both are ready."

"Then ready yourself."

The blond's eyes narrowed. A sliver of wind whipped past Lon's face and cut his tattooed cheek. "I said be patient."

Lon didn't flinched. He gazed at Chasym, eyes narrow. "You've never been one to act so childishly."

Chasym scoffed but said nothing. He shot forth another sliver of wind, this one slicing through Lon's left shoulder. It tore the cloth of his purple robe and revealed the tattoo there; blood trickled from the cut, dripping down the sword blade.

The corner of Lon's mouth twitched. "You think to seal my power with this ritual? These markings no longer effect me."

"We shall see."

He cut Lon's left arm again, revealing a second tattoo further down. At the same time two slivers of wind cut two places on his right arm. Why Lon didn't move away, I couldn't understand. He only stood there, watching Chasym with an unreadable face. As blood trickled from the cuts, the five tattoos began to glow red.

Lon flinched, but his eyes remained fixed on his traitorous friend. "You cannot control me now."

"Actually, I can." Chasym raised his hand and swiped it downward. Lon collapsed to his knees, slamming them hard against the stone. His eyes glittered with confusion. "You may have beaten the ritual before, my friend," Chasym said as he stepped toward the Seer, a gentle whirl of air circling his slender form, playing with his long hair, "but things were different back then. I only had the same power as everyone around me. Since then I find myself—what's that word you used, Jase?—omnipotent. The rules don't really apply to me anymore." He towered over Lon, who only watched him mildly.

"What is your point, Chasym? So you can disable me—do you think I'm the only one you're facing?"

Before Chasym could respond, a dark form jumped through the air and knocked him to the ground. With one hand Jenen's claws sank into his stomach, while he used his other hand to slash across Chasym's eyes. He leapt up to stand on Chasym's shoulders and wrapped his toe claws around them. He stared down at the man with fire in his metallic eyes.

Chasym lay on the platform in stunned silence for moment, but then a smirk crossed his bloodied face. "How ever did you get free?"

"You're not the only one with power," Lon answered. "I unchained him while you were monologuing."

I would've laughed had things been different, but now I sat very still, trying to feel through my shock. Faintly, I felt grim satisfaction at Chasym's situation. Taking my eyes from the fight for a moment, I saw Crenen still cradling Sasha, his head buried, though he'd stopped crying. I rested my hand on his shoulder. He didn't respond.

At the sound of a gasp to my right I looked over to find Menen clutching Haeon's throat. Hatred flared inside and I silently urged Menen on. Haeon struggled for air desperately, but then a smile spread over his face and he laughed between gagging breaths.

Menen's red eyes narrowed and he squeezed harder. "What's so funny?"

"You can't...kill me..." he wheezed.

"Don't be so certain," Menen said between gritted teeth. Then he lurched forward a step as his eyes widened. Kirid stood behind him, his clawed hand thrust into Menen's side. Kirid's eyes were vacant.

"Menen!" I cried out as blood spattered the ground.

Crenen jerked his head up and looked around for his cousin. When he found him he pushed Sasha into my arms and stood abruptly. "Menen?"

The tall man's eyes narrowed and, despite the large wound in his side, he spun around and knocked Kirid forcefully to the ground. Somehow he managed to maintain his stranglehold on Haeon, who dangled a few inches above the ground.

"It will take more than that," Tall Strong Jerk said calmly.

Kirid lay still, though he was conscious. His gray eyes found mine and he stared at me imploringly. His lips mouthed a silent question: 'Why?'

I could give him no answer.

Crenen was standing quietly now, his blood-stained face paler than ever and streaked with tears. His eyes were haunted as he watched Haeon struggling while his life drained away. Menen showed no sign of relenting and no one moved to stop him.

From the corner of my eye I saw Chasym send a wind current toward Jenen, who was pushed into the air and landed with some grace near Lon.

"Ideas?" Jenen hissed.

Lon was frowning. "None yet."

"That helps," Jenen replied sardonically.

Chasym leapt to his feet and ran a hand over his eyes, healing the scratches. He opened them and grinned. "Think fast now." He raised his palm. Liitae broke free of Kirid's grasp and flew to him. "Now then—"

"Cha...sym," Haeon choked desperately.

The blond paused, glancing at Haeon. A frown touched his lips. "All right, Jason. I think you've stood aside long enough." He glanced at Jenen and Lon. "Hold still." Tendrils of shimmering air snaked up from under their feet and wrapped swiftly around their bodies, binding them before they could move.

I looked up at him. "You're pretty eager to die."

"You misunderstand. I'm destroying you, not fighting you." He smirked, gazing at Liitae. "It will be a simple task, using this." The ball's light flickered and then went out.

Pain shot through my heart and I gasped, feeling as if half of myself had been snuffed out.

"This ought to work," he said.

Suddenly Liitae flared to life again, but its blue light had darkened as if clouds swirled within. My eyes narrowed. Blue mist. The disease.

"Now," Chasym said, smirking as he lifted the shawl from his shoulder with one hand. "Who would've thought it would be so simple?" He ran a hand along the silky material, and, grabbing Liitae, he shoved the orb into the shawl. In seconds the orb was absorbed. The silver cloth crumbled to dust.

"Jenen?" I heard Lon say quietly.

Glancing at them I saw Jenen slumped over, held up by the airy tendrils, his pale face contorted in pain as blood seeped from the corners of his mouth. The Paradisaical disease had struck with paroxysmal vengeance, as though making up for Jenen's miraculous escape for so long.

Then it fell over me. A strange tingling sensation crawled up my legs, then my arms, until a numbing cold had swept over my body. The disease was claiming me too, though not as quickly. I shivered as I laid Sasha gently aside. I forced myself to stand and face my enemy.

"It's not enough," I said quietly. "All this—it's not enough to make you hurt. I don't know what sort of monster you've become, but it's a far cry from the man Veija loved once. You're..." Pathetic? Cruel? Heartless? What word could describe the atrocities which he had inflicted? "You're...crying," I whispered, seeing an image that shouldn't have been there. Behind Chasym, like a dying flame, I saw him again, doubled over and sobbing uncontrollably. Invisible chains held him captive, wrapping around his arms and legs, and even around magnificent black wings.

Chasym scoffed at my words. "You've lost it, Jase. I suppose it makes sense, after all you've been through. It's probably best to finish you off now."

My eyes followed the chains that imprisoned the fleeting image of Chasym until I saw Menen holding Haeon as the former Seer was strangled. My eyes went to Haeon's clenched fists, where the chains ended. Then I looked into Haeon's face. He wasn't really dying. It was all a ploy, all a setup. We'd been tricked.

"KEY!" Veija screamed just as I felt Chasym plunge Liitae into my heart. I felt the taint take immediate effect, coursing through my body like scalding water. Stumbling back, I placed a hand over my heart as darkness crept in from the corners of my eyes.

Was I dying?

"Key," Lon's gentle, desperate voice said from a great distance.

Would I ever see him again?

With that thought, I watched through the growing darkness as I fell away from the core, away from my friends. My body was still laying on the ground, as I both fell and flew, beneath and above, until finally my world spun away and I was standing in a beautiful meadow. A single puddle shimmered in the noonday sunlight, three butterflies danced around the wildflowers, and a soft breeze swept through my long hair.

Not far from where I stood I saw two other people in the meadow. The first was Lon, kneeling before a young child. Lon's face was sorrowful as he cupped his hands around the boy's face. The boy—me—gazed into his father's eyes with all the trust of an idolizing son.

I didn't know if I was alive or dead; I hoped for the former. But one thing I was certain of: My life was about to pass before me. The finals answers were finally here.

38
The Heir Of Vendaeva?

As I watched the silence was finally broken.

"It's all right to be afraid," Lon said softly to the four-year-old. He took his hands from the child's face and placed them on his shoulders. "Everyone is afraid sometimes."

The boy nodded, his gray eyes shining with unshed tears.

Lon opened his mouth to say more, but closed it again. Swallowing, he tried once more. "Be brave, Key. You have all the power you need."

Again the boy only nodded vigorously, as if that would keep the tears from falling.

A rustle in the thick brush to the right of them made both look up. Chasym emerged from the foliage, brushing off his silken forest-green garments as he approached. "I'm sorry I'm late," he said. Crouching down, he ruffled the boy's hair. "Ready to go?"

At first the boy nodded bravely, but then the tears fell and he threw himself into Lon's arms, sobbing. Lon held the child with a gentleness I'd never seen in him. He allowed the child to stay there for several minutes while Chasym looked on with a sad smile.

"It's not too late, Lon," the blond said after a while. "Choose another child."

The Seer shook his head. "How can I ask it of someone if I'm not willing, myself?"

Chasym sighed. "The chance that he can succeed is slim. Are you willing to take that risk?"

Lon met his gaze evenly. "If you are there to guide him, how can he fail?"

Chasym hesitated, but finally nodded. "Very well. Though I'll never know how you talked me into this."

"You're a good friend."

"No, I'm not," Chasym said as he stood, "and the sooner you figure that out, the less pain it will cause you. Besides, if I really was a good friend, I'd put a stop to this nonsense."

Lon pulled his son away and met the boy's eyes. "Time to go." He got to his feet and guided his son to the gleaming puddle where they watched the water for another moment. "Take him, Chasym."

"No," Chasym said crossly. "I'll protect him only after you've done your part. I don't agree with this, so don't ask me to do it for you."

Lon sighed heavily and nodded. "I understand. Sorry to give you such trouble."

"I'm used to it," Chasym replied. Then he frowned. "How is Meyana?"

"Better off," Lon answered. "Open the portal."

Chasym waved his hand and the puddle rippled, then stood still again. "You mean you sent her away."

My younger self reached up his tiny hand and slid it into Lon's.

"Yes," Lon said as he stepped with little Key into the water.

"Why? You need her now more than ever."

As the puddle churned at his feet Lon turned back to meet Chasym's gaze. "She never belonged in this world anyway. I had no right to bring her here."

"But you're sending your child to another world? You're a hypocrite."

"The one thing about myself for certain," Lon replied. He glanced down at the child. "One stop before I take you to your new home."

"Please, Lon. There must be some other way," Chasym burst out, taking a single step forward as though to stop them.

This time Lon didn't bother answering.

The three of us—Lon, myself, and the little me—were swept away from Chasym, swallowed by blinding golden light as we traveled to some unknown destination. We appeared in a conspicuous puddle in the middle of a hundred-degree desert. The sun beat down on us mercilessly, drying up the puddle even as Lon guided the child from it. Somehow I'd been knocked over in transit, so I clambered to my feet and joined them.

They walked some distance from the drying puddle until they stopped before a single, equally out-of-place tree. Its majestic branches extended high into the sky, providing shade for several dozen yards. On the branches were countless bunches of the most plump and purple gerani I'd ever seen. My mouth watered as I eyed them.

Because of this distraction I didn't see the person sitting beneath the tree until he started speaking.

"This is the one?" a soft, young voice inquired.

"My son Key," Lon said.

I pried my eyes from the glorious sight above and set them on the small, lithe stranger before me. He looked like a child no older than ten and his silvery eyes danced with the shadows playing across him in the shade. White hair sprawled across his shoulders and half way down his back. He wore a knowing smile, as if he knew every secret contained in the world. Slowly he stood and his long, overly large black robes dragged across the ground as he approached the boy. He knelt before my younger self, though he wasn't much taller. Looking into each other's eyes, both boys said nothing, as if words weren't needed.

I felt oddly drawn to the white-haired youth, like I knew him as a friend. Stepping closer, I tried to recall this same memory from the eyes of my self back then. I took one more step, and the youth pulled away from little Key's gaze, glancing in my direction. He stared for a moment, his silver depths unfathomable, and then he smiled.

"Yes, Lon. I was correct to choose your son and you were wise to listen. It is for the best." He slowly took his eyes from mine. I found my lungs and breathed deeply. The youth turned back to the boy and his smile turned kind. "Little one, do you know what great task you are to perform?"

The boy nodded. "Father says I've got to save Paradise."

"Yes, that is exactly right." The white-haired youth beamed. "You are a smart one. You may yet succeed." He glanced pointedly in my direction as he spoke. "Now then," he set one pale hand on the boy's head, "I give you my blessing, heir of Vendaeva." Ruffling little Key's hair as he straightened, he turned his focus to Lon. "His memories must be suppressed."

"Chasym said he would—"

"No," the youth snapped, then blinked at his own angry tone. His expression softened. "No, no, that will not be sufficient. Such precious memories need special care." He placed his hand over the child's heart and, with a startled gasp from the boy, the youth pulled forth a blue orb. "Contain his memories in here. All the ones which are important—like this meeting. Only this orb must have these, do you understand? Do as you like with family memories; but all the knowledge of Vendaeva will be kept in this and this alone. Do you understand, Seer Lon?"

Lon nodded curtly as he took the blue orb and slipped it into his robes. "I do."

"Good." The gentle smile returned. "You must hurry along; time is not slowing down, even for me." He slid his hand under the child's chin and raised his head. Their eyes met. "I declare you my heir." With a flash of blue light, everything vanished, and then returned. The only difference now were the two silver eyes blinking rapidly in little Key's face.

Lon and his son bowed and turned away from the youth, who had retaken his seat under the tree. Before they got far, however, the youth called after them. "Lon, do not forget—he is mine now, you have forsaken him."

An emotion flitted across Lon's face, but then his expression hardened and he bowed again. "Of course."

I ran after them as they approached the cracked ground where the puddle had been. With a wave of his hand, Lon filled the parched earth with water and they stepped into it. As I followed I glanced behind me to where the tree had stood so tall. All that remained was a barren desert floor. I kept my eyes on the empty spot until the golden light swallowed us again.

It was raining when we found ourselves standing on a familiar street. Glancing around, I saw a few vacant lots where houses had yet to be built, but my own white home appeared the same as always—except for an older car sitting in the driveway, and a different mailbox (Jana had run this one over when she first acquired her driver's license).

Lon headed straight for the white house, taking my shivering shadow with him. I trailed slowly after them, gazing around at the gloomy street.

As we reached the front lawn we halted and Lon bent down to meet his son's eyes. "Your new family lives here. They are good people and you will be loved. Stay here until you are summoned."

The boy nodded bravely as tears began to roll down his rain-wettened cheeks.

Lon pulled the blue orb from his robes and touched it to the boy's forehead. The orb pulsed and Lon slipped it back in his pocket. He reached out and wiped the tears gently away and stood up. "Goodbye, Key." He walked down the street toward the same puddle we had arrived in, but rather than follow him, I felt compelled to stay. Turning back to the small child, I saw him watching Lon leave with rising panic. Suddenly the boy ran after the Seer.

"Father! Don't leave, please!" he cried, slipping along the pavement as he hurried to catch up.

Halting, Lon glanced back, his expression stony. He flicked his hand. Little Key stumbled backward and sat hard on the ground. Fresh tears spilled down his face unchecked as he watched his father vanish in a brilliant glow of gold.

"NO!" he screamed. He scrambled to his feet, ran to the puddle, and splashed around in it, as if that would reopen the portal and bring his father back. He slipped and landed on his face, sobbing into his scraped hands.

Another form appeared, this one seemingly out of thin air. Kneeling down, Chasym drew the child into his lap and held him while he cried. Chasym patted the small back as he gazed into the distance. Finally the blond sighed and placed his hand on Key's honey-colored hair.

I knew what was coming even before it happened. And though the scenery didn't change around me, in my mind I saw what Chasym was giving the boy: fake memories of a life I'd never really lived. I saw a party, celebrating my fourth birthday that supposedly happened only a week before. I saw a child, dark-haired but still my older sister, laughing and teasing me as we played a game in the backyard. My parents, stern but loving. And a baby, perhaps one year old, who would grow up as my younger brother Jeremy. Countless memories I'd always cherished played like a movie in my head. All of this had been a lie; my family wasn't my family; my memories weren't my memories; my life had never really been my life.

Finally Chasym pulled the child to his feet and smiled at him. "Well, Jason Sterling, I wish you a wonderful life." He stood up and the rain fell off of him like feathers. He stood in the downpour still, but the water couldn't touch him. "I'll visit from time to time." He waved his hand and the boy's Paradisian garments changed into denim jeans, a little red jacket and a white t-shirt underneath. The pointed ears vanished, the eyes changed back to gray, and the honey-colored hair became short.

Then Chasym was gone, as if he'd never been there.

Both my younger self and I stood in the rain for a long time, and then, with a sullen expression, the young child trudged through the heavy rainfall until he reached the front door to the house and, after some difficulty, managed to open the door. As he entered I could hear my mother's exclamation of surprise and then a scolding about being out in the rain, especially by himself.

I smiled to myself, recalling the occasion from the boy's perspective. Of course, before today I'd never known why I didn't care at all that she was so angry. Now I didn't doubt that with such a change, and such a loss, it would leave a boy much more...closed.

I remembered a lot of my childhood, but the events that played before me now in rapid succession were things I didn't recall. I saw myself as a sullen boy who didn't want anything to do with his family. Several years passed by in seconds, and my eight-year-old version sat in the backyard, swaying slowly in the swing hanging from a giant oak tree. Now time slowed down and I watched as a dark-haired boy approached my swing, his arms folded.

"I've been watching you," the boy said.

Young Jason looked up with an indifferent expression. "So?" he said quietly.

"So. Why are you always pouting?"

"I'm not pouting."

"Then prove it."

"I don't have to." Once upon a time I hadn't been so easy to provoke.

The other boy clenched his teeth. He lurched forward and grabbed Jason's collar, dragging him from the swing. "See? You're still pouting."

"I'm not," Jason said, unaffected.

"Fine," the youth's mouth twisted, "you're sulking then." He shook the collar for emphasis.

"What's your name?" Jason asked gently.

"My name doesn't matter."

"Oh." Jason turned his eyes to watch a bumblebee circle a flower.

The other boy scowled darkly. "What's wrong with you anyway?"

"I don't know."

They stood there for a while; the dark-haired boy clutching Jason's collar, while the latter merely gazed into some unseen realm. Then the older boy released Jason and slammed his fist into the eight-year-old's face. Jason stumbled and fell, holding his cheek with a startled expression. He looked like he'd finally woken up. As what happened sank in, Jason looked up with a glare.

"The only way to make you stop sulking is to beat you up. How pathetic!" the older boy taunted.

Tears welled up in Jason's eyes, but instead of wiping them away, he scrambled to his feet with a scream of rage and threw himself at his enemy, flailing his fists in the hope that he might actually hit something. Several times his fists struck their target, and by the time he stopped to catch his breath, the older boy lay on the ground, grinning arrogantly as he wiped his bloody nose. A deep cut under one eye started to bleed as it swelled.

"That's better. That's the man I know," the boy said with a laugh.

Jason gritted his teeth and clenched his fists, feeling both angry and hurt. "I'll beat you. No matter what, no matter where, no matter how—I swear, I'll beat you at everything."

"That's the spirit," Chasym's youthful form said, sitting up. "Keep that up, and you'll stop sulking."

The image of those two boys on that distant summer morning was whisked away then, and I saw more shadows of my despondent days as a child. What baffled me was that I couldn't remember being such a sullen boy; in fact, my childhood memories had always been a blur—all but the very happy ones. I'd always assumed that was only natural, until now.

I saw Chasym in many different forms, helping me when I was the most disheartened, reminding me that I was somehow going to make it. These memories confused me the most—who was Chasym, really? What side was he on?

As if to answer this, the kaleidoscopic mesh of memories fused into one and formed my bedroom. It was dark, the crescent moon gave only a little light, and my twelve-year-old self slept fitfully in his bed.

A figure appeared on the floor before my bed, staring at the stirring form inside of it. Stepping around the bed, the figure crept to the headboard and rested a slender hand on it. Slowly, gently, he reached his hand down and set it on the boy's shoulder. Raising the other hand, a white flame burst forth and cast light in the room. The light revealed the figure to be Lon, who gazed at his sleeping son with mixed emotions. Sliding his hand from Jason's shoulder, he stroked the boy's hair once.

"You shouldn't be here." The hoarse whisper came from the window.

Lon jerked his hand back and spun to face the newcomer.

Chasym stepped into the light, a frown on his face. "If he so much as sees your face the memories I've suppressed could return. Can you take that chance?"

Lon glanced at the bed. "I had to. Just once, Chasym. Even if I cannot claim him as my own now, I had to see how he's grown. It's been so long."

Chasym's face softened. "I understand that, but this was your choice. The family he has now is wonderful and he has a mission to accomplish. It could be his end. Don't let yourself become attached again."

Lon nodded once. "You're right, of course. I won't come back again."

The blond stepped nearer and set his hand on Lon's shoulder. "It will be all right, my friend. He's a strong boy, he'll be fine. He's got a good fist, too. I don't know how many times he's punched me in my different forms, but I swear I still feel every one." He slid a finger down his cheek as if to emphasize his words.

A fleeting smile touched Lon's lips, then it vanished. "Care for him, Chasym. Keep him safe as long as possible. He's..." Lon glanced at the bed, "...so young."

"I promise," Chasym said, smiling. Then he grinned. "I hear you altered your own prophecy."

"I did. Mind you, I didn't alter fate—the consequences would be dire—but I did rewrite the record of the prophecy and spread it around. Coming through a puddle will make things simpler. It will be easier to spot who Vendaeva is."

"...How will that be easier?"

Lon smiled. "I have found Key a mentor."

Chasym arched a brow. "I'm intrigued."

"He's still young yet, but Prince Crenen of Yenen Clan shows promise. And his brother has some strange connection to Vendaeva. I'm not sure what."

"Princes Crenen and Jenen, eh? Are you positive they're that's the best choice?"

"I'm not very positive about anything."

Chasym snorted. "True." He stretched his arms out. "Who am I to question the workings of a Seer?"

Lon's smile faded. "She's awake, Chasym."

The blond froze mid stretch and looked sharply into Lon's eyes. "What?"

"It happened the day we brought Key to Earth. I wasn't sure whether to tell you or not. She...isn't well. Her mind, it seems, is lost. Not completely; she remembers me. But, I wonder if it is best to leave her this way."

Chasym turned to the window and gazed into the darkness beyond. "Probably. She doesn't need to know everything."

"Will you be all right?"

"I...don't know." He laughed darkly. "For now I'll stay on Earth then. I...don't want to risk stirring painful memories..."

"How long will you avoid confrontation?"

Chasym continued as if he hadn't heard. "...I'll stay in the shadows until Key turns fourteen. Then, I'll join him in his school. We'll have to be in different cliques. Close association would risk too much." He faced Lon again. "Why would she wake up the day Key came here? Coincidence or fate?"

Lon shook his head. "I wish I could say."

The blond glanced toward the bed. "So, she has no idea about your son? ...Or even about your wife?"

"No. And it will remain this way. I had no right to a family anyway, not after all she suffered."

"Somehow I doubt she'd see it your way." Chasym gave Lon a pointed look. "But, enough idle chat. You have to leave."

The Seer sighed and nodded. "Of course." He turned to the bed, ran his hands through Jason's hair one last time, then vanished.

Chasym stared at the bed long after his friend had gone. "I am sorry, Lon," he whispered. Stepping close to the bed, he knelt down and reached a hand before him, hovering it over the sleeping boy's heart.

I held my breath, scared for the young Jason even though I knew something would prevent him from dying—otherwise how could my present self exist?

Long moments passed in which Chasym kept his hand suspended above Jason, his eyes intent, his lips pursed. Then, he relaxed and set his hand on the bed's edge, smiling sadly. "I can't do it, kid. I just like you too darn much." The sleeping form turned over, mumbling something that sounded like "shut up" as he shifted his covers and fell into a deeper sleep.

Chuckling softly, Chasym stood up and brushed his long blond tresses aside. "Unfortunately, I will have to kill you eventually." His yellow eyes flicked to the window. "Haeon will see to that."

More images flashed before me; days at school in which I sat alone and indifferent to everything. Then the fleeting images melted into a street I recognized as a route from middle school to my home. The weather was chill and the leaves on the elms overhead were bursting with bright autumn colors. My younger self was trudging slowly down the sidewalk, dragging his backpack along behind him, wiping at a bloody nose with his long-sleeved shirt as he went. He was limping a little, and one dirt-smudged cheek hinted of tears.

I didn't remember this event, even though I should. I couldn't be less than thirteen in appearance, yet the memory escaped me completely.

Suddenly Jason halted, glancing around the quiet street, as if listening. Then his gray eyes rested on a tree on the other side of the road. A figure stood beneath it. Long, golden hair floated around the purple-robed man, whose golden eyes peered at Jason intently. Then the form stepped from the shadows and his appearance was altered: short, honey-colored hair, light blue eyes, rounded ears, and a dark gray business suit. He walk toward Jason, his eyes concerned. The illusion wavered slightly as the nippy breeze passed, but the boy might not have noticed with his eyes still full of tears.

Lon, in human form, crouched down and eyed the boy was a gentle smile. "Bullied?" he whispered.

Jason was wary, but he nodded after a moment. Realizing what he'd admitted, he then shook his head vigorously. "N-no." He halted as his voice cracked and tried again. "No," he said more firmly. "I tripped."

"Quite a fall," Lon said softly. He stood back up. "Be more careful. Sometimes it is best to choose an alternate route, if what you have taken leads to this."

The boy sniffed, rubbed his bloody nose, then dropped his backpack strap to rub at his teary eyes. "I'm fine," he assured Lon. Then, through much clearer vision, he looked up at the man and his eyes widened.

Time seemed to stand still as father and son examined one another. Then, with a shiver and a shallow gasp, the boy collapsed. Lon caught him quickly, pulled him up into his arms, grabbed the discarded backpack, and hurried toward the white house a little way off.

I followed them, pondering this chain of events. Lon had come to see me, had come to console me in a time of need. But I'd recognized him. Chasym was right; the memories he suppressed had returned—but on what scale?

Lon reached the house, pounded on the front door with his foot, and waited impatiently. Finally the door opened to reveal my mother, who gasped and beckoned Lon inside. I hurried in after them.

Jason was laid on a couch. My mother asked for details as she grabbed a first-aid kit and started dabbing at the boy's cuts and bruises. Lon explained that several bullies at school were picking fights with the younger kids until I stepped forward and told them off. For such defiance I alone had suffered.

"You found him unconscious?" Mom asked.

Lon barely hesitated. "Yes." He turned toward the door. "Please excuse me. I'm late for a meeting."

"I'm sorry for the inconvenience. Thank you so much for your help," she called after him. He didn't pause or even acknowledge her. He merely stepped out of the house, closed the door, and vanished.

The next few days passed rapidly. Jason was feverish and more despondent than ever. He refused to acknowledge anyone, nor would he eat. During his fitful slumber he called out for "father" though whenever my dad was called in, Jason ignored him completely. The family grew even more scared when Jason started talking in his sleep about being abandoned.

I was ashamed of my display. The pain I'd caused my family was too much, yet I'd been oblivious to it. A fresh pain stabbed me as I recalled a similar experience in the not-too-distant past, when I first returned from Paradise. No wonder my family had been so afraid; so determined to restore my sanity. It had been a relapse.

The memories slowed and it was nighttime in my bedroom once more. Two figures appeared near the window.

"If you'd come to me sooner this might have been avoided. Look!" Chasym hissed. "He's a mess. You can see the chaos all around his aura."

Lon glanced at the bed, and quickly looked away. "Do not lecture me, Chasym. I am ashamed enough."

"Is it really enough? Perhaps. Now will you heed my advice?" He approached the bed and placed his hand on Jason's head. "I'll have to remove this memory completely. It's the only way to restore his mind and keep him from recalling anything." He closed his eyes. Silence fell across the dark room until Chasym opened his eyes and exhaled slowly. "Done." He turned on Lon. "Never. Never do something so idiotic again. You could destroy him."

"What of when he returns to Paradise?" Lon asked, refusing to be cowed. "I cannot avoid him then if I am to help him."

"Adopt a new persona," Chasym suggested. "Do not act fatherly or his memory suppression could again be jeopardized." He sighed. "Maybe...if he is successful...you can reclaim your role."

"You said before that the family he has now is wonderful. I reconfirmed that the day I brought him to...his mother." Lon's smile was bitter. "I will not steal from him anything more."

Chasym shook his head. "Would you make up your mind whether you're selfish or not? This constant shifting is wearying," he said. "Ah well, I suppose it's for the best that I never had children of my own. I doubt I'd be much different." Before Lon could respond, Chasym vanished.

Lon turned back to the bed and smiled sadly. "Farewell. Until we meet once more. You will be looked after." He hesitated. "I'm sorry." And he too disappeared.

Something confused me. A few of these memories had taken place during times when I couldn't have been conscious to experience them, and Chasym had removed the incident with the bullies and Lon. So, where were these coming from?

"I was hoping that you would ask," the youth's voice said with a smile in his tones.

My eyes widened with realization. The youth from the desert, the one who declared me his heir, was the white orb. No wonder I knew the voice. I spun and found the youth standing before me; long, over-sized robes of white hanging from his lithe form. His silvery eyes danced with light, though his expression was grim.

"These memories come from three sources besides your own mind. The first is Seer Lon. The second is from Orb Liitae. And the third, as you can guess, comes from Chasym Verenvey of They." He spoke with his mind; his mouth remained closed.

"And why are you here?" I asked.

The youth smiled again, his eyes brightening even more. *"I am a part of you. I claimed you as my heir, and with the world's close, I escaped inside of you. It was the only way I could survive. When you entered the water in the Realm of Yenen, you took my physical manifestation with you."*

"Physical manifestation?"

"The form you see now has long since been destroyed in the real world. When you left Paradise as a four-year-old, I entrusted to you my energy. As the world began to descend to its own destruction, my body gradually disappeared as all of my energy transferred to the new core—to you."

"What?"

"The place where your body now lies is only the threshold of my domain; the entrance to the misty plains. Once, those plains were glorious to behold, but now they are ravaged by the disease. And the misty plains are only my lair. I am—no, I was *the core. But now,*

when you are finally ready, you may become the core instead, and save all of Paradise—or, if you so choose—destroy it."

"I don't understand. How...? Why...?" I stopped to collect my thoughts. "Please explain everything."

The youth nodded. *"To best explain, we shall journey backward to a pivotal moment in Paradise: Chasym's choice."*

39
Chasym's Choice?

The wind was fierce on top of the Hykyae Ridges. Winter was coming early, and it promised to be harsh; already the bite of frozen snow made Chasym's cheeks raw. He pulled his robes tighter and glanced back at his servant, Haeon. The Verenveyan smiled encouragingly and Chasym nodded back and went on. If they could just find the gateway by nightfall they would be all right.

Ten minutes later they reached a gorge and gazed into the dank, tree-strewn fissure.

"This is it," Haeon whispered, smiling with excitement.

Chasym closed his eyes. Three years. It had taken three years to find a way in—and now they had it. "Let's not waste more time. We have precious little."

Chasym tied a rope around his waist and Haeon lower him into the crevice, then he waited as Haeon secured the rope to a sturdy pine and followed after his master. When he dropped to the gorge's uneven floor, he joined Chasym and they walked to the far wall.

Several dozen deeply carved runes adorned the rock surface and Chasym traced them earnestly. "This is amazing, Haeon. These runes—I've never seen anything like them."

"I have," Haeon frowned. "Ancient Seeric runes."

Chasym arched his brow. "How could you have seen them, if I have not?"

"You have. They adorn the Seeric Temple. Now the building is only a ruin, but there are still traces along the high rises."

"Ah, I recall it vaguely," Chasym said with a single nod. He ran his finger along an especially swirly rune. "But you cannot read them?"

"If I invoke my power I might."

"Try." Chasym stepped aside.

Haeon placed his own fingers on the runes with a look of concentration. After a moment the runes began to glow blue. Haeon pressed his hands against them and smirked. "I understand only a little, but it is enough." He let go of the wall, causing the runes to stop glowing, and turned to Chasym. "There is a price."

Chasym blinked. "To get in?"

"Yes. You must have something to sacrifice."

"I expected as much. It is just as well," Chasym said.

Haeon glanced at the runes. "You have something to offer?"

"Yes."

Haeon nodded firmly. "We may enter." He touched his heart and drew forth a blue orb, touched it to the runes, then placed the orb back inside his body. "The pact is made."

The ground rumbled as the rock wall slid open before them. Darkness stretched out from inside to greet them. They stared for a moment, but Chasym gathered his nerve and entered the cave, Haeon following after him.

They walked on for what seemed hours, until they reached a sheer drop into nothingness. Chasym examined the walls on either side, then his glowing yellow eyes flicked back to the drop. "We jump?" He stepped off solid ground and fell without waiting for an answer.

The darkness receded swiftly, replaced by blinding light. It took a moment for his eyes to adjust, but that moment was long enough that he slammed into the hard ground. He winced, startled that he was still in one piece after such an impact, but gingerly got to his feet, shockingly unbroken.

He stood on a circular platform high above an endless ocean of hot lava. Several other such platforms rose above the fiery ocean some distance away. The red sky was filled with a thick haze. As he studied his surroundings, Haeon landed hard against the ground and climbed slowly to his feet.

"Not quite what I expected," Chasym mused.

"Nor I," Haeon murmured as he brushed his magenta robes free of the clinging ash.

"Why have you come?" *a voice spoke from nowhere and everywhere at once.*

Chasym glanced around for the voice's source and his yellow eyes fell on a floating white orb. "We come to ask for aid."

"You presume that I will aid your cause?"

"We presume nothing. We only beg," Chasym replied.

"With the presumption that it will give me reason to help you."

Chasym smiled wryly. "Very well. You're right. I'm desperate, and I want your help."

"Help." *The orb bobbed thoughtfully.* "How can I help you, Chasym Verenvey of They?"

Haeon stepped forward. "We seek justice."

Chasym shot Haeon a reproachful look. "And something else," he added.

"Justice. Other beings like yourselves have sought justice, and gotten only that for their trouble."

Haeon looked confused.

Chasym smiled again. "It means they never received mercy in return. What they gave, they got back."

"Exactly."

Haeon scoffed. "So be it. I have nothing to fear."

"Nothing to fear?" *asked the orb.* "To demand justice of another is to risk your own damnation. If your perception of their deeds is skewed, then you may be more in the wrong than they to misjudge them. Remember: one only receives hurt for hurt."

Haeon threw Chasym an exasperated look. "Never mind that."

"Very well, Seer Haeon. How would you have me serve justice?"

At this inquiry Chasym and Haeon exchanged knowing glances. "The fall of Renocahn," Chasym answered.

"By madness," Haeon added.

"Renocahn is a great people. Without them, Paradise may fall into chaos. You ask too much."

"We're not finished yet," Chasym said, his yellow eyes flashing. "You misunderstand, Core, that is exactly what we want. Chaos."

The orb was still for a time. "What do you mean?"

"My choice of sacrifice when I entered has overcome your power, Core. I've outsmarted you."

Haeon blinked, but then an evil grin crossed his face. "So, you chose that route after all."

"I don't care about the consequences—I only know that I must spare Veija and cleanse this world."

"What are you going to do, Chasym Verenvey?"

"The sacrifice I chose to make when I entered your domain was enough to destroy you."

"Impossible."

"I beg to differ." Chasym reached out and grabbed the orb, knowing that for him it would be solid now. "I chose to become your destruction."

"Impossible," *the orb repeated, sounding much less confident.*

"Take me to your real *domain." Chasym threw the orb before him and a portal appeared, showing a realm of brilliance; a place of pure light. As he stepped into the realm, the light began to fade and alter. The white swirls of brilliance shifted and dulled to murky blue mist. "The easiest way to kill off a populace is to infect its core."*

Haeon laughed with delight as he stepped up to join his master. As they gazed at the growing taint, both men caught sight of a child kneeling amid the chaos. White hair flew about the boy's face as his silver eyes glistened with tears.

"What have you done in your madness?" the youth asked aloud. "You've damned yourself, Chasym Verenvey."

"I'm still not finished yet," Chasym said. "You already agreed to serve justice. As Haeon requests, you must destroy them with insanity."

"You already hold me captive, you have tainted my power. I am useless to you," the core said coldly.

"I doubt you're as helpless as you say. But you are right about one thing—I own you now. You will do my bidding."

The core stood up, ignoring the glistening tears streaming down his face. He slowly, laboriously, approached Chasym and, while the blond watched with curiosity, the youth placed his hand on Chasym's heart. Closing his eyes, he frowned. "I see. That is the secret to your madness." He opened his silver depths and gazed up into Chasym's own eyes. "All this for a love already lost? You have my pity, Chasym Verenvey." He touched his own cheek. "So, it is your tears I cry?"

Anger flared inside Chasym and he struck the child, throwing him aside. "You know nothing. You have never lived."

The core looked up at Chasym from the puddled floor, his eyes reproachful. "I am not the first to be here. I was alive once, too."

Chasym scoffed and turned to Haeon. "Our work here is done."

The Seer bowed to his master and they turned to leave. The core watched them sadly until the portal closed.

They said nothing as they left the core's threshold; Chasym sprouted feathered wings of black and carried Haeon up the pit, then landed in the gorge. Leaving was a simple matter; after all, the sacrifice had been made.

Haeon finally spoke. "Master, what is the sacrifice you gave?"

"I became the disease that will wipe out Paradise. Only four of us will survive in the end, Haeon. You, me, Veija, and Lon."

"Lon? Is that wise?"

"I hurt him. This is my payment for that." Chasym reached the rope and tugged to make sure it still held tight. "I can't carry you any further. Climb up. We'll camp in the cave we saw above."

Haeon approached him from behind and smiled wickedly. "Sleep," he whispered, magic lacing his voice, and Chasym immediately fell back, unconscious. Haeon stepped aside to let his master fall hard against the ground.

"All of that time I spent on you, yet you still managed to have some control. No matter. I will deal with Lon." He bent down and placed a hand on Chasym's forehead. "I'll take your memories of this event. It would be horrible if you found some way to stop the disease now, right, Master?" His tone was mocking. "Especially after your noble *sacrifice." He barked with laughter as he straightened and climbed up the rope.*

The memory faded and I blinked as my eyes adjusted to the dim light of the misty plains.

"Do you understand now?"

"No. Not completely." I took a deep breath. "So, Haeon was controlling Chasym?"

"In a sense," the core said. "He really only rearranged Chasym's emotions to manipulate him. Haeon was never clever enough to come up with the Paradisaical disease; he only mixed Chasym's desire for justice with a hot anger, causing Chasym to create a way to 'cleanse Paradise.' This, as well as his romantic tragedy were what I saw when I looked into his heart. I knew Haeon was manipulating him, yet it was Chasym who condemned Paradise."

"But Chasym doesn't remember that, right?"

"He does. After Haeon left Chasym for dead on the Hykyae Ridges, I appeared to him in a puddle shortly after he awoke with no memory whatever, and I unlocked his memories. Haeon could only suppress them—something he had learned from Chasym in years past. He could not fully remove them. So it was a simple matter to slowly restore Chasym's to him."

"Why didn't Chasym use memory suppression on Veija instead of 'killing' himself?"

"Chasym secretly hoped Veija would be distraught enough to bring Lon around. He never expected Veija to act so rashly. By then, the damage was dealt. Chasym was half-mad with grief when Haeon first attacked his emotions and then told him of ancient Seeric legends about a planet's core and its limitless power. As clever as he knew Chasym to be, he was confident that if anyone could harness my power, it was him. And, sadly, Haeon was correct. Mostly."

"Mostly?"

The core smiled. "Chasym came to himself on the Hykyae Ridges, and while it was too late to stop the disease, he proposed a solution. You."

"Me?"

"Well, an heir, at least. Originally we chose a boy whom we both felt could handle the power and be..." He trailed off.

"*Be*?" I urged, feeling like an echo.

"...Manipulated." The core smiled sheepishly. "We knew that any headstrong boy would fight his fate."

My eyes narrowed. "What fate is that?"

The core sighed wearily. "Originally the plan was to have the heir simply sacrifice himself to restore the balance of Paradise. I would keep my place, Chasym would be redeemed, and—"

"Kirid would be a hero, dead and gone," I whispered.

"We were wrong to think it. Both of us. But it was the only thing we *could* think of." The core paused. "Then Haeon intervened. He found Kirid and stole him from Lon—"

"Where does Lon fit into all of this?"

"I sent him visions of Kirid's role—though not the *end* of that role. He wrote the prophecy concerning Vendaeva even before anyone knew the disease was a threat. Your father never knew Kirid was supposed to die. When Yenen Clan branched off from Kirid Clan, Lon found the Realm of Yenen and stayed close to protect Vendaeva; the infant named Kirid. But Haeon manipulated fate—not only to locate and steal Kirid, but to have power over his mind at any given time. This is why you see two different people inside of Kirid; the child, lost and confused, and the young man, noble and independent. Haeon's manipulation tore Kirid in two. Unfortunately Haeon—somewhat cleverer this time—saved both his Seership and immortality because he used Kirid's power to restore it, and...to recapture Chasym."

"I see," I whispered, thinking of the image behind Chasym—the form in chains. "So, he is a prisoner."

"He is."

"Where do I come in?" I asked, folding my arms and silently daring the core to try explaining his way out of this.

"You were the downfall of everything." The child smiled fondly. "And we could not be more grateful to you."

"Expound."

The core continued to smile, unaffected by my attitude. "After Haeon stole Kirid, Chasym and I both panicked. If Haeon wanted, he could used Kirid to overpower us and finish destroying the world. Fortunately Chasym thought of a plan. It was reckless, and most likely ineffective, but as desperate as we were—"

"I thought Chasym was under Haeon's control now," I interjected.

"I will come to that." He raised his hand as if to calm my impatience. "As desperate as we were, it was something at least. Lon came to me, asking for some new means of saving Paradise. His willingness to sacrifice himself was noble—but he was too old to receive such power. I knew of his son; Chasym had mentioned the boy before. So, without considering how Chasym might feel—though I should have—I ordered Lon to sacrifice his son. I assured him you would be fine, which was most likely true. Your job was not to replace Vendaeva—only to nullify his power."

"Wait. Stop. Lemme get this all straight." I closed my eyes and mulled over his words. "Basically I was the first victim that popped into your twisted little head, so I was chosen as the 'next heir' only because it would lessen Kirid's power. You never expected me to save Paradise."

"At first, no," the core admitted. "More correctly, we dared not hope for such an advantage."

"So, Chasym's plan didn't actually include saving the world, just keeping it from dying faster?"

"Precisely. It would perhaps cause Haeon to realize Kirid's uselessness and abandon the boy, giving us back the heir. But things did not go as planned."

"Obviously."

"Haeon still had Chasym under control, as you pointed out. It wasn't that Haeon had control over his mind this time; Chasym would only follow direct orders, and then, grudgingly. Chasym could still plot behind his master's back. However, Haeon suspected something was amiss when Lon didn't come after Kirid. He ordered Chasym to find out what your father was up to and to truthfully report what he discovered. Of course, Chasym knew nothing of the agreement Lon and I had made, and so he was very angry when he found out—which I suffered for later. Under orders he gave the information to Haeon, who then ordered Chasym to play along until he could dispose of you.

"At the same time, I accepted you as my heir, and Kirid's power lessened. At that moment Haeon's grip on Chasym lessened as well and the latter was able to battle against the command to kill you. As you can imagine, it was very painful for him, but he succeeded for years. Haeon was furious, naturally. He now only barely retains his Seership and feeds on Kirid's life to stay alive and keep a firm grip on Chasym's body."

I stared at the youth. "What now? What happens now?"

"That is up to you. For some reason you have access to all the power of Paradise—even that which I could never tap. It is a mystery why you overpowered Kirid and took his place as Vendaeva." He cocked his head to the side, gazing at me intently. "But some things have no explanation. Or, perhaps the reason is that you simply defy fate. There is only one other in Paradise who ever truly defied fate—even Chasym Verenvey and Lon were subject to its whim. Perhaps that is why Lon chose Crenen as your mentor. He is just as rebellious."

I smiled despite myself, thinking of Crenen; his antics, his leadership, his sacrifice, his loss. A twinge of pain knotted my stomach as I thought of Sasha's death. I inhaled deeply, pushing down the pain. Not now. Later.

The core went on. "I remember seeing you that day in the desert. I sensed a fourth presence and saw your shimmering image looking on. It...gave me hope."

I blinked. "You mean I was really there?"

"In a sense. Even memories have power." He fell silent.

After a time I spoke. "You say it's up to me?"

"It is," the core said.

I glanced around the misty plains. "Am I dead?"

"You are between life and death. Your body is finished, but I am sure the true Vendaeva would have no trouble constructing a new one."

I arched my brow. "*True* Vendaeva?"

The youth shrugged, smiling. "I told you before I am but a Remnant. My time has finished. Without even my consent, you have surpassed and succeeded me."

"How do you know? So far I've managed only a few miraculous things on occasion."

"Then remove occasion."

I raised my other brow. "Remove...?" Of course. The only thing limiting me was *me*. "Liitae," I whispered.

The core beamed as my orb appeared, bobbing with excitement.

"Hi," I said, stroking the orb. I cupped Liitae in both hands and gazed at it closely. "I'm really trapped inside of you. I just have to get out. It's where I've been all along."

"You're sounding rather cryptic," the core said.

I grinned. "It's about time *I* got the chance." I turned my focus back to the orb. "Liitae, it's okay now. You can let me out."

The orb wiggled its understand.

Memories filled my mind. It wasn't like my previous encounters with memory gain. It was sudden, clear, painless. I simply knew...

...Everything.

40
To Heal The Broken?

Power; untamed, untainted. It wasn't good, nor was it evil. It simply was. Countless possibilities soared through my mind. The second thing I must do was clear: create a new body. It wasn't the only option I had. I could simply become the core and solve everything that way. And it was tempting. But I knew instinctively that such a course would cause pain.

Before I created my new body, I needed to do something else. I became the mist around me, sweeping through it, coming to understand it. Cleansing the mist now wouldn't end the disease because it was only a manifestation of it; like the youth was only a remnant of the core now—simply a symbol. The disease truly dwelt in the core itself—and the core was not really me. Not yet.

Hadn't Chasym himself admitted he was the disease? The sacrifice he made so many centuries before wasn't quite as he'd phrased it. He sacrificed his past life to become the core—the previous core hadn't known it, but they were both the core after that, which was what initially caused the taint to occur. Which was why the disease was unstoppable.

Until now.

Because I was the heir of Vendaeva.

Pulling away from the mist, I began to construct a new body with my mind. As I worked, I reached out and summoned the image of what was occurring on the threshold of my domain. It was easier to do than pressing a button or flipping a switch. And much more effective. I was standing among them, invisible, invincible, undetectable, but while all of this, I had no trouble seeing or hearing or feeling. In fact, all of my senses had been heightened at least one hundred fold. I could taste lava, smell blood, hear the pounding of many hearts, see every bead of sweat, and feel every emotion on the platform. Yet it wasn't overwhelming.

Time hadn't passed here. They were all very still, staring at my limp form on the hard stones. Suddenly Veija screamed and Lon and Jenen broke free of their bonds—or perhaps Chasym released them—and ran across the platform, skidding to my side. Crenen stared, his weak body shaking with sickness and horror. Menen took a moment to snap Haeon's neck and toss him aside, then he hurried to the broken body, standing just behind Lon. Kirid, sitting on the ground, watched blankly, staring at the three bodies littering the ground with unfocused eyes. Chasym stood in the back of the crowd, and while he seemed completely blissful to the pain so thick in the air, the shadow-form in chains behind him was racked with grief too strong for tears.

Lon slid his hands under his son's neck, lifting him and holding him tightly. "No," he whispered too quietly for anyone to hear, though my enhanced hearing caught the word effortlessly.

If I didn't know everything now I would've found myself confused about how I could die though I was immortal, but now the answer was simple. Just as Haeon lived through Kirid's power, I died through Chasym's. The core wrote and rewrote the rules.

Now it was my turn.

Grinning with anticipation, I fixed my spirit-eyes on the dead boy who had once been me, and would be again. The process would be painful, fixing my soul to both the old and new bodies and fusing the three together, but it was necessary. I must return.

Especially since Haeon wasn't dead.

I glanced around the mourning group one last time and my eyes fell on Veija. Tears shone in her eyes as she stared at my dead form. If there'd been any doubt that I would revive myself, it disappeared at the sight of her. It was true, I loved Veija. Not in a romantic sense, but as family. I knew then, as I gazed at her fair face, how best to end it all.

Turning toward my limp form resolutely, I approached it, gazing down at my pale, lifeless face. The pain would be excruciating; with all the power coursing through my soul, the idea of being confined to such a small body was uncomfortable.

Still, there was no better way. Especially if I wanted to pay Haeon back for everything he'd done.

I could've made the experience flashy and exciting, but subtlety seemed the best approach; both because the shock of a person coming back from the dead was usually better handled without the special effects, and because I figured it would hurt less.

I'm still not sure how well that second bit actually worked.

As I slipped into my body and began knitting the old and new bodies and spirit back together, I felt and knew little besides pain. It was as if my existence was only pain. Cold, uncomfortable, clammy. My body felt like a prison as I finished the fusion. But I was alive.

Apparently Lon noticed.

Gasping, he nearly threw me to the ground in his shock, but fought off his natural reaction and held me more tightly.

I opened my eyes slowly, blinking away my blindness. As expected, I could barely move at all. But I couldn't afford delays. My vocal cords were reluctant to work, so I locked eyes with Lon and, through my mind, asked him to help me up.

Nodding, my father pulled me to my feet, and held me as I tried to gain my balance. It was no use, I couldn't feel my legs at all. Sensing this, Lon wrapped my left arm around his shoulders and placed his arm around my waist for support. Hopefully this setup wouldn't last too long, or my plan wouldn't work very well.

In the meantime I wandered through my mind, making certain the transition from spirit to body hadn't ruined my perception. I wasn't all-knowing now, but I'd retained what I needed to fix this situation, and that was what mattered. To keep my knowledge of everything was impossible inside the body I'd reconstructed. It would overwhelm my material senses and driven me mad—and who really wanted to do that to themselves?

Satisfied, I turned my focus to those around me. My friends. And Haeon.

"Hi," I said, finally locating my voice.

"Key," Jenen whispered from beside me. I tried to glance at him, but didn't have the strength. Lon aided me by turning slightly. "What happened to your hair?" the feminine prince asked.

I blinked. "Hair?" Of all the questions he could ask—?

"It's white," he explained.

"It is?"

He nodded solemnly.

Surprised, but unconcerned, I smirked. "There are bound to be a few changes when a person comes back from the dead."

I want to see Chasym, I thought.

Hearing me, Lon again turned us to face the blond standing quietly in the background. Chasym's face was unreadable, but I didn't need an expression to know how he was feeling. I'd seen his sorrow. The prisoner inside of him was my friend, as he'd always been. The form now possessing his body was nothing more than a disease—one about to be purged.

"Chasym," I whispered.

He met my eyes defiantly. "You just don't die, do you?"

"I manage to beat death a lot," I said. "I just won't stay dead."

For a moment Chasym merely watched me, then a smile flickered across his lips. "Should I be flattered that you use my own words against me?"

"Not against you. Against your master."

Chasym's eyes flicked to Haeon's still form, then back to me. We both knew he was still alive and still in control.

"Veija," I said, turning from Chasym's impassive face to the beautiful woman. "I need to show you something."

She stepped forward without hesitation, her eyes still glistening. "I thought we had lost you," she said softly.

I grinned. "You know me better than that." A tingling sensation started in my arms. "Veija, I need you to bear with me while I do something, okay?"

She nodded. "Of course."

"Look at Chasym."

She turned to face him, features growing hard as she eyed man who had betrayed us.

Chasym's eyes narrowed. "What are you planning?"

"Hold still," I said, knowing my word would be law. Watching Veija, I decided on the best way to perform the task I must do. *Veija. I want to show you the truth. All of it. And it will be very painful, but you must see it through. All right?*

Again she nodded.

Good. First I'm going to show you the real Chasym. The one I *see.*

Chasym was struggling. Outwardly he only watched, but I could feel the pull of his considerable power. He reached out to Kirid and tapped his power as well. I ignored his efforts, unconcerned. Instead I raised one weak, tingling hand and placed it on Veija's shoulder, willing her to see what I saw.

She drew a strangled breath as the image of Chasym bound with chains unfolded before her. Cupping her hands to her mouth, fresh tears fell down her face. *He is still our friend. Haeon is the true villain then.*

Yes. We both followed the chain that ended in Haeon's still-clenched fist. *Chasym is chained by a fate he made for himself, and even though he wants to break free of it, one thing keeps him from finding the strength he needs.*

Veija looked at me questioningly.

Veija. I know you lost someone you love. I know it drove you insane. But I also think it shouldn't have.

Her eyes became confused, distant, as if she couldn't grasp what I was saying. I only smiled reassuringly, then I sent a silent order to Chasym's body. It wasn't easy, breaking through the chains that held him prisoner, but my determination went a long way. With a cry of surprise and pain, Chasym doubled over, his long hair falling in his face as he clutched his chest. Despite the pain, he transformed; his hair became black, his eyes green, and his build shrank a little. Even his clothes changed from black to a midnight blue robe in the cut and fashion once common among Kirid merchants.

"No," he whispered, though he knew it was too late to hide the truth.

"Stand straight," I told him gently.

He resisted, but finally he straightened, glaring at me with vehement hatred.

"Reji!" Veija stepped back as she began to sob. Her eyes were filled with horror, but as she stared and the vision remained, her eyes gradually grew gentle, hopeful. She stepped forward, reaching out her hands to this man whom she loved.

Chasym pulled away. "Stay back." He found me, his eyes frightened. "She was never supposed to know."

I said nothing, only gazing calmly at him. For the wrong he had done, the souls of the dead demanded justice. It was my duty to see it done. But Chasym deserved more than justice; he deserved a second chance, and this was the only way he could have one.

"All this time," Veija said, bringing Chasym's eyes back to her. "You've been alive all this time." I watched with satisfaction as a near-invisible set of chains which had been wrapped around her mind began to fall away. Haeon's grip on her was diminishing.

When I learned that Haeon had controlled Chasym, I suspected the truth. Veija would never have considered manipulating fate unless someone had suggested it was only means of saving Reji. And only one person would sacrifice her so. Haeon's own motives were unclear, but I knew he was the cause of Veija's fall from Seership and the madness that had plagued her until now. Only when I'd become heir of Vendaeva did Haeon's power fade enough for Veija to awaken. And now, as cliché as it sounded, the power of love would undo the last of Haeon's manipulation.

"You've lost," I whispered to the man laying motionlessly on the ground.

Still bound by my power, Chasym couldn't escape from Veija's embrace. She held him, clinging as though if she let go he would vanish. His green eyes were fearful and ashamed. The form behind him, still chained and immobile, looked up from his weeping and gazed around as if seeing for the first time in years—no, centuries.

"Clever," a familiar voice said, but from the wrong place.

My eyes narrowed. Rage filled my body and I found myself strong enough to stand on my own. Pulling away from Lon, who let me go calmly, I turned to face the man who had, for his own selfish reasons, caused everything.

"Get out of his body, Haeon," I demanded quietly, my voice betraying none of my anger.

Kirid smiled a smile not his own. "I think not, Jason Sterling. This is the best way. If only I had considered it sooner—it would have saved so much time."

"Time for your monologue now, eh?" I asked.

"Why yes, I believe it will have been my first chance—I don't dare pass it up." He brushed a lock of black hair from his face in annoyance. "Besides, you deserve to know why I will win despite all you have accomplished."

I shook my head, smiling patiently. "Why? Because Chasym can't undo what he's done? Because you're immortal since you've stolen Kirid's body? Because you destroyed the core? Or is it because your desire for justice is stronger than that of the countless lives destroyed by your disease?"

Haeon laughed. "You have done your research. But I must correct you—this is not my disease. Chasym came up with it all on his own. I must admit, it was a brilliant concept and a beautiful execution."

I grinned. "Considering how much you admire it, I think it only fitting for you to experience the fullness of its execution, don't you? As they say, one can't expect to fully appreciate what they haven't experienced for themselves."

Haeon laughed again. "And how do you propose to go about doing that?"

"I'll just borrow Chasym's little trick."

Haeon grinned. "Shove your little orb into my gut? It won't work. I have full access to Kirid's power. I can control Liitae as easily as you can."

I scoffed. "Use Liitae? As much as I should like to honor him with the taking of your life, I'm afraid there are a few others who have already claimed that right."

"Oh?" Haeon sneered.

"Oh," I confirmed. A hum started from above. Hundreds of thousands of glowing orbs descended from the smoky sky, swarming around Haeon before he could even think of moving. His screams filled the air as he was hidden from view by countless spheres, bobbing in and out furiously, until finally his screams died away. I waved my hand and the floating orbs vanished, the illusion fading away.

I stepped weakly to Kirid, kneeling down and placing my hand on his shoulder. He would live, of course. The orbs were only supposed to scare Haeon out of Kirid's body through threat of disease, and, with no other choice, Haeon returned to his own. But now came the difficult part.

I placed my hand on Kirid's forehead, closing my eyes and willing my consciousness to enter his. I needed to convince him to relinquish his power so I had full access in my limited form. When I'd died I could tap all power, borrowing from anyone, but that would leave a toll on the borrowed, so I chose instead to return and gain my rightful power with the permission and willingness of Chasym and Kirid. I delved deep into the boy's mind, until I located him huddled in the darkness, sobbing uncontrollably.

"Kirid," I whispered as the light from my presence rested on the young man.

He looked up, winced at the brilliant light and shielded his eyes with one hand. "Kiido," he whispered back. More tears welled up in his deep black eyes. "Haeon betrayed me. He stole my body and locked me in here. I thought he cared about me."

I stepped forward, smiling at him. "I know. He betrayed a lot of people. But it's okay now. Your body is your own again. I can take you back."

He hesitated, wiping at his eyes. Then he nodded.

"Before we can go, though, I must ask a favor. It would be hard, and painful, but—"

"Anything, Kiido." The trust in his eyes startled me. "You were right all along. I will do anything to help you stop Haeon."

My smile returned. "You're a good person, Kirid. Thank you."

He didn't smile back. Instead he shivered. "I...saw something when he entered my mind. It was dark and...evil."

I crouched down and placed my hands on Kirid's shoulders. "I know. Haeon has only used you, but I can stop him from doing that. Okay?"

He nodded vigorously. "Anything."

Standing up, I beckoned Kirid to join me. "I need your power. All of it. Vendaeva's power has been spread out too much; I have to contain it so I can use its full strength. Will you do that for me?"

Again he nodded. "What must I do?"

"Just let it go," I replied. "Give it up willingly and I can handle the rest." I glanced around. The atmosphere in his mind had been dark, but as I comforted Kirid, his own light had begun to appear. Now the white aura around me was much less blinding because Kirid was glowing too. "That's the way," I said. "I have to go back out now. I can guide you, if you want?" Extending my hand to him, I waited. After a second's pause, he grasped it and we disappeared.

I opened my eyes and removed my hand from Kirid's face. He blinked slowly and smiled at me. "Why did your hair turn white?"

I grinned. "Because I'm cooler than you." His expression clearly indicated that he had no idea how white hair would make me less affected by the lava's heat, but he didn't press the issue. I let him wonder.

"Key?" Lon murmured from above me.

I glanced up and nodded. "Yeah," I answered, knowing what he was asking. He took my wrist and pulled me to my feet, where I wavered a second before gaining my balance. "I think I need a nap after this."

He nodded. "Just a little while longer."

"Yeah." Using one of Crenen's favorite words reminded me of the prince. I sought him out and found him kneeling beside Menen, who was allowing his master to bandage his wounded side.

"Haeon is still not dead." Lon wasn't asking a question.

"I know." I pulled away from my father's support and, still wavering, stumbled toward the Seer's motionless body. "What is your goal?" I whispered to him as I stood above his broken body.

To destroy Paradise, he answered in my head.

"Why?"

Because it must be punished.

"What about everything you've done? Through you more people have died than by anyone else. But you don't think yourself condemned?"

I do not worry about my own condemnation because I am doing what is right.

"No. You're not." I wondered why Haeon had become such a man as this, but I wasn't curious enough to enter his mind. Whatever the start of his reasoning, he was wrong and would pay the price. "I'm going to kill you, Haeon, but I won't make you suffer. I won't prolong your life to humiliate you."

And why is that?

"Because I know you'll get what's coming to you soon and I don't want your soul on my hands." I bent down and whispered in his ear, "Because I choose mercy."

Haeon's hand flew at me and snatched my throat. "You are a fool, Jason Sterling. An idealistic fool." His grip tightened.

"Kirid," was all I said, feeling no need to duel with this man anymore. He was about to die.

In response to that single word Haeon's hand lurched and fell by his broken body. His eyes grew wide with terror and he shouted another name: "Chasym!"

I turned sharply in time to see Chasym break away from Veija and charge toward me, his eyes cold. He was on me in seconds, grasping my hair and pulling me to my feet, dragging me away from Haeon's corpse.

"Too late to stop me now," Haeon's voice whispered in my ear through Chasym's lips.

"Get out of him," I snarled. In the moment Kirid relinquished his power, Haeon's hold to life had failed him in his true form; I had suspected his next move, but hoped he wouldn't have time. Apparently he did.

"No," Haeon replied. I heard the slight echo of Chasym's voice in his. "I rather like this form."

"You planned this all along, didn't you?" I said as Haeon pulled my arms behind my back. Luckily my humerus bone had healed when I reconstructed my body.

"I knew my other body could not handle all the power I'm about to receive."

I scoffed. "And how are you going to 'receive' power?"

"Simple," he answered. "You're going to give me yours, just as Kirid gave you his. I would have preferred it in reverse, but...this will do."

I grinned. "Except you miscalculated one thing, Hae-Hae, and it's going cost you more than you can afford."

"I don't believe you, Jason Sterling. You are a liar after all."

"Jason Sterling was a liar, yes. But Key isn't, and *that* is who I choose to be." I closed my silver eyes. "Hold *really* still, or this could hurt more than it has to."

Chasym. Reaching into his mind without being detected wasn't easy, but I knew I'd managed it.

Jason? he answered back quietly.

I need your help.

I felt his hesitation. *How do you know I will help you?*

Because, I said with a mental smirk, *you want to.*

Regret, anguish and guilt rose up inside of Chasym. *I've betrayed you. All of you.*

I'll admit you've done some pretty stupid things, but how about I help you try again?

I felt his hesitation.

Chasym. Veija's waiting for you.

A new feeling entered the fray of Chasym's mind. Fear.

Don't. Don't run away this time.

He was silent, then I felt his nod. *Very well. What do you want me to do?*

I couldn't help but grin. *You're a shapeshifter. So, shift.*

Into what?

Two people. You and Haeon.

I can't. That would be impossible.

Why? I had trouble hiding my excitement. I knew his answer and I had a comeback.

Because, I need two... He trailed off, finally understanding.

Souls? I finished gleefully. *Okay, you've got them, what next?*

Chasym couldn't hold back relieved laughter. I felt it, rather than heard it, but it was there all the same. *You astound me, Jase.*

I know.

All right. It won't be easy...

But you'll be fine, I thought reassuringly.

I felt Haeon's grip tighten. "I don't have time for your games, boy." My mental conversation with Chasym took significantly less time than it would had we used real words, rather than thoughts. Only a second had passed.

"Don't worry. The games are over," I replied casually.

Now? Chasym inquired.

Now.

Haeon gasped as the change began. Releasing me, he threw his head back and screamed, clasping his hands to his stolen face. He stumbled and Veija ran to his side, placing her delicate hands on his shoulder.

"Reji?" she whispered fearfully, then slowly stepped back.

The image of one man splitting into two wasn't what I would call pleasant, but it wasn't as bad I feared. One half of the face that belonged to Reji became Chasym while the other changed into Haeon. Blond hair spilled down his right shoulder, while vine green hair fell down the left side. One yellow eye watched me trustingly, while one green eye was full of pain and terror.

"What have you done?" Haeon's voice screamed.

"Destroyed you," Chasym's voice replied from the same mouth.

Blue light ripped vertically between the two faces in one body, splitting them entirely in half. Then the light filled in the missing halves of each man. Tears fell down their cheeks and they silently screamed as the pain heightened.

"Reji?" Veija repeated as Chasym fell limply to the ground, whole in form. She stepped over Haeon's prostrate body, walking slowly toward the blond.

"No," I said quietly, causing her to stop. "Reji didn't exist, Veija. His name is Chasym."

She stared at me in wonder, then smiled gently, her ditsy presence gone entirely. "Of course," she said in a soft, understanding tone. She knelt down, her silken gown laying gracefully around her as she pulled Chasym's head onto her lap and began stroking his hair. "Chasym."

Haeon groaned and pulled himself into a kneeling position. Staring around in shock, he raised a trembling hand and slowly looked at it. "No," he whispered hoarsely.

"Yes," I said.

He looked up at me, his eyes a muddy brown color.

Lon stepped beside me, placing a supportive hand on my shoulder as he fixed his coldest glare on the pitiful man before us. "You're finished. You are now condemned to the life of a mortal man. You'll die, Haeon. It seems justice has a certain sense of irony."

I glanced up at my father's face and blinked. His eyes were gold.

"She'll die," Haeon said. "Without my aid, Veija will die as well."

"No," I said calmly. "Just like you fed off Kirid for so long, I'm giving Veija new life. Only, this is for real. She'll be fully restored to her Seership forever." I turned my eyes to the couple on the ground. "Chasym?"

He opened one yellow eye and smiled. "With pleasure." I felt him relinquish all of his power taken from the core. Then he passed out.

I drew his power to me, letting it trickle into my soul. It was familiar, like an old friend. Then the rush came, like adrenaline through my veins, only this was spiritual. Welcoming the surging pulse, I closed my eyes and raised my hands before me. I formed a new orb by taking a small portion of my Seeric power and encasing it. When I opened my eyes I saw the gold orb bobbing contentedly above my opened palms. "Go home," I said. It glided across the air toward Veija.

Haeon cried out, standing clumsily and wobbling toward it, but the orb passed through him and slipped inside Veija's heart. She gasped, her eyes fluttered, and then she gripped Chasym's shoulder tightly. As I suspected, her violet eyes changed to gold.

"It's the mark of a Seer," I said. "That's why my eyes changed."

"Striking eyes are one distinction of an eternal being. For a Paradisaical Seer, both hair and eyes match. For someone like you, Key," Lon brushed a finger through my white hair, "it is similar, but also unique."

Haeon crumpled into a pathetic heap on the floor, sobbing into his arms. I could've killed him then, ending his pain, but something told me it was more merciful to let him live a while. That, or my own sense of justice was a little ironic. Either way, Haeon had certainly gotten what he gave.

"I did warn him," the core's voice whispered somewhere inside my head.

He most certainly did.

41
Death?

My body was completely exhausted, but my soul surged with power. Good thing, since there was one last order of business. "Lon," I said, feeling weird as I called him by name.

"Hm?" He looked at me.

"Whe—" I broke off as I heard Crenen cough violently. Turning from Lon, I saw Menen holding his master with a stricken expression. The Yenen prince was clutching his chest, coughing blood onto the stone floor. His eyes were glazed. "Crenen?" My own eyes widened as I remembered another who had succumbed to the illness. Spinning, I found Jenen kneeling on the ground, barely able to hold himself up. He looked up as he felt my eyes on him, and smiled weakly.

"Beautiful work," he said as blood slipped from the corners of his mouth. "Lon must be very proud." His dark hair fell in his eyes and he bowed his head, coughing raggedly.

"Jenen," I whispered.

"I think this is all you could have done. One cannot fight against nature."

"No." I shook my head. "No, Jenen. Shut up. Don't say that. I can fix this."

Jenen smiled patiently.

"Jase."

I turned to see Chasym looking up at me from Veija's lap.

"The power I gave you was slowing the disease down. There's no more time. Act now."

I nodded slowly. "Okay." I walked to him, crouched down, and placed my hands on his heart. "Give it to me."

Chasym shook his head. "Use me. I won't let you take it. Just use me."

"No."

"Jason!" Chasym shouted, then his body slackened. "Just. Do. It."

I winced. "I...can't." I was about to take my hands away when Veija set hers on top of mine.

"Key, he needs to do this. Let him atone, use him." Her golden eyes held my gaze steadily until I finally had to break away. "They will die if you don't hurry."

I glanced at Crenen, then Jenen. They were both so nearly gone. "I— Okay."

"Thank you," Chasym whispered.

I glanced up at Lon. "Get everyone else out while I work. And...find me a thesher."

He raised an eyebrow but nodded without hesitation. "I will."

"Thanks."

Wordlessly he turned and walked to Jenen, helping him up and motioning for Menen to do the same for Crenen. As they aided the twins, Kirid got to his feet and walked to Haeon, pulling him up and leading him firmly after the others.

"Go, Veija," I whispered.

"I won't leave him," she said, tightening her grip on Chasym's shoulder. He winced as her nails penetrated his skin, but said nothing.

"Veija." This time I held her gaze. "I need you to do something for me." She looked ready to protest. "No. Listen. It will be hard, but I need to you take Sasha with you. She can't stay here. Please?"

Closing her mouth, she nodded. "I understand." Slipping from beneath Chasym, she carefully laid his head on the ground, brushed his forehead with her hand, and then hurried to Sasha's body. As the others began to disappear from the threshold, I turned my entire focus to Chasym.

"Think I'll survive?" he asked quietly.

"Considering your history I'd say it's fairly likely."

He laughed, closing his eyes. "Time to get started then, Jase."

"Call me Key," I said. "Jason is gone."

"But I liked Jason," he said softly.

"You'll like Key better," I assured him. "Now shut up so I can concentrate." He obeyed, and I began one last journey into the core, leaving behind the stone platform raised high above hot lava.

We were standing on the misty plains, feeling the moisture on our faces and inside our clothes. Chasym gazed around with a pained face. "I knew what I was doing when I overpowered the core. I was well aware of my emotions, well aware that Haeon was manipulating them. I didn't care. I was willing to do anything for Veija, anything to make myself worthy in Lon's eyes. And, with them, who needed the rest of the world?"

I watched him. "What made you change your mind?"

He looked at me thoughtfully, then smiled. "You. You and your father. Until you were the one chosen to become the new Vendaeva I had no quirks with any sacrifices made in the attempt. I knew by then that what I'd done was foolish, but since I knew there was no way to fix it, I didn't worry. The core and I made plans to fix everything, but we both knew better than to hope.

"Then Lon intervened. The core suggested you without realizing what you meant to me. And, while I wouldn't have thought it possible, Lon actually agreed. He felt responsible. Him! After everything *I* had done. But even then I didn't have the heart to tell him the truth. I wasn't willing enough to stop him from sending you away, because I was selfish."

He laughed bitterly. "But you, just like Lon, had to mess it all up. You had to go and earn my respect, and even my love. Your stubbornness, pride, and your nobility grew on me. I began to think of you like a little brother, so even after Haeon told me to kill you, I couldn't bring myself to do it."

I considered him thoughtfully. "That's when you met Jenen and me in the forest right before the furapintairow attack—when you refused to listen to Haeon anymore. And that's why he attempted to kill you." A drop of liquid mist fell from my hair, rippling in the puddle near my feet.

"It was never an attempt to kill me—only to remind me who was in charge. When you were captured, I went to save you, knowing very well that Haeon would be furious. That's why he locked me in the cellar. Haeon couldn't kill me—to do that would undermine his plans because I was the disease—but he could punish me. He had a hold on Veija's mind in case I went too far."

I frowned. "So you always knew why she was insane?"

"Not always, but when she finally woke up only after you were declared Vendaeva's heir, the puzzle piece fit into place."

Something clicked. "That's why my power was never consistent, and why I was always so tired."

He blinked.

"You held some of it, as did Kirid, which kept it from working right every time. It threw off the balance, and when one of you used it, you robbed my energy." I laughed. "Man, it's really kind of simple when everything's finally laid out."

"I always thought it rather complex."

"Some of it," I agreed as I gazed up into the endless mist above. "Enough about that though. It's time to gather it all back up." I glanced at Chasym. "Are you su—"

"Positive. Just do it."

"All right." I reached out with my mind, seeking every tiny piece of the Paradisaical disease, beckoning it to come to me. Finally the disease relented, slowly pulling away from wherever it clung. I felt its touch leaving the victims of Paradise, reluctantly at first, but then eagerly, sensing the presence of its creator.

Closing my eyes, I sought out Crenen and Jenen. An image formed and I saw them sitting with the others in the throne room. The only one missing was Lon, undoubtedly seeking out a thesher. Enhancing my senses, I felt Crenen's slowing heart beat and heard Jenen's shallow breathing. I pulled at the disease inside of them, beckoning it to leave and follow me. It took only a little coaxing for the illness to pull away from Jenen, but when I entered Crenen's center I had to retreat.

"What's wrong?"

I opened my eyes and looked at Chasym. "I can't heal Crenen. I can't touch him."

His face darkened. "I was afraid of that. The pact he made was binding, thus his body wasn't the only thing infected. It's tearing apart his soul. While the souls of the other victims are trapped, his...is being destroyed."

I stared, panic pounding against my chest. "That can't happen, Chasym. You're the one who caused the bloody thing—tell me how to fix this."

He cringed at my tone and lowered his head. "I'm sorry, Ja—Key. I don't know what to tell you."

I stared at him as I racked my own brain for any ideas. As I concentrated, I felt something brush against my hand. Glancing down, I spotted the white orb hovering by my thumb.

"What must one do to bring back a soul?"

I blinked. "I...don't know.

"Bargain."

"Bargain? With my soul?"

"That depends... I would not be the one to decide."

"But you *are* the one who bargained with Crenen to begin with," I growled.

"That is because I was in charge at the time. But before I bargained with Crenen, I had to bargain with someone else..."

I glanced at Chasym.

"Not him," the core said.

"Then, who?"

"Who is keeper of the dead?"

I was at a loss. "I dunno, the Grim Reaper?"

"Precisely."

I gave the orb a skeptical look. "You're kidding."

"Not at all."

I continued to stare at the orb, unable to comprehend. As I stared I felt the moisture in the air evaporating as the disease was collected by my subconscious beckoning. At last I looked at Chasym. "Is he—it—kidding?"

The blond shook his head. "No."

I gawked. "Unbelievable. I have to bargain with Death?"

"Yes. Unless you would rather Crenen stopped existing."

I furiously rubbed my head with one scarred palm. "No." I paused. "Okay, fine. How do I...meet with Death?"

"You're the core now, it can't be too hard to summon him," Chasym said.

"Merely do as you always do when summoning."

"Hold out my palm?" I scoffed.

"No, not when you summon Liitae."

"Stop being cryptic," Chasym chided. He met my eyes. "Send Liitae to get him."

I watched him blankly and finally shrugged. "Okay. You heard them. Go on, Liitae." My blue orb bobbed with excitement and vanished on the spot. "This is crazy," I commented after a moment.

"In Paradise, what isn't?" Chasym replied.

"Yeah, but this is way beyond Paradise-crazy. This is..."

"Universal structure," the core finished.

"Not quite what I was going for." I absently watched the disappearing mist. As it departed, the plains were brightening. The puddles around me were drying up. Suddenly the puddle by my feet turned to ice. Puzzled, I glanced at another puddle to find it freezing over with a shrill crackle. A chill spread over me, like a winter morning. My breath came out in little clouds as I sensed a new presence before of me.

"You summoned?" a soft voice whispered.

I looked up slowly, as if my joints were half frozen, until I saw him. It was like he stepped straight out of a horror movie. He was instantly recognizable for what he was.

Dressed in black from head to toe, complete with a billowing, hooded cloak, he held a scythe in one gloved hand; the blade hovered several inches above his head, while the wooden haft extended to the ground. While his appearance was profoundly intimidating, it wasn't until I found his eyes under the shadow of his hood that my breath caught in my lungs. Black. Pure, deep, fathomless eyes that bore into my very soul.

I couldn't speak.

He seemed to understand my silence. Raising a slender hand, he brushed back his hood to reveal a surprisingly human head. He was very pale and his face was angular and flawless.

Long pale-blond hair fell down his shoulders and disappeared beneath his cloak, and peeking out from his hair were pointed ears. He wore no emotional expression, he only watched me, knowing, seeing.

I wasn't the only one at a loss for words. I felt Chasym's fear like a tangible thing. It was then that I knew why the puddles had turned to ice—it was a manifestation of the numbing terror we felt. Despite the fact that this creature in many ways resembled a movie's depiction, there was nothing comical about his presence.

It seemed like forever before I finally got up the nerve to speak. "I—" And that was the extent of my efforts.

Death's black eyes had not left my face, and only now did he blink; slowly, patiently. "You wish to discuss the life of Prince Crenen." It was a statement.

I nodded vigorously, feeling like a tiny child under his gaze.

"You wish me to keep him alive."

Again I nodded. I should have felt embarrassed, I knew that. Normally I would have gotten very angry at myself by now and taken it out on him, but this man—Death—I knew better than to disrespect him.

Death glanced around the plains, taking in the frozen water and halted mist. "You are saving this world."

I wondered if that bothered him, but made no reply.

"Your sacrifice is enough," he said, closing his mesmerizing eyes. When he opened them, they flicked back to me. "I will help you."

My breath returned in my relief. "Th-thank you."

He made no response. Instead he pulled the hood back over his head and, propping his scythe against his shoulder, pressed his thumbs and index fingers together. A small light appeared before him and gradually grew. I winced as the light formed a near-blinding tunnel of swirling light and shadow.

He stepped into the brilliant opening hovering just above the ground.

"W-wait!" I called. "Don't you need some sort of payment?"

He glanced back and again I felt like my soul was exposed. "Your sacrifice to enter the core was enough of a price for one day. Besides," he turned away, "I do not accept payment." The light swallowed him whole and vanished, leaving a gloomy atmosphere behind.

"What did he mean?" Chasym asked.

I glanced at him as my limbs tingled with new feeling. The ice beneath us began to thaw. "What?"

"What was the sacrifice you made to enter the threshold anyway? You never said."

I smiled sadly. "I...will never live with my family again."

"Jase—sorry." He hesitated, then spoke again. "Key. That was too much."

I shook my head. "Not really. I can still visit them from time to time. I just chose to live in Paradise. So, it's not that bad."

He watched me, unconvinced. "Is that really the extent of it?"

"Yeah," I lied easily. It wasn't true. I had chosen to lose my family. It was the only way I knew we would get into the core, so I broke my ties with them. They would never remember their oldest son. Jason Sterling would no longer exist in their memories. With my appearance as it was, along with my position as Vendaeva, there was no way I could return to Earth. It was better if they forgot me. I would never see them again. Such a price had been enough to enter the core, and through that sacrifice I would save Paradise.

A image appeared in my mind's eyes, drowning my thoughts. I saw Crenen resting against a stone wall beside Menen. The former was unconscious, barely breathing, while the latter watched him sadly, knowing the time to say goodbye was soon.

A tunnel opened before Crenen. From its swirling depths emerged Death, standing tall and silent in the dark throne room. No one could see him, or they certainly would have reacted. He raised his hands and Crenen's spirit rose from his body. Crenen looked around curiously in his spiritual form, but I could see the corrosion that had taken hold. Parts of his transparent figure were darker than the rest, like oil poured into water.

Menen stiffened as he saw his master's body grow lax. Leaning over the still form, he clutched his shoulder. "Master?" He shook him lightly. "Master?" He grabbed his wrist and checked the pulse, knowing there would be none. "Crenen," he said despairingly.

Jenen opened his eyes and stared at the still form of his twin. "No," he whispered weakly, bowing his head. "No, please."

"Now, Seer Key," Death's soft voice filled my head. *"While I have his soul, remove the sickness. Then I will return him to his body. After that, it will be up to Crenen how much his soul can be repaired."*

I smiled softly. "Thank you." Reaching out, I grasped the ugly disease and wrenched it from Crenen's body. It was reluctant, but finally gave way. As I brought it into the core, I saw Death return Crenen's spirit to his body. Crenen drew breath immediately and Menen jerked away from him, startled and afraid.

"*Crenen*?" Menen exclaimed.

"Hush, Tall Strong Jerk. We were sleeping of being dead, yeah?" he mumbled, then slumped over and slept.

Jenen blinked, staring in wonder at his brother's revival. Slowly a smile touched his lips. "Key."

"It's been collected," I said as the image faded from my mind. I looked at Chasym. "Are you ready?"

"I am," he answered firmly. "Hit me."

I hesitated for a moment, torn between the horror of what I must do and Chasym's need for redemption. "If you die..."

"It would be better than what might have happened otherwise. But, like you recently pointed out, my friend, I tend to cheat Death better than anyone. He and I—we go way back." He winked. "Do it."

The disease was gathered; now all I had to do was give it all to Chasym. I looked at him. "Merry Christmas." I thrust the entire sickness into his heart.

He laughed at my words, but as the disease entered his body he doubled over and sank to his knees, vomiting blood. He hugged his chest as tears of pain leaked from his eyes. Again he vomited, then wiped his mouth with one hand, smearing the blood across his chin. "It hurts...so...much," he whispered with a tiny laugh.

I stood in silence. "Is it all there, Chasym?"

He hesitated, then finally nodded. "Yeah. I'm gonna have to say yeah," he said through clenched teeth.

I knelt before him, placing my hands on his shoulders. "Thank you. Now let me kill it."

"Please, by all means, do," he managed to gasp.

I pushed in on the disease, containing it inside of Chasym so it wouldn't spread anymore. Focusing, I explored my possibilities. I had to be the one to destroy it, but as weak as I was in this frail body, doing so here and now was impossible. I had only one option—as I'd suspected. I pulled the blond to his feet. "Let's go." I glanced around. The mist had completely left the plains. Instead a realm of purest light surrounded us. Opalescent swirls of color had taken the blue mist's place, dancing around us airily.

"This is your home now," the core whispered.

I shook my head. "Nah, I don't think I like it. Maybe I'll visit from time to time, but I feel like I've had enough of the core to last me a while."

"But you *are the core. This is merely your domain."*

I smiled, but said nothing. Domain it might be, but home it certainly wasn't. Besides, the place would be safer if I wasn't in it. Not many would know I was the core, so the desperate would seek out this place in the hopes that it would grant their wishes. It was definitely better if this domain and I stayed far away from one another.

Pulling Chasym's left arm over my shoulders, I vanished from the swirling lights, and we found ourselves back in the core's threshold. The platform showed recent signs of battle; several tiles had been badly chipped, while the blue ring around the circular floor was charred and blackened. Blood pooled the ground in several spots. But for these, the threshold held no sign of being disturbed. The lava below bubbled contentedly, the smoke rose lazily, and the red sky gazed down in disinterest.

"What's up with this place anyway?" I asked.

"It is more intimidating than a swirling mass of light, do you not think?" the core answered with a child's laugh.

"True." I glanced at Chasym. "Hang in there."

He nodded weakly. "I always do."

I walked to the portal leading away from the threshold. While I somehow liked this scenery better than the plains, I never wanted to see it again. Too much had happened here. We left the platform and found ourselves standing on the throne's dais. My friends all looked up, except for Crenen, who was probably sleeping more comfortably now than he had in six long years.

"Key," Menen said. He glanced at Chasym. "What happened?"

Standing in such a normal place took its toll on me. I hunched under Chasym's weight and felt my legs begin to shake. "Where's Lon?" I asked, suddenly too tired to answer any questions (while it seemed I was never too tired to ask them).

"Here," the Seer said, entering through the double doors across the long room. He led a giant horse in after him. "I've brought your thesher."

I tried to smile but was certain it looked more like a grimace. "Thanks." I stepped from the dais, aiding Chasym, and we started across the room toward our ride. Lon met us somewhere in the middle.

"Help me get him mounted," I said, and Lon pulled Chasym onto the carnivorous horse, while I pushed a little, probably not being much help. I tried not to think about what I was doing as I pulled myself into the huge saddle. The horse was my friend; it wouldn't eat me.

"Where are you going?" Lon asked.

"The Healing Pool."

"That's a long ride," Lon said as he handed me the reins.

"Yeah, well," I patted the thesher's head, then quickly drew my hand away, "this guy's only taking us to the nearest body of water. From there, we travel my way."

Lon shook his head. "You don't have enough energy for that."

I shrugged. "I'll think of something."

"Jason," Chasym said behind me, "I'm not worth all this trouble."

I snorted. "I'm not going to listen to you until you stop sounding stupid."

"But—"

"Nope." I turned the massive beast around and nudged him forward. "I'll be back."

"Key," Lon said from behind me. "The Pool does not have the properties to heal anything more than the body. Your energy won't be renewed."

"I know." But I wasn't worried about me. I snapped the reins and the horse rushed forward. Within seconds we'd left the throne room far behind, and not long afterward we reached the front doors. "Liitae!" I called, and the orb bounded forward and thrust the heavy door open before we had to stop. Flying down the several hundred steps, almost like they weren't there, the horse reached the ground in minutes. Then we rode across the ground more swiftly than I'd ever traveled in my life.

I squinted my eyes against the wind, looking for signs of the lake we'd come by before, or anything that resembled water. It wasn't long before I caught sight of a shimmering something in the distance. "Just a little longer," I called back to Chasym.

"Right," he mumbled.

Something jarred my memory and I remembered the large fissure the earthquake had formed that separated us from the lake. I hoped theshers could jump as high as they could run fast. "Hang on," I called as I spotted the crack. We reached it fast, leaped, and then we were over it. For being such a large and cumbersome creature the thesher could certainly manage a graceful landing. We hardly moved in our saddle as the horse hit the ground and kept running. As we neared the lake I finally took the time to glance at our surroundings.

The captured army of Kirid warriors had disappeared by now, along with its furapintairow guard. My instructions had been to take them some place out of the way, and I now wondered vaguely how the Small Red Fuzzies had interpreted that.

The world still seemed like it was dying, but I knew it wouldn't take too long before it was restored to the Paradise I'd first come to know. (I wondered with a smile when I'd started to consider that a good thing.)

The thesher finally halted at the lake's edge, and I slid from the saddle and helped Chasym off. He could hardly stand now, but we managed to walk into the water. Glancing at the thesher, I nodded my thanks. I might have imagined it, but I could swear the creature nodded back before tossing its head and galloping back toward the Kirid castle.

Wading deeper into the water, panting under Chasym's weight, I gathered my remaining energy and summoned the watery portal. "Here goes."

The golden light circled us, wrapping the glistening water above our heads like a blanket, and then we landed in the Healing Pool. Satisfied, I released Chasym and sank into the water's depths. It didn't burn this time, and I was grateful for that. Oblivion touched the corners of my mind, but I fought the urge to sleep. That could wait until I knew whether Chasym would be all right or not. I fought my way to the surface and gasped for air as I looked around for my friend. I couldn't find him.

"Chasym!" I cried, kicking my legs as I struggled to stay above the water.

"Here, Key," he said calmly from behind me.

I slowly turned around and saw him sitting on the shore, dripping wet and smiling.

"You're okay?" I asked.

"Yes, I'm okay. Thanks to you." He got to his feet. "You tapped into your power through the Pool, because your body was too tired to take it directly—am I right?"

I only grinned.

He smiled. "Shall we go?"

I nodded, relieved everything had worked. I swam toward the shore, eager to get back to the others.

"Jason!" Chasym called in warning just as I felt a sharp pain on the left side of my back. It spread like a burning fire through my entire body. I heard the splash of water and then Chasym pulled me from lake and laid me down on the muddy bank. "Talk to me."

"I'm..." I took a moment to cough, "...alive, I swear. What...happened?" I winced as the pain pulsed through my body again.

"Snake."

"Snake?" I repeated.

"Yes, snake." He turned me onto my stomach. "They are pets of They." I felt him rip my shirt open. "Paradisians call them serecu."

"Lemme guess, Paradisian snakes are especially harmful?"

"Well, they hurt like insanity itself."

I laughed dryly. "Insanity, I'm told, doesn't hurt too much."

"You'd be surprised," he mumbled. I felt him press his fingers against the skin around the bite.

"Anything else, 'sides a lotta pain?" I inquired, noting that my speech was slightly slurred.

"Fever. Delirium. The basic symptoms of the Paradisaical disease. Where do you think I got the idea?"

"Only the disease was...worse," I concluded.

"Yeah. That killed. This is only really uncomfortable. It's meant to make an enemy weak so it's easier to destroy them."

I felt my mind swimming toward unconsciousness. "Where—how'd...the snake...come...?"

"These snakes swim."

"Huh." Poisonous water snakes. Charming. And...why'd it strike me...?"

"You saved my life. Snakes don't like me much."

I snorted. "Seems pretty common, Chazzy." My vision was gone. Or were my eyes closed? "Kinda like...my...weakness —"

—Was getting to be rather redundant.

I felt Chasym rest his hand on my head and ruffle my long hair. "This time you earned it, kid. Now, sleep. I'll get you home."

As I felt myself drifting toward that familiar friend called oblivion I was lulled by the sounds of the water's gentle waves and the wind through the branches overhead. Then all was gone.

42
Tying The Ends?

Somehow I knew I'd slept for three days. No one had to tell me, because for once in my life my internal clock was working properly. I wasn't bothered by the fact that I'd slept so long. With as little rest as I'd received through my adventures, I felt justified. Still, three days was long enough. So, as I felt the sun's warm rays on my face, I swam up from the depths of my mind and forced my eyes to open.

"Good morning."

I turned my head carefully and saw a bed near my own in which rested Crenen. He was propped up against several plump pillows, his black hair was loose, hanging at uneven lengths around his shoulders, and he watched me with a quiet smile. He wore untattered white robes—something I never expected to see him in.

I smiled back with more energy than he was exhibiting. "Hey."

He watched me for a moment longer, then turned to look out the panoramic window covering the entire wall near the end of our beds. The scenery beyond was spectacular, showing a green valley with lakes dotting the landscape. In the distance I could see thick forests, and beyond that, the sea; blue and endless.

"Where are we?" I asked.

"Kirid palace," he said.

I glanced at him, raising an eyebrow at his reservation. "How're you feeling?"

"Strange," he answered softly.

I felt an ache in my heart as I watched him. "Crenen." I waited to speak until he finally looked at me. "I'm sorry."

He blinked his mismatched eyes. "Why?"

"I couldn't save her."

Crenen's smile deepened. "You tried."

"Yeah, but—"

"Don't," he whispered, shaking his head. "Don't."

Silence resumed as we both turned back to the view beyond our room. I could easily hear the breeze beyond the glass and I watched the birds fly back and forth as they collected breakfast for their young. One brought back to their nest what looked like a little bunch of gerani. My mouth watered.

"I would rather die than witness someone else's death—at least of those I care about," Crenen said after a while. "Perhaps I am a coward."

I picked at my furry blanket. "Then I'm a coward, too. But," I looked up, "that doesn't mean you can start calling me one again, okay?"

He tried not to, but ended up chuckling. "You've been out for a long time."

"Three days," I said.

He nodded.

"You really are Vendaeva," Crenen stated after a pause.

"Took you that long to finally admit it, eh?" I laughed. "So, how is everyone?"

Crenen glanced at the door on the other side of his bed. "They're fine. Lon comes in occasionally to check on you. Sometimes Chasym comes too. And both Veija and Nithae have been nursing you back to health. Menen is stationed at the door, along with your friend Kirid."

I waited for the rest, but when he stopped I decided to press him. "What about Haeon and Jenen?"

"I don't know. Haeon obviously doesn't visit, and Jenen hasn't been here either."

I watched Crenen closely, looking for any sign of emotion. "He was crying for you," I said.

"Haeon?" Crenen asked.

"When you died, Jenen was crying for you," I said, refusing to let him dodge the issue.

"I did die, then."

"Yeah. It was the only way to break your little deal with the core."

Crenen abruptly turned his head to look at me. "Deal?"

"I know about it. I *saw* it. So did Jenen."

"How?"

"Chasym showed us. He and the core were sort of working together, so he knew." I let this information sink in. "That was a really cool thing you did, Crenen."

He cocked his head. "'Cool'?"

"Er, good. I meant good." I didn't want to explain more slang. "Anyway, I mean it. Jenen was really touched. Angry—but touched. And grateful." I felt awkward as I praised him. He was the type of person one always admired, but never out loud.

Crenen watched me thoughtfully now. "You still have that second question. I will answer it wholly if you want."

I paused, considering his offer. Then I smiled and shook my head. "It's okay. I'll save it." There really was something I wanted to ask, but the issue was too painful to address at the moment.

"Are you sure?" he asked.

"If I knew everything today, there'd be nothing left to discover tomorrow," I offered a grin, "and that'd be boring, yeah?"

Crenen slept after that. But while my body screamed for more rest, I found my thoughts too active. I reflected on the question I'd almost asked. It was painful even to think about, but remembering Sasha's last words made me feel responsible to ask.

Did Crenen love Sasha?

And while I felt that the question should one day be answered, some part of me never wanted to know. The real question was, had *I* loved Sasha? It was the first time in my life I realized some things should never be answered. Especially since it wouldn't bring her back.

I turned over and shoved my face into my pillow, squeezing my eyes shut. I didn't want to think about it. Ever again.

...Or, at least, not until tomorrow.

"How are you feeling?"

"Still drools, yeah?"

"Yes, Master."

I opened my eyes and found Menen's wife Nithae looking down at me with beautiful pink eyes. Hers had been thc first voice I heard.

I managed a smile. "Better, thanks to you and a lot of sleep."

"I am glad," she said as she reached forward and ran her fingers along my hair. "It is very beautiful, this new color. It suits you much."

I'd forgotten about my white hair. I hadn't even seen it yet. "I'm going to have to take your word for it." Turning my head I saw Menen standing at the end of Crenen's bed, while Crenen grinned toothily at me.

"Still drool," he told me.

"Yeah, I heard you."

"We brought you a gift, Menen and I," Nithae said. She held up her left hand and my mouth began to water. Plump gerani dangled from her graceful fingers. She took my hand and placed the bunch carefully into it. "Be sparing or Menen will never allow it so again." She stood up. "You have visitors waiting outside. We will leave you to them now." She walked to Menen, who took her hand and led her from the room after nodding to me.

I heard voices murmuring from outside the door, then it creaked open to reveal Veija dragging Chasym inside.

"Don't be silly. He saved your life—of course he wants to see you!" she was saying.

"No, Veija, let someone else in," he protested, grabbing the door's frame and forcing Veija into a game of tug-of-war.

"Stop being so stubb—"

"Don't be ridiculous, Veija," I interjected. "I want nothing to do with the moron."

Chasym's hand slipped from the frame and he turned his yellow eyes toward me. "Moron?"

"You heard me. Now, get out, idiot."

He scowled. "Idiot?"

"Oh, great. Now you're a copycat." I scoffed. "Honestly, how pathetic can you get?"

His eyes narrowed and danced with an eerie light. "*Pathetic*?"

"Yeah. Pathetic. You going deaf too?"

He crossed the stone floor in seconds and stood above me, arching an eyebrow.

"Chasym," I said, adopting a serious tone, "I owe you something." Grabbing the pillow beneath me, I yanked it free and slammed it into Chasym's stomach, making him stumble backward. "The only way to make you stop sulking is to mock you. *That's* pathetic." My hand fell limply to my side. "Now...shut up unless you have something smart to say."

He held the pillow in his hands as he stared at me in wonder. Finally he smiled. "You're one strange kid."

I smirked. "Of course. I'm Paradisian. Hate to say it, but it's one giant asylum around here."

"Amen," he said as he handed me the pillow. "So, how are you?"

"I'm okay. It helps that I finally got some real sleep."

Chasym chuckled, then glanced at the door. "Well. Everyone else is waiting. I'll...see you later."

"Right." I stuffed the pillow behind my head and watched him leave with Veija, who waved gracefully in parting. I returned the gesture with a small nod.

Kirid came in next, watching the floor nervously as he approached. Finally he looked up and managed a tiny smile. Even now that our hair was completely opposite our resemblance was uncanny.

"Hey," I said. "What news from the outside world?"

He sat down on the bed's edge. "There have been a few skirmishes. It seems a lot of Kirid Clan followed Haeon, not me. And since I lost my powers, I...haven't had a lot of influence. Fortunately Lon has been helping out."

I chuckled. "That would be interesting to see."

"I had no idea he was your father!" Kirid exclaimed, and my smile turned lopsided. "You certainly look alike, now that I think to compare, but he just seems so young. Somehow."

"The beauty of immortality, I think."

We grew quiet for a while, then Kirid shifted. "Kiido?"

"Yeah?"

He paused and took a breath. "I don't think I deserved to live—no, hear me out."

I closed my mouth and nodded.

"I've done things you say are wrong. And the fact that I never felt remorse, fear—anything I think I ought to have felt—makes me believe that I have a lot to learn. So, even though I don't deserve to live, I'm going to make the most of it. And," he swallowed, "I would like you to guide me."

I smiled. "I'd be honored."

He looked genuinely relieved. "Thank you." He stood. "I'll go now. Lon seemed a little anxious, but he wouldn't come until everyone else had."

"Wait, Kirid. I've been curious about something. What *does* Kiido mean?"

He laughed uncomfortably. "It's... Never mind."

Before I could interrogate him further he was at the door, and then through it. I wrinkled my brow. "I hate being left in the dark."

"It means 'brother,'" Crenen said.

I turned to look at him. "Really?"

He nodded, then raised his arms above his head and stretched. "Well, Strange Reckless Dolt, we going for walk now, yeah?" He tossed his blankets aside and pushed himself from the bed.

"Are you feeling well enough?" I asked.

"Always plenty well enough. Have more important things needing done right now than staying inside." He walked to the door, perfectly unconcerned about wearing his robes. The outfit almost resembled a Japanese kimono, with the wide sleeves and the way it folded in the front, but the difference between this and a man's kimono was that Crenen's robe dragged a little on the ground behind him.

"Hey," I said.

Crenen glanced at me.

"Uh. What's with the clothes?" I asked. "You look like you're wearing a dress."

He grinned pointedly. "Not dress, Strange Reckless Dolt. When not traveling always we wear formal attire, yeah?"

"Formal?"

"Formal sleepwear," he explained as he pulled the wooden door open and stepped into the corridor beyond. "Strange Reckless Dolt wanting speak with Mysterious Girly Guy. Go in or die like tiny worm," and he shoved Lon unceremoniously into the room. Apparently, if he'd been anxious, it certainly didn't keep Lon from hesitating when his turn finally did roll around.

As the door closed behind the Seer, he stood stock-still, watching me from across the spacious room. His hair was pulled back in a ponytail, and he wore a purple headband on which a single red eye had been embroidered. His robes were much more elaborate than I'd ever seen them. At least five layers thick, they were each a varying shade of purple; lavender, plum, periwinkle, violet, and crimson. The topmost layer was sheer, with gold thread trim on every hem.

"Ever seen a peacock before? I think you'd find you have a lot in common," I remarked, unable to stop myself.

Lon blinked his golden eyes slowly and then a slight smile touched his lips. "It is the traditional garb of a Seer."

"Huh. Well, don't get any ideas. I like my current gender, thanks."

More silence. It seemed everyone was feeling a little awkward. I almost wanted to ask if there was something on my face, but that was a stupid question. It wasn't how I looked (so much), but what I'd done. Looking from their points of view I could understand. Here I was, a tiny, reckless, whiny boy who suddenly hopped up and saved Paradise right after dying. And now I was the core. I was having trouble swallowing everything myself.

"How are you feeling?" Lon asked at last.

"Good, really good." I smiled to let him know I meant it.

"Good," he said, looking everywhere but at me. I almost laughed at his nervousness, but thought better of it. "Well," he found the door handle behind him, "I'll let you rest."

"I don't understand you people at all," I blurted.

He hesitated.

"I mean, when I first arrived in Paradise I thought the natives were hostile, controlling, inconsiderate jerks all out for themselves. Everyone had his own agenda. Nobody really cared about anything else."

Lon cast his eyes to the ground. "About that, Key—"

"But then," I said over him, "I find out every single person here is a melodramatic, selfless twit. Chasym; bent on revenge for his lost love, and searching for a means to redeem himself. Crenen; desperate to help his brother and his clan by sacrificing himself. Jenen; as angsty as they come, but for a surprisingly good reason. Veija; insane because she—don't interrupt me, Lon—because she is being manipulated by just about the only person without a good cause. Sasha—" my voice cracked for a moment, "—determined to save Crenen regardless of how impossible it seems. And Menen; probably the most selfless out of the lot! Can't even spend a decent amount of time with his wife for it." I paused, watching Lon's stricken expression. "Then there's you," I said gently. Lon met my eyes and I saw fear in them. "The biggest idiot of all." I smiled, hoping I could convey my feelings. "I don't hate you for it." I swallowed. "Father."

He stared as if my words were incomprehensible. Then his eyes filled with tears and, for the first time, I watched him cry. He stood quietly, though his body shook with emotion and his head was bowed. Tears fell to the ground. I waited in respectful silence until he'd composed himself. After a while he wiped his eyes dry and straightened.

"Whether you blame me or not," he said in a strong voice, "I am not deserving of that title."

"Do you think Meyana would agree?" I asked.

He started. "How do you...?"

"That's the name of my mother, right?"

"Yes."

"Well—do you think she'd be fond of the idea that you still forsook your son when you didn't have to anymore?"

"I... Key, listen—"

"You sent her away when I was four."

Again he stared. "How do you know all of this?"

I shrugged. "Oh, just one of the many voices in my head giving me a tour of my memories." I raised my hand and Liitae appeared. "Of course, this li'l guy's the one who opened everything back up." I laughed. "I even remember Meyana a little bit. She had red hair, right?"

Lon absently watched the blue orb soar around. "Yes," he said. "Like fire."

"And she had gray eyes," I said. "Actually, I saw her a while ago. When you restored my memory after I escaped from Haeon I think you accidentally opened a few more than you planned."

Lon grimaced. "Yes, I'm...not as good as Chasym at memory manipulation. He is what one calls a Keeper of Memory."

"What's that?" I shifted my blankets around me.

Lon crossed the room at last and sat on the empty bed which had formerly held Crenen. "On each world a Keeper of Memory is chosen to hold every significant event of the planet inside his mind. You might call them historians. A Keeper has countless stores of memory, most inaccessible even to him. One advantage to such an appointment is a perfect recollection. Another is long life—unless you're immortal already, of course. And lastly, memory manipulation. Chasym can give or take memories at will, and he can also alter or even create new memories to replace true ones."

"Like when I was sent to Earth."

"Yes, precisely."

"Why was he picked for the job?"

"I don't know." Lon shook his head. "One day a creature called Ter N'Avea arrived and appointed Chasym. Since then Ter has visited Paradise frequently."

"He even taught Yenen Clan how to speak English," I said.

"You *are* well informed."

"*Finally*. So, this creature—a woodelf, right? Did he teach Kirid Clan too?"

"He did. Ter never picked sides while visiting. He only did what he 'came to do' and then vanished."

"Is that how you met Meyana?" I asked.

Lon arched an eyebrow. "What makes you ask that?"

"Well, in one memory you mentioned that she didn't belong in this world." A wild thought struck me. "Did she come from Earth?"

"No, not from Earth. Actually her original home is called Sirinhigha. It is also the home of Ter N'Avea."

"Yeah, I think Jenen mentioned something about it. Is that where she is now?"

"I believe so." He met my gaze. "She couldn't stand to watch you leave, but she understood the importance of it. Still, I was afraid to watch her suffer, and in case Paradise grew too dangerous...I didn't..." He closed his mouth to compose himself again. Then he stood. "You really should rest now. The final preparations for Sasha's funeral are nearly complete. This evening is the time of her farewell."

I nodded and watched him turn and head for the door. "Lo—Father?"

He halted. "You have a habit of last-minute questions."

"Yeah," I laughed, but then grew serious. "You loved her. Meyana. Didn't you?"

"I did," he whispered.

"Why don't you bring her home?"

"After fourteen years I think she will have probably moved on with her life. I don't want to uproot her again."

"I think you're wrong about that. But," I shifted again, "don't worry. I'll find her and bring her back."

He turned his head to look at me. "She's not on this world, Key."

"I know. So, after Sasha's farewell... I'll look for her."

"How do you plan to go about that?"

I grinned. "Well, considering what I've heard of this Ter fellow, he seems pretty interested in affairs pertaining to our family. So..." I shrugged.

"You may do as you please," he said after a moment. "After all, you are finally a man." He opened the door. "Tonight, after we say farewell, we will also release the souls of those still bound to Paradise."

I blinked. "They weren't released before?"

"You cannot expect everything to conclude in one moment. There are always ends yet to be tied."

"Ain't that the true," I mumbled as he closed the door. I listened to his footsteps fall away down the stone corridor as I watched the scenery outside. "Meyana of Sirinhigha," I whispered.

I'd given up my home on Earth forever, and I'd lost a close friend as well. The idea that somewhere out there was a woman who also felt this pain, who almost certainly missed her own family, and that there was a chance I could bring her here—it made the hole in my heart a little smaller. For her, for Lon, and for myself, I would bring her home.

After I said goodbye to another.

43
A Last Departure?

Whether I liked the idea or not it seemed I was doomed to wear a peacock's attire.

It was a little less ornate than Lon's—for which I was certainly grateful—but it still felt far too extravagant for any man to wear. *Walking* was a chore. I wore three layers; a black under-robe wrapped tightly around my torso, then a midnight blue robe opening up to reveal the black beneath it and which trailed across the ground behind me, and lastly, a shimmering silver cape attached to each shoulder. The material of the cape was light and airy, easily caught in the tiniest breeze. It was probably made that way for dramatic effect. My feet were wrapped in black cloth strips, while my white hair was brushed, but kept down, and a winged headdress was set on my head.

I wanted to run away and hide. How could these people give me a hard time about a hospital robe when they wore only more flamboyant versions? But no matter how much I protested, I was eventually forced to resign myself. It was only for the funeral, so I used that reason to console me.

Since my legs were still disinclined to move on their own, Menen helped me from my room, through the massive castle, and eventually down a flight of stairs on the west side of the mountain. The stairs led down into a garden where flowers of every color bloomed and where ancient trees stood high above like sentinels. In the center of the garden rested a coffin. By each corner of the coffin stood a lighted torch, and surrounding the coffin were all of my companions. I spotted Jenen after a moment and indicated to Menen that I wanted to speak with him, so the tall man headed in that direction. As we neared the quiet twin I saw that he was speaking with Menen's wife.

"Thanks for all your care," I told her as we approached. Menen allowed me to stand on my own, after making certain I was balanced.

Nithae looked at me and smiled warmly. "It was my honor."

I recalled something I'd meant to take care of earlier. "Uh, Nithae?" I spotted Kirid sitting beneath a tree, watching the setting sun. "Kirid. He's...he's your little brother."

Nithae blinked as a frown creased her brow. "What?"

"It's true. Your brother was supposed to be Vendaeva, but Haeon captured him when he was a baby. So, um, basically...he never died."

"This is certain?" she asked.

"Yes," I answered promptly.

She stared at Kirid for a moment, then her lip curved upward. "Well then, if you shall excuse me, I will be speaking with my little brother." Inclining her head, she took Menen's hand and headed for the tree, leaving Jenen and me alone.

We both watched her sit beside Kirid on the grass and strike up a conversation. He looked uncomfortable, but smiled shyly.

"You look better," Jenen said after a moment.

"You didn't visit," I pointed out.

Jenen shrugged—a strange sight without his shawl. "I was guarding Haeon. While he is mostly harmless, I...wanted to be certain."

I raised an eyebrow. "And?"

"And what?" he asked.

"And why else were you guarding him?"

He hesitated. "I wanted to know his motive. While I do not like the man, I know most people start to do things out of necessity."

"What did you find out?"

Jenen sighed. "That some men simply do things because they can, and because they feel justified. His grievances were great, but not more so than any other Verenveyan. More than anything his vengeance was toward Chasym, for abandoning his people. That is how it started."

"Funny how as soon as he got power he became a hypocrite," I murmured.

"Most are overcome by the power they believe they possess. In reality it is controlling them and they are only slaves." Jenen rested his eyes on me. "But then, some prove that power is also tamable. Key, thank you. For saving my brother. For saving us all."

"You're welcome," I answered. I turned to face the coffin. "I just wish I really saved everyone."

Jenen placed a consoling hand on my shoulder. "You did. Even if not her life, you still saved her from dying alone." The meaning in his words was evident. I smiled appreciatively. Then we stood in silence as the ceremony began.

It was a simple service, but fitting. No one spoke elaborately of her accomplishments. We merely bade her farewell, most of us in silence. Sasha lay peacefully inside the casket, her dark brown hair spread softly around her fair face. Her eyes were closed as though she only slept. She wore a white dress, elegant in its simplicity. Her dying smile still touched her lips.

I thought of her life; of the story she'd shared with me about the loss of her family. Seeing her smile now, remembering her words about one day smiling forever, I felt strangely happy for her, even as a tear escaped my eye.

After a while Crenen stepped forward and closed the lid. He rested his hand on top of the casket, stroking the wood. "Goodbye," he whispered.

Lon stepped up from behind me and nodded toward the setting sun, a somber smile lighting his face. "No matter how many times it sets, the sun is always sure to rise again. Isn't it amazing?"

I was surprised but touched by his words. I felt hope kindle that one day, if not soon, I would see Sasha again. In the meantime I would keep her memory close. I turned my eyes to look up at my father, smiling. "It is."

After the funeral Lon helped me walk to the edge of the garden, where a clear pool of water sparkled up at us, glistening in the twilight.

"That would've been helpful a few days back," I murmured.

"It wasn't here a few days back," Lon replied.

I stepped closer and gazed down at my reflection. It was a startling sight. White locks of hair trailed down past my shoulders and striking silver eyes watched me calmly, despite my inner surprise. With the Paradisian apparel and headdress, the only trait still remaining of my former life was my unchanged five-foot-six height (with shoes), yet I still felt somehow taller. Perhaps it was because my shoulders were erect and I held my head high. I was no longer Jason Sterling the liar.

"Look," Lon said.

The pool began to glow with golden light and a figure emerged from the circling water as I stepped back to give him room. He was short—shorter than me. But it only made sense as he looked about ten years old. This child wasn't the core, however, but someone else entirely. He had short blond hair and the biggest, brightest blue eyes I'd ever seen. His attire was a simple gray tunic and white britches beneath, with brown leather boots reaching up to his knees. His ears were long, pointed, and seemed to twitch as he watched me with open curiosity.

"Key," he said cheerily. "It has been far too long, you've finally outgrown me. If only a little."

"You're Ter," I deduced.

"I am. I hear you've been busy." His left ear twitched.

"Just a little."

He chuckled. "I told the former Vendaeva that you'd been underestimated. I'll bet he finally believes me. But now isn't the time for sport." His tone didn't quite agree with his statement. "Now, in fact, is the time for you to finish your task."

I nodded. "By releasing the souls?"

"Indeed," he nodded back.

"Then what?" I asked, voicing the biggest question weighing on my mind.

He'd been studying the pool as if it held the secrets of the universe, but at my words he looked up and met my eyes, his own brimming with understanding. "Whatever you like, methinks. This world is a big place, and the universe is bigger still! With such a space opened up to you, what will you do?"

"Well." I hesitated. "I want to see Meyana."

Ter's blue eyes slid from me to rest on Lon. "Ah. Yes. It has been quite some time since last she had Paradisian contact. Perhaps she is long overdue for a visit. What, then, will you do about seeing her, Key?"

"I was wondering if you could take me?"

"Not I," Ter said, laughing. "You would need better companionship. But I will certainly help you." He bent down and twirled his finger around in the water. "Be patient, Key, and I will send you aid. In fact—I know just the lad!" He chuckled. "But for now," the water started to glow again, "let us journey to the Realm of Yenen."

The journey through the water was uneventful. By now I was finally able to keep my feet for the entire experience, and it wasn't long before we arrived at the pool in the clan's forest home. The trees were still charred and fallen, the ground was black and muddy, and Crenen's Holy Bridge Thing had been completely broken, laying in pieces across the murky earth. The only thing unchanged was the grandfather tree towering high above us, the Hierlek watchtower still eyeing the sea of trees around the Realm.

"They say this was the first tree planted in Paradise," Ter said conversationally, his own eyes on the ancient tree before us.

"Is that true?" I asked.

"Yes indeed. The core's realm once dwelt inside it, but with the presence of man, Vendaeva detached his home from the trunk and now it rests between dimensions."

I felt the threat of a headache coming on. It seemed I was never going to run out of mysteries to solve and histories to discover.

"That is called life," Lon murmured.

"Hm?" Ter glanced back at us.

"Nothing," Lon said.

We walked up the battered steps and into the hollowed-out tree.

"Key, if you would?" Ter said.

I raised my palm and summoned Liitae. Continuing on, we eventually descended the steps and came to the double doors. I breathed in, smiling with anticipation, and pushed one heavy door open. Countless orbs still hovered inside, but this time they were perfectly still, as if waiting. Which, of course, they were.

"Hi," I said. My voice rang through the chamber. "Ready to go?" They bobbed in reply. "Then," I grinned, "go!" As if my words unlocked invisible chains, the orbs burst toward the doors. Ter, Lon and I dodged aside as the massive swarm rushed by. I watched them leave with mixed emotions. I almost wished I could have brought them back to life, but I was happy to see them free at last.

Again it was goodbye. I felt like the entire world was flying by, leaving me behind.

Liitae was very excited by the commotion. Several times the orb almost followed the line of departing souls, but as it finally lurched forward Lon reached out and snatched it. "No, Liitae. Key has already parted with too much of his soul."

I laughed. "Yeah, it's definitely feeling a little emptier in here." I tapped my heart, wondering if multiple Liitaes really had anything to do with it.

The last of the orbs finally darted by, and the heavy doors closed with a boom.

"Goodbye," I whispered for what seemed the hundredth time.

"Until again we meet," Ter added. I glanced at him and he beamed back. "It is but a second in time in which we mourn. Soon all shall be reunited."

"But what if you're immortal?" I asked.

The woodelf's smile deepened. "Did Lon never explain?"

"I did not," the Seer said. He turned to me. "Each immortal can, at any point, choose to die. They must truly desire it, but they are allowed to forsake their mortal eternity."

"Mortal eternity?" I asked

"As I said once, we are half-immortal. If we are killed or choose to die, then after our death is when we truly live forever, in the realm beyond this life."

"In that sense, this life is but a single step on a very high ladder." Ter's ear twitched. "Isn't it a beautiful thing?"

I stayed silent for a while as we headed back to the lake. Finally, as we approached the water, I caught sight of Lon's arm and remembered something else I hadn't found the answer to yet. "Hey, uh, Father?"

Lon glanced down at me. "Yes, Key?"

"What's up with your tattoos? Chasym used them to control you before."

He rested a hand over his forearm. "Yes. They were a brand of sorts. They were a magical sign to show that the Renocahn owned us. When we disobeyed, the tattoos were used to punish us and force us to adhere."

We reached the water and Ter began opening the portal to the west, humming as he swirled a stick through the moonlit water.

"And it wasn't supposed to work anymore, but Chasym somehow forced it anyway?"

"Yes. Since Chasym's trick I've pondered this and concluded that when They went mad they couldn't control their own minds, let alone that of another. Because Chasym still had his senses—mostly—about him, he could at any point use the marks to bend our wills. The fact that he has never done so before is one reason I haven't killed him."

"He feels really bad about everything," I said.

Lon sighed. "I know. And, because he is both a friend and even possibly soon to be my brother-in-law, and because you chose to save him despite his betrayal, I will let him live. For now."

I smirked. "You've always struck me as the reserved but prideful type."

"You're a decent judge of character."

His words sank in then. "Wait. Wouldn't that make Chasym my uncle?"

Lon smiled. "I'm afraid so."

I moaned softly, thinking of all the ways Chasym could abuse that authority. "Let's never say anything and hope he doesn't notice."

Lon only chuckled.

"Ready," Ter said, who had been ready for a while now but seemed perfectly content to stand there and watch the night's insects flying around aimlessly.

The three of us stepped into the water and soon arrived at Kirid's castle.

"Probably the best way to travel," I stated as we waded out of the water, "except for being wet."

"Easily remedied," Lon said with a casual flick of his hand. Instantly his clothes were dry.

I glanced down at my own. "Dry," I mumbled, satisfied when my command was obeyed.

"Well then, I shall be on my way," Ter said, stopping to gaze up at the starry sky. "There is so much to be done."

"Like what?" I asked.

He looked up at me. "Anything to help. Including locating your guide to finding Meyana. But, Key, please rest while you wait for your companion. I believe you will start this new adventure of yours very soon; in the meantime be patient. If you become bored, Paradise could always use a strong hand in rebuilding itself." He nodded his head. "Key, Lon, until again we meet." Then, without the use of water or any Tunnels of Light, he vanished.

"There goes one of the most powerful forces alive," Lon said as we watched the empty space where the peculiar woodelf had disappeared.

"Until again we meet, huh?" I whispered. "Am I doomed to associate with weirdos all the rest of my life?"

"If you're not used to it by now, perhaps Crenen should remind you."

I laughed. "Maybe tomorrow."

Tomorrow came quickly, and while I tried my best to sleep through it, Crenen had other plans. This time he did manage to dump icy water on my face and, while I coughed and sputtered, he bounced on the edge of the mattress.

"Up, Strange Reckless Dolt! Sun has been risen in sky for nearly hours!"

I moaned and attempted to turn over, then decided against it. My pillow was sopping wet. "Crenen, I'm exhausted."

"More sleep now won't make less tired more," he said. "Only make grouchy." He tugged at my blankets. "Up, up!"

"Come on, people, don't any of you ever sleep? You seriously *are* felines."

Crenen bounded off the bed and I heard him pad across the floor. Seconds later he returned and sat on my bed. "Bring you breakfast," he said. "Been long time since Strange Reckless Dolt eat gerani yesterday, and we though—"

I sat up and pushed my white hair aside. "Where is it?"

Crenen held up the tray and I eagerly snatched it, then paused as my eyes rested on the contents. "Gerani?" I asked as I studied the plump, green spheres on the platter.

"Green gerani, yeah?" Crenen said, showing his pointy teeth.

"*Whoa.*" I was in awe. It only made sense there might be green ones, of course, but I'd never considered it before. "Are they as good as the other kind?"

"Some like this kind more better."

I eagerly selected a green gerani from among the bunch and popped it in my mouth. As I bit down, flavor exploded on my taste buds and I gasped, chewing faster as tears welled up in my eyes. Swallowing, I made a gagging sound. "It's sour." It was unquestionably the most sour food I'd ever tasted.

Crenen cackled. "Keep Strange Reckless Dolt awake for long hours now!" He stood. "Shifty Cocky Man enjoy green gerani, but he always sour like that anyway." He winked his silver eye and headed for the door. "Now we go for important gathering."

"Important gathering?"

He nodded and flung the door open. In came Menen, holding a familiar set of clothes in his arms.

"No." I shook my head. "I just wore those. Never again."

"Would Strange Reckless Dolt prefer different Obnoxious Shiny Drapings?"

I grimaced. "No, I think...these will work."

While Menen helped me dress (both because the clothes were difficult to get on and because I refused to be a part of it), I stared out the window. At some point Crenen deserted me, cackling as he left the room. After a while Menen finishing securing the headdress and stepped back to examine me.

"It will do," he said.

"Great. Let's get this important gathering over with, so I can stop wearing dresses." I gathered the bulk of my ropes and trudged toward the door.

Menen caught up with me in a few steps and slowed to my pace. "I have news," he said.

I looked up at him. "Yeah?"

A full fledged smile spread across his face—possibly the first I'd seen. "Nithae is with child."

I blinked, then laughed. "That's great, Menen! Congratulations."

"Thank you." He looked very proud.

We didn't speak again as we headed for the main doors of the castle, but we didn't need to. The excitement and happiness we felt was greater than words, and somehow the emptiness I felt at Sasha's death, while still present, had ebbed a little. It was true; the sun would always rise again, no matter how many times it set.

While I reflected on this news, Menen pushed open the doors and sunlight flooded the entryway. I blinked until my eyes adjusted to the morning light. As my gaze focused I saw hundreds of Paradisians, of Yenen and Kirid clans both, gathered on the steps leading up toward me, watching me with unreadable expressions.

Veija swept into view, gowned in gold. "Here is the man who saved us!" she cried. "All hail Vendaeva!"

The crowd broke out into shouts and applause, as if the curtain had been raised to reveal some wonderful surprise. How long the joyful noise lasted I couldn't say, but I stood there for a long time, staring in awe at the multitude before me.

"You be hero from now and onward," Crenen said in my ear, and I jumped at his voice. "They revere you like Great Noble Hero." He grinned, metallic eyes twinkling.

"But...why? I didn't do any more than anyone else."

"You saved Paradise, rescued all Paradisaical leaders, and defeated Delusional Broken Man. What not to worship?"

"W-worship?" I was having trouble wrapping my head around the fact that, while once I'd been a nobody, now I had legions of followers. "I'm...only a man."

"At last, yeah?" Crenen said wickedly.

I laughed. "Yeah, well, it takes longer for some to grow."

"And with such mental growth, the physical matters little," Jenen's voice came from behind me.

I turned and saw the second twin, and beside him stood Lon, Chasym, Menen and Nithae. With Veija to my left and Crenen to my right, our party was nearly complete. Liitae and the the white orb circled contentedly several inches above my head. I spotted Kirid standing near the top of the steps, holding my two little furapintairow. I smiled at him. He returned my smile brightly.

Between the unwavering support of my friends and the crowd so happy below me, I felt a little overwhelmed. "What the heck?" I muttered, shaking my head to try and quell my emotions.

"Not in Land of Heck anymore, yeah?" Crenen said.

It was true. After fourteen years of walking among strangers, I'd finally returned to Paradise.

I was home.

Epilogue
An Adventure Called Life?

You've probably been expecting with some apprehension for me to halt my narrative and admit this was all a lie. That my adventure was just a story imagined by a bored college student who had little else to do with his spare time. From the beginning I made it a point to remind you I'm a liar—or at least, that I was.

I won't deny that I still tell the occasional lie. Old habits die hard, as they say. But I'm not the same boy who first landed in a puddle and got swept away on some bizarre adventure. I'm not the same boy who ran back home when he couldn't handle the truth. Now I'm a man, and while I will continue to grow (hopefully physically, too), I can at last stand before the truth as a friend, unafraid to see it.

Is this story a lie?

No.

That said, I'll move on.

The funny thing about life is that when one adventure ends, it doesn't mean everything is over. Unlike the fantastical stories written in books, real life keeps on going. So, all the things that would usually be answered, aren't. Life is the great mystery; our curiosity won't be sated with the turn of a page. Some things are better never answered. At the same time, there are certain things I will not let alone.

I plan to meet my real mother, Meyana, and with time I will. But as Ter suggested, I'll wait with patience. Crenen is slowly recovering from death and continues to lead Yenen Clan (though he refuses to be called Yenen), and Kirid leads his clan while also bonding with his sister. Jenen has been appointed as a diplomat between the two clans and, given time, we hope to unite the factions.

Lon recently left with the promise to return. He volunteered to travel all across the island and gather every Seer who may still live. Chasym travels with him in search of any remnant of They to make his peace. And Aunt Veija, who refused to part with him, has gone as well. The three are finally together.

Menen and Nithae are well. She is several months along and the signs are beginning to show. If the child is a girl, they'll call her Sasha. If the child is a boy, they'll call him Yenen. Kirid hasn't quite grasped that he'll be the infant's uncle.

As for me? I've kept busy. Now that I've finished writing my story I feel certain Ter will soon make good on his word. In the meantime I'll just kick back and share my purple gerani with Grump while Liitae teases my venomless furapintairow dubbed Fuzz.

I've heard rumors of another race of people in Paradise. They live in the desert and, because of that, are called deserters. According to Kirid they're actually the Valaj. They've kept to themselves, miraculously avoiding conflict. It makes me wonder whether they were also affected by the disease, or if it somehow passed them by. I want to find them, meet them, befriend them and learn about their part to play in this insane world. Aside from curiosity about their history, something else motivates me to visit them. Haeon has disappeared. His last sighting was near the desert border. Somehow I doubt he's up to any good.

Rather than relax, maybe I'll find Crenen. He's probably ready for another adventure too.

The End?

The Paradex

A few notes on the language of Paradise—

As there are many rules in the Paradisian language, it would be impossible to give a definitive guide on the exact science behind it; however, there are basic rules which make it easier in the attempt to sound fluent (or at least proficient).

First, a little tip: remember that hard sounds aren't as hard as English words. Emphasize the soft; soften the hard. Like Veija—you emphasis the 'V', and you soften the 'J' (although there *are* exceptions to this). It should be noted that the 'J' is always soft except at the beginning of a word or name. Thus, Veija versus Jenen. The first is a soft "J', while the latter is hard.

Bear in mind that Crenen is *not* a good guide to the language. His broken sentences are not in keeping with the phraseology of the native tongue. He intentionally sounds unique. A more accurate demonstration of literal translations comes from observing Jenen, who speaks both excellent Paradisian *and* English. Sentences are generally structured the same in both tongues.

The Paradisian language is the sole surviving language in Paradise. There have been, through time and wars, variations on words and phrases, but generally the language has remained true. Its roots come from the Renocahn and were eventually adopted by all other cultures. Over time every language save this were forgotten, with the exception of Seeric runes, whose magical properties spared them the dissolution of other alphabets.

Knowing this, and paying close attention to the following pronunciation guide, should help the reader to familiarize oneself with the basics of how words sound in Paradisian. The Paradisian tongue has fairly precise rules to its vowels and consonants (mostly the latter), but like in English, they do vary from time to time.

1. 'A' is usually either "uh" and "aw" sounds, which makes the name **Jason** seem to Paradisians very peculiar in its spelling. A good example of both common sounds is the name Sasha [saw-shuh].
2. 'E' often makes an "eh" sound, though occasionally it can be an "ee" (as in "need"). The former is the case in the name Crenen [kren-en].
3. 'I' can also be used for the sound "ee", but usually sounds like in the word "in", such as the name Kirid [k-eer-**id**].
4. 'O' can be either "oh" or "aw." The first is rare, while the latter is so in names like Haeon [hay-on] and Lon [lawn].
5. 'U' is almost always "uh", but can be "oo". The latter is the case in serecu [sare-eh-koo].
6. And lastly, "Y" sounds like the word "eye.". This occurs in the word Hykyae [high-KAI-ay].

The real difference lies more in the consonants. The most prominent example rests with the word gerani, which is often mistakenly read as jer-on-ee; it should instead be gur-ON-ee. (*Gur* as in "grrr" like the growling sound a furapintairow makes.)

Paradisian is not an easy language to master, unless one is raised with it. In this regard it is very much like English. The occasional exceptions to rules is one cause of this. However, once the basics are mastered it is only a matter of vocabulary, as the sentence structures are the same as in English.

People & Pets?

BEASTIE **[bee-stee]** – Key's pet dog, an American Eskimo.

CHAS **[chaz]** – An arrogant jock in Key's high school. *(Also see Chasym)*

CHASYM **[chaz-im]** – “Shifty Cocky Man” – A shapeshifter who masquerades as Key's classmate for a while. *(Also see Chas)*

CRENEN **[KREN-en]** – Leader of Yenen Clan.

FENIK **[Fenn-ik]** – “Gross Smelly Man” – A warrior of Yenen Clan.

FREKET, FYAR **[frek-eht, fai-air]** – Fire-breathing frogs that occupy the swamps.

FREKET, WAYA **[frek-eht, wai-uh]** – Acid-spitting frogs that live near the ocean.

FURA **[furr-uh]** - Nickname for the furapintairow. *(Also see Furapintairow)*

FURAPINTAIROW **[fur-ah-pin-TAI-row]** – Venomous animals considered sacred to Paradisians.

FUZZ – A venomless furapintairow.

GRUMP – One of many furapintairow leaders.

HAEON **[hay-on]** – “Delusional Broken Man” – A male Verenveyen Seer.

HISKII **[hiss-kee]** – "Quiet Sneaky Thing" – A warrior of Yenen Clan.

JACOB STERLING – Key's youngest brother.

JANA STERLING – Key's older sister.

JASON "KEY" STERLING – *(See Key)*

JEKIS **[JEK-iss]** – Menen's deceased father.

JENEN **[JEN-en]** – The first Paradisian to encounter Key, expect for two furapintairow.

JEREMY STERLING – Key's younger brother.

KEY – "Strange Coward Boy" – The main protagonist.

KIRID, elder **[k-eer-id]** – Leader of Kirid Clan.

KIRID, younger **[k-eer-id]** – The only son of Kirid (*see Kirid, elder*).

LYDIA STERLING – Key's mother.

LIITAE **[LEE-tay]** – Key's Essence—or soul—personified (sort of).

LON **[lawn]** – Seer Veija's protector and elder brother.

MENEN **[MEN-en]** – Personal servant of Crenen.

MEYANA **[mee-yan-a]** – A mysterious woman.

NITHAE **[nee-thay]** – A woman of Yenen Clan.

SASHA **[saw-shuh]** – Female doctor of Yenen Clan.

SERECU **[sare-eh-koo]** – Venomous snakes.

SIKEL **[sick-ELL]** – A member of They Clan.

TER N'AVEA **[tare n-AH-vay] –** The ever-present.

THESHER **[thesh-er]** – Carnivorous equine beasts.

VEIJA **[vay-zhu]** (Hint: rhymes with *Asia*) – A female Verenveyen Seer.

YENEN, elder **[YEN-en]** – Deceased leader of Yenen Clan.

YENEN, younger **[YEN-en]** – The eldest son of Yenen (see Yenen, elder).

Places, Powers & Palatables?

APINAIKEAL **[ah-pin-AI-kee-all]** – A very sweet apple-like fruit.

CORE, The – The core of Paradise, location unknown.

DESERT – The desert which occupies the middlemost area of Paradise, to the east of the swamps (*see Swamps*), to the west of the Hykyae Ridges *(see Hykyae Ridges)*.

GERANI **[gur-on-ee]** – An intoxicating, vision-inducing, tree-clinging grape.

HIERLEK **[high-er-lek]** – A watchtower over the Realm of Yenen, which can view miles around.

HYKYAE RIDGES **[high-KAI-ay]** – A massive mountain range separating Kirid lands from the desert, swamps and Yenen lands.

KIRID CLAN **[k-eer-id]** – A division of Paradisian people who dwell in the east.

KIRID, Realm of – The capitol city of Kirid Clan.

PARADISE – The world on which Key appears through the puddle.

PARADISIAN **[pare-uh-dis-ee-an]** – Term used in reference to the people of Paradise, as well as its language.

PARADISIACAL DISEASE **[pare-uh-dis-AI-uh-kal dis-ease]** – The life-threatening epidemic sweeping across Paradise.

PHUDEL **[fuu-del]** – Paradisian word for "Puddle." *(Also see Puddle, The)*

PUDDLE, The – A portal which carries Key from Earth to Paradise.

RENOCAHN **[renn-oh-kahn]** – An ancient shapeshifting people which once ruled Paradise; now only a remnant remains. *(Also see They Clan)*

RESEJ **[ress-ej]** – A meadow in the west of Paradise, where medicinal herbs grow, including the cure for a furapintairow's bite.

RYDI **[ree-dai]** – A village one day's travel from the Realm of Yenen (*see Yenen, Realm of*).

SWAMPS – The marshy lands between the Realm of Yenen (*see Yenen, Realm of*) and the Desert (*see Desert*). *(Also see Uzadob Swamp)*

SWENSIE **[swen-see]** - Sugar

THEY CLAN – A once-elite organization within Renocahn; now a maddened, violent people.

UZADOB SWAMP **[ooz-uh-dob]** – A particular swamp where "Walking Dead Things" are said to dwell.

VALAJ **[va-laj]** – A desert tribe of people, of which little is known.

VENDAEVA **[venn-day-vuh]** – The prophesied hero meant to save Paradise from the terrible Paradisaical disease.

VERENVEY **[vare-en-vay]** – The Seeric people of Paradise.

YENEN CLAN **[YEN-en]** – A division of Paradisian people who dwell in the west.

YENEN, Realm of – The capitol city of Yenen Clan.

Paradisian Phrases?

"Vais! Sa Vais!" – "Prince! My Prince!"

"Eyia sovei cir hej slovej. Veys irefen ii cran yas." – "The men have been worried. We're relieved that you're alive."

"Sa Vais, eyias deshe ii cran yas." – "My Prince, I'm glad that you're alive."

"Cra yas en veikes. Teishne." – "You live as well. Excellent."

"Keis lavun taka lem." – "It would take more [than that]."

"Cra vener eyia baskyne, Lon!" – "You left the barrier, Lon!"

"Vener miek diay kryn." – "You never came back."

"Daja vener soraj ihi kryn keis levieshna jaer lanya deirsh eyia baskyne liish cra liiv, Domi Libin Kag? Se braryr hem." – "Do you know how hard it was to get through the barrier without you there, Stupid Thoughtless Fool? Thanks for nothing."

"Sa Vais, eyia Rydi veren—" – "My Prince, the Rydi village —"

"Vonenae havun." – "One of a kind." – A unique Paradisian saying that has no literal translation; "one of a kind" is the closest equivalent.

BONUS STORIES

Afterward

The history of *Liars Go To Paradise?* is a long one, at least when measured in the life of its writer. The story was conceived during a creative writing class exercise when I was sixteen years old (that's where the prologue comes from). After a year collecting dust in a boxed-up notebook, the story was uncovered and out of sheer boredom, I sat down to continue the silly bit of prose.

I'd just signed up for a DeviantART account and, aside from a few pathetic attempts at visual art, I had nothing to share—except said silly bit of prose. So I posted it and waited. There was a response. Oh, nothing amazing. My writings skills were sadly lacking, but the few who chose to ignore my shoddy work and read on were amused, at least.

It was enough for me. I kept writing. And writing. And writing. I finished what I lovingly dubbed my "novelette" and what was ultimately the skeletal structure for part one of the book you're now holding. By then I'd garnered a small circle of readers who wanted more.

So did I. And so I kept on writing. Part two was easier to write than the first, and by part three I was in love. I took chances, pushed the boundaries of my mind, and weaved a world I'd never dreamt I could—until I already had.

After over a year and a half of diligent updates to my deviantART account and a readership larger than I ever hoped (comprising over twenty people by the end), I sat back with over 180,000 words of a zany, magical, fulfilling story. What had I done?

I'd proved to myself I could write. Reading back through the entire story, I saw vast improvement from when I'd begun.

Determined to set things to rights, I rewrote the entirety of part one, asking for feedback and receiving oodles of help from the readers.

Then I attempted to publish, confident I'd done enough to earn the right. After several form rejections, I grew discouraged and moved on to other projects. But this story lived on in my heart and I tried several times to rewrite it from scratch, hoping to turn its potential into something greater.

Alas, each time I tried to improve upon the prose, I lost some of its essence, its life, and at last I threw my hands up. I knew this story would never see the light of day again. It was, simply put, *badly written*.

Several years later, feeling nostalgic, I thought to turn *Liars Go To Paradise?* into a webcomic. My sister (a.k.a. illustrator) agreed to give it a go, and we started the process of converting everything from prose into visual art. To recapture the heart of the story, I returned to the manuscript and began to read it.

And I fell in love again.

I know I have a natural bias towards my little monster. I know its writing *does* leave something to be desired. But as I read, I began to smooth the prose, cut out excess words and bad descriptors, and eventually brought the 180,000-word novel down to 169,000.

I'm not saying it's perfect. Far from. I continue to improve my craft and I'm happy to say I've come a long way from the place where this story resides, but I did pore my heart into every character, every plot twist, every inch of the world called Paradise. As a growing writer, this story carried *me* to where I am and where I will someday be.

Knowing that, in gratitude I can't simply bury the prose and forget. The story should be accessible to those who read it that first time; those beautiful people who stayed on-board and encouraged me to press on and finish what I started.

This novel is dedicated to them, and to Key, who taught me how to refine a novel's voice by letting me borrow his.

Thank you.

– M. H. W.

The following was written years ago, purely in answer to the question, 'How did Key get his name?'

Naming Key

When Chasym entered the Seer's home he spotted the child's crib. It rested near a window filtering the light from the setting sun. Lon stood over the crib, watching his infant child with the tender smile of a father. He stood with a quiet pride, shoulders erected. Chasym approached silently, rousing dust motes visible in the orange light of evening. It wasn't until he reached the crib that Lon stirred, long golden tresses twisting as he moved.

"Chasym," he said. "I have a son."

Chasym looked down, merely to glance, but something stopped him dead. His yellow eyes locked with those of the infant boy; the baby stared back earnestly. Chasym couldn't break away. "Lon," he said with disbelief. "He's..."

"Beautiful," Lon said. "It's the only word for him."

Chasym's mouth quirked. "I wonder if he would appreciate such a reference."

Lon only laughed quietly.

"What is his name?" Chasym asked.

Lon hesitated. "I'm not sure. Meyana has made several suggestions, but she asked me to name him." He shook his head. "I don't dare name a pet, let alone a child."

"When was he born?" Chasym asked, watching the gurgling child wave a chubby hand in the air, a bubble forming at his mouth.

"Three days ago," Lon answered. He leaned over the crib and wiped the boy's mouth. "He seems to like you."

"Mustn't be a good judge of character, then," Chasym murmured, smiling wryly.

"Or perhaps he is a better one than the both of us. Do you want to hold him?"

Chasym stiffened, taking an unconscious step back. "Absolutely not."

Lon ignored him, reaching in and pulling the infant into his arms. The child was tiny; just a little bundle of arms and legs. "Here." He held him out.

Chasym backed up again, shaking his head. "No, Lon. I don't know how..."

"Neither did I," Lon said. "He doesn't weigh more than a bunch of gerani. He'll—"

"Break," Chasym finished firmly.

Lon scowled, his gold eyes chastising. "If you do not take him, I will drop him, and you'll be to blame."

Chasym took a third step back. "You're lying."

"Try me," Lon said, offering the baby again. "I'm counting to three, then he falls. One...two...three." He released the child as Chasym reached forward frantically, blond hair flying, and grabbed him. The tiny boy seemed unfazed by the wild exchange, only blowing more bubbles and beaming up at his new retainer.

"He's so small," Chasym whispered, awed by the child's fragile strength. "How is he alive?"

"Despite your misconceptions, you came into this world around the same size," Lon said flatly. "Although he is small for an infant. He wasn't expected for another month."

Chasym gently bounced the baby up and down, listening to his cooing and gurgling sounds. Finally he looked up. "Is Meyana all right?"

"She's fine," Lon said. "She will rest for a few days and then be on her feet again."

"I'm relieved to hear it." Chasym glanced back down at the child laying contentedly in his arms. "He's certainly a happy tike."

"Right now," Lon said dryly. "You should hear his vocal range sometime. He's very adept at screaming."

Chasym chuckled. After a moment he remembered the second reason for his visit and carefully balanced the child in one arm as he retrieved a key from his shoulder pouch. "This unlocks the doors in the *Rekani* tree." Lon looked impressed as he reached for the key. Another tiny hand grasped it first. Both men looked down with surprise as the tiny child pulled the key toward himself. "Should he have the strength to hold that?" Chasym asked.

"I...don't think so," Lon replied, utterly bewildered.

The child clasped the key to his chest and hugged it tightly.

"Strange," Lon said. "I'm certain newborn babies do not notice objects like this. I tried to gain his attention earlier with Meyana's necklace, but he was indifferent."

"Maybe he just really likes keys," Chasym suggested mildly.

"Do you?" Lon asked the child, laughing softly as he ran a finger along the boy's slobbery cheek.

The child gurgled back. He dragged the key to his mouth and began to suck on it.

"That can't be sanitary," Chasym pointed out.

Lon reached forward and tried to pry the key from his son's mouth. When he finally succeeded the infant decided to demonstrate just how loud his voice could be. Very.

"Hush him," Chasym said as he tried swinging the baby back and forth in his arms. He only continued to cry. Finally Lon returned the key and the boy immediately quieted down.

"I guess he can keep it for now," Lon said. He seemed ready to say more, but hesitated.

"What is it?"

"Chasym, would you mind...?" He stopped again.

"I will mind if you don't finish the question," Chasym said flatly.

He smiled. "Would you like to be his godfather?"

Chasym started, nearing dropping the child and his key. "*Me*? You've lost your mind, Seer. Don't you recall what I've done to you already? I would cause your son nothing but pain. I can't..."

"Consider this your chance to redeem yourself," Lon said. "Not in my eyes. You've already done that. This might be your one chance to forgive yourself, Chasym. Don't pass it up." Chasym bit the inside of his lip and glanced down at the child as he drifted off to sleep, one fist clutching the key tightly. "I..."

"A simple yes will suffice."

"...Fine. Yes," Chasym said, surprised by his words. "But never say I didn't warn you..."

"It is settled, then," Lon said. He watched his son for a moment. "And as such, you must help me name him."

Chasym laughed shortly. "Don't jest."

"I'm very serious," Lon said, his smile gone. "If we don't name him soon, he'll have an identity crisis."

"Fine." Chasym sighed. "How about Gerani?"

Lon couldn't suppress a chuckle.

"No?" Chasym thought for a moment. "How about Key? He seems to like it an awful lot, and if he ever wants to blame us for how stupid it is, we can just tell him he sucked on his first key when he was three days old and wouldn't let it go."

Lon laughed softly and leaned down to gently slip the key out of the boy's loosened grip. "Key, huh? It's somehow appropriate."

Chasym blinked, but when his eyes found the child he

smiled. "It really is."

"Very well. His name is Key," Lon said. After a moment he looked up. "Your second task as his godfather is to inform Meyana."

Chasym scowled. "Don't press your luck, Seer."

The following silliness was written for a deviantART event I hosted called Gerani Fest. It was posted in five parts over five weeks. It's not considered canon, per se.

Gerani Wars

Part 1

I awoke with a craving.

This was not unusual. I always awoke with a craving anymore. Not for chocolate, not for ice cream, not for anything typically addictive. I wanted gerani. (I know, you saw that coming. Obviously. The story's freaking called "Gerani Wars" for crying out loud. How could it be anything else?)

Sliding from under my coverlets, I stepped onto the plush carpet surrounding my bed, and eyed the cold flagstone floor beyond the edges of the soft carpet. The floor spread out before me like a harsh sea, separating me from my kitchenette where a bowl of gerani rested on the counter, beckoning.

I eyed the luscious spherical grape-like delights, salivating.

Be brave, I told myself. *A cold floor can't come between you and your gerani. Go get it, Key.* Gathering my nerve, I embarked, taking that first awful step from warm comfort to frozen shock. The floor was as cold as I'd feared, but the first step was over with. I could only go on from here, though each subsequent step would be agony. For my precious gerani, I would endure the harsh flagstones. It was worth any hardship.

I was halfway there, wincing at each, equally alarming touch to the icy floor, when the heavy wooden door to my chambers flew open. Freezing mid-step, I turned and beheld—!

To Be Continued?

Part 2

Freezing mid-step, I turned and beheld—!

—Crenen. (Let's pretend you didn't see that coming a mile away, for melodrama's sake.)

Before the door had finished banging against the inner wall Crenen was leaning lazily against the frame, mouth spread wide in his unique toothy grin, black ponytail lopsided as always, mismatched eyes gleaming with feral intensity. As our eyes met, silent communication passed between us. Had it been translated into words, the dialogue would have gone something like this:

Crenen: "We knowing what you up to, Strange Reckless Dolt, and we planning to stop you. But be guest and try to reach Paradisaical Purple Fruit before us, yeah?"

Key: "Crap."

Yeah. That about sums up our mum exchange. (I know. Pathetic, but hey! *you* try finding a better retort when faced with Crenen's megalomaniac deportment.)

Outwardly, nothing was said. But Crenen knew my mind and his grin widened unnaturally. You know the look.

All at once we moved, sprinting toward the kitchenette at full speed. Heck, Captain Picard would've been proud to use us for his warp drive.

The only aspect missing in that moment was the stars shooting by like tiny streaks of white light.

Except, those were coming, too, because suddenly—

To Be Continued?

Part 3

The only aspect missing in that moment was the stars shooting by like tiny streaks of white light.

Except, those were coming, too, because suddenly—

—The furapintairow called Grump leaped out from behind the big bowl of gerani, rows of razor teeth gleaming maniacally in like-manner to his humanoid brother Crenen. With a growl that sounded disturbingly like a cackle, the Small Red Fuzzy lunged at me, flying through the air like a streaking bullet covered in blood-colored fur. I tried to dodge, and only managed to slip on the flagstones (stupid gravity), arms flailing. I went down backward, slamming my head hard against the unyielding surface of the cold floor.

And yes, this is where the stars come in. They were there above me, twinkling like that bloody little star in the children's song. Accompanying the scene was a dull throb just behind my eyes as an egg formed on the back of my head.

Grump was sitting contentedly on my stomach; I could feel his weight and the dull thump of his slowly wagging tail. While my vision was still swimming in a sea of effervescent stars, I could easily imagination his triumphant grin. No doubt he and Crenen had been in cahoots all along. Rotten little traitor.

A dark blur appeared among the stars as I lay there seething, and—blinking rapidly a few times to clear my vision—the blur began to take proper form. Unsurprisingly, it was Crenen, holding the bowl of precious gerani, his own impossibly-wide grin plastered to his pale face.

"We win again, Tiny Loser Boy."

Scowling, I opened my mouth to retort, but—

To Be Continued?

Part 4

"We win again, Tiny Loser Boy."

Scowling, I opened my mouth to retort, but—

Someone at the doorway into my bedroom cleared their throat.

I turned my head at the same time Crenen straightened, and we both laid our eyes on the newcomer. Only that should be plural. There stood Jenen and Menen, twin scowls fixed to their angular faces. Their eyes were glued to the gerani in Crenen's hands.

"This is getting ridiculous," Jenen said, stepping fully into the room, Menen at his heels. "It's four o'clock in the morning and this is the third time this week you've raised a ruckus over those—*things*."

I opened my mouth to argue a case in favor of gerani and how they weren't "things" but Crenen beat me to the punch. Like always.

"Not 'things'," he said. "Best food in whole of Wide Strange World. We think you only jealous we not give you some." His grin stretched nearly to his ears (or so it seemed). "Want?"

"No," Jenen said flatly.

Menen didn't bother saying anything.

Crenen shrugged mildly. "Missing out, yeah?"

"Not likely." Jenen took another step. "I'm serious about this, Crenen. Your fetish with gerani is your own business, but using it to manipulate Key—as well as waking the entire castle—is mine." He raised a hand. "Now hand it over."

Crenen blinked slowly, unimpressed. "Give good reason."

"Because I *said* so."

Crenen hissed. Then he perked up. The grin dropped, then returned looking more wicked than I'd ever seen before. I shuddered from my spot on the floor. I was glad he wasn't fixing that devilish smile on me.

"All right," Crenen said, shrugging again. "We hand it over."

I gawked. What did he have up his figurative sleeve?

To Be Continued?

Part Finale

"All right," Crenen said, shrugging again. "We hand it over."

I gawked. What did he have up his figurative sleeve?

Jenen seemed suspicious as well. He stepped back once. "Don't you dare—"

"Tall Strong Jerk hold Sick Nasty Dog in place, yeah?" Crenen ordered of his cousin.

Menen didn't hesitate; he only laced his arms through Jenen's, and pinned the smaller man against himself as Crenen stepped lithely forth, brandishing his torture implement: Gerani.

"Are you serious?" I asked as I sat up, watching in fascinated horror.

Was this the fateful day when I would learn *why* Jenen despised gerani? I'd always wondered if it affected him especially ill, and thus he avoided it like the plague. In my mind's eye came the involuntary image of him giggling like a little girl and prancing around with rabbit ears. As we were connected, Jenen also saw the image, and he managed to break away from his dilemma long enough to shoot me a scathing glare. Then he was once more entranced by the Paradisaical Purple Fruit coming his way like a private apocalypse.

I was torn between cheering Crenen on and looking away in respect of Jenen's final moments. I found, however, that I couldn't look away no matter what. Pinned as he was, Jenen never stood a chance. It had been long coming; Crenen was, after all, the Gerani King. There was no disputing his position. He hailed supreme.

It was over in a few moments. Like it or not, Jenen ate the gerani; chewed and swallowed because it was the only way Crenen wouldn't stuff more down his gullet.

Did Jenen giggle like a little girl or hop around like a rabbit? Did he pass out? Did he break out into operatic soprano? Or stare into the distance seeing things that weren't there? Did he turn violent and start karate-chopping people?

On pain of death, I cannot say. The worlds may never know.

Fin

The following is a Halloween special and is the most recent prose addition to the world of Paradise. In the official timeline it takes place after the end of the novel, before the beginning of a never-completed sequel. The references to Beastie herein are semi-official. Key's dog does eventually join him in Paradise, drastically changed in appearance and large enough to ride.

The Horrors of Uzadob Swamp

Paradise is full of what one could describe as "unholy creatures." e.g. My first encounter with a furapintairow taught me that pink eyes do not a friendly creature make, nor does a round, furry body always promote warm fuzzies. In fact, fur is a really good way to conceal a deadly weapon, like sharp, pointy, venomous teeth. As for bendy tails with fluffy ends...I'm waiting for the fatality hidden there to reveal itself. In short, I've learned on a very personal level not to judge a book by its cover.

But nothing prepared me for the horrors of Uzadob swamp.

For those who don't know me very well, I'm Key, prophesied savior of a crazy world called Paradise. I didn't grow up here, but was pushed by a kindly classmate into a magical puddle and sent as a result to be drowned, maimed, humiliated, worshiped and even killed for the sake of a variety of sadistic jerks who treated me like a servant at best, and a pack animal at worst and most often. (Here's looking at you, Crenen.)

I'm not one to spoil a good story, though, so I won't go into the details here of my efforts to save everyone from a horrific fate. This narration is apart from that; a little experience I'm assured is worthy of holy writ (don't ask). I agree it's an interesting story, at least, and maybe even appropriate to the season (the leaves are peculiar shades of pink and lavender, the Paradisian equivalent of deciduous changes in the Autumn).

I looked up the definition of adventure once, and the word fits (something about hazardous undertakings), so I'll use it to explain our journey. That said, our adventure began when Crenen had a metaphorical itch he couldn't scratch. That moods befalls him an awful lot, and as a result I usually end up in some sort of trouble, but not allowing him to do as he pleases usually makes things worse, so I just go along with whatever schemes hatch inside his creepy little head.

This instance began in the dining hall of Kirid Castle, where I was enticed by the scent of gerani. He was waiting, perched like a cat upon the long table, a grin stretched across his face, pointed teeth flashing like his mismatched eyes with some grand idea. I knew I'd been caught; a flailing trout on a hook. He held aloft a bunch of luscious gerani and I came forward. As he sat up and plucked a purple sphere from the bunch and gnashed it between those teeth, I did my best not to salivate. He plucked a second and offered it to me. I reached out, fingers twitching, but had just enough sense to halt.

"What's this about?" I asked, eyes fixed on the gerani, my one, lovely addiction.

"We going out for seeing of Dead Walking Things, yeah?"

I jerked out of my trance. "Sorry, what?"

"Heard first time," Crenen said, popping my morsel in his mouth before I could snatch it. He offered another, which I stubbornly refused.

"What, dare I ask, are Dead Walking Things?"

"No idea," he said, shrugging. "Never seen one, only *heard* about."

"If you've never seen one, why does it have one of your special names?"

"Not one of our special names. Is only name of Dead Walking Things in Smelly Wet Lands."

"Smelly...wet...lands..." I laughed shortly. "I'm not going."

"Sure you is, Strange *Coward* Boy."

It had been some time since he threw that particular insult at me. I'd proven my bravery in spades, but Crenen's memory is only as good as his manners when said memory impedes his whim. "I'm not," I said.

"You not going or not coward?"

"Both, neither." I frowned. "Go by yourself, if you want. Take Menen with you, but leave me here."

Crenen gnashed another gerani between his teeth. "We thinking Strange Coward Boy coming or might regret."

I sighed. "Are you threatening me?"

His eyes widened and he blinked (which isn't innocent like it sounds, but actually appears twice as creepy as anything else you might've seen in your life). "We not threaten, yeah? Only warn."

"Is there a difference?" There was a time, upon first meeting Crenen, when his temperament made me adhere to his every desire, but we were friends now, and I wasn't going to cave so easily.

"We thinking so. One being evil, other being friendly."

"Er, okay. Sure.

The far doors into the dining hall burst open and Jenen entered, a startling expression of excitement on his face (meaning his eyes were bright). He crossed the flagstones quickly, hands clutching his white shawl. "When do we leave?" he asked, looking between us.

"Not," Crenen said. "Strange *Coward* Boy not inclining to leave comfort of home for sake of discovery, like Wee Sissy Girl." (Chasym had been teaching him new words for 'small' lately.)

"Hey now," I said, scowling, but my scowl slipped away as realization dawned. Crenen had mentioned Smelly Wet Lands, not anyone's favorite vacation spot, but Jenen appeared to be coming and, what's more, eager to be off for those foreboding lands. I frowned at him, eyes narrowing. "What is all this?"

"Did he not explain?" asked Jenen, shooting Crenen a disapproving look.

"We explain plenty," Crenen said, folding his arms.

"He said he wanted to go to Smelly Wet Lands to see Dead Walking Things."

"Yes, exactly." Jenen arched a brow. "Don't you want to come?"

"Um, no. Have you gone mad or are you Chasym in disguise?" I looked him up and down to spot any inconsistencies in his appearance.

"I'm not mad, nor am I Chasym, which would amount to the same thing."

Definitely Jenen, I decided with growing perplexity. "Do you want to explain to me why you, of all people, intend to visit Smelly Wet Lands?"

"For science."

I stared at his feminine face for a long moment. "Are you serious?"

He nodded. "Of course."

"We not going for science. We going for fun," Crenen said, acting entirely like himself, which was really no comfort.

"Since when are you a scientist?" I asked, crossing my arms to study the specimen before me.

"I am not," Jenen said. "Crenen and I have been petitioned by scientists to fund an expedition to Uzadob Swamp, and I want to be certain we are not being taken advantage of, so I am going as well."

Again, definitely Jenen. "Right. So why do you both want me to come?"

They exchanged a glance. "In truth..." Jenen began.

"Small Furry Pests like Strange Coward Boy," Crenen added, grinning.

"Yes, exactly," said Jenen. "You attract trouble, and we are seeking just that."

I gave him a hard look. "That's both not funny and really kind of mean."

"But true, nonetheless." Jenen turned back to his twin. "The last of the essentials are being packed. Is Menen to come as well?"

"Tall Strong Jerk come even if we say not coming, yeah?" Crenen tossed the gerani shoot, now devoid of the little fruits. I stared at it, then sighed. It seemed I was coming along, like it or not. An old, familiar feeling of uneasiness settled in my stomach, assuring me with lurching caresses that things were going to turn ugly very soon, not to worry.

So, of course I worried more.

~~~

Uzadob Swamp was an uneventful four-days' march from Kirid Castle, heading north-east, beneath the stretching shadow of tree-clad foothills. Crenen, Jenen, Menen and I were accompanied by a small contingent of warriors and a dozen black-cloaked scientists from both Yenen and Kirid Clan. The latter stayed to themselves, mostly, standing in clusters to whisper with open glances in my direction. I had the distinct impression they wanted nothing more than to dissect me, so I gave them a wide berth.

I will note that I learned several traditional Yenen campfire songs, which, when translated into English, make less sense than any abstract song I've heard in my life, though I suspect Lewis Carroll would be thrilled to learn them. I personally refrained when Menen offered to teach me, though that was more because I was tired from the day's journey. Even riding Beastie, I had been long enough away from camps and travel that I was sore inside
~~~

and out. (Politics make the body and heart atrophy if you're not careful.) Despite my exhaustion, I was glad to be free of the demands normally plaguing my life, even if the price was an impending encounter with Dead Walking Things.

The first signs of swampland appeared on our third day, when the seyaming birds ceased their warning cries, replaced by the sound of freket frogs coughing fire. Crenen ordered several caught to make building fires easier, as the days were chill and the nights were freezing.

On the fourth day we reached the border of Uzadob Swamp. I crested a bald rise and stopped to study the lay of the land. The heavy stench of rot and mildew filled the dreary sky, while miles of dark blue- and maroon-leafed willow-like trees covered the land like a lumpy carpet. A peculiar noise crept up from the bog, eerie on the foul wind that carried it. I glanced at Jenen, whose knuckles were white as he clutched his shawl, eyes fixed on the sight. Crenen didn't seem to care about the general ambiance, intent instead on complaining to the cook about his food selections, which didn't meet at all with the prince's approval. But then, few meals ever did.

The cook argued with him for only a moment (being a Kirid Clan member, he thought he didn't have to listen to Crenen), but Crenen inched nearer to the man and whispered something and, pale-faced, the cook bowed and murmured apologies. Crenen cackled and moved to stand beside Jenen and me, surveying the swamp. He took a deep whiff of air and grinned. "Smell like Dead Walking Things."

"Yeah, about that," I said, grimacing. "You don't mean zombies or anything, right? You don't *have* zombies in Paradise, right? Because I am *not* good with handling zombies."

"What are zombies?" asked Jenen.

"Dead people who come back as mindless corpses to eat the brains of living people," I said.

They regarded me for a long moment.

"Brains?" Jenen asked.

"You meaning like Hungry Rotten Men?" Crenen asked.

I gave him a flat stare. "You just made that up, right?"

He grinned at me.

"Rest assured, Key," Jenen said, pulling his shawl tighter still. "Brain-eating corpses are not what we seek here."

A shrill scream cut through the swamp. Everyone went still, hearts and breaths cut off. I searched the treetops for movement, waiting for another death cry, but all was silent, even the wind. Glancing at Crenen, I recognized curiosity on his brow. Sensing my gaze, he looked at me and flashed a grin.

"Smelly Wet Lands plenty dangerous enough for Strange Coward Boy, yeah?"

"Yeah. Plenty."

"We go in now," he said, and turned to the forces standing by. "Forget Nasty Pig Slops for lunch. We go into Uzadob Swamp."

The cook said nothing to the contrary, still pale from whatever image Crenen had planted in his mind. The warriors appeared unperturbed by the scream, and they immediately moved to break up the pavilions arranged only moments before for the midday meal. In one regard I was fine skipping my meal; between the stench and the scream, I had no appetite, though I'd been famished moments before.

"Well," I said, grimacing. "Might as well face doom before dinner."

"If it is any comfort to you," Jenen said, "I am assured that the creature we seek is mythical."

I gave him a sidelong smile. "All the creatures existing here would be considered mythical back home."

"Very well, perhaps a better word would be 'false.'"

"Did the scientists tell you that?"

"Yes."

I sighed. "That doesn't mean anything. Scientists back home think I'm descended from monkeys." I couldn't help but wonder what Lon would think of that theory.

"What are monkeys?"

A movie reference came to my mind, but I pushed it down. "Let's just say they're kind of undignified animals."

A faint smile haunted Jenen's lips. "Scientists can be quite observant."

"Not funny." I turned back to the swamp. "You came to keep Crenen out of trouble, didn't you?"

"I came to keep you *both* out of trouble."

"You dragged me into this."

"Crenen would have either way."

I couldn't dispute that. I might be considered a hero by most, but to Crenen I would always be his lackey. I smiled. I preferred it that way. Being worshiped is miserable, and he was always there to rub that in my face. Funny how some abuses are worth tolerating.

Crenen strode over to us, scowling. "We going now. Don't keeping still."

I shrugged. "Ready whenever you are, captain."

He shot me a flat look, then turned around. "Move out!"

Menen signaled his men and we started down the hill towards the source of smelly scents and shrill screams. I was thrilled.

~~~

Have I mentioned I don't do well with horror films?

Back on Earth my sister took me to see a movie that will, for the sake of my dignity, remain undisclosed. I may or may not have screamed like a little girl and fainted. In short, my imagination takes an extra hand in things, guiding my inner mind to the darkest, scariest realm possible whenever it can. After encountering many surprises in Paradise, I thought I had outgrown this special condition, but as we entered Uzadob Swamp, I realized with the closeness of the trees that some things are not to be overcome.

Willow trees have never scared me, nor have they featured actual faces on them outside of cartoons, but the trees of Uzadob managed both. (I do stand by the claim that Beastie was the one whimpering, not me.) I gripped my mount's ample fur very tight as we moved through the leering grins of wrinkled, bark-covered faces, and tried to imagine they were grandmotherly, like a certain animated
~~~

movie portrays them. But these grins were more Crenenish, and I failed to comfort myself. Beastie glanced up at me with doggish concern, but his glowing blue eyes only creeped me out more. Once, Beastie had been an ordinary-looking American Eskimo, but Paradise alters what enters its domain and now he was a very large, rideable creature with teal markings and an oversized appetite.

Fortunately he's still a very nice fellow, unless he gets annoyed.

The swamp's wildlife annoyed him. I can't really blame him. Who wouldn't be annoyed by blood-sucking hummingbirds?

They swarmed down from the trees, their angry hum a cacophony of death. One of the scientists screamed. I let out a more manly yelp as several birds charged me, then ducked down, letting Beastie take a direct hit. He, well, bucked. I flew off his back and landed in a pool of rancid water, head submerged. I tried to resurface, but vines wrapped around my wrists and dragged me down. Reflexively I tried to call for help--which might be the dumbest thing I've ever done. Foul water filled my mouth and my lungs burned. The vines shot up into my mouth, trying to wriggle down my throat. I choked, writhing, fighting against them. Blackness smothered my mind. Death hovered nearby.

And I got mad.

Release, I commanded the vines, and they shrank back, burned by my power. *Rise,* I told the water, and it let me surface. I gasped for air even as I hacked up a gallon of fluid, then blearily looked around to see brave Yenen warriors engaged in battle with a flock of birds. It might sound ridiculous, but several men had been downed and were being fed upon by the blood-sucking monsters. Beastie was bounding about, knocking down young trees and clan warriors as he barked and growled at the flittering pests.

I spotted Jenen against a tree, slashing with claws at any bird who dared approach. Crenen was up in the same tree and climbing higher. I realized his intention. There must be a nest several branches above him, probably containing baby humming-monster eggs.

The humming sounds drew nearer and I spun to deflect a second attack. As my eyes narrowed on a hummingbird, it froze and dropped to the ground, encased in ice. I turned away and spotted Menen approaching from across the way, batting off the occasional killer bird in his quick march. When he arrived he looked me over, frowning.

"Are you all right?"

"Fine," I said, looking way up at him. "I was attacked by killer vines, though, so don't let anyone fall into the water."

He glared down at the nearest pool. "Noted. Where are Crenen and Jenen?"

"There." I pointed to the tree and blinked as I saw its carved eyes glance in my direction, then return to watching Crenen. "That is really, really creepy..."

Menen looked between me and the tree. "What is?"

"The tree. It's watching Crenen."

"The tree is?" He looked hard at the trunk.

"Yeah. I think—" Before I could voice my thought, it happened. The tree moved, sweeping the branch Crenen stood on out from under him. He tumbled down, hands scrambling for purchase, claws shredding through bark until a trail of blood ran down the trunk. Jenen tried to catch his brother and crumpled under Crenen's weight. They both lay still for a moment, and as the birds moved in, enticed by the scent of blood, Menen took off to rescue his cousins. He barreled into the flock of birds and knocked them away, ignoring the piercing wounds they inflicted on his limbs. Kneeling beside Crenen, Menen pulled him into a sitting position and I heard snatches of the prince's tirade of Paradisian curses. Menen next helped Jenen up, simultaneously smacking a hummingbird aside with his free hand.

I moved towards them, dodging around the birds. I considered calming Beastie, but he was doing such a good job chewing birds up, I decided to let him continue to vent.

"Are you both okay?" I asked, stepping around a few twitching twigs.

Crenen shot me an are-you-that-stupid look, holding his bloody fingers to his chest. He glowered at the tree, then frowned. "We never have tree move from under before."

"It's laughing," I said, taking an involuntary step back as the strange, rumbling laugh shook the ground. My voice brought the tree's eyes down on me, and its leering smile stretched wider, causing the trunk to moan. The ground trembled again. Roots broke free of the muddy earth, snapping up and wrapping around my ankles to pull me upside-down into the air. I let out a cry, blood rushing to my head. Strands of white hair hung in my face.

"Let him go!" Menen said in a commanding tone.

My shock subsided and I pushed my hair up out of my face to stare at the world dangling around me. "You heard him, lemme go!" You must understand, while I am a very powerful person, power is new to me and, well, I don't know what to do with it half the time. My mind just draws a blank. So it was now, as I swung upside-down in the grasp of an evil, animated tree who wasn't grandmotherly.

Crenen sauntered forward, picked up a twig with bloody fingers and prodded the roots holding me. "We thinking you release Strange Coward Boy or we grow annoyed, yeah?"

The roots shuddered and gripped me tighter. I gritted my teeth. "Not. Helping. *Crenen*."

Crenen laughed and snapped the twig in two. The tree didn't like that. I went flying through the air and plunged once more into the murky pool of nastiness. Fortunately the vines knew better than to imprison me, and I emerged from the depths, gasping and spluttering. I turned in time to see Crenen fending off the tree roots with a large stick, moving as gracefully as any fencer, parrying and thrusting, dodging and ducking around the lashing roots. Dirt flew everywhere as tendrils of the tree tried in vain to catch their new prey. Menen and Jenen were battling against a large force of hummingbirds, throwing rocks and pebbles with deadly accuracy.

My eyes turned back to the tree. Crenen had been going for a nest up there. I pushed up my sopping sleeves and tiptoed across the battleground. After witnessing me freeze the last hummingbird who tried to stab me, none of the others seemed inclined to block my path, and I reached the tree unscathed. Its beady eyes were focused hard on Crenen as I moved behind it and jumped up to catch the lowest branch. The tree bucked (which is a really interesting sight, I'm assured by eye-witnesses and my own strained arms). I gripped the branch as I was pitched back and forth by the mighty trunk trying to dislodge me. My pride kept me from being thrown a third time, and I lifted my legs mid-pitch, locking them around the branch as my fingers began to slip. Clutching the branch for dear life, again hanging upside-down, I waited and prayed for the tree to settle down. At last it did, roots redoubling their efforts to kill Crenen, who had taken to name-calling as he snatched at willowy tendrils, ripping leaves free and scattering them across the boggy ground.

I clutched the limb for a moment longer, then eased myself up into a sitting position. I caught my breath, smoothed my hair, and stared up. Through the canopy of weeping willows, the sun filtered down in shafts of golden light. I studied the higher branches and spotted a large knot colored different from the tree's bark. The nest. I smiled to myself and got to my feet, balancing carefully on the trembling limb. I caught a higher branch and pulled myself up, paused to be sure the tree wasn't going to throw me, then continued to climb. Crenen was doing an excellent job enraging the willow's roots, and I was forgotten.

Climbing trees was one of my favorite childhood pastimes, right next to reading novels. They were both hobbies I could do alone, and I often preferred solitude. It had been a long time since I'd last climbed a tree this size, and my muscles ached, but it felt good to go higher and higher. At last I reached the nest and, peering inside, I found three tiny eggs. Drawing a breath, I hoped this would work.

I shut my eyes and concentrated on sending my thoughts into the minds of the enemy. *I've got your nest. If you want it to remain safe, cease your attack and form a circle around the trunk of this tree.* I sent images with my words, making sure they saw which tree to approach. The humming drill faltered, then increased as the birds flocked to the tree and circled it in little darting motions. The roots of the tree stopped their attack, confused by the birds' attention.

I sighed and looked down, relieved to find many of my warriors getting to their feet, expressions sour.

The tree bucked again.

My fingers slipped free of the bark and I fell backward, arms flailing for purchase. Such is my life. As I fell, wind rushing by me, stomach lurching, I heard a strange, eerie song in my ear. A child sang it. The words were unintelligible, but seemed to speak of death.

Claws caught me and I dangled, arm straining. I winced as blood trickled from wounds made by those claws. They weren't the same as Yenen Clan's sharp nails, but were three inches long and curved, with two opposable thumbs on each furry paw. Looking up, I stared into an adorable face. I don't use the word lightly. Heck, if there was a word more manly than 'adorable' to fit this critter's description, I'd use it instead, but, well, there isn't. A shaft of sunlight lit up its green eyes as it blinked at me, making a little cooing sound. It resembled a koala, with rounded ears and soft grey fur, though it was only around fifteen inches long. And, I realized, it was somehow holding me up on its own. I stared back at the little teddy-bear-like animal, forgetting my pain in the face of cute.

And then the sun hid behind a storm cloud. The plush sea of cuteness turned into a creature of horror. Its face was skeletal, eyes blood-red, mouth fanged and salivating in a sneer of wicked pleasure. The cooing sounds turned into a horrible nursery rhyme sung by the voice of a child.

My reaction was a scream, and I batted free of the monster before I remembered it was keeping me from falling.

Darkness, that old, familiar friend, caught me in a cold embrace.

~~~

It was night when I awoke. A fire blazed close by and a gap in the trees overhead allowed me to see glimpses of twin moons behind whisps of grey cloud. Something warm and smelling of dog panted beside me, so I reached out to stroke it. Beastie's giant tongue licked my fingers. I felt the bruises all over my body, as I lay there assessing the damage. My head felt intact, only pounding dully. That was something. I could also wiggle my toes and fingers. Another plus.

Jenen's head appeared above mine, eyebrows arched.

I smiled through my general discomfort. "We need
~~~

to stop meeting like this."

He let out a brief, humorless laugh. "You hit your head harder than I believed."

"Actually it feels surprisingly unimpaired." I winced as I tried to sit up. "At least compared to the rest of me." I looked around and my sense of humor fizzled up and died. Where the trees had been eerie before, now they were downright horrible. A faint mist hung like green smoke in the putrid air, and the trees were in black relief against it. Worst of all were the myriad glowing eyes, red and twinkling in the firelight.

"Jenen," I whispered, voice breaking. "Why are we still in Uzadob?"

"We have been separated from the others," he said, "and the trees will not let us leave."

"How did that happen?"

"As soon as you fell unconscious, everything attacked at once: the trees, the birds, even vines in the water."

"And evil teddy bears," I murmured.

He arched a brow. "Evil...teddy...burrs?"

"The thing in the tree. Did you see it?" I shivered with the memory.

"I saw nothing in the tree."

"It was what caught me."

"Nothing caught you."

"Yeah, when the tree threw me off that branch and I was caught before I fell."

"Nothing caught you, Key. You fell straight away."

"No, the evil koala caught me, but it didn't look evil then, and then its face changed and I..." I couldn't bring myself to say anything synonymous with 'freaked out.'

"Cried out," Jenen said, nodding. "But nothing was holding you up. You caught yourself."

I started to protest, when the eerie child's song struck up again from the trees. A chill ran down my spine as goosebumps formed on my arms. "Jenen," I whispered.

"I hear it," he said, eyes fixed on the trees. "It's beautiful."

I glanced at him, frowning. "Come again?"

He stood, pulling his shawl close, and moved towards the trees.

"What are you doing?" I asked, rising unsteadily to snatch his arm.

Shadows danced across his face and his eyes remained steadfast on the dark shapes of the forest. "Let me go," he whispered.

"Go where?"

"They're calling me."

His eyes had lost their focus. I jerked him around to face me. "Snap out of it."

The song rose higher, chilling my bones. My breath caught and I wondered how he could think it beautiful. Why was he so affected? Or was it me? I hesitated, loosening my grip enough that Jenen pulled free and walked towards the foliage again. I caught the end of his shawl and tugged. He released the cloth and I stumbled back, falling into a thorny bramble, because Beastie had moved.

It wasn't me, it was definitely him.

I rose and caught his arm again, yanking him around to face me. "Jenen, fight." I considered punching him, but well, he really does have a feminine face and my hand just wouldn't respond to my command. Instead, I met his vacant eyes and focused on our soul-bond. *Jenen, stop listening.*

Remember that disclaimer about my powers not quite being under control? My silent command was too much. He flinched and his ears began to bleed, even as his eyes cleared. He lifted his hands and felt the trickling blood, then grimaced at me. "What was that...?" His brows drew together and he shut his mouth and swallowed. He cleared his throat, then looked at me with eyes wider than I'd ever seen them.

"What have you done?" he whispered.

"Sorry," I said. "I didn't mean--"

His eyes widened more. "What did you do?" His voice was panicked as he felt his ear. "I can't hear you!"

Drat and bloody blast it all. The horror of what I'd done set in as the song hit a shrill note, then cut off. I looked into the trees, neck-hairs tingling as silence smothered the night. Jenen was watching me with mixed fear and concern. He said nothing.

I held his gaze. "Jenen," I said, speaking slowly and exaggerating my lip movements. "I will fix what I have done. Promise. Also, we might be in trouble."

He nodded, understanding (unless he'd misread my lips and thought I was a lunatic talking about bubbles).

Beastie let out a low growl, hackles rising. His eyes were vibrant in the night as he padded forward. I reached out and caught a handful of fur, shaking my head. "Easy boy. Don't stir up the wildlife."

He glanced at me, thumped his tail to communicate

his annoyance, but decided to heed his master's command. At least someone in this place listened to me (you know, without going deaf). I stroked his fur, trying to subdue the beast within as I concentrated on the problem hidden in the trees. I'd faced crazed Seers, murderous shape-shifters, the devil's own horses and gerani-induced visions in the past, but nothing was quite like the horrors of Uzadob Swamp. I was petrified, and worse, mortified at my petrification.

Running came to mind, but I squelched that at once. There was nowhere to run.

The singing started up again, creepier than any nursery rhyme in any horror flick ever filmed. My shivers turned into tremors. Aside from running, my greatest desire at the moment was to see Crenen. He would never be intimidated by a song, even as creepy as this was, of that I was (almost entirely) certain.

Jenen caught my sleeve and I jumped out of my skin. When I was whole again, I glowered at him. He nodded to the trees. "What's that?" he whispered rather loudly.

Finding what he referred to was against my survival instinct, but curiosity wins more often than good sense. I squinted my eyes to see amidst the gloom and found the unmistakable form of a person standing there. That chilled me more than the idea of zombie teddy bears and goosebumps pricked my arms like needles.

The figure shifted, then approached, faceless in the shadows. I took a step back even as Beastie's growl deepened and he inched forward. I caught his fur again and tugged. "Stay," I said, fighting the panic building inside. I was on the verge of hyperventilating. Visions of zombies danced in my head, and worse, a serial killer from some slasher film. My heart hammered through my body (pumping ice-for-blood must be a chore). We were going to die. We were going to die. We were going to die.

There comes a point when fear reaches such heights that all you feel is numb. That numbness set in now and my head tingled. I felt my limbs only from a distance as the approaching figure loomed nearer and nearer, but I had enough presence (or maybe absence) of mind that I flexed my fingers and prepared to defend against the undead. Somehow.

I expected something horrible to step into the firelight. What I got startled me silly. The figure who emerged was tall, slender and clad in flowing layers of white streaming out behind it. Black hair hung in its face. A grin stretched wide across its pale face as it stroked an evil koala nestled in its arms. The little creature eyed me, its skull-like face mirroring the white-clad figure's grin, fangs bright in the firelight. The figure let out an eerie cackle.

Whatever act of defense I was half-prepared to conjure was forgotten. I scowled. "Crenen, what the *heck* are you doing?"

His answer was a laugh.

~~~

The little zombie teddy bears were called kookanin and apparently Uzadob Swamp was their refuge as they were in endangered species, once highly coveted for their fur. In
~~~

the sunlight, kookanin were adorable, but in the darkness they had a second face used to defend themselves against predators. All in all, they were harmless herbivores, whose claws were used only for foraging and climbing trees. They were not mythical and the scientists didn't give a fig about studying them.

In fact, the entire thing had been set up for one reason: me.

"Strange Coward Boy enjoy tricker-treat?" Crenen asked when he was finished laughing.

My eyes narrowed and I folded my arms, both to show annoyance and to ward off the chills coursing through my body. "Who told you about trick-or-treating?"

"Shifty Cocky Man," Crenen said, scratching the kookanin's head with affection.

"Chasym did? That little jerk..."

"Strange Coward Boy call no one else little, yeah? Delusional self."

Jenen sat beside me, arms also folded, eyes flicking between me and his twin. He said nothing as he concentrated on reading our lips. I turned to him and very slowly asked, "Did you know about all this?"

He hesitated (*he* actually hesitated!) and gave a little nod. "I confess I was intrigued."

I stared hard at him, looking for some ounce of regret. "Then it's your own fault you're deaf."

His expression went flat. "I am not the one who cannot control his powers." His eyes flicked to Crenen. "Though I confess the jest may have gone too far."

Crenen snickered, scratching the kookanin's chin. The creature gurgled appreciation, features shifting between horror and cute in the flickering light.

Turning to Crenen, I struggled with the image of him in white, his hair laying around his shoulders. I'd always seen him in black and red, with a lopsided ponytail high on his head, and the two images didn't coalesce well. No wonder Beastie reacted poorly to him; he looked creepier than ever.

"So Chasym told you about trick-or-treating and you decided to, what, create a Paradise-style spook-alley?"

"Shifty Cocky Man say would make Strange Coward Boy feel at home for holladay," Crenen assured me.

I snorted. "Yeah. Yippy. Being scared is so much fun." And then the magnitude of everything struck me. "We traveled over a hundred freaking miles and injured how many warriors just to scare me?" I tried to fight the high note that sneaked into my tones.

Crenen nodded with enthusiasm. Jenen remained still. I'm not sure which reaction angered me more.

"So, what, the scientists were for show?"

Crenen shook his head, grin widening. "Pokey Lurky Men want to see Great Vendaeva when he put in bad spot in Wet Smelly Lands, so we say yeah, yeah?"

"Yeah," I murmured, feeling my face heat. "They must've been so impressed."

"That," Crenen said, "and all this idea belonging most to Tall Strong Jerk."

That took a moment to register. "Sorry, come again?"

"Tall Strong Jerk ask that we doing all this."

I shook my head, wondering if Jenen's hearing trouble was somehow contagious. "Sorry, for a second I thought you were accusing Menen of plotting to make me travel for four days straight, enter a smelly bog and engage in battle with the local wildlife, including the undead, all to make me die of a heart attack."

Crenen bobbed his head yes and no, strangely indecisive. Then he shrugged. "All so, except for last bit. Tall Strong Jerk do all that for Strange Coward Boy's *good,* not heart attacking. We never seen heart attacking anybody, yeah?"

"Oh, oh, right. Riiight. I forgot it was for my good, sorry." The ice in my blood was melting in my growing wrath. "How the heck to you expect me to believe Menen would do any of this on his own?"

"Crenen isn't lying," Jenen said.

I shot him a look. "How do you know? You're deaf!"

"And whose fault is that?" Jenen retorted after sorting out my accusation.

"Gee, let me think. How about the devil's own twins, who led this hunt into Hell!"

"We are not in Hell."

I jumped to my feet. "I wasn't being literal!" Okay, maybe I was.

Jenen's eyes flashed with anger. "Is this gratitude after all we've done?"

"GRATITUDE!?"

The kookanin let out a mournful singsong sound and I flinched. It regarded me with burning eyes and I looked away.

"That is enough," said a new voice.

I whirled, relief washing all the ice and lava from my blood. "Menen, they're accusing *you* of this nightmare."

"And rightly so," he said simply. "I am responsible."

There was a long silence. "Come again?"

"You heard me."

"I didn't," muttered Jenen.

"I'm not sure I did either," I said.

Menen smiled. "Chasym was enlightening us on one your Earthling customs called Halloween. Crenen was, unsurprisingly, enraptured, especially with the concept of tricker-treating."

"It's trick-OR-treating," I said.

They all regarded me. "What that meaning?" asked Crenen.

"It's where little kids go around to all the neighbors to get candy. But I bet Chasym left that part out."

"Ah." Menen shifted. "We were led to believe it was the act of a tricker being treated to the chance of scaring someone."

"Nice. But there's no such word as tricker. It would be trickster-treat, but either way that's a ridiculous idea." I left out the origins of the holiday's rituals, thinking it best not to give them any more bad ideas.

Menen nodded. "I agree with you, and I initially attempted to persuade Crenen *not* to harass you in this fashion."

"I appreciate your efforts."

"But then I was struck by a realization."

"I'm beginning to hate those."

Menen went on. "Every time you encounter a challenging experience, your powers grow, as does your ability to wield said powers. I thought this the perfect chance to push you further, to make you grow stronger."

I ran a hand through my hair. "You gotta be kidding me. You did all this so I could *grow stronger*?"

"Precisely."

The hand dropped to my face. "I suppose I should thank you."

"What did he say?" asked Jenen.

I dropped my hand. "I said I'd like to *kill* you."

"I don't blame you," said Jenen. "Though, to be fair, we chose Uzadob Swamp solely because Crenen wanted to select a kookanin to take home with him."

I pursed my lips and counted to ten. Then I looked at Crenen. "You can't keep it. You're not bringing it with us. No freaking way."

He eyed me with a level of indifference only a god could conjure, then returned to pampering his new pet.

I had the distinct feeling that the journey home was going to be about as unpleasant as my night in Uzadob Swamp.

I was wrong. It was far, far worse. But *that* is a story for another day.

This last tale was the first 'bonus' story I ever wrote for Liars Go To Paradise? *It was composed shortly after the original part one was completed, so the writing suffers somewhat. It's silly and pointless and entirely unofficial. As will be evident as you read on, it's a twisted take on the fairytale* Rapunzel *and is narrated by Key. You may want to read it around two o'clock in the morning, when everything is funny.*

Vendaezel

Once upon a time, in a kingdom that doesn't actually exist, there was a tower. Which isn't uncommon in most kingdoms, seeing as how each kingdom seems to hire the same architects for the basic design of the buildings—castles for kings, mansions for rich snobs, straw huts for peasants, and huge leering towers for villains.

Back to the story.

In this particular tower, there was a beautiful maiden who had been captured by Evil Witch Crenen. This maiden—hey, whoa, wait a second! This *maiden* is me! I'm not a girl. I'm a guy!

To rephrase that last paragraph, there was a handsome young man stuck in a tower, held there by the Evil Witch Crenen. This handsome guy, by the name of Key, sat each day at the solitary window inside the tower's one room and gazed longingly at the abundant gerani trees far below, desiring to taste one. Alas, the only way Key could eat one was on the rare occasion Evil Witch

Crenen came to his room and felt slightly generous, which wasn't very often.

Key was well aware that the only reason Evil Witch Crenen kept him locked away in the tower was to lure his prey near. Evil Witch Crenen had begun a rumor—or, more accurately, he had sent his crony, Tall Strong Servant to begin the rumor. (Evil Witch Crenen wasn't the kind of person to do his own work unless there was no other choice. And yes, though the name is deceiving, Evil Witch Crenen is male. This is a fairytale, and fairytales have evil witches, not evil wizards…)

The rumor claimed the great Vendaezel was trapped in Huge Leering Tower and could never be released. Now, Key knew it was a ridiculous rumor, and he couldn't imagine anyone would actually fall for such a story. But it seemed no one was nearly as intelligent as Key.

The kingdom believed Vendaezel was a being of tremendous power who would someday save the kingdom from some kind of 'certain doom' scenario. And who was Key to point out their stupid, primitive falsehoods as being just that? Besides, for several years now Key had been stuck in Huge Leering Tower, isolated from humanity, subjected only to the antics of Evil Witch Crenen and his crony, Tall Strong Servant.

Once in a great while, princes from several different kingdoms would come to free *Vendaezel* from Evil Witch Crenen's clutches, each under the mistaken impression that only a princess could be trapped in a tower. Could Key help it if during a late night excursion to raid Evil Witch Crenen's gerani trees he'd been caught and forced to play the charade of 'damsel in distress'? It had hardly been optional.

The most depressing part of Key's situation was, as soon as the princes realized the prisoner's gender, they were quick to depart.

Each weekend Evil Witch Crenen would go to the bottom of the tower and say in a taunting voice, "Vendaezel, Vendaezel, catch Big Long Rope, so Crenen can come up and hover gerani under nose, while eating, and Vendaezel watch with drool coming from mouth in disgusting manner."

To which Key always replied, "In your friggin' dreams."

Evil Witch Crenen would then proceed to unlock the door at the bottom of Huge Leering Tower and climb the steps, his crony, Tall Strong Servant close behind him, carrying a bowl of gerani in his hands.

When the two evil men reached the top of the stairs, the door would open to reveal a relaxing Evil Witch Crenen in Tall Strong Servant's arms, while the latter strained to carrying his Master and the bowl of gerani safely into the room.

As before mentioned, Evil Witch Crenen did nothing that could be done *for* him, including ascending very narrow, steep steps. Key couldn't help but sympathize with Tall Strong Servant's situation.

The same pattern had lasted the past several years, and Key had grown accustomed to the idea that he would never get away.

That is, of course, until our hero arrived. King Jenen, ruler of Nearby Neighboring Kingdom heard of

Vendaezel, and grabbing his only child (a female), forced her to dress as a prince and ordered her to rescue Vendaezel or Jenen would have her executed for high treason.

Jenen's daughter, not the brightest crayon in the box, told her father she had no idea who 'High Tree's son' was, but that she would certainly go in his place and she happily marched from the throne room, mounted her steed, and rode off in the wrong direction.

Key continued to watch hopelessly from his window, eyeing the ripe gerani trees mournfully.

Evil Witch Crenen received word that King Jenen of Nearby Neighboring Kingdom had sent his son to rescue Vendaezel, which was exactly what he intended. Evil Witch Crenen had been trying to barter with King Jenen for a long time, hoping Jenen would take Huge Leering Tower off his hands. Key had suggested Evil Witch Crenen just leave the tower if he hated it so much, but Evil Witch Crenen would hear of no such thing. He wanted Huge Leering Tower in the hands of someone trustworthy.

Apparently King Jenen was somehow trustworthy.

Anyway, when Evil Witch Crenen heard the news, he ordered Tall Strong Servant to release Mighty Ominous Dragon, whose actual name was Lon.

This red-eyed beast was Key's number one enemy, even over Evil Witch Crenen. Mighty Ominous Dragon had been the one to catch Key sneaking into the gerani trees, and now Key couldn't forgive him—ever. It was an eternal feud. (Never mind it's pointless to have a feud against a dragon, not to mention unhealthy.)

Tall Strong Servant released Mighty Ominous Dragon as ordered, and Key watched as the duel began; for Princess Veija, daughter of King Jenen, in the guise of a prince, was coming along the wide pathway (which Tall Strong Servant had cleared for easy access to Huge Leering Tower.)

The 'prince' halted, gasping at the sight of Mighty Ominous Dragon. "Oh my!" she exclaimed, sounding a touch too feminine. "It's a cute ickle dragon!"

Mighty Ominous Dragon had been about to conjure fire with his hands (while Evil Witch Crenen claimed Lon was a dragon, he more resembled a person who just happened to have white fire at his disposal)—but at Veija's exclamation of 'cute ickle dragon,' he hesitated and stepped backed.

The 'prince' slid off the white steed and approached the dragon. "Do you want to be my pet?" she asked, giggling.

Lon stepped back again, then darted away, defeated by the girlish laugh.

Evil Witch Crenen emerged from his secret hideaway (which adjoined Huge Leering Tower) and grinned with sharp pointy teeth. "You did good when fought Mighty Ominous Dragon, but what happen when you go against Tall Strong Servant?"

Tall Strong Servant stepped out from behind his master, holding a wooden spoon in one hand.

"Are we baking something?" Veija asked, looking at the spoon excitedly.

"You bad boy," Evil Witch Crenen cackled. "Get punishment!"

Veija gasped as Tall Strong Servant turned her over his knee and swatted her behind several times. She squealed in pain until he released her, then stumbled to her horse—and decided that mounting might not be the best idea. So she ran, pulling her horse by the reins until they disappeared.

Key sighed, depressed. "Can't I have just one gerani?" he called down to the two evil men.

Evil Witch Crenen shook his head, grinning wickedly, and returned to his secret hideaway. Tall Strong Servant followed behind him.

While Key believed the 'prince' would give up and go home, Evil Witch Crenen knew better (somehow). He made plans for the coming day and Tall Strong Servant painted a sign for him, working through the night.

The following morning arrived, along with 'Prince' Veija; her jaw set determinedly. She crept up to Huge Leering Tower and glanced at a new sign set before it, which read:

Evil Witch Crenen and Tall Strong Servant gone until you rescue Vendaezel. Don't steal Bright Shiny Key.

The key to the door just behind the sign was hanging by a nail on the sign itself. Veija clapped her hands in delight and gazed up at the tower. "Oh, but Bright Shiny Key would help get up there much more easily," she remarked, shielding her eyes from the sun with her hand. "Oh well, I'll think of something."

She stepped back and spotted Key watching her from the solitary window. "Oh, are you *Vendaezel*?"

He nodded, going through the routine with decided indifference.

"Might you have some rope which I could use to climb up?" she called.

He shook his head.

"Oh, well, that's okay. I'll discover another means to achieve my goal."

She took to scouring the grounds until Key could take it no more. "Just take the stupid key and open the blasted door!"

"But," she whimpered, "the sign says not to steal it!"

Key sighed and then snapped his fingers. He knew how to deal with her. "You'll only borrow it to get up here. You'd never actually take it with you when we leave, right? So you're not stealing anything."

"Oh, of course. You're very smart, Vendaezel," she shouted, then happily removed the key from its nail and proceeded to unlock the door.

Key waited until the 'prince' reached the top of the stairs, dreading the reaction he would get when the 'prince' discovered his gender (since Key had yet to know that Veija was, in reality, a woman.)

At long last Veija reached the tower room and burst in, sword drawn and ready for combat.

"I have come to plead for High Tree's son's life!" she exclaimed.

Key watched her blankly. "Say again?"

"My father, King Jenen, has sent me to plead for High Tree's son in exchange for rescuing you. Will you not kill him, please?"

Key was bewildered, but recovered quickly. "Yeah, sure. Whatever you want. Let's just get outta here."

She beamed and allowed him to lead her from the top of the tower, down the steps, until they reached the base. Just as they exited Huge Leering Tower, Evil Witch Crenen and Tall Strong Servant stepped out of nowhere and blocked their path.

Veija screamed and Key halted, his eyes narrowed as he calculated a means of escape.

"We have bargaining tool now, yeah?" Evil Witch Crenen pronounced gleefully.

"You just wanted the prince?" Key inquired, seeing his chance.

"Not prince. Princess, yeah?" Evil Witch Crenen replied.

Key glanced at Veija and nodded. "Guess you're right. So you needed the, er, princess to use as a real bargaining chip for dealing with King Jenen, and I was just the bait for the bait for the King, right?"

"Exactly."

"Why go to all this trouble?" Key asked.

"More fun, yeah?"

"I guess so…" The former-captive said. "So, since I'm no longer needed, can I go now?

Evil Witch Crenen hesitated for a moment, then nodded. "Farewell False *Vendaezel* Dolt."

"So long," Key replied, and took off at a quick jog. Gerani, or no gerani, he was never coming to Huge Leering Tower again.

Princess Veija blinked. "Well, I hope he saves High Tree's son."

Evil Witch Crenen nodded to Tall Strong Servant. "Take her to top of Huge Leering Tower."

"And the false Vendaezel?" Tall Strong Servant inquired.

"False Vendaezel Dolt's use has run dry as village well. Kill." And Evil Witch Crenen went back to his secret hideaway.

Key wasn't very far away when he heard the distinct sounds of pursuit. Turning around, his eyes widened and he quicken his step to avoid the deadly clutches of Mighty Ominous Dragon.

When Evil Witch Crenen later contacted King Jenen, he received a 'thank you' note expressing the King's delight of being relieved of his child. The note concluded with his condolences.

So much for happy endings.

COMIC SAMPLE

The following is a sample of our comic version of Liars Go To Paradise? *You can read weekly updates by visiting AvianSkies.deviantART.com.*

Liars Go To Paradise?

BY AVIANSKIES

W-WHAT IN THE WORLD?

PAGE 1

. . . . .
HM...
I CAN'T REMEMBER HOW I GOT HERE!!
. . .
WAIT.
IT WAS RAINING.
SSSSHHHH
PIT
PAT
PAGE 2

RMMBL
FLASH

YO JASON!
OUT ENJOYING THE SPRING WEATHER, ARE WE?
THAT'S RIGHT.
THAT'S WHEN *HE* SHOWED UP.

UGH.
SLIP

S'UP?
THIS IS CHAS, LOCAL HIGH SCHOOL CELEBRITY, CHICK-MAGNET, AND LIVING PROOF THAT LIFE ISN'T FAIR.
HE'S ALSO NEVER SPOKEN TO ME BEFORE.
I MEAN, WHY SHOULD HE? I'M A
NOBODY.

PAGE 3

I MEAN, C'MON.
WITH LOOKS LIKE MINE, WHO NEEDS AN EDUCATION?
NEVER MIND.

WELL, JASON . . .
THIS IS THE PART WHERE WE SAY GOODBYE. I CAN'T SAY IT HASN'T BEEN INTERESTING.
HALT
SSSSSSSHHH
MAYBE, IF YOU SURVIVE, WE'LL MEET AGAIN.
?

HUH?

PAGE 4

PAGE 5

ABOUT THE AUTHOR

M. H. Woodscourt has been a writer since she was twelve and a storyteller all her life. Twenty moves through her youth provided opportunities to see the world, experience people and cultivate a highly (sometimes overly) active imagination; thus, the fantasy genre called out to her, demanding her attention. Story ideas haunt her in the night, characters demand birth, and she loves every disturbing moment.

Printed in Great Britain
by Amazon.co.uk, Ltd.,
Marston Gate.